to Alan
with all

CW00447922

A Sound Like Angels Weeping

by

Jeremy Hilton

Jeremy Hilton (signature)

Brimstone Press

First published in 2013
by
Brimstone Press
The Mount
Buckhorn Weston
SP8 5HT

www.brimstonepress.co.uk

Author contacts:
xtendthepoem@gmail.com

Printed in Times New Roman by ImprintDigital.com

Cover by Linda Reed & Associates
lindareedassoc@btconnect.com

Cover photo by Patricia Field

ISBN 978-1-906385-39-2

Dedicated to all those troubled and
damaged young people struggling
to make sense of a hostile world

With thanks to –

Keith Walton for his assistance in
preparing this book for publication

Linda Reed for designing the cover

Patricia Field for the cover picture

and last but not least thanks to
Kim for her love, forbearance and support
during both the writing and the preparing
for publication of this book

A SOUND LIKE ANGELS WEEPING

A SOUND LIKE ANGELS WEEPING

"And from a battered guitar came

A sound like the angels weeping

For all the restless spirits in the night"

(Bob Childers)

1. SHE'S LEAVING HOME

Marcus Sullivan drove his brother's large estate car southwards into the late morning sun. Beside him sat his wife's stepfather, and on the back seat sprawled Katy, his wife's younger sister, a nineteen-year-old slightly taller than average blonde girl in a black sweatshirt and pale blue jeans. On the seat next to Katy but with his head in her lap, lay her beloved rough-coated mongrel terrier, Greg. In the foot-well below the seat where Greg lay, Katy had placed his basket, rug, bowls, and the various other bits and pieces he would need. In the large rear space were crammed all Katy's worldly goods, two cases of clothes, a smaller bag of accessories, several boxes of books and CDs, a number of framed prints and posters, a small TV, a small sound system, a kettle, a laptop computer, her cello, her paints and easel, carrier bags containing food items, and various items of footwear scattered loosely among the rest.

    Katy was reading a book, or attempting to, and had her personal stereo plugged into her ears. Her only communication was with the dog, which was by touch, smiles, and possibly by submerged sounds which only the two of them could hear. The two men in the front occasionally attempted to engage Katy in conversation by remarking on the weather (sunny), the state of the motorway (quite busy), or asking her how she was feeling in a conciliatory tone, which she answered as briefly as possible before turning back to her book, her music, and her dog. It had been clear from the beginning that conversation was not part of the agreement she'd made for this trip. So the two men talked among themselves about cricket (the season had just concluded and Lancashire had been relegated to the second division, a source of great consternation) and the football season, which was getting under way. It was not that these subjects held no interest for Katy, who had played and followed several sports over the years, had been to Old Trafford with her stepfather and her brother-in-law many times to watch both cricket and football, it was just that she didn't like to talk much, especially at times like this.

Katy was off to university in a town about ninety miles away. This was not in itself a remarkable event for a nineteen-year-old bookish girl on a bright September morning, but it had caused a degree of speculation among people who knew her, at school, in her neighbourhood, or among her family, even among those who knew her best.

A younger sister by some years (her mother having suffered one miscarriage and one stillbirth in the years between), Katy had been a very treasured child. She had grown up into a somewhat home-loving teenager - not to an extreme, not worryingly so, she'd been out with boys often enough, sometimes in a foursome with her best friend, sometimes just her and a boy, but nothing had ever developed further - and had managed to avoid most of the pitfalls of turn of the millennium teenage girlhood, unwanted pregnancies, binge drinking, drugs. A generation or two earlier, her sort of girl would have found employment locally when she left school, in a respectable position such as a clerk-typist in a solicitor's office, in the local library, or perhaps as a nurse, where she would have stayed until she married, for marry she surely would. In fact, Katy seemed more like a girl from an earlier generation in some ways. It was not that she stood out as being old-fashioned, she didn't stand out at all. She was not unattractive, but she wouldn't cause anyone to stop and stare. She never seemed to want to make the effort to cause anyone to notice her.

Those who only knew her slightly would have thought that Katy would continue to live in her home town when she finished school, whether she continued her education or found work, because of her mother. Sharon, Katy's mother, it was generally considered, had had a hard life, what with losing two babies, a difficult break-up with Katy's father, a retreat into depression, and now being confined to a wheelchair with the fairly rapid onset of multiple sclerosis. Katy, it was further considered, had been a devoted and loyal daughter through these difficult years. In contrast to her older sister Samantha, who had gone through some problem years as a teenager, though she'd turned out all right now, hadn't she, with her marriage to that Marcus Sullivan, seemed like they were making a go of it, unlike so many young marrieds these days, and two lovely kids as well. And wasn't her sister Katy devoted to those two little mites, you were always seeing her with them, round the shopping centre, or in the park with the dog, or at the play area, didn't she babysit them at least twice a week, so's the couple could have their nights out together, it warmed your heart, didn't it, to see a teenager putting her family first - not many you could say that about.

Even to those closest to her, Katy's decision had come as something of a surprise. While they understood, and supported, her need to get away, they wondered if she was quite ready for independence yet. They feared that, away from the closeness of family, she might not find the strength to resist getting sucked into the darker underbelly of teenage life. Or, in contrast, she might get lonely and depressed, trapped in her little flatlet, too scared and shy to venture out and develop a social life. Or that her devotion to her nephew and niece might bring her back home every weekend on the train, her student railcard put to maximum use, so much so that she would have gained little by moving away. And then there was Greg, her dog. They couldn't quite believe Katy's assurance that she'd been told she could have Greg with her at college, that she'd found accommodation where the dog was accepted. Steve, Katy's stepfather, was quite prepared for the possibility that he would have to bring Greg back with him, and to look after the animal in term-time for the three years his stepdaughter was studying. But whatever their doubts, Steve and Sharon, Samantha and Marcus, none of them had said a thing to discourage Katy, and now the day had arrived.

Steve and Marcus decided they'd like to pull in at a service area for a coffee and perhaps a bite to eat, an early lunch.

Hey Marcus, what you doing? We're not there yet! piped up Katy from the back, as the driver pulled into the slip road and braked. It was the first sign that she'd taken any notice of the journey.

We thought we'd stop for a coffee, love, and perhaps a bite of early lunch, said Steve. And let Greg out for a run, he'll be needing it before we get there.

No, Dad, I mean Steve! She stumbled as she grew more distraught, she used to call Steve dad when she was smaller but had refused to do so for many years now, and this was the first

3

sign of inner anxiety she'd shown. We must go straight there, please! I mean, I promised the landlady I'd collect the key before lunch! Greg will be OK, I promise, there's a park near my flat which is miles better for walking him. I mean, service stations are, like, just so gross! For dogs, I mean.

Marcus drove the car straight back onto the motorway. Katy seemed to have been startled by the incident into a more talkative mood, something that was quite rare for her.

It's just a minuscule patch of grass, she went on, apparently intent on a further justification of her intervention. And anyway, the coffee's always gross! And the food! There's good cafés near my flat, I promise. You'll get a much better lunch there. You two can go and find somewhere while I sort out my key and let Greg have a run in the park. You'll like that, Greg, I promise. She now turned her face to the dog and spoke in a quieter, more soothing tone. No service area for you.

I don't know where you've got so much knowledge of service stations from, grumbled Steve, addressing Katy but turning to the driver of the car.

I've been there loads, Steve, you must be suffering memory loss, said Katy, adopting an unusually withering tone. Not just with you and mum, but I've played basketball all over. And there was that marching band, remember, when I was a kid, right?

Steve glanced at Marcus and smiled inwardly to himself. For something like three years between the ages of eleven and fourteen or thereabout, Katy and her best friend Sophie had been inseparable and had dedicated themselves to being the star turns in a local band which had played all over the north of England and won numerous prizes. Katy had played a side-drum which hung from her neck, and Sophie twirled a baton. Sophie, without a doubt, had been the performer, the chief enthusiast, the seeker of accolades, but on the quiet there had been many parents who believed it was Katy's drumming which had got the band their prizes. When Sophie moved away from the area with her foster-parents, Katy had left the band. It had been a hard decision for Sophie, she could have remained in the town and been placed with new foster-parents, but no members of her birth family were in the town any more, and she'd been with this foster-family for some years, so she decided to move with them. She and Katy kept in touch by phone and text message, and met up once or twice. They still were in contact, but much less so now. The interesting thing was that as soon as Sophie had left, Katy had taken down all the rosettes and shields which decorated her bedroom, and put them away in a drawer, and had taken her drum up to the attic, and posters of pop stars, artwork, and her cello, replaced them. On the one occasion when Sophie came back to visit, the drum and the trophies had been temporarily retrieved from their seclusion. Steve was remembering the amusement with which he and Sharon had reflected on this, at the time, four or five years ago. They had not said anything, and Katy rarely, if ever, had mentioned the marching band since, and Sophie only very occasionally.

And of course they had thought, as had many others, but no-one had ever said anything, that it was to replace Sophie that for her fifteenth birthday Katy had insisted on being given a puppy to which she'd become so devoted.

We'd like to have lunch with you, love, said Steve gently as Marcus finally left the motorway. We can wait until you've walked Greg. We can be unloading your stuff first, then we can all have lunch together.

No Steve, I'm gonna unpack the car myself, I promise! Then I can decide where to put everything! Please. Look, I'll just get the key and make you a cup of coffee. I'll walk Greg while you're drinking your coffee, then we can have lunch and I'll unpack the rest of my stuff after lunch.

Safer to get your things out of the car before we go off for lunch, chipped in Marcus. There's valuable stuff in the back there.

There's not. Like, it's all cheap stuff.

Even so, it's not my car and I don't want it broken into.

OK then. But if Greg's in the car then I don't think a thief will wanna break in there somehow.

The university was on the outskirts of the city, a former higher education college which had recently been upgraded. They drove past it and in towards the city centre, with Katy giving clear and careful directions. After an area of large residential houses, they turned off the main road and the houses became smaller, semidetached, and somewhat rundown, though still solid and prosperous enough in their time.

I thought you were near the university, grumbled Steve.

It is near! It's the next street on the left, protested Katy. Look, the park's just over there, and the other side of the park there's the canal and the river which have paths along, so it's a good place for Greg.

And where are these shops and cafés? queried Steve.

They're back on the main road.

I didn't notice them.

We turned off just before we got there. This is it, Marcus! she suddenly shouted, as the car was about to drive past her flat. It's 17, with the bike propped outside. That's my landlady's bike, she added.

I thought you said she didn't live here!

She doesn't, but her house is only about, I dunno, about half a mile away, so she bikes it over.

In fact, Katy allowed the two men to help her unload the car while she waited for her landlady to open up the flat and then for the kettle to boil. They sat on the wall at the front in the sunshine, drinking their coffee, while Katy took Greg to the park, and then they drove the car back to the main road and found a place to eat.

Well I hope you'll be happy, Katy, said Steve rather feebly.

Sure I will.

Phone us soon and let us know how you're doing.

Sure. Give mum my love and tell her not to worry. And Marcus, tell Neil I owe him a million thanks for letting us use his car, and give my love to Sam and loads of hugs and kisses to Lara and Liam.

They'll miss you. And Sam and me'll miss your baby-sitting.

I'll come back and babysit if you need it, like if you can't find no-one else. And I'll do more in the holidays to make up.

OK, I'll hold you to that.

She retrieved Greg from the car, put him on his lead, and they kissed awkwardly before she set off for her new flat, waving frantically as they drove off. Only the dog would have known whether she then allowed a few tears to fall.

She called Sharon and Steve on her mobile within the

week to let them know she was fine, she was settling in, but she seemed to have little specific news for them and didn't want to talk for long. She said she would write, but all she sent were hand-drawn cards for her nephew and niece, they had several weeks to wait, it seemed an age to them, before a letter arrived.

Dear Mum and Steve, everything is fine here, I'm sorry I haven't written, I've been very busy, I think of you a lot but I don't have time for letters. The flat is great, me and the landlady get on fine and she likes Greg. The courses are going OK, sociology is more practical than I expected, I only have one essay this term. I have two art projects to do, and two English essays. I mostly work at weekends apart from lectures and classes. Some lectures are crowded but most are nearly empty. Not many students go to lectures I've discovered, I still go to a few myself, I can tie Greg to the cycle racks outside the lecture hall. Classes you do have to go to, and I have to leave Greg in the flat then, because they can go on over their time. I have six classes a week, two in each subject, every few weeks I have to prepare a topic for a class, you do get some choice, you can sign up for the topics you want, but I didn't put my name down in time, because I couldn't decide what I wanted to do, so I didn't have the choice. I'll know better next term. For my sociology practical I'm helping out at a children's home which is quite near my flat. I got in first on that one, some of the others thought they might have chosen it if I hadn't. It's great but it's hard work. The kids need heaps of attention, I usually go there twice a week. As well as that, I've joined the women's basketball team, we practise one night a week as well as matches every two or three weeks, and a choir and an orchestra. The choir is very good and sings folk music from other countries and things like that, the orchestra's not so good but the music they play is really difficult. So I've got to practise, usually at weekends, and then I try and go running two or three times a week to give Greg some exercise and keep fit myself. He only gets short walks in the week, sometimes I give him a longer walk at weekends. I don't go out much otherwise, but I've made some friends, both men and girls. I invited one friend back - a girl - for a coffee at my flat and I said I'd cook her a meal at a weekend. I don't usually have time to cook in the week. Most students go to the pubs a lot but I don't, I don't know how they have the time.

Lots of them also do blogs, you know, on the internet, I don't know how they have the time to do that either, but I thought, if you got onto the internet, Mum, which you should, because of all the information they have about disability and all that, then I would do a blog which you could read instead of me sending you a letter, so you could find out what I was doing every week. The other thing is I can't find the time to come over to Longworth during term so why don't you come and see me here? It's not that far in the car, and tell Sam and the children to come too. I know there's football for Marcus but Sam can drive now and if she doesn't like driving on the motorway she can come on the other roads, it's a bit slower but not if the motorway's jammed up. Or they could come with you, Sunday morning's the best time and we could have lunch together here. If you want to come, just phone me on my mobile first, it takes messages if I'm busy or I've switched it off. I miss you a lot and want to see you soon, give my love to everyone, ESPECIALLY LIAM AND LARA.

Lots of kisses from Katy.

They didn't get round to arranging a visit. It was the weather, mainly, cold dark mornings and dark nights. In the spring, they thought. Not long after the letter arrived, it seemed Katy's end of term was approaching. She called to say she was coming home on a Friday night, and would be bringing a friend, just to stay the weekend. She would try and bring all the stuff she needed for the holidays but might need to go back for more. Steve said he would come for her but not on a Friday evening. Could she wait until the Saturday? No, she would come by train on the Friday, with her friend. They would walk up from the station. She would call when the train got in.

They thought it might be a boyfriend. They even hoped. She never said much about boys, but then she was inclined to be secretive.

Sharon was expecting them, because Katy had called from the station. She was waiting by the front door to let them in, sitting in the hall chair with her stick by her. Steve hovered in the background. When Sharon opened the door, her mouth fell open. Katy looked the same as ever, with her largest case in her hand and a pack bulging on her back. Beside, or rather slightly behind her, holding Greg on his lead, stood a strange waif-like creature, female undoubtedly, but not like any girl they had seen before, with untidy dirty-blonde hair, a stud in her nose, a large ring in one ear and a small one on her chin.

Aysha, this is my mum and this is Steve, my stepdad. Mum, this is Aysha, my friend from the children's home I help at.

2. THE MERCY OF THE FALLEN

Katy and Aysha would always remember, both of them, how and when they had first met. Or rather not exactly met, but had passed each other by. It had been Katy's first visit to the home, her first evening as a volunteer helper. She hadn't done much helping but she'd been asked a lot of questions about herself, both by children and staff, and been given a lot of information about the home, some of which she'd asked about and more which she hadn't thought to ask but had just been told. And one of the things she'd been told was that one of the kids was missing, and it was much quieter without her because this kid was by some way the most disturbed they had living there.

She's the older sister of that girl you sat next to at tea, who was asking all those questions, and that girl with the mass of dark hair that you thought might be a boy.

How long's she been missing? asked Katy.

Since last night. She goes out most nights and doesn't come back at the time she should. Sometimes she's back late and sometimes she doesn't come in at all. If she's not in by midnight we have to notify the police, and they're out looking for her, but they haven't found her yet today. They know the places she's likely to be, so it's not often she's gone more than 24 hours, sometimes she strolls in of her own accord, sometimes the police bring her back. It's always worse if they do, because she hates the police and makes a big scene and gets in a terrible mood back here, and we have to try and sit on her and make sure she doesn't bunk off again.

How do you stop her?

Well, the doors are locked after nine o'clock so it's a bit harder to get out then. But we're not a secure establishment, we're completely open, kids can come and go as they wish, so we really don't have any redress when we're up against a determined absconder like Aysha. Grounding her would be useless because she wouldn't take any notice and that would make us all look foolish to the other kids. There really isn't any appropriate punishment other than removal to a more secure place, or perhaps the threat of it. We've tried the positive approach, using rewards, trying to build relationships between staff members and her, but she's been here over a year now and none of it seems to be working. She isn't here enough, and when she is, she's actively fighting our attempts to engage. All her relationships are being built on the city's streets, and those are the worst possible relationships as far as we are concerned. Really she should be placed out of the area in somewhere more secure, but there are her two sisters to consider. If it weren't for them she would have been moved on before now, but there is a bond which none of us is wanting to break.

But if she's so close to her sisters why is she out all the time? Don't they miss her, or her miss them?

Well it's not true to say she's out all the time, just at the wrong times and more than she should. She does spend time with her sisters and she can be very protective of them. A lot of the time Aysha's out missing is at night when Charly and Zoë are in their beds fast asleep.

Don't they worry about her? asked Katy.

They seem to be used to it by now.

The rest of the evening had passed uneventfully without further mention of Aysha, and then as Katy was leaving, having put Greg on his lead, she heard a commotion at the front door. Cassie, the care worker who had talked with her earlier, was seeing Katy out and opened the door on two uniformed policewomen who were dragging and restraining a young girl, struggling, swearing and shouting. A third adult woman, not police it would appear, was attempting to talk to the girl and calm her down. The girl was just wearing a thin sleeveless top and a short skirt, inappropriately dressed for a cold October evening, Katy thought, and she couldn't help noticing the tattoos on both her arms.

The girl broke off from her struggle to stare at Katy.

Who's that? she asked, and for a moment her tone seemed less querulous, she seemed genuinely interested, but before Katy could answer the girl had been whisked along the hallway and into the office. Cassie indicated to Katy it was best that she and Greg leave.

The second time Katy visited she decided to leave Greg at her flat. She was worried that the staff at the home hadn't really wanted a dog in the house and had only asked her to bring him in out of some sort of politeness or generosity. But there was such disappointment among all the children, especially the younger ones, that she had to, with the blessing of the staff, promise she would bring him next time and if possible on all subsequent visits. She did not see Aysha on this second visit, strangely, said Cassie who was again in charge that day, the girl had not gone missing this time but was on an outing with her educational unit. She normally could be relied on to not turn up at the unit if the school day was going to be longer than the minimum.

The third time Katy went was on a Friday after school. Tea at the children's home was half an hour earlier on a Friday, it had been explained to her, because some children would be going home for the weekend, some having an evening out with friends, relatives, social workers or volunteer befrienders such as Katy. So she had to rush after her college class to collect Greg and then get to the children's home in time for tea. It was warm and still light and the sun was beginning to blaze orange low in the west, so Katy tied up Greg by the bike rack, knowing the children's tea would have already started and not wishing to cause a distraction in the middle of the meal. She explained this to them all as she found her place, found some food and sat down, promising to bring Greg inside as soon as the meal was over. But in less than five minutes Greg appeared in the room, panting frantically and pulling in behind him the girl Katy had just caught the briefest glimpse of on her first visit, Aysha.

I had to bring him in, miss, there was some kids gonna let him off his lead.

Oh, well, thanks, Aysha, said Katy, momentarily caught by surprise, a little embarrassed and confused. But in her con-

11

fusion she was quick to notice there was no place set for Aysha. The children's meals were served on two tables which were placed at right-angles to the kitchen hatch. Each table was set for six children, three down each side (there were twelve children in the home) and one adult at the end facing the hatch and therefore also facing the two doors in the room, the door on the right of the hatch into the kitchen and to the left of the hatch into the reception area, that being the door Aysha had just entered. But on both tables there were six kids, and Katy realised that on the table where Aysha's two sisters were sitting, and where Teresa, who was one of the two staff on duty tonight, presided, one of the older boys must have brought a friend, unless there had been a new admission, for there were three older boys sitting next to one another instead of the usual two.

Taking all this in as she jumped up to rescue Greg from Aysha, she moved her chair across.

You sit next to me, Aysha, I'll make an extra space. I'll just put Greg over here and then I'll get you some tea.

She gave the girl her chair, settled Greg in a corner, and pulled another chair over to the table, seemingly all in one movement. She then went to the hatch, found a plate, cutlery, drinking glass.

There's shepherd's pie, vegetables, gravy. You want all that?

Just vegetables. And lots of gravy.

Are you vegetarian?

Nah. Just don't like shepherd's pie.

Do you want some mashed potato off the top?

Yeah!

So it's just the mince you don't like?

That's it, miss.

You want a cup of tea? Or glass of water? Or both?

Just water.

Katy brought the girl her plate of tea, poured her a glass of water, and sat down next to her to continue her own meal. Before starting eating, Aysha took off her jacket and hung it over the back of her chair, revealing her bare arms not just with their tattoos, Katy could see now, but full of scratches and old half-healed scars.

Well, Aysha, you've got the royal treatment today, interjected Teresa from the other table. You're not used to this, are you? What do you say to Miss Owen?

Thanks, miss, Aysha mumbled inaudibly as she tucked hungrily into her food. She certainly seemed a little bemused by the situation, and kept glancing at the other kids, as if unsure how they would react to her being given a privileged position, clearly something she wasn't used to.

Don't call me miss, Aysha, call me Katy. That's my name, Katy Owen. I'm a student, I've just started helping out here.

How d'you know my name, miss, I mean Katy?

Well, the first two times I came here you weren't here, the first time you'd run away and the second time you were on a school trip, so I heard about you then.

Not school, miss, it's a unit. Pupil referral unit. For bad kids like me.

I'm sure you're not bad, just a troubled kid.

Did you see them policewomen bringing me back in?

I did, yes. I was just leaving at the same time.

I know, I seen you. Didn't you think I were bad then?

No. I thought your life must be terrible, like in turmoil. All over the place.

Their chairs were touching, squeezed together at the end of the table. Katy could feel the child inching herself nearer without ever making physical contact. She could sense the thin body got up like a teenager but still a child, with its tensed-up energy beginning to thaw just a fraction, she could sense the rapid pulsing of Aysha's skin, she could feel something tingling on her own skin also.

So who were these kids then, Aysha? persisted Teresa. These kids outside, who were they?

I dunno. Just kids.

It was probably just her imagination, but Katy felt some kind of enhanced mood had just been broken.

Were they the kids you know from the estate?

No.

Well, it's funny they should turn up outside at the same time as you.

Aysha did not deign to answer this, but just shrugged her shoulders.

You know those kids are not supposed to come round here. You know you're not allowed to see them. It isn't us so much as the neighbours round here. If they complain too much about undesirable teenagers hanging around, we might get closed down.

I don't care if you do, retorted Aysha under her breath but loud enough for Katy to hear.

Katy was getting the picture. With hardly any sanctions they could impose for Aysha's aberrant behaviour, the staff here had resorted to verbal sparring, a kind of determination to keep one step up on her, not let her grind them down. It made sense really in terms of maintaining their credibility with the other kids as well as their own sense of confidence, but what was it doing to Aysha? Katy felt she might have crossed over some unspoken boundary by having Aysha sit next to her at the head of the table and by giving her a free choice of food. Maybe such unorthodox initiatives would be seriously frowned on, a black mark on her eventual report.

In fact, none of the staff called her to account over the incident, and later, thinking back, it seemed to Katy that it was that moment at the children's home, sitting the child next to her and in particular offering her just the potato from the shepherd's pie, which had brought them close together.

After the meal was finished, Aysha hung around, seemingly not sure what to do with herself, while Katy and two of the children did the washing-up. When they had finished Aysha had vanished, and Katy got involved in playing dominoes with a few of the younger children including Aysha's sister Zoë. After a few rounds, Katy noticed that Aysha had sidled up and was watching them play.

D'you want to join in? she asked her.

Nah. I was thinking, miss, like -

Katy.

Katy. Aysha put her face right up against Katy's. D'you wanna see my room? she whispered.

Yeah, I would. Very much. But only after we've finished playing dominoes. Look, why don't you join in?

Cos I dunno how to play, miss, I mean Katy.

Why don't you join in with your sister? She's good, you can learn off her.

Can't I play with you, miss, I'll learn better off of you.

Charly's best at games, out of us three, said the wide-eyed, dark-haired Zoë.

Where is Charly? asked Katy. D'you want to find her and ask her to join in?

She's listening to her music in her room, said Aysha. She likes being on her own, right.

OK, you play with me then, Aysha.

Again she felt the ticking fuse of the young girl's body close to hers, as she tried to explain each domino piece she played, and why.

It's Zoë's bedtime now, Aysha announced after they'd played two more rounds.

No it ain't! It ain't, Katy, not on Fridays, I promise you! complained the younger girl. I'm allowed half an hour longer on Fridays.

When's we gonna finish then? I wanna show Katy my room.

Just be patient, Aysha. Here, you take my place. See if you can play without my help.

Bet you I can't. I just know I'll lose.

Well, give it a try. I'll sit right behind you if you need help. Katy drew up another chair.

Aysha kept turning to Katy during the next game, despite every encouragement not to, but after that she managed to play without help, and soon went out first, amazed that she had won a round.

Right, we'll stop there, said Katy. I've got to go soon and I've promised to see Aysha's room first.

I'm sorry for you, miss, said another of the girls who'd been playing.

Why?

Seeing Aysha's room. It's a terrible sight, miss.

Fuck off, Poll, exclaimed Aysha angrily, grabbing the other girl's wrist and twisting it behind her back.

Ow, ow! You let go of me, you!

Aysha! Stop that, or I won't see your room after all, said Katy, alarmed, feeling that the tensed up fuse of the girl was

15

starting to blow.

Sorry, Katy. Aysha let go at once, but seemed a little dubious at having done so.

Any problems here? Teresa had heard Polly's shout and appeared in the room.

It's OK, said Katy. Aysha's just going to show me her room now and then I'll have to go, so could you look after these other kids? Thanks, I'll come again on Sunday.

She went with Aysha and found a room with dark curtains and a black bed-cover, and mostly covered with posters of 'goth' or death-metal bands. There was a chest of drawers - the only item of furniture besides the bed - with various nick-knacks and accessories on the top, and a CD player with a small pile of CDs by the bed. Some clothes were strewn on the bed, and others had been piled, somewhat hastily it appeared, alongside the chest of drawers. The room was neither over-tidy nor desperately untidy, and Katy commented on that.

The posters are interesting too, like expressing your personality or something. Not my taste in music, though.

Why, what d'you like, miss, I mean Katy?

I dunno, like ordinary pop music, charts and stuff. Retro stuff, soul, world music.

Charly likes world music. And indie rock.

Does she? I also like some classical. I play in an orchestra, not a very good one, and sing in a choir. It's good fun.

D'you really, miss?

Katy.

I keep forgetting your name, no I don't really. Aysha gave a little giggle, the first time Katy had experienced even a smile from her. Katy?

Yes?

Can I take your dog for a walk?

Well, not now -

No, I mean, like some time, either with you or me on my own.

If you took him on your own, how do I know you won't bunk off?

No, I promise I won't. If I were gonna bunk off, like I wouldn't take Greg then, would I, right?

OK, but maybe the first time I'd better come with you

so's Greg can get to know you a bit better first. And I guess I'll need to check it out with someone first.

They won't mind, miss, I mean Katy, as long as I'm keeping out of trouble and not bothering no-one, they don't like me much so they wants me out of their hair.

Oh really, well, I tell you what, I'm coming for tea on Sunday so why don't I come earlier in the afternoon and we could walk Greg together. I've invited a friend over for lunch so I can't come earlier than about two-thirty, so I'll see you then. Sunday, ok?

Yeah, miss - you going home now?

I'm gonna have a run with Greg first, he needs some exercise, so do I. Then end up at my flat - but let's find Greg, we left him sitting under the dominoes table, but we may need to look for him.

Ain't it dangerous, running in the dark?

Not so much when there's a dog with you.

Is that why you wears a track-suit?

Yes, well, sort of, I just like track-suits, right. Now I need to find my track-suit top, and I'll see you Sunday, Aysha.

I'll find your top, miss, and I'll find Greg for you.

Katy had arranged to cook lunch for a girl from her art course, Briony, a slightly weird-looking girl in bright-coloured clothes who, Katy thought, was actually rather shyer than she at first seemed. She decided on a chicken stir-fry, and called Briony on her mobile asking if she could make it a bit earlier than first arranged, so that she could go out after lunch. After a light breakfast and a short walk with Greg in autumnal sunshine filtering through mist, she practised her cello for half an hour - there was no way she could get stuck into course-work, and then started preparing the lunch.

She'd got in a pack of beers but no wine, thinking that Briony might bring wine, but all the time she was thinking of Aysha, and all her decisions, like should she drink beer, or wine, or neither - she had fruit-juice in as well - were based on what would be best for later that afternoon. The thought of walking Greg with the girl was inexplicably thrilling for her, and however hard she tried to concentrate on the lunch, and entertaining

17

Briony, she could only think of getting out of her flat soon after two, and heading to the children's home. Thinking about the Friday evening, she was sure when Aysha disappeared she had gone to tidy her room before asking Katy to see it.

As Aysha had suggested, the staff were only too happy for her to be outdoors with Katy for the afternoon, and so they headed off for the canal and thence the countryside on the city's edge. For such a slight person, Aysha walked well and was happy to hold Greg on his lead, pulling him back whenever he got too energetic. At first they both seemed a little embarrassed, and what talk there was seemed stiff and disjointed, with Katy commenting on places she'd noticed when she'd walked this way before, and Aysha admitting that the only places in the city she knew were one or two of the roughest estates and 'down the city centre'.

I thought you were from this city, said Katy.

Yeah, I was, but like I were moved around a lot when I were a kid.

Katy wanted to ask her more about this, but Aysha seemed reluctant to say more, and Katy couldn't find the words to help her open up. It was Aysha who finally found the opening to a more meaningful conversation, but not so much about herself.

I didn't think you was gonna come today. I were ready to bunk off if you didn't.

Why would I not turn up?

Cos you had a friend coming for lunch and I thought that must be your boyfriend and so you'd wanna stay with him the rest of the day. Or even if it weren't your boyfriend you'd, like, get talking and be late.

Well, it wasn't my boyfriend, it was a girl from my art course and we did our talking before and during lunch.

Is you good at art, Katy?

Not very, I just enjoy painting.

So does my sister Charly. Has you got a boyfriend, miss?

No.

Why not?

I dunno really, I never met a boy I liked enough.

Has you never, like, been with a boy?

Well, I've been out with boys quite a few times. I've been kissed now and again. But I'm still a virgin, if that's what you mean. She blushed as she said this, acutely aware that she had probably transgressed some rule about how much of your personal life should be revealed to a child in one's charge.

Aysha looked at her wide-eyed. All the teenage kids I knows has done it, she said.

Including you?

I ain't a teenager yet -

Aren't you?

Nah, not til December. But why don't you like boys?

I do, I do, well sort of, I mean I'm not a lezzie or anything, Katy protested but was beginning to doubt her own protestations. I've just never been keen on going out with boys. I like doing things, me, and boys just wanna hang around pubs and stuff. To me, that's like a waste of space and time but if a boy asked me to go out with him to do something interesting and he was, like, cool and hunky, then that's different. But it hardly ever happens.

So what's, like, the best thing to do on your date?

Oh, I dunno, go to a film maybe, or even better a concert, a gig, I like music, or play tennis, or go running or something.

Or take your dog for a walk?

Yeah, of course. Any boyfriend, or any friend at all, would have to like Greg.

I like Greg. I don't like sports, but I do like going to gigs. But I hardly ever goes cos I ain't got no-one to go with.

I could take you some time.

That would be cool, miss.

I used to have this best friend, went on Katy. She was called Sophie and she was in care too, but different from you cos she was fostered. Long-term. We did things together and went everywhere. When we was about, like, thirteen and a half, we started going to gigs, maybe once every two weeks. Sometimes we went with my older sister Sam, other times my stepdad would take us or Sophie's foster-dad, but they wouldn't go in, they'd wait outside, or go home and the other one would come and collect us. Oh Aysha, that was the biggest fun ever, and I think that's why I never had a boyfriend cos it would never be the same as me and Sophie. I don't hardly ever talk about her now.

What happened to her?

She moved away, with her foster-family. She didn't have to, but that's what she chose. I wanted her to move in with us, but my mum had just been diagnosed with multiple sclerosis, so no-one thought we'd be allowed to foster her. So she moved away, up to Scotland.

Why did they go up there?

Cos her foster-dad moved his job. He worked in a prison, he got a better job.

He worked in a prison?

Yeah, well someone has to, don't they, and it's kinda, like, well paid. He never talked much about his work to me or Sophie but what he did say was, you'd never ever wanna go there.

Did he work in a women's prison?

No, but he had been in women's prisons, he knew about them too. And he said prisons were terrible places with violence and drugs and horrible people and you could never get away from it.

The magistrates would've sent me to prison, y'know, only I were too young. So I had to stay in a children's home instead.

Well, thank your lucky stars.

So is that why you're like such a good girl cos you's been too scared to get into trouble?

Well, I dunno, that's one reason perhaps, but there's probably lots of others.

What's the other reasons?

Well, like I would never wanna disappoint my mum cos she's had a hard life. An' my nephew and niece, I love them to bits and I couldn't bear the thought that I was gonna become a bad example to them -

D'you think I'm a bad example to my sisters? Cos I loves them to bits too.

I know you do. Katy realised she'd said the wrong thing. And I don't think you're a bad example cos it's just your way of trying to deal with your life.

But ain't that the same for you? Like, has you never got drunk or took drugs or stuff?

No, never, I mean I've had a few drinks now and again but I never got drunk cos it seems so, like, pointless or something, and I never took drugs.

But if you did, that would be just your way of dealing with life like you said for me.

No, it wouldn't, that wouldn't be me, I've turned out a certain way and I'd be letting down the people I love the most if I acted different.

Aysha turned away, looking sad or maybe cross, Katy couldn't quite tell. The younger girl called to the dog and picked up a stick for him to chase. They were beyond the edge of town now, walking through woodland, the leaves half off the trees with a few more floating down, sunlight filtering through. Aysha was ahead, wearing a black jumper, creamy-white short skirt, black tights. She was chasing around with Greg and had removed her jumper and tied it round her waist. As usual, she just had a thin top with shoulder-straps underneath, and the sunlight flashed on her scarred arms and her tattoos, Katy could see, including one on the top of her back, she noticed for the first time, a skull with the words HELL to the left of it, and RULES to the right. On one arm was a serpent, on the other a scorpion. She was tumbling and playing with Greg, who was licking Aysha's arms and face excitedly, and Katy reflected on how good Aysha was with the dog, and how Greg was oblivious of Aysha's physical idiosyncrasies or her troubled history. The picture of Aysha moving in and out of the filtering sun ahead, the strange beauty of it, Katy knew would stay with her for ages, and that she loved this girl, as she hadn't loved anyone for years, not sexually, not a physical thing, but like a younger sister or even as a child of her own.

But Aysha now turned to face the waiting Katy, and something in her look made Katy rush forward to her.

What is it? What is it?

It ain't no good.

What isn't?

I never thought I'd like someone like you.

What d'you mean?

Like, a nice girl like you. A good girl. None of my other mates is good. They's always in trouble like me. And I bet that Sophie were a nice girl like you, right. And you come round here

21

to our place looking for another kid in care to replace your Sophie and all you find is a bad kid like me, right.

Aysha, Aysha, that's not true, never! It's ages since Sophie went away, but I've got over that, and I'm not trying to replace her, I promise! I do want to help kids in care, that's true, and I know we're very different in lots of ways, but I like you, I really do, I mean, I would never have expected it either, but it doesn't matter about, like, you being in trouble so much, I still like you.

Even if I stay bad, would you still like me?

Yes.

Cos I ain't sure I can ever change now. Like, I think it's too late for me.

It's never too late. You're so good with Greg, I can see the good in you.

Aysha clutched her arm.

We'd better turn back, or we'll be late for tea, said Katy.

Come on here, Greg! called Aysha. I love coming out here, she said. I never ever thought I would like coming out in the country like this. I'll tell Charly and Zoë.

Perhaps they could come another time. What do they like doing when they're not in school or at the home?

I dunno, really. They both like going on trips with staff. Like swimming and stuff. 'Specially swimming. Zoë does dance at school, she loves that. Charly likes reading and listening to music, she reads books about wildlife, and outer space and, like, prehistoric stuff and all that - what d'you call them?

Science? Non-fiction?

Yeah, non-fiction.

And what about you?

Nothing me. 'Part from music, I'd love going to gigs!

Don't you like going on the trips? Or swimming?

Nah, I hates all that. She turned and showed her bare arms to Katy. How can I go swimming with these? Everyone would stare.

But you don't mind showing them in the home?

That's different, that's like saying to the rest of them, look at me, remember I'm trouble. But in a swimming-pool, I'd hate it, it would just be so embarrassing.

And you went on the trip last week with your education

unit?

Yeah, that took them all by surprise, that did. Look, Katy, can you come to my open day at the referral unit?

Well, I can try. Katy felt an unexpected thrill at being asked. When is it?

I dunno. It's coming soon, I'll find out when.

If I can fit it in round my classes, I'll come.

Good.

I think it's gonna rain soon, said Katy, pointing to dark clouds building up in the west. We'd better hurry on back. Aren't you cold?

Nah.

Best get Greg on his lead now.

I'll do it, miss. Give me his lead.

OK. Try and remember to call me Katy. I hate being called miss.

OK, Katy! You mad with me, Katy?

No, of course not. They both laughed as they hurried on to beat the rain.

3. LIFE'S OTHER SIDE

Katy tried to go to the children's home three times a week. She tried not to miss Aysha on the other days. She tried not to let her feelings for the girl affect the rest of her life. She knew she should not get too emotionally involved, but thought she probably already was, and the important thing was not to let her feelings show, not to Aysha or to anyone else.

She bought music papers and looked up gigs. The college had a few, every now and then, but she felt a strange reluctance to take Aysha to one of those. Better to go out of town, as long as there was transport back. She got hold of all the bus and train timetables. It would have to be a Friday or Saturday night, for sure. A lot of the bands listed she'd never heard of, she wondered if Aysha would have. The child's taste in music was way different from hers. Should she give Aysha the choice, and risk going to some terrible gig full of head-bangers with violent music and lyrics that she, Katy, couldn't stand. In the end she made a list which included two chart bands playing at big venues within reach, and three unknowns but whose names did not suggest they would be too dire.

Now and again she was selected for the women's basketball team matches on a Saturday. There was an away match coming up, and that meant leaving Greg in her flat for several hours, most of the day in fact. Should she ask if Aysha could look after Greg while she was away? She was sure Aysha would be willing, but what about the staff at the home? No harm in asking, she thought.

So she went to the home a little earlier the next visit, skipping a not very important lecture and hoping to get to speak to whoever was in charge that afternoon before the kids got in from school. But it seemed Cassie had the same idea.

Come into the office a minute, Katy, she said.

Her heart sank. She would be told she was getting too involved, that she'd better not come any more, that she wasn't suitable for working with children. Already she'd begun to realise she didn't have what the rest of the staff had to help them deal with the kids, which was a kind of brazenness, a projection of personality, an extroversion bordering on charisma. All she had was her quietness, her steadiness, her patience, a little insight, perhaps a little potential for empathy, and her dog. It wouldn't be seen as enough.

We've been very impressed with how you've knuckled down here, interacting with the kids on their level, Cassie was saying. Most of all, we're really encouraged with how you've begun to befriend Aysha, to offer her the possibility of a meaningful relationship with an adult. It's something, as you know, that we've been in despair over, her absolute refusal to relate to any of us at all, and while she's still a load of trouble to us at times, there are clear signs of some improvement in her since you've started coming. I do hope you can carry on with your commitment, for all our sakes, not just Aysha.

Don't worry, I won't stop coming. I'm gonna try and come three times a week, and in the holidays except when I'm visiting my family.

Good. Well, there's one thing come up which I need to

ask you. Are you familiar with life-story books?

No.

All the children in long-term care, and over half the children here are long-term, should have a life-story book. It's theirs, they own it, they do it themselves, but with help from an adult, usually their keyworker here or their social worker or both. It's to help them remember and make sense of what is often a very confusing childhood. All the children here have one, more or less completed up to date.

She paused.

Except, of course, Aysha. If there's one kid who really needs one, it's her, but in typical anti-authority attitude, she's always refused point-blank to start one, I'm sure just for the hell of it. But we regularly ask her, and lo and behold, perhaps you can guess what's coming next?

I think so. She wants me to do it with her.

Absolutely. She suddenly seems keen, provided you'll do it.

Of course I will. Katy felt an immense thrill. But I haven't a clue where to start.

You'll have to read her files, the one here and the one at the social worker's office, and probably talk to Aysha's social worker, who's known her a few years, since before she came here. And you'll need to look at one or two of the other children's life-story books, to get some idea. The best place to start would probably be her sister Charlotte's since I don't think she would mind you looking, and obviously they share a lot of history, but you'll have to bear in mind Charlotte started hers over a year ago, soon after she arrived, when she was only nine, although quite a grown-up nine in many ways.

Just like Aysha's very grown-up for not quite thirteen.

Yes, it seems growing up too fast's an occupational hazard of damaging childhoods. So you'll need to phone Aysha's social worker, Ruth Barnes, here's her number, went on Cassie, scribbling it down. Of course she's social worker for Charly and Zoë as well. Charly keeps her life-story book in her room, most of the kids don't, but she does, so I'll have to ask her for it.

There were a couple of things I was wanting to ask you, said Katy.

Fire ahead.

First of all, I was wondering if I could ask Aysha to look after my dog Greg on Saturday when I'm playing in a basketball match away from home. She's very good with Greg, and I thought it would be good to give her some responsibility.

Sounds a good idea in theory, but how would it work? I don't think you should trust her in your flat on her own yet.

No, I was thinking of bringing Greg here and Aysha looking after him here. She could give him quite a long walk so you wouldn't have to put up with a dog on the premises for much of the time. If one or both of her sisters wanted to go along as well, that would be fine with me. And I'll feed him before I set off, so there's no need to bother about that, I'll just bring his lead and his water bowl. I'm sure Aysha will be fine with him, but I'll go out with her again this week first, just to make sure.

Have you said anything to Aysha yet?

No, I thought I'd better ask you first. And the next thing is, Aysha wants me to go to her education unit's open day, and I said yes as long as you agreed, and it didn't clash with anything important for me.

When is that?

I don't know, but soon. Aysha's finding out for me. And there was one other thing.

What's that?

We were discussing what else we could do together as well as walking my dog, and we thought maybe I could take her to a gig. A music gig. It's one of the few interests we share.

Isn't she a bit young?

Well, not for the music gigs I've been to. I started going when I was thirteen with a friend, and at most I've been to there's been even younger kids than that. When my friend moved away I went with my sister sometimes, or another kid from my school, or sometimes on my own. I was lucky living near Manchester where there's loads of venues.

Well, ok, let's say yes to the open day, no problem there I'm sure. About having the dog here on Saturday, I think I need to speak to whichever of the staff are on duty that day before I give an answer, so don't say anything to Aysha yet. And I think I need to think about, or consult someone, about music gigs before I give a clear yes, although I agree it seems a good idea as long as Aysha's behaviour warrants it.

Aysha's open day was in two weeks. Katy arranged to go for lunch and the afternoon, as she had a morning English class. In the meantime, she phoned up the social worker and arranged to meet her at the children's home on the Friday before her afternoon class. On the Wednesday, having been given the go-ahead for both the music gig and the dog-minding, she arranged to meet Aysha straight from being dropped off by her unit minibus, and they again walked Greg together for an hour before tea. As she anticipated, Aysha was thrilled to be able to go to a gig, and at being asked to look after Greg.

Now you must let Charly and Zoë help out, right, if they want to. Including taking him for a walk.

I'm gonna take him for two walks, Katy, one in the morning and one in the afternoon. One I'll do on my own, the other with one of my sisters. Or both, if they wants. It depends on what else they're doing on Saturday.

Well, don't give up completely what you would be doing. If you've got homework, or want to listen to music, or read, or watch TV, Greg will be happy to sit quietly with you. He's good like that.

Yeah, I know. But apart from listening to music, there's nothing I like to do. Saturdays is dead boring. I never does homework, I know I should, but I never does.

How much do you get from the unit?

Well, they've stopped bothering giving me any cos I never does it.

Well, we'll have to look into that when I go to the open day.

Fucking hell, Katy, that's not what I asked you for!

I know, I'm going as your friend, not as a parent or social worker or anything, but as your friend, we need to discuss homework. And after tea we need to discuss going to a gig next week and decide which, so's I can book tickets.

Yeah, yeah, she brightened a little but still grumbled.

Katy met Ruth Barnes, who was not the social worker she had seen with Aysha on that first encounter but an older woman in her fifties, seemingly harrassed and stressed. She rushed in with Aysha's file, shook hands and apologised that she was in between two urgent appointments, and asked Katy to phone her next week, Tuesday would be the best day.

Katy asked Cassie if Charly had agreed to loan her life-story book for her to look at.

Yes, she has, it's here somewhere.

Well, I'll look at that first rather than the files. Then you can give it back to Charly.

Also she had a strange reluctance to look at the files for fear of what she might find there. And although she had talked to Aysha about agreeing to start the life-story book, Aysha had seemed a little reluctant to be pinned down, so no starting-date had been arranged, nor details of what it would entail. She didn't want to look into the files without Aysha's clear knowledge and agreement.

Aysha wandered through the outskirts of the city with Greg on his lead. In the morning she'd taken him out with Charly and Zoë as well, but that was only to the park. Now it was just her and she had the afternoon to herself. She decided to walk the same route she walked with Katy the previous week. Why? Because she wanted to remember. She kept remembering Katy's words, You're so good with Greg, I can see the good in you. No-one had said that to her before. OK, loads of bastards like shrinks and psychologists had tried to make out there was good in her, somewhere hidden inside, that all the bad stuff was just her act-ing out stuff from her childhood, but that was a load of crap, it were no good saying she were good if they couldn't see it, if all they saw was bad like all the grown-ups ever in her life. Katy was the first who liked her as she were, who saw good in her now. Katy trusted her to look after Greg for a whole day, so she must like her. She were gonna stay out as long as she could, it weren't gonna matter if it got dark or if she were late for tea, as long as she got back by quarter past six when Katy said she should get back to the home. She must be there then, it would be awful if Katy thought anything had happened to her or Greg.

Aysha wanted to go round the estate and see her mates. She could get some ciggies, smoke a bit of weed, drink some lager, get a kick from being there like she always did. She hadn't got no money but she had mates who might help her nick some or give her some if she nicked something for them. She hadn't been round the estate or down the city centre for quite a few days and she wanted to go again soon. She didn't want them calling her a fucking stranger. But they might laugh at her or ask awkward questions if she took Greg. Or they might treat Greg badly and she'd hate that. Or she might not be able to get away in time. Or worse the fuzz might raid the estate, they was always doing that. They knew her and the bastards wouldn't believe it were legit for her to be in charge of a dog. They'd put her in a fucking cell at the nick like they'd done loads of times before. She hated it at first but she'd stopped caring now. The first time she were only nine and her social worker had to tell the police they weren't allowed to lock her up, they'd had to take her back to her foster-home that she hated so she'd just bunked straight off again. In the end they moved her to another foster-home where she weren't with her sisters so she'd run off from there back to the first one. Another time she'd smuggled a razorblade into the cell and slit her wrists. They had to call an ambulance and take her to hospital. They brought Charly and Zoë to see her in hospital the next day. She felt bad then but when she did it she remembered not caring if she died. She hated the fucking cells but she couldn't stop doing the things that got her put there. She kept going down the estate or the city centre and getting into punch-ups or bigger gang fights. It gave her a kick but it were scary too. There was drugs, there was knives, even guns sometimes. Guns really scared her. The police was always coming round, and one time she were given a gun during a police raid. That really did shit-scare her, having that cold metal in her hand, she didn't know if it were loaded or not. The guy what gave it her told her what address to take it to, he must've thought they wouldn't stop a girl her age but he must've not known how well the police knew her. She were scared what she'd do if the police did stop her, would she point it at them and be in heaps more trouble than even she'd ever been in before, or would she pull the trigger by mistake and shoot someone? She kept it under her jacket, holding it careful as she could, it seemed miles and miles to the flat she'd been told but she got it there without being stopped and weren't she relieved to hand it over. Knives was more common than guns and more than once she'd had hold of a knife. If you were in a big fight you needed a knife to defend yourself. But once the police nicked her in a gang-fight with a knife on her, and weren't she in mega trouble then? She were locked in a cell overnight and taken to court. But when her lawyer told the magistrates she'd only been lent the knife to defend herself and never used it and never would've, which were more or less true 'part from the last bit, they let her off with an absolute discharge for possession of a weapon.

Why were she thinking of all this now? She tried never to think 'bout the past, most of all when she were really little, she were never ever gonna think 'bout even less talk 'bout any of that no matter what any of them shrinks and psychologists and social workers kept saying.

She were just trying to tell herself how it were better taking Greg where she were taking him now, instead of the estate. She never thought she'd like the country better, but having a dog with you made you see things different. Aysha tried to think good thoughts. Freedom! She let Greg off his lead, they were on the canal bank now. She were more free here than down town or on the estate. No cops around for one thing. Freedom! Greg were running off ahead then coming back. Freedom! She took off her jacket and whirled it above her head. It nearly flew out of her hand and landed in the water. Greg got excited and tried to jump up for it. No Greg this ain't for you, I'll find you a stick soon, she said to the dog, trying to calm him down a bit. It was cloudy and windy and cold, but she didn't mind. She'd got used to sleeping out and never felt the cold any more. There she was, thinking bad thoughts again, sleeping on park benches or down the underpass with the drunks and homeless old men and bag ladies, she hated that and they didn't like her much either, said the police always came around and gave them aggro if there were a child sleeping with them. She never stopped out in winter any more unless she could kip at a mate's place, summer it were different, she could wander around the city all night or smoke ciggies and drink a few cans of lager on Green Common or in St Mary's Park, the only park in the city which were open all night, but the police usually looked there first and found her.

She liked the feel of the wind on her arms, she were in the woods now and she found sticks for Greg to chase. She kept whirling her jacket round her head like that were the only way she could believe she were free. There was no-one here to see the scars on her arms. She never thought she'd like being out in the country on her own. She'd be scared if it weren't for Greg.

Suppose she met a perv or a rapist or murderer, would Greg protect her? Katy said when she went running at night, having a dog were good protection. She tried to keep thinking of Katy. They were gonna go to a gig. A band called Test Icicles. Katy hadn't heard of them but she, Aysha, had. It were their name. Katy hadn't got it. She bet Katy would be shocked, but there you were, she needed to learn a few things. Life weren't as sweet or innocent as Katy thought. She liked Katy all right, but she needed to harden her up a bit, a gig would be a good way to start. She would drink a beer or two. Or lager. That would shock Katy too, but it were only what she did with her mates. She would tell Katy she wouldn't need to go down the estate so much if she could get some booze at a gig. Katy were gonna start this life-story with her. She'd already lent Charly's so she must already've found out some stuff. Aysha didn't mind Katy knowing more about her, what had happened when she were littler, but what she were scared of were having to talk about it, even with Katy. Well, perhaps she did mind her knowing in case Katy weren't gonna like her no more once she found out her past, she didn't know what she wanted, she were all mixed up, but Katy'd said she were gonna like her whatever bad stuff were in her life so perhaps she'd just gotta trust her. Charly said did she like Katy? She said yeah, she were kinda OK. Zoë said she liked her too. Charly said Katy must like her, Aysha, or she wouldn't't've trusted her with Greg all day.

Aysha knew many of the streets of the city and thought she was pretty good at finding her way, and all she had to do was turn round and go back the way she came, and anyway she'd been here before. But woods was different. She'd hardly ever been in woods before and she thought there were only one path in these woods but there was lots. And you couldn't see where the woods stopped. She began to think she must be lost. The wind was getting up stronger and making a howling noise through the trees. She saw two people up ahead with another dog which Greg chased after and played around with. Aysha put her jacket back on so they wouldn't see her scars but she was still too embarrassed to ask the way. She turned down a different path and called Greg after her. The trees were creaking and groaning and it looked like it were starting to get dark. The wind felt rougher and colder. She got to feeling quite scared in a fun sort of way and she needed a pee. She went behind a tree and then called Greg again. She thought maybe Greg would know his way back. She said to him, go home Greg and I'll run after. She got Greg to run ahead and she followed, running. She never liked running but she loved it now. Greg kept stopping for her to catch up. She said it again, Lead on Greg and set him to run ahead. Then she'd catch up. They came to the edge of the wood and she could see the canal ahead in the fading light. She knew which way to go down the canal because she could see the lights of the city in the distance. But all the bridges over the canal looked the same and she hoped Greg would know which one to cross over by. Then she thought Greg might take her home to Katy's flat instead of the children's home, but she let him lead on, over a canal bridge until they came onto a lit road on the city's edge. Now she knew where she was, and put Greg on his lead to follow her. Half way back to the home she stopped to hug him and let him lick her face. You're a very good dog, she said, slightly embarrassed even though she was on her own, but less than she would have been if she'd waited to praise him until they got back.

Katy took Aysha to the gig, and found she'd had her hair done up in something like an afro.

Where did you get that?

At my unit. They have a hair salon room, it's the only way they get most of the girls to go regular, some of the boys too. If you've gone every day for a week you can go in on a Tuesday, if you've gone for two weeks you can have a Friday, did you know I've had full attendance for two weeks? That's the first time ever.

Good.

D'you like it?

Very much. It's certainly different. Makes you look older. Although I'd never have thought you were still twelve, even before.

She wore a black jumper, faded blue denim skirt and black tights. In the gig she took off her jumper and wrapped it round her waist. She didn't seem to mind her scars showing but then, it was quite gloomy in there. Katy wore a green peasant-style dress, nearly ankle-length, and a cream jacket, and since it was in a smallish club-like venue and was hot and stuffy in there, she envied Aysha being able to wrap her top garment round her waist while Katy had to carry her jacket over her arm as there didn't appear to be a cloakroom for coats. The main band, the Test Icicles, were noisy and disjointed but produced occasional snatches of brilliant instrumental work. Before them there were two support bands who were quieter and more nerdish, one had a girl singer with a wispyish voice, the other played numbers which had more instrumental work than vocals in them. Katy liked these earlier bands better but the one on second had a struggle to be heard as the crowd were getting restless for the main attraction, and the Test Icicles certainly had the ability to whip up fervour in the audience.

Half-way through the first set, Aysha wanted a drink of beer or lager, and Katy refused.

Sorry, it's gotta be Pepsi or lemonade or something.

No way! I ain't drinking kids' stuff! I must have a beer, Katy! I'll go mad if I don't!

What, are you addicted or something?

No I ain't addicted. But I'll run away before we get back and go down the estate where I've got mates will give me a beer. And I'll be in a foul mood the rest of tonight. You don't know me yet, Katy, and if you did, you'd let me have a beer.

It's because I know you I'm not letting you have one.

Oh come on, you know I ain't been down town in Burs-field for what, two weeks or more, nor round the estates, and you know why, it's cos of you, cos you've been good to me but you gotta let me have a beer now, or a lager, cos I've been thinking you would, like you'd carry on being kind, and helping me and all that.

It doesn't mean I won't keep on helping you.

It does though, cos for me like, what's the good of help, what's the good of coming to a gig like this if I can't have a proper drink.

Non-alcoholic drinks are proper drinks too.

But Katy's quiet resistance was not having the desired effect, she could see Aysha's disappointment was causing her to get more and more worked up and threatening a real rift between them. Aysha had turned away but there was smouldering anger and resentment there, Katy could tell, and something in her heart gave in.

OK, Aysha, she took hold of the girl and turned to face her. I'll let you have one beer. Only one.

Oh thanks. Aysha brightened at once. You have one too, Katy.

No, I won't, I'm not feeling like one tonight.

Oh, go on.

No, but you go and get yours before the bar gets too packed out. Do you need money?

Yeah, but like, you've gotta go and get the beer, Katy. They won't serve me, I don't look that old.

Oh my god! Katy regretted at once having given in. But there was nothing to it now but to fight her way to the bar, having asked Aysha what she should get.

Lager, and get a pint, Katy, then we can share it. A big glass. I'll wait right here.

I told you I didn't want any.

However, she thought sharing some beer might be the best way of keeping Aysha quiet. There was no way she would agree to go to the bar again. So she bought two bottles of lager and two medium-sized plastic glasses and returned to the waiting girl just as the first act was finishing.

Good one, Katy. Aysha immediately took a large swig. Now Katy noticed she had lit up. There were no smoking signs scattered around the walls of the venue but nobody seemed to be taking any notice of them, and the bar staff did not seem bothered. Nevertheless, Katy was even more worried, as this was the first time Aysha had smoked in front of her, she was concerned about what the staff at the home would think if she returned the child with booze and tobacco on her breath, or worse, what other substance was in her roll-up?

Aysha appeared to have sensed her anxiety. Don't worry, Katy, it's only a normal roll-up, she said, waving the lighted end in front of her. Like, just tobacco, right.

Aysha was now on a high, and Katy felt on a downer, as though she had relinquished control to this unpredictable, maverick twelve year old. She took a sip of the lager and that made it worse.

Ugh! This stuff is vile.

It ain't. Aysha took a much bigger swig. It's quite strong, but that's wicked.

It isn't its strength, it just tastes gross.

It's prob'ly the glass, advised Aysha. They leaves the soap in sometimes. Here, try my glass.

That's no better. How d'you know they leave the soap in?

I just do. Not just gigs like this, bars and stuff they do. Everyone knows that.

In fact these were plastic beakers off a clean stack, and Katy knew, or thought she did, that it was unlikely these plastic things would get washed and re-used, but she decided to let Aysha have her head tonight. She was acting like the one in charge, the one in the know, and that was OK for once. Still, Katy couldn't drink this vile stuff.

Sorry, I can't drink this.

That's cool. I'll drink yours.

She gave Katy a look of such wicked complicity that the older girl felt drawn in despite everything. Was this the way to relate to a kid like Aysha? Her rational mind should be telling her no but her heart was saying yes.

OK, but if anyone asks, I bought the beer and let you have one or two sips. They might smell it on your breath, you see. Beer and smoke.

They won't, I promise.

Where've those roll-ups come from?

In here. Aysha pointed to the pocket in her denim skirt.

How many more've you got?

Just one more. I'll light that one up when The Testicles come on. She grinned complicitly at Katy again.

The Test Icicles?

Yeah. That's what I meant.

Where d'you get the smokes?

Oh, from mates on the unit or on the estate.

Katy felt pulled along onto her own high by the spirit-edness and complicity of the younger girl. She did her best to enjoy the music even though The Test Icicles, which was the band Aysha was clearly most into, were difficult to Katy's ears.

They had to run to catch the last train back to Bursfield. Flopping down onto adjacent seats, they laughed like a pair of naughty sisters.

What a wicked night!

Who did you like best?

Test Icicles were, like, total!

Total what?

Just total!

I liked the second band best, but you could hardly hear them for all the noise of the crowd.

What were wrong with Testicles?

Nothing much but I thought the good music in them was in battle with their need to make noise, and the noise won.

But that's what good gigs is about, the noise winning!

Not all gigs, I'll take you to one where the noise doesn't win.

When?

When I can find one, December or January.

That's ages off!

Well, they won't pay for us to go to a gig every week!

Can you pay for some eats? I'm famished, complained Aysha, loudly. Ain't there a fucking trolley on this train?

Shush! I don't think so, not this time of night.

Will the café at the station be open?

That's unlikely too. Won't they give you some food when we get back?

Nah, I don't want their food, no way.

Anyway we can't really stop for food, it's way past your bedtime. She grinned at Aysha, realising she'd said a foolish thing. Bedtime was not a word in Aysha's vocabulary.

Fuck that! I needs some eats!

And remember I need to get back to Greg. He's been sitting in my flat on his own all this time.

Oh yeah, sorry, but I still need food. If we pass a chip-shop that's open, can we go in? I can eat them on the way back.

Yeah, of course, as long as you'll let me have a few.

Yeah, we can share them. It's your money.

What d'you do about money? Don't you have pocket-money of your own?

Nah, if I needs money I nick something or go round one of my mates on the estate and scrounge some.

What d'you have to do to scrounge some?

Nothing mostly. Sometimes do an errand with some, y'know -

Drugs?

Aysha shrugged her shoulders.

What about pocket money from the home?

Nah, that gets all taken, nearly all, in comp, what d'you call it? Compensation. From fucking court, for damage.

Damage?

Yeah, criminal damage, they got me on that.

What did you criminally damage?

The fucking custody desk at the nick. They took me there when I ain't done nothing at all, just for the hell of it, and I just blew a fuse. I picked up a chair and smashed their computer screen and then threw the chair at a window. Hard. The window didn't smash but it kinda cracked. And buckled. And the chair broke. So they got me on criminal damage when they'd brought me there with no other fucking charge they could bring. And that's a big lot of money, a window and a computer and a chair. Like, it's gonna take me mosta the rest of my life to pay off that. So you see why there ain't too much point in being good?

I can see how annoying that is. But it was rather stupid when they would've had to let you go anyhow.

Yeah, but they wasn't gonna, was they? They was gonna lock me in their fucking cell. And anyhow, they can't expect me to always think first, not when I'm only twelve. Like, it's just exploding inside so how'm I expected to think first?

OK, so it's me paying for the foreseeable future.

Don't you claim it back?

For the gig and the train fare, yes. But I can't claim for late night chips and even less for beer.

Aysha grinned at her.

Remember what we agreed. I bought a beer and let you have a few sips.

A few days later Katy went for lunch at Aysha's education unit. Aysha was waiting for her and she was greeted warmly by the teacher in charge, and then found herself in a dining area where a buffet lunch had been provided. Katy felt a bit out of place as she glanced round. There weren't many people eating, but there were a couple of teenagers clearly with parents, three others in a group among themselves, and the remainder of the people in the room were obviously professionals, teachers, social workers, psychologists. Katy felt out of place in either category, but Aysha didn't seem to mind.

The teachers wanna meet you, Katy.

The one in charge came up while she and Aysha were eating lunch. Has Aysha offered you a cup of coffee? Or tea?

Could I have a black coffee?

Run along to the machine, Aysha, your lunch won't walk away.

The change in Aysha is unbelievable, she went on straight away as the girl sprinted off. She says it's since you came into her life. She hasn't missed one day, and has worked conscientiously all the time she's here. Of course we still get bad language, insolence, and flashes of temper, but it wouldn't be Aysha if we didn't, and the point is not only are these occurring more infrequently, but they're over in a flash and she's back to her work, whereas before, any incident involving Aysha would last the whole day and throw everyone here out of kilter.

What work is she doing now? asked Katy as Aysha returned with her coffee.

Well, she wants to show you the work she's done in recent weeks. Big improvements in reading and writing. Projects on the local environment, involving science and history. You've found it quite interesting, haven't you, Aysha, whereas you never used to take much interest.

Aysha looked tongue-tied.

How would you describe your work before this big improvement?

Aysha shrugged her shoulders. Bad.

To say patchy would be expressing it kindly. But we all know you can do it, Aysha, you're an intelligent person, and it's amazing when you think how much school you've missed through truanting, suspensions and other factors, that you're not too far behind in your basic skills.

Aysha hung her head.

Can we discuss homework for her later this afternoon? asked Katy.

Shut up, Katy.

We can discuss it now if you like. I'm likely to be occupied with other visitors most of the afternoon.

Well, can we bring the rest of our lunch into your office? I think we should be somewhere more private.

No, I'll tell you what, you both finish your lunches and then come and find me. Bring in another coffee by all means, and one for me too. And after our discussion Aysha can show you some of her work.

She seems nice, said Katy.

Why d'you have to ask 'bout homework?

I told you I would.

But Aysha's protest only appeared to be a token one. She readily agreed to do two pieces of homework a week for the rest of this term, and then three next term. That brought up another issue from the teacher.

Aysha, I may be jumping the gun here, but have you thought about trying to reintegrate into mainstream school before you start GCSEs?

No.

Well, do start thinking about it. Because it's much easier to start in September than any other time, and if you thought next September might be possible, we'll need to start working on it very soon.

What d'you mean, working on it?

Meeting a teacher from the school, looking at the work you've been doing here and what they're doing at the school, and trying to bridge the gap.

I ain't wearing a school uniform, said Aysha defiantly. No way, right! It would have to be a school that don't go in for uniforms.

Most schools have uniforms but some are more strict than others about it.

Well I'd only go to the one that's, like, totally unstrict.

These are the things we need to be thinking about, said the teacher.

I'll talk to Aysha about this before the end of term, said Katy.

Good. Now show Katy your work, Aysha.

Katy felt more comfortable in many ways in this situation with Aysha than she had at the gig. But thinking about it, she decided that what happened at the gig was just as important a part of their relationship, possibly more so.

Katy tried to give some time to her own life. When she went to the children's home she tried to spend time with other children and not just Aysha. She made a decision that she had to get home as soon as term ended, or she would find herself caught up in Bursfield for ever. Aysha would have to accept her being away visiting her family for a few days at least. She found there was a Richard Thompson gig in Bursfield the week before Christmas. He was one of her favourites. She booked two tickets before telling Aysha, and when they arrived she knew that meant she'd have to spend some time between end-of-term and Christmas back in her adopted city.

Meanwhile she also tried to spend some of her available spare daytime hours at the home when the children were at school, so she could look through Aysha's social work file without distraction. She was prepared to find some pretty awful stuff, but she couldn't help be shocked by some things. For instance, soon after Aysha had arrived at the children's home, she'd gone round the nearby council estate on a Sunday rounding up a posse of younger children, who'd then gatecrashed a church on the edge of the local park, disrupting the service which was taking place and causing mayhem. She'd been taken to court for this, and made subject to an ASBO (which seemed appropriate and justified, Katy thought) for a year forbidding her to associate with any of those children or go within a hundred yards of the church. She appeared to have kept to this, even though she'd been in court since that time on a number of occasions - for resisting arrest, possession of a knife, theft, and the criminal damage episode she'd talked to Katy about last week. The ASBO had expired a month before Katy met her. There were reports of a number of suspensions from her primary school from the age of eight, until she'd first gone to an education referral unit at the age of ten. At the first unit she'd gone to, she'd stolen a knife and climbed onto the roof of the building on a cold January day, threatening to slash her wrists if anyone approached. She'd stayed up there all day, and only came down when everyone else had gone home. She had never yet attended a mainstream secondary school, and from what she was reading, Katy doubted if any secondary head would be willing to take her. She had twice made suicide attempts, or gestures at least, once when she was nine in a foster-home when she'd gone into the foster-parents' bedroom which they normally locked but on this occasion had forgotten to, and found paracetamol tablets which she'd over-dosed on. Fortunately the foster-mother was in and called an ambulance in time. The second time she'd smuggled a razor blade in her shoe when she was locked in a police cell, and slashed her wrists, and on this occasion she risked bleeding to death, as it was only by chance that they checked the cell soon after she did it. This was when she was eleven.

But it was the earlier, chronologically, parts of the file which concerned Katy the most. She found that after Aysha and Charly's father had died, social services had first become in-volved because their mother, a known drug user, was attempting to look after them on her own, and they were considered "at risk". They first came into foster-care during this period when their mother was in hospital having overdosed on heroin. Aysha was four and three quarters at this point and Charly just two. Soon after this Zoë's father, a serial child abuser who had changed his name after his most recent prison sentence, came on the scene and it appeared started abusing the two girls, both physically and sexually, once their mother became pregnant with Zoë, but it was ages before this was picked up. The two older girls came into foster-care again and were put on care orders, but they were returned to their mother once her relationship with Zoë's father appeared to have terminated and she claimed she was no longer using drugs. She then moved away from Bursfield and changed her name, started living with Zoë's father again and the abuse recommenced. She was also getting more and more into criminality at this point, dealing as well as using heroin. Again it was some time before the authorities picked up the child abuse, but finally all three girls were brought back to Bursfield and placed in foster-care, with Zoë also on a care order this time. Not long after this their mother went to prison for the first time, and had spent all but a few months of her life since that time, behind bars.

This was in 1999 when Aysha was seven and a half, Charly nearly five and Zoë two and a quarter, and it could have marked a turnaround in their lives, the start of a period of stability. But unfortunately all three girls were too emotionally and behaviour-ally disturbed at this time for the foster-parents they were placed with to cope with the three of them at once, and frequent breakdowns occurred, with the girls having to be moved several times. At only one foster-home was an extended commitment made allowing the girls to stay for over six months and for Zoë and Charly to achieve a period of stability, but Aysha seemed determined to sabotage this placement by continual absconding and outbursts of violence towards her foster-parents (though not her sisters or foster-siblings), leading eventually to Social Services placing Aysha on her own in a different foster-home. This however caused even more serious disruptions to all three girls and led to their eventual placement in the home where they were now. Recent reports on the file concluded that neither Aysha nor Charly were ready to be considered for family placement at present, and that it was difficult to envisage how Aysha was ever going to be. Referral of Aysha to a Secure Unit for placement there was frequently discussed but up to now deferred in order to try and keep the girls together.

Katy tried to take all this in, to hold onto the detail in some rational part of her mind, when the overwhelming effect it had on her was to make her want to reach out to Aysha, to hold her tight, to cry for her, cry Aysha's tears as well as her own, to never let her go. When she put the file down, she had to sit for several minutes to recover herself before she could face seeing anyone.

But later, when she went back in her mind through what she had read, she realised that she couldn't start Aysha's life-story yet, and it wasn't just all the pain lurking behind the stark facts in the file that made it impossible, though that was a real difficulty. There had been no mention of sexual abuse in Charly's life-story - how much of this trauma should one leave out? But most of all, what should have glared out from the file but probably didn't because of all the other harrowing detail, was the lack of any information about Aysha's early childhood until she was four.

She tackled Cassie about this the next time she saw her.

How can I start this life-story when I can't find any information about Aysha's birth and early years. Surely we have to start there?

Ideally, yes. But you just have to go on what information you've got. There should be a birth certificate somewhere, in a separate envelope in the filing cabinet. Or maybe it's a copy, but still, it should have the basic info on her birth. But her mother's the only other possible source for those years, her father being dead.

Well, maybe I need to go and visit the mother in prison.

Are you sure you'd want to do that?

Anything that would help Aysha make sense of her life. Do the girls still go and visit her ever?

Not for ages. I think Zoë would, given the choice, but the other two are adamant they won't, and I'm not sure Zoë should go on her own.

The rest of November flew past and although she saw Aysha frequently Katy found no chance to even think about this further, let alone talk to the girl about her past. At the beginning of December, with her term drawing to a close, she received a surprise message on her mobile from Ruth Barnes, Aysha's social worker.

She called Ruth back as quickly as she could, fearful that something awful had happened to Aysha.

Can we talk for a few minutes? said the social worker, a little hesitantly.

Yes, is Aysha all right? gulped Katy in one breath.

She's fine. We've provisionally set up a meeting next week which we'd like you to come to, but we haven't told Aysha yet.

Why not?

It's about her future, where she's going to live. You probably know that the children's home want to move her on. She's wasting a valuable place because they're not helping her in any way, and there are other children on the waiting list who could make better use of the place, one in particular who's desperate for a placement there.

But - surely - where will they put her, and what about her sisters? Katy's heart was sinking fast.

What would you think about suggesting she comes to live with you?

Katy gulped. She needed to sit down. Her heart had

sunk into her ribs and now it bounced back up as though she'd almost been given an electric shock. She felt dizzy with both astonishment and something close to elation.

Of course she can. I'd be really pleased to give her a home.

Well, there's a lot to think about and discuss before we can finalise a decision. That's why we're having this meeting. You'll need to consider your accommodation, and how it will affect your studies, and we would need to fast-track approving you as a carer and take up police and health checks. But I hope you can see our thinking, it would free up a place, it would keep Aysha in Bursfield and in close contact with her sisters, and most of all it would keep her in the community, we none of us want to lock her away in a secure unit, but we've been despairing of finding any alternative. Your arrival has given us that possible option.

What will happen to Charly and Zoë?

For the moment they'll stay where they are, but we need close and regular contact, with a view to reuniting them as soon as possible.

With me?

If it all works out and circumstances allow it.

Whose idea was it?

Well, it was Aysha that asked, actually. She asked one of the staff at the home, and they said she would have to ask you direct and get permission from me, but Cassie then contacted me because she thought it was worth exploring and we set up this provisional meeting - so Aysha hasn't said anything to you?

Not a thing, but I'm sure she would do. She was probably trying to pluck up courage. She's easily intimidated about some things, surprisingly, but on the other hand she's also impatient to get answers.

Yes, she is, and that's why we haven't said anything to her yet, and we won't do until the evening before the meeting, in case you change your mind when you've given it some thought.

I won't change my mind.

Well I needed to run it past you and let you consider it before we went ahead with the meeting. If you'd ruled it out straight away we'd have cancelled the meeting without Aysha knowing and things would have carried on as they are while we thought again.

And she might have gone to a secure unit.

Possibly.

Even though she's made big improvements.

That's got a lot to do with our approach to you now. Much of the improvement is down to you.

It's not, it's down to Aysha herself. When is this meeting?

Next Tuesday or Wednesday, to fit in with your schedule.

Well, term will have almost finished. Tuesday afternoon will be fine.

Good, let's say two-thirty. Remember this is just exploratory discussion at present, there's no commitment on either side until we've discussed it more fully. We may not even reach a decision next week. Have you finished with the file, by the way?

Oh yes, over a week ago. I left it with Cassie for you to collect, didn't she tell you?

I think she might have left me a message, I've been very busy.

Do you have Aysha's birth certificate? I couldn't see it on the file.

Yes, it's in my filing cabinet. Do you need it now?

Yes, I want to see it before I start the life-story work.

Oh yes, well Katy, you don't mind me calling you Katy do you? - there is something I need to tell you.

What's that? Katy's heart was suddenly sinking again.

According to her birth certificate, Aysha's birth father was different from the man she thought of as father. He was the father only to Charlotte.

Why has no-one told Aysha this?

There never seemed the need. It would upset her even more and that was the last thing anyone wanted.

Did she never want to see her birth certificate?

Not as far as I'm aware.

So how come she's been constantly encouraged to start a life-story book under this - this misapprehension?

Well, the staff at the home don't know, there's really no need, but you're right, it was up to me, I should have said something before that work started.

It's Aysha who should be told.

Perhaps I should tell her at the meeting.

No I'll tell her, said Katy. Let me have the birth certificate, then I can show her.

Katy came away from that conversation amazed at her
new-found assertiveness. She would never have spoken like that
to a professional before now. Aysha must be having a good
effect on me as well as me on her, she thought. She knew how
protective she was feeling towards the girl, how determined she
was to be an effective advocate for her, and that was shaping her
approach. But she also told herself to be careful in front of Aysha. The last thing she needed to do was to turn Aysha against
her social worker even more than she was now.

The following Monday Katy obtained the birth certificate and
went round to the children's home to join them for tea. Monday
was her orchestra evening and it was the final rehearsal before a
concert performance the following Monday, so she would have
to leave straight after tea to drop Greg back at her flat, pick up
her cello and get to her rehearsal. She had decided that the following day she would take Aysha to visit her flat and have lunch
there before the meeting. That would give her the chance to talk
in private about the information on her birth certificate and the
need for Katy to visit Aysha's mother. Now was about letting the
child know about tomorrow's meeting which she did as soon as
she saw her.

There's a meeting tomorrow which we've both gotta be
at. You'll have to have the day off from the unit.

Yeah, I know. About me coming to live with you.

How did you know?

Charly heard one of the staff talking and she told me.

Right, well that is what it's about, but nothing's been
decided yet.

But you've said yes, right.

I'd be very happy for you to come and live with me. But
there's a lot to sort out. I have to be approved as a foster-carer
first which can take some time although they've said they'll do it
as fast as they can, and there's my studies, and stuff like that, and

then there's Charly and Zoë and plans for them, anyway, all these questions are for looking at tomorrow, but what I wanted to ask was if you could come to my place for lunch tomorrow before the meeting so's you can see my flat.

Aysha looked a little taken by surprise. But how'm I gonna find my way?

No, no, I'll come for you here. I've got my last sociology class in the morning but then I'll collect Greg, come on here and we can walk back with Greg through the park. I'll get some lunch ready before I go to my class. Are you ok with that?

Yeah, sure thing.

Good. Well, since I'll be seeing plenty of you tomorrow, can I spend some time with the other kids? D'you wanna take Greg for a short walk on your own before tea?

'Course I will, right.

But you must be back for tea, right!

Katy wanted to spend some time with Zoë and perhaps one or two of the other younger children. But as soon as Aysha had gone, she was cornered by two of the older teenage girls, Stacey and Donna. Katy got on better with the younger children usually, indeed there was no child older than Aysha with whom she had formed any rapport, and certainly not these two.

Is it true Aysha's gonna move in with you? Stacey asked.

Nothing's been decided yet. But we're discussing it.

Well, we think we should warn you, miss. You don't know what Aysha's like, said Donna.

And we do know her, went on Stacey. And she's taking you for a ride, miss.

You's too soft on her, said Donna. You'll let her walk all over you.

No I won't, protested Katy. I know her better than you think, and I can be as tough as anyone in dealing with someone like Aysha.

The two girls looked at each other.

That ain't what Aysha says, said Stacey. We weren't gonna say this, but it's Aysha what says you're a soft touch.

Oh come on, I'm no pushover.

Well, how come you bought her a beer then? went on Donna. She's still twelve and she got you to buy her a beer.

No, all I did was let her have a couple of sips of mine.

That's not what she says, said Stacey. We don't mean no harm, miss, but we think it's only fair to warn you about a kid like Aysha. You're too new to this, you ain't had the experience to stop her running rings round you.

You're too nice, miss, for a kid like her.

Well, thanks for the warning, I'll keep all this in mind.

She was devastated, and she had to struggle really hard not to show it. She was that close to fleeing the home and never coming back to it, indeed she might have done if Aysha hadn't been out somewhere in the fading light with her dog. She fought back tears and couldn't think straight. But she knew there must be some truth in what the girls had said to her, though how much truth she couldn't be sure. She wasn't equipped to deal with a damaged kid like Aysha. She was too nice, too sensitive, too easily led. But what was worst was that Aysha had betrayed her. She had told these two hateful girls about what had happened at the gig. It had been their special secret that had bound them in complicity, and Aysha had failed to honour it. A seed of mistrust, of hardness, had been sown in Katy's heart. She was not sure if she could ever feel quite the same feelings for Aysha again.

She got a grip on herself before the children's tea was served. She let nothing show, not to Aysha, who brought Greg back on time, or to any of the other children. She went off to her rehearsal and played her cello better, more forcefully, than she ever had before. But later, after she'd got into bed, she cried and cried for the loss of something beautiful and fine which had now become tarnished and ordinary.

In the cold light of morning, and it was a cold morning, the ground gleaming white with frost, Katy found her perspective had changed. She still had the deep desire to see Aysha, to be with her. She was still looking forward immensely to bringing her back to the flat for lunch. She was up early, preparing the lunch, wrapped up in many layers over her pyjamas for the flat's heating was not the greatest, before she showered, dressed and ate her breakfast.

She even began to see that those girls had done her a

favour. She had been too idealistic about Aysha and the relationship between them. She was only beginning to realise just how damaged the girl was, and from a kid like Aysha, consistency, loyalty and trust were an unrealistic expectation. She couldn't give any because she'd never received any, and it was her, Katy, who had to show those qualities if she were to see Aysha through. How many more let-downs, many of much greater import than spreading the story of Katy's purchase of beer for her, were there bound to be over the years if she stuck with Aysha, as she was determined to do. No, she thought as she set off to her sociology class through the bright and still frosty morning, the important thing was that she loved this girl and would stand by her whatever happened, because no-one else ever had. She felt surprisingly strong.

She walked Greg to the children's home, and took a longer route back with Aysha along the canal and through the park, where she stopped to talk.

Listen, what have you been saying about you and me?

Nothing.

Donna and Stacey were telling me you thought I was a pushover.

They's lying, miss - Katy.

She shuffled, turned away, and began calling Greg.

So how come they know about the beer I bought you?

It was lager -

I don't care what it was, the fact is you're too young to drink and nobody should've known about this, especially other kids at the home.

But they all knows I drinks beer, even the staff knows too.

But we agreed, did we not, that we would both say you'd just had a sip of mine.

Aysha shrugged her familiar infuriating gesture by which she had no need to actually say the words "so what" or "I couldn't care less". She seemed to be quivering more than shivering, stood still in her thin clothes in the cold of the morning like a dog just dying to be given the signal to rush off, to chase around. Katy went to face her, holding her shoulders. Aysha's eyes appeared to have glazed over in order to avoid direct contact, but Katy looked right into them all the same.

Listen, I'm gonna make this work, I'm totally committed, right.

Make what work?

You and me, coming to live with me and all that.

So?

You've gotta help me make it work, I can't do it without your help.

I will help, I promise.

Good. There's gonna be lots of mistakes from both of us -

I can't be good all the time.

I know you can't, nobody can, but especially not you. But if I'm crap at looking after you, they're not gonna approve me, d'you understand. They won't let you move in.

You ain't crap at looking after me.

But if you tell people I bought you a bottle of lager they might think so. It were a stupid thing to do.

The staff doesn't know.

How can you be sure those two girls ain't gonna go snitching on you?

They's just jealous, that's all, protested Aysha. They kept going on and on at me, they did, calling me names, making out how dumb I were hanging out with a posh kid like you -

Posh? Me?

Y'know, what with being at college and all that.

If you wanna know, I'm the first one from my family to go to uni. OK, Steve my stepdad is a teacher, or rather was, cos he just does evening classes now, but my mum and my real dad are both, like, solid working class. One granddad was a car mechanic and the other worked in a factory.

Yeah, well it weren't me that called you posh, right, Katy. It were them two girls just having a fit of jealousy and going on at me. I never said you were a soft touch, I just said you weren't hard like the staff and you'd let me get what I wanted and I did say 'bout the beer yeah and I know I shouldn't but they got me worked up, right, and it just came out.

Ok, let's hope it doesn't make them turn me down as a carer.

It won't, will it? Aysha suddenly seemed agonised. It'd better not, right, or I'll throw a fit right in that meeting. Like, you never knew 'bout being my carer when we was at that gig.

That's not the point, I had responsibility for you that evening and I acted irresponsibly.

They can't expect you to act responsible all the time. Like, not on a night out, right. I mean, that's what I likes 'bout you, Katy, you ain't like staff, you'll let us kids have fun.

I'm sure the staff let you have fun.

Not my sort of fun they doesn't.

Well maybe you need to change your idea of fun.

No way, Katy.

Anyhow you go off and play with Greg and get yourself warmed up a bit. The dog had been chasing off after other dogs but kept returning to the two girls pleading for some fun with them. I'm going to that entrance over there, went on Katy, pointing. I'll wait for you there if you haven't already caught me up. My flat's only a few yards from there.

Why were Stacey and Donna jealous anyhow? she asked when Aysha and Greg caught her up.

I dunno. Aysha shrugged. Cos I get on well with you and they wish they did, right. They can't see why you should've picked out the worst kid in the place for your, like, special friend. And when they finds out I might be leaving to, y'know, live at your place then that makes it worse, I mean for them it does, cos they wants to leave and they knows the staff wants kids to leave cos there's other kids waiting, an' when it's me, the baddest kid in the place who leaves first, I mean, they's bound to feel bad, right. But it's their own stupid faults cos they both could've got out of that place by now right. Donna were gonna go back home but she goes for like a weekend's trial, and the first night she has this huge fight with her mum, and her dad brings her straight back. And then Stacey, right, she made it up that her stepfather had, like, interfered with her cos she wanted to split him and her mum up -

How do you know she made that up?

Cos she said she did, right, when she decided she wanted to go home after all cos her mum and stepdad had stayed together. But of course they wouldn't have her back after that, y'know, in case she said it again, and you can't expect any foster-dad to want her either, so she's stuck at the home. And even at the home, right, there's a rule that none of the men must be on their own with her. But they found a foster-carer for her, a woman on her own like you but older, but Stacey wouldn't go, said she hated her.

How do you know all this?

Oh well, kids tell each other things, and sometimes I hears or Charly tells me stuff she hears. You gotta keep your ears open in a place like that, right. Everyone's desperate to know what's going down. Like, whenever I'd bunked off and got brought back, it was like, where've you been an' who've you been with and how did they find you and that's staff as well as the other kids, all wanting to know. But don't tell anyone I'm saying all this, right, Katy.

No, I get the picture. But going back to Stacey, I mean suppose she was being, like, abused by her stepfather? I mean, that's tragic right, that in the end she retracts it cos her mum don't believe her, nor anyone else, and now no-one will trust her alone with a bloke.

Now don't start taking her side as well, Katy. You've taken on more than enough with me.

I know, I know, and I don't regret it one bit. They were in her flat now, and Katy broke off from putting lunch on her table, to look Aysha in the eye. Welcome to my flat, kid.

She'd made several rolls that morning, had bought a cream-cake and some fruit at the weekend. She put out plates and knives. Sit down and help yourself to some lunch.

Aysha ate hungrily, she always did. She was making up for meals missed during her abscondings, Katy thought. Her thin frame needed a bit more padding out, her breasts were beginning to develop. Katy had assumed she'd reached puberty because in most ways she looked and behaved like an adolescent, but she would need to check with Aysha before she moved in. She didn't seem to have much to wear, wore the same clothes most of the time, and nothing very warm. There were a lot of questions to ask but they would have to wait.

How d'you like my flat? she asked.

It's great.

Would you be happy in somewhere as small as this?

Course I would.

D'you think you might get bored? There's not much to do, no-one else around besides me.

Who lives in the other flats?

I don't know them, older single people who go out to work.

Well I like being with you so I won't get bored. I like talking and going for walks and we could go to gigs sometimes.

We could, but only now and again, like one a month, right. And remember, I've got my studies and other things I like to do some evenings.

Yeah, I know, you plays the cello and sings in a choir and plays basketball.

And I have to do college work in the evening, like after you'd gone to bed. I mean, I could get some of it done in the day-time while you're at the unit, but I might have to do some at night.

I'd take Greg for a walk every day so you wouldn't have to so much.

Yeah, that would be a help. But I like taking him for walks or runs myself sometimes but you could come with me.

That's like, even better. But I ain't ever gone in for running.

You could learn. It's pretty easy.

What else would you find to do here? Katy added after a pause.

Homework. Listening to music. I could brush and comb Greg. And do the washing-up.

Yeah, good, but brushing Greg would need to be done outside, in the back garden. And by the way, there's strictly no smoking in the flat. I won't stop you smoking but you'd have to go outside.

Yeah, that's cool, I could light up when I go to the park with Greg.

You could, but try and be discreet about it.

What's that mean?

Don't advertise the fact you're smoking, in case anyone complains about your age. D'you read books or magazines?

Not much.

I've got a drum at home. Would you like to learn drumming?

Yeah, cool!

It's not drums like they have in rock-bands, it's what's

called a side-drum like they have in marching-bands. Katy mimed how it worked. I used to be in a marching-band with my friend Sophie, and I played the drum, but I play the cello now instead. But I could show you how to play the drum, and if you got good at it we could see whether there was money to buy proper drums, cos the principle's the same.

That sounds wicked, but wouldn't the neighbours object to the noise?

Not in the daytime when they're out at work, if you practised soon after getting back from your unit, cos you always seem to get back early, right?

Yeah, we only have one class in the afternoon.

It's funny, we're talking like it's already been decided when the meeting's still to come. I only wanted you to see the flat in case you said, no way, I ain't moving to that dump.

It's the home what's the dump. This flat's great after that place.

OK, here's some juice, while I have a cup of coffee. Now there's one more thing I need to mention. Here. She produced Aysha's birth certificate. D'you know what this is?

Aysha studied it for a moment.

It's a birth certificate?

D'you know whose?

She studied it again.

Mine. How d'you get this, Katy?

I wanted to see it for starting your life-story work. I asked Ruth, your social worker. She let me have it. Have you seen it before?

Nah, don't think so.

Well, read it carefully, look at the names.

She studied it again, time and time again.

Can you read your father's name?

It's got my name, and my mother's name.

Can you read your mother's name?

Janine Estelle Stanton. That's her all right.

What about your father?

I can't read it, Katy. You read it.

Milton Orlando Jewell, it says.

Yeah, that's why my middle name's Jewel. I remember my mam telling me once.

That's not the name of Charly's dad, is it? Or Zoë's?

Nah, Charly's dad's dead, that were Kenny, Kenny Harrison. And Zoë's dad's in prison. I think. I hope.

Did you know you had a different dad from Charly?

No, Kenny were like my dad when I were little. When he died it were like I lost my own dad. But I think my mum did tell me once he weren't my real dad. But I never knew who my real dad was, and anyhow, like I kinda stopped thinking about all that family stuff right? I mean, apart from my sisters. But mum and dad, never. Once my dad died, that were it.

Except he weren't your dad.

But he were the only person before you come along who treated me right. Like, who was good to me.

But what we've gotta take on board is, you've got a dad, this Milton Orlando Jewell, who might well be still alive.

Well I don't wanna go to him, Katy. I wanna stay living with you.

I know. I don't mean live with him. But if we could find him, you could start seeing him.

But he might make me move in.

Not likely. By the time we've found him, you'll be at least fourteen, and you'd have more say about where you wanna live. I mean, you've got some say, even now.

How d'you know it would take so long?

Cos I don't even know where to start just now. But what I was gonna say is, none of us knows much about the first two or three years of your life, apart from the names. So how's about I go and visit your mum in prison and see if she can fill in a bit more detail from those years.

I don't think it's worth it. She's been out of it from heroin for ages.

Well, she'll be off heroin now, and being cleaned out may have helped recover some of her memories.

I wouldn't be so sure, said Aysha. There's lots of prisons where drugs gets smuggled in.

Another reason to never get sent there. D'you ever wanna visit your mum in prison?

Nah, never. I hates her.

Why?

Cos they used to write to her and tell her how we was

getting on, all three of us. And she would write back, but then when I started getting, like, in loads of trouble, she stopped writing. She didn't write to any of us no more. I hate her for that cos it made me feel bad like I were the reason she stopped writing, and it just made me badder. Badder and madder.

Because you wanted to punish her?

Yeah, well, that were one reason, Katy, but like you said there were loads of reasons why you turned out good, there's loads of reasons why I went bad. Bad to worse.

I'm sure you're right. D'you know the other reasons?

Nah. Well, one of them's the way people went on at me. That made me worse, right. You're the first one that don't do that.

So I can't persuade you to go and see your mother, then, right? But what about Charly and Zoë? If I went to the prison would they want to come too?

Zoë might. But why d'you have to go at all?

Well, first of all, if there's major change to your life, she will need to know. Now I -

What d'you mean, major change?

Moving in with me, right.

Oh yeah.

We could just write to her, but I'm sure she'd prefer for me to go in person to tell her, so she can meet me. And I think she might be willing to co-operate in giving more information to start your life-story book, even something which might help us start looking for this Milton guy.

My real dad?

Yeah.

If you think she'll co-operate, you don't know her.

Of course I don't know her, and I'll need to ask Social Services but I think it's worth the effort.

If they say yes when'll you go?

I guess I could go the first week of next term because my college probably will start a week later than you so I won't have much to do that week.

But Charly and Zoë will be at school that week. Anyhow if you wanna talk to our mum I don't think you should take any of us kids with you.

But maybe I could offer to take one or more of you the next time, like, just in a spirit of co-operation. But I can't understand why Social Services haven't tried to contact your real father before.

They prob'ly didn't know.

Well, they only had to look at your birth certificate.

So when did you get hold of this? Aysha queried.

Yesterday.

So you only found out my real dad's name yesterday?

Yeah. But I did know you had a different dad at the end of last week, when Ruth Barnes phoned me about the meeting tomorrow and I asked to see the certificate. She told me then, but I said I wanted to have the certificate in front of me before I told you.

Oh.

Look, we'd better get moving or we'll be late for this meeting.

They both became very nervous as they got to the home and turned to each other in mutual anxiety. Katy tried to encourage Aysha who clearly felt very uncomfortable. There was someone senior from Social Services in charge which didn't help.

OK, so you're Aysha, he started off. I've heard a lot about you but never met you before. I'm Frank Johnson, Deputy Manager for Children's Services. Now your full name is - Aysha Jewel Stanton, is that right?

Yeah.

That's a very lovely name. And your date of birth is December 12, 1991?

Yeah.

So you're about to turn thirteen?

Yeah.

And we're here to discuss a new placement for you. It is suggested you be placed with Katy Owen, who is a student at the University on a volunteer placement here, and who has formed a good relationship with you.

She's a good friend to me, mumbled Aysha anxiously.

Nobody has any objection to this proposal, Frank Johnson went on. But we need to sort out the details, what needs to be done first, and by whom, and the timing. First, we need to recap on the reasons. Cassie?

Aysha has always been difficult here. She doesn't like

us and she makes it hard for us to like her. No-one has been able to make any progress with her until Katy Owen started helping. Since Katy has befriended her Aysha has stopped absconding and has attended her education unit every day. There have been no incidences of violence here, or self-harm, although she is still difficult and insolent with staff here when Katy isn't present. We desperately need to create vacancies for other children, and we have said for some time that Aysha's place is a wasted one because she hasn't responded to anything we have tried to offer her.

Ruth?

I basically agree with that, but as you know Aysha has been tried with several of our foster-families, along with her sisters, and these placements have broken down. I have resisted moving her on because up to now that could only be to a Secure Unit or an Out-County Placement, which is a very severe step to take for a child not yet thirteen, and most of all because it would split her up from her sisters.

And there is also the cost to consider in such a move, added Mr Johnson.

So this presents us with an alternative option which in many ways seems ideal. Close contact with Charly and Zoë can be maintained, as can Aysha's attendance at her unit. But I'm worried that we've landed this on Katy with undue haste, and that the longer term implications need to be thought through.

What do you say to this, Katy - is it ok to call you Katy?

Yes, fine. Katy looked at the girl. I like Aysha very much, I think we get on pretty well, and I've read her file, so I can see that all this disturbed behaviour she's shown, it means her life's been in chaos and turmoil from all the moves and the things that happened to her when she was younger, so I'm, like, prepared for anything. I won't give up on Aysha. I want to provide a home for her and I'm determined to make it work. I hope Aysha will help to make it work too, and from the big improvements she's shown the last few weeks, well I believe you'll work with me, Aysha, to keep it up.

All this time Katy had looked direct at the girl she loved, who seemed to be squirming in her seat, whether from anxiety or embarrassment or both, Katy couldn't be sure.

What d'you think, kid?

Yeah, I'm gonna do my best. I wanna move in with Katy, I've seen her flat, I likes it. I don't wanna stay here but I do wanna live near enough to see my sisters.

What will happen if you two fall out, if you decide you don't want to live with Katy any more, Aysha?

I ain't gonna think that, cos I knows if I does it means a secure unit which I'd hate. I'm always gonna stay friends with Katy.

And the same with me, said Katy. Whatever happens I won't let her go.

But you will have to draw the line somewhere, surely?

What d'you mean?

Some behaviour will be unacceptable?

Well yes, especially if repeated, I mean if you start continually running off or self-harming, Aysha, or if you harm Greg, which I know you won't, I know how fond of him you are - that's my dog - or if you cause distress to my niece and nephew, then yeah, that's serious, but the point is, whatever happens, I think I can talk to you, Aysha, and get you to stop. If you won't, that's a different story. But the other thing I need to check out -

Yes, go ahead?

I'm new to all this, I'm still young and inexperienced, I haven't learned the rules yet about dealing with children in care. I think that's one reason Aysha likes me, like I don't represent the care system. But I'm having to learn on the job, I feel like I'm on a very steep learning curve, and I'm gonna have to stay on it for a long time, and I'm bound to make mistakes, I've made some already and I'm sure I'll make quite a few more, and I hope Social Services won't hold that against me -

No, don't worry, we'll make allowances for that.

For instance, I let Aysha drink alcohol the other night when we were at a music gig, and I realise it was wrong, but it's important I'm still allowed to take her to gigs, it was my mistake, and the other thing is even after I'm approved as her foster-carer or whatever and I've gained a lot more experience, I'm never gonna be like part of the care system, because I'm just not that sort of person, I'm a person who makes friends with kids - like I will with her sisters as well as Aysha - I'm no good as an authority figure.

That's fine, said Ruth Barnes. There's room for befrienders within what you call the care system, which isn't really a system at all. I'm sure someone like you will get the best out of Aysha and her sisters.

And we accept there will be mistakes, added Frank Johnson. Cassie or Ruth or even myself will always be ready to talk over any problems and advise as best we can.

Is this ok, Aysha? asked Ruth.

Yeah. What you's just said is true, 'bout why I likes Katy.

Because she's not an authority figure?

Yeah. She's like, more of a friend.

Yes, good. Well, we need to start thinking about details and look ahead. First of all, about approval as a carer.

Before that, interrupted Ruth. Can I ask you, Katy, if you've checked out with your landlady and with your college tutor about this?

Not yet. I was waiting til after this meeting, but I'll phone my landlady tonight and my college tutor tomorrow morning. Or even this afternoon if I could phone from here.

You certainly can.

But it won't stop it happening, whatever they say. If I can't carry on with my courses, then I'll drop some of them, or if necessary pull out altogether and do my degree part-time or on the Open University or something, but it won't stop me being Aysha's carer. And if my landlady objects, I'll just have to find another flat.

Well, if that happens, then we in the council will take the responsibility for finding suitable accommodation. Which brings me on to the question of the other two girls, let me see - Charlotte Jade Stanton, date of birth September 5th 1994, and Zoë Amber Stanton, date of birth April 27th 1997 - what are your views about their future, Ruth.

I think we should ask Aysha and Katy if they've thought about this.

I would like the three girls to be reunited as soon as possible, said Katy. I don't know what you think, Aysha, but if things work out well with you living with me, I think we could take on the care of Charly and Zoë as well, don't you?

Yeah!

It would be a question of when. And of course we'd

need a bigger flat, said Katy.

Of course. Or a house. Well, that's what I'm pleased to hear, and I think we need to start the ball rolling as soon as possible on finding a bigger property. Could you alert our property section, Ruth, as soon as possible?

Yes, but I'd like to check out with Katy about other things in her life as well as accommodation and her degree course, said Ruth.

What d'you mean? asked Katy, somewhat on the defensive.

Well, Cassie has told me you're quite busy with other hobbies?

Yeah, I'd like to keep going with those, but I've talked to Aysha and she doesn't mind. She'll stay home and look after Greg, my dog.

But there may be times when Aysha needs supervision - care - support - and shouldn't be left.

Sure, I wouldn't leave her if she needs me.

And you'd be contactable if a crisis arose?

Sure.

What are these activities?

Orchestra - I play the cello - choir, and basketball. And I go running two or three times a week, but Aysha's said she'll join me on that.

Could she join you on any of the others?

Well, not for orchestra or basketball. But choir's a possibility if you've got a reasonable singing voice, Aysha. There are a few younger members already.

I ain't no good at singing.

Well, let's check some time.

The other thing is about relationships, Katy, went on Ruth. Family, boyfriends, and the like.

This will come up in her assessment as a carer, surely? asked Mr Johnson.

But we do need to know now. If your family object to this, Katy, or if you have a boyfriend, now or in the future, who objects, what difference will it make?

None at all, said Katy. I don't think my family will object but if they do I'll go ahead with Aysha anyway. As for boyfriends, I don't have one, but if I ever did, he would have to accept Aysha, and the other two girls if they was placed with me.

What about sleeping over?

If I had a boyfriend, and there weren't room for him and Aysha sleeping over, he would have to go back to his own place.

Good answer.

Now back to the matter of approving you as a carer, Katy. We want to fast-track this, do it as quickly as possible. I'll take responsibility for ensuring one of the fostering team gets on with this. We must have police and health checks done, at once, if we haven't got them already. Cassie?

I think they've been done at the college.

Did you sign a permission, Katy?

I don't remember doing.

Well, Ruth, Cassie, you must jump to on this one. Chase it up, I want to see those checks on my desk by the end of the week. Anything we should know, Katy?

What?

Any police record hidden away? Or health problems?

No, nothing, I promise.

Any health problems in the family?

Well, my mother has MS. Just the last couple of years. And when I was a child she had depression. Quite bad. But she's not had it for many years, not since she remarried, and no-one else in the family ever has. I'm not the kind of person to get depressed.

I agree, said Cassie. I don't think Katy's the depressive type.

Nevertheless we need to take some note of this. Katy, please let Ruth or Cassie have the name, address and phone number of your GP - and your mother's, if different from yours. And you will need to let us have three referees, one can be a tutor from your college, another a family member, but we must have one independent referee. And I want all this to be done with maximum speed. There's a form to be completed - have we got one here, Cassie?

No.

Ruth, you must put one in the post to Katy tonight, first class. But let us have the names of your referees as soon as possible, Katy, before you complete the form. Aysha, I'm very sorry for all these procedures and formalities, but they must be done.

When do you want to move?

Soon as I can.

We have to complete at least some of these formalities first. But we want you moved in before Christmas, ok. Katy, where are you expecting to spend Christmas?

At home with my family.

I thought you would. Will Aysha be able to come?

I think so. What about Charly and Zoë?

Let's decide about them nearer the time.

Can I ask one other thing? said Katy.

Yes?

Well, I haven't been home all term, and it's end of term this week and my family will be expecting me home this weekend. Can I take Aysha to introduce her? Would you like that, Aysha, to come to Longworth near Manchester and meet my folks?

It seems a good idea, very important in fact, Aysha, said Ruth Barnes.

OK then, yeah, said Aysha, shrugging her shoulders and looking as if she were nonplussed and just wanting to get out of the room. Can I visit the loo?

Of course.

It is Aysha's birthday on Sunday, said Cassie. We were planning a birthday tea for her here which we hoped also would be a little farewell do.

Yes, and I wanna come to that, said Katy. But if she could come home with me Friday evening, I'd come back to Bursfield on Sunday afternoon. If you're agreeable, can I claim her train fare?

Of course. Please see to it, Ruth.

One other thing, said Cassie. I hope Katy will still agree to help as a volunteer here, she's been very good with some of the younger children as well as with Aysha.

Yes I will, definitely.

But time might be a problem, said Ruth. But at the same time, it will be important to maintain the contact with Charly and Zoë.

Yes I know, said Katy.

I also just want to say that I did invite someone from your unit, said Ruth to Aysha who had opened the door but not come inside. But no-one could come, it's such short notice and a busy time of year. But they will be ready to change the transport arrangements at the start of next term.

What d'you mean?

Reroute your minibus to Katy's flat.

Many thanks for coming, Aysha, said Frank Johnson. Good to meet you. We'll move ahead with this, I promise, as quickly as we can.

4. TIME WILL BRING YOU WINTER

Sharon Owen had kept her own surname when she married Steve Mountfield. She explained to anyone who asked, as well as herself and Steve, that it was for the girls. She felt she needed to have the same surname as Samantha and Katy. She and Steve could have adopted them of course, or changed their names by deed poll, but it was clear neither of the girls wanted to change from being Owen, even though they'd had no contact with their birth father for many years. So Sharon remained Sharon Owen. Lately, though, with the onset of her disability, she'd taken to trawling through her memories. There was little in the present to engage her, and even less the future, and despite some desperately tough periods in her life, there were enough good memories to make it worth recalling them.

She now thought there was another reason why she had decided to remain Owen. It came from one of the happiest times of her life, in the two years before Sam was born and a year or so afterwards. Those were the years Sharon drove her taxi. She and Rodney, her first husband, had set up the taxi firm from scratch soon after they got into their relationship, when Sharon was twenty-four. They borrowed money from the bank to buy a car and fit it with a two-way radio. Sharon's dad was a motor mechanic who in middle-age branched out on his own, and he found the car, fitted it out and kept it serviced. A year later they could afford a second car. Sharon still remembered their logo:

They'd printed cards and flyers and blitzed just about everywhere in Longworth and neighbouring towns and villages, phone boxes, newsagents and other shops, take-aways, rest-aurants, pubs, clinics, hospitals, schools and colleges. Sharon did most of the driving at a time when there were very few women taxi-drivers in the north of England, and the response had been amazing. They quickly built up a loyal and regular clientele who wouldn't use any other firm. They bought a second car, but rarely used more than one at once except in an emergency. When Sharon fell pregnant, she carried on driving until she was close to full-term, when they swapped over and Rodney drove while she manned the office and the phone and did the paperwork - all run from their home. Soon after Sam was born she returned to driving, Rodney and her mother sharing the baby-minding while she filled bottles with her milk. But problems with the next two pregnancies, frequent tests, hospitalisation and enforced rests eventually put paid to what she loved the most.

They struggled to keep the taxi-firm going during her pregnancy with Katy. Sharon remembered it as a time of great frustration, but their need, their desire, Rodney and her, for a second child, outweighed everything else. Katy's arrival ought to have signalled a return to normality but it didn't. Sharon became obsessed with Katy and her survival. She ignored Rodney and she ignored Sam, and when either of them demanded attention from her she became bitter and angry. It didn't help that Katy was an incredibly difficult baby, unlike Sam who'd been placid and easy, sleeping little at night, and constantly demanding her

65

feeds. She suffered colic and later, painful periods of teething. Sharon always said that Katy had got all her problems out of her system in that first year and a half, whereas Sam had saved hers up for later.

Both her husbands had been good men and treated her well, Sharon thought, but the difference was that Steve had stuck around and seen her through her troubles, while Rodney couldn't in the end stand it any longer. Sharon blamed him at the time but looking back now, she felt the fault was mainly hers. What did surprise her though was that Rodney hadn't taken Sam with him, since he had got so close with their older daughter during those troubled years. Not only that, but he hadn't even bothered keeping in touch, and she knew how upset Sam had been to lose her dad not just from the family but from her life completely.

Sharon still felt terrible pangs of guilt thinking about this now. She'd had pills and she'd had counselling but the guilt remained. She'd got to love both her daughters to bits but she still felt guilty whenever she saw them. And the strange thing was that it was Katy who aroused the most guilt in her. Sam had, outwardly, suffered most throughout her childhood, with a mostly absent mother in her formative years, a father who'd done most of the parenting and then disappeared, and then from the age of about seven to twelve she'd had to keep the household together with the help of her grandmother, when Sharon was too depressed to do much at all. But the arrival of Steve had freed Sam up to become the rebellious teenager, and she appeared to have got all her troubles out of her system that way. She no longer caused her family any worries and seemed to be a much better mum than Sharon had ever been.

But Sharon continued to worry about Katy. It was partly that she knew that inwardly she had particularly blamed Katy during those difficult years, and she felt sure that Katy had in some way been aware of this. And Katy had been still a toddler during those years of Sharon's depression and couldn't have really understood in the way Sam appeared to understand, what was going on. But the main worry was that Katy had never really got herself much of a life. OK, she had always been on the shy side, a bit of a loner, and she'd always found plenty of activities to involve herself in. At school she'd got on pretty well without making any real friends other than Sophie, who'd been her bosom pal almost from the first day at high school, and her quiet friendly nature, her conscientiousness with her work which had kept her in the top stream throughout, and her sporting abilities, had all held her in good regard with her peers as well as her teachers. What was it then? She'd had no real friend since Sophie, and she'd never as far as Sharon knew had a boyfriend. Sharon herself had had a number of boyfriends in her teenage years in the late sixties and so had her older daughter Sam when she was a teenager in the early nineties. Sharon had lost her virginity at seventeen and Samantha at an even earlier age, she was sure, but Katy was apparently still a virgin at nineteen and Sharon sometimes wondered if she might be secretly gay. Sharon was aware that most girls' lives were very different from Katy's, much more like the sort of life Sam had had before she married, however much anxiety it caused Sharon and Steve. With her tracksuits, sweatshirt tops and jeans, even her clothes, while fashionable and contemporary enough in their way, seemed quite different from the trend of most of her peers to wear outfits that showed off their legs their midriffs or their shoulders or all three. Sharon saw these girls walking past on their way to a night on the town, or coming back merry and unsteady in threes or fours in the early hours, and wondered why Katy was never among them. And then there was her dog. It had seemed the right thing to get her for her fifteenth birthday, the puppy she had been so desperate to own, and there was no doubt Katy had taken her responsibilities as a dog owner very seriously, spending all that summer holiday when she'd just turned fifteen, apart from texting the recently departed Sophie and working on the couple of school projects she had to complete, training Greg and in doing so developing the devotion the dog had shown her ever since. There was no doubt Katy had done right by the dog and by everyone else, because a better behaved and more friendly dog you couldn't hope to find, and he was wonderful with Katy's nephew and niece, but was that really how a fifteen year old girl should be spending her entire summer holiday? Was Katy happy? She seemed to be living the life she wanted to lead, but Sharon Owen had her doubts. And these doubts about Katy had now trebled when she'd appeared with this so-called "friend", this waif of a girl called Aysha from that children's home in Bursfield.

67

That first night she and Steve hardly saw the two youngsters. They had disappeared into Katy's room with muted giggles and whisperings, and even though Steve had already made up a bed for her friend in the spare room, Sam's old room, Katy had retrieved a mattress from the attic, and made up a bed in her own room. A blanket for Greg was taken in there too. Sharon was seriously concerned that the girls might be wanting to share a bed, but it appeared that both beds had been used, although it appeared that Katy had given her own bed over to the girl and had slept on the mattress herself, which again Sharon wasn't happy about. She cursed her disability which meant she couldn't keep such a close eye on what was going on - she couldn't expect Steve to take the same interest.

After she and Steve had gone to bed and all the lights were out, she heard the two girls emerge from the bedroom in that way girls have of trying to keep quiet but never quite managing it, and go downstairs with much shuffling, whispering and muted laughs. Sharon had, despite the difficulty and pain, and despite Steve's admonishments, insisted on going to the door and peeping out, waiting for them to return upstairs, which had taken some time, despite the late hour, and when they had, Katy had seen her mother and spoken crossly to her.

What is it, mum? Don't you trust us?

I just wondered what you were doing.

We're just getting a drink, that's all.

But Sharon had seen, in the second before the girl had crossed the landing and disappeared while Katy had stopped to remonstrate, the cuts and scars on the girl's arms, and the tattoos, though it was the scars that bothered her most. Aysha had on a long sleeveless shirt which she appeared to use as her nightwear. The rest of her stay with Sharon and Steve she'd always kept on her jacket.

In the morning the two girls had appeared late for breakfast. Aysha hardly said a thing but Katy tried to be bright and cheerful.

Sorry we're so late, mum. We were really tired last night.

They both ate breakfast hungrily but Aysha declined tea or coffee and Katy admonished Steve for not having any fruit juice in the house.

Really, Steve, I'm away for one term and this place goes to pieces. We'll have to do some shopping, Aysha, while we're out.

Where are you going?

Well, first we've gotta give Greg a walk, and then I want to take Aysha to meet Sam and Lara and Liam. And Marcus, if he's there, but I guess he'll be busy with his football. I'll phone Sam straight after breakfast and check when's the best time for her.

There probably won't be a good time at present, said Steve. Because they've had some bad news. Marcus's mother's been diagnosed with cancer.

Oh my god! Poor Marcus!

Yes, it's incurable apparently. They've given her about six months.

And it wasn't too long ago his dad died, was it?

That was about four years ago, wasn't it, Steve?

Nearly four, yes. A climbing accident in the Pyrenees.

Yes, I vaguely remember, said Katy, turning to her companion. Sorry, Aysha, that there's sad news on your first visit here. But I don't think that should stop us going to see Sam and the kids. I'll phone her in a minute. Will Marcus still be doing his football this weekend, despite the news?

Oh, I think so, said Sharon. There's no crisis yet. Although Marie isn't well, she's said she wants to carry on with her teaching until the end of this term.

What will happen after that? asked Katy.

I think Marcus is helping her find a place in a hospice for early in the New Year. And Neil will be coming back home to help look after her over the Christmas and New Year period, so Marcus will be able to spend most of the holidays with his own family. They'll have Marie and Neil to visit on Christmas Day, I think, and then they'll come to us Boxing Day.

Neil's an odd fish, said Katy, turning to Aysha again. He's Marcus's older brother and he's a real loner. He spends all of his time up in the Scottish mountains or in the Lake District training mountain rescue dogs. If you think I'm a bit shy you should meet him. When Sam and Marcus got married he was the best man and I was the bridesmaid, and I chatted to people heaps more than him. He made a speech but hardly said another word, did he, mum?

Some people hoped you two might hit it off, bridesmaid and best man, and both of you a bit shy and lonely.

Oh really, mum, I was only fourteen for god's sake, and he was nearly twice my age and, like, quite gross really, I know I shouldn't say it.

And when he lent you his car to take your stuff to Uni, interjected Steve.

Yeah, I know, he's kind and all that. But he's got this huge beard. Katy turned to Aysha and giggled. Sharon couldn't help noticing how Katy appeared to have regressed to an earlier point in her teenage years. But Aysha just stared at her, clearly struggling to take all this in.

Anyhow I'm sorry about Marcus's mum. But if Marcus is still doing his football then I think Sam will be glad if me and Aysha calls round and keeps her company. And I'm dying to let Aysha meet Lara and Liam. They's my nephew and niece, she turned to Aysha. But I've told you 'bout them already, ain't I? Lara is four, is that right, mum?

Coming up five. She starts school after Christmas.

And Liam is nearly three. He goes to a playgroup. And Marcus my brother-in-law, as well as his job, he plays Sunday football every week and runs these kids' teams on a Saturday, so -

He doesn't run them, love, corrected Steve. He helps out. It's a proper kids' football club with three boys' teams and two girls' teams and a proper management committee and all that.

Yeah, but he's on the committee, right?

That's true. But also remember they have a break in the winter. This is the last Saturday they'll be playing for over a month. So Sam and the kids will see more of him.

But his Sunday team carries on playing, right?

They only stop for Christmas and New Year. But you fix a visit with Sam, and then I'll drop you round.

No, Steve, we'll walk, honest. I've got a late birthday present for Sam I've got to collect, and Greg will want a walk.

I thought you said you would walk Greg first. I can easily drive by the shops.

Two walks is fine, ain't it, Aysha? Greg likes as many

as he can get, especially this time of year. And it ain't raining. And anyhow, it's a place in Corporation Road I've gotta go, and you know what the parking's like there.

But that's miles out of your way.

No, it ain't. If we take Greg to Mountpleasant Park then it's, like, almost on our way to Sam's.

Rain's forecast for later.

Well we'll get the bus back if it comes on.

When's your sister's birthday? whispered Aysha hoarsely.

It were about two weeks back, November 27. Yeah, you and her's quite like each other in lots of ways, you's both Sagittarius and I'm sure you'll get on. I only sent her a text, that were all, on her birthday, but the present we's collecting will have a card with it.

What is the present? asked Aysha.

Ah, that's a surprise. You'll find out soon enough.

When's your birthday, Aysha? asked Sharon.

Katy and her friend looked at each other conspiratorially.

Well, it's tomorrow, actually, mum. December 12, but -

Oh, so you'll be here for your birthday, pet! You should have told us earlier.

No, mum - you don't need to worry - the children's home are giving Aysha a birthday tea, we've just gotta make sure we get the 2.15 train back so's we won't be late.

Well we'll give you a special Sunday lunch.

Yeah, OK, but don't call Aysha pet for god's sake, right? Greg's my pet and Aysha's my friend.

She's not always like this, you know, said Steve, turning to Aysha.

Like what? asked Aysha.

Like a bit of a stroppy young madam.

I like it, me, said Aysha.

It's nice for Aysha to have someone else throwing the strops, said Katy.

Shut up, Katy, right, mumbled Aysha.

Anyhow, you wait till you meet Lara and Liam, they're the experts at throwing strops, both of them are. I always love babysitting them, but there's loads of times they've acted up 'specially when I've tried to get them to bed. I reckons they take after their mum.

They take after Marcus too. They're both mad on football, said Steve. Lara would join his girls' under10s, but there's a lower age limit of seven, so she's two and a bit more years to wait.

It's sad to think you'll be their only grandparent by then, said Katy to her mother. I mean, one dead already, one gonna die soon, our dad disappeared, that just leaves you.

Yeah, and who knows how long I'll carry on.

Oh, mum, you've quite a few years in you yet.

But not years of being able to help much as a gran. Sharon felt this effect of her disability most acutely.

It's not doing much, it's just being there that counts.

Anyway you'll know how it feels, Katy, won't you, so you'll be in a good position to help them through it.

What d'you mean?

Well, you lost three of your grandparents when you were very small.

Yeah, but two of them died just after I were born. And your dad died when I was, what, two years old? I can only just remember him.

I think you were three.

So there's only your mum I remember.

Well, I should hope so, said Sharon. She looked after you a lot before you started primary school.

Yeah, but let's not start thinking of them days too much.

All I meant was, you could be a good help to your nephew and niece when Marie dies, if Sam and Marcus is too upset.

Yeah, OK, mum, but we must let Greg out now, or he'll die from waiting. If Sam phones, tell her we'll be back in twenty minutes and I'll phone her then.

5. THE BEAUTY OF THE RAIN

Katy lay awake in her bedroom at home listening to the rain. It hammered on the roof above where she lay and it streamed against the window she so often had spent time looking out of when she needed a break from her homework or was trying to find inspiration for a painting or was just idly dreaming about life in the future, away from Longworth. She had spent her whole life in towns and cities, mainly in Longworth itself, and her dreaming had always been of other towns, but she loved skies and changes in weather and going running or walking with Greg out beyond the edges of town, all of which she attempted to include in her paintings.

This rain was something else, though. There was no venturing out in this, and Greg, curled up on the end of the bed, seemed to know that his morning walk wasn't going to happen for a while. Katy herself was on a not very comfortable make-shift mattress, and in her bed slept Aysha, her hair tousled, her eyes shut, her mouth relaxed and everything about her suggesting the peace of a sleeping child. Greg seemed to understand the need to contribute to the peacefulness by curling up around Aysha's bedclothed feet.

In the morning's quiet Katy was overwhelmed by her love for Aysha, which seemed to be growing stronger all the time. Surrogate child, surrogate younger sister, friend, foster-kid, something of all four came together in the love she felt, and which had swept her through the last few days in a whirl of activity.

She thought back to the meeting and what had happened since. A rush of filling in forms and phone calls about getting her approved as a carer. Preparing Aysha for the travel, a train ticket, help with packing. In fact, she brought very little but had tried to pressurise Katy into buying her some more clothes, which Katy had resisted. Neither she or Aysha had any money at this stage of the term, and Social Services had promised Aysha a clothing grant when or just before she moved, but it hadn't come through yet. Aysha was disappointed but accepted the situation. In fact, Katy thought, there were plenty of items of clothing previously owned by her and her sister Sam, which their mother, who hated throwing things out, still kept at home, perhaps in the hope of their being useful for Lara or other granddaughters when they reached their teens, though god knows what outlandish out-fits would be the fashion then. These might be acceptable to Aysha, or to Charly or Zoë for that matter, but Katy decided not to raise this just yet, best let her mother get used to the sudden appearance of new family members first.

So Aysha had made the trip with only the small back-pack she took to her education unit, and even that not full. Katy meanwhile had had to find time to pack a lot of her stuff, and Greg's, amid everything else going on, including preparing for a final sociology class and a rehearsal with her choir. Basketball matches and practices had finished, thank god. In the middle of all that, she sent her first two Christmas cards, and found time to scribble a letter to her old friend Sophie.

Dear Sophie, she wrote, I'm very sorry I haven't written for at least a year, or e-mailed or texted or phoned. My life has taken off in some strange directions, I've started at Uni, studying Eng. Lit, Art, and Sociology at Bursfield. I became a volunteer helper at a local children's home, and now I'm being approved as a foster-carer - would you believe it? - for three sisters, starting with just the eldest. Could you let Andrea know that I've given her name for a reference, I hope she doesn't mind.
Don't tell her the rest of this, though, PLEASE, this is very pri-vate. The girl I'm fostering first, she's called Aysha, is, kind of very special to me. VERY special. I love this kid to bits, not les-bian or anything, but just like she was my own kid sister or my own child. I guess I've been a bit lonely since you left Long-worth and here is the first person I just want to be with, like, all the time, since there was you. Do phone me on my mobile so we can talk some more, and like I say, don't tell anyone how smitten I've got. Let me know how you've been doing and how many boys you've been with and has one got serious yet? Happy Christmas and New Years, lots of love from Katy.

She'd put this note in the smaller of the two cards, sealed it up and addressed it to Sophie, and sent the larger card to Roy and Andrea, her foster-parents, with the smaller one inside, and the envelope addressed to all three. Then she'd taken all her stuff and Greg to the children's home after lunch on the Friday, posting the card on the way. Aysha, who always got in from her unit early on a Friday afternoon, would look after Greg, give him a short walk, while she, Katy, jogged to her last sociology class, jogged a little faster back to the home, and then with her bags, her dog and Aysha, caught the bus to the station.

And that train journey! Not much more than an hour, and a crowded train, but she'd barely been aware of any other fellow-passengers. She'd asked if Aysha had ever been to Manchester before, and the girl had said no, but she nearly did once, when some of her mates in Bursfield were going but she'd chickened out at the last moment, mainly cos of her sisters, she'd no idea when she'd see them again if she did go. She had gone to Birmingham one night, and stayed there most of the night, but then she knew the car-driver were coming back.

Then Aysha said to her, Well d'you have another name, Katy, cos you knows my middle name now?

Yeah, Aysha Jewel, I really like that, she'd said.

So go on, tell me yours.

You'll have to guess. It begins with a V, so you should guess easy.

Val?

No.

Viv?

No.

Virginia? Aysha laughed.

No.

Vera? Aysha laughed louder.

No.

Not Veronica? Aysha was now giggling hysterically.

No. What's up with you?

I knew this kid called Veronica Anne, she spluttered. It were when I got moved to a foster-home on my own, there were this older girl there, I musta been ten and she something like, fourteen. She said I gotta call her Anne, but the stupid foster-mum would insist on calling her Veronica which she hated. So anyhow I got her to bunk off with me lotsa times, it weren't hard persuading her. We used to nick stuff and the fuzz would pick us up and take us in, and the foster-parents blamed me and, like, blew a zillion fuses. But the thing were, when the fuzz asked her full name, she goes Verona Anne, and I goes, why's you giving a false name, and she said, really my name is Verona, that's what's on my birth certificate. Then she told me how her mum had always wanted a girl called Veronica, but her dad went to register her and whether he were stupid or wanted to get his own back on her mum, no-one knew, but he put Verona instead. And her mum were furious and soon after, threw him out cos he kept calling the baby kid Verona, and the mum wanted Veronica. So when she grew up a bit more, she decided to use her other name, like, Anne, right, and that were more rows with her mum and she ended in foster-care. Course I soon got moved and I never knew what happened to that kid, but it shows you how much trouble the name Veronica caused, which is why I laughed so much but I knows I shouldn't really.

Still shaking with laughter, she leaned across to Katy, grabbed her shoulders and whispered in her ear, There was a young woman called Veronica / Whose wardrobe contained only one knicker / When her friends asked her where / Was the other of the pair / She said she left it under a Japonica.

Where d'you learn that? asked Katy, both repelled and drawn to the smuttiness.

Charly and me made it up. When I told Charly what I just told you, she said we gotta make up a lim - what's it called?

Limerick.

Yeah.

You've not guessed my name yet.

Vanda?

No.

Vonnie?

I think that's short for Yvonne.

Vanity.

Vanity? What sort of name's that?

I mean, Verity.

Verity? I verily name this baby Verity!

I verily name this very tiddly baby Verity!

By now both girls were totally hysterical, clutching each other, rocking around in their seats, whispering loudly in each others' ears, and causing more than one disapproving glance from fellow passengers which they were hardly aware of.

Come on, you've gotta guess it!

Tell me, I give up!

No.

Vanya?

No.

Velocity?

Now you're getting crazy! You've missed one out, think of football.

How d'you mean?

Well, my surname's Owen right. Think of a footballer?

Michael Owen!

OK, so think of another footballer more famous than Michael Owen.

I dunno any footballers. Hang about, Wayne Rooney!

Nah, more famous than him even. He plays in Spain now, but he used to play in Manchester, near where I live.

David Beckham!

So who's his wife? Used to be a Spice Girl.

Posh Spice? Oh I know, Victoria Beckham! You're called Victoria!

You got there! I'm Katy Victoria Owen.

Oh wow! That's some name.

I was christened Katy. Not Katherine or Kathleen or anything. Katy Victoria Owen.

Me, I think that's better than mine.

No, it ain't, Aysha Jewel Stanton's miles better.

Yeah, you's just saying that, right!

No.

By now, they were drawing into Manchester Piccadilly, and had to change to a local train, with Aysha holding Greg on his lead and Katy carrying her case, each with a pack on their back, but still managing to clutch each other with their free arms. It was only as they approached Katy's house that Aysha grew more serious, more nervous, dropping behind Katy, loosening her hold but still reaching for the older girl's fingers as though scared she might disappear.

She hadn't said much in the house that evening as Katy tried to help her feel at home, but after they'd got into bed she said,

What's Manchester for sick?

What d'you mean?

Like, d'you say vomit or puke or throw up or what?

Well, any of those - why?

Cos I always throws up whenever I'm taken to a new house.

Why?

I dunno.

Maybe it's a kind of protest or something?

Could be. Maybe I just don't like being moved.

You've enjoyed today though?

Oh yeah, that's totally different, like, wicked fun.

So let's hope you won't need to throw up tonight.

And Aysha hadn't.

Yesterday had been rather a strain for Aysha, it had seemed, trying to relate to new people. They had gone to Sam's for lunch, picking up a large outdoor pot for Sam's birthday on the way, which Katy struggled to carry the half mile from the shop to her sister's house, Aysha as always with Greg.

Katy was relieved that Aysha immediately got on with her young niece and nephew, chasing around with them, playing peek-a-boo and monsters, as she must have done many times, Katy reflected, with her own younger sisters, and thinking how it was always older kids or adults that Aysha had her brushes with. And now, it was Katy's sister and brother-in-law where things seemed less easy. Not so much Marcus, who was already half-way through his lunch when they arrived, and went off to his football straight after, but with Sam, Katy sensed at once a tension between her and Aysha, even though she had come to believe there was a lot in common between the two of them, and that tension seemed to be getting in the way of her own relationship with her older sister. It bothered Katy, who had always set great store by her older sister, the support she'd had from her over the years, and which she could repay now, she hoped, by babysitting and in all other ways being a hands-on auntie. She must talk to Sam, assure her that none of that would diminish because of the new responsibilities she was taking on.

While they were at her sister's house, it had started to rain and soon turned into a Mancunian downpour. They got to the bus-stop only half-wet, but from the bus back to her own house, even though it was only a short distance, and even though Katy had her umbrella, they both got soaked. Aysha, whose thin jacket gave her little protection from the rain, and who insisted on holding Greg's lead, and who therefore Katy could not properly cover with her umbrella even though she tried, was the more drenched of the two as they scrambled into the house to meet Katy's mum, again waiting in the hall for them.

Oh look at you two! Sharon had exclaimed. Aysha, my angel, you must have a bath straight away and put on some dry clothes. And we'll put what you're wearing through the spin dryer and try and get them dry for tomorrow.

But Aysha had insisted that she must dry Greg before she had her bath even though Steve had offered to do that.

Where d'you want me to go to dry him? she asked.

Well, you'd better use the front porch, said Sharon.

Have you got an old towel I could use?

I've got one, said Katy. Upstairs with his things.

Eventually Aysha agreed to a hot bath, but apart from underwear and tights she had no spare clothes with her, so Katy had to find some of hers from earlier years and bring them into the bathroom. Aysha wanted her to stay, but Katy felt uncomfortable, she sensed her mother feeling concerned about them sleeping in the same room and didn't want to do anything to heighten that concern.

She went downstairs and was drawn into talking to her mother and stepfather.

So you've really taken on this girl, have you?

Yeah, I'm being approved as a foster-carer. Just for Aysha. And maybe, later, if it all works out ok, for her sisters.

She has sisters?

Yeah, two younger sisters called Charly and Zoë. They live in the children's home too, but only Aysha will move in with me to begin with. If they give agreement for the other two girls to join us, they'll find a house, or a bigger flat for us.

Isn't this all a bit sudden? What's going to happen to your studies?

It's a big change, I know, all a bit unexpected, but I'm going to do my best to keep on with my degree as well.

Are you sure you've thought it through? I'd hate it for you to be let down, or get out of your depth. I know she's a poor little mite of a girl, but - I can see -

Sharon hesitated.

We think she may be more disturbed than you realise,

put in Steve. In the past, that is.

Listen, mum, I've read her file, I've talked to her social worker and Cassie at the home, and to Aysha herself. My eyes are wide open. I KNOW this is the right thing to do, I have no doubts at all. This is what my life's meant to be about, helping kids like Aysha. When she and her sisters are grown up, I'll carry on fostering troubled kids, I know it's what I want to do in life. I would give up my degree if I had to, and everything else - well, apart from my own family - but not caring for Aysha.

But it all seems the wrong way round, said her mother. Get your degree, find a steady boyfriend, get a job, get married, that's the time then to think about fostering.

No, it don't work like that. Aysha needs me now, not in five or ten years' time. You have to do it when the need arises.

All right, so what about Christmas? Will you and Aysha be here?

Well, I hope so. Are we invited?

Of course you are, my love. But what about the other two girls?

I don't know. I guess Aysha would want to spend Christmas Day with them, but she wouldn't want to go back to the home, no way.

Well, could we invite them as well? asked her mother.

Are you sure?

Of course, Sharon turned to Steve. We'd be happy to have three extra kids at Christmas, wouldn't we, Steve? You could cope with Boxing Day lunch? For ten?

Bloody hell! Poor Steve. Would you really cope? What if Neil and Marie were coming too?

They won't come. Christmas Day with Sam, Marcus and the kids will be as much as either of them could take. I'll cope somehow.

Well, as long as you're sure, I'll ask Aysha, and I'll ask Social Services. But I'm sure they'll all say yes.

Then Aysha had appeared in Katy's old clothes, a pale lilac top and her brown knee-length school skirt. Katy could hardly stop herself from emitting something between a laugh and a gasp, the child looked so different, so out-of-character.

You sure you wanna wear that skirt? I've got an old pair of jeans with holes in.

Nah, this skirt's fine.

For travelling back to Bursfield in?

Yeah.

We'll try and dry your own clothes as much as possible, my angel, said Sharon. But I don't think they'll be dry enough to wear.

They had a long supper in which the Christmas arrangements were discussed. Aysha was now becoming more talkative, and interested in Sharon's family background and childhood memories. When the two girls finally escaped upstairs, they put some music on, lay on the bed facing each other and talked more.

Who's this man with the beard, Katy? asked Aysha.

What? Oh you mean Neil, he's Marcus's older brother.

Why d'you call him gross?

I dunno, he's just a bit odd, gross ain't the right word.

What's odd 'bout him?

I've only met him, I dunno, three times, he ain't down here in Longworth very often. But it were Sam's wedding, right, that's what brought this on -

Brought what on?

Like, calling him gross instead of just odd. See, he were best man and me, I were the bridesmaid. Just me, right, but I really wanted my friend Sophie to be a bridesmaid too, but Sam wouldn't agree. Sam's got all these girlfriends she's made over the years, and she wouldn't ask any of them to be bridesmaid in case it upset the others. She said none of her friends would mind if it were just me, but they would mind a lot if Sophie were a bridesmaid. I kept hoping she'd change her mind. Anyhow, before the wedding Sam and me went to be fitted for our dresses. Sam wanted lemon yellow, like made of thin lacy stuff, so I had the same, right, but mine were, like, bare shoulders. It's not my usual style but I chose it for Sophie, right, she were the one used to flirt with the boys and, like, show her flesh and stuff. But it were so dumb, right, to choose that dress cos the wedding were in January and it were a freezing cold day -

Why did they get married in January?

Cos Lara were on the way, right. Sam was already beginning to show it but not too much. Well, they took ages to decide if they wanted to get married before Lara were born, and when they did decide, they had to arrange it quick and January were the only month. Anyhow I were, like, totally frozen solid. The church were cold and then we was all waiting outside in the freezing wind while the photos were taken and stuff -

Why did they get married in church?

God knows, just to create a good impression I guess. I mean, none of my family's ever gone to church, right, but I think Marcus used to go before he started going out with Sam. Anyhow I asked Steve if he could go back to our house and fetch me a jacket, but he were needed for photos too, so by the time he did, we was all in this hotel for the reception and it were like, boiling hot in there and I didn't need a jacket at all. Anyhow, that was the first time I met Neil, right, and I had to stand right next to him for some of the photos, with me like shivering and turning blue. You could tell when the photos came out. It were just so embarrassing -

Have you still got the photos?

My god, Aysha, I dunno, they just make me cringe!

Katy, I'd love to see them!

You're a wicked kid, if you want to see what's just the most embarrassing pictures of me ever.

Nah, I just wanna see what you looked like when you was something like my age.

Not so brilliant that day, I'm telling you, kid. Anyhow, this Neil came and, like, put his arms round me and kissed me on the cheek with his bristly beard, y'know, when we was first introduced, after the church but before the photos, and then he were stood right by me on some of the photos, and he were sat next to me at the reception, but he never said a bloody word. I were too embarrassed to ask him anything, all I said were, like when he finished his speech, that it were a good speech and made me laugh, but all he did were mumble thanks and look the other way and that were about it. So later when I told Sophie we decided that meant he were ten out of ten gross, and after that whenever we saw a man we used to give him a mark for grossness, we had fun doing that. But fair dos to Neil, he did lend his car for me to get all my stuff to Uni, and he did put us onto the place where Mum and Steve got Greg for me, so he can't be all bad.

Were Greg a puppy then?

Oh yeah, he weren't trained or anything, it were me had to do all that, right.

How come Neil knew places to get dogs from?

Cos one of the things he does is train mountain-rescue dogs, right. And if any of the dogs don't make the grade for mountain rescue, they go to this home where we got Greg.

Were Greg s'posed to be for mountain rescue?

Oh no, he ain't big or strong enough for that. But the place we got him's a good place for dogs, and they have unwanted puppies there as well as older dogs that ain't made it for mountain rescue.

By this time, Katy noticed, Aysha was virtually asleep. Katy got down off the bed, turned the music down very low, and lifted Aysha like a toddler, the same as she'd done many times with Lara and Liam, into the bed. She then scribbled a brief note which she left on her own bed in case the younger girl woke, and silently signalled the dog out of the room.

Now the sleeping child slept on, apparently undisturbed all night as far as Katy could tell, making up, Katy suspected, for years of disturbed nights, nights of not enough sleep, nights of no sleep at all. It was her birthday, of course, and later in the day they would return to Bursfield for her birthday tea. In the meantime Katy could hear sounds of her mother and Steve downstairs, but she would let Aysha sleep on while the rain outside beat an accompaniment to her breathing.

Sharon Owen was beginning to think she would take to Aysha. She didn't know anything about her two sisters yet, Katy had only just mentioned them, but Sharon was already looking forward, feeling a degree of expectation, about a Christmas with three new children, almost new additions to the family, being part of the proceedings. Steve seemed remarkably unfazed by all the extra cooking.

Aysha didn't seem to have minded getting soaked in the rain, nor having to borrow some of Katy's old clothes. In fact, dressed the way she was seemed to have brought her closer to her and Steve, and over supper, Aysha had seemed genuinely interested to hear about Sharon's childhood and especially her grandfather.

I remember visiting my granddad quite a few times when I were small, she told Aysha. He was my mother's father and he worked in the mill all his life. His wife, my grandmother, had died before I was born but he were still alive, living on his own in this little back-to-back terrace house.

What's back-to-back? asked Aysha.

It's like most housing was for working people back in the old days. It were probably the same in Bursfield. There was a row of houses opening onto the street, a front room and a back room and upstairs, two small bedrooms. There was no bathroom and the toilet was out the back. The front room was kept for entertaining visitors, and the back room was where the family lived, cooked and ate all in a tiny room. Upstairs all the kids however many there was, had to share one bedroom. There were a tiny yard at the back but no garden, and the yard backed onto an alleyway. Across the alley were the back of another terrace of houses, that's why they was called back-to-back. This was the old days when they didn't have council houses, or hardly any anyway, and working-class people couldn't afford to buy houses, so these back-to-backs were owned by the mill-owners. Everyone worked at the mill, including my granddad. My mum and dad did too when they was younger. But just after I was born, in 1951, the mills all started closing down. Well, actually some closed before the war, in what was called the Great Depression.

What were that? asked Aysha.

Not depression like feeling really down like I did after Katy were born. This was economic depression, nearly everyone lost their jobs and was unemployed, in them days it were called being on the dole. It was in the nineteen thirties.

Was your granddad on the dole?

I don't think he was. He told me he worked at the same mill all his life. It closed the year after I were born, in 1952. But he was sixty-five that year, so he didn't need to go on the dole, he could retire and get his old-age pension. But he would have gone on working if the mill hadn't closed down.

Did he fight in the war?

Not in the last war, he were too old, he were fifty-something when it started. And my dad were too young, he were only twelve when the war started, but he were called up in 1944, but he never got to fight in the war because the war ended a few months after his call-up. But I had two uncles, one on my father's side and the other on my mother's who both died in the last war. And my granddad fought in the first world war and he were one of the lucky ones who got through alive. My other granddad was too young for the first world war, he were born in 1905 I think it was, but he were killed in the second world war, here in England, in one of the bombing raids.

So what happened to your granddad's house, where you went to see him? asked Aysha.

Well, they got pulled down, didn't they, them back-to-backs. There's flats built there now, or offices, or stores, you know, like Argos or Homebase, I don't remember now exactly where them houses were, even the streets have disappeared, but next time you come to Longworth, Katy can show you roughly where they was -

I don't know, Mum, do I? You never showed me, complained Katy.

Well, there's nothing to show. It's only in my memory now, but it's still clear as daylight in there. There can't be that many of us left remember them back-to-backs.

The mill is there still, though, said Steve. For years that mill was a derelict building, a real eyesore in the town. Now it's been done up and it's a museum and craft centre and there's a café and a small-scale arts venue there.

Yeah, so Katy could take you there, my angel, and you could hear some music and look round the museum, and remember it was once where Katy's great-grandfather worked.

I played there once, said Katy. There was about ten of us from school playing string instruments, orchestral suites and stuff like that. I tell you, Aysha, it were terrible, I were just so embarrassed, I said I were never gonna go back in that place again.

Well, now you've got a good reason to change your mind.

I don't think that place will put on the sort of music Aysha likes.

They have folk music as well as classical, stuff from around the world, said Steve.

My sister Charly would like that, said Aysha. But I'll go

as well. I'm keen on music gigs, any sort of music.

But what Aysha likes best is loud discordant music, added Katy.

Well, there's places in Longworth has that, said Sharon. You go down the town centre on a Saturday night you can't help hearing it coming out of every other building. And you see the teenage girls with hardly anything on going from one place to another looking for the loudest music.

Yeah, mum, they call it clubbing, said Katy witheringly.

But Katy never got into that, did you, love?

No, and I'm not about to start now, Aysha. But live bands I'm on for, like that gig we went to the other week.

And that had given the girls the cue to retire upstairs, and soon the music could be heard from their room, though not too loud. Sharon was sure it was not Katy's music, and assumed that Aysha must have brought two or three of her favourite CDs with her. Later Katy had reappeared, saying that Aysha was fast asleep and she would have to take Greg for a short walk in the heavy rain, for which she'd put on layers of waterproofs and wellies. She asked Steve to listen out in case Aysha woke up and got upset. When Katy came back in, she asked Sharon where the photos of Sam's wedding were, because in the morning Aysha wanted to look at them. This was another pointer for Sharon that she thought she would get to like Aysha, poor little mite that she was.

It was still raining the next morning and it was ages after she and Steve had got up before the girls appeared. Sharon didn't want to have her breakfast without them, so she busied herself finding photos, not just the wedding photos but others as well. When, finally, the girls did appear, Aysha wanted to walk Greg before breakfast but everyone cajoled her to wait.

It's your birthday, my angel, happy birthday!

Yeah, many happy returns, Aysha! called Steve from the kitchen. Sorry I've already eaten my breakfast but I've got to start cooking lunch if you're going to catch that train!

Happy birthday, kiddo, whispered Katy in Aysha's ear. To Sharon, Aysha was beginning to seem more and more uncomfortable, and for a moment Sharon wondered if the card and present by the girl's place at the table were a mistake. It was only a box of chocolates, quite a fancy box, but really nothing special.

Katy had rushed back upstairs and appeared with her own card and present, a CD.

Oh my god, it's the Testicles!

There was some embarrassed laughter, clearly some kind of private joke. Sharon heard Aysha whisper to Katy, Why didn't you wait and give me this later?

I were gonna, but when mum had a present for you, I had to give you mine too, right. Didn't I? Katy whispered back.

Aysha opened her presents and cards, drank two large glasses of orange juice and ate some breakfast. She seemed like a foreign child struggling to adjust to a new culture.

Katy said you wanted to see some photos, said Sharon to her. I've got some wedding photos here, and some other photos. Katy, can you clear some space on the table, so's I can sit here and show these to Aysha.

But what 'bout giving Greg his walk? mumbled Aysha, unhappily.

I'll do that, said Katy. I hate seeing them photographs, I do really, and anyway, it's still raining and I've got better water-proofs.

But I must walk Greg, you know how I likes to.

There might be time just before lunch or just after, and the rain might have eased off by then.

Some hope! called out Steve, emerging from the kitch-en. I'm taking you down to the station, by the way, no argu-ments, rain or no rain, that'll give you a bit more time. And I'll call at the Old Mill Centre on the way back and pick up a pro-gramme for the Christmas period. Better doing it on a Sunday, you can park on the street outside without risking getting a tick-et.

I thought they had a car park.

They do, but you have to pay. It's not much, but I'm blowed if I'm going to pay anything if I'm only there for a couple of minutes.

Oh good, so there might be time for me to do the wash-ing-up, said Katy. While Aysha takes Greg out just before we go back.

Steve retired to the kitchen, Katy went out the back door, and that left Sharon sitting with the bemused child explain-ing the photos. Aysha wanted to know who everyone was, on the wedding photos and on the other ones. When she saw pictures of Katy aged fourteen (at the wedding) aged twelve (with Sophie in their marching band outfits) aged ten (a primary school photo) and finally aged six at Steve and Sharon's own wedding, Aysha kept clapping her hand over her mouth in disbelief. It was clear she was trying to piece together who everyone was in Katy's family, and this endeared her to Sharon even more. The only one she showed no interest in was Sophie, and Sharon, who had always considered that Sophie was rather over-indulged by her foster-parents, sympathised with that too.

It was one of those mornings where lunch followed breakfast with indecent haste, and by now Aysha seemed thoroughly relaxed again and ate her lunch hungrily unlike both Sharon and Katy who were used to eating breakfast much earlier and had had more breakfast than Aysha anyway.

A shame you've got to go back so soon, Sharon said.

Well it is Aysha's birthday. Her sisters will want to see her.

And me see them.

Will you come again before Christmas?

Yeah, I'm gonna come on my own, said Katy. I'm playing my cello in a concert tomorrow night but I'll come Tuesday. Steve's said he'll collect me so's I can bring some more of my stuff home. I think I can stay till Thursday and I'll go back by train. We think Aysha'll move in Friday if it all goes through, I mean if I'm approved as a carer. We're going to a gig Friday night and then my choir's singing in this kind of alternative pre-Christmas festival thing next Saturday. After that I don't know. I'd like to come soon after, but I don't want to land all three kids on you for too many days. I might even come with Aysha first and then go back for the other two. I'll let you know.

We'll just be glad to see you that week before Christmas. And Aysha, my angel, we're really pleased to have met you, and we'll look forward to seeing you again soon.

Thank you for the card and present, stammered Aysha, looking embarrassed again, her only wish being to get out of the house with Greg, into the slackening-off rain and the promise of clearing skies.

6. PASTORAL CARE

It was just after lunch on the Saturday before Christmas and Samantha Sullivan was walking with her two children half-way across town to visit her mother-in-law, Marie. She would have liked to have walked faster but the small children forced her to adopt a slow pace. She would in some ways have preferred to come without the kids but she knew that was selfish. Marie would want to see her grandchildren, however bad she was feeling, and the children should be seeing their grandma even if they didn't fully understand.

Where are we going? complained Liam, though for two-and-a-half he was a good walker.

To grandma's house.

Why can't she come and see us at our house? It was usually at their own house that the kids saw their grandmother, indeed they saw her most days as she called in after school, either on her way home, or between end of school and one of her many meetings when she would grab a cup of tea and a sandwich, but however long she stayed, it was always the grandchildren to whom she gave her attention.

She ain't well enough to come out today, said Samantha. She's gotta rest.

What's the matter with her? asked four-year-old Lara.

This was the more difficult question, and Lara was old enough to sense the seriousness behind the lack of a clear answer. But their mother could not bring herself to tell them yet that their grandmother was soon to die.

We don't know. The doctors are doing tests. But she had to come home early from school yesterday.

Why? persisted Lara.

She kinda collapsed at school. She's been ordered to rest.

This was true. Another teacher had brought her home, Marie refusing to allow them to call an ambulance. She was trying to deal with this situation with minimal fuss. Samantha felt bad that it wasn't until now that she was getting to visit her since her collapse yesterday. Marcus had been round yesterday after work and made up a bed downstairs, made sure the heating was turned up and that there was food ready and prepared for the evening and the next morning. But she could have visited this morning, changed their schedules.

There were times Samantha felt like a football widow, what with Marcus's near obsession with the game, but that was a bit unfair. He was a good husband, a good father, and a good son to Marie. Every Saturday morning in the winter months, and sometimes in summer too, straight after breakfast, Marcus would take the two children to the supermarket and do the weekly shop. Since the news of Marie's diagnosis, he would include shopping for her as well. He made it a fun time for the kids and they loved going with him. While he was gone, Samantha held open house for her friends, it was really her only chance to see most of them. Usually it was coffee and biscuits, though she never referred to it as a coffee morning. Some only called in briefly, some only made it every now and again, others came every week and stayed the whole morning. Sam, as everyone - husband, family, friends - called her, though she still thought of herself as Samantha, the name she'd been called as a child, had accumulated many friends since about the age of sixteen, ten years ago. Her group of teen-age friends had mostly remained good friends despite the lack of chance to meet up now, and there had been additions from her work, when she was working, from Marcus's work colleagues' partners, even a couple of other football wives. The most regular of all though was the partner of Marcus's best friend from school, Iona, who wasn't from the town and really welcomed the chance to meet other young women since she'd moved in. Their lives had taken many different directions, some, such as Iona and Samantha, were at home with small kids, one or two were trying to combine children and jobs, others were married or had part-ners but no kids, some were footloose and fancy-free, some were on the paths of high-powered careers, others were in dead-end jobs. But one thing you could say for all of them was that life was not the same as it had been in their carefree teens, Samantha would have been very surprised if any of them now used canna-bis or ecstasy, though a couple of them were regular takers of cocaine, she was fairly sure. Nights out together were very much the exception now, whereas in those days she and her friends were out on the town more nights than they stayed in. And alcohol - their collective intake must have reduced by more than ninety per-cent, since the years of getting drunk, getting high and getting laid, those years of one-night-stands and eyeing-up the opposite sex. If any of them were without husbands or steady partners now, they either were trying to find one or had decided men weren't bothering about at all. And only Tanya, no children, unhappily married, and in a high-powered marketing job, was a heavy drinker now and that was something she tried to keep secret. This morning, the last time they'd met up before Christmas, it had been wine or sherry instead of coffee and Tanya had turned up, the first time for several weeks, and her drink problem was clear to everyone if it hadn't been before, even though her job and her marriage were the problems she actually talked about.

No, she couldn't have cancelled this morning, Samantha thought, even if she had little time for any of her friends' problems. Samantha felt she had enough problems of her own right now, in fact a combination of grief and anger kept bursting up inside her. She was not one for keeping her feelings in, but she did try hard not to show her feelings to her kids and now she would have to do the same with Marie. Marcus would have to receive the brunt of it although some of her friends were receptive this morning, Iona especially, and would be willing to listen over the phone.

She had to force her attention onto her kids who were disrupting her progress through town. Lara had decided to walk on the top of every low wall they passed alongside, and Liam wanted to do the same. But he kept falling off. Lara was trying to help him up onto the wall and then hold his hand, but it wasn't working because Liam couldn't keep up with her. Samantha helped Liam along for a while but then told them they must stop playing this game because they were getting late for their grandma's, and wouldn't have time for the party afterwards.

What party? asked Liam.

The party at daddy's football club, Lara told him. Daddy told you, remember. He's coming to grandma's to collect us, isn't he, mummy?

That's right. Later, after it gets dark.

So how come we'll be late for it? It's not dark yet, protested Lara.

Because we all want to spend quite a bit of time with grandma, seeing as she's not well.

And daddy's bringing grandma's shopping which we helped him with this morning, chipped in Liam. We left it in his car for later, didn't we, Lara?

Good, said Samantha, encouragingly. You're good kids and let's hurry on, it's not far now. And she took both their hands.

Have you got grandma's Christmas card? asked Lara.

Yes, it's in my bag.

Samantha reflected on how Marie was not a normal mother-in-law. She regarded her as somewhere between mentor, surrogate mother, and almost a saint. Certainly her relationship with Marie was a lot better than that with her own mother, and had been since she was a teenager. She had indeed known Marie for quite a lot longer than she had known Marcus, and the degree to which she had fallen in love with Marcus must, she thought, have been connected to how she felt about his mother. She could still remember as clear as if it were yesterday the first time she met Marie. It was near the end of her first year at High School and was in one of the small offices off the main corridor. It was Steve who'd told her to come and it was Steve who'd told her the news which she could still remember now him saying,

I'm going to move in with your mum at the end of term, Samantha. We're going to get married soon. It means I can't be responsible for your pastoral care any more. I'm going to be your stepfather instead.

And he'd introduced her to Marie, a teacher she hadn't met before although she'd been at the school a long time, longer than Steve even. She must have seen her around, but she hadn't been taught by her.

Samantha had taken a shine to Steve ever since he'd been the one to coax from her all the problems she'd been facing. In fact, for the just turned twelve schoolgirl it had soon turned into a fully blown crush. She'd been proud that Steve often used to take her home at the end of school, or call by at other times to see how she was coping. She hadn't been doing at all well, what with having to help her grandmother deal with Katy, having to look after her mother who was often in bed all day, Samantha was frequently late for school, sometimes not making it at all.

Her academic work was suffering badly, not that she was ever going to be that kind of kid; she was tired in school, moody, prone to outbursts of temper and easily riled by other kids. Steve had understood all this, had taken a genuine interest in helping her. He had offered a referral to Social Services, but Samantha had refused, saying her mum already had a social worker, which was true, with her being under the mental health services. So Steve had undertaken the help himself and had got to know Samantha's mother and sister quite well. But this had not prepared her for the shock of finding that lately his visits to the house had only been the pretext for seeing her mum. But Marie had quickly understood the situation, realised that Samantha's feelings for Steve, childish crush though it was, were strong enough to mean life was going to be difficult for her. The jealousy and resentment had been bottled up at that time, only to resurface as Samantha hit the mid-teens and her final year at school. Marie had stuck with her through those years, had helped settle her back into regular school attendance and a reasonable academic performance, and was still there to show understanding and support during the years of teenage rebellion, when Marie's house became a refuge for Samantha from the frequent rows with her mum, the stormings out and angry words. In those days there was also Marie's husband, Jack, and her sons, Neil and Marcus, living there, it was the same house Marie lived in now, on her own, but for how much longer? She had often pondered over the strange coincidence that of the two teachers who had helped her through school, one had ended up her stepfather and the other her mother-in-law.

Samantha felt devastated at the prospect of Marie's impending death. Anger brimmed within her like nausea. What had she done to deserve this, after all the trouble she'd had as a child and adolescent, an absent mother, a father who deserted her, a mother who became so depressed that she, Samantha, had to care for her and her sister and who then married the one adult she trusted and turned to for support, and then started fighting her over her teenage bids for freedom. Only in the last five years or so had Samantha found, through the support of Marie and the son whom Sam had married, a degree of stability, but even this period had been beset by tragedy, with Marie's husband Jack dying in that mountaineering accident and then Samantha's own mother developing multiple sclerosis, and now an even greater tragedy impending. And then, when the one person who seemed an oasis of calm in the middle of all this grief, the one person whose quiet trustworthiness would lend Sam a sympathetic ear, who had always been there for Sam and her kids, her younger sister Katy, what should she do but turn up with this orphan child she'd met while at university, a strange misfit of a girl who Sam had taken an immediate dislike to and felt so angry about now?

Yes, this girl had been good with Lara and Liam, she grudgingly had to admit. She played with them as though she herself were not much older than Lara. But Samantha could see through this, she knew. She had always considered herself as a "person" person who could tune into others with a strong intuitive sense, unlike her younger sister, whom she thought of as being naive and lacking any judgment about people. And Samantha now had a strong instinct that this kid spelt trouble. She was too grown-up for her age in some ways and too childish in others. She didn't want her streetwise ways influencing Lara and Liam. She was going to cause nothing but trouble to the family and what did Katy think she was doing bringing her into the family especially at this difficult time? She needed to talk about this to Marie, even in her poor physical state.

They were at Marie's house now, and Samantha let herself and her children in with the key which Marcus had given her. She called out, Marie! It's only us!

Come in, Sam, come in! Make yourself a cup of tea, and there's juice for the children.

How are you, Marie? Lara, Liam, say hallo to grandma!

Marie was sitting in a chair, swathed in blankets, a makeshift bed along the wall near her chair. She switched off the radio, and tried the television with the remote on the table by her bed.

I'm not sure there's anything but sport on the TV this time on a Saturday afternoon, but I might find a children's channel.

You've not stayed in bed, then?

No, I can manage to get about a bit.

How are you feeling?

Not as bad as yesterday. The doc's increased my pain-killers. A little bit. I don't sleep well, but the rest has helped.

Samantha emerged from the kitchen with a pot of tea.

Will you have a cup, Marie?

Oh yes, dear. Have you found the juice?

Yeah. Here, Lara, take these and go and sit with Liam and watch TV, while I talk with grandma.

What you gonna talk about?

Never mind.

When's daddy coming to take us to the party? chipped in Liam.

Not yet, we only just got here! Grandma will want to hear what you've been up to, after we've had grown-ups' talk for a bit.

You lucky children, having a party to go to later! Whose party is it? asked Marie.

It's Marcus's football club, didn't he tell you? He's there now, helping get it ready.

He may have mentioned it. Everything from yesterday's a blur.

Of course. Was that your last day at school, then?

I'm going to take Monday off, but I must go in Tuesday, if I can. Not to teach, but to say goodbye to everyone, and I believe they've planned some sort of presentation.

Well, that's no more than you deserve. How many years have you been at the school?

I think I counted it up as thirty-three. Those five years you were there were a small proportion, but a very significant one.

Is there any news of Neil?

In the next few days, he says he'll arrive. He can't be sure which day. He's phoned me up twice. He's on the final stage of a dog-training programme, so he can't leave this weekend.

I guess Christmas holidays is a busy time for the mountain rescue.

Yes, especially if there's snow or ice. He'll have to be on call when he does come down to Longworth. They may send a helicopter for him, he said, if it's a dire emergency.

Well let's hope nothing like that happens. We want you both with us on Christmas day, and we want someone to look after you full time.

Oh, I'll manage. You know we've got a place fixed, so

95

it's not for much longer.

Yes, Marcus said.

So what about your folks, Sam? What's happening to them over Christmas?

Funny you should ask, Marie. Katy's gone and be-friended this family of orphans. She's persuaded mum and Steve to have them over Christmas. It'll be full house. If Marcus throws me out I'll have to come here.

Why, how many are they?

There are three sisters, or half-sisters, or something. They normally live in a children's home, but Katy's being ap-proved as their foster-carer. Would you believe it? Quiet Katy, with so little experience of the world.

I think behind her quiet persona there's lots of strength of character. And kindness. But then, I wouldn't claim to know her.

Well, I think I do, and I think she's making a big mis-take. But I don't know what to do about it. Apparently she's won mum round to the idea, and Steve's gone along with mum, as usual. And Katy had the cheek to put my name down for a refer-ence, would you believe?

Well, you can't deny her a reference.

No, of course, I did the reference, and they wanted it, like, by return of post. And then Katy was back home for a cou-ple of days in the middle of the week, and came round both nights to babysit and wanted to know what I thought. You know I've never been one to keep my opinions to myself.

Sure, so what did you say?

Well, I did keep my mouth shut, more or less, but it was tough. I just said I was a bit worried if she was taking on too much, and if she could cope with kids like that.

Do you know what these kids are like?

Well, I met the oldest one last Saturday. I haven't met the other two yet, Katy just brought the one to meet us, her folks, but it's this one that she's made a - what d'you call it - "special relationship" with, apparently. It all sounds very unhealthy to me, and I must admit I didn't take to the girl at all -

Does this girl have a name?

She got on better with these two than me. Lara, d'you remember the girl who came with Auntie Katy, what her name was?

Aysha, her name was Aysha.

What about her sisters, d'you remember their names?

No, mummy, I don't remember. Are we gonna meet them too?

Yes, I think so, on Boxing Day, when we go to your granny's house.

So did you like Aysha? Marie asked Lara.

Oh yes, she was good fun, she played with us lots.

What did you think, Liam?

I liked Aysha too.

Good, well I hope you'll like her sisters too. Marie turned back to Samantha. Try and give this a chance, Sam. Don't condemn it before it's started. Katy has to make a few mistakes in life before she gets much older, this may be one of them, but we mustn't automatically assume so until we see how it works out. And even mistakes can sometimes turn out to be blessings in disguise.

Well, that's how this Aysha struck me, all disguise. But a blessing, no way! Friendly with the kids, but under all that, god knows what horrors lurk. When Katy came on her own, she all but admitted it. Told me how she'd had a terrible childhood this Aysha, had been going off the rails since she was about eight! She didn't tell me the details, but you get the picture. Can you imagine our Katy dealing with that?

But you mustn't condemn this girl because of a terrible childhood, Sam! Remember you didn't have that good a time yourself, you needed a lot of help to get through it.

I know, Marie, but I never hid my problems and I think this girl is. And there's a big difference between you, with all your experience as a teacher, or even Steve, helping me, and Katy taking on this Aysha.

Well, in a sense you did hide your problems. It was only Steve and me you made aware of them. And we don't know she's hiding hers. She may just have learned some self-control for when she meets new people such as Katy's family, and that surely is a good sign?

Yeah, well self-control's definitely up her street, but me, I think it's for all the wrong reasons. It was Katy who said to me, If they'd never invented the word "streetwise" they'd have had to invent it for this kid, and I had to laugh when she said it, but I have this feeling it will all end in tears.

Marie couldn't help laughing herself, but ended doubled up with pain.

Oh god, Marie, what is it? Are you OK?

Lara and Liam came up. What's the matter with grandma?

No, I'm all right, it just hurts when I laugh. So tell me what you children have been up to.

We played with Auntie Katy's friend Aysha, said Liam.

You had a party at playgroup, Liam, didn't you, and you had one at nursery school, Lara.

Father Christmas came, grandma, and I got some coloured pencils and a balloon.

It was one of them helium balloons, explained Samantha. And what happened to it, Liam? The boy made a skyward gesture with his hands. Yeah, it floated up in the sky, didn't it? He would insist on holding it while we walked home, I knew he were bound to let go.

And me and Hayley's going up to big school, added Lara.

Is Hayley your best friend?

Yeah!

We've got to have a shopping trip after Christmas, haven't we, Lara, to get stuff for primary school, said Samantha.

And have you seen your other grandmother?

Not this week, have we, kids? Maybe tomorrow we'll go and see her and Steve. I want to see her before Katy and these three girls of hers arrive.

But I want to go when Aysha and the other girls is there! complained Lara.

She's taking after you, Sam, already, said Marie, managing a weak smile. Always wanting to be part of the crowd. How is your mother, I was wondering?

Not too bad as far as I can tell. It's you we're worried about now.

Don't worry about me.

Well, we will come again soon. Tomorrow or Monday. Can we do anything? Get you something to eat?

No thanks dear, really. There is food in, but to be honest

I've no appetite at all. And though it hurts, I must move around a bit every now and again. Is that Marcus arriving?

Lara had gone to the window. It is daddy, mummy! Time for our party!

Can you help daddy to bring in grandma's shopping?

There was only one bag, mummy, he don't need help. And you've forgot to give grandma her Christmas card!

7. BLESSINGS IN DISGUISE

Back in Bursfield, Katy was preparing to collect the three girls for the trip home. But Katy was not a happy person either just now. She was determined to continue with her venture but the fates seemed determined to make this difficult. The start of her troubles had occurred first thing on the Monday morning, the day after Aysha's birthday, when she'd been phoned by a man called Tom Jameson, a social worker in the fostering team, who told her he was dealing with her application. Katy had reacted badly, partly because she felt uneasy with most men, and also because she had not realised that she would need another person on her case. The conversation had not gone well, this Tom Jameson had said she needed to stay in Bursfield that week to process her application, while Katy insisted that she needed to go back to Longworth, she had promised her family, she had promised to babysit for her sister, and she needed a few days away from Bursfield on her own. Mr Jameson said he needed three appointments with her that week, including an "inspection" of her flat, a full discussion in his office, and a meeting with a small group of existing foster-carers. He also said Katy would need to produce a four-page report to back up her application form, one page should describe more fully the qualities she could offer as a foster-carer, another should concentrate on the three girls and what she could do to help them specifically, a third page should look at her motives for wanting to foster these girls, and a fourth should concentrate on what problems and pitfalls she could expect to have to deal with. Katy's heart had sunk, it was not that she lacked the ability for such an exercise, but how much of her real motives should she reveal, she needed time to think this out. And time is what she did not have. She had her concert that evening, she had a final practice with her choir on Thursday evening, she had promised Aysha, Charly and Zoë to have tea with them at the home before her choir practice, and Aysha was expecting to move in on the Friday afternoon. She had also been encouraged to join in parties and pre-Christmas social events by various of her colleagues - she could not really call any of them friends - on her university courses, and in her basketball squad. There were also parties for her orchestra and choir after the concerts. Katy suspected that she was regarded as being too stand-offish, a bit of a loner, and she wanted to try and fit in as best she could, even if she didn't like or feel comfortable at most of these sorts of events. She also had three longish pieces of work, one for each of her subjects, to complete during the vacation. It would have made sense to cancel her trip home but she'd stubbornly refused to do that. Instead she'd phoned Steve to ask him to collect her after lunch on the Tuesday instead of before, and she also arranged to return earlier on the Thursday afternoon than she'd originally planned. She arranged with Tom Jameson for him to visit her flat the Tuesday morning, for her to meet the foster-carers Thursday afternoon, and for her lengthy discussion with him to be on the Friday morning. She'd fitted in two lunchtime parties on the Monday and the Tuesday, one of them being with her basketball team, and she'd written one page of her report on the Monday afternoon and another on the Tues-day before Mr Jameson arrived. Altogether Katy felt that that week she'd been hit by a whirlwind, and poor Greg had been terribly neglected.

You will approve me, won't you? she pleaded with Tom Jameson as soon as he arrived.

I can't promise that, we have to follow procedures even though they're being streamlined in your case, or rather in Aysha Stanton's case, because of the unusual circumstances.

But they told me it would just be a formality.

They had no right to tell you that.

But Aysha's supposed to be moving in on Friday! She'll be devastated if she can't.

No-one should have promised her that, at this early stage. He looked around the flat.

Where will she sleep?

Katy's heart sank. In my bed, she mumbled, indicating.

Where will you sleep? He looked at her quizzically.

In a sleeping-bag, on a spare mattress. My stepfather's bringing them both this afternoon when he collects me.

In this room?

Yes, there's no other option, the kitchen and bathroom are too small.

He didn't comment further, but then he raised another matter which had Katy reeling.

You do realise you'll need some induction and training into the whole range of issues concerning becoming a foster-carer.

Yes, I mean, no, I hadn't really thought - but yes, I can see that would be helpful, she stammered.

With you being so much younger than most of our carers, and with the process being speeded up for these special reasons, I would say immediate training is an absolute must.

Yes, she said, but she must have betrayed the doubts in her mind.

When are you available?

I don't know - this is all happening so fast - I feel I can't draw breath.

I know how you feel, I too think it's happening too fast, I think both you and I are being steamrollered here into meeting other people's demands.

But we can't stop it now! she protested.

I'm not suggesting that. What I am saying is that your willingness to undertake training as early as possible will be a crucial factor, the most crucial factor, in the outcome of your application.

Oh I will, I will! she exclaimed, relief evident in her voice. I'm sorry I seemed doubtful, you caught me by surprise, no-one had mentioned training, but I can see now how important it is.

Good, he said, a lot more gently. I do know the press-ures you are under, with studying for your degree, and I under-stand you are an active person with a number of hobbies, and your dog, which, by the way, I'm pleased to see you have trained so well. And then there will be Aysha's care, and possibly before long two other children, and of course I note that you're intending to continue as a volunteer at the home. So I'm offering you a choice. There is a training course for new foster-carers next term, one evening a week for ten weeks, that would mean you being part of the group - many of whom won't yet have had placements - but if you prefer, and I'm offering this not just to suit your schedule but because I believe it will benefit Aysha, you, and all of us, for you to get the training as quickly as possible, I'm prepared to set up a crash course geared to you individually as soon as possible after New Year. The choice is yours, but I will need to know soon, by the end of this week in fact.

There's a week when school's started, I mean Aysha's unit, and my courses haven't. Were you meaning then?

I guess that was my thinking.

Would I be needed all five days? Because I have said, though I haven't fixed it yet, that I will visit Aysha's mother in prison that week, in order to try and get some of the vital information for starting her Life-Story book.

No, I think that's a most important task that week. If you choose to have the training that week, I'll make sure I keep one day free. I'll let you know which as soon as possible.

Before he left, Katy handed him the two pages she'd completed and promised the other two by Thursday, and felt somewhat relieved after he departed. It sounded as if he were inclined to approve her, now that she had agreed to the training. But when she was going to get her three course projects done this vacation, she had no idea.

But she had two other shocks in store that week. The meeting with the other foster-parents was not one of them, in fact it seemed to go very well, although Katy found it difficult to concentrate on what was being said, what with having just returned from home and still smarting a little from the fact that her sister, even though very grateful for the babysitting, still felt negative about what Katy was doing, but it was more that her mind could not stop straying to Aysha who she'd be seeing very soon for the first time since Sunday.

And that was her first shock. When she got to the children's home Aysha wasn't there! Charly and Zoë were, and greeted her, Zoe affectionately, Charly in her customary non-committal way, and Cassie was there and said that Aysha had gone out earlier, as soon as she returned from her unit. Cassie apologised but said Aysha had been quite determined and there was no stopping her.

She's been to the unit every day, and until tonight she's stayed in here, but to be honest, Katy, since you've been away she's been an absolute pain to the staff here. She's been mouthing off, winding us all up, knowing she won't be here by the end of the week. To be quite honest when she walked off earlier we were glad to see the back of her. She did promise she'd be back, but my view is that she's determined to kick over the traces this week before she moves in with you, so I wouldn't hold your breath tonight.

Katy felt desperately disappointed but tried her hardest not to show it. Tea was about to start so she joined the other children at their tables, having Charly and Zoë sitting each side of her, but acutely aware of the vacant space further down the table. She began to see now why the staff at the home had never set a place for Aysha in the days when Katy had first started coming, it drew attention to the fact of a wayward resident who was beyond everyone's control.

Then half way through the meal Aysha breezed in, high as a kite. Apart from that first meeting when the child was struggling with two policewomen, Katy had never before seen her like this. She could smell her breath, what was it, alcohol, tobacco, cannabis, a mixture of all three and what else, before Aysha even opened her mouth.

Sorry, Katy. Here, Zoë, move up, kid, I'm gonna sit next to Katy.

No, that's not fair, complained the tearful younger child.

Aysha, you can't come in late and take your sister's place. And I'm not having you sitting next to me with your breath smelling like that.

Well, Katy, fuck you, then. Aysha seemed startled for a moment, her face almost crumpled, and then hardened again. Fuck everything then, I'm gonna go back out. And as she reached the door she threw out a parting shot, loudly.

So, you never bothered 'bout my breath when we went to hear Testicles, right!

There was a subdued snigger from some of the other children round the tables. Katy felt her face redden, she felt a sense of utter humiliation and despair. She forced herself to finish the food on her plate and the tea in her mug even though she didn't really feel like eating any more. As soon as the first child left the table, she got up, saying to Charly and Zoë that she'd be back soon, called Greg and took his lead, and went outside.

She didn't have a problem locating the missing child. She was standing on a patch of grass just down the street kicking her foot against a tree and banging her head as well. When Katy got closer she could see tears in her eyes which Aysha quickly wiped away on her sleeve. Greg went rushing up to the girl, straining on his lead so that Katy released him and he jumped up at Aysha who gave him a hug and let him lick her face.

Is that it then? Aysha whispered.

What?

Blown it, has I, me?

Blown what?

Coming to live with you.

Of course not. Come here, you daft kid. For the first time she hugged Aysha, held her tight.

I'm sorry, the child whispered. I just had to go off and see my mates on the estate and say goodbye. Cos I knew you weren't gonna let me go there no more. I never meant to get plastered with stuff but, like, that were their way, y'know, one last time and all that.

It's all right, Aysha, I understand. I'm sorry I reacted the way I did but I didn't think it was fair on Zoë.

No, you're right, it weren't. But if you'd just said that I wouldn't've minded so much. It were you going on 'bout my breath.

OK, my fault that, I'm sorry. As I've told you, I'm gonna make plenty of mistakes. But you don't know how worried I were when I got there and found you missing. I was in a right state. Why couldn't you have gone and said goodbye another day when I were away?

Because, see, Aysha was stumbling over her words and seemed close to tears again. I might not've come back if I'd gone another day, when you wasn't here, right. I can't trust myself without you, Katy. I'd've prob'ly stayed out all night and all that stuff would've started over again, like, missing school and the fuzz and the fucking cells and all that, and next thing I'm in a secure unit and I've blown my whole fucking life. But, like, tonight I knew you was coming, and Greg, and she turned again to hug the dog, so I knew I were gonna get back, whatever happened, even if I were drunk or out of it, even if I were hours late, I would get back. I were never gonna lose this chance you've gave me, and then I thought I had.

Well, you haven't. You're still coming to live with me. Mind you, I haven't been told I've been approved yet, but don't worry, I'm sure I will be.

Y'know, you ain't like any other foster-mums or staff or anything.

Yeah, well, look, I've got my final rehearsal with my choir tonight and I'm gonna be late. And I said I'd go and talk to Charly and Zoë again - look, if I get the OK from Cassie, can you look after Greg, Aysha, until I get back? I know it'll be a bit later than usual, but I'm sure you won't mind staying up, and it means I can go straight there instead of back to my flat first.

Course I'll look after Greg. When is - like, your concert?

Our performance. Saturday afternoon. There's a kinda party afterwards.

Can I come?

What, to the concert or the party?

Both. What kind of music is it?

It's a kind of non-religious, or rather multi-religious Christmas concert and there are groups from lots of different countries.

Charly would like that too.

Well, it might be better if she came too, then you won't be sitting all on your own. But won't it be a bit unfair on Zoë?

Zoë could look after Greg. She'd love that, then she wouldn't mind.

But is she sensible enough? I'd hate anything to happen to Greg.

Yeah, I know. But I could teach her tonight, while you're at your rehearsal.

Teach her what?

Like, how to call him and get him on his lead, and how he needs water and stuff.

OK, sounds a good idea, let's check with Cassie.

So a number of arrangements were made with the home and the two younger girls, and Katy left for her rehearsal feeling on more of a high.

The second shock came the following morning when she went for a long talk with Tom Jameson in his office. She had already decided Mr Jameson was someone to respect, even quite nice. He came straight to the point.

Well, I'll say straight away that you'll be approved as a foster-carer for Aysha Stanton as from today, subject to your agreement to undertake training. I was impressed with what you wrote and your contribution at the interview yesterday. But there are a few further matters I'd like to discuss.

What are those? asked Katy.

Well, two straightforward but important points, first. The sleeping arrangements are not ideal - Aysha really should have her own room.

Yes, I know that.

So I'm going to recommend that you be rehoused in a three bedroom property as soon as possible, and when you are, it's important that you and Aysha each have your own room, and the two younger girls are the ones to share.

OK.

In the meantime, could I suggest that you make up a proper bed for yourself on your spare mattress rather than using a sleeping-bag which makes it seem that you've renounced your creature comforts too much. And, even more important, can you put your bed as far from Aysha's as possible within the room, if necessary by moving round some furniture?

Why?

Because young people of Aysha's age, boys or girls, just reaching puberty, need a lot of privacy, as much as possible.

She hasn't seemed to need much up to now.

I assure you she does, or will. The other point concerns the Life-Story book. When you start this, which I hope will be as soon as possible after you visit the mother, you should set aside a certain time each week for it. It could be an hour, or even half an hour would be OK, but my experience is that if you just wait for you both to feel ready to do it, and have the time, it will never get done. This really is important, and should have priority over virtually everything else. So sort out with Aysha a time when you can both guarantee being available, and stick to it.

Yeah, I get the message.

Now, is there anything arising from our discussions or from what you wrote, that you'd like to discuss further?

I can't think of anything.

Well, let's look a bit more at the page you wrote about possible problems. You mentioned the children's troubled childhoods and how you were prepared to face up to anything they might present you with, resulting from what they'd gone through?

Yes, I've thought about that quite a lot.

Does that include the sexual abuse?

Yes, it does, I know they might show problems in that area?

What problems do you have in mind?

Well, problems of a sexual nature, nightmares, being scared of men, becoming withdrawn, I'm sure there are lots more, I'm still learning about all this.

Yes, of course. Do you think there's any risk of aberrant sexual behaviour from any of these girls?

What do you mean?

Inappropriate sexual play with other children?

Katy was beginning to sense where this was leading.

Oh no, I don't think so. There's no record of anything like that in any of their files, and I'm sure the children's home would have mentioned if -

The risk of such behaviour is very very small, higher in boys but very low indeed in girls. But a history of sexual abuse does increase the risk significantly, even though it still remains low. Now with these three girls, we know Aysha and Charlotte were both abused, but there was no evidence that Zoë had been.

No.

She was very small at the time and the natural child of the abuser, and there was no medical evidence, so let's leave Zoë out of the picture for now. Have you noticed anything in either of the two older girls?

What sort of thing?

To do with behaviour, or physical contact, for example?

Not really. Aysha makes physical contact by grabbing - no, that's the wrong word, kind of clutching my arm, or snuggling up close side by side, but nothing untoward that I'm aware of. Charly I don't know so well but she seems very aloof, avoids physical contact.

Yes, good, that's what I've understood also.

How do you know so much about them?

I've read through their social work file. Not in detail, but when you've been around quite a while, you learn how to pick out the salient points.

They don't talk about having been sexually abused, either of them, and there's nothing about it in Charly's Life-Story book, which did surprise me.

No, it's common for that kind of experience to get repressed, which is why I'm raising it now.

Because it might show up in other ways?

Exactly. Now I understand from what you wrote that you have a close bond with your niece and nephew?

Yes, I do. It was them that first made me think I wanted to work with children.

That's good. But I imagine there will be contact between your niece and nephew and the three Stanton girls?

Yes, Aysha's already met them, and they got on very well.

I just think you need to be aware of the dangers, only a very slight risk, I must add, but one you have to try and prevent -

What do you mean?

I mean, inappropriate sexual behaviour from Aysha or Charly towards your niece. Or nephew. You see, once it's happened, it's too late. Several lives become ruined. I repeat, the risk is so small, but you need to think about what you can do to prevent it.

Well, short of stopping them seeing each other, I don't know - I mean I would supervise closely anyway.

That never works. Children will always find ways of playing together, out of adults' sight or earshot.

Well, I could warn Lara when she's a bit older. Or even

now. Tell her not to let them touch her in the wrong places, when do you think a child is old enough to be warned?

I think it depends on the child - and the parents. I'm very impressed with your thinking on this but I hope you weren't thinking of telling Lara without consulting her parents first.

But if I tell the parents they're not going to let Lara see the girls, are they? Or Liam.

Probably only Zoë. But this is your huge dilemma, taking on girls with this background. If you tell people, you risk finding that the girls, and even you, are ostracised. If you don't, you are faced with a much smaller, but far more serious risk, of something occurring which can destroy lives, and not just of the children either.

Why are you telling me this now?

I'm sorry to be so negative, but I really did think this needed to be discussed. I know it's left you with some very difficult decisions, but I still think it is right that you are fully aware.

Well I think I was aware already, just not of the full implications.

Quite so.

Katy was upset and angry for hours afterwards, even as she was helping Aysha move in, though she hoped nothing showed then.

She had grown to trust Tom Jameson, thought he was straight and helpful, now all he had done was cast her under a dark cloud of anxiety, facing an impossible dilemma. She was sure it was deliberate on his part, someone had told him he'd got to approve her in order to get Aysha out of Social Services' hair, and do it quick, and he didn't like that, so he'd got back at her right at the end. Of course, she knew that there was truth in what he said, and it was a truth that yes she did need to be aware of, but this could have waited until she did her training in January, surely? Now she would spend Christmas under this shadow of fear and doubt. Still mulling over the situation that night, after she and Aysha returned from the Richard Thompson gig, unable to sleep long after Aysha was peacefully slumbering, tucked up in her new bed, Katy came to see the best answer. She would need to help the two girls face their abuse, accept it, come to terms with it, work through it, come out the other end to a place where the risk to others no longer existed. If she could get that process started, other people could then know. She beat her fist on the pillow and almost called out, Yes! and wished she'd thought of it earlier so that she could have told that Mr Jameson before she left his office. Of course, she realised, pursuing these thoughts, that this would be too difficult for her alone, she would need expert help, there were experts in this field, surely? She could ask when she was doing the training. Aysha, she decided, was not likely to accept anyone else and it would have to be her, Katy, who helped her through, but she thought she could get to it in Aysha's case through the Life-Story work. With Charly it would be more difficult, she did not know Charly well, but from what she did know, she was resistant to any close or intrusive relationship, and Charly's Life-Story book had already been completed.

Finally she fell asleep, determined to hold on to what she'd decided when she woke the next morning. Then she and Aysha were back at the home, handing Greg over to Zoë and collecting Charly for the concert and the party afterwards. Both girls stuck close to her at the latter. Katy had tried to tell as many people as possible about her new situation, but still there were people who came and asked if these were her younger sisters. There was no longer a simple reply, "friends" would not seem appropriate now. Fortunately both girls were more interested in talking about the music than their relationship with Katy, it was gratifying that they had taken so much interest, had decided which pieces they liked best, and that they were full of enthusiasm for something that was an alternative to the normal "carol service" which they did not hesitate to express their disdain for. Katy felt hopeful she might have made a small breakthrough with Charly.

After a quiet restful day, Katy and Aysha had spent most of Monday shopping. Katy wondered how strange it was for Aysha to be traipsing round the city centre in daylight, working hours, amid all the festive lights and pre-Christmas crowds, after her many evening and overnight escapades here. But other than matter-of-fact comments, such as, That were the bench I spent the night on once, or, That were the shop Dean and me used to nick stuff from regular, she did not seem to be perturbed by memories or nostalgia. They bought clothes, for Aysha, Christmas presents and after a long lazy break for lunch in a café, they went into a main high-street chemist, where, having established that Aysha had reached puberty, but unable to find out from Aysha or from anyone at the home, when her periods were due, she made sure the girl had the necessary supplies.

She also, after some argument, reluctance on her part, and pleading on Aysha's, bought the girl a pack of twenty cigarettes. The problem was that Katy had very little available cash. She was going to be paid a fairly reasonable allowance for Aysha's care, but only the clothing grant had arrived so far, and what with the Christmas post, Katy could not be sure the regular allowance would come before the girls travelled to Longworth. Aysha said cigarettes, and other things such as presents, could come out of the clothing allowance, but Katy said no, she had to account for everything she spent out of that, and anyway Aysha needed lots of clothes. She had chosen a somewhat warmer jacket than her current one, which was at least partly waterproof Katy hoped, for the girl had no wet weather protection at all, and a tracksuit to wear when she joined Katy for running, but she adamantly refused to wear jeans or trousers of any kind. They bought two extra skirts, two more pairs of tights, some extra underwear, and several new tops, long-sleeved, short-sleeved, sleeveless, winter, summer, warm, thin, and in-between. More than a third of the allowance went on footwear, Aysha insisted on expensive trainers and an even more expensive pair of boots. A bag, quite a lot larger than her present one but still at Aysha's insistence, to be worn on her back, was also seen as necessary, and what little was left after all that went at the chemists. Katy said that once the allowance arrived, she would give Aysha two pounds fifty a week pocket money out of it, and Aysha would have to buy her cigarettes out of pocket money, so this now was a one-off. Katy would put a small amount, smaller than the home had been paying, aside for paying the Court for the Compensation, but she wouldn't take it off her pocket money. But she told Aysha that she was having to go into a Bank and negotiate a small loan facility, because she, Katy, wouldn't get any more student grant until the beginning of January and basically she had run out of money.

How's you gonna pay it back? asked Aysha, concerned.

I'll pay back some when your allowance arrives, and the rest when I get next term's grant. But I've still got to pay for my own train ticket home, as well as buy some more presents, so there's absolutely no chance of any more cigarettes.

What about me and Charly and Zoë's tickets?

Social Services are paying that.

Now, the following evening, she was doing final bits of packing, ready to collect the other two children after breakfast tomorrow and get a morning train to Longworth.

8. POOL OF SORROW

Steve Mountfield was glad to have extra visitors for Christmas. He didn't mind all the extra cooking and other housework involved. He had slipped into that role quite seamlessly, and knew it was an extension of the commitment he had made to Sharon and her daughters all those years ago, and which had always been quietly appreciated even when nothing was said. In any case he found it easier to stay on the periphery of these family occasions, even before Sharon's disability had been diagnosed, he had taken quite naturally, even with some relief, to the kitchen as his main domain. Thinking about this, he decided it was a combination of reticence and a disliking of emotional complications. He'd kept his own family at some distance both geographically and emotionally once he'd escaped to college, to the point that he rarely saw them now, and he was determined to ride light over the emotional complexities that had accompanied his becoming part of the Owen family, and which now seemed to be particularly brought into prominence by the sad news about Marie.

Steve knew how devastated Samantha would be by this news, and that when Sam and her family came on Boxing Day they would have just had Marie to visit, possibly for the last time, certainly her last Christmas. Steve couldn't help but be reminded how important both these two, Maria and Sam, were still to him, not in the same way as Sharon, who still meant the whole world to him, but in a more difficult, complicated way which he couldn't talk to anyone about, even Sharon, and that was why, over the Christmas period as a whole, he welcomed the distraction of Katy's visitors, and on Boxing Day specifically, that he would be entirely focussed on cooking for ten.

When Steve had arrived at Longworth High School in 1972, aged twenty-two, from his home town of Bristol, Marie and Jack had been there just one year. Marie taught geography, Jack taught science, and Steve was a wet-behind-the-ears historian. The school, previously the secondary modern for the town - as against St James High School, where Katy went, and Marie's two boys, which was the old grammar school - was still very much the poor relation, results weren't good, and even though the divide was supposed to be geographical, it was surprising how few of the brighter students ended up at Longworth High. The new intake of young teachers in the early seventies, of which he, Marie and Jack were leading lights, had in a relatively few years, changed all that round, mainly through commitment and enthusiasm, and a willingness to give up loads of their own time to encourage out-of-school activities. Marie and Jack organised many school trips, at weekends and in the school holidays, and Steve had joined in more than half of them. Quite a number of these were to the Lake District or to North Wales, as Marie and Jack shared a passion for the mountains, and Steve also was a keen hill-walker and came on most of them too. There were others, though, with scientific or geographical interest, Ingleton, Malham Cove, Morecambe Bay, the Conway Valley, Anglesey, the Dark and White Peaks. What was most amazing about Marie was the number of teenage girls from years nine and ten that she got climbing the mountains with enthus-iasm. This may have had something to do with the fact that from a very early age Marie would bring her boys along too. Steve had to admit that in those days his feelings for Marie were something more than just admiration and friendship for a colleague. Not that he would ever do anything, of course, and he knew that Marie and Jack were devoted to one another, which only increased his admiration. Thinking back to those years, Steve felt a combination of pride, at how a small group of teachers, and Marie most of all, had turned the school around, and a nostalgia, which was not about his bachelor feelings and yearnings, but about what they did together, with groups of children and sometimes on their own, a small group of staff on a hiking trip to the mountains, it had been something like a substitute family for him.

Eighteen years of a life, a living, a lifestyle which had really felt far too good to Steve for him to want to change by applying for new jobs or even making serious efforts to find a wife or a steady girlfriend, though he'd met, been with, been out with, a number of women both within and outside the school teaching community, but the thought of commitment to anything other than his existing commitments always deterred him from taking it further. But he had taken on additional responsibilities at school, and this had led him into the life of Samantha Owen aged just twelve, for whom he was history teacher, class teacher, and year head for year seven.

He was drawn to Samantha, and he could see later that it was her feelings for him that had drawn him to her. But at the time he thought it was mostly how he had coaxed out of her the troubles she faced at home, that drew them together, troubles which she'd been trying to deal with for at least two years, and which nobody at her primary school or in the mental health services who looked after her mother, had given any attention to.

Steve was not a trained counsellor, he took on his role in the school with only a half-day induction, but he felt he had given Samantha the support and counselling she'd needed at the time, when she was failing in her work, falling further and further behind, was overtired, moody, prone to temper outbursts, undervalued, and just plain sad. Much of that he'd turned around by the individual counselling he provided at school, but it was clear that the real help Samantha needed was at home, and wasn't being provided there by anyone else. He soon realised it was very foolish for him to offer this, untrained as he was and way beyond his remit, but a revitalised Samantha had been very persuasive! So he'd been drawn beyond Samantha into the Owen family, where he'd found a grown-up version of Samantha, his own age, still attractive, but like Samantha when he first knew her, a very sad person, depressed for some years, with periods in psychiatric wards. Steve lacked the emotional defences for this experience, children with problems yes, but the mother's pool of sorrow was something else, it sucked him in, out of his depth, and for the first time in his life at the age of forty-one, he knew what it was to fall in love.

He was sure he'd done the right thing, as he and Sharon Owen cemented their relationship and planned to marry, not just in making his commitment to Sharon and her daughters, but for Sam, as he was now calling her, that he called on the person up until now whom he'd liked and admired most in the world, to take on the continuation of the counselling which he knew Sam would still need. And Marie had not let him down. Steve, of course, was still a teacher at the school and still saw Marie regularly, but he no longer joined her and Jack on their trips, no longer gave up his free time, no longer took on additional responsibilities such as pastoral care. He was head of history by now, and that was enough. The rest of his life was his devotion to Sharon. But the link with Marie continued through Sam. Through Sam's turbulent adolescence, through the drinking, drugs, staying out too late, the frequent rows, even fights, between Sam and her mother, sometimes over virtually nothing, it often seemed to Steve, and how similar they were, he continued to think, neither of them willing to give an inch, through all this Marie was there in the background for Sam, often taking her in overnight and returning her the next day, which were the only occasions now, outside school, that Steve ever saw Marie. Until Sam and Marcus fell in love. Steve could remember that strange sense of almost physical pain when he realised what was happening. But why shouldn't it? He of all people should have seen it coming, it was so similar to him and Sharon, only twenty years younger. Sam and Sharon were so alike, although Sam didn't suppress her guilt and anger like Sharon had done, she wore her emotions on her sleeve, and Steve knew that this was why Marcus, very like him, not a teacher for sure, but a placid caring guy who was already into sharing his enthusiasm for football with young kids, found Sam so attractive.

All these emotional entanglements which Steve liked to stay clear of now! He relaxed mostly by going to cricket or football matches with Marcus or Katy or both, but during all those years he had longed for the relaxation of the mountains, and hoped he'd one day be able to return to them. But why, he mused as he prepared the big Boxing Day lunch and half-heard all the excited squeals of children running in and out of the downstairs rooms, did he never include Katy in his mulling over the past? Quiet, sensible Katy, diametrically different from her older sister yet so loyal to her, Katy who had just turned six when Steve moved in with her mum, who had been so much part of his life, such a constant presence, since that time, Katy who had been the stepdaughter every man like him would have wished for, friendly but not too close or demanding, leading her own life but helpful when she could be, stroppy at times in a humorous sort of way but never a real fight or emotional outburst either with Sharon or him, Katy who had accompanied him many times to football matches at Old Trafford, or Maine Road, or Burnden Park - before those latter two grounds made way for newer ones - and to cricket at Old Trafford, who would chat happily about sport all day as a boy would have done, rather than get onto anything more personal, Katy who was just like Steve himself in so many ways that he wondered about having had an undue influence on her in those first years of being part of her family. Sharon used to worry about Katy, still did in fact, that she was different from other girls, had never had a boy-friend, and he would reply, jokingly, that she shouldn't worry, Katy was just like him, stayed away from emotional entanglements, after all he'd never had a long-term girlfriend until he was forty-one!

Still, even Steve had to admit surprise about Katy now. Not that they weren't expecting Christmas to be like this, after all they'd already met Aysha and Katy had told them a bit about the other two girls. Katy had said, soon as they were in the door virtually, that she and Aysha would help with the cooking and Zoë and Charly would help with washing-up. But Steve hadn't wanted this, the kitchen was his domain now and he wanted to preserve its sanctuary effect for him, especially today, Boxing Day, the big family occasion. He did accept help with washing-up, and agreed for Katy and Aysha to cook a meal the day after Boxing Day, when even he expected he would need a break from cooking. And Katy had taken all three girls and the dog, all the way to the centre of town on Christmas Eve to get a bit of last-minute shopping. Sharon was in her element, with an addition of three more girls to the family, even if she couldn't do much on a physical level with them. Katy's closeness with Aysha was even more noticeable than on their first visit. He, Steve, stayed in the background to observe. Charly was more like a boy and very quiet, Zoë was shy but affectionate, Aysha was, well, just Aysha. They didn't seem, any of them, to know quite what to make of Christmas Day in a strange household, but there was genuine enjoyment and appreciation and Steve felt the day had passed well.

The difference today, apart from the increase in numbers, was Steve's sense of Marie's ailing spirit, hovering there. He knew Sam would be aware of it too, and probably Marcus. And what about Neil, looking after Marie at home? Or Jack even? Funny how many players in this tangled-up drama slipped from Steve's mind all the time. He thought back to that critical year and a quarter when so many changes happened. It was 2000 into 2001, start of the foot-and-mouth crisis, before 9.11 and the world changed forever. First, the wedding, Sam and Marcus hitched, and all the feelings that brought up, followed soon after by Lara being born. Then Katy's best friend had moved away, and soon after that, on Katy's fifteenth birthday, a puppy called Greg became part of their household. Fast forward to the following March and there was the shock of Sharon's diagnosis, and a month later the shock of Jack's death.

At least Jack had a year of seeing one grandchild, but he never saw Liam and he would miss them both growing up, as Marie now would too. Jack would never know what happened to change the world the September after he died. Marie was there when the accident happened, but he, Steve, wasn't, and neither of course were Neil or Marcus, both leading their own lives, one married with a small child. Steve might have gone abroad with them if Sharon's diagnosis hadn't come when it did, but mountain walking in the Pyrenees in April was always going to have an element of risk to it, and that higher-risk type of walking wasn't for him, really. Still, he might have plucked up courage and gone, and who knows, it might have been him instead of Jack. At the time he'd thought of this and then thought, thank god it's Jack, not on his own account, but because he thought Marie would cope better on her own than Sharon ever could, even without the MS diagnosis. After all, Sharon had already lost one husband and hadn't dealt with it very well. But now Steve could see he'd been entirely wrong about that, beneath her coping exterior Marie had in fact been devastated by Jack's death, and had lost the resistance to prevent the creeping onset of her own.

What troubled Steve was that Marie had seemed to avoid him ever since that time. He would have felt he should have been able to take some kind of consoling role with her after Jack's death, he had been a good friend to them both for all those years, after all. Marie had steered clear of him at the funeral; and at school, during the one term they had there together between Jack's death and Steve's resignation to take up part-time evening lecturing because of Sharon's future needs, their paths hardly crossed at all. He had hardly seen her since, and had to admit to a huge disappointment when he found there was a presentation for her at Longworth High the day before Katy and the girls arrived, and he had not been invited. Memories were so short these days, he had devoted so much of his life to the school, alongside Jack and Marie, OK so it seemed it was very much an internal school event, neither Marcus and Sam, nor Neil if he'd arrived back in time, were expected at it. He had thought about just turning up uninvited, but decided that wasn't the done thing. But he did puzzle about Marie and what was in her mind. Did she resent him for surviving when Jack had died? Did she think that any kind of emotional contact between her and him would be showing disloyalty to Jack? Steve felt a burning need to see Marie soon, before she became too ill and before she died, to find some sort of closure on how things were between them, but wasn't sure how best to make this happen.

What he did remember, trying to focus his mind on happier thoughts, was that things had been good between him and Marie in the year 2000, that year when Steve finally returned to the mountains again. Sharon was happy in her life more than Steve had ever known, she had returned a few years earlier to driving taxis again, though not her own business this time, Sam was married, settled down, and most of all there was a small grandchild, apple of Sharon's eye. Katy was growing quite mature, even with the moving away from Longworth of her friend Sophie, she did not need Steve around that much, and certainly did not want his help with the training of her new puppy. Only once had he persuaded her to come to watch Lancashire at cricket that summer, and even then she'd insisted on bringing the damned dog, which meant she was wandering off every few overs to find a patch of grass behind one of the sightscreens. So that year, firstly at the May half-term, and then for much of the summer holiday, Steve had returned to the mountains of the Lake District and Snowdonia. Two or three days at a time, or sometimes just a day, starting early, returning late. Sometimes with a small group of teachers from school, sometimes just with

Marie and Jack, sometimes on his own, the hills had become something like an addiction for him, a craving he'd had for many years without being aware of it. He could remember every single walk almost as clear as if it had been yesterday. The long horse-shoe ridge above Mardale and Hawes-water, and the sight of a golden eagle from near the top of Ill Bell. Crinkle Crags and Bowfell from Langdale, returning over Harrison Stickle as the sun began to set over Sca Fell Pike. Sca Fell Pike itself from Seathwaite by the direct steep ascent to Sprinkling Tarn, and returning along the Corridor Route. Haystacks and the Pillar Traverse from Honister Pass, returning from the summit of Pillar by Black Sail and Moses Trod - that was some walk, remember-ing the tiredness in his limbs as he trod the Trod, as he and Marie joked that evening. And he remembered the Welsh walks too, only he forgot, much to his chagrin, the Welsh names of valleys and villages, even sometimes, though not so much, of the moun-tains themselves. And it was not for Steve just the joy of the mountains them-selves, but that when Marie and Jack were with him, things were back to those years before he married Sharon, when his friend-ship with them, and the teaching, the success of the school, the expeditions into the hills were all part of a life lived, seamlessly, purposefully, what he felt his life was meant to be.

But that was the only year. Sharon's impending dis-ability, along with the foot-and-mouth, ruled out 2001 and the years since. It was foot-and-mouth that indirectly caused Jack's death, because that was the reason the short-notice trip to the Pyrenees had been arranged for the small group of teachers that enjoyed the mountains, none of them were open in England or Wales that Easter. And that was Marie's last experience of the mountains. She had not returned to hill-walking since Jack died, and surely would not now.

But there was something else. When he got together with Sharon, he had not been able to tell her, for he sensed that when he entered that deep pool of sorrow with her, and only with difficulty succeeded in pulling them both clear, this would have been that one extra thing, that one straw, which would have kept them both there caught in a hopeless love, sad and drowning for ever. And ever since, his failure to say had haunted him. He kept saying to himself, Some day soon .... but it never happened.

Most of the time he forgot, ignored it, that was why he kept to himself, busied himself with household duties and Sharon's needs, lost himself in other memories, happy or sad. But now, all the family were here and he was very tempted. He could have easily placed the turkey and the vegetables on the table and then said, Just wait a moment, there is something I need to say to you all. But there were these three new members of the family here, still struggling to adjust. And two small grandchildren, too young to understand. And the presence of the dying Marie hovering over them all. No, he could not say anything now.

Charly volunteered to help with the washing-up after the Boxing Day lunch. Aysha and Zoë were busy playing with the little kids, Aysha with Lara mostly, and Zoë with baby Liam. Katy was talking to her mum and her older sister, and Marcus was helping Steve clear the table, and Charly decided that she liked Marcus and especially Steve best of the new people she'd met this Christmas. She liked the idea that the men would be doing the washing-up and talking about sport, even though she didn't do sport apart from swimming herself and didn't know much about it. She hated women's talk and didn't much like small children either. So she took a tea-towel they offered her and started drying the dishes as they were handed to her, half listening to the men's conversation and half thinking her own thoughts. Charly had used to worry a lot about Aysha. For a long time she had hated it when Aysha went missing overnight, wondering what might have happened to her, although after a while she got used to it, knew somehow that she would always come back. But then she thought that Aysha would get sent a long way away, by the police or the courts or Social Services, who had already once put her in a different foster-home to Zoë and her, and she worried a lot about that. Sometimes she talked to Aysha about her worries but that weren't any good, Aysha didn't seem bothered, although Charly knew Aysha loved her and always came back mainly to see her. Aysha had looked after Charly when they lived with their mum, because their mum took drugs and couldn't look after them proper which was why they was took into care. Charly tried in return to help Aysha now. How she could help her was with her schoolwork and by telling her things. Charly mostly went about on her own, she tried to look like a boy and have a scowl on her face because she thought boys were stronger and could be alone without getting teased or bullied. It worked, no-one bothered Charly. She liked doing things on her own, like reading, listening to music, painting, writing, walking and even swimming she liked doing on her own when she could. But Charly also watched and listened. She went round the home with a book and with music playing in her ears, and the other kids thought she were in a world of her own but she weren't. She knew what were happening, she always listened and watched. Even in her room, she left the door open and listened out for other kids. Just now there was no kids in the home who liked to go in other kids' rooms and nick things, but there had been in the year and a half she'd been there, more than one kid who took other kids' stuff, which Charly hated. She had loads of her own private stuff in her room and she wanted it to be safe there. There was special books about science and wildlife, there was special albums which were hard to get, and there was her Life-Story book. Charly liked looking at it, not because she wanted to read about her own life but because she'd done coloured drawings in it, and so had Teresa who'd helped her with the book and also helped her with her art, so it were as much an artwork book as a Life-Story book. She was the only kid who kept theirs in their room. When she first came Charly thought the rooms should be kept locked, but staff said that in that case kids would not be able to go freely into their rooms unless they had their own key which was dangerous because bullies could steal your key, lock you in and throw it away, or kids could lock themselves in their rooms and be at risk from fire or self-harm. So Charly had agreed this were best but she watched and listened for any nicking going on or a kid going in someone else's room. When this happened she told Aysha. If Aysha weren't around she waited for her to come back. Then Aysha would get in a fight with the kid that did the nicking until either the kid gave back what they nicked or a staff intervened. Aysha would tell the staff why she were fighting the kid and the staff would tell Aysha off for fighting and said she should've gone straight to them but Aysha didn't care. Anyhow the nicking had stopped and Charly didn't feel so worried.

Charly also used to tell Aysha what staff had said and things other kids had said while she were out. Aysha used to tell her what she'd been up to, and Charly used to laugh because she knew that were what Aysha wanted but inside she felt worried. She also worried about Zoë. Her younger sister had a friend called Ambrose. Ambrose weren't real, he were Zoë's imaginary friend. His name was made up from Zoë's middle name, Amber. Zoë didn't let anyone else know about Ambrose, only her, Charly. He only came to see Zoë in her room, and she would be always talking to him in whispers. Some day someone would find out, and Zoë would get teased. She were coming up eight and was too old to have a secret friend. Charly told Aysha about it, and Aysha said she already knew and that Zoë would grow out of it, but she weren't growing out of it. Charly wondered if Katy knew about Ambrose, whether Aysha had told her. She kept meaning to ask, but there was always other people around.

Charly liked Katy. She liked her because she did running and music and painting and had a dog. She liked her because she weren't a girly girl. Most of all she liked her because it were due to her that Aysha had stopped running off or getting arrested. That were a big weight off Charly's shoulders. She missed having Aysha around the children's home, but at least they was spending six days, all of them together, over Christmas. Charly hated meeting new people, but if these was Katy's family she hoped they'd be like Katy. And they was, especially her step-dad Steve. She dried the stuff from the washing-up in silence and thought how this were much better than listening to the women's talk or trying to entertain them screaming kids. It were good to have time to think, and listen to men's talk.

Everything OK, Charly? Steve asked her.

Yeah. Charly never smiled, and spoke as few words as she could get away with. She thought Steve understood.

Good, we've nearly finished. You've been a fantastic help, hasn't she, Marcus?

It's about time you got a dishwasher, Steve, said Marcus.

Can't afford it. Anyway I enjoy washing-up when it's just the two of us. Dishwasher would be a waste.

So what's on for you tomorrow, Charly? asked Marcus.

She shrugged.

Charly's a kid of few words, aren't you? said Steve. But intelligent. Nearly reading grown-up books, eh? And good at art.

Got some new paints for Christmas, didn't you, kid? And no chance to use them yet. So let's get you doing a painting tomorrow while Aysha and Katy are cooking the meal. And then I think we'll have a quiet, restful day. And the day after you'll be going back home, won't you?

Yeah, said Charly.

9. DREAMING WITH EYES WIDE OPEN

When she got back to Bursfield, Katy found among a plethora of mail, the first month's allowance for Aysha's care, and a note from Tom Jameson with the schedule for the training course early in January. On that basis she got in touch with the prison the girls' mother was at, and arranged for them to send her a visitor's pass. On the train back from Longworth she had talked to the three of them about a visit to their mother, and whether, the next time she went, which would be some months off she assured them, any of them were going to want to come too. She left Charly and Zoë thinking about this, knowing with some certainty that it would take much longer to persuade Aysha to come.

Meantime she was faced with almost two weeks with Aysha. On one level Katy felt a sense of profound joy that it would just be the two of them sharing their time, blissing out, but when it came to the nitty-gritty she hadn't a clue what she could do to keep the restless thirteen-year-old from getting bored and therefore risking a return to her old ways. It was the opposite problem from before Christmas, when there was so much happening, so much to do, that she was lucky to seize an occasional hour with Aysha on her own.

She contemplated a further few days back in her home town. She still felt the need to make things up with Sam, but to take Aysha back yet again might only make things worse. Aysha and Lara were getting on like a house on fire, but the fire was threatening to get out of control. Anyway she'd visited three times already this vacation, and would be doing so again at the end of January, when there was a performance by a group of African musicians at the Old Mill Arts Centre, which both Aysha and Charly were keen to go to. Steve said he would get the tickets and Sharon said she was happy to look after Zoë. However, when Marcus and Sam and the kids had arrived on Boxing Day they had plenty of presents for Katy, Sharon and Steve but none for "Katy's three girls" as the family started calling them. Who noticed this and who felt bad about it was not entirely clear, but it seemed none of the children allowed it to spoil their day. Katy, however, was mortified, and put it down as further evidence of her sister's hostility. Marcus was very apologetic, and Katy hoped very much he was speaking for Sam as well as himself, and so it had been agreed that he, Marcus, would buy the tickets for Aysha and Charly. It only remained for him to do a quick trawl of the shops the following day and find a present for Zoë - a book on ballet with an attached DVD, ballet wasn't Zoë's favourite form of dance and they didn't have any equipment which played DVDs, but the intention was there - which Marcus dropped by with later that day.

So Katy and Aysha found themselves running together with Greg in tow, or giving him walks, which Aysha was happy to do on her own, so as she could light up, Katy was sure, and this despite a spell of dull, miserable, and sometimes quite wet, weather. There was nothing on around New Year, apart from a firework display in the city centre on New Year's Eve itself, which they went to, but only briefly because Greg's dislike of fireworks meant leaving him in the flat.

Aysha had never, up to now, taken to reading books, or even magazines, nor was there anything on television that appealed, apart from the occasional music programme which featured her kind of music. She was happy to listen to her CDs, and one or two of Katy's, in the evenings, learn to bang Katy's drum in the daytime once the others in the neighbouring flats returned to work after New Year, and brush and comb Greg endlessly. And she was always happy to talk, about her sisters, about Katy's family, about music, about things they'd seen on their walks, the latter two subjects being the source of endless jokes and laughter, but she never talked about herself unless pressed. It appeared that not only the sexual abuse in her childhood, but all the other trauma and erratic behaviour, she had now put behind her and did not wish to raise up those spectres any more. It did not bode well for the Life-Story work.

Katy was keen to get her three course-work projects completed and explained this to Aysha. The child offered to take Greg for even longer walks on her own to give Katy the time - she did not seem bothered about weather conditions, and had better outdoor gear now in any case. Even so, there were some evenings when Katy needed to get down to serious writing and Aysha, with no schoolwork of her own to do, and no need to be up early for her Unit, showed no inclination to retire to bed until Katy did. So she spent some evenings with the headphones on listening to album after album and Katy worried about this. Aysha tended to sleep late as long as Katy could stop Greg licking her face to wake her up for his first walk of the morning, and that then allowed Katy a good hour at course work. Katy got all the meals and Aysha washed up, and they did the shopping together. One or two college friends of Katy's called her up, although most weren't in town at this time, and were invited round for coffee or lunch, or they arranged to meet up in town, when Aysha was happy to try and join in the conversation as long as she was allowed to ask what words meant or for explanations about the topic of discussion. They had Charly and Zoë round for a meal, and went to the park on another occasion with them, but Aysha did not want to revisit the children's home otherwise.

One of her projects required Katy to spend quite a lot of time in the College library, and if Aysha were to be left at the flat, she would need to have a key, so that she could take Greg out and let herself back in. Katy felt, for some reason, reluctant to lend the girl her own key, and wondered at what point she should get a spare cut for Aysha's own use. It proved no problem persuading Aysha to come to the library with her, show her where she would be working, and then let Aysha wander round the campus with Greg for an hour or so, come to join her for a quick drink and snack in the library's cafeteria, and then repeat the process for another hour. Dogs weren't allowed in either the library or the cafeteria, and the only difficulty with this arrangement was Aysha's unhappiness at having to leave Greg tied up by the front entrance for more than a few minutes. But they did this successfully twice, to Katy's satisfaction, and she completed the piece of work.

On the Saturday night before Aysha's new term started,

there was another gig at the same place where they'd been to see the Test Icicles all those weeks ago. The headline band was unknown to both of them, but they decided to go, Katy making a very strict stipulation that it would be coca-cola only, no alcohol. Aysha had agreed with this, but it did not stop her trying it on once they got there. In fact the evening followed the pattern of the previous one at that venue with eerie sameness, Aysha even wore just about the same outfit, eschewing for once the new clothes bought before Christmas for her old black jumper and denim skirt, but Katy went for jeans and a jumper this time. At this gig the noisy outfits were the support bands, while the headliners, The Have-Nots, gave out a quieter, gentler, more harmonious sound which Katy, but not Aysha, liked a lot better. The other big difference this time was that Katy stuck to her guns over the no alcohol rule despite all Aysha's protestations and pleading. Despite this, the younger girl seemed in just as high spirits on the train journey back as on the previous occasion.

On the Sunday Katy judged it the right moment to ask Aysha if she'd thought any more about preparing to transfer to a mainstream school in September. Of course Aysha hadn't. Katy was beginning to see that this was a kid who lived in the present, tried to forget the past and had no concept of thinking about the future, or at least not more than a few days ahead.

D'you wanna think about it now?

What's I s'posed to think?

If it were a school which didn't insist on uniform, d'you think you could settle in there? Catch up on the work?

I dunno, do I? How's I s'posed to know?

Well, we could talk a bit more about it with your teacher at the Unit, what's her name?

D'you mean the one in charge?

Yeah.

Julia Flowers.

OK, Julia Flowers. Shall I ask to have a discussion about it, you me and her?

OK then.

Shall I write her a note, or shall I take you in tomorrow?

Just write her a note. Is the minibus collecting me?

It should be. What time does it come?

Half-past eight from the home. But I dunno what time

from here.

Well, we'll have to assume about the same time. When d'you get back?

Half-past three, but quarter-to on Fridays.

Right, well remember to give Ms Flowers the note, right.

Ms Flowers, you don't call her that.

What do I call her?

Mrs Flowers, or Julia. She's got a husband who's a teacher.

What, at the Unit?

At the junior one I went to before, right.

OK. Now listen, I've got a spare key for you, right. You won't need it tomorrow or Tuesday cos I'll be here when you get back. (She would have to leave her training ten minutes early, but never mind, it seemed important the first two days.) But on Wednesday I'm gonna see your mum and I won't be back till later. So I'll give you the key breakfast time and you'll have to let yourself in and give Greg a walk straight away. Cos he'll have been on his own all day in here, right. Remember you'll need to take the key with you when you take him out, otherwise you'll be locked out. I'll remind you again Wednesday morning when I give you the key.

So, three trains and a bus journey had taken her to a women's prison near the east coast of Yorkshire where she'd been shown into a friendly enough interview room but whose door had been locked with a woman officer standing inside the door and another one just outside. A third officer had brought along the girls' mother, Janine Estelle Stanton, and they had sat down on comfortable chairs around a coffee table, one of the other two officers then being dispatched to bring cups of coffee and biscuits.

You don't mind me being here? said the third officer. I'm specially assigned to Stella, and she asked me to come along with her.

Stella?

I don't call meself Janine any more, said the prisoner in a rough Midlands accent. I'm Stella now.

Right. Well, my name's Katy Victoria Owen, call me Katy. I've taken on Aysha, first as a befriender, and now I'm approved as her carer. She's moved in with me, and her two sisters probably will soon too. I thought you'd want to know, and to meet me. Also I wanted to meet you.

Why?

To understand the girls better. I think I do understand Aysha, but there's always more to know.

Aren't you a bit young for Aysha?

Yeah, I'm only a student, and I'm nineteen. But the thing is, Aysha can't or won't relate to older people, but she will to me.

How's she doing then? I heard she were in loads of trouble.

She was. But she's turned that around. Too early to know for sure how long it will last, but the signs are good at present.

Well, just like me. I'm on the mend, ain't I? She looked at her officer.

Trying your best, Stella.

Stella looked ravaged and worn out. Her voice was harsh, rough and tired. She could have looked attractive once, Katy thought, but it would be impossible for anyone not knowing her to judge her age.

Charly and Zoë are fine, too, said Katy. All three girls came to stay with my folks for a few days at Christmas. They had a good time.

I'm sorry they can't stay with me, said Stella. Maybe one day. I never even sent them a card or a present.

I want to encourage contact with you, said Katy. But it's up to them. I can't force them to come. But you could write if you wanted to. Social Services are going to move me to a bigger place soon, before Easter I think, so that all three of them can be together. And they'll put in a phone. I'll come again then and let you have the address and phone number.

Where are Charly and Zoë now?

Still living at the children's home. They'll be in school just now. Charly only has one term after this one before she moves to High School.

Is Aysha in High School?

No, she's still in an Education Referral Unit. But we hope to get her a transfer to High School next September, so she'll start the same time as Charly, but not necessarily the same school.

See, I know nuthin 'bout my kids, their mother said in a sad but resigned voice, turning to the prison officer and back to Katy. They sent me letters but I blocked it out. I never wanted to lose them but they told me I had to. I thought I were never gonna see them again. So I stopped bothering.

It's never too late to start bothering again, said Katy.

That's right, said the prison officer.

I did love them, said Stella Stanton, in a torn voice. I still do, really. I'll never stop loving them, you don't, do you, when it's your own kids. But I should never have had kids, I wasn't right for being a mother.

It weren't you, it was your circumstances. Mixing with drug addicts and all that.

D'you know a lot about me? the woman asked Katy.

No, not much at all. That's another of the reasons I've come.

What's that?

I wanna help Aysha go through her life. Understand what happened to her when she were small. Staff at the children's home have done that with Charly and Zoë and it helped them settle down. But Aysha wouldn't do it. I'm hoping she will, with me. I want to start next weekend.

I can't help you much. It's all gone from my mind now.

Well, to start with, are there any photos? The girls have no photos at all.

I've got one or two photos in my room. But I don't have any spare ones.

Could I borrow them, do you think, to make copies? I promise I'll look after them, and get them back to you.

I could go back to the wing and get them, said the prison officer.

But can you get copies done here? asked Stella.

No, that's not likely. Best give them to this lady like she says.

I promise I'll put them back in the post straight away. Registered post. Have you a photo of Aysha's father? Katy asked.

Kenny? Yes, he's on one or two of them.

No, I was meaning this guy Milton Orlando Jewell who's on her birth certificate.

Oh him. No, I've none of him.

He is Aysha's birth father, is he? Katy persisted.

Yes, he must be. I guess. It were a long time ago, I were only fourteen.

Fourteen?

Yeah, he were a lot older. I were still living at home then.

With your parents?

Yeah.

So they knew Aysha?

I guess they did.

What were their names?

Katy scrabbled for her notebook and pen and started getting as much down as she could.

My dad were Alan Roy Stanton, he worked on the railways. My mum were called Barbara Pauline Stanton and she worked in a shop. They were quite a lot older than my friends' parents, and kinda very old-fashioned.

D'you know what happened to them?

No. They moved away, they retired somewhere down south. We lost touch, they gave up on me.

But they may be still alive?

Maybe, but I dunno.

Did you have any brothers or sisters?

I had one brother but he died.

What was his name?

Peter. Peter Charles.

How did he die?

On his motorbike. Aysha must have been a few months old then.

He was older than you?

Yeah, but only about a year and a half. Seventeen when he died. He should never have ridden a powerful bike like that.

Right, so going back to this Milton character, d'you remember anything about him?

He were a darkie, not black, but dark. From somewhere in Asia, I can't remember where. That's why I called her Aysha Jewel.

What was he doing over here?

Driving. Van driving it were, he used to be a sailor, he'd sailed round the world, he wanted to go back to his folks in wherever it was, but he had to earn some money first. He were on a regular run to Bursfield, so I got to sneak out to meet him, my parents didn't know, they'd've thrown a fit, with him being so much older, and a coloured guy too.

Aysha don't look coloured.

No, but then nor did he, only a little. But you could tell he weren't English. He acted and spoke like a darkie.

Can we try and think where he came from.

Well, it were Asia, I do know that. And not India or Pakistan.

South-east Asia? Thailand or Malaysia?

No, somewhere more like India. Nearer India but not India.

Nepal? Sri Lanka?

Sri Lanka! I'm sure that were it.

You don't remember the names of any of his folks.

No way, I didn't know him that well, I only met him a few times but one of them times produced Aysha. I only know he wanted to get back to see his folks. Oh, and he were a great one for weed, so he never got that much saved.

But did he go back?

Maybe, I dunno that. He stopped coming to Bursfield's all I know.

Did he know you were carrying his child?

No, he had no idea.

See, Kenny's dead and Zoë's dad we've gotta write off, but I think it's worth the effort to try and trace this Milton. Any idea of his age, date of birth, any birth marks or tattoos or anything about him which might help us trace him.

What are you, a detective or something?

No, I just think it will help Aysha to find her real father.

Well, he did have tattoos, if I remember right. On his arms. And two big scars, one on his belly where he'd had his appendix out, and another big one on his shoulder where he were stabbed.

Stabbed?

Yeah, he'd got in this massive fight on the docks.

Panama Canal I think he said. How come I'm remembering all this?

It's good you are, said Katy. So this Milton disappeared, and Aysha were born, and then what happened?

Well I were with my mum and dad then. And my brother, before his crash. They kinda looked after the baby so I don't remember much about her. I used to go out all the time and got into drugs, not just weed, the real stuff like, and when they found out they chucked me out. So I were on the streets -

With Aysha?

No, no, my parents kept her then. But I got put in this place, this home, sort of, and they gave Aysha back to me. That were when mum and dad moved away. But it were terrible there, it were with this woman who looked after a few of us girls with babies, but she were awful, a right, er -

Battleaxe?

That's right. But I couldn't do anything or they'd have took my baby off of me. Anyhow I got my own flat when Aysha must've been, one I think. And Kenny, that's Kenny Harrison, moved in and helped me look after her and then I had Charly. But I were taking more and more drugs by then and doing god knows what, selling myself, stealing, you name it, to feed the habit. Kenny stood by me, or rather, stood by the kids, but then he died.

From an overdose?

Well, not an overdose, cos he never were taking much like me. I think he must've been sold some bad smack.

Contaminated?

Whatever.

And he's definitely Charly's father?

Oh sure. I never started seeing other men till after Charly were born, I am sure of that.

How old was Aysha when Kenny died?

God, I've no idea, she must've been about four.

And what happened to Kenny? Is he buried somewhere in Bursfield?

I really don't know, I think they cremated him, but I were just out of it and his brother took over the arrangements and it were only his family, they wouldn't let any of us go.

So the kids stayed with you?

No, cos I wanted to go, I tried to go, I left the kids with a neighbour but I collapsed on the way there and someone brought me home.

The woman officer returned with several photos. She removed the coffee cups from the table and spread the photos out. This is Aysha and me when she were a little baby, said Stella. This one's me and my brother Pete with Aysha. She must've been a few months old then. Pete, in long hair and black leather, held her on his lap.

Here's Pete with me and my mum before Aysha were born. My dad must've took it.

A very young and visibly pregnant Stella, or Janine as she was, stared wistfully at the camera. Katy had to gulp back a tear.

This one's Kenny, with Aysha and Charly. Here's me and Charly. Here's the four of us, I don't know who took that. Here's Zoë and me, when she were just born. Here's Zoë on her own. Here's the three girls together, that's the only one of them. This one's Kenny and Aysha, a nurse took that at the hospital when they came in to see Charly for the first time.

What about Kenny's brother? Katy asked, leaving the photos where they were for the moment.

What about him?

Did you know him, or anyone else in Kenny's family?

No, they would never have anything to do with me. I might've met his parents once, or his brother, I don't quite remember.

D'you remember their names?

Oh god, I should, shouldn't I, I'll try and remember - he did used to talk about them sometimes.

Did no-one ever show you where he were buried, or if he had a grave or a memorial stone or anything?

No, not that I remember, but I were getting more and more out of it. If it weren't for Aysha, and then Vic, Zoë's dad, I wouldn't have coped with the kids at all.

What happened then?

It all gets a blur after that. I know now that Vic abused them girls and I should've stopped him, but I were too much out of it. I know I could've had them put in care, but no mum wants to do that, do they?

But they've ended up in care anyway.

Yeah but you never think that at the time, do you? You just wanna keep the social workers away. That's what Vic always said, and I know why now.

Katy felt that she'd got as much from this visit as she could have hoped, and that Stella looked as if she'd talked enough. She started collecting up the photos. I promise I'll keep these safe and get them back to you very soon, she said. I think the girls will be very grateful for having the chance to have copies. I'll come and see you again in a couple of months or so, and I might have one of the girls with me then, but I can't promise. Thank you for seeing me and talking to me.

Stella mumbled her thanks before she was led off looking exhausted.

One of the officers offered Katy some lunch, but she declined, thinking now only of Aysha waiting at the flat, and wanting to get back quickly. She picked up a sandwich at one of the stations, bought crisps, chocolate and coffee off a trolley on the train. But every few minutes waiting on a platform, every time a train slowed down, she died with frustration. She checked her bag frequently to make sure the photos were still there, but did not look at them, wanting to share that with Aysha. Finally she got back at five-thirty, relieved, overjoyed, to find the girl sitting in her flat with Greg, brushed and clean, resting his head on her lap. Aysha looked cold, nervous and hungry, had touched nothing apart from Greg's things.

I've got these photos to show you, Katy declared, hugging her briefly. But I'll get us some tea first, right.

Did you see my mum?

Yeah, I did, it went OK. I'll tell you all about it later.

So they went through the photos, Katy explained she'd be getting copies made tomorrow, so Aysha could have some for herself, and told her about her mum, how she was, the things she'd said. Then Katy told her they now needed to start the Life-Story book, and they fixed an hour every Sunday morning to work on that.

She negotiated her training course, and asked the man running it, who wasn't Tom Jameson, but announced himself as one of the department's training officers, about dealing with sexual abuse. Again she was asked about picking up on signs of this.

Aysha had in the last week or so on a couple of nights started waking in the middle of the night screaming from nightmares, and Katy had woken up and had to comfort her, and Greg had run over to her and licked her face, and she'd settled down again. In the mornings she couldn't remember anything about her dreams or waking from them. Katy mentioned this, but said that apart from possibly not wanting to have close contact with men, there was no other behaviour that could be linked to her past abuse.

It's difficult unless there's anything to go on, said the training officer.

But if I get to that part of her life in the Life-Story work and she gets disturbed, what do I do? I want to help her through it if possible, rather than backing off, but I don't know if I could do it, certainly not on my own. Are there any experts in the field I could refer to round here?

There are, both within the department, and outside. But the best ones, including those who work for us, are always incredibly busy and have long waiting lists.

But that's no good, I'd need the help there and then.

All I can suggest is you go through the child's social worker, or their line management. Raise it at the child's next review.

This did not seem, to Katy, very much help.

Nor did things start very well with the Sunday morning sessions. Aysha liked to lie in as long as she could at the weekends, and spend the rest of the morning walking Greg. If the dog licked her awake quite early, she could be gone more than half the morning. She was eating very well, putting on a fraction more weight, but she did not seem to need to eat at regular times, which Katy assumed must be the result of her previous lifestyle. So she often ended up having a late breakfast on Sunday, and there was little time left for the book. Katy tried to insist on breakfast before dog-walking, but this was no help as Aysha would stay out all morning, and come back laughing and joyful, even if soaked with rain, full of stories about what had happened and where she'd been.

One Sunday early in February, Katy made the mistake of taking Greg out herself, having drunk a mug of tea and eaten a weetabix, and prepared the rest of breakfast for them both, and left a brief note for Aysha to start breakfast without her. It was a horrible morning, grey and heavy with sleet falling which gradually turned more like snow. Katy just gave Greg a run in the park for little more than ten minutes but when she got back Aysha wasn't there. She waited nearly two hours getting more and more frantic until the child finally let herself in with her key, wet through and shivering. She'd put on the first garments she found, hadn't even worn a jacket, had gone to look for Katy and the dog, or so she said. Katy thought if Aysha had gone straight to the park she couldn't have possibly missed her, and said so, but the child swore she'd been wandering round the park the whole time. A hot bath, a large breakfast, left no time or inclination for Life-Story work.

Katy decided Sunday morning, however good a time it had seemed, was not working - moreover the point that Tom Jameson had made about a fixed time was utter crap, in their case, anyway. From now on she decided she would get out the book in an evening whenever Aysha was at a loose end and Katy had no pressing assignment.

So with half-term approaching, not much was in the book apart from the photographs and a few words about Aysha's mother, birth father, maternal grandparents and maternal uncle dead in motorbike accident. Still, Aysha gradually was showing more interest, and seemed impatient to move onto talking about Kenny.

10. MIXED BLESSINGS

In a small cottage on the shore of a West Highland sea loch, Duncan Keith was holding a letter in the fading light of a late January afternoon. Duncan had no need to raise himself from his chair and go to switch the cottage light on, for he knew what the letter said by heart. Since it had arrived the previous week he must have read it at least a hundred times.

Duncan was preparing to make a journey. At his stage in life this was some undertaking, in fact since he had stopped driving and sold his car five years ago, he had not travelled more than the half mile into the small town of Lochrana at the head of the loch. He walked this distance most days, or sometimes along the shore of the loch the other way, with difficulty, with the aid of his walking-stick, to give both himself and his dog the exercise they needed. Only in extremely wet weather, and if he required some provision urgently, did he resort to a taxi. He couldn't really afford the expense, for a start. But tomorrow, before dawn, a taxi would call to take him into town. Not really a town except by the standards of this very remote part of Scotland. Two buses a day to Glasgow, the second one much too late, so he had to catch the early bus. He'd booked a ticket, and a train ticket from Glasgow. He'd packed an overnight bag, rescued from a store cupboard, not used for god knows how many years. And he'd arranged to drop his dog off with one of his old drinking pals in town.

Duncan had the appearance, and led the life, of a man older than he actually was. In fact he was in his early sixties but a combination of physical troubles had reduced him to a reclusive, hermit-like existence, in the dwelling he had chosen many years earlier. He had osteo-arthritis which made getting around difficult, diabetes which made it essential that he took regular exercise, and angina which prohibited anything too strenuous or tiring. But it was his failing liver, result of half a lifetime's heavy drinking, which was the clincher among his ailments. He'd had to stop drinking alcohol, which made his struggle with depression and loneliness all the harder.

Yet Duncan Keith was not a man initially cast into this solitary, depressive mould. When younger, he had led just about the most active life of anyone he knew. He had travelled all over the highlands of Scotland, walking, climbing, exploring, he had sailed the inshore waters under sail and on the ferries, he knew all the islands like the back of his hand. He had driven beaten-up land-rovers, his body withstanding the jolting and the elements. And, why he thought of this last on the list he did not know, he had taught geography at Oban Academy for nearly thirty years until failing health forced him to stop.

The letter he held now, and placed on the table by his chair, as he finally made the effort to give the room some meagre light, had been sent to Oban Academy before Christmas, and forwarded on after the new term started. He had not moved house, but he guessed his address was not easily found, and even his name no longer well known, more than nine years since he retired from teaching there. At any rate, the letter had only reached him nearly three weeks into the term. Duncan was at a point in his life when any life-changing news, any emotional tug on his heart, was both potentially dangerous and totally unexpected, but that was what the letter contained.

Dear Duncan, it read, I am contacting you after all these years for two reasons. The first is that I am soon going to die, I have ovarian cancer and have only a few months to live. Do not grieve, because my husband Jack died nearly four years ago and since then my main wish in life has been to join him. But the other matter I need to tell you is that you have a son. My oldest boy Neil is your child. I would like to introduce him to you. If you could come down to Longworth as soon as you can, I will see to it. From January 4th my address will be - The Mount Pleasant Hospice, Mount Pleasant Road, Longworth. I will have a phone but I don't know the number yet. I'm sorry I haven't told you this before but I hope you will understand the reasons. I do hope this letter will find you (whether you are still teaching at Oban or not), that you have not entirely forgotten me, and that I will see you soon, a friend from your youth, Marie Sullivan (formerly Hodgson).

It was only in the last few years that Duncan had stopped thinking about Marie Hodgson. For all of his lonely bachelor life it was Marie his heart had held some sort of torch for, even though he knew that he would never see her again, that she would not contact him and on no account should he attempt to contact her. All he held, until this letter arrived, to link him to Marie were his memories.

The earlier memories, of when she was a senior student at the Academy, studying geography although in a class mainly taught by his senior colleague Ian Colquhoun, were the strongest ones. She was then, when he first arrived at the Academy at the age of 23, a seventeen-year-old with dark brown hair, slim, medium height, with an attractive, open face, but quiet, unde-monstrative, never seeking attention. The talk at the school was of her brothers, hardly ever of Marie. The boys had both left, the one the summer just before Duncan arrived, on a scholarship to Oxford, and the other the year before to study medicine at Edinburgh. The family lived on a housing estate in one of the poorest areas of the town, and the school took an immense pride in these achievements, but left Marie to, or so it appeared, hide in her brothers' shadows.

When Duncan, soon after he started teaching, had put forward the suggestion of organising school trips for the senior students, it had been assumed he was thinking just of a group of the more enthusiastic boys. The trips would include mountain walking, visiting the islands, and learning to sail, and in those years in the mid-sixties, it was assumed not many girls would be interested. But Duncan felt very strongly that girls also should be encouraged in these activities, and he was helped in his initiative by a woman colleague, a science teacher, married but no children, a prim and energetic woman in her thirties of the sort that had kept the Scottish education system going for so many years. She too thought these educational activity trips were not only a good idea but should be open for girls too, and she was willing to give up time to make this happen. So for the months of September, October, and March through to early July, weekends during term-time, half-term weeks, and parts of the Easter and Summer holidays were given over to groups of usually between seven and twelve students walking over mountain, moor and rocky shore, crossing the waters to the islands, walking sandy beaches, cliff-tops, and machair grass, camping wild or on camp-sites, or staying at youth hostels or field centres, studying the plants, the birds, the otters, the sea-life, the geology, the history of cultivation and crofting, of fishing communities, of island culture, the influence of weather and the sea. Girls never quite making equal numbers with the boys, but nevertheless always at least three or four girls, and always, on every single expedition, there was Marie Hodgson, first to put her name down and pay up the small fee, keen to escape the poverty and deprivation of home-life, as her brothers had done, so the old hands among the teachers suggested, nodding their heads to indicate they possessed the wisdom of experience.

And how Marie flourished! From a rather shy, undistinguished girl, in not much more than four terms, she grew visibly more confident, a bright and beautiful girl whose eyes danced as she talked, and she talked a lot, eager to learn, eager to question, eager to share her thoughts. Always walking with him, leaning on every word he said, and he on her, and then in school, giving him the sweetest smile whenever they passed. Nothing happened between them, of course, the freedoms of the sixties had not yet reached the west of Scotland. Nothing, on a personal level, was said, even, but he knew she was in love with him, without anything needing to be said, it was more than a schoolgirl crush, and he soon knew that he also was in love with her, and was sure they both knew how they felt.

Then she got a place at Dundee University to study geography and education, and would be away from Oban for four years. She came to his classroom in the school on her final day, and spoke the only personal words that had passed between them.

Goodbye, Duncan, I'll miss your expeditions and I'll miss you. But we mustn't be in contact while I'm away, please understand. I hope to qualify as a teacher and return to teach in Oban after my four years, and I hope you'll still be here and still unattached, and we can see each other again then.

He would wait for her, he knew. Her words were enough of an encouragement, ambivalent though they were. He thought of her all the time while she was away, and tried to be nonchalant when one of his colleagues asked if he'd heard from her and he had to say no. In the meantime his life at the Academy continued, the trips out and the teaching became his whole life.

Before the end of the third year after Marie's departure for Dundee, Ian Colquhoun, his head of department, the one who had taught Marie, announced his impending retirement, and encouraged Duncan, though he was not yet thirty, to apply. They could advertise his post at the same time, if he was willing to put himself forward. Duncan mentioned that in a year's time, Marie Hodgson should be a qualified geography teacher wanting to return to Oban, and would it be possible to hold the vacancy for her?

I thought you hadn't heard from her? said the older man.

No, I haven't, she told me this before she left.

Well, you'd better check this out. Not a bad idea, especially as I like the thought that I could help out, fill the gap while there's a vacancy, it will ease me into retirement.

Not such a good idea for Duncan, though, he soon realised, almost impossible to develop a relationship if he was going to be her head of department. But he had made the suggestion now, and had to follow it up. So he went up to the council estate and called at her parents' address. He knew where they lived, because he had frequently dropped her off there after the expeditions - they always met up at the school when they started off - but he had never been inside the house.

Marie had never talked much about her family, but he knew her father was a working man, in the forestry. He spoke now to her mother, who, despite where they lived, seemed a cultured woman from the way she spoke, and the interior also seemed cultured, with several bookcases on view, and no sense of undue poverty.

I've just called by, he started off nervously. Because before she went to Dundee Marie mentioned to me that she might be interested in coming back to Oban to teach. And in fact there's a vacancy coming up, to teach geography, and we wondered if she might still be interested.

Oh, you're the teacher who organised all those trips she went on, aren't you? said the mother. Oh yes, she had a soft spot for you all right. But no, she won't be coming back home. She's engaged to be married now, and after the wedding she and her husband are planning to teach abroad, in Africa probably.

Oh really. Well, that's good, but I didn't know.

No, I'm sure she would have told you at some point. The wedding will be in Oban of course, so if she never thought to tell you, you would see the notices, find out that way.

When is the wedding?

Next summer, after she finishes her courses.

Well, thank you.

My pleasure.

A note arrived at his home address soon after this. Dear Duncan, I understand my mother has given you my news. I have met the true love of my life, and we will marry next summer, possibly going to teach abroad after that. This summer you may see me and Jack around Oban, as we're spending most of the vacation meeting each other's families and exploring both our home areas together. Then Jack will be going abroad and will just return for the wedding. So I won't be back in Oban much after this summer, but if our paths cross I hope we can still be friends and I hope you will understand, with best wishes, Marie Hodgson.

Duncan had done his best, when commitments allowed it, to be away all that summer. Those were the years he had his old land-rover, and he simply threw a load of stuff in the back and took off north-eastwards, to explore the Cairngorms and other parts of the eastern highlands. The last thing he wanted was to meet Marie and her fiancé on the streets of Oban. He had not put in for the Head of Department post.

A year passed and he tried to forget her, to think about and even meet other young women. But he found he could not. Perhaps he would have done in time, but the following July, just before the end of term, he received a telephone call one evening.

Is that Duncan? This is Marie Hodgson.

Hallo, Marie. How are you? You're not married yet, then?

No. Soon, but not just yet. Can we meet up for a coffee?

Yes, of course. Where? When?

Tonight, or tomorrow night?

So they'd met that night, at a coffee-bar in town. Marie told him that Jack was still in Africa, would be returning a few days before their wedding, which was to be the middle weekend of August. After the wedding they would not be going abroad, but they both had obtained teaching posts in a school near Manchester.

Why are you not going abroad? Duncan asked her.

Oh, lots of reasons, but I guess the main one is that we both want children. It would be difficult to raise a child in Africa, and it wouldn't be fair on the kids we'd be working with out there if I got pregnant quickly and had to leave. Jack's staying as long as he can, and I went out there at Easter to join him, so I've had my little taste of Africa.

What was it like?

A bit kind of overwhelmingly different. I didn't find it

easy to adjust, but at the same time I do think it's important that when I teach about Africa I've had the first-hand experience, even if not so much as Jack. We both studied Africa as one of our special topics.

So which country were you in?

Zambia. A big country. Near the Angola border. Right in the hinterland.

What are you doing now, back in Oban?

Final preparations for the wedding. It's all fixed up now. That's why I've contacted you. I need a short holiday.

Aren't you having a honeymoon?

We're not sure. It depends how much there'll be to do in our new place before term starts. We're hoping to get away for a few days but we haven't booked anything. I need a holiday now and I don't want to go alone.

But what about friends? College friends?

No, they've all made their plans already. I can't go abroad because I've got to find us accommodation in Longworth.

Longworth?

That's where Jack and I will be teaching. What I've decided is to stay in the Lake District for two weeks or so, and go down to Longworth from there. I'd love you to join me, Duncan. Do say yes.

But I have some commitments, school trips.

We'll fit around them, she said, in a manner both straightforward and final.

Are you planning to camp? Or Youth Hostel?

I was thinking of finding a small Guest House, or Bed and Breakfast, or something. I'll pay, Duncan, for us both.

No, no, you mustn't, I'll share payment. But places are probably booked up by now, you'll be lucky to find anywhere.

That's my point. We must get on with it. But I insist on paying, Duncan. I'd saved up some money, my own money, for the wedding, knowing my parents would be hard pushed, and now Jack's parents have come up with all the money. As long as me and my family do all the organising, they will pay. So I've got this money to spend on myself, apart from putting down a deposit in Longworth, because I know Jack's got enough money to keep us going until we get our first teaching salaries.

But doesn't it sound terribly ungrateful of you, to return

your in-laws' favour by spending your money on a holiday with another man?

No, Duncan, that's nonsense! Listen, Jack's who I love and who I'll spend the rest of my life with, make him happy and I hope provide children, grandchildren for his parents. I don't owe them anything beyond that! I don't have to spend my whole summer being kept on the straight and narrow while he's half-way round the world. I just need to think of myself, and you! It's you I owe a lot to, you gave me so much, helped me believe in myself, we had such a good thing going but because you were my teacher we couldn't do anything about - couldn't consummate it, and then I let you down when I owed you so much, by falling in love with Jack, so now I'm making up to you for it.

She could sound very convincing.

And no-one will ever find out, she added. Look, I'll go in the Tourist Office here in town tomorrow and get phone numbers of places in the Lake District. Then I'll come round your place after school and we'll make phone calls. That's all I'll let you pay for, the phone calls.

So they went ahead, despite his misgivings, booked a small guest house in Staveley - he still remembered turning to her, saying, They only have double rooms left, and she hissing at him, That's what we want, you idiot! - for nearly two weeks, between the two school trips he had organised, arranged that she would travel to Crianlarich by train and he would meet her there with the land-rover. Booked in as Duncan and Marie Keith. It all seemed cloak and dagger to begin with, as far as he was concerned, at least. But that all disappeared in the flowering of his love for Marie, the physical expression of it, the first and only woman he had ever loved, ever made love to.

In the daytime they walked in the mountains, sometimes gently, sometimes taking strenuous hikes. Early in their adventure she said she would need to take a day trip down to Longworth and insisted that he should not come with her.

You have another walk up here, Duncan, on your own. You can drive me to the station but that's all. It would complicate things too much if you came down to Longworth. So he took her immediately after breakfast to Oxenholme to catch the Manchester train and met her off the last one back, when she announced she hadn't got round to all the prospective places to rent, and would need to go back early the next week.

She was the more clinical about the whole enterprise, not just about fitting in the finding of accommodation, but phoning her mother almost every evening, telling her she'd found a place in Longworth and was now in the Lake District, having a walking holiday, asking about the wedding arrangements, had any problems come up, and had Jack phoned, and was he still planning to return on the eleventh?

She told Duncan that if Jack suddenly changed his flight and came back early, she would need to break off and return at once to Oban. But she thought that was unlikely. She spoke nearly all the time to Duncan of her love for Jack, apart from when they made love when she seemed to reserve all her passion for him, Duncan.

He asked her which of them she really loved. Or loved the most.

Jack, of course, she said. You must understand that, Duncan. This is just a temporary interlude in my affections. Promise me you understand.

I'm not sure I fully understand. But I do accept what you say, I promise you that.

And you must promise not to contact me after this. You can come to the wedding if you like, but that is all. Can I trust you on that, Duncan?

Yes, of course you can. And I don't think I'd want to come to the wedding, even if it didn't coincide with the second school trip.

One final night of passion and he'd driven her to Crianlarich, dropped her off some way from the station, she would get the train to Oban. She had pressed his hand, kissed him briefly, and thanked him for everything. It was he who should have thanked her, he reflected. That was the last time Duncan had seen Marie, had heard anything of her, over thirty-three years ago. Until tomorrow. And not just see her, but see his son, his son by her. It was difficult for Duncan to take all this in. And that she was not for long in this world, joy crossed with sorrow, mixed blessings. His heart pulled in so many directions. He had lived with those memories, of Marie, of their two weeks together, they had sustained him in his loneliness for a large part of his lifetime, his bachelorhood, his gradual descent into heavy drinking, male only company, deteriorating health, reclusiveness, an end to his teaching, the company of his dog and the four cottage walls. He looked around the cottage. How could he explain all this to Marie? What would she think of his existence now? Only a small collection of books, fewer than he'd found that one time he'd entered her parents' house, most of them sold to fuel his drink habit. His minimal items of furniture cheap and battered. A small ancient television, and radio likewise. A log fire burning, well at least he still could afford logs, a stack of them beside the cottage. He put two more on the fire, those would be the last for a while, he'd let the fire burn down overnight. Just keep his one storage heater on low while he was away. He would only be away a few days, his pal in town wouldn't agree to have his dog for longer than that, but it seemed as if he was going away for a lifetime, a whole new life, a son, what would he make of his meagre, lonely, impoverished existence? Had Marie told him, the son, this Neil, and if so, what had she said, would he now be a disappointment?

He went to the front window of his sitting room, and pulled back the curtain a few inches. The window looked over the loch, and by turning his head to the left he could see the lights of the town. Not a town to Marie or Neil, more like a village. Just a scattering of lights, really. A moderate wind had got up and blown away the heavy cloud of the afternoon. Stars were now out, and a half moon, reflected in the gently rippling water of the loch. A few boats at anchor, outlined against the moonlight, their faint lamps swaying tipsily. He momentarily stopped to pray that harsh weather did not come overnight, though this seemed unlikely, the climate here was generally mild, it wasn't too bad tonight, and in any case the Glasgow buses usually made it through. He had everything ready, he would retire early. He looked out one more time, as he usually did before stepping into the back room where he slept. One only had to look out, and see that the life here was not that bad. In his darkest moments of depression, loneliness, despair, this was all he had to do to ease the worst of it. Surely Marie, Neil, would see it the same way.

11. A MAN SHE ONCE DID OWN

Marie Sullivan lay back and tried to sleep. Pain, grief and a troubled conscience had conspired to make sleep difficult for her since her Jack had died. It was probably best that he had died not knowing the truth, but now Marie tortured herself wondering if she should have told him. Thinking back over her life, Marie knew that everyone thought highly of her, even those closest to her, her husband and sons, her daughter-in-law, all that she had achieved in her life, had worked so hard to achieve, all the children she had helped, the sons she had raised, the husband she had loved, the colleagues and friends she had supported, all the praise and kind words that had been spoken when she returned to her school for the last time a few days before Christmas, all had been built on lies and nobody knew, nobody guessed. Everything she had done had been to cover up the deceit at the core of her life.

Now half the task had been achieved. The other half could wait for the moment. She wondered if Duncan would return before she died. He had always been reliable in that way. In many ways it was the more difficult bit that had happened. Duncan and Neil had met, and knew they were father and son. She knew it had been difficult for Neil. She had only told him after Duncan had arrived in Longworth. Fortunately, Duncan had let her know his travel bookings so she'd been able to telephone Neil and ask him to come to see her the day after Duncan arrived. She rarely telephoned any of her family any more, found the phone too much effort, so Neil had realised it was important.

Neil talked very little, even to his mother. He asked how she was, but he could see that Marie's health was failing and there was little in her life to report on any longer. She tried to dredge up news of the rest of the family.

Sam comes quite often with Lara and Liam. They're lively little kids. Lara's started at proper school, seems to be getting on well.

Neil nodded.

Sam's annoyed with her sister, who's taken on a family of three girls in care. The oldest one's already moved in with Katy. Sam doesn't like this kid. But I've told her to try and accept her. Lara and this girl in care have really hit it off, it seems.

Hit it off? queried Neil.

You know, bosom pals. Marie sank back. She had said too much already, she had no energy left for the important bit. She wished Neil would say something of his own accord about his life, his wood-carving, his dog-training, the mountain rescue, his wildlife photography, rather than asking things which required an answer from her, or forcing her to ask him before he ventured any information. She felt her pain level increase beyond what was bearable. She leant over the side, ready to retch from the pain. Neil came up close and held the bowl steady but nothing came.

She managed a weak smile at him. I'm eating virtually nothing now.

You must have something, he said.

I know. Listen, Neil, I have something very important to tell you. I should have told you before, ages ago, but I'm telling you now before it's too late. Jack wasn't your father, Neil. Jack was in Africa when you were conceived. Your father is a man called Duncan Keith. I had a brief – er, relationship with him before Jack and I got married. She paused. She couldn't work out how Neil was taking it. Maybe he wouldn't believe her, think she was rambling, delirious, the illness talking.

She attempted to reach for her son's hand. He had never been an affectionate child. Caring but undemonstrative. Talkative when younger but not sociable. Relating to Neil had always been a somewhat haphazard business, a matter of mind and heart crossing in unfamiliar ways, colliding, her feelings fragile, easily hurt, because of his origins she supposed, and his too, causing his mind to shut out his heart. Jack had always been better at dealing with Neil than she had, two minds he could keep on track together while avoiding the collisions of the heart. Now her hand could not reach his and sadness overwhelmed her. It was always so.

With great effort she turned to look at the clock at her bedside. She had to speak on.

I wrote to your real father, Duncan, before Christmas. The letter finally reached him a week or so ago. He has come down to Longworth to meet you, Neil. I told him to come between two and quarter past today. He could arrive any time.

It was all too quick, she could tell. She hadn't done this right. All the mistakes she'd made in her life, how had people not realised? A life full of error, sin, deceit. Neil might just walk out, he would be quite justified in doing so. He might walk away for ever. She couldn't bear the thought, she needed her family to stay with her now. Until she died. All of them. She started to cry, as the pain returned and the nausea rose up in her.

Don't cry, mother, said Neil, gently.

He would not be used to her crying. The one quality she had in abundance was strength, and the ability to hide her failings. That strength had seen her through, even through Jack's death, which zoomed back into her mind, as vivid a picture as ever. But that strength had gone now, reduced her to a pathetic sinner. Now she was vomiting, bringing something up.

It's OK, mother. These things happened a long time ago. Don't feel bad about it now. If this Duncan wants to meet me, that's fine.

All the rooms in the hospice had en suite bathroom and toilet. Her son took the pot through the connecting door and she heard him empty it, flush.

He lives in Scotland, in the Highlands. She watched his face register a new interest. But he's quite old and disabled now. He arrived last night, I saw him briefly, he was going to stay at The Greyhound.

He could have stayed at Kitchener Avenue, if he didn't mind the chaos.

No. She realised Neil would stay there tonight, although the house had been sold. She knew Sam and Marcus were busy clearing out the place. This was another picture she tried to keep from her mind, because of all the pain. It was the house where she and Jack had lived all these years, raised a family, happy years, despite her guilt, years bathed in love, it was also the house where she'd lived on her own, trying to cope with the emptiness, not coping, though people thought she did. Too many chickens were coming home to roost now, and Duncan could not sleep in that house.

Please keep this confidential, Neil. I don't want Sam and Marcus to meet Duncan, it makes things too complicated. Sam is upset enough already, she has too many things to worry about without finding a strange old man staying at Kitchener

Road.

She paused again. Her chest was tight, her breathing difficult and irregular. Where was Duncan?

Sam and the kids usually pop in here after school, quarter past or half past three, something like that. I don't want them meeting Duncan. He will need to have gone. If you want to talk some more, get to know each other, you'll need to leave at three.

She fell back on her pillows. Why did she still need to exert this control on people, still be the teacher, manipulating what could be done or said? Did any of it matter now anyway? Neil had got away from all that, lived his life as he wanted, didn't want to come back to visit his mother and find the patterns of his childhood being re-enacted. Marcus had married someone who, like his mother, wanted to be in control, but he'd found a good balance between the life he wanted to lead and the love he felt for Sam, just as Jack had done with her.

Jack appeared in front of her yet again, larger than life. He was big and strong and she was a tiny being, and he would carry her off, across the mountains, to a new country, only he never did. Don't leave me again, Jack, she whispered.

Another part of her heard voices in the room. Jack was still there, looking out of the window.

You must be Duncan!

You must be Neil. Is Marie asleep?

She's very tired. She drifts in and out.

Duncan was there! She didn't want to banish Jack, who seemed reluctant to leave, but she tried to focus on Duncan. Jack had come back to witness this meeting between Neil and his real father, it would seem her conscience had ordered it to be.

She doesn't want you to meet the rest of the family, Neil was saying.

Perhaps we could go somewhere else to talk?

Duncan! she whispered hoarsely. Don't go yet! She had loved Duncan, she remembered, it had been a long time ago, but despite the years, he was still the same Duncan. But was she the same Marie? Better perhaps if she wasn't, since she had treated him so badly.

This is your son, Duncan. She was not sure if the words had been spoken aloud. To say them aloud was to betray Jack. She only wanted to join Jack, but would he let her join him now?

150

Did he know her secrets already? Would he think better of her if she finally told them, or would he prefer them to stay secret, and she go to her grave with them troubling her still? But either way, she could not escape her deceitful past, and Jack could not help her now.

Duncan was her first love. It was more than just a schoolgirl crush. Why had she been so ashamed? Why had she wanted to compartmentalise her life? Why had she told no-one about Duncan?

She could hear him talking to Neil.

Duncan!

Marie, are you OK?

I think, said Neil. It's more difficult for her than it is for us.

When are you going, Duncan?

Back to Scotland?

Yes.

I must go tomorrow. My ticket's booked. And I must relieve my friend Jock from looking after my dog. And I can't really afford another night.

I could pay.

No, Marie.

What are you doing the rest of today?

Getting to my know my son, I hope.

But I've seen so little of you!

But we spent most of this morning talking, Marie. Catching up on things.

She was losing her mind. Of course he'd been with her this morning, talking about his life, asking about hers. But there was more yet to tell.

She remembered he'd asked how could she be sure Neil was his. She said just wait until you meet. He reminded her that she had said she was on the pill. She was! she remonstrated. That must have been bad timing, it wasn't part of the deceit, although she could see how it must have looked now. He had asked after her family. She had told him about her parents, how they'd retired to the Island of Mull under a special Forestry Commission scheme, a year after she married. They'd lived in a forestry house by a loch among the hills for all those years, her father cultivating his cottage garden and keeping a supervisory eye on the nearby forestry, her mother taking in paying guests. Every summer they'd gone there, Jack and the boys and her, when they weren't running a school expedition, for a week or a fortnight.

This came back to her now, those years. Why had she followed her brothers in wanting to rise above her parents' simple lifestyle? Was that not the crux of the problems in her life, ambition and rejection of her parents' values? Whenever they went back there, as a family, Jack and the boys would embrace those values more than she ever could. She could never entirely relax, wanting to plan next term's lessons or next year's trips. But now, she could see where she went wrong. Her parents had lived on in that house well into their eighties, only in the last few years before their deaths had they moved into a bungalow in Tobermory. Her father had died a month before his ninetieth birthday, her mother had just passed ninety-one. She envied their quiet and simple devotion to each other now.

It was Neil who kept in touch with my parents right through until they died, she'd told Duncan that morning. She hoped he'd heard her, it suddenly seemed important. She hadn't given it any thought for years, but both her sons had got a lot from those trips to Mull, especially Neil. Neil had called on them whenever he went up to Scotland. She had stopped visiting, so had Jack and Marcus when Marcus got married. Her father was on his deathbed at the time, so they hadn't been able to come to the wedding, and only Neil had been to see them. They'd been to the funeral, Jack and her, and to her mother's, and in between had been up to see her mother later that year, after Lara was born. But her mother had never seen her great-granddaughter, only photos. She might have grieved her mother more, she now thought, if Jack hadn't died so soon after. But they hadn't been close for years.

Neil used to go and see my parents every summer, didn't you Neil? she said out loud to the room. How old were you when you started going on your own?

Fifteen, I guess. I sometimes went at Easter too. The sea eagles started breeding close to their house.

Oh yes, Mull, said Duncan. An island I used to know well.

Which parts? asked Neil.

All over, just about. The south and the west coasts, the

mountains.

Ulva? Gometra?

Yes. And Iona, Jura, Colonsay.

Marie needed to rest. Memories of family visits to Mull were flooding back in, in a confused way. Neil as a boy, Marcus as a boy, Neil as a young man, Jack just before he died, Duncan when she went on those school trips with him. Mull seemed to be the link. She wished she could have been more like her mother. Mull had turned her into a woman, a man, a woman like a man, an ambitious and controlling woman, but she had no place there. Duncan had set her on the road to independence and self-confidence but she had not known how to stop. She'd gone too far. Competition with her brothers. Not content to be the quiet unassuming little sister. Duncan had asked her about her brothers. Both doing well in their careers, she had replied. Both wealthy. But not much contact, although one has been to see me here, and the other one's supposed to be coming next week.

Sam's younger sister had been content to be quiet and unassuming. What was her name? She couldn't think.

What's Sam's sister's name, Neil? She was Sam's brides-maid, remember.

You mean Katy? Why do you ask?

I couldn't think of her name. I was thinking she was like your grandmother. I was thinking of Mull, and your visits there.

I don't think she's anything like grandmother, said Neil.

Can I have a few words to Duncan on my own? she asked Neil. Could you wait outside?

Will you come back, Duncan? she said. I've booked one of the guest rooms here, second half of February, so you won't need to stay at that pub.

Do you want me to?

Yes, very much, that's why I booked that room.

Can you explain to your family? I don't want to keep hiding from them.

I will, but it's so complicated. There's something else I'll tell you then. Please come. I want to get to know you better now we've met again.

Yes, me too. But there's not much more to know about me.

But I've forgotten already.

I rebuilt a semi-derelict cottage by a sea-loch. I used to drink heavily for many years. I had to retire from teaching on health grounds. I live in the cottage with my dog. Full stop.

There must be more. I won't go until you come back and tell me.

Go?

I'll stay alive, I promise.

Well, that's a cue for me to stay away as long as I can.

No, I've booked the guest room for you, remember. I want you to come back before the pain gets too bad.

I'm sorry about that, Marie. But what can I do?

Can you bring painkillers, Duncan? Are you on them?

I'm on a whole cocktail of pills, but not painkillers as such.

A pity. Diamorphine would be good. More of it. They're very tight with it here.

With good reason, I should think.

Get to know Neil. Make the most of your time together.

Duncan slipped out. She slipped in and out of delirium. The pain grew terrible again. She needed a pill. She rang for a nurse. Finally she slept.

Jack came to her. He told her they needed leave at once. Where are we going, I'm not ready, she complained. The ferry's about to leave, he said, and started putting her things into a small back-pack. Leave out my wash-bag, she shouted. I must have a shower. There was vomit down the front of her dressing-gown. They were in Oban, but Oban had changed. There was a health-spa where the harbour office used to be. Go and take your shower in there, Jack advised her. But when she went through the door, she found herself on the ferry. It was already sailing. She couldn't see Jack. She hadn't got enough on. She put down her pack, reached inside for a coat. The boat lurched, and the pack slid away from her, across the deck and over the side. Then she saw Jack, running to the rails, diving in after her pack.

When she woke she saw Jack again. He had come to her in her dream and he was still there. She wanted to join him but she also wanted to see Duncan again. All her life, she now thought. See Duncan again. Those school trips, such a short space of her life. How she wished she could stop time. Why had she not come back in her college vacations and offered to help

Duncan with his expeditions? Her whole life might have been different. No Marcus, no Samantha, no Lara or Liam. She could not regret this, although she had no good reason for not doing it, other than her college friends might laugh at her, raise their eyebrows, and that she already had her eyes on Jack. If only she could stop time when Jack was alive, if only they had not gone to the Pyrenees, or had gone a week later, or had taken a different route that day. If she could have stopped Jack leading, stopped time at their lunch break. The scene had played itself in slow motion at the time, and every single day for three years she had seen it played in front of her mind. It still came back to her, though not, she thought, every day any more. They were traversing a high-level route, a designated one, in snow. They had carefully navigated the difficult bits with the help of crampons and ice-axes. They stopped, exhausted, for a longish lunch-break. Nothing very difficult now, so they removed their crampons before having their lunch. When they started again, Jack led. After a mile, the path crossed a snowfield, gently sloping downhill, but pretty flat mostly. Ahead they would drop below the snow level. There was nothing to worry about. Then Jack stumbled on a patch of ice on the path, lost his balance slightly. She could still see it all so clearly, she was a few yards behind him. She had not rushed forward, there seemed no need. Jack seemed to right himself, but his stumble had taken his right foot a foot or so off the path. The snow was icy, and he couldn't get purchase. He put his hands on the ground to steady himself, but in doing so he couldn't keep his other foot on the path. It slipped off too, but still no-one was concerned. The ground was almost flat, and he had his ice-axe. Jack was trying to steady himself with hands and feet. He didn't immediately reach for the axe. He slipped slowly further away from the path. She, and the rest of them, were level with him now, but they could not reach him. Two of them got out their ice-axes and started to form a chain on the field of frozen snow. But Jack was slipping away from them faster now, struggling to reach for his axe. Further off, the slope steepened. By the time he had his axe out, it was too late. He was sliding at speed towards a precipice, a chasm. Marie was screaming. The others were trying to comfort her. It had all taken place in slow motion, but then suddenly speeded up at the end.

They never found Jack's body. She guessed vultures and

ravens would have eventually cleaned it out. In western India, she knew, the Parsees chose that way to leave the world. But it was hard for her to grieve. Not hard to grieve, but hard to work through it. She grieved all the time, every day, and relived the incident never knowing if she could, had she run forward quickly, have saved him. It would have only needed a hand, someone to get close enough to take his hand, or hold his left leg.

She said to people afterwards that if they had both lived longer, that is the way they would have both liked to die. But Jack's death was too early. She should have been the one to go first, she thought, Jack would have coped, better than her. And she would have been saved this terrible dilemma about her past. She sometimes wished she had followed him down that slope. But she remembered that as Jack disappeared from her sight for ever, the others were holding her, trying to calm her down.

She had never returned to the mountains. She had continued to teach, and occupy a senior position at the school. Her grandchildren were her only interest outside school. Even though her heart was grieving, and there was this terrible emptiness at the core of her, she had never thought of ending it all until now. She remembered Steve had sent her a note, delivered it by hand through the hospice's letter-box a week or so after she moved in. He had asked did she want to go back to the mountains one last time? Llanberis Pass perhaps, or somewhere in the Lake District. He would be willing to take her. He even suggested a trip up the Snowdon Mountain Railway. She had to laugh. It was the last thing she wanted, and if she had, she could have asked Neil, couldn't she? She supposed Steve meant well, and she knew he had a soft spot for her, always had done, but she had no feelings for him and he was never in her thoughts any more. She didn't even reply to the note. Perhaps she should have done.

Now she wondered if the idea of going up Snowdon by the railway had been so that she could follow Jack, walk off the edge up there at the top of the mountain. But no, Steve couldn't possibly have thought that. How could he have gone back to Longworth, to Sam and Marcus and the kids, having given her that opportunity? No, he must be more stupid than she thought. In any case, she could not have coped with the long car journey, let alone the buffeting of a mountain train. Even in those first weeks of being here, she had only left the hospice twice, or was it three times, to go to Marcus and Sam's, less than a mile away. And for three weeks now, she hadn't left her room.

She would wait for Duncan, but perhaps he wouldn't return. Perhaps he only came to Longworth to meet Neil, had no interest in her any more. She couldn't blame him, after the way she'd treated him. She thought of him twenty years earlier, still a bachelor in early middle age, still holding a torch for her, still stuck in the same old teaching job at Oban, rebuilding the walls of his cottage nearly every weekend with his own hands, and then, tired and thirsty, repairing to the nearest hotel and drinking his nights away with the local heavy-drinking crowd. She thought of him now, a wreck of a man but still something of the Duncan she had known and loved. Had she made the wrong choice all along? Jack would never have let her draw him into a wasted life. She couldn't face the thought of letting Jack down, the possibility of their marriage breaking up, but that was for her sake, not his. And the two boys, of course. Not that Jack would have ever done anything to jeopardise their marriage. He was entirely to be trusted, she was sure of that, not like her. Not that he was perfect. He had his faults. His humour could be draining, particularly given his propensity to come out with it when the matter was serious, and she, or others, were wanting a serious response from him. Lighten up, would always be his message, even if he didn't use those words. But in her eyes his biggest fault was how he appeared to favour Neil. Marcus was the easier child, but she always did her best to treat them equally. Jack appeared to think he could protect her from any difficulties dealing with Neil by taking a special interest in his eldest. Both boys in the end reacted against this, but it was Neil whom it had affected the most. In his twenties he had kept Jack at a distance.

Duncan phoned, left a message on her answerphone while she slept. Marie, he said in his soft Scottish burr. I will come back. I'll arrive next Tuesday evening, and stay for a week this time. She confirmed with the matron that an old friend from her childhood in Oban would be staying in the guest room. She held herself together one final time.

Duncan slept late after his journey. He missed breakfast at the hospice. When she finally saw him, he said he would go into town and find something to eat. She felt terrible, but she tried to stay calm. She would tell him when he came back. She wondered if he'd brought her any pills. She'd already managed to secrete some diamorphine but not enough, she thought. Her life was juddering to its close. Duncan took ages coming back. She thought he must have walked into town and back. When he finally arrived, he said he had. He had to walk every day because of his diabetes. She asked about his dog. He said he'd arranged kennels this time.

My daughter-in-law Sam has a younger sister who's devoted to her dog, said Marie. Sam is scornful, says it's not natural, preferring a dog to boyfriends.

There are advantages to having a dog.

I'm beginning to think you're right. What's your dog's name?

Why was she avoiding what she needed to say? She needed to gather strength, avoid these diversion tactics.

Barney, Duncan said.

She paused, preparing herself. Then the door opened and a small person pushed her way in. She recognised Lara.

Grandma! Grandma! Look what I've brought you!

Grapes! Oh that's good! I've run out! She turned to Duncan. Grapes, soup and jelly's about all I can eat now, and not much of that. A bit of scrambled egg now and then.

Lara had noticed Duncan. Who's that man, grandma?

Hallo, said Duncan. I'm an old friend of your grandmother's, from when she was a girl in Scotland, I've come to see her before she dies. I'll go now, Marie, and come back tomorrow.

Are you gonna die, grandma? asked the small child, as Duncan was leaving the room.

Hasn't mummy and daddy told you? The child shook her head. Where is mummy anyway?

She took Liam to do a poo. Lara held her nose and grinned. She told me to come on ahead.

Aren't you early? Why aren't you in school?

It's half-term, grandma! Have you forgot? Why are you gonna die?

People die when they get old. Their bodies don't work properly any more.

You ain't old, grandma.

But my body isn't working all the same. That's why I've got to live here, and stay in bed. But listen, don't say anything

158

until mummy and daddy tell you. I'm sure they will soon. Until then, it's a secret, right, Lara. Pretend you don't know.

All right, grandma.

12. ONLY ONE ANGEL

Aysha lay in bed. She tried to sleep some more. It was the Friday morning of half-term, yesterday Katy and her, but not her two sisters, had come here on the train. She was in Katy's old bed, and she loved sleeping in this bed. She loved sleeping and dozing, half-asleep, half-awake, well into the morning. She could hear the faint voices, downstairs, of Katy and her mother and her stepfather but she dozed on. Last night was the first night since she left the children's home that she'd slept on her own, without Katy in the room. Katy had moved into her older sister's old room, said it was time they had separate rooms. But she'd let Aysha continue to sleep in her bed, for which the younger girl was grateful. And let Greg be in with her, although soon, she said, Greg would need to be back in the kitchen at night. Even so, last night, without Katy close by, Aysha couldn't get to sleep for ages. She kept going over in her mind all the changes that had happened to her, that had led her to this strange house in an unfamiliar town. She remembered when she first saw Katy. She'd been feeling so totally fucked up, violently foul, lashing out against the whole fucking world, hating being brought back to the home but not caring where she was or what she got up to or even whether she lived or died when she saw Katy with her dog. Katy had looked tall, then, taller than she really was, to Aysha, who was bent down to fight off her captors, and her blonde hair, way up above, had seemed to shine. Aysha had a sudden thought that she was an angel, an angel in a tracksuit with a dog. The picture had stayed in her mind that night. It wasn't that she was bothered about an angel or anyone in a tracksuit, but it were the dog. The dog were what drew her, made her want to be that angel-person. But then she threw it out of her thoughts. She, Aysha, could never ever be like that, she were a bad girl for ever now and no angel would even go near her, so no use thinking 'bout it. But then a funny thing happened. She'd been to the   estate and none of the kids she were special mates with was there, they were all gone down town. So Aysha were taking a walk from the estate into town and she went past the home. It weren't the only road she could take, usually she hated the place so much she went by a different way. But this time she happened to go past the home and there was the dog. Tied up outside. She went up to the dog and she knew straight away this dog were her special friend from the way it nosed her and licked her and looked at her and made excited noises. So she untied the dog and took him into the home. She knew it would be cruel to him if she took him off somewhere else. So she invented a story about kids who was about to untie him. And there was the girl with the blonde hair whose dog it were who had looked like an angel and she, Aysha, were sitting right by her and she were getting her some food. It all happened from there and who would have thought it and everything in her life had changed.

Sometimes Aysha missed the old life, which were full of excitement and huge highs and lows. Trouble were, the lows got worse and lasted longer, and there were no-one she could trust apart from her sisters and the whole world had a down on her. Fighting the world were fun for a while but then you couldn't stop. Everyone had it in for you. Fighting meant fucked up and fucked up meant pissed off. And total piss-off were a terrible thing. You had to take more and more stuff. And then you couldn't look out for your sisters no more and then you would die. Aysha still couldn't believe how it had changed for her. She had to keep asking Katy was she still in a dream. If it weren't for Katy she'd've gone back to the old life, just for the buzz, for the highs. She knew that, it weren't that this life were better, not really. But it were so different from her old life, she had to try living Katy's kind of life, and now she were in that life she mustn't let herself slip back out of it. Katy had rescued her and Katy were a wicked angel she loved being with, they had some great laughs together, even if she didn't do much in her life now 'part from schoolwork and walking Greg and going to a gig now and again and visiting Katy's folks.

Aysha didn't usually think much 'bout any of this stuff but last night what with just her and Greg in the bedroom and not getting to sleep for ages, she were thinking these thoughts and there they were again in the morning when she wanted to doze. Now she could hear footsteps scrambling along the landing outside and door handles being rattled. Aysha were trying to make sense of this when the door opened and that wicked little kid Lara burst in. Lara, she knew, had just learned how to open doors and this made her so much more of a handful. Aysha totally liked this kid, more than any small kid 'part from her sisters, in fact if Zoë hadn't been her sister she'd've still liked her but she'd've liked Lara more.

Aysha, Aysha! You gotta get up! Listen, I've got this secret! It's a BIG secret!

Oh, right, kid, that's wicked.

D'you wanna know my big secret?

Yeah, 'course I does!

My grandma's gonna die! I ain't s'posed to know but a man told me. It's a secret.

Oh, right. Aysha didn't want to tell her she already knew, everyone knew this. She couldn't bear to deflate the small child.

Aysha, what will happen when grandma dies?

Well, she won't be around no more. You won't see her no more.

Where will she have gone?

Well, no-one knows that, but she won't be alive on this world. Listen, it's like if someone goes away, right, like moves house or goes on a journey or something, and you ain't gonna see them for ages and you's sad. That happened with Katy, your auntie Katy, right, she had this friend she used to go round with all the time, every day, and then her friend moved house a long way so she couldn't see her and Katy were sad. Well, dying is like that only for ever.

Has anyone you've known died, Aysha?

Yeah, my dad died, well he weren't my real dad, he were Charly's dad, but I called him dad cos he looked after me and Charly right -

Did he look after Zoë too?

Nah, Zoë weren't born then, but listen, Lara, it's really important that you's gotta say goodbye, right, when someone like your grandma dies -

Did you say goodbye to Charly's dad?

161

No, that's it, see, I never did. And I'm always gonna wish I had.

What happened?

I were with him see, cos my mum used to take drugs so he were the one to look after us, me and Charly, and I were four and I thought my dad, Kenny, that were his name, I thought Kenny were asleep, so I stayed with him through the night, I didn't know what dying were then, and Charly were just a baby and when she needed feeding I tried to wake Kenny up but he wouldn't wake up.

So what did you do?

So I waited for our mum to get back but she didn't, so I went round a neighbour's flat. And after that I never saw Kenny again. And they has a thing called a funeral which is when everyone who knows the person what's died, right, like family and friends and stuff, can go along to this place and say goodbye before they goes away for ever, but they never let me go, so I never got to say goodbye.

And was you sad, Aysha?

Yeah I still am, right, so you must say goodbye to your grandma before she dies or when they has the funeral for her or both, OK?

OK. Aysha, you could say goodbye to Kenny when I says goodbye to grandma.

Nah, that would be just for your grandma, not for no-one else.

But yes, Aysha, I want you to come with me so you say goodbye to Kenny while I say goodbye to grandma, both of us the same time! pleaded Lara.

Well, you get along downstairs now while I gets up. Is Katy and Greg downstairs?

Yes, they is. Can I stay and watch you get dressed?

Nah, I'm gonna dress in the bathroom, kid, ok?

Aysha took her time in the bathroom. However much she liked Lara, she didn't much feel like encountering her mother so early on in her day, and hoped they might have left. When she got downstairs she found Katy's mum, the two small kids and the dog, in the breakfast room.

Katy's gone into town with Steve and Sam, reported Katy's mum. She didn't want to wake you up. I'm looking after the kids and Katy says could you give Greg a walk after breakfast.

I'll give him one now, said Aysha. I would've got up earlier if I knowed he were waiting for his walk.

Are you sure you don't want to get some breakfast inside you first?

Nah, I'm ok.

She stayed out a while with Greg, torn between wanting to see Katy and hoping the others might have left and gone back to their house. When she got back she was starving hungry and although over half the morning had gone, she started putting slices of bread into the toaster, poured herself a large glass of orange juice, and tucked into a huge bowl of cereal. Katy's step-father had gone out again but the rest of the family were still there, the three women sitting at the other end of the table with steaming cups of coffee. Lara and Liam both came and sat beside Aysha, who asked if they wanted some of her juice.

They can just have a little sip, said their mother.

Mummy! said Lara loudly - she was a kid, Aysha decided, who knew nothing between a whisper and what was close to a shout - Mummy, Aysha says I must say goodbye to grandma and go to her funeral. It was clearly an outburst she'd been saving up and could hold onto no longer.

What? You bloody cow, what've you been saying to my kids? yelled Sam, rising from her place so fast she spilled some coffee, and rushing over to where Aysha and the two kids were, pulling Lara and Liam away so that she was between them and Aysha, and raising her hand virtually in the same movement, beginning to bring it down to slap Aysha on the head.

Sam! Sam! Aysha heard Katy scream, and the two children scream as well, but Aysha wasn't there to see what happened next. Once Sam had raised her hand, Aysha was off. Years of exposure to all sorts of violence had quickened her reactions. She darted out of the room and upstairs, slamming her bedroom door but then realising that Greg, very concerned, had followed her upstairs, she opened the door again before jumping on her bed and curling up in a ball. The dog jumped up also and pawed her, licked her face.

After a few minutes Aysha became aware of the noisy argument going on downstairs, and couldn't help listening. She heard Lara crying and keep repeating like a mantra, Mummy, it were me what told Aysha about grandma! It weren't Aysha!

She heard Sam raving on. I won't have that little slut in my house any more!

Katy kept saying, Sam, whoever's fault it is it's no excuse for physical violence. Raising your hand is inexcusable.

I was angry, right!

Katy's mum kept saying, Listen to Lara, Sam. I don't think any of this is Aysha's fault!

Who else could've told her? Lara's just trying to stop that slut getting the blame!

No, I'm not, mummy! she heard Lara wail. Liam was crying too.

For god's sake let's calm down and find out what happened, she heard Katy say.

We need Aysha down here as well, if we can get to the truth of it, said Katy's mum.

She'll need Sam to apologise first, she heard Katy say, which caused Sam to erupt again.

I won't apologise to that cow! She can stay in her room all day for all I care!

Aysha thought she heard Katy crying now.

Then she heard nothing. She thought Katy's sister and the two kids might have gone, or maybe they were trying to comfort the kids and calm everyone down. She decided to stay put until she knew what the score was down there.

Katy came up to the room, her face tear-stained. I'm sorry, Aysha, for my family, for my sister I mean. None of this is your fault and I hope you'll come down so that we can sort this out.

Aysha went down, one hand clutching Katy and the other stroking Greg.

Lara was looking very upset, with her face in her chest, and refusing to look at Aysha or anyone else.

Sam's gonna apologise, said Katy's mum. And then we'll try and sort out what happened.

I'm only apologising for raising my hand to you, Aysha, said Sam, reluctance obvious in her tone. I don't need to tell you I've never liked you, and when you start telling my kids about their grandma, which has nothing to do with you the slightest bit, then I'm gonna see red, and I did, and I'm not apologising for that.

Did you tell Lara about her grandma? asked Katy.

She told me her grandma were dying, said Aysha. Which I already knew but I pretended I didn't. So I told her 'bout my dad dying and how I never got to say goodbye to him or go to his funeral, right, so I said how Lara must, like, make sure she says goodbye to her grandmother.

See, Aysha's done nothing wrong, protested Katy.

But no-one at home's told Lara about Marie.

I think you should have done by now, Sam. It would have saved all this trouble.

Tell Lara what, Granny? whined Liam.

Katy's mum sat Lara down on her knee. Now tell us, Lara, who told you about grandma?

The child started to cry. It were s'posed to be a secret.

Secret my foot! exploded Sam. We've had too many -

Sam! Shush a while, for god's sake! Lara, continued Katy's mum, who told you it was a secret?

Grandma, said the tearful child.

I can't believe Marie would do that!

Well, she is getting in quite a state.

So, Katy's mum continued asking Lara. Grandma told you she were gonna die and asked you to keep it secret? Did she, Lara?

No, said Lara. There was an old man in her room said he wanted to come and see grandma before she died, and grandma said to keep it secret. She said you and daddy were gonna tell me and Liam soon, mummy.

Tell me what? pleaded Liam.

Well, Marie's a dark horse. I wonder who this guy is?

I'm gonna phone her up about this, asserted Sam, taking out her mobile from her bag.

Yeah, but first, let's agree this, Sam, said Katy's mum. Aysha done nothing wrong at all, in fact she made a helpful response.

Yeah, well, I've already said sorry, muttered Sam, dialing.

There was a pause. Katy gave Liam a hug, Lara were still on Katy's mum's knee.

Marie's asleep, they're telling me, said Sam. Not to be disturbed. They did say she had a visitor staying in the guest-room, an old friend from Scotland, didn't give his name. I bet that's who's with her now.

Did they say how long he were staying?

No. I'll ask next time I phone.

Maybe you should leave off from visiting just now?

Should we? I wanna meet this guy.

Sam, Marie needs a bit of space, a bit of privacy. You've done wonderful visiting nearly every day, but you concentrate on explaining to Liam, let Marie have time to herself and her private affairs.

Well, I'll see what Marcus says, said a reluctant Sam. I guess we'd better get home for some lunch.

Stay and have some here if you want.

Nah, I'm still feeling a bit sore about all this.

Katy went to the door with them, and whispered something to her sister. They seemed to be having a bit of an altercation on the doorstep. Then Katy came back in and spoke to Aysha.

Try and not be too angry with my sister, Aysha, please. Try not to hate her.

She hates me!

She's always had a temper. But she's finding life tough just now, she's normally a warm and kind person.

Why can't she be warm and kind to me, right? Like, I couldn't care less, Katy, but Lara likes me and she's a great kid, but I don't have to like her mum, right.

The thing is, when Katy were a baby, said Katy's mum. Their dad left and I got, like, real depressed. I even had to go to hospital a few times. Well, it were Samantha kept the family together then, even when she were still at primary school. Then at senior school she had some problems cos she'd got behind with her work and some of the other kids used to give her a bad time. And Marie helped her a lot then, helped her get through. And then in her teenage years she got to be a bit of a rebel and her and me used to fight, so she'd end up at Marie's house and sometimes stay the night there. That's how she and Marcus got to like each other.

So now that Marie's dying, continued Katy. Sam's really

upset and it's a very touchy subject. I know it's no excuse for raising her hand or speaking the way she did, but that's the reason she lost it just now.

Steve and me's trying to support her all we can by helping out with the kids, said Katy's mum. Where is that Steve, by the way? He's supposed to be home making lunch.

Aysha and me can do that, said Katy. And then I think we'll need to get out of the house this afternoon. And I hope Sam will let us babysit this weekend, even after what happened, cos I think she needs a break from the kids.

13. LAST CONFESSION

Marie was dying now and could only speak with difficulty. Duncan felt desperately sad for the girl he had once taught and loved. He wished he could, however remotely, however occasionally, have known her in the years between. But at least there was Neil, her son, his son, their son. Neil was not a sociable or talkative man but then in recent years circumstances had forced Duncan into the same mould. Two crusty blokes at home in the wild places, trying to make some connection, which should have been made from Neil's birth or childhood, trying to make up for lost time now. The worst of it was that ten or fifteen years ago they could have gone together walking, climbing, camping, exploring the mountains and islands of the west of Scotland, father and son together, but Duncan was no use now, except in dredging up memories of those places. But Neil, already a frequent visitor to the West Highlands, had promised that after Marie's death he would start coming even more and accept Duncan's invitation to call in, stay overnight or a few days at his cottage, whenever he travelled north.

Marie's death? There was that shadow hanging over them both. Neither of them felt comfortable trying to deal with it, but despite the whole situation being so strange for Duncan, he could see it was harder for Neil. It was his responsibility, as the older son, to try and cope with his mother, before she died and afterwards, and on top of that, he had this bombshell presented to him, the presence of Duncan in his life. Duncan tried to be supportive and gentle with him, ease their way into some kind of father-son relationship.

He had phoned Neil at his place in Grasmere before travelling back to Longworth. Neil had volunteered to come and spend more time with him, and of course with Marie as well. Duncan had expected this time that he would meet the other relatives and friends, but that didn't happen, apart from that little girl, the granddaughter, who'd suddenly and unexpectedly appeared the first day he was back. After that he spent time with Marie on his own, or with Neil, but no-one else. Marie seemed now too weak and incapable to be keeping her visitors apart, so he could only assume it was Neil's doing.

Marie was in a lot of pain nearly all the time, and rarely slept well. Instead she drifted in and out of a troubled and restless delirium, unable to concentrate for more than short periods and often barely able to speak. Duncan knew that there was something she needed to tell him, and also that once that was said, she only wanted to die. She had secreted some of her diamorphine tablets in a sock in one of her drawers, and she had wanted Duncan to find some more, thinking she did not have enough to have the desired effect, but Duncan did not want to take this responsibility, did not feel it would be wise to give her any of his own tablets, have her mix them with the diamorphine. Yet his heart felt torn, his love for Marie had sustained his whole adult life and yes, it could be said that all she had done was to use him, and this would be the final instance of this, but on the other hand he had done little enough for her out of his love for her, and surely this one last deed? He sympathised with her wish to die. On the other hand, he did not know how her family would feel about it, should it become evident who had given the helping hand. He did not want to alienate any of them, particularly of course Neil. It wasn't something he could discuss with him. There was always the terrible problem with the dying that the longer the process went on the more unable the dying person was to take the action entirely on their own initiative, without someone else's help. This was the case with Marie, now, but he shrank from the position he was being placed in. She had asked him to move the sock from her chest of drawers into the cabinet by her bed, which he had done, pretending he didn't even know what the sock held. But even assuming there were enough tablets in there to finish her off, would she be able to find a final surge of strength sufficient to reach for them and swallow them down unaided?

How long would it be before Marie died? This was a matter he could discuss with his son. Neil thought his mother could hang on for some time yet. He offered Duncan the use of his place at Grasmere, as none of the guest-rooms at the hospice were available beyond the week booked for him, and there wasn't anywhere else in Longworth, other than the hotels. The family home, Marie's home, in Kitchener Avenue, having finally been sold and vacated, Neil himself was staying with Sam and Marcus, in a house which was really only big enough for their own family of four, Neil said, and Steve and Sharon often had this family of orphan kids staying. If Duncan wanted to attend Marie's funeral, Neil suggested, Grasmere would be a good place to be based. Neil himself would return there to await his mother's death. Duncan said yes, he would take Neil up on the offer, but probably best to return to Scotland first. There was his dog Barney in kennels up there, first time he'd had to place him in kennels. He'd keep in touch with Neil by phone. Neil said he'd try and be at his mother's bedside when the time came, but would return to Grasmere once he and Marcus had sorted out funeral arrangements. He would phone Duncan and meet him off a train at either Penrith or Oxenholme.

Oxenholme! He'd passed the station, of course, travelling between Glasgow and Manchester, but suddenly the mention of Neil meeting him there brought back a flood of old memories which he found he could hardly bear, especially as they related to Neil's first inception in this world. It would all seem too much of a squaring of the circle, and too painful a one.

With great effort, great difficulty, Marie had said to him, in snatches, pausing frequently.

I need to tell you this, Duncan. There's no-one else I can tell. Neil must not know this. Only one other person knows.

Jack and I were desperate for a second child. But it wasn't happening. Nothing wrong with our relationship, the sex was good. We couldn't understand it, but I began to realise that

Neil was yours and Jack must be infertile. Low sperm count or something.

We thought of tests. I had to do something to prevent there being tests. I couldn't bear for Jack to find out Neil wasn't his. Neil was over two by now.

I talked to a friend at school. Steve Mountfield was a nice guy, single, no complications, similar age to Jack and me. Not gay. Could be trusted, I was sure. I knew he liked me. I explained my predicament to him.

Steve was willing to help. This was the mid-seventies, HIV wasn't around then, but I needed him to have tests, sperm count, any hereditary stuff, the lot. Meantime I persuaded Jack to try for a bit longer.

It wasn't hard to get it done. I went to Steve's place. It helped that he lived a few miles out of Longworth at that time. Then I was pregnant with Marcus. Jack was delighted. So was I, in a way, but also I knew the deception had been compounded.

I told myself that if Jack died first I would put the record straight. But it wasn't that simple. Steve has been very good, I'm sure he's told no-one, not even Sharon, his wife. But with hindsight I should have sought out someone miles away from here.

Marcus is so like Steve, for one. Not so much in looks, although there is that, but in personality. But it was how things turned out later I could never have predicted.

Steve seemed the typical bachelor type. Wedded to his job, plenty of brief girlfriend relationships, never got serious, nothing lasted. Then he counselled a girl in his first year set who was having problems. Through her he met the mother and next thing he and the mother are in love and about to marry.

He asked me to take over pastoral care of the girl. How could I deny that request? The girl got over her problems, more or less, for a couple of years, but of course I still saw her, asked how she was getting on.

Then she hit the teenage years. Big time rebellion, rows with her mother, all the usual. My home became a refuge for her. Only ever one night at a time or at the most two. Neil wasn't home much by now, but Marcus was. Our boys were at a different school, so he hadn't known Samantha before.

Marcus and Sam fell in love. What could I do now?

There was no blood-link, so we couldn't stop them marrying. But how could we tell Marcus now? That his wife's stepfather is his own father. It was impossible. But I just had to tell someone before I die. I can't leave it just with Steve.

What am I supposed to do with this news, Marie? Duncan asked her.

Marie just shook her head. Duncan could not be sure if she'd heard his question. After such an effort she sank back, she seemed close to death, but she did seem now more at peace than at any time since he had been visiting her at the hospice.

Why have you told me this, Marie? he muttered to himself. But he only needed to look at her to know the answer. It wasn't the last time he saw Marie alive, there were three more days before he would return to Scotland. There was a faint brightening in her eyes, in her demeanour, when he visited her over those three days. He could tell she was pleased to see him, but she spoke virtually nothing to him, and certainly nothing of import, after that.

13. TRUST IN INSTINCT

Lara and Liam were told about their grandmother. It was Marcus who told them, sat them down just before tea on Friday, spoke seriously for, what, ten minutes, maybe a bit more. Lara already knew, of course. But Marcus felt she should be told by a parent and that, in fact, she appreciated this. Liam, on the other hand, did not fully understand. To be sat down and talked to like that felt a bit like a punishment to him.

Now it was Sunday and Marcus had been playing football, as he invariably did on a Sunday morning. Instead of having a shower at the playing-fields, he'd come home for a bath. He'd sat down with the kids first and talked with them for a few more minutes. Now he lay in the bath, contemplating. He rarely allowed himself much time for that, probably it was deliberate.

He worried about his wife at times like this. He didn't usually worry that much about her, because her emotional hotheadedness, her quickness to anger, her wearing of her feelings

171

on her sleeve, were all things that he loved about her, that had made him feel attracted to her in the first place. He deferred to Sam in all matters of the heart, he trusted her instincts, her intuition, and while there were some matters, money for instance, holiday plans, on which he'd put his foot down, take the lead in decision-making, if it was primarily a feeling thing, he gave in. But he wished on this business of informing the kids about their grandma's impending death, that he'd insisted on going ahead before now. Sam would normally be the one to tell them these things, and she'd kept wanting to put it off. He could understand how difficult it was for her, but he should have stepped in. Although Marie was his mother, he was aware how much harder Sam was finding it to deal with her dying. Initially, before Marie went to the hospice and for the first week or two she was in there, Sam had been pleased to visit her mother-in-law regularly, but now she found it very painful and would come back upset and crying. She left the kids with her mother when she could, so they wouldn't see her so upset. Marcus was going to have to take them now. Sam wasn't going to stop visiting Marie, but Marcus hoped she'd go less often. He didn't like to see her tearing herself apart like this.

There were three things important to Marcus, his family, his football, and his work, in that order. If there was stress in one of these, he could always absorb himself in one of the others. In particular football was a useful diversion if either family or work matters were causing him stress, and they were just now. So Marcus lay in the bath, thinking of football. There were the teams he watched, the two Manchester teams or Bolton Wanderers, only if one of these was playing a weekday evening however, because his weekends were taken up with lower-level games. There was the team he played for, whom he had just helped salvage a vital draw against the league leaders with a crucial tackle in the last few minutes as the opposition had pressed harder and harder for the winning goal. But it was the kids' teams he thought about most. The last couple of years he'd been coaching the boys' under 15 team, and the girls' under 11 team. He didn't do it on his own, but he was regarded as the senior coach, with lead responsibility. And he particularly needed to keep thinking of the boys' team. The girls' squad was expanding slowly, with younger girls coming in all the time, but there was a fairly settled team, the only question being when to 'blood' each of the younger girls in a league match, rather than the practice or friendly games which he arranged to help them all feel involved in the club. But the boys' team had presented two real dilemmas. The squad had grown this year from eighteen to twenty-one, which was good, gave him more options, and this was not just from more boys coming up from the under 12s, but there had been four boys new to the club - two had joined from other clubs in the leagues because of parents having disputes or being unhappy with the way their sons had been treated, one had moved to the town from elsewhere, and another had only now, at the age of 13, decided to put his enthusiasm and aptitude for football to the test. This latter was an Asian lad who liked to play an old-fashioned left-winger's game, and had the skill to bring it off, not just with the ball at his feet, but with the ability to place pinpoint crosses into the goalmouth, including taking corners from either side. Marcus thought this was an important addition to the side, but it meant restructuring the way the team played, which up to recently had involved a combination of forward running by the strikers, moving the ball forward with short passing, or at times the despairing hoof upfield towards the penalty box. If a corner was awarded, or the ball ended near the corner flag, it had been invariably played short to a player backing up. Now it was necessary to persuade more of the boys with scoring potential to get into the box and get onto the end of crosses. To begin with, when this Asian boy was selected, that didn't happen, chances were wasted and games lost. There was the temptation to drop the boy and revert to the more limited options, and Marcus had on two occasions done that, but over the season as a whole he'd stuck to his belief in this boy, and it was now paying off with good wins the last three games in which Naheed had laid on a number of important goals. The other problem he'd had was with the goalkeeper position. The regular keeper over the last two years was a tall boy who kept shots out of goal with alacrity, but who never left his line. Up from the under 12s this year had come a younger, smaller lad, agile and with a tremendous leap for his size, and who had the courage and instinct to come out off his line and take the ball from an opponent's feet or jump with good timing to catch a ball in the air. But of course this was a risky strategy at boys' level, when the defenders were not used to having to protect the goalkeeper by dropping back onto the line whenever the keeper came out. Marcus had felt it important to ring the changes, give both keepers the chance to play, sometimes within the same match by a substitution at half-time. It had not been a successful strategy at first, mainly because of defenders' struggling to adjust to the different styles, but finally in the last few games the policy seemed to be working.

Marcus reflected on these matters with satisfaction, which was something he could not feel when he thought of either his work or his family. Normally his work was satisfying. He was an electrical engineer designing the circuits for electric wheelchairs at a factory which manufactured them in town. Part of his job involved going out to user groups and talking with them about ways the design could be improved, and then helping them understand the working of a new prototype when one appeared. But two weeks ago a major fault had appeared in the latest model, and he'd had to spend all his working time "back at the drawing-board", literally, with no chance of a break and no opportunity for getting out of the factory.

Then when he got home, he had to try and cope with his wife. It was bad enough coping with the upset that her visits to his mother brought about, but two days ago, when he got home on a Friday after a very stressful week, he found Sam tearing herself up over an incident at her mother's that morning.

I made such an idiot of myself, she moaned. That wretched girl Katy's taken on, she makes me so furious, she really does my head in. I couldn't help it, I raised my hand to hit her, I know I shouldn't -

Did you hurt her?

No, she shot out of her chair like greased lightning when she saw my intention, and was out of the door before I could move my hand. She's been hit before, that's clear from her reaction. And of course Katy's all holier-than-thou, about how with an abused child you should never show even the smallest hint of violence -

Well, she's right of course, but no-one can be expected to think out what's the right thing every time they react to a situation. What had this girl done, for god's sake?

Well, that's the thing, I thought she'd been messing with Lara's feelings, talking about Marie and how she were gonna die.

But it turned out it were Lara who told her and not only was that slut blameless but had actually said good and helpful things to Lara. Can you imagine how I felt?

I dunno, not good for sure. Bad situation.

You can say that again, Marcus! For Christ's sake, you know how I hate that kid Katy's taken on. And now I've lost face completely and I can just imagine that little cow smirking away at how she put one over on me. Katy said she'd need to explain to her why I get so upset about Marie, but I dunno what's worse, having this kid frightened of me cos of my temper or having Katy trying to get her feeling sorry for me by telling her all about my past. I mean, is nothing sacred these days -

Well, the most important thing is not to blame Lara in any way, said Marcus, trying to soothe.

Of course not. You don't think I'd blame Lara, do you?

No, no, that's what I meant, I know you wouldn't.

Mind you, I'm sorely tempted to blame Marie. It were some old bloke she had visiting her, god knows who that was, who let it slip to Lara that Marie were gonna die, and then Marie made Lara promise to keep it secret. You know how I hate secrets, and I can't stand the thought that Lara and this Aysha kid are getting thick as thieves and Lara's letting her know things she's keeping from me, her mother, for god's sake!

Don't blame Lara for that, it's pretty normal for kids her age to share things with other kids rather than parents.

Not something important as that, Marcus! Jesus Christ!

She wouldn't realise its importance.

Anyhow, it's one thing to whisper to your friends at school, quite another to get thick as thieves with an older girl like this Aysha. I mean, what do we know about her background? We know it's dire, Katy's said so, but she hasn't told us any details. There may be all sorts of stuff coming out which could have a terrible influence on Lara. And Katy has the cheek to say this kid reminds her of me when I was younger! I mean, I were nothing like this Aysha! I had a temper, yes -

You still do.

OK, but I had justification, everything I'd been through with mum -

I'm sure Aysha has reasons for being the way she is -

Yeah, but she don't have a temper. Sweet as pie most of

the time, but she's sly, that kid, I can tell. God knows what's lurking underneath. Not like me at all. And the worst of it is how Katy's taking a back seat to her. I mean, Katy was developing a brilliant relationship with both our kids, and now she's kinda handed it over to this Aysha -

I think that's a bit unfair, Sam. Katy still gets on very well with both of them, tries to see them when she can.

Well, with Lara at least, it's all Aysha now -

Just a temporary phase. And Liam still looks mostly to Katy. And to us, of course.

Mummy, mummy, it's Neighbours on now! came a cry from the other room.

Well, you can watch Neighbours if you want. Daddy and me's having a talk.

You always talking, mummy, said Liam, barrelling in. Marcus scooped up the little boy.

Grown-ups do need to talk some time. And I need to have a talk to you two. In a little while.

What about, daddy? asked Lara who stood in the doorway, her eyes on the television but her ears listening out for her parents' words. Is it about what happened at granny's this morning?

No, said their mother.

It weren't Aysha's fault, you know, mummy.

No, we know that, said Marcus. And not your fault either, Lara, you're not to blame in any way.

Who is to blame, then? Was it that man?

No, sometimes things like that happen, without anyone being to blame. But I do need to talk to you about grandma, said Marcus.

In a few minutes, kids, go back to the TV and close the door. I feel such a jerk, she went on to Marcus, almost in the same breath, and cranking up her emotional pitch. I've lost all credibility with that Aysha kid, I can't stop her coming here with Katy or they'll just say it's sour grapes, or revenge, or something. God, it's infuriating! And what I said about her and Katy's true, you know. Katy gives in to her, lets her take over from her. Everything. I mean, letting that girl have her bed, not just back here, but in her flat as well I gather, and now Katy's moved out into my old room, would you believe! And that wretched dog of

176

hers! I mean, Katy was devoted to that dog, and now what happens? Aysha looks after the dog. All the time, she does. And the dog don't sleep downstairs now, and don't sleep with Katy, oh no, it's Aysha what has the dog in with her at night! See what I mean!

But it's because the kid's insecure, protested Marcus. Lots of kids don't like being on their own at night, she'll feel more secure with the dog in there.

Insecure, my foot! Just selfish, if you ask me! I mean, why should she be insecure now, she's got Katy running around after her all the time, got a good home, everything she wants -

I meant, insecure from her previous life.

Yeah, well, that's exactly my point. And now I've lost any advantage I had. How can I tell Katy now that she can't bring Aysha when she comes?

Well, no, you can't, Marcus had said. Are they coming tonight?

Yeah, in about half an hour, I think. And tomorrow night. At least we've got two nights to ourselves.

I'm gonna talk to the children now, then, said Marcus. Listen, kids, he opened the door and called through. Switch that off now and listen to me!

Are Auntie Katy and Aysha coming soon? asked Lara, too innocent in her tone. She must have been keeping her ear to the door, Marcus thought.

Quite soon. Mummy's getting your tea.

What about Uncle Neil? chipped in Liam.

No, he's not coming tonight. He's gone back to Grasmere 'til Sunday. He'll be back here Sunday night and staying with us next week. Probably.

Assuming your grandmother hangs on another week, he thought to himself.

15. ACROSS THE GREAT DIVIDE

She was aware of the light, and the voices. A blur of presence. She slept a lot, uneasy sleep, pain and nausea intruding. She was doped up, she knew, couldn't focus, couldn't even concentrate her thoughts. She wanted only to die, she was ready now, but she had no strength to reach for those pills, she could hardly remember where they were.

Nurses needed to come and deal with her bodily functions. She hated that. She wanted only to die. To join her Jack. To be forgiven.

Marcus came with the two children. She lay with her hand at the side of the bed. She heard him whisper, Touch your grandma's hand.

She couldn't remember their names, but she felt their small fingers. It was enough. Duncan had gone now. He had said goodbye.

Duncan, Duncan! but she couldn't speak the words. She'd said what was needed. He'd come back, a light in the darkness.

Both her brothers had been now. They'd been close as kids, how had she let them drift away? Samantha came and cried. She'd buried her face in Marie's hand, Marie had felt her tears, but couldn't hear the words. Neil had been there, grave and silent, a shadow in the room. She knew it was Neil. All the important good-byes, but where was Jack?

She was going to Jack, she clung to that thought. Leaving all the others and going to Jack.

Consciousness drifted. She was back in her childhood, with her brothers, tagging along behind their drive and ambition, chiding her parents for their simple life, their unwillingness to change. Going to primary school, the three of them. The salt air and gulls' cries of Oban. Her love for Duncan, trying to make sure she sat next to him in the minibus. A love discarded for no reason. Meeting Jack at Dundee. One love overtaking another. But whatever memories, pictures, drifted through her subconscious, there was always one stronger, clearer than the rest. The moment of Jack's death still came back to her, as it always had done, even as her own approached. For a geography teacher, she had gone abroad remarkably little. But she lay back now, all the time, no longer having anything other than the vaguest awareness of the room she was in, the light or darkness outside, those closest to her by her bedside, hardly aware even of sleep or pain or nausea, and she was back on a high mountain path in the Pyrenees, crossing a snowfield, watching the man she loved slowly sliding away from her.

16. COLOURS OF THE WORLD

By the time of the February half-term, Katy felt she had got into a reasonable routine in her life with Aysha.

On Tuesdays she walked with Greg through the park and to the children's home. If either Cassie, who she knew best and who was Zoë's key-worker, or Teresa who was Charly's, was on duty, she went a bit earlier to have a talk about the girls and when they might move in with her. Otherwise she tried to arrive when the girls got back from school, and would take them straight back with her to have tea with their older sister and her. If they hurried, they would beat Aysha back. Katy knew that she, Aysha, hated getting back to an empty flat. A couple of hours later, they would all walk back to the home, and Aysha would then take Greg for a walk while Katy spent a bit of time helping out with some of the kids. On Thursdays Aysha had started coming with Katy to her choir evenings. This had seemed a big step forward. It meant that only when Katy had orchestra and basketball was Aysha left on her own, and basketball practice was now only once a fortnight, so this meant only three evenings in each two-week period. The original idea had been that Aysha would go back to the children's home on these evenings, but she had insisted on staying in the flat. There was no real difficulty. Aysha caught up with her homework on these evenings, and when she had finished, or at least done as much as she could, she took Greg out for his evening walk. The two girls normally gave him an afternoon walk together, or sometimes went for a run, as soon as Aysha got in from the Unit, apart from Tuesdays. Katy wasn't entirely happy about Aysha wandering freely around the city, on her own apart from the dog, at that time of night, and she couldn't help wondering if the girl was being entirely honest when telling Katy where she'd been, but she was always back when Katy got in, was never high, or smelling of alcohol or cannabis, only tobacco, and she had to admit Greg was contented, as well as Aysha. On the other Wednesday, when Katy had no basketball, the girls stayed in together, and Katy made sure they did some of the Life-Story work on these evenings. Every Friday they went out together, to a music gig or concert if they could find one, otherwise to a film or to have a meal out if there was no music or film. Aysha was prepared to be flexible about music, even though her tastes remained the same, she even came to one or two classical events, but she was very adamant about films. She would only watch comedy or horror. As Katy couldn't abide horror films, this only left comedy. Katy hoped films such as The Lord of the Rings trilogy would fit the bill as far as horror went, but not according to Aysha's thinking.

At the weekends, things were a bit more flexible. They usually went for a run together Saturday mornings, or if Katy had a basketball match on a Saturday, Sundays instead. As Aysha rose late, these runs took them through almost to lunchtime. Sometimes they took in a visit to a supermarket at the end of the run, Katy insisting that Greg be left tied outside and that Aysha come and help her shop. Once a fortnight approximately, on Saturdays when Katy wasn't playing basketball, they had Charly and Zoë for lunch and for a good part of the afternoon, going to the park if weather permitted. Katy and Aysha would normally stay in on a Saturday evening unless there was a particular gig they wanted to go to. Katy had four basketball matches during the term, but only one of them involved travelling any distance from Bursfield. On this day she insisted Aysha went to the children's home for lunch, yes she could take Greg with her, but it was not acceptable for the girl to be left on her own almost all day.

Sundays were quiet, relaxing days. Aysha caught up with homework, Katy with coursework, they listened to music, they went for a walk, Katy practised cello, Aysha drum, Aysha gave Greg a brushing, sometimes a bath. They each had an early night. Katy had decided it wasn't possible for her to stay up doing her coursework, after Aysha was in bed. She tried to do as much as possible while Aysha was at her Unit, and always managed an hour or so on Saturday and Sunday mornings while the girl had a lie-in, and then caught up a bit more on a Sunday evening.

This routine, however, did not leave much space for various matters which Katy was aware of pressing for her attention. The first was Ruth Barnes, Aysha's social worker, wanting to see Aysha regularly, which Aysha didn't want at all. A compromise was reached whereby Ruth Barnes called once every three weeks or so at about three-thirty, and saw Aysha briefly when she got in from the Unit. Aysha would take Greg for his walk as soon as she could get away, leaving Katy to have a longer talk with the social worker. The two main issues as far as Katy was concerned were a transfer to mainstream high school, and reuniting Aysha with her two sisters. Progress on both issues had been slow. The Life-Story work had gone slowly too, and attempts to find Aysha's real father, or the grave of her stepfather, had been put on hold. Ruth Barnes wanted to hold a case review. Katy agreed, but thought the two issues should be discussed separately. Eventually it was agreed to hold two reviews, one at the Education Unit focussing on Aysha's education and her future transfer, and the other at the children's home, looking at the prospective move to a larger property and the three children being together. They agreed it was necessary to hold both meetings before the end of term, and because Easter was so early the timing was going to be tight. Katy felt strongly that a move of flat would have to happen in the vacation, to attempt it in term-time would be crazy. She also had it in her mind to organise another visit to the prison, but she couldn't get either Charly or Zoë to make their minds up whether they wanted to come or not.

For someone who liked horror films Aysha was surprisingly full of phobias. She was scared of spiders and of thunderstorms, but her worst phobia was of the dentist. Katy discovered that she hadn't been to a dentist for some years, not since one of her previous foster-mothers had taken her courage in both her hands and dragged Aysha along. Katy wondered if the fear was not so much of the needle or any aspect of dental treatment, but of being totally subjected to an adult's power, and particularly if that adult were a man. She had an appointment with her own dentist back in Longworth in her Easter vacation, and she knew there was a woman dentist in that practice, so she hoped it might be possible to get her to take on Aysha, even though her connection with the town was tenuous.

All these matters were on Katy's mind, and the pressure on her time to sort them out, when she had a call on her mobile from Sharon, to say that Marie had died. Katy felt sad for her sister, brother-in-law, nephew and niece, who would all find it a sad loss, and she worried about how her sister would cope, but she hardly knew Marie herself, knew a lot about her of course, but had only met her a few times, her sister's wedding and a few other occasions, but none recently, so she kept an emotional distance from the news and merely thought she had better phone up Sam in the next couple of days.

She mentioned the news to Aysha that evening after they'd had their tea.

Marie died during the night, y'know, Lara and Liam's grandma.

Oh my god! exclaimed the younger girl. That's terrible. Lara's gonna be very upset. When's the funeral gonna be?

I dunno. There's no reason for me to go, I know they'll take Lara and Liam, the rest of my family will be there. I hardly knew her, me.

But Katy, you must go. Lara and Liam's gonna need you, right!

No, I don't think so, they'll have my mum, she'll probably go, and Steve.

But your mum's disabled, so Steve will be looking after her. You and me's gotta go and look after them kids!

You, Aysha? But you never even met Marie!

But that Lara told me all about her! I've gotta go there, Katy, so's when Lara says goodbye to her gran, then me, I can say goodbye to my dad the same time.

Where've you got that idea from?

Nowhere, it's just like really important and stuff.

Well, I'm not sure Marie's family will want us there, you or me.

Why not? You mean cos your sister don't like me?

No, I don't mean that, I mean cos it's normally just close family and neither of us is close family.

Well, you's close to your sister, right, and me, I'm like

close to you and your mum. And Lara, right, and she's Marie's grandkid.

It ain't the same as being close to Marie.

It is, Katy, it is! remonstrated Aysha in an anguished tone. Look, I gotta go, right, for Lara to help her, and for me, so's I can say goodbye to Kenny. So I'm gonna go, Katy, and if you ain't I'll just like go on my own! So you phone up and find out 'bout the funeral and if you don't I will.

How're you gonna find the place if you go alone? queried Katy, laughing despite the seriousness.

Look, it ain't funny, Katy, Aysha protested. What d'you mean, place?

The crematorium or whatever, how're you gonna find it?

Well, I'll just go to your house, right. I know the way now. I'll go with your mum.

If she goes.

You said she were.

Yeah, probably.

Anyway, she'll give me directions if she don't go, or your stepdad would give me a lift or something. I'm going, any-how, so.

So?

So I'm going, right. It'll help me, like, work through some of my problems.

It was true that in the Life-Story book they'd got a bit stuck on Kenny and his death. Aysha wanted to visit his grave and Katy had said that would have to wait til the Easter holidays. Trying to trace Milton Orlando Jewell would have to wait until then, too.

I'm sure it would help you, Aysha, I'm just not sure whether Neil and Marcus would want to open it up wider, y'know, beyond immediate family. And also, we've got so much happening here the next week or two.

Fuck that, Katy. This is more important.

Is it?

Yeah, it is, right! Anyway, what else is there happen-ing?

Well, on top of the normal things, there's a review at the children's home next week. Then we're going to visit your new

High School the Monday after -

What d'you mean, my new High School?

Remember, at the meeting at the Unit the other day, they said they'd found a suitable High School, willing to have you, no uniform, and we need to start introductory visits, so that you'll get used to going. The first is Monday week.

Bloody hell, Katy, that's scary, right. I ain't ready for that yet.

On this idea, it was true that things had suddenly taken off and were moving ahead quickly. And Katy was aware that she'd allowed the professionals to twist her arm so that she was to be the one to accompany Aysha on these visits. On the one hand, Aysha would probably be happier if it was Katy went with her, but on the other, it was an awesome responsibility for some-one with Katy's lack of experience.

OK, then, here's a deal. I'll come to the funeral if you'll come on the visit to the school.

Aysha looked at her, as though she were not sure which of them had outwitted the other here.

What if they's on the same day? she ventured tent-atively, hopefully.

Well, you can't rearrange a funeral, so we'll have to hope the school will rearrange the introduction. Katy's love for the girl overflowed on these sorts of occasions, and she went and gave Aysha a hug, knowing she really needed it. Mostly the girl was quiet enough, but once she got the bit between her teeth, she could go on for ever. Then when she finally gave up, ran out of steam, or was forced to accept a compromise, she was at her most vulnerable.

So I'd better phone my mum, right?

She looked at Aysha, who seemed totally tongue-tied now and just nodded her head.

Katy got through on her mobile. Mum, Aysha and me's been talking 'bout, y'know, Marie's death and, like, we've decid-ed we ought to come if we can. Y'know, to the funeral.

Oh, Katy, I think everyone will be very grateful, and pleased to see you, and Aysha, but you don't have to, you know.

Well, y'know, we wanna show solidarity, with Sam and the kids, sympathy and all that, and help look after Lara and Liam, so that Sam and Marcus can concentrate on, like, the other people who've come.

Well, I was thinking it was gonna have to be me taking on that role with Lara and Liam. All help welcome, there'll be lots of upset folks, I'm sure.

Yeah, so when is it, mum?

Well, I don't know, Katy, they haven't fixed it yet, or if they have, they haven't told me yet. You could phone Sam, she would know.

Can you find out, mum, and let us know, in case we need to rearrange or cancel any appointments? I will speak to Sam, but I don't want to just yet, leave it a couple of days. Is she very upset?

She didn't seem too bad when I spoke to her, but it may not have sunk in yet. I'll be having Lara and Liam a lot over the next few days, so I'll see plenty of her, even if briefly.

Well, mum, do tell her if she wants to speak to me, she can phone me any time, and just leave a message if my mobile's off and I'll phone her back. I just don't know who she'll want to lean on just now. I mean, Marcus obviously, but apart from him.

I'll let her know, love. We'll look forward to seeing you, both of you.

The funeral turned out to be on the Monday before Easter, which meant the planned first introductory visit of Aysha to her high school had to be rearranged to the Tuesday. The two girls travelled back to Longworth on the Sunday afternoon. There had still been no news of a larger place, but on the Saturday before the funeral, Charly announced, when she and Zoë came for lunch, that she'd like to go to the same High School as Aysha, and since they didn't know where they would be living, then why couldn't she choose any High School. She and Zoë also said they would come with Katy to visit their mother in prison. Some things at last seemed to be happening. The two younger girls returned to the home a little earlier than usual that day, as Katy and Aysha had to go into town to find something for Aysha to wear at the funeral.

17. CALLING ME HOME

Neil hated himself at times like these. He wasn't cut out for dealing with death or dying. He had from time to time been called to rescue a dead or dying climber from the mountains. It was a terrible experience. If they were already dead, the whole operation could be more clinical, emotion kept out of it, but if they were still alive, you had to somehow tune in, keep them positive, keep them awake, pretend they still had a chance. Which perhaps they did, but if they then died, that was ten times worse. Build up hope, only to have it snatched away. Neil wasn't good at all that feeling stuff. Most mountain rescues weren't like that, climbers lost or trapped and unable to move, injuries, broken limbs, all these he felt at home with, the relief at being winched or stretchered to safety. An emotion he could deal with. But dying, no. Dying should be like the animals or birds, Neil thought, just a part of the cycle of life. A momentary panic, survival or not.

But the long drawn-out dying of his mother was a terrible thing. He did not know how to deal with it, what he should say to her. He would have felt uncomfortable talking about his own life, the very active, physical living of it, when his mother had no way of participating, sharing. All his life, since he first came to love the mountains and wild places, initially sharing them with his family, and later on his own, this was the main thing, often the only thing, he talked to his mother about. And his father too, until they started talking less and less as the years went by. But their conversations, his mother and him, were predicated on her sharing of the experience of the mountains. Even after his father died, and his mother lost interest in the outdoor life, he was able to revive it a little by recounting his experiences. But not when she was dying, he thought, what would be the point of rekindling that interest now?

He sat by her through love and duty, and the strange experience of finding he had a father four years after his father died. He recognised the bond at once, the likeness, things shared. He would get to know this stranger who was part of him, but they both had to negotiate his mother's death first. His brother Marcus was probably a lot better at these things than him, but Marcus had a wife and children, had to cope with their distress

186

as well as his own. The house had been sold, at least. A will had been made, most of the legacy left in trust for the grandchildren. Not much chance of any grandchildren from him, he thought. His mother had put her affairs in order in that week and a half between Christmas and her move to the hospice. So there was only the funeral now, or cremation rather, but that was the worst ordeal of all.

He had been with her through her last hours. Before he went to the hospice for the last time, he had called his father, said she was expected not to last out this night. No chance of Duncan getting there, instead he would await details of the funeral. When Neil got to the hospice, his brother and sister-in-law and their children were already there. He stayed with his sister-in-law while Marcus drove the children, after they'd whispered their loving good-byes to their grandma, to their other grandmother. Funny, when he came back a few minutes later, Marcus had Steve with him. Not right that, it should be just the three of them. Steve seemed to realise this after a few minutes and left again. So between the three of them they'd kept watch for several hours until she'd slipped away. None of them could have been sure how much, if at all, she was aware of their presence. They took their turns in holding her almost lifeless hands. He wasn't used to physical contact with her.

He needed to refer to Marcus and Sam over a lot of matters, but he basically did most of the arranging of the cremation and a get-together afterwards, for which he booked a room in a local hotel and a buffet lunch. None of this came naturally to him, but easier to arrange in advance than deal with on the day. He put his faith in his brother and sister-in-law for the day itself. He would speak, in his stiff awkward way, at the service, but that would be it.

His mother had not been religious, or particularly artistic or musical. A passage from one of Ella Maillart's travel books, and her favourite hymn from childhood, had been her own choices, and she also wanted their father's favourite pieces of music, a section of "Fingal's Cave" and the song "Carrickfergus" which had been played at his funeral also. Neil had remembered, when these pieces had been played before, a family holiday on Rathlin Island and a day trip to the island of Staffa, both of them when he and Marcus were boys. Holidays were for him treasured interludes in the painful struggle of his boyhood. Now he faced the final struggle, the culmination of the pain, because while he still had Marcus as a link to his childhood and Duncan as a new-found parent, neither of them were directly, or even indirectly, part of that unsuccessful process of adapting him to the social world.

The chapel was pale varnished wood and plain white walls. It seemed cold and lifeless despite the plentiful displays of flowers in various mixtures of colour. In a side-room were displayed more flowers and a whole range of cards, not all for his mother - there were two other cremations happening that day - but it was noticeable how many there were for Marie Sullivan. And the chapel, cold when Neil entered among the first few mourners, soon filled up almost to capacity and took on a different feel entirely. The service was led by the school's head of religious studies, a good friend of his mother and a man of ecumenical leanings. Neil's anxiety almost overwhelmed him at times. Would anything go wrong, had he forgotten something important? It all felt foreign, not alien but foreign, to him. Marcus would be the first to speak. That was reassuring, his younger brother seemed like a safe pair of hands in this situation. Then some music, then Neil's turn. He was to read from the Ella Maillart, but he needed to say a few words as well. He had them jotted on a card, tucked into the book at the appropriate page. Later, Samantha would speak. She had insisted, although Neil wondered if his sister-in-law was feeling even more anxious than him. She was tearful and couldn't keep still, but then, even Neil recognised Sam as one of those people who needed to make an open display of her emotions.

He went to the front when the music ended, holding the book, hands shaking. Before I read one of my mother's favourite passages, he said, I would like to add a few words. I am not a man for whom, since I reached adulthood, family ties have been particularly important. Those of you who know me will know that I'm a solitary man who has carved out a solitary life for myself. There is a contrast, not only between me and my brother, but also between my adult life and my childhood. Family ties were very important in my childhood, and what has happened to me since is not about rejecting those childhood ties but about expressing the person I've turned out to be. I have many many happy memories of my childhood, and now no longer have either of my parents to share these with, to help me remember. It is important to keep those memories alive, and I hope my brother and I will be able to, separately and together, not just for my parents' sakes but also for our own. I'm sorry if I've spoken more about me than my mother, but those memories of family life together when I was younger were important to my mother, and an important part of our relationship in recent years. I never felt my mother was disappointed in me. She would have had every right to be, but she wasn't. She understood the way I turned out to be, and she understood that making my own very different sort of life was not a rejection of her values. I will for ever hold dear those values of hers and the generosity and understanding which went with them.

He gulped. It was difficult to proceed with the Ella Maillart. His mouth was dry and crackly. He stumbled on, nevertheless, almost dropped the book but got through it.

More music, and Samantha got up to speak. Her voice was cracking too. Her register was all over the place. His little nephew Liam was clearly upset to hear it. A wailing sound interrupted his sister-in-law's words. Both the children had done well up to now to keep still and quiet. His brother shifted into the aisle and took his nephew's hand. Neil turned round to check what was happening. He saw Samantha's sister, grown-up now but still recognisable from the adolescent girl who was bridesmaid at the wedding, move into the aisle as though to take the child, but then a younger girl in a black dress, moving quickly and wraithlike, took the boy into her arms and hoisted him on her fragile-looking shoulders, bouncing him up and down as she moved to the back of the room. Neil had never seen this girl before and wondered who she was, what she was doing here, but then remembered mention of an orphan girl that Samantha's sister had befriended. They appeared to have been sitting together, that must be who she was.

His sister-in-law got through her tribute with no further problems, and then the hymn and the final words and people were spilling out into the bright cold March air. Now he felt even more awkward, everyone else talking, sympathising, a few people coming up to him and offering their condolences or expressing appreciation of what he said, but he had no words left. He'd caught a glimpse of his father at the back, slipping out before him, and nowhere to be seen now. They'd agreed to stay apart for the duration of the event. He noticed the girl in the black dress who now had both his nephew and niece with her, holding each by the hand. His niece spotted him standing on his own. Uncle Neil! she called out, with no thought for the hushed tones most were using at this point in proceedings. Come and meet my friend Aysha! And she pulled a seemingly reluctant adolescent girl towards him. His nephew meantime had pulled away and run on ahead to greet him.

This is Aysha, said Lara. She's a friend of Auntie Katy.

Hi, I'm Neil.

Hi, mumbled the girl. Yeah, I know, I heared you give your talk. That were good, that were cool. Yours were the best, 'part from the song.

The hymn, you mean, or the folk-song?

Nah, the folk-song, I meant. Magic, that were.

My mother and father both loved that song.

Who were your father?

Jack, he was called. He died a few years ago, in a mountaineering accident. That's when I decided to do mountain rescue. You don't remember him, Lara, do you?

No.

You were only about a month old when he died.

When grandma died, I were five years old.

Just turned, weren't you?

Well happy birthday kiddo, said the girl in the black dress. Sorry if I forgot before.

That's ok, Aysha, said Lara. Have you said goodbye to your dad?

Yeah, I did. But shall we say it again, together?

Yeah, let's!

Let's go over to them flowers.

Can you look after Liam a moment, Uncle Neil?

No, I wanna come too. Let me come, Aysha!

OK, let Liam come, said Aysha.

You just have to say goodbye to grandma, Lara explained to Liam. You can come too, Uncle Neil. Cos she was your mother, weren't she?

Neil found himself facing a colourful bed of flowers

with the three children, all bowing together.

Goodbye, grandma.

Goodbye, grandma, echoed Liam.

Goodbye, Kenny, my dad.

Goodbye, mother, said Neil, moved beyond anything he would have expected.

Afterwards, there was silence.

There were fewer people outside the chapel now.

I guess we'd better get along to the lunch, Neil said to the three children. Are you all coming?

I'm starving, said the older girl. Funerals is hungry work, right.

Neil laughed.

Can we come in your car, Uncle Neil? asked Lara. And Aysha too?

I think your mummy and daddy will expect you to go with them, said Neil.

No they won't.

I must find Katy, said Aysha. Cos neither of us has a car to go in, 'part from Steve's. I think he's already taken Katy's mum.

She wandered off, still with the children holding each hand. Then Katy came up to him.

Could you take Aysha and me to the hotel, Neil? My mother needed to get back home, she ain't gonna make it for the lunch. Steve's hoping to come once he's got mum settled down, so I just need to phone him to tell him to bring me and Aysha's stuff so's we can go straight to the station.

Fine, said Neil.

While Katy was on her mobile, Aysha came back, still with Lara and Liam.

Mummy and daddy says we can come in your car, said Lara to Neil.

It's true, said Aysha. They did say yes.

They piled into the Volvo Estate, Katy in the passenger seat, the three children in the back.

Is this the car you moved all Katy's stuff to Bursfield in? asked Aysha.

Yes, said Neil.

But it weren't Neil that drove, it were Marcus, Lara and Liam's dad, explained Katy. Neil just lent his car, which was real good of him.

Will we need it again when we move to a bigger place? asked Aysha.

I've not even thought that far ahead, answered Katy.

Are you moving again? Neil asked Katy.

Aysha's two sisters are s'posed to be moving in with Aysha and me, but we'll need a bigger flat or a house, and Social Services haven't found us one yet.

Well, if you need this car, just say, and I'll be happy to help out. This time I'll come and drive it myself, said Neil.

Well, thanks, but what about all your other commitments?

They can wait. Any idea when it's likely to be?

Next term some time, I guess. I were hoping it would be the Easter holidays but they're leaving it too late for that.

Well, just get a message to me as soon as you know the date.

Now we need to get you two to mummy and daddy, said Katy to Lara and Liam as Neil pulled into the hotel car park. Aysha, can you watch out for Steve? He had to take my mum home cos she weren't feeling up to the rest of it, and he's coming back with Greg and our stuff, which one of us'll need to get from his car.

OK, said the girl, trundling along a little reluctantly, it seemed to Neil, after Katy who had her nephew and niece firmly by the hand and was seeking out her sister. Neil was left on his own in the car park. He made his way slowly, feeling a degree of reluctance himself, to the area of the hotel where the buffet lunch was set out, all of which he'd arranged himself. He looked for Duncan but couldn't see him. He saw one of his uncles and a couple of his cousins and stopped for a few words, took a mineral water from the drinks table, waited for a bit more space to appear at the food queue, looked for a seat, somewhere to put his drink. Somewhere where he wouldn't be expected to make casual conversation.

That girl in the black dress appeared again, what was her name, he should remember, with Steve. They appeared to be looking for Katy, but the girl, who he could now see was holding a dog on a lead, stopped by him.

This is Greg, she said to Neil. Has you met him before?

I don't think I have.

He comes from a place you told Katy about, where your rescue dogs goes if they don't make the grade.

Really, I don't remember telling Katy -

Neil was beginning to feel confused, disorientated. The occasion was finally overwhelming him. He needed food, but could not face all the people milling around. And now this girl had a dog. Neil loved dogs, but not in here.

One of the hotel staff came over and politely told the girl that she wasn't allowed to bring the dog inside. Neil felt some relief, he had been about to tell the girl the same thing, but it would have been an unpleasant task.

Where can I take him? the girl asked, innocently enough.

He can go in my car, Neil answered, coming to the rescue, allowing the member of staff to disappear back to the bar area.

But he's just been in Steve's car, and before that shut in the house. I can't shut him up again, I've gotta give him a walk first.

Don't you want to eat some food first? I thought you said you were starving.

I am, but I'll have to wait. I don't mind, as long as there's some left.

Where will you walk him, round here?

Is there a park anywhere near?

I don't think so, no.

So, I just gotta walk him round the streets then. Listen, I'll have to get a bag for scooping his poo, right. I've gotta ask Katy where his things is. Can you hold onto him while I goes and asks.

Neil noticed for the first time that the girl was holding a glass of red wine. He handed her his own glass.

Look, I'll walk him with you, I need the fresh air. Can you put my glass with yours, and ask them to save some food for both of us? This way, we can put him straight into my car when we get back.

The girl was back in no time with a plastic super-market bag.

Won't you be cold? Neil asked her.

Nah. Oh my god! she exclaimed. I think I left my jacket back at the funeral place. Bloody hell!

Shall I drive you back there to find it?

Oh no, no thanks, I can't remember where I left it, like, it might be in Steve's car, or back at Katy's mum's house. Any-how, I'm coming back here in a few days cos it's gonna be Easter and Katy comes home for Easter, and I've got a spare jacket back at home, I mean, at Katy's flat.

But you don't want to leave it at the crematorium if it is there.

I'll ask Steve when we get back here.

She let the dog lead her out on to the street, with Neil following.

So what did you say the dog's name was?

Greg. And Katy did say, or it might've been her mum, how they got him from this place you knew.

Well, now I do recall letting Samantha have the details of this place outside Lancaster.

That must be it. So d'you work with dogs a lot, on mountain rescue?

Yes, quite a lot. I train at least one new team of dogs each year, and most of the rescues I go on, I take a couple of dogs with me, dogs I've trained, that is.

So you must like dogs, then?

Oh yes. I sometimes think I must like dogs more than people.

Oh me, too! the girl agreed in a heartfelt tone. Since my dad died, Katy's the first person, apart from my sisters that is, but they're just kids, who I've really liked, and I wouldn't've liked her only she had a dog. And that were Greg.

She bent down to let the dog nuzzle her.

See, dogs never criticises or judges you or anything. They never bothers 'bout what you did last week or what your mum or dad did to you last year, or what this or that poxy social worker or shrink or teacher's put in their report. You's just you to a dog.

Quite right. It sounds like you've had your fill of that

sort of person.

Yeah, you said it. That's why I likes Katy, she ain't like any of the rest of them.

They'd turned down a quieter residential street. Aysha stopped to scoop up Greg's deposit from near the base of a tree.

I need to find a bin now.

And wash your hands soon as we get back.

Sure. You don't need to tell me, Katy's done already.

It's very good you do that. Many dog-owners don't.

Katy said, if it were on the street or in a park or on the canal bank or the river bank, then scoop it up, but if it's in the country or in the woods then that's ok.

Sounds like Katy's a responsible dog-owner.

Oh yeah, she's like, very good with Greg and good with me too, right. I never ever thought I'd get on with a good, y'know, responsible, person 'til I met her.

There's not many around.

Too right there ain't. The girl seemed to be getting into her stride. But you must be good too, what with training dogs, and mountain rescue, and what else is it you do?

I do some wood-carving, mainly on winter evenings. But what I love most is going to wild places and observing wild-life. And photographing wildlife when I can.

Where d'you go for that?

Scotland, mostly. The highlands and islands. Some-times the north of England, the Lake District -

We's in the north of England now.

Not much wildlife round here, I'm afraid. Unless you count the Friday night drunks.

The girl laughed, and paused. Yeah, I've been one of them before now. But tell you what, you must meet my sister Charly. She's really into all that wildlife stuff, y'know, she loves to read books with it in, photographs and stuff, she'd love to meet you. When you come to move us, you must make sure you tells her 'bout your work.

Well, I don't really call it work. I might make a bit of money from selling a photograph now and again, but it's pleasure really - a kind of hobby.

I wish I had a hobby, said the girl a little wistfully. Walking dogs and going to gigs is the only things I likes. Oh, and I is learning drumming, I s'pose you could say that's a hobby.

Sure it is. Look, we'd better take this road, to get back. Need to have our lunch.

Yeah, Katy and me's gotta catch a train soon. But can Greg go in your car while I has my food?

Sure. Well, I enjoyed our walk. I'd have hated it being stuck in there all the time.

Me too. All those people!

I can't stand crowds of people either.

Dogs is best. Kids is all right, but grown-ups, nah! Can you open your car up then? Now I must find those two kids before we goes for our train.

And get some lunch?

Oh yeah, and finish my drink. And wash my hands first.

So what did you say your name was? I'm terrible with names.

Aysha, she said, and went inside with a skipping motion and looking happy. Then Neil noticed Duncan just inside the door.

I've been looking for you, said the older man. Where have you been?

Getting some fresh air. With a girl and a dog.

I thought you'd gone without me.

Of course I wouldn't. My car's still here. Just hang on, Duncan, while I find some food.

18. CAN'T FIND A REASON TO CRY

On the train back to Bursfield with Katy and Greg, Aysha felt strangely happy. It wasn't the same buzz she used to get from taking stuff with her mates and getting high, it might have been the wine she'd drunk, it might have been from helping out with those two little kids, it might have been from not trailing along with Katy all the time, she couldn't be sure what it was. She knew that somehow she weren't s'posed to feel like this after someone's died, but deep down she'd begun to feel she were glad to be alive, for the first time ever in her life. She wanted to say this to Katy but thought Katy might still be sad about Marie so she'd better wait. Katy weren't saying much and did seem a bit sad, so Aysha wanted to try and cheer her up. She took off her jacket, which she'd located in Steve's car, and wafted it around in front of her friend. She was still wearing the dress she'd worn for the funeral. Aysha couldn't remember when she'd last worn a dress, but was pleased with this one, felt good in it.

That Neil were cool to talk to, he loves dogs more than people, just like us.

He always seems shy and awkward to me.

He just don't like people much. But he does think good of you, Katy, he said so.

But he hardly knows me.

Well I went and told him how good you was, y'know with Greg, and with me, treating us both good. The other thing is, Katy, Aysha spluttered on, realising she was seriously embarrassing the older girl. That Neil, he's mad 'bout wildlife, he goes to Scotland to find stuff to photograph. That's just like our Charly, she's mad 'bout wildlife too, didn't you know?

I did know that, yes.

Well then, she and that Neil should meet up, shouldn't they, talk about wildlife and stuff?

Sounds a good idea. He's said he'll come and move us, whenever that happens.

Yeah, I know.

I wondered what you were doing when you went missing while the rest of us were eating.

I were just giving Greg a walk. I did tell you.

And having a chat with Neil. Hooking him up with Charly. Katy started smiling at Aysha in the way the younger girl loved, and this was the first time since they left the hotel that she had smiled. But still Aysha felt a bit confused, doubts entering her mind about how much to tell her friend.

And how many glasses of wine did you have, young lady? Katy continued.

One! I only had one! Aysha protested.

You made it last a long time, for you!

Well, I were out walking, weren't I?

How many would you've had if you'd stayed in the hotel?

I'd still only have one!

I saw you pouring some more just before we left! Katy was grinning at her now, she seemed to have completely recovered her cheerfulness.

I just had one little swig! Aysha protested even more vehemently. I had some cake crumbs in my mouth and I had to wash them down!

You could have drunk water.

No way! I'd had the wine in my glass!

Yeah, you'd got that quick enough, before I had a chance to watch out!

I mustn't follow you around all the time, Katy. You gotta let me do my own thing sometimes.

Yeah, I know, kid, I think that too. But taking wine at a buffet lunch weren't exactly what I were thinking. I only hope it was one glass -

It were, I promise.

Cos we're going to that school tomorrow and I don't want you going hung-over.

Hung-over? What me? Aysha laughed. Fucking hell, Katy, don't remind me of school, or I'm gonna make out I is - "hung over". She exaggerated the words, making Katy laugh too.

You're going, kiddo, whatever. We had a deal, remember.

Worse luck.

She wore the dress again the next day for the visit to the school but wore a white top over it - it was the only top she had what weren't black. She had her new jacket on, too, it were a freezing cold morning and they had to go into town and change buses - the bus station in town were always just about the coldest place in the whole world. The school were miles away, in a part of Bursfield she'd never been before, right on the edge, miles from the centre, and the other side of the city from Katy's flat.

She felt very strange. She thought everyone was staring at her. She wanted to hide behind Katy, but knew only little kids did that. She forced herself to not look at the floor the whole time. Katy said to her not to look down or up. If she couldn't look straight at a person, to look to the side. It were difficult to take in the rooms they was being shown into, or even what the teachers was saying. Too many other kids would keep looking at her and it all seemed a blur. She could only think geography, that Marie who just died had taught geography. Otherwise, all she could say were yes or don't know. Katy came to her rescue all the time.

History and science you like, don't you, Aysha, as well as geography. And English. You're interested in the environment, aren't you?

Yes, she mumbled.

What subjects did she dislike?

She shook her head. I think that would be maths, wouldn't it? Katy said, encouraging her.

What about languages?

Have you learned any French yet? persisted Katy.

She shook her head, mumbling.

You would have to learn a language here, but you could join a beginners' French set. What about sport?

She shook her head again. Sport was unknown territory.

Running, prompted Katy yet again. You like running, Aysha.

Oh, right.

Art? Design? Music?

Music, yeah, she muttered.

She's learning drumming, said Katy. You enjoy drumming, don't you?

She shrugged.

And you've started singing in a choir. You've not a bad voice.

What about the visual arts?

Aysha turned to Katy, in desperation. What's that mean? she tried to express by facial glances, but beneath that there was the appeal, Get me out of here.

She's quite good at art, said Katy.

Nowhere near as good as you, said Aysha finding at last something she could say.

But you lack confidence, don't you?

You'll need to think about which year to join, said the

teacher. Year 9 is your age-group. Or you could start in Year 8.

We'll talk about that, said Katy. I'll phone again at the start of next term and arrange another visit.

Oh no! she thought.

You should stay longer next time.

No way! she said to herself.

Yes, said Katy. That's a good idea.

On the bus back, she said to Aysha, Don't worry, first time's always the worst. You'll get used to it, I promise.

No way, bet you I won't, Katy, she said, turning her face away and looking intently out of the bus window. The high she'd felt yesterday had well and truly disappeared.

But later, back at the flat, she told Katy she wanted to push ahead with the Life-Story book now. Katy gave her a hug and said they had tomorrow evening and all day Friday.

Ain't we going to your mum's Friday?

No, Saturday morning. Hardly any trains Good Friday, and we have only just seen her.

19. DARKEST DAY

This had to be the worst week of her life. Two weeks, rather. In fact, Samantha reflected as she lay awake next to her sleeping husband but unable to sleep herself, it must be exactly two weeks to the hour since Marie died. Well, she'd had unhappy periods in her life before. When she'd left school and felt her mother hated her because she'd left at sixteen when her mother had wanted her to stay on, get better grades, and then tried to stop her doing what all sixteen year old girls were doing, staying out late, drinking, smoking dope, doing ecstasy, partying, discoing, and getting laid when an opportunity with the right sort of boy came along. And her mother trying to force her to be home by ten-thirty like she were still a schoolkid. What was the point of leaving school, earning her own money, if her mother were punishing her, taking it out on her, getting her revenge, giving her less freedom than if she'd stayed on in the sixth form? She never actually said that but Sam was sure it were true. She was full of anger then at life being so unfair. But even before that, at a time which was a bit hazier in her memory, she knew she'd been even more unhappy, when her mum had kept sitting around the house taking tablets and leaving her, Samantha, to look after her little sister, and getting taken to hospital every now and again.

She didn't like to think back to those times, not when her life had been happy and fulfilled for all those years since, a good marriage, two lovely kids, but that's what made it seem so much worse now, that it had suddenly come after the best years of her life. Two terrible weeks. Constantly shouting at the kids, and sleeping so badly. She must be depressed, she knew, but that were what made it so much worse, the fear that she were turning out just like her mum, that fear that must have lurked just below her consciousness all these years.

Marcus had been great, but he still had a big problem to deal with at work, and couldn't take much time off, apart from the actual day of his mum's funeral. Marie was dead, and her own mum had been taken ill at the funeral, and were still in a bit of a bad way at home. Still, tomorrow were Good Friday, and Marcus was taking the kids to her mum and Steve for the day. They'd have them overnight in fact, only for one night cos Katy and them three girls was arriving Saturday for the rest of the Easter weekend. But they'd have them during the day. Steve said he didn't mind, that once Katy and Aysha was there, they'd be helping out a lot with Lara and Liam, which was true of course, but Sam felt bad so much was landing on Steve, when she should be pulling herself together and dealing with her kids herself. The real problem was who could she talk to? Marie was dead, her mum not well, Katy away, Marcus had had to soak up so much of her negative emotion already, and had to step in so often when she were losing it, and Steve was doing more than anyone could've expected of him.

So she'd been phoning up friends and sounding off to them. Some of them were coming round for coffee in the morning. Friday wasn't the usual day, but then it was Good Friday, and she'd missed seeing them last week out of respect for Marie - although a few of them had been at the funeral - and the week before, which it had been too late to cancel, Marie had only just died and that had put a damper on the whole morning.

She hoped those of her friends that did come wouldn't

mind the state she were in, but she really did need to sound off now, or she might never get over this downer she was going through. Marcus was trying to stay loyal but how much longer would he put up with her, and she could already sense her two kids flinching from her, looking to their dad or their granny when they would normally seek out their mummy. And wanting their auntie Katy and that friend of hers, that Aysha kid.

When she thought of Aysha, it made Samantha feel worse. It was partly that incident a month ago when she'd ended up looking a fool and been put at a complete disadvantage. Then when her mum had said that Katy and Aysha were coming to Marie's funeral she hadn't known what to think. Her mum had said that well, if Katy wanted to come then Aysha would have to come too, or otherwise she'd be sent back to the children's home for the day. Well, let her, Sam had thought, but said nothing, as she was trying hard not to be still seen to have a down on the girl. She was even beginning to think she might have been wrong about Aysha, which was very galling because Sam thought of herself as always a good judge of people, and she'd been quite sure that girl spelled trouble. But the funeral had begun to raise doubts in her mind.

She could still picture that moment when Liam started his howling. It had been so important for her to address the gathering, give them a personal perspective of how important Marie was in her life, how good she had been, and then Liam was going to wreck it all. She couldn't have carried on. But within seconds of the wailing starting up, she could see the little boy being bounced up and down on the shoulders of that Aysha, at the back of the chapel, and all gone quiet again. OK, Marcus or Katy could have dealt with Liam, but could they have quietened him down so fast? Sam thought not, and anyway if it had been Marcus it would have meant leaving Lara on her own and she might have started up. But how had that girl known the best thing to do, and how on earth had a little skinny strip of a thing got a boy of Liam's size up on her shoulders so quick? Even Marcus found him difficult to lift now, he was a big kid for his age, not fat, but lots of muscle on him. So it was beginning to seem that Aysha could do nothing wrong, and after Samantha had got through her speech, with no further interruptions but it had still been a bloody ordeal, she, Sam, were out of it, totally drained, and Marcus, knowing it, had let Aysha and Katy, but mostly Aysha, look after the kids in order to protect her. That was what really got her, that she couldn't cope with her own kids and a brat like Aysha was taking over. She wouldn't have minded anything like so much if it had been Katy. But typical Katy, she always took the back seat, let Aysha be the star. And Aysha had made a great impression, no doubt about it, loads of people had said, Who was that girl? That dress she wore, for a start. Nothing wrong with it, black was right, anyway the girl always wore black, but it made her seem more alive somehow. And what a difference from how she was that first time she came to Longworth in December, which must be to Katy's credit, though her sister never seemed to want to claim any. Perhaps it was just that everyone else at the funeral were affected by Marie dying apart from her. And of course little kids would always go to someone who was lively and happy, unlike her, Sam. Mind you, Katy had had the good sense to bring the kids to Marcus and her when they got to the hotel, knowing they'd be getting tired by then, which they were, so they'd both been able to have a rest with their mummy and daddy, with Liam falling fast asleep. And Marcus had pointed out that Liam's reaction in the service had shown that at heart, his mummy was the most important person to him. But even so, when they'd livened up again after their rest, who did they want to see but Aysha, make sure they saw her again before she and Katy went off for their train. And what had Aysha been doing all this time? Walking that dog, chatting to Neil, and drinking glasses of red wine! Really, Katy needed to keep a closer eye on that girl! Trust Lara to have noticed, nothing much escaped the attention of her older child, and then she's wanting a glass of the wine herself. Fortunately Marcus was able to deal quietly and firmly with that one. If it had been left to her to deal with Lara, there'd've been one almighty row.

And so it had been since. When Marcus was at work, or a football practice, she'd been constantly rowing with the kids, Lara especially, losing it every time they tried it on - and these were two kids who were always trying it on. And Lara, thinking she knew better than her mother, just like you at her age, Sharon would tell her. No, Marcus had to deal with them whenever he was home, and he told her she needed as much of a break from the kids as she could get. And she knew what that meant. Once

Katy and those three girls arrived, it would be Aysha taking over her kids and there was nothing she, Samantha Sullivan, could do about it, in the state she was in now, and after everything that had happened. And she still couldn't sleep for thinking about it, wondering how life had turned from being so good only a few months ago, to being so miserable now. Was it Marie dying, or was it Katy bringing that Aysha into their lives? Or was it the combination of both? This was what she was longing to ask her friends when they came in the morning.

20. NEXT YEAR BETTER

The flat in Bursfield was quiet. Aysha was listening to one of her favourite CDs but had her headphones on. Only a very faint thumping beat could be heard. Katy was reading a novel, Small Island by Andrea Levy. She loved reading, but this was a rare chance in her present life. She wished Aysha would show more interest in books, but hoped that if she started reading a bit more when they were together, something might rub off onto the younger girl. Her mind kept drifting from the story on the page, good as it was, to the child in the room. How she'd seen two sides of her this week, chatty, full of life, taking the lead with Lara and Liam, at the funeral, with Katy not needing to support or encourage her at all, and then the next day on the school visit the child was a tongue-tied bag of nerves, totally relying on Katy to see her through. Overall, Katy reflected, it was amazing how little trouble Aysha had given her, and the only thing that weighed on Katy's mind was the antagonism between her sister Sam and Aysha.

They were travelling to Longworth tomorrow morning, the three girls and her. Katy had kept in touch by phone this week - not only had her mother been unwell, but, she gathered, Sam was in quite a bad way and the two small children were with Steve and Sharon today, and for most of the Easter week-end, apart from overnights. Katy would be pleased to see them, but it sounded like there would be a lot to do, and she would have to help Steve out, when really all Katy wanted to do was veg out and let someone else have the responsibility for a few days. Well, Aysha would look after the two little ones, that was for sure, and Charly and Zoë were never much trouble.

Greg was dreaming. He quivered, shifted his paws and made muted squealing noises. Aysha, headphones still on, bent down to fondle the animal, who sighed in a satisfied sort of way and went quiet again. Greg was happy to have the two of them to share his devotedness, and the intuitive rapport between Aysha and the dog was amazing. He always lay at her feet in the evenings, or alongside her bed during the night.

Katy had wanted to do another Life-Story session with Aysha that evening, but was glad now that she'd given in to Aysha's reluctance. They'd had two attempts this week, but had got no further than talking about "her dad Kenny", writing things about him, deciding where to place the photographs, and thinking about his death. They'd been doing this for some time now, and it did not seem possible to get any further with it. Katy would have loved to be able to help Aysha find Kenny's grave, or any surviving members of his family, but his surname, Harrison, was such a common one, and no-one seemed able to put a firm date to when he died. But she had decided to offer to go with Aysha to a local registrar's office and look through the records, when they were back after Easter. Perhaps moving on in the Life-Story would have to wait until then. The next bits were going to be difficult - the mother's increasing drug addiction, including overdoses, foster-care and being "at risk", and then Zoë's dad, Vic, coming on the scene and the start of the sexual abuse. No, the start of the Easter weekend was not a good time for broaching those issues - it would need to be when offices were open, professionals available, in case she needed to call for help.

Already it seemed as if her Easter vacation was going to be swallowed up with so much to do, another reason why she'd hoped her few days at home over the Bank Holiday could be devoted to dossing. She'd decided the visit to the prison would be after the kids were back at school. This was a compromise she'd only agreed with great reluctance, not happy to have to ask the head-teacher at Charly and Zoë's school to allow them a day off. Also, she only had a few days' window between their term starting and hers, and during that time she needed to get to

Aysha's Unit to sort out a programme of introductory visits, and possibly make another one herself, to her High School. However, she'd been forced into this compromise by Aysha's refusal to either come with them to the prison or to go to the children's home for the day. She was not prepared to leave Aysha on her own all day, and while Aysha had agreed to go to the home on the occasional Saturday when Katy was away most of the day for a basketball fixture, Katy could understand the difference - on those Saturdays, Charly and Zoë were at the home. She had suggested to Aysha that she could spend most of the day walking Greg and only need go into the home for her lunch, but Aysha had countered by asking why, in that case, Katy couldn't leave some lunch for her in the flat. Hence, the compromise.

The most pressing development, however, which she hadn't yet mentioned to Aysha or anyone else, resulted from a message she'd had on her answerphone yesterday from Frank Johnson, the manager who'd convened the meeting at the children's home at the end of last term. Something had prompted her to phone him back when Aysha had gone out with Greg (Aysha's term had finished on Wednesday, and they'd celebrated by going to a gig together, so Aysha had spent most of yesterday morning in bed). Mr Johnson had told her that a property had been located, but there had been such a tone of hedging in his voice that Katy realised that there could be problems.

It's the only place our property department has been able to come up with. So I'd like to sound out your views before we go any further. And maybe not mention it to the children until we are nearer a decision.

Why, what are the problems?

It's not furnished, and in need of decoration. But we can remedy both those problems, he went on fairly hastily. I guess the main problem is location. It's an old school house, in a village.

A village?

Well, it's part of the city now, a place called High Chapel, the area includes two housing estates, one private, one council, but the old village where this property is, it's right on the city boundary, edge of the countryside, the other side of the city from where you are now -

Well, it can't be too far from Aysha's new school, then -

Which school is that?

Andrew Wheeler High School.

Well, no, they're both south side of town, but Andrew Wheeler is south-west whereas High Chapel is on the eastern boundary. The issue really is that no-one at the school is interested in living there any more, and the council really wants to sell it, but we're trying to get them to give priority to your situation.

So why the reluctance? asked Katy.

Well, it's the usual thing, the neighbourhood, most of all the school itself. They'd prefer to have a so-called "normal" family living in their midst than children in care. And that's before knowing anything about Aysha's background. So there'll be a lot of pressure on you to get the girls to conform, if you do move there. It's quite a small primary school in what was a fairly exclusive sort of village, though I think this is people living in the past.

Well, what do you want me to do? asked Katy. I mean, we do need a bigger place.

Yes, I know. I suggest you go and have a look, on your own initially, maybe after Aysha's gone back to school next term.

She's still at her Unit for one more term.

Of course.

How will I find the place? How will I get access?

One of our properties team will meet you there.

Where?

At High Chapel Primary School.

Can't we go in the holidays initially? Me and Aysha? Firstly, to speed things up a bit, secondly to suss out the place while it's quiet? But Katy was also aware that she had too much happening around the start of the new term.

Well, I don't see why not. You'll need to link up with a man called Alan Grosvenor in properties. And he gave Katy the phone number. Katy decided she wouldn't say anything to Aysha until the night before they went. She'd tried to phone this Alan Grosvenor as soon as she'd finished the call to Frank Johnson, but he wasn't available, she'd have to wait until after Easter, and she was left with a strange mixture of excitement and anxiety over this development.

She switched back to the present. One more chapter of

her book. Everything was packed and ready. An early start to-morrow morning, collecting the other two girls straight after their breakfast. Aysha might not be tired, after her lie-in. Perhaps take Greg out for fifteen or twenty minutes, the two of them, and then to bed, and pray that Aysha was also ready for sleep.

21. LIVING IN YOUR LIGHT

The sounds of so many children about the house made Sharon feel better, in herself and about herself. She felt that despite her physical condition, she could be a helpful, hands-on granny to Lara and Liam, and could be supportive to Katy's tough venture. She knew, of course, that she could be none of these things with-out Steve's willingness, and it made her feel all the more certain that she'd made the right choice in taking Steve as a husband, that she was lucky to have found him. She needed to hold onto these thoughts because in the bad moments of this last week when she'd been unwell and confined to bed she had found her-self thinking of Rodney Owen, her first husband. She wondered what would happen if Rodney suddenly reappeared at the house he had left all those years ago. She and the girls had remained in the same house, so if he had been the least bit interested in them, he had no reason not to seek them out. Whereas they had no idea where to find him. She was sure he was either dead or had re-married and had a new family of his own, there was no other explanation of why he had stayed absent all these years. So in fact it could not be imagined that he might present a threat to the stability of her relationship with Steve, even if he did reappear. But what had preyed on Sharon's mind this week was that her increasing physical incapableness along with Marie's death meant a severe lack of grandparents for those two little mites. Steve couldn't really be counted in that respect, whatever com-mitment he gave, he wasn't a blood relation, and however impos-sible it would be for Rodney to resume a relationship of any kind with her or Sam or Katy, why could he not come back and take on his rightful role as a grandfather with Lara and Liam?

Fortunately, Sharon was feeling a lot better by the time

first her two grandchildren, and then Katy and her three proté-gées, came to stay. With Steve's help she could get downstairs, and even move around a little bit without her wheelchair. So she could take an interest in the kids, and hoped she'd be able to do this for many years yet, despite her inability to help in any prac-tical way. And it was looking more and more as if those three girls Katy had taken on were going to be around for the duration. All of them now seemed pleased and relaxed the minute they stepped in the door. Of course it helped that Lara and Liam were in the house. That young girl Zoë, she just liked having other kids to play with, but she also enjoyed any one-to-one attention she could get from an adult, whether it was painting, reading stories, playing games or just talking, whether it was from her, Sharon, or from Katy. The next one up, Charly, kept her dis-tance, always seemed to hold back, but this time there was no sign of that grim, hostile expression she'd worn the first time she came. Non-committal, yes, but reasonably pleasant with it. And as for Aysha, well Sharon could remember very well the fright-ened insecure little waif who'd hid behind Katy that first time, and the transformation was quite remarkable. She still had that odd expression of not quite believing what was happening, but she treated Sharon, and even Steve for that matter, like genuine friends whom she was pleased to see and could relax with.

Sharon still worried about Katy, though. She thought her daughter must be giving too much of herself to her charges, Aysha in particular. Because it seemed that in exact proportion as Aysha had come to life, then Katy had lost some of hers. She seemed on this visit drained, hollow, with little energy left, on the way to becoming a mere shell of her former self. With her dog, with her niece and nephew, all three of whom had been so important to her, she now stepped into the background and let Aysha take the lead role. And she still seemed to have no friends, and no sign of a boyfriend, and little spark left to ever attract one.

On Easter Monday, Steve offered to take the children on a day trip up to Rivington Pike. The weather seemed to have taken a turn for the better, and he thought Sharon must be tired of them all falling over her and each others' feet as they dashed around the house. It was going to be rather a squash in the car, however, with Greg to fit in as well, until Katy offered to stay behind and keep her mum company. She and Steve were a bit shocked - Katy had always liked the outdoors, and even though she hadn't been up onto the moors much with Greg because of not having a car, it was all the more reason to go now when she had the chance. But no, she insisted she preferred to stay behind. Sharon hoped at least that this would be a chance for Katy to talk to her, but instead Katy disappeared upstairs saying she wanted to be on her own, and Sharon began to wonder if there was anything wrong with her, some creeping illness of some sort, or depression. After an hour or so, she reappeared in her track-suit, saying she'd been finishing an urgent piece of coursework which she needed to hand in during the vacation, and now she was going for a run. This reminded Sharon of how her daughter had been in the two years before she went off to college, the sixth form years, and she began to feel a little reassured.

When Katy returned from her run, she went straight into the kitchen and started making some lunch for her mother and herself.

What would you like, mum? Something on toast? Soup out of a can?

Soup would be nice, love.

Soup it is then. And rolls and butter - do we have any rolls?

I think so - did you enjoy your run, love?

Great, yeah - it's such a relief to have a break from the kids, you know. I can't remember when I last had a run on my own - and just think how I encouraged Aysha to start running when she came to live with me.

You're not growing tired of her, are you, my love?

No, mum, of course I'm not, I still love her dearly, and still would even if she'd caused me a lot more grief which she hasn't, I've been surprised how little. But there's always so much to do, and now there's two more kids as well, sometimes I feel I can't find the space to breathe. I'm not tired of them, I'm just tired, full stop.

You don't seem to spend much time with Lara and Liam any more.

Well, there's no need, is there, Aysha and Zoë are both keen to spend time with them, and that eases the pressure on me.

That Charly seems rather a solitary kid.

Yeah, she's no trouble, but she's gonna be hard work in terms of getting through to her, building any sort of relationship.

Katy, said her mother, pausing and trying to adopt her most serious tone. I do still worry that you're taking on too much. Seeing you so tired like this, that you don't even want to join a trip up to the moors. It's just not like you.

I'm all right, mum, I just need a break from kids now and again. Any kids, and only now and again. And I'm looking ahead, there's a lot happening over the next two weeks. I'm not that tired, I'm just trying to conserve my energy. Also getting my most urgent bits of coursework done, in case I don't have a chance until the kids are back at school.

Well, I can see you're being sensible, love, but what are all these things?

Well, it's, like, all things to do with the kids. First of all, there's a possible bigger place we've gotta go and look at. Then there's things to do with Aysha's Life-Story book. We want to try and trace her natural father, who we think may be in Sri Lanka, and find her stepfather's grave, which might mean tracing some of his relatives. And she may have grandparents somewhere on the south coast. Then there's a visit to their mother to fix, and take Charly and Zoë - Aysha won't go. Then there's Aysha's transfer to High School in the summer to prepare for. The other two also may be starting new schools.

I think all this is too much, Katy. You must hand over some of it to other people, there must be social workers and professionals who could do it.

They're all too busy, mum, and you know Aysha, right - she'll only go along with something if I'm fully involved.

But that's not right, love, the child shouldn't be so dependent on you.

I know, but she is getting less so, I mean, like how she's gone off today without me. But things to do with her background or her education, she still needs me, right.

I'm worried that you're taking on too much, trying to do all this on your own. I'd hate for it all to fall apart because you don't get enough support. I'll try and help, and I know Steve will, too, but we're limited in what we can do. As for Sam, I'm not sure what we can expect of her.

Yeah, I'm sorry Sam feels the way she does, and that

she's in a bad way now. I thought I might drop round to see her after lunch.

The thing is, Katy, I know from my own past experience how hard it is to deal with all these problems in life when you're on your own. When I was left on my own with you and Sam I couldn't cope at all. It was only after I got together with Steve that things started working better. And Sam's like me, she's got Marcus, thank god, but I think you are struggling too. I wish you had someone in your life -

I know you've always been dying for me to find a boyfriend, mum.

Well, any friend, love, if, y'know, it's girls you, er, like better, then there's nothing wrong with that - we would accept it, it's just we don't want you facing life alone.

I'm not gay, mum, please don't think that. There's plenty of time yet, I'm only nineteen for god's sake. And now I've got Aysha and her sisters, I don't feel alone any more.

It's not the same, love, it's not even the same as having a close friend like that Sophie. These children are a responsibility, you know that, and I can see how much it takes out of you.

But Aysha's who I want to dedicate my life to, that's just the way it's happened. It doesn't mean I'm a lesbian, it doesn't mean I won't ever find a husband or boyfriend, all it means is I've got a commitment, a bit like being a single parent, which is going to have to come first.

Have you ever thought about finding your real father?

What's that got to do with it?

I dunno, my pet, I just thought when you said about trying to trace Aysha's father, maybe you need to trace your own - I mean, you're in the same situation as her, with regard to birth fathers, and why should all your efforts be directed to helping her? It could be beneficial to find Rodney, someone who could give extra support to you, and to Lara and Liam, who are being seriously depleted of grandparents, and now of their auntie as well -

They are not being denied their auntie! All I said was, when there's Aysha to give them her attention, it lets me ease off a bit.

Well, all right, but I have been wondering if it would be a good thing for your father to be back on the scene.

Well, he's never been interested in supporting us for all these years, so why should he be interested now? And how could we trust him to stick around if he did come back? I really don't see why I should make the effort to find him. With Aysha it's different, her birth father doesn't even know of her existence. He may not be any good either, but it's at least worth trying to find him. I've had a happy childhood without my real father, and Aysha's had a terrible one, and what would Steve think if I tried to contact Rodney, I mean, it would seem awfully disloyal, right?

Mother and daughter had finished their lunch by now. Sharon had to accept the truth of what Katy had been saying, or most of it, anyway. She nodded, feeling pretty exhausted herself by now, and told her daughter she would rest for a couple of hours before the house was invaded again by the younger generation.

Katy went to phone her sister, and came back saying while she washed up the lunch plates that she would go over on the bus, but might appreciate a lift back, and could someone phone her if she wasn't back before the others.

The children all seemed really disappointed that Katy was out, but she was back in no time at all, it seemed, delivered by her brother-in-law, who gave his two children a quick hug and told them he'd be back later to collect them. All of them were then clamouring for Katy's attention, wanting to tell her all the exciting things they'd done, and all the chasing around Greg had done, and while an exhausted Steve was confined to the kitchen making their teas, none of them would let Katy escape to help him or to do anything else, although Charly, by far the least demonstrative of them, soon went to the kitchen to help prepare tea. Sharon felt a little reassured by this, as she could sense how important Katy was in the lives of these children, and that Katy herself appreciated this and felt all her efforts were not being wasted. But at the same time Sharon's highly-tuned emotional antennae could sense some tension between her daughter and Aysha, which lay unexpressed until Lara and Liam had been collected by their dad, and Charly and Zoë were upstairs in their room.

What's up with you, kiddo? said Katy softly, gently, not in a whisper but half teasing, half exasperated.

Nothing.

Come on, kid, I know you well enough to know something's bugging you.

Well, you should know what then.

Because I went round to see my sister?

Why didn't you come with us? We had a great day, and you missed it.

I'm sure you didn't need me, it were best I stayed with my mum.

We missed you a lot. Me, the most. It's hard work trying to be like you if you're not there.

Katy laughed, and playfully tousled the younger child's hair.

It ain't funny, Katy.

It would have been too much of a squash in the car. And I had a seminar paper to prepare for the first week of term.

So why d'you go round your sister's then?

Cos I finished the work, right, then I had a run on my own, then I had lunch and a talk with my mum, and I still had time left so I went to see Sam. She's been struggling since Marie died, that's why the kids are spending the days with us. Marcus was involved in his kids' football, so she were on her own.

So, why d'you take her side, against the rest of us, right?

I don't, Aysha, I don't! I'm sorry you don't like her -

That's only cos she don't like me!

Well, whatever, she is my sister, and if she thought you were turning me against her, were wanting to stop me seeing her, then how d'you think she'd feel then?

I dunno.

Well, I do, she'd dislike you much more, and with some reason. If she talks about you, says negative things about you, then I always defend you, I totally disagree with her view, but in other ways I need to be there for her, especially now when she's struggling so much. I don't want her and me to fall out over you, I want her to get to like you, and the best way is for me to continue to see her regularly, and in fact she doesn't dislike you anything so much now.

I bet she's just pretending.

If you knew Sam better, you'd know she doesn't do pretence, right. She's a person who always speaks her mind.

Yeah, I know, I do, really. But ain't it best if, like when you goes and sees her, you takes me as well, right, then she can see I'm an OK kid now, I ain't like I were before. If you goes on your own, it's like you don't want her to know nothing 'bout, y'know, me, us, only what you tells her.

Katy went over and gave the girl a hug. Sharon, over on the other side of the room, was a little surprised and embarrassed by this show of intimacy.

I think you're right, kid, said Katy gently. It is best normally if you comes with me. But just at the moment my sister can't even cope with her own kids -

I ain't a kid!

Yeah, that's true, but you know what I mean. It's less stressful for her just to see me.

Nah, it ain't right, Katy, it's like you sneaks off to see her when I's out of the way. It's like, she thinks I's trouble and you's agreeing with her, right?

Absolutely not! I promise you that's not how it is, it isn't what I think, you must know that! I promise you I'll go with you next time I call round there.

She hugged Aysha again and the girl seemed pacified.

Sharon had kept quiet, even wondering if they realised she was in the room, but could now begin to see more clearly what there was that held this relationship together. For a start, they were able to be open with each other, and she had to admit some surprise at how much awareness and insight the younger girl had. Most of what she'd said, Sharon couldn't help agreeing with. Katy obviously was helping the child express herself, and yet Katy was always willing and able to argue her corner, she wasn't letting the girl dominate their discussions. Sharon thought she would like to convey this to Sam, how well Katy could handle Aysha, encouraging her to come out with things, working through them. She mustn't say anything about what they discussed, just convey the process. And yet, some doubt still lingered in Sharon's mind as Steve appeared and started helping her to climb the stairs to their bedroom, at which Katy and Aysha both jumped up to give Steve a hand. It was just that sense that Katy was trying to be, no she was, mother and sister and friend to Aysha, all at the same time, and Sharon could sense the confusion there, the blurring of boundaries, and with a lingering degree of anxiety wondered how it would all work out.

They'd all gone on this outing, to the moors, to a place called Rivington Pike. Her two sisters and her and the two little kids and Greg, Katy's dog. And Katy's stepdad, who'd driven the car. But Katy hadn't gone with them cos the car was too crowded and everyone was sad she'd stayed behind, 'specially Aysha.

Aysha weren't bad any more. Zoë was pleased she didn't get in trouble. She liked Katy for letting Aysha live with her and keeping her out of trouble. On this outing Aysha were really good and took charge of the little kids. She went ahead with them up to the top of the hill and carried little Liam on her shoulders some of the way. Zoë and Charly played with Greg on the way up. Katy's stepdad were tired from all the cooking and housework so he went the slowest. Before they got to the top Aysha let Liam down so he could run ahead and be first to the top. She took Lara by the hand and they pretended they were gonna catch Liam up but they let him win. Lara said he weren't first cos Greg had run ahead and got there first but Aysha said dogs didn't count and Liam were first. Zoë knew it weren't true cos Ambrose had joined them and he'd got to the top before Liam but she didn't say anything.

If she had said, Aysha would have said invisible children didn't count either. But Zoë thought they did count. Charly thought so too. Charly and her and Ambrose threw sticks for Greg after they left the top of the hill. But Greg never chased the stick Ambrose threw. And when Zoë told Greg to go give the stick to Ambrose he never did, instead he looked at her in a puzzled way and went to Charly instead. Charly said dogs didn't understand about magic children.

Katy stayed at home because it would be too much of a squash in the car but Ambrose was magic and came along without riding in the car. When it was time to go back to Katy's mum's house Zoë said see ya to Ambrose before she got in the car. But she didn't say it out loud cos Aysha said not to let Lara and Liam know about Ambrose cos they'd think it were funny peculiar and so would Katy's stepdad. But Ambrose could hear things she said inside her head, so she tried never to have bad thoughts in case Ambrose got cross with her.

216

Everyone had real good fun on the outing and when they got to the house everyone wanted to tell Katy about all the fun they'd had but Katy weren't there. She'd gone to see her sister. Katy's sister is the mummy of Lara and Liam. That means Katy's their auntie. Lara says Auntie Katy. All the kids were sad when they got back to the house and Katy were out. Aysha were the most sad. But although Katy came back very quick, Aysha were still upset. Zoë wanted to tell Aysha not to be sad now Katy was back but Charly said not to interfere, it would make it worse. So Zoë went to bed and in the morning everything were ok.

Ambrose did not come and see her at Katy's mum's house. He only came on the outing. One day Charly and her were gonna move in with Katy and Aysha. She would still have to share a bedroom with Charly and maybe Ambrose would come and see her there like he did in their room at the children's home.

On the last day at Katy's mum's house Katy's mum got them to do some painting, and she put Ambrose in her picture but she never told anyone who it were. She just said it was a picture of a boy playing with a dog. Katy said her picture were very good and so did her mum.

In Scotland, life for Duncan had returned to its previous pattern after the disruption of three visits south in quick succession, two to see Marie and one for her funeral. In the most important respect, however, his life had changed for ever. He now had a son, and what is more a son who liked to visit the west of Scotland regularly. The Easter holiday was over and Neil was expected to arrive later this afternoon. He'd explained that he was committed to his mountain rescue duties during the Easter period, but would be taking a trip to Scotland as soon as he could and would stop by.

Duncan wished he could have known Neil earlier when he was fit and able enough to join his son on his excursions. One evening and night together in a small cottage, and then another when the younger man was returning south, did not seem a great deal of contact, but was better than his life had been before. He was well stocked with food and drink, and fuel, a makeshift bed in a corner of the living-room. He was prepared in a fashion for his first visitor in many years. What would his son think of this small cottage, rebuilt largely with his own hands?

Duncan was surprised by the knock on the door. He had been thinking of his recent visits to Marie, how much she had suffered, not just the physical pain, but the guilt and the struggle to make amends, and how his heart had reached out to her again, all these years after his younger self had been smitten by the seventeen-year old high school student. Drifting in reverie, time had passed, and now Neil was at the door.

Welcome! he said. Come in, and I'll put the kettle on.

Neil just nodded gruffly.

He showed Neil the cottage, not much time needed for that, and the makeshift bed. The younger man needed the loo, and a quick wash. Duncan made tea. Cake and biscuits appeared for the first time for ages. They got to talking, though for Neil it seemed an effort, after his long drive.

Neil asked his father if there were places he'd like to be taken to, which he couldn't normally get to, on some of these visits.

I'm sure there are, Duncan replied. Let me think about that a bit more. There are places down the coast, beautiful sea lochs, and there's the little road all the way up Loch Awe. And there are ferries to the islands, Gigha, Islay, Jura, even Arran you can get to. I've taken all those ferries in my younger life, but I'd sure like to take them one more time.

They took a walk along the loch between tea and supper. Neil was a watcher rather than a talker, he had his binoculars and used them frequently. Conversation was sparse and desultory and stayed like that after they returned to the cottage.

Over supper, Duncan got round to asking the younger man about the funeral.

I was nervous as hell, but I thought it went well. Did you get to talk to people?

Neil had already asked him this, on the drive from Longworth to Grasmere. But Duncan's answers then had been evasive, perhaps he was still too overcome with the enormity of the situation, or maybe he'd thought Neil was. At any rate, they'd both, willingly it seemed, soon switched what conversation there was to topics relating to Grasmere and Neil's activities there.

Now Duncan felt an opportunity was arising to sort out in his mind some elements of Marie's life in all the years between.

I did talk to a few people. Explained I was an old friend of Marie's from Oban, recently back in touch. Didn't seem anything wrong in saying that, though I tried to avoid contact with her brothers. But it was extremely difficult working out who everyone was.

Sure thing. Even I was finding that bit hard. Of course I recognised the relatives, or most of them. But there were quite a few friends, teachers from school mostly, that I hadn't seen for years and completely failed to recognise. And then there was a bunch of her current or recent students.

Yes, said Duncan, beginning to warm to it at last. Sorting out the younger generation was really difficult, for me. The young woman who spoke near the end of the service, who was she?

Samantha, my sister-in-law. Marcus's wife. Mother of the two small kids, they're my niece and nephew, the only small kids there. Marie's only grandchildren.

Yes, I remember meeting the little girl by accident the last time I saw Marie. She burst into the room unannounced.

Yeah, she's like that. Great kid, though.

Now, are you sure there isn't another grandchild somewhere, Neil? You don't want the same thing to happen to you, you know, a son or daughter turning up after all these years when you've got too old to really appreciate it.

No, I'm quite sure I've never conceived a secret child, but I sure wouldn't want to wait to find out if I did. But I thought you did appreciate it, said Neil in a puzzled voice.

I do, yes, I wasn't being entirely serious. But tell me, who were the other young people at the service? That girl with the dog, you were with quite a bit, who was that?

Oh yes, her. She's a nice, but rather strange kid who I'd never met before. Let me try and map this out for you. There's the Hodgsons, that's my mother's folks, that's my uncles who both came, one, Uncle Graham with his wife and two of his three children, my cousins, same sort of age as me, the other, Uncle Ross, came on his own, tall, red face, black moustache.

I never met Marie's brothers - they'd left Oban Academy before I started teaching there. I only called at her house once that I recall, and only met her mother then. Your grandmother, that would be.

I really liked both my grandparents, said Neil. Came up to Scotland as much as I could, stayed with them until they got too old.

Anyway, carry on with the family tree, said Duncan. Sorry about my interruption.

Well, after the Hodgsons, there's the Sullivans and the Owens. The Sullivans are my dad, I mean, Jack, my mother's husband Jack's family. And me and Marcus of course. Jack had a younger sister and brother, we really only knew his sister who never married, was a career civil servant, came and visited when she could, but it wasn't often. She came to the funeral, though, hair dyed blonde, kind of wine-red jacket and skirt, quite striking, talked with my brother quite a lot.

What's her name?

Ellen. Ellen Sullivan.

So who are the Owens then?

Well they're my sister-in-law's family. She was Samantha Owen before she married Marcus. They're part of the set-up. For one, Samantha was a kind of protégée of my mother, came to the house quite a lot around the time I was beginning to spread my wings, trying to leave the nest. Then, Sam's mother, who came to the service in a wheelchair, but didn't make the lunch, married a friend of my parents, Steve, another teacher at their school. Steve was there too. And the other thing is, they're a local family, the Owens, Sam's mother can trace her family back through several generations of Longworth working people, although of course she wasn't born an Owen -

What happened to Mr Owen then?

I've no idea. And then there's Sam's younger sister, Katy, who was at the funeral but I hardly know. She's at university now. She was at the same school as my brother and me, but I'd left before she started, I think Marcus had too. She was bridesmaid at Marcus and Sam's wedding. But that girl you mentioned, that I walked the dog with, is a kind of protégée of Katy's, so she's been kind of adopted into the Owen family. I don't know the whole story, but she's very close to my niece and nephew, seems very good with them. And with the dog, though the dog is in fact Katy's.

God, said Duncan. Aren't families complicated?

I never thought ours was, said Neil. Typical mum, dad and two kids, grandparents, a few uncles, aunts and cousins. Still needed to get away, mind, but that was clashes between my dad and me. Now I know he wasn't my dad, it makes things more complicated but also simpler in a strange way.

Yeah, I can see that. Me and you kind of exist in a different dimension.

Exactly! said Neil. And it's a dimension that somewhere inside me I've known I belonged to, or wanted to belong to, all my life. Does that sound strange?

Not at all. Look, said Duncan. Come to the window, and you'll see why.

They went to the front window and looked over the loch. Light streamed across the water in silvers and golds.

In the spring, said Duncan. The sun slides down the line of the hill behind before finally setting. The light changes colour all the time, whether there's cloud or not. I'll never ever get tired of looking out across the water. Morning, evening, or night. This cottage may not be much in itself, but as long as I can see out of this window I'll treasure my life here.

I understand, said Neil. I'm glad I've found you, late as it is.

22. PLEASE DON'T EVER DIE

After they got back to Bursfield, and took Charly and Zoë back to the home, Katy got a bad cold. Some days she was up and about, but there were some days she just lay in bed. Aysha got worried about her, thinking about her mum being ill, and Sam her sister in a bad way, and that Marie who'd just died.

You ain't gonna die, is you, Katy? she said.

Course not, said the older girl but in a weak, not very convincing tone of voice. It's only a bad cold, glandular fever at the worst. I'll soon get over it, I'm hardly ever ill.

I dunno what I'd do if you died.

I won't do. Come here.

Katy wanted her to sit on the side of the bed. Sometimes she wanted to talk, sometimes to just sit there looking at each other. Aysha felt uncomfortable. She wanted to do everything she could for Katy, take Greg for his walks, make food for her, and cups of tea, tidy and clean the flat, but not just sit there on Katy's bed. Aysha hadn't got far yet in learning to cook, so on most days, unless it was pouring with rain or Katy was feeling really bad, they went to a café for lunch and had their cooked meal there. Sometimes Katy was hungry, sometimes she weren't. Aysha was always hungry. Usually Aysha made the breakfasts and suppers. Katy never wanted to go out in the evenings so they didn't get to any gigs, much to the younger girl's disappointment. She didn't go to her orchestra or choir, but she did get Aysha to go on her own to choir, Aysha felt very proud. She had, at least temporarily, quit smoking, and her singing voice was getting better.

Katy read a lot of books and sometimes got out her paints and did a painting. Aysha went for walks and runs on her own with Greg and was happy then, but in the flat she couldn't stop herself feeling sad, there weren't much to do apart from watch the TV or listen to music with her headphones on. Greg was sad as well in the flat, he didn't like Katy being ill, he didn't like it that she never came running or on their walks. He sat looking at Katy all the time with a mournful expression. Aysha thought quite a few times of going off, back to her old life, which would be loads more exciting, but then the thought of leaving Katy on her own and leaving Greg with no-one to take him for walks, stopped her.

Katy wrote a letter to the Sri Lanka High Commission, which she showed Aysha.

Dear Sir / Madam,

I hope I can enlist your help in tracing a man I believe is a Sri Lankan national, and resident in that country. This is nothing to do with the tsunami - I have waited until now to write as I realise how busy you will have been following that disaster.

I have in my care a 13-year old girl called Aysha Jewel Stanton. Her mother, who is in prison in UK, is Janine Estelle Stanton, and her father is Milton Orlando Jewell, believed to be Sri

Lankan. There was a brief relationship early in 1991 in Burs-field, UK. Mr Jewell I believe is unaware a child resulted from this relationship, and may have returned to Sri Lanka in 1991 or subsequently. The only other details we have about Mr Jewell other than his name is that he had tattoos and two scars, and had worked as a sailor.

I am not concerned to exact financial or other responsibilities from Mr Jewell, but simply to make sure he is aware that he has a daughter here in UK, and to enable daughter and father to be put in touch with each other if that is what he wants.

I would be grateful for any information and help you can give.

Yours faithfully,

      After she had read this, Aysha went out to post it.
      Even though Katy was ill, they did go out twice, once to look at a new house, and once to look at the death records in the registry office. Katy thought Aysha's dad Kenny must have died in 1996 if Aysha had been four. But they spent hours looking through without success until they tried December 1995, and found that Kenny had died on December 6th that year, six days before Aysha's fourth birthday. They didn't get much further, though, because the name and address of the person who'd regis-tered Kenny's death, possibly his brother, could not be found in the telephone directory, so Katy told Aysha they'd have to look on a map and go round there when she was feeling a bit better.
      Aysha liked the house, and she thought her sisters and Greg would like it too, even though it was right next to a school and was right out of town, on the edge of the country. It did have a railway station, as well as a bus service, so you could get into town fast, faster than from the flat they was in now, as long as you worked out the times of trains. It had two big downstairs rooms as well as a kitchen, and a staircase that went up at the back from the kitchen. There was three bedrooms and a bath-room upstairs. There was a garden at the back which the kids at the school used for growing flowers and vegetables - Katy said she'd let them keep on doing that. The house were totally empty, and the man left a kinda magazine thing, a brochure, Katy called

it, that they had to choose furniture out of.

Aysha wanted Katy to get better before they did anything about moving. She wanted to help all she could but it were hard enough trying to do the stuff in the flat what Katy normally did. Aysha didn't like doctors but she wondered if Katy should see one. But Katy said no, she'd soon be better.

Is it looking after me's made you feel bad? Aysha asked one time.

No, of course not. I mean, I have got rather run down and tired, but that's because I've been doing too much and I've had a bit of a struggle adjusting. But I'm strong, I'll get over it, don't worry. And please don't let anyone know, Aysha, I don't want anyone worrying about me or thinking I can't cope.

What about Charly and Zoë? They's gonna wonder why they's not coming over like before.

Well, let's have them tomorrow. Can you walk over and fetch them? Take Greg with you.

They were due to go back to Longworth the day after, just the two of them this time. It was Katy's dental check-up, and she was hoping to book Aysha in at the same practice. But Katy wasn't feeling up to a visit to the dentist. Aysha thought she should go to her mum's all the same, anything to break the depressing routine they were in now, but Katy didn't seem to be up to the train journey. Aysha thought maybe Steve would come and collect them, and asked Katy to let her have her mum's number.

Why? asked the older girl.

So's I can let her know 'bout how you is and, like, not up to the train journey.

I don't want to worry her.

Well, she's expecting us, right?

OK, I'll phone her. I'll phone while you're out fetching your sisters. I'll get up and have a shower and phone her.

No way, Katy, I'll phone before I go. She handed Katy her mobile. You dial, and then I'll speak to your mum or Steve.

Katy wants to come home, said Aysha into the phone after Katy had dialled and passed it to her. Like we arranged, and I want to come too. But Katy ain't feeling too good, and not feeling like a train journey. She needs to cancel the dentists, she ain't feeling like that neither.

Steve agreed to come and collect them.

Aysha knew that in the early days of going round with Katy, she liked to touch her, just clutch her arm or brush against her, it was like she needed to know her friend was still there, hadn't run off like everyone else in her life. And when she moved in with Katy, it was like just so important to be in the same room at night, to hear the other girl breathing, that she weren't on her own in life any more. When Katy first slept in a different room at her mum's house, Aysha felt weird and couldn't sleep. But now, and especially now Katy hardly went out from the flat, Aysha were just dying to sleep on her own, she didn't understand why, she just were. That were one reason why she wanted them to go to Katy's mum's house without her two sisters, and she wanted the move to the school house to happen soon too. And she didn't like it that Katy touched her quite a lot more now, often hugging her and tousling her hair. It weren't that she'd stopped loving Katy or thanking her for taking her in and believing in her when no-one else did, it were just that Aysha didn't feel like a kid any more, she'd grew up a lot and she weren't sure what Katy's feelings were. She wanted to ask her, but when she were feeling bad weren't the right time.

Did Katy not want a boyfriend? Aysha were starting to think about boys, secretly look at them when they was out. She thought of Katy and that other friend she had, that girl, what were she called, Sophie, right? Aysha had felt jealous but now she were bothered more than jealous. If Katy wanted a girl to be instead of a boyfriend then Aysha weren't on for that. All this sitting on the bed staring at one another just did her head in. Streets was better in lots of ways, plenty of boys, more kids to choose from, kids in gangs. When could she talk? Perhaps tomorrow night after Charly and Zoë had gone, before they went off to her mum's.

When he would start grieving his mother, or whether he ever would, often crossed Marcus Sullivan's mind in the weeks after she died. Her absence, certainly, was deeply noticeable in the life of his family, for him, for his children, but most of all for his wife. He knew she would be the one to feel it most, but even he was not prepared for the degree of depression she had descended into. It had, however, brought Sam and him even closer as he'd spent as much time and emotional energy as he could listening to her, supporting her, seeing her through it. They had needed time without the children for this to happen, when the children were home his attention had to be at least partly on them because Sam was handling them badly, and they were tending to play up all the more because of that. So it had been a real blessing that Sharon and Steve, despite Sharon having been in a bad way herself for a few days, had agreed to have them over the Easter weekend, and the presence of Katy and her girls had made the prospect exciting for Lara and Liam. They came back each evening happy and tired, full of the things that they'd done, full of Auntie Katy this or Zoë that, but mostly it was Aysha this and Aysha that, and asking when was Aysha coming back to stay at granny's house. Marcus feared the children's enthusiasm for Aysha might upset their mother, make her angry or bring about a setback, but if Sam was upset or concerned, she didn't show any outward reaction, and by the weekend after Easter she seemed to be almost back to her old self, and life had returned to normal, more or less.

This was a relief for Marcus because the football season was beginning to near its climax, and although the team he played for was ensconced in mid-table, the two junior teams he was involved in helping, were both challenging for honours, the girls' team with an outside chance of winning their league, the boys' team looking as though they should manage second or third. So his focus was needed to switch to the teams, confidence-boosting, team selection, and he hoped he could balance this with maintaining a reasonable level of support to Sam and the kids. Fortunately the big problem he'd had at work was now resolved, and life in that quarter was a little easier on him.

On the Friday two weeks after Easter, he'd got home from work a bit earlier than usual, and was looking forward to an evening at home - there was no match that evening at any of the big clubs in the Manchester area, all the junior teams were resting prior to their weekend exertions, and Sam had had the kids all day, the new term not having started yet. It was a very beautiful spring evening, warm enough for the children to play out in their back garden while he and Sam relaxed with drinks, debating which of them would cook or whether he should go and fetch a take-away a bit later, Sam having already given the kids their tea. The sun was still high enough to bathe their garden in evening brightness and for the first time for some weeks Marcus felt that they were back to being a happy family again.

When the doorbell rang and he went to answer, he did not think that any disruption to this mood could be possible. But when he recognised his sister-in-law's foster-kid Aysha, and dog, Greg, he was more than a little surprised. But he invited them through to join the family in the back garden as he would have done if it had been friends or neighbours of either or both of Sam or him.

Let me get you a drink, Aysha. What would you like?

Juice, please. Any sort of juice.

The children of course were excited and wanted Aysha to join their play, which she readily did.

Let Aysha sit with us and have her drink, Sam said to Lara and Liam.

The girl played for a few more minutes and then joined the adults, Marcus having added an extra chair for her.

So what brings you here? he asked.

I can't stay long, said the child, stammering slightly. I just came this way to walk Greg, Katy and her mum don't know I've come, right. But Katy ain't too good just now, and, like, I thought you oughtta know.

What's the matter with her? asked Sam.

Like, she's had this bad cold for more than a week, some days she just wants to stay in bed, y'know, like depressed or something.

It must be in the genes! exclaimed Sam vehemently. First my mother, then me, and now Katy!

Shush, said Marcus, aware that Lara had stopped what she was doing and was listening intently. She hung on every word of her parents and even more of Aysha. You don't know that, it's more likely to be exhaustion, both on your part and on Katy's.

That's what Katy says, agreed Aysha.

Well, I always said she was taking on too much, Sam said, switching from alarm to self-justification.

We all take on too much at times, said Marcus. It's a common problem nowadays.

It were hard work for her taking on me, agreed Aysha. All them meetings and training courses and stuff for foster-parents, right, and then meeting my mum in prison, and now we've gotta move to a bigger place before my sisters can move in.

Is it really necessary for that to happen? asked Sam. Couldn't they stay in the home?

Nah, we all of us wanna live together. They tried to separate us before and it were terrible –

Who did?

Social Services. Anyway it ain't fair on them, right, if they let me move out of the home and make them stay.

Maybe not, went on Sam. We can all see how good you and Katy are together and how much she's helped you. But perhaps you don't need to live with her, still stay good friends but live somewhere else.

Nah, there ain't nowhere else for me, stated Aysha categorically. 'Part from a secure unit what they was gonna send me to if Katy hadn't come along.

What's a secure unit? asked Lara, listening avidly again.

Never you mind, young lady, I think it's nearly your bedtime, said Marcus. Liam! he called out. Upstairs and get ready for bed now! Lara, you go with him, make sure he cleans his teeth.

Can I come back down again?

No, you'd better stay up there.

But that ain't fair! wailed the five year old. I should stay up later than Liam, he's only two!

I'll come up and read you a story, said Aysha. And you, Liam.

Lara brightened up. And watch us clean our teeth?

OK, then. Greg! said Aysha. You be a good dog and stay down here while I see to the kids.

Well, that's good of you, said Marcus to Aysha. It's usually much harder to get Lara to bed if one of us is trying.

Sam and he found themselves inevitably discussing the problems of Katy and her protégée.

I don't think it's fair on Katy, said Sam. It's as though she's given all her strength to help this kid, and now she's got nothing left and it's Aysha thriving.

It is a bit weird, agreed Marcus. She's just grown up so much since we first saw her.

Why can't she give back some of this energy to Katy, I wonder?

It's not easy to see how.

Or otherwise live somewhere else, and let Katy recover on her own. They could still be close friends.

But I'm sure Katy wouldn't want that. It would seem like a failure to her.

It's just that Aysha seems the dominant one in the relationship now, which has been a complete turnaround. And I don't want my sister, or anyone else in my family for that matter, being dominated by a kid like that.

She seems a decent enough kid now, though.

Seems! But what about her background, Marcus? We can't ignore that.

Sshh. I think I can hear her coming downstairs.

In fact Aysha appeared holding Lara's hand. Liam's asleep, she pronounced.

He must be very tired, said Sam. He won't usually go off without a goodnight kiss from mummy and daddy both, if we're both in.

It's prob'ly the way I reads stories is, like, very boring.

I don't think Lara would agree, said Marcus.

Anyhow, Lara says she'll go to sleep, won't you kid, if I tells her what a Secure Unit is. So can I tell her?

I don't see why not. But in front of us, please, said Sam.

We wanna know too, joked Marcus.

Oh my god, I don't know any more than you, said Aysha. All I knows, Lara, is before I met your auntie Katy, I used to, like, get in loads of trouble, y'know with the police and stuff, and they used to put me in a police cell at the nick -

That's the police station, said Marcus to Lara, interpreting.

But then there weren't nowhere they could take me, right, 'part from back to the children's home, and I just kept bunking off again and getting in more trouble. So a Secure Unit, right, is where they can put kids so's they can't bunk off, it's like a children's home, right, but with locked doors and bars on windows like a prison for kids. Only there ain't one anywhere near where Katy and me and my sisters lives so they'd have to send me, like miles away right, which I'd hate.

She paused. She could see that she'd worried Lara, possibly upset her.

So I ain't gonna get in any more trouble, right, now that your auntie Katy's let me live with her.

Ok, now it's bed, young lady, said Sam. I'll take Lara up, and you talk to Aysha, darling, about options, she added, looking meaningfully at Marcus.

Options?

Well, we none of us wants Aysha in a secure unit, she said as she disappeared into the house. But there must be other options.

We'll go inside now, said Marcus. It cools down quick once the sun's gone.

I's gotta get back, said Aysha. Has you phoned them?

No, I'd better do that, hadn't I, then I'll give you a lift home.

No, I'll walk, Greg'll like another walk.

Won't you be cold?

Nah, I'll run, right, or, like, walk quick.

Hot drink before you set off?

No thanks, but could I have a bit more juice?

Of course.

He poured her another glass and went to find his mobile. Samantha came back down.

See, Sam, there ain't nowhere else they could put me, said Aysha, seemingly aware of what was on the older woman's mind. None of the foster-carers in Bursfield will have me after what happened before, right? And I'd, like, hate it, and I'd just bunk off and get in trouble, I knows I would. Katy knows too, she's never gonna let me go nowhere else. But what she should do is like -

Aysha hesitated.

Yes, what? asked Sam.

Well, it's like leading more of our own lives, not always doing everything together. Giving the both of us more freedom. And Katy trusting me, right.

Hard to trust you, Aysha, after all you've done.

Yeah, yeah, I knows, but I don't think it's good for Katy

to be, like, on my back all the whole time. Can you tell her?

I could try. But can't you tell her?

Nah. I has tried. Anyhow, she said, draining her last drop of juice, I's gotta get back. Thanks for the drink. Greg, come on here, we's going home to Katy now.

23. CHANGE FOR ME

Slowly Katy started feeling something more like her normal self, and, back in Bursfield with Aysha, tried to plan out a schedule which would cover all the things she needed to do, but wouldn't get her too exhausted again. Aysha, she realised, was beginning to make a bid for some more freedom, and Katy realised that being ill had caused her to show her feelings in a way which she never should have done, and which Aysha had felt stifled by. The kid had been happy to help out in the flat whenever she could, and take Greg out endlessly for his walks, and feed and brush him, but she was not into being nursemaid in all the more intangible ways that Katy had hoped for. Of course, what thirteen-year-old would? Katy should have known, but she hadn't been thinking, or rather her thinking had been clouded by a combination of tiredness, illness and heightened emotion. She'd been in a state of labile passivity unusual to her, normally such a self-controlled person. She just wanted Aysha there in the room with her for her eyes to follow around, or sitting close so that she could sense the vibrancy of the girl's blossoming strength and physicality. For without a doubt she was growing, and Katy's feelings were struggling to keep up. There was pride, there was love, there was gratitude, but there were twinges of less admirable feelings also, jealousy, envy, possessiveness. Aysha seemed to be maturing so rapidly and in so many ways, but most of all in the ripeness of her young body, she was becoming a sexual being. And however hard Katy had worked at convincing herself and everyone else that there was no sexual, no lesbian, element in the love she felt for the girl in her charge, every day that went by now made it harder for her to keep to that conviction as the girl's physical presence grew more and more overwhelming to her feelings. And Aysha herself had clearly begun to have some sense of this.

Katy? she'd said in a hesitant, questioning tone the night before they went to Sharon and Steve's. Why d'we have to spend, like, all the time together?

I thought you liked that. The shock, the disappointment, that hit Katy could probably be sensed in the tone of her reply.

I did, yeah, I still do, like, gigs, going on walks, yeah. But not indoors, Katy, that's boring, right.

Well, normally we'd go out more, ok. I'm not ill very often, I'll try not to be again for a while.

Yeah, but it ain't just that, right. Like, why can't I go out on my own? Like, with new friends. Like, kids my own age. Like, boys? She ended tentatively, questioningly, appealingly.

Where are you gonna meet these new friends?

I dunno. Gigs, I guess. But what I mean is, Katy, like you's gotta meet new friends too, like your age, right. Like, p'raps boys, p'raps girls, whatever, right?

Katy was beginning to get the drift.

You want me to get into a serious relationship with someone my own age?

Well, yeah, I think so, like I think that's gonna be so much good for you, Katy, like not having to cope with all this stuff on your own, right? Someone to share the load, right?

But what if it were someone you didn't like? Or didn't like you?

Nah, like you said once, it would have to be someone who liked us, I mean Charly and Zoë and me. I mean, we's good friends, right?

'Course we are.

But we's also like, you's my older sister looking after me, right?

You could say that.

So, when you lived at home with your older sister, right, and you were 'bout my age, you would never've gone 'round all the time with Sam, would you? She'd've gone 'round with her friends and had boyfriends, right, and so would you. You had that Sophie, right?

True, but that was a bit different -

Yeah, ok, but it's like, I don't care if it's boys or girls, right, Katy. Like me, I don't think I wanna a girlfriend like that, I think it's boyfriends I'm gonna want, right. Katy felt she didn't have the strength just then to interrupt the younger girl's flow. And amid the shock, there'd been some pride too, some recognition that Aysha was right, that it said a lot for her increased confidence that she'd been able to come out and say all this. And Katy knew that not only did it make sense, much of what Aysha had been saying, but that she, Katy, would need to stay strong now, keep her feelings in check, let her "child" spread her wings and become independent, even though she'd been hers for only such a short time, and show no loss, no sorrow about this. But she had serious misgivings, all the same. However much she loved Aysha, Katy knew that realistically she couldn't be sure how much she could trust her. The young girl had done fine under Katy's close guidance and supervision, indeed she had surprised everyone by causing so few problems, but was this just a front to justify claiming more freedom now? And what would happen if Katy loosened the rein?

Katy had suffered a short period of acute anxiety when she found out that Aysha's long evening walk with Greg had included an unscheduled visit to her sister's house, and on top of that had included her putting the two children to bed unsupervised. She still remembered that awful session with Tom Jameson when he had sown the seeds of doubt concerning sexual abuse. She had tried to make sure Aysha was never alone with the kids, especially at their bedtime. She wished Marcus had never said how Aysha had got them to bed more successfully than he or Sam usually could. She had dreaded the angry phone call that might have followed, that would have blown everything apart. But nothing had happened, and she began to question her own anxiety and distrust, why could she not believe in the innocence, the essential goodness, of the child in her care? And of course she could say nothing, even when Aysha had asked her.

What d'you think of me calling on Sam and her kids?

Well, it's OK, but I were a bit surprised, cos I thought you didn't like Sam.

No, I keeps saying, it's her what don't like me, the girl

protested. I wants to get her to like me better, so that's why I called.

Katy left it at that, but couldn't help thinking that it had some connection with her own solo visit a couple of weeks earlier.

Back in Bursfield, and with one day left of Aysha's school holiday, they took a bus journey across the city to the address they'd found from the register of deaths, possibly that of Kenny's brother. The woman who answered the door said Mr and Mrs Harrison had lived at the house before them, and they'd been there nearly four years. They'd moved to Wolverhampton, she seemed to remember.

We still get one or two Christmas cards for them, she said, and called through to her husband. Jim, do you still have the Harrisons' address? Why are you looking for them? she said, turning back to Katy.

His brother died some years earlier, and this is the brother's stepdaughter. Katy indicated Aysha. She wants to try and find her stepfather's grave.

After they'd been given the Wolverhampton address, and said their thanks and goodbyes, Aysha asked Katy, Was he really my stepfather?

Kenny? Well, not officially, if he and your mother never got married. But unofficially, yes, it's the best way of describing him.

Can't we, like, just call him Kenny?

'Course we can, but with strangers like them we need to try and explain the connection.

Oh, right. So, is we gonna go to Wolverhampton?

I dunno, it's quite a long way to go when we don't even know if they'll be in, or they might even have moved again. So maybe I'll try and find a phone number and call them first. Remind me to do it tonight.

Taking these excursions with Aysha was never any problem, Katy reflected. Things were just as they had been on those early occasions, their first gig together, the first trip back to Longworth, her first visit to Aysha's unit, that pre-Christmas shopping expedition. The girl was happy, joking, grateful, willing to learn. At home, though, Katy felt tension, a sense of a coiled spring in her charge waiting to unwind. Greg could help relax the tension better than she, Katy, could. The drumming helped too, but the times Aysha could drum had to be restricted. If only she could get the girl to develop more interests, apart from listening to music, drumming and dog-walking. Reading seemed a non-starter, and even TV held little interest, the only programmes that perked Aysha up were the sort of films shown very late and mainly on Channel 5 which had poor reception in their flat.

Maybe the move to the school-house, and the arrival of the other two girls, would help. Katy was getting all this sorted, not without problems, as she'd found that the first two first-year exams from her course were on the Thursday and Friday of the school half-term, when she'd hoped the move would happen. She decided to ask Neil to help them move on the Tuesday of that week, if possible, or the Wednesday, and make sure Charly and Zoë were with them to help with the move, but they would have to have two more days back at the home and then finally move in for good on the Saturday or after tea on the Friday. Meantime she was busy ordering furniture through the guy called Alan Grosvenor, and telling him which room to put which furniture in, and asking him to let her know when items had been delivered.

On the first day of Aysha's term (her two sisters had started a day earlier), Katy went over to the unit after lunch and took the girl into town after school. Before that, though, she and Aysha sat down with Julia Flowers and hammered out a firm programme of visits to Aysha's new High School, not just dates, times, and who would go with her, but what the purpose of the visits were and what the child would need to do in order to best prepare herself. Aysha was reluctant to be tied to such a firm programme, but Katy felt very relieved, and was sure Aysha would also be in due course.

Then there was her visit to the prison with Charly and Zoë. It was not easy, Zoë was nervous and tearful, Charly was even more morose and uncommunicative than usual. Stella was trying her best but still inclined to be defensive when asked something that she found uncomfortable. Katy felt torn between attempting to intercede between the mother and her kids, and leaving them to it. It was hard enough for her attempting to justify Aysha's absence to the brittle mother, clearly grieving the loss of her children beneath her tough, life-hardened exterior. She would have liked to have asked more about the children's fathers, but it did not seem appropriate in front of Charly and Zoë, and there was no other opportunity. Katy felt she'd done as well as she could have expected, better in fact, on the first visit to Stella, to have begun to get the mother on side, but she hadn't made any further progress in that respect on this visit, and indeed had used up some of the goodwill she'd previously established with the incarcerated woman. Would it require her to persuade Aysha to come, to mend things?

She dropped the younger girls back at the children's home after the exhausting train journey, and got back to Aysha and Greg feeling tired and miserable. Aysha made some half-hearted attempts to cheer her up but soon gave up.

You ain't phoned that Wolverhampton number for Kenny's brother, she said finally and somewhat reproachfully.

I have tried more than once. I'll try again tomorrow. Not tonight, she added.

Were my mum, like, shitty to you?

No, not at all. Just a very tiring day. Katy decided not to say that Aysha's absence had cast a shadow over the visit.

We's gotta go to a gig soon. Cheer us up, right? ventured the younger girl.

We'll get music papers tomorrow and find something.

Soon, right.

Yes.

Aysha relaxed and peace prevailed for the rest of the evening.

Katy was strong physically now but struggling emotionally. She was suffering some sense of loss with Aysha. She'd forced herself to let go of her obsession, to try and readjust to feelings which were more appropriate to her role as carer, and which were more in tune with the girl's feelings towards her, it was clear. She still loved the girl, but was worried that her feelings might dwindle further. The 'specialness' of the relationship was gone, and it all seemed uphill work from where she was now. At her most vulnerable moments she tried to recall the way she'd felt in those early weeks, the thrill of a new love, how her life had changed, it had been like a dream but the dream had been real and now she was left with the reality without the dream. But she thought of Aysha, her tough vibrating body now filling out and softening, her hard little face, the smiles that came so reluctantly, the way she avoided eye contact, her dirty blonde hair often such a mess but sometimes beaded like a hippy, spiky like a punk, blackened like a goth or puffed out in an afro, her tattoos and piercings. There were times she almost wished for the old Aysha, or at least for the girl to have given her a harder time of it since she'd taken her on. There seemed to be a hollowness now at the core of their relationship, and it caused Katy to worry that she might be losing the child completely. There was no question her commitment to Aysha would continue, but she feared that all the girl's past damage was being shut in, dammed up, waiting to show itself in some terrible crisis when least expected and everyone's guard was down.

And then there were the sexual elements. Katy had not yet attempted to try and tackle the issue of Aysha having been abused, even though she remembered clearly how she saw this as such an important element in her mission, and until it was done there would always be that niggling anxiety about what Aysha, or Charly for that matter, might do. But the truth was that it was her, Katy, who seemed the more sexually confused of the two, and who, just as much as Aysha if not more so, had tried to suppress this by pretending there was no sexual element in her feelings towards the girl. So how could she possibly at this point in time justify trying to deal with Aysha's sexual damage, when she was struggling with her own orientation? She thought of Sophie, and now Aysha. Did her having never had any other close friends besides them mean she was lesbian? Surely not. Was she ready for any sexual relationship yet? Aysha clearly thought she should be, but Katy was unsure. Why did she have this problem? And was it why she'd become so smitten with a child?

Thinking about it didn't help. There was no-one she could talk to. She had started writing or texting to Sophie again, but she did not reveal her inner feelings or thoughts, just gave progress reports on her career as a carer. She couldn't tell Sam, or her mother. She knew life was dreary for Aysha, knew she had to try and inject some spark into both their lives while avoiding getting too smitten again. Friends would help, but the age-gap made it hard. There were people she liked on her courses, in the basketball squad, in the orchestra, her own age, but there was no-one in the choir, no-one suitable for Aysha. Maybe at her new school?

She felt there were so many balls she had to try and juggle, even without her inner turmoil. Helping Aysha prepare to transfer to her new school, get ready for the move, continue with the life-story work, build a better relationship with the other two girls, maintain contact with their mother and continue tracing other relatives, as well as her own activities and course-work. And until something else added a spark to their lives, she and Aysha must get to gigs more regularly as the girl had quite rightly suggested.

They went back to the venue of their first gig together. This time the music was more up Katy's street, K.T.Tunstall with Richard Hawley opening for her. Aysha didn't think much of Hawley but perked up for Tunstall. She spent part of the opening set searching around for possible mates, and during most of K.T.Tunstall's performance she danced, not well but frenetically, crazily at times, with whoever she could find, including Katy when she let herself be persuaded. By the time the gig ended a small group of admirers had formed around Aysha, but as before, the two girls had to run to catch the last train, so nothing came of it. Aysha didn't seem to mind though, and was fired up, laughing, joking and teasing Katy for the whole of the journey back. Katy felt both pleasure and relief at seeing her like this again.

More gigs followed, some of them at seated venues, others following the pattern of the K.T.Tunstall one. Aysha started getting noticed, making one or two brief or casual acquaintances. Her cuts and scars had almost disappeared now but she continued to cultivate a subversive and disrespectful look which Katy assumed must be quite appealing and "cool" for many of these fellow gig-goers. As for Katy, she assumed that most of these kids that Aysha hooked up with thought that she was the shy and respectable older sister, which was near enough the truth.

After several failed attempts to speak to Kenny's brother on the phone, Katy wrote a letter:

Dear Mr and Mrs Harrison

I am about to become full-time carer for your niece, Charlotte Jade Stanton, aged 10, the daughter of your late brother, Kenny. I already care for her older half-sister Aysha, and there is a younger half-sister, Zoë, also soon to come into my care. These girls have had troubled childhoods and spent much of their lives so far in Social Services care. Their mother is serving an extended prison sentence with no release date at present.

It would in my view be helpful for Charlotte (known as Charly) to have some contact with her father's family, and likewise Aysha for whom your brother provided the only stable parent-figure in her early childhood, and who always thought of Kenny as her father. Even if you feel unable to assist with any direct contact for these girls (remembering that if your parents are still alive Charly is their granddaughter), I hope that at least you can help with some information about the life and death of your late brother, and in particular let us know where he was buried or cremated.

I look forward to hearing from you in due course.

Katy wrote this shortly before Charly and Zoë were due to visit, so that she could let all three girls see it before she put it in the post. But Charly was singularly non-committal and Zoë did not appear to fully understand. Only Aysha responded with warmth and enthusiasm to the one further step taken.

Sharon's condition seemed to be causing her life to disintegrate into a plethora of disconnected states. Her day-to-day life with Steve began to seem less important and less integral to who she was, although she hated herself for thinking this. When other members of her family visited, Sam and the grandchildren for instance, who came at least twice a week, or the more occasional but longer visits by Katy and the girls, as she now referred to them, Sharon seemed able to get into a different space and find reserves of energy and emotional commitment which were no longer an element in her life at any other times. When friends or neighbours called by, which seemed to be happening more and more, her response was different again and more mixed. She was pleased to see them and their news gave some added interest to her day, but she also felt their presence as somewhat intrusive, and perhaps as a reminder that her days were now limited, not quite in the same way as Marie's had been, but even so she was only fifty-three and would be lucky to see her sixtieth birthday. She and Steve did not talk much unless there was family news or problems to discuss. In the evenings, unless Steve had a class, they watched TV together, or a film on video if there was nothing interesting on TV. Sam or Marcus often came by when Steve was out but sometimes Sharon sat on her own dreaming or remembering. Even if the TV was on, she tended to lose herself in her thoughts. She found herself unable to share these thoughts which seemed to come from a separate corner of her being, and mostly dwelt on Rodney and the early years of her relationship with him, and the years they set up the taxi firm together.

Rodney was not from Longworth but he drove a van around the Manchester area delivering dairy products to shops and restaurants and came to Longworth at least twice a week. Sharon was a shop assistant in a grocery store, and he must have noticed the cheerful, pretty young girl who always seemed to be there to help him unload. If it wasn't her, he started asking where she was, and on the rare occasions when a different van-driver came, she also made it clear she missed Rodney. In this way, the romance had become a story on the lips of those that worked alongside both of them before they themselves had taken any steps. Rodney had had to be virtually dragged in front of her before he asked her out, not because he was unwilling but because he was shy of making the first move and thought Sharon seemed more confident and more likely to take the lead. But in those days that hardly ever happened, and a girl just had to wait.

So it could hardly have been called a blind date, but it was soon apparent how much more there was to get to know about each other once they started dating. Both were only children and lived at home, Rodney with his widowed mother, Sharon with both parents. Both of them drove but neither of them owned their own car so had to rely on buses or parental generosity to meet up. There was not much apart from the cinema to do together then, they liked listening to music but would not have thought of going to live music unless it was a local dance. Eating out didn't happen much, and neither was into exotic food. Pubs seemed to be for people not like them. It was, Sharon thought now, an old-fashioned courtship which had vanished completely now and was beginning to even then, but which she looked back on now with feelings of great joy and happiness, and regrets for the loss. They would walk out together, holding hands, into their respective towns, not for any special reasons other than to be together and be seen together by friends, acquaintances and work colleagues. They spent a lot of time at each other's homes, listening to pop-music singles on old-fashioned record-players, watching TV and getting to know each other's families, but each returning to their own homes for the night. It was not until she and Rodney announced their engagement that they started staying overnight together, and even then in separate beds. Sharon remembered many moments of intimacy in the back seat of a car or behind the bushes in a park before they got to spend the night in the same bed. And before that happened, they had already hitched their life together not just with an engagement ring, and the deposit on a house, but with a registered taxi, and a whole batch of printed cards.

Sharon rarely left the house now. This house, the same that she and Rodney had purchased together and somehow made into a home for them and later their daughters, despite having little skill and even less experience of homemaking. How had they done it? Youthful enthusiasm she supposed and little else, yet in her memory now she felt nearly all of her own enthusiasm had been for driving the taxi, and she had refused to let this be diminished even after Samantha was born. There were still pangs of guilt about this and about the burden she'd placed on her older daughter in the years she was so depressed, but then Sam had paid her back all right in her teenage years. Now they had a pretty equal relationship. Neither of them owed the other anything, and thank god Sam had found a steady and devoted husband. And two great kids. She, Sharon, would still do what she could to help out with Lara and Liam, for instance over Easter when Sam herself was going through a down period after Marie's death. A pity she couldn't take the kids out anywhere, though, had to leave that to Steve. No, the bad turn she'd had at the funeral had really knocked her back as far as going out went. The best she managed at the moment was sitting out in her wheel-chair, but Steve wasn't happy to leave her outside when he left the house. Still, summer had almost arrived and it was nice to sit out in the sun while Steve pottered about doing odd gardening jobs, or worked in the kitchen from where he could keep an eye from the back window. She preferred sitting out in the front, mind, where she could watch the world go by and people she knew might stop for a few minutes and talk.

On wet days, or when it got cooler in the evening, or when Steve was out shopping or at one of his classes, she liked to sit in her wheelchair by the front window. She kept her memories at bay by watching the life of the street. People came home from work on their bikes, the older folks usually wheeling them slowly up the slight incline, younger men and women pedalling vigorously. Before the factories and shops closed, there would be a straggle of high school kids, most of them on foot, many messing around, pushing each other into gateways or off the kerb. She recognised many of them, from families who lived nearby, or because Katy used to keep a protective eye on some of them when she had made the same journey to and from school not that many months ago. They shouted or they whispered to one another but seemed incapable of conversing in any tone in-between. That was another way Katy was different from most of her peers. When there were few people passing or waiting at the bus-stop just across the road she would watch the houses opposite to see who was coming or going or what activities were being played out. There was rarely anything salacious, nothing more interesting than the arrival of a new washing-machine here or a man repairing a roof there, or a stranger who she assumed must be a new home-help calling on Elsie Venters. More interesting was if one of Elsie's relatives made one of their rare visits. A few doors up a new family with small children (two or three?) had just moved in, she sometimes heard them from the back garden but rarely saw them. Once they had walked past and another time she'd seen mother and two kids waiting for the bus, but she had no chance to speak. There were too many back gardens in-between, she'd asked Steve to wheel her up to introduce themselves, but he'd so far been reluctant to do this. She thought the children must be a similar age to Lara and Liam, although there was an older boy (or were there two, one at school perhaps) and a younger girl.

She watched the sun going down over the buildings in towards town. She used to know every building, every street, even until quite recently. But the town had changed so fast, and she'd been into the centre so infrequently in the last year or two. Now she might see the sun glinting off a high window in a block the other side of town, more than a mile away, and could not name the building. Five years ago she could have done, not of course that she thought of that then, she had little time for idle reflections like she had now. She also liked to watch the flocks of chattering starlings that flitted from one front garden to the next, or sometimes hopped about on the pavement, especially near the bus-stop where the kids would throw crisp packets or styrofoam from take-aways when they left their bus, or while they waited. Steve scattered breadcrumbs in both the front and back gardens for the birds, but the starlings always came to the front garden while all the other birds preferred the back, and rarely came when she was out there, so she generally only saw the sociable starlings.

When the birds had gone silent and darkness had crept over, she might stay by the window and watch the girls of about Katy's age sauntering into town for the clubs and gigs, squealing with laughter as they strutted their stuff. It was at these times that memories overtook her. She had been a sixties teenager, part of the liberation of the young, but it all seemed old-fashioned looking back now, the lives of her and her contemporaries in a place like Longworth. They all waited for the right boy to appear, some couldn't wait long enough, some waited too long, but she had found Rodney, and he was mister right and he'd come at the right time. Why had she lost him, why had she pushed him away, why had she failed to cope with the problems of kids, difficult pregnancies, business failings, loss of her livelihood? Why had he never got back in touch, never wanted to see his children again? There could be only three reasons, he was dead, a lonely undiscovered death somewhere, or he'd gone abroad, put too much distance between him and his former life and family, or, perhaps most likely, he'd remarried, started a new family, and never told them about his old one. All these possible reasons made it seem rather futile to try and find him after all these years, but still Sharon kept thinking that was what she should do, even if it did seem disloyal to Steve. After all, if he had kids of his own with a new partner, they would be half-siblings to Sam and Katy, teenage uncles or aunts to Lara and Liam. Surely they had a right to know about each other. But Katy showed no interest in attempting to find out, even though she was constantly putting her mind to tracing relatives of these three girls she'd taken on. It didn't seem fair, Sharon thought, when there was such a big hole in Katy's own past. She wondered who she could talk to when Katy showed no interest and it didn't seem right to burden Steve with the question.

24. CHASING RAINBOWS

Riding on the bus from her school into the town, sitting with some of the other kids, Aysha could not stop thinking how much her life had changed. Who would've thought she'd ever be sitting here with brainy kids talking 'bout homework and stuff? Most of the kids who travelled on the bus with her were friendly enough, one of the boys enough to make her think he might soon ask her out. Sometimes she sat next to him and talked 'bout music, but mostly she put in her earphones and kept to herself, even if she were sitting among them. Lots of kids did that. Katy said she should be friendly to these kids, and she tried to be, but there were nothing 'part from music she could talk with them 'bout, not homework or computers or TV shows or other kids at the school. And even with music, they sometimes laughed or gave her looks over what she were into.

She were going to this school two days a week now, and after half-term it would be three days, and then when her year finished their exams it would be four. She never thought she'd be doing this. She never thought she'd fit in. It weren't easy, mind, and without Katy she'd never've done it at all. The staff at her unit had helped too, but it were mostly Katy. Every time early on she'd hated it or got scared, Katy'd come along with her, talked to teachers, stayed with her a while. It were Katy who'd got her in the school choir, got her drumming in one of the school bands, got her running 2000 metres in games lessons.

Those were all things she liked, and it helped her fit in. She would've never dared do it on her own. Not all the kids were friendly, but Katy said there was always some gonna be skanks. Even the friendly ones thought she were a bit weird, but that were ok, she was weird. Some thought she were stupid cos she knew hardly anything 'bout the work they was doing, so she had to try and show them she might be a bit weird but she weren't stupid. She was working hard now. She did English, Maths and Geography on the days she went, as well as music and athletics. When she were going full-time she would do Science as well, and Computer Studies and either History or French, she had to decide. But now she were mostly working to catch up, on English and Maths. She tried never to ask for help, even off Katy, she wanted to work it all out herself.

She wore white tops and black skirts for school. She'd grown a lot in the last few months and could wear one or two of Katy's old tops if none of hers were clean. She preferred long-sleeve tops cos she were still embarrassed 'bout her arms with the tattoos and the faint remains of scars, but kids saw them when she changed for athletics and she thought most kids in the school knew 'bout them by now.

The worst thing 'bout her life now was when she got off the bus in town she sometimes saw kids she used to know from the estates and one or two of them wanted to check out what she were up to. And the kids from her school often went in a café for a drink or something to eat before going their different ways to their houses and they asked her to join them and sometimes she did cos she were usually starving hungry. So she were caught between the two and she hated that, 'specially when her new mates asked who her old mates were and she never liked to say. Sometimes she did walk part of the way back with one of the kids from the estate, and tried to explain 'bout her new life now and her new school and how Katy and her was moving to a new house soon, and how she had to get back and feed Greg and give him a walk so she couldn't stay long.

Now, with Idlewild playing fast and loud on her stereo, she were thinking all these thoughts and glancing at the other kids now and again, and she took out her ear-muffs cos that boy were saying,

Hey! Aysha?

Yeah?

They all knew her name but she could never remember any of theirs, which were just so embarrassing.

What you doin' over half-term, then?

Well, we's gotta go to Katy my carer's folks for the weekend, an' then we's moving from our flat to a house, an' my two sisters is gonna move in with us.

Who d'you say this Katy is?

She's a friend. I told you how she looks after me cos my mum's in prison an' I ain't got a dad.

Where's her folks live?

Manchester. Near Manchester.

What's she doing in Bursfield?

She's at uni.

She's cleverer than you then, said one of the other kids, a girl, with a childish giggle.

She sure is.

You ain't stupid, is you, Aysha? the boy persisted. You in care or what?

I were, but now I lives with my friend Katy.

Why's your mum in clink? asked another of the kids.

Drugs. Drug-dealing.

Don't you wish you lived with your mum or dad?

No way! The thought of Kenny flashed through her mind. Katy'd written to his brother, Charly's uncle Phil, and he'd written back to say that Charly's gran were still alive, and they would all, that is Charly's gran and her uncle Phil and his wife, would come to Bursfield to see them , but Katy'd phoned and said wait til they was settled in their new place.

I hates my mum, she went on. And the only dad I knew were a guy called Kenny who weren't my real dad, and anyhow he's dead, right! An' I hates, like, foster-carers an' children's homes an' all that stuff, right! Katy's cool, an' the only place I wants to live!

She never liked getting animated, always tried to avoid it, but she could tell the other kids were at least a tiny bit impressed. She were about to tell them all 'bout the last gig her and Katy went to, but then remembered she'd told them at least twice already, and she didn't wanna keep going on, so she shut up. They were nearly at the bus station, so she put her stereo in her school bag, told the other kids she had to get home quick today, and got ready to make a dash for it, not talk to no-one else.

She were much later getting back on days she went to her new school. The bus into town were slow, and then she usually walked from town. Last thing she felt like were another bus-ride, even a much shorter one. Katy stayed on at college working, and Greg would be impatient, desperate to be let out, so she walked fast. It were almost half-term, her last day at the new school before they got a week's holiday. They were going to Katy's mum's Saturday, all of them, and then next week Neil were coming down to help them move. That were good, it would be wicked to see Neil again, he were weird like her. Charly would like him too, what with all that wildlife stuff he went in for. And the rescue dogs, she'd like him for that too. She were gonna make sure Charly and Neil could meet up and talk, but it were gonna be harder than she'd thought, cos Katy said Neil weren't staying over, but going back to his place the same night. They would have to give him a meal, Aysha'd said to Katy, not at the new house, but take him out to a café or somewhere, and Charly and Zoë too. Katy agreed, said that were a good idea. She were gonna have to get Katy sitting next to Zoë and Neil next to Charly. She were getting all worked up 'bout this, cool it Aysha, she told herself, don't keep thinking 'bout it, think about something else.

She thought of Greg, how he would jump up when she opened the door of the flat and walked in, how much he loved his walk. But you couldn't keep on thinking 'bout a dog, dogs was simple and most things in life was more complicated like getting Neil to talk with Charly, and going to gigs, and making friends, and getting more freedom.

Katy were letting her have a bit more freedom, all right, but she were never gonna let her go to a gig on her own. Not for a long time, anyhow. It weren't so easy talking to other kids, 'specially boys, when Katy were there with her. She liked going with Katy and they'd been going once, sometimes twice a week, to a gig since Katy recovered from being bad. But Aysha would go even more if she could, there was bands on at clubs and other places in town most nights. But Katy said she weren't old enough to go to these places 'part from with her, and anyhow they could only afford to go once or twice a week. She'd asked Katy what would happen 'bout going to gigs when Charly and Zoë were living with them, and Katy said some of the gigs they could all of them go to, but those at clubs and places like that well even Aysha shouldn't really be at them and ok she looked quite a bit older than thirteen and being with Katy prob'ly helped, but if the doorman ever asked for proof of age, well Aysha was gonna have to be disappointed. So unless they could find someone to look after the two younger kids, they'd have to stop going to gigs like that. Katy had phoned their social worker and asked her to find a babysitter or a family or volunteer who would look after Charly and Zoë now and again. Before she phoned, she'd asked Aysha if she thought the girls would wanna go back to the home or go to someone else's house, or have a babysitter come to look after them. Aysha said she were nearly sure they was never gonna want to go back to the home. After they moved, Katy were gonna get a proper drum-kit for Aysha. She'd got her social worker to send for some money. Katy'd make a deal with Aysha, she said, and Aysha knew Katy liked making deals. You carry on with going to your new school, she said, and staying out of trouble, and the drum-kit's yours. There was one at school but with Aysha only being there two days and lots of kids into drumming, she never got much chance to get on it, and only had Katy's old side-drum to practise on at home. This would be miles better.

Aysha often thought 'bout running off. Not for ever, just for a night. She wanted more freedom, she missed the high of the streets. But she never did. She knew Katy would have her back, she could run off three, four, even five times and Katy would have her back. But would the cops or the magistrates let her back all those times? Once p'raps, and after that Secure Unit. And then there would be Katy's disappointment and sorrowfulness which would be a hard thing to face after all Katy'd done for her. And there'd be Greg, missing her like mad even for one night. But the main thing were, she knew if she ran once, she might not be able to stop. It weren't the mates, it weren't the crime, the booze or the drugs that she might get back into being addicted to. No, it were the running away itself, it were the freedom, that were the addiction, she could see it now. So she stayed with Katy and would do when they moved. It would be better then, they wouldn't be on top of each other all the time.

Neil set off early from his place in Grasmere on the last Wednesday in May, hoping to beat the morning rush-hour and get to Bursfield in time to make an early start with Katy's move. He wasn't quite sure how long it was going to take, there was stuff belonging to the two younger children to be moved from their children's home, he knew that, but he hoped with his big estate car, two trips should do it, and with a bit of luck, he could be back on the road back to Grasmere soon after lunch. Katy had given him directions over the phone, and the paper he'd scribbled these down on was clipped to his map on the passenger seat beside him. He remembered Aysha from his mother's funeral, wondered if the other two girls would be anything like her.

The spring half-term was a busy time of year for mountain rescue, and he'd been out the previous day and before that a rescue in the dark, a group of three had got stuck on Jack's Rake on their way down from a high level walk, but hadn't attempted to call for help until darkness had fallen. They had no torch and were very frightened, but otherwise unharmed. Although it sometimes seemed annoying to be called out in such circumstances, Neil much preferred those situations to dealing with the pain of a serious injury or the grief of someone whose companion had died. Nothing of that nature so far this week, the only injuries a twisted ankle on scree and bruised ribs from a partial fall. His colleagues on the team had jokingly bemoaned his absence today, saying this was the day there was bound to be a serious incident. Neil was determined to be back on call tomorrow, ready and prepared, and the dogs too.

Katy, when she'd spoken to him on the phone, had said they would pay his petrol money and for a meal at a local café, before he set off on the drive back to Grasmere. She said she was being given an allowance by Social Services to pay for the move.

When he got there, he found Katy and Aysha waiting at their flat, everything packed and ready. It took two journeys to move all their stuff to their new place, and then they directed him to the children's home where the other two girls were also waiting with their belongings. This took longer than he'd anticipated because there were forms to fill in and protracted farewells but at least they didn't have to go there more than once. Aysha seemed to have a downer on the place and was clearly relieved to have no need for further contact with them. By now it was well past lunch-time and Neil, after his early start, was starving hungry. It was Aysha who seemed to sense this and suggested they went straight to an eating-place before they unloaded her sisters' stuff. He was very grateful for this proposal.

It won't be anywhere posh, mind, said Katy. Just a cheap café. There's plenty of those in this town. We might have thought of a pub, but I think most of them will have stopped serving by now.

That's OK. I'm not going to be drinking today.

So they found a reasonable café which was by now nearly empty, and Aysha organised it so that he sat between her and her sister Charly, and almost immediately got into asking him about his wildlife activities in Scotland. She seemed to be indicating that her sister had a particular passion for wildlife, although Neil would not otherwise have been able to sense this, as the girl herself was almost silent. In fact it was the youngest of the sisters who seemed the most chatty, although even she, and Katy as well, all four of them in fact, seemed to genuinely want to listen to his accounts of his searches for sea-eagles, otters, corncrakes, red-throated divers and other creatures.

The lunch went on and on, several pots of tea and soft drinks, lots to eat, and Neil talking as he'd rarely if ever done before. He, such a shy, solitary, awkward man, began to feel a connection to the world that he'd rarely if ever felt before, even with his own family or work colleagues, or indeed his new-found father, good though that connection was, it was slow going building it up.

But here were four young females who seemed in their different ways to be hanging on to nearly every word he spoke. He did not know how genuine their interest was, and suspected with Katy at any rate that it was mainly politeness and gratitude for the help he was giving her today. But these three young sisters were an unknown quantity, except that he'd already seemed to hit it off with the older one, this rather strange teenager Aysha. Two misfits somehow acknowledging a connection, he conjectured later. But the silent Charly whose sharing of the interest in wildlife did seem genuine enough, what could he make of her? Somehow, before they left the café about two hours later, and without his quite understanding how it had happened, but it did seem that it was that Aysha girl somehow behind it, he found he had offered to take Charly with him on one of his wildlife expeditions. The girl had suddenly livened up, surprised, encouraged, eager, but also a little anxious and not sure whether to say yes or no.

They had a new place to live, her and Zoë. Aysha'd been to see the house a few times, but not her and Zoë cos it were a long way to go when you didn't have a car. This man with a beard came in his big car to move her and Zoë and their stuff out of the home and into this new house where they was gonna live with Aysha and Katy and Greg. Aysha were different now. She were more grown up and didn't bunk off all the time. She'd always liked Aysha and she still did, not less and not more, but she still worried 'bout what she were gonna do next, were she gonna start bunking off again, now she and Zoë were living there? The man with the beard was called Neil. Katy knew him and so did Aysha. Charly asked Aysha if he were Katy's boyfriend, and Aysha laughed and said no. Aysha said she met him at a funeral, she said he were ok.

The man went on trips to Scotland where he watched eagles and otters. There were nothing Charly wanted to do in the whole world better than that. When the man said she could go with him some time, she didn't know what to say. It were, like, awesome and scary at the same time. Just her and this man she didn't even know. If the others could come as well that would be much better, but it meant camping out in wild places, the man said that, and Zoë might be too small. They'd been camping before, with staff and other kids from the home, but that was to the seaside and proper campsites. Wild camping sounded fun, but not just her and that man.

Everything seemed to be happening all at once. There was a new house to get used to and being back living with Aysha again, and then there were school. She were in her last term in top juniors. Aysha told her 'bout her new school, she didn't like it at first but now she did, well she said like it weren't too bad, which Charly knew meant if Aysha said that she must like it which meant it must be a good school. So Charly asked her teacher in top juniors and she asked Cassie at the home and she asked Katy who was gonna be her foster-carer now, could she go to the same High School as Aysha, but no-one had done anything 'bout it yet, or if they had they hadn't told her. Aysha'd told her she were doing cool music at her school and if Charly went there she could learn guitar. Then Katy told her she'd talked on the phone to her uncle, she had an Uncle Philip and a granny too, and after her and Zoë was settled into their new house they was gonna come and see her. All these things happening was too much to take in. Then there was Zoë, going on 'bout her friend Ambrose and how he was gonna come and live in their new house too, and when Charly tried to explain Ambrose couldn't come cos there weren't room and he were an imaginary friend just for the children's home, Zoë got all upset and said well anyhow she were gonna let Ambrose visit her and no-one could stop her.

So who's gonna tell Katy 'bout Ambrose, then? Charly asked her younger sister. Cos I don't think Katy knows about him and someone's gotta tell her.

Aysha! said Zoë, with sudden inspiration. Aysha knows Katy best so she can tell her. You tell Aysha and Aysha can tell Katy!

No way, so. You gotta ask Aysha, right! Don't tell her, you gotta ask her. Aysha don't like being told what she gotta do.

There were already a problem between Zoë and her over the visit they'd made to the prison to see their mum. Zoë wanted to go again and kept going on about it, but Charly didn't. Aysha were right, Charly thought, refusing to go. Their mum had never cared much about them before, why should they bother caring for her now, prisons was horrible places and a long train journey away, and why should she put up with all that just to please her mum.

Charly had always looked out for Zoë all the years they'd been together in foster-homes and the children's home, and she'd tried looking out for Aysha too whenever she could, cos Aysha'd looked out for her when she were very little and still did when she could. Now, Charly thought, there was Katy to look after Zoë so she could start doing more stuff with Aysha. But Zoë and her was still sharing a bedroom. Charly didn't wanna start fighting with Zoë, just wanted to be more on her own. She decided she would try and spend time in Aysha's room, listening to music, asking about school.

It weren't the best time for that man to ask 'bout a camping trip to watch wildlife. She had so many other things to think about, she didn't know what to say. That were another thing to ask Aysha 'bout, Aysha would know what to do.

Samantha, Marcus and the children spent the half-term week in Cornwall. Although the weather was a bit mixed, they had some warm days on the beach, and on the only really wet day they went to the Eden Project. They got there early, before it got too crowded, but even later in the day when it was jam-packed, Lara and Liam seemed happy.

Sam seemed to be over her depression. It was as though her own personal cloud had been hanging above her, blocking out the sun and sky, and it had finally lifted. At last she could enjoy the company of her children, give them her full attention, and they seemed themselves happier now, better adjusted. She still missed Marie, but missing her no longer seemed to have taken over her life.

She cherished Marcus all the more now, and while they were away, with the children happily exhausted each evening and ready for their beds and their sleep, Samantha wanted nothing more than to talk with Marcus, expressing her gratitude and her love. Talking as a prelude to rediscovering their physical intimacy after it had been temporarily mislaid. Marcus, of course, didn't really see the need to talk now, he was more into talking when there was the real need to support Sam through the worst of it, and now it embarrassed him to talk and he would prefer to cut straight to the physical expression of desire.

Sam, however, cherished his patience with her, his understanding, his willingness to deal with the children, and she needed to say so.

I'm glad you're through it, he replied.

Well, I hope it won't happen again. I remember our mum, she were depressed for years, I sure to god hope I'm not gonna turn out like her.

You won't, you're not the depressive type. It was just

your own reaction to losing Marie, we all react to these things in our different ways.

She was your mother, so how come it were me got so depressed?

I had a happy childhood, more or less, you didn't. That makes a lot of difference.

Sam thought about this. It was true, she couldn't remember ever feeling happy until she was in her relationship with Marcus. She thought of her mum, Steve, Katy, Marie, even her dad who'd left her all those years ago, there was sadness associated with all of them.

It's great to see the kids so happy again. Can't have been much fun for them. Or you, she added.

Well, you've told me what it's like being a kid with a depressed mum.

And they haven't mentioned that Aysha the whole holiday! Perhaps she shouldn't have said this, she knew Marcus didn't share her dislike of the girl, and indeed hoped she had got over it, as perhaps she had. Still, Sam wasn't one for buttoning her lips and she was really pleased that no shadow of anyone else was hanging over their enjoyment of a holiday just the four of them. They had of course sent postcards, and they had to think hard when they sent Katy's, to remember that when the card reached her she would have the other two girls with her as well as Aysha, and then to remember their names, which required Lara's help. Then of course they realised they didn't have the new address, so Sam had to phone her mum to get it. To tell the truth, before they left for Cornwall she'd been a bit worried about Sharon whose condition seemed to be deteriorating quite rapidly, and how she'd cope with the influx over the Bank Holiday, and if she coped with that, how she'd be with just Steve and her for the rest of the week, so Sam was glad of an excuse to phone without giving her anxiety as a reason. What she did find of concern, well slightly odd anyway, was not her mother, who seemed to have bucked up a bit from having her visitors, but the fact that, according to Sharon, it was Neil who'd driven all the way over from Grasmere to move Katy and her girls to their new place.

Did you know Neil was doing that? Driving all the way down to Bursfield to move them? she asked her husband in the presence of the kids, when she came off the phone. They were in the lobby of their small hotel, taking a short evening walk to include the post-box.

No, no idea. Maybe I should have made myself available again -

Again?

Well, I did drive Katy over there when she first took her stuff. Me and Steve.

Oh yeah, of course. They walked out onto the road, each taking one child by the hand.

But Katy probably didn't want to ask me again, even if I'd been around.

Why not?

Well. Marcus paused. I have had rather a lot on my plate. But anyhow, she must have known we'd booked this week away.

Even so, why Neil?

It's cos uncle Neil met Aysha at grandma's funeral, said Lara. And we all said goodbye to grandma together, and then uncle Neil told Katy he would help them move. Didn't he, Liam?

Her brother seemed puzzled, but nodded.

Really, said Samantha. I wonder what that was about. Can you put these cards in the post-box, Lara?

25. A PLACE I HAVE LEFT BEHIND

Although Charly and Zoë had never presented the problems associated with their older sister, it took Katy completely by surprise how much her life changed compared with when she took on Aysha on her own. Then, she had continued to lead the single life but with a younger teenager to share it, some of it, with. Now, she was head of a family, somewhere between an older sister and a mother figure. Her studies had to be encapsulated within the times the girls were in school, her social life, such that it was, was dependent on finding babysitters, something all three girls were scornful about, claiming they could look after themselves, that Aysha was old enough, sensible enough, to be left in charge.

Life became a constant round of planning meals, shopping, working out rotas for household tasks and making sure they were kept to, getting the girls to school on time, making sure homework was done, making sure Greg was fed and watered and walked - all three girls competed to look after him, but it wasn't always clear who was doing what. Life had without doubt changed for ever.

From day one, Katy found that it was Zoë who needed her most, who was most often her companion. Charly and Aysha paired off and became thick as thieves, and although Katy wasn't entirely happy with this, she realised that there was little she could do. Deep inside herself she mourned the gradual diminishing of the special relationship she'd had with Aysha, but knew she must not show it in any way. She'd already shown too much and that had driven Aysha apart from her, so it was natural now for Aysha to link up with Charly. Neither girl presented any outward problems, but Katy could not help wondering what they got up to all those hours spent in Aysha's room, listening to music, talking together, sharing secrets in a way she and Aysha very rarely had. She had only agreed to take on the two younger girls because of Aysha, Katy reflected sadly, but now Aysha seemed the most distant, separate, of the three of them.

There were some teething problems. There were a few shops in the "village", but they were expensive, and not entirely suitable for the weekly shopping, and the nearest supermarket was a short bus-ride away. At first all four of them went, but then Charly and Aysha offered to do it on their own. Katy wasn't happy letting them have such a large amount of cash on them, but neither was she happy leaving them if she took Zoë on her own. School was another problem - the two younger girls continued to attend the same primary school as before, but it was a difficult journey which Katy had to help them with initially. Aysha also had a complex trip on the days she went to her new school, she had to get a train into town and then a bus out, and do the same in reverse in the afternoons. Meantime Charly was, understandably in the circumstances, pressing to be given a place at Aysha's school and at the same time it seemed to make sense for Zoë, once her sister was at high school, to move to the school next door to where they lived rather than continue the difficult journey.

They went running, all four of them and Greg, together. Aysha had developed a talent and an enthusiasm for middle distance at school, so she needed no persuading, and Charly was happy to go with her. Katy had to do a bit of leaning on Zoë, but it was, at least, something they could all do together. There were occasional concerts also which they attended as a foursome. But for many of Aysha's sort of gig, Katy had to find a babysitter for the other two, or, occasionally and very reluctantly, allow Aysha to go on her own. Along with the running, it was one of Aysha's only real enthusiasms, which Katy couldn't bring herself to deny the kid.

Aysha restricted her drumming practice to the weekends, or days when she was still at her Unit and was brought back on the minibus before the other two returned. A delivery van brought the anticipated drum-kit one Saturday morning as they finished breakfast, and it was squeezed into Aysha's room where she had to be leaned on hard to prevent her succumbing to its attraction at times which disrupted homework or television.

The TV was on a lot more now, and likewise Katy's computer was in constant use. Charly watched wildlife programmes and documentaries, Zoë watched some children's programmes, early evening soaps, and they both enjoyed quizzes and one or two other "Celebrity TV" shows. Even Aysha started watching a bit more, but as far as Katy could see, she wouldn't be drawn onto the computer even though at the Referral Unit she was supposed to be concentrating on improving her computer skills in readiness for taking up Computer Studies at school next term. Charly, in particular, and Zoë both used the computer for homework and for more general information and entertainment.

The uncommunicative Charly was, Katy soon came to see, the lynch-pin of their world. Zoë still looked to her out of the habit of years in care together, while Aysha, Katy knew, had always seen her as an ally, and now all the more so. Unfortunately Charly was the one whom Katy found it almost impossible to relate to in any meaningful way, yet she knew she had to keep her on side if the arrangement was to work. Fortunately Charly, for all her moroseness, never showed any desire to derail the set-up in any way, and in addition Katy had two big advantages. Charly was really keen to learn the guitar, and Katy had promised her one in the summer holiday as an advance birthday present, and she was also desperate to go to Aysha's school, and Katy was working tirelessly at this on her behalf.

Aysha would not have been happy for Katy to continue to come to Andrew Wheeler High School, but Katy was desperate to know how her protégée was getting on, which Aysha was becoming reluctant to divulge. Once the two younger girls no longer needed accompanying on their journeys to and from their primary school, Katy made the trip across town to Andrew Wheeler. Katy no longer was required at Uni on her courses, she had projects to complete and a long reading-list in all three subjects to prepare for next year, but her time was her own as far as university went. Basketball practices finished a while back, and the orchestra only met once a month. Only her choir still met weekly. So she could go when she liked to the girls' schools, and she had a very good reason to present to Aysha for visiting hers, namely to press them for a place for Charly, but still she was really disappointed when Aysha wanted her to go to her school on one of the (now rare) days when she still went to the Unit.

You don't need me there, Katy, right? she pronounced in that way she had of forestalling any possibility of argument or discussion. You can tell them all the stuff 'bout Charly.

You know her a lot better than me.

Yeah, but you knows how to say it, like what'll go down with teachers and stuff, which I don't, right?

Aysha could still call on her friendship with Katy, the element of intimacy, complicity even, but only when the younger girl had something to gain from it. The rest of the time she was casually distant, keeping to Katy's rules, more or less, without fuss, but making little effort to communicate. However, Katy found that at her school they were generally happy. Aysha, it appeared, was mixing quite well and causing little trouble. They were pleased with her running, singing and drumming, but they felt she wasn't making as much effort as they would have expected to catch up in her academic subjects, ready for next term. Katy told them that her younger sister Charlotte would almost certainly be a good influence on Aysha in this respect, particularly if she was also coming to the same school. Although the girl lacked some social skills, she was academically minded and a hard worker. She showed the head and the head of year seven some of Charly's recent reports from primary school, which backed up her argument.

Summer arrived and the weather grew warmer. They now lived on the edge of the country, and Katy took the girls and the dog out for walks at weekends across the fields and beyond. Charly was the most enthusiastic, keen to spot any wildlife, which she would then try and identify from a book or a website after they returned. Katy made a mental note to try and find an old second-hand pair of binoculars for her. The other two girls came along either because they were drawn to Charly's enthusiasm or because they liked walking Greg, or in Aysha's case because she might meet up with other local teenagers. If she did, it didn't usually deflect her from the walk but on their return she would frequently stay out longer, hanging out with whoever was about, sometimes even if no-one was. It was the same with returning from school, she'd often stay out talking and smoking with another kid who was on her train, or had met her by the station. And if she went with one or both of her sisters, taking Greg for a walk or a run, Charly or Zoë would come in on their own with Greg, and Aysha could be seen outside their front gate or just up the road, smoking with one or more of the local kids.

Katy had made firm rules about drugs, alcohol and smoking. Nothing was allowed in the house, and drugs and alcohol were forbidden anywhere. Once or twice she suspected she might have smelt a touch of alcohol or cannabis on Aysha's breath, but she wasn't sure enough to risk a confrontation. But the girl made no secret of smoking outside, though she told Katy and her sisters that she was cutting down because of her running. The reduction didn't seem obvious to Katy.

The fact was that Aysha had reached adolescence. She had grown taller, filled out, and while no-one would have called her physically attractive, she had a certain physical presence in her brash, alternative style. With the warm weather came skimpy tops and bare legs like many teenage girls, and Katy worried about what might happen next. On the one hand, it was gratifying that Aysha, in such a short time since she was running amok and in and out of police cells, should now be apparently behaving like so many adolescent girls, but on the other hand she was presenting, it seemed to Katy, as older than her thirteen and a half years, and the kids she was talking to, mixing with, were probably older than her although it was impossible to be sure, and Katy was beginning to feel a huge generation gap even though it was less than seven years. But where had all the disturbed behaviour, all the damage gone, was it going to start showing again, and if so, when and how?

The Life-Story book had been put to one side, before the move, and since. Katy's exhaustion after Easter, Aysha's new school, the move of house, tracing relatives, their life together in their new home, all seemed to have got in the way. Katy remembered how she had reacted to Tom Jameson's cruel warning, how she had been determined to help Aysha, and perhaps Charly too, deal with the sexual abuse, how ambivalent the girl had been about it until that wonderful moment when she'd said she was ready. But nothing had happened and Katy was left wondering when the damage would show up. Aysha had moved away from her since then and it might even be better, Katy thought, if someone else took over with the Life-Story work. Someone more skilled, more experienced. She'd continued, from time to time, to contact Ruth Barnes and others at Social Services about how she could get guidance on this, but very little help had been forthcoming, which was perhaps another reason for putting it to one side. In the meantime, she was having to reassess her own feelings for the girl. Sometimes she felt she had been used, that Aysha had latched onto some sense that Katy was smitten by her, in order to find an escape route out of her terrible life, that even that period of intense joy of being together, short as it had been, was fake. If she could just believe that it was real, Katy could hold onto everything else, their new life now, the very different relationship between them, Aysha reaching adolescence, wanting more freedom like every adolescent, growing more independent and detached, and wherever this was going to take her, Katy could go with this, be there for her, stay with her through any troubles ahead, only as long as she could still believe that for a few short months they had had something special, shared feelings which might be called love.

One hot Sunday around midsummer, Charly's uncle and his wife came for lunch, bringing Charly's grandmother too. Katy had spent all morning making the house look welcoming and preparing the lunch, assisted by the mostly willing Zoë. Charly herself, and Aysha, had gone out together with Greg after breakfast, seeming even more secretive than usual and with

Aysha dressed to flaunt herself in front of any of the boys that might be around, so that Katy, while they were out, was really anxious that they might not return for the lunch with the visitors. But return they did, in plenty of time, and set about tidying their bedrooms, and showering, and changing, in Aysha's case, into more suitably modest gear. She wore the same black dress, now a fraction small for her, she'd worn for Marie's funeral, Charly had put on a clean tee-shirt and jeans.

The visitors arrived and introduced themselves, Phil whom Katy had already spoken with on the phone, his wife Ruth and his mother, Charly's grandmother, Joan. Both women seemed uncomfortable, quiet, self-effacing, Uncle Phil was a little more relaxed but even he struggled to talk much. Katy busied herself with being hostess, trying to make them comfortable, offering drinks which they declined, putting the final touches to the roast lunch. She herself did not feel it was right for her to raise family matters with these strangers to whom she had little direct connection, even if she'd felt confident which she didn't, her innate shyness having returned and could only be covered up by staying busy with serving lunch.

So things were stiff and awkward as they all sat down in near silence. The girls helped bring food to the table, Zoë sticking close to Katy, overawed and confused and having temporarily lost her friendly side. Charly was her usual morose self, hardly even looking at the guests. Katy was desperately hoping one of the visitors would rescue the situation, but it was Aysha who finally broke the ice.

I remember Kenny, she said, looking at the older woman. He were good to me when I were a little kid, he were like a dad to me.

Yes, I remember you too, said Joan, Kenny's mother. And your sister, Charlotte. She looked at the middle child. I met you a few times. I remember Kenny brought you to our house, both of you, just after baby Charlotte was born.

I was still living at home then, mother, said Kenny's brother Phil. Do you remember, you called dad and me at work and told us to get home soon as we could. Kenny waited until we finished work.

Do you remember that, Aysha? asked Joan. Coming to our house in Bursfield?

I dunno.

Having a baby sister was probably all you could take in at the time.

Where were our mam then?

I don't know, said Joan. She never came to our house. We never met her more than once or twice. To be quite honest, and I hope you won't mind me saying this, she wouldn't have been welcome in our house. We were never happy with Kenny taking up with her, we knew she had a problem with drugs, and then of course we blamed your mother for his death. But please believe me, we never had anything against you girls, my husband and I, Ted his name was, bless his memory -

Joan petered off, stuttering and swallowing, her neck seemed to bulge out and she put one hand on her grey permed hair. Her knife and fork rested on her plate, and Katy noticed that so far she had eaten very little. Katy worried and felt bad, even if the older woman was all right, this was clearly an ordeal she was being put through. But then, Phil and his wife didn't have to have brought her.

Joan took a sip of her apple-juice. Katy asked if she wanted water as well, but she declined.

I'm sorry about that. She took a few mouthfuls of vegetables from her plate, and leant across to Charly.

Ted and I would have liked to adopt you, Charlotte. And even you, Aysha, as well. Kenny said to us many times that he would not allow you two girls to be separated. When we got the chance, we talked to Kenny about leaving Janine, your mother that is. He told us he'd been trying to get her off taking drugs, but it clearly wasn't working. But we never said anything of this in front of you, Aysha, it wouldn't have been right for you to hear what we said.

What did Kenny say? asked Aysha.

He told us he wouldn't leave Janine unless he took both children with him, and he didn't think he would be allowed to look after you, Aysha, since you weren't his real child. So that's why he stayed. He did talk of going to a lawyer, applying for custody or something, we don't know if he did. But then he died.

So it were cos of me he died, then? queried Aysha. If it weren't for me he'd've gone back home to you, and taken Charly, and still be alive now?

I don't think we can say that, interrupted Uncle Phil.

But he did love you like you were his own kid, said the grandmother.

He should've stayed alive, said Aysha quietly. Even if it meant splitting me and Charly up, we could've lived together later, and Kenny would still be here.

Joan was now sobbing silently.

Ted and me, we did go to a lawyer, she said. We asked about adopting you two girls, but he told us we might have a chance with our own grandchild, that was you, Charlotte, but hardly any chance with you, Aysha. So remembering what Kenny had said, and thinking at our age we might struggle raising two children, and not wanting to face Janine in a battle in the courts, we decided against it, and so Janine kept you two girls and we gave up trying to see you. But we always remembered we had a grandchild and not one day went past only we wished we'd done something -

It wouldn't have been much fun for Zoë, Katy interrupted, thinking that the youngest child would be feeling left out in all this. I mean, if Aysha and Charly were taken from their mother, then she would've been on her own from when she was born.

Yes, said Phil's wife Ruth, speaking for the first time. That's a good point. And she smiled at Zoë.

Katy started carving some more chicken and asked Aysha to serve second helpings of vegetables.

Make sure you get some yourself, she said to the girl, and turned to the guests. Aysha has a huge appetite these days. When I first met her she looked half-starved but she's making up for it now.

Shut up, Katy, said Aysha with a rare smile. You're like just so embarrassing sometimes.

So what have you girls been up to, then, since my mother and I last saw you? asked Uncle Phil. How long ago was that?

Aysha shrugged, and looked at Katy. How long ago, Katy?

Katy still couldn't help feeling a thrill when Aysha looked at her like that, summoning some shared memory of the work they'd done together. Must be more than nine years, she said, trying to sound as casual as she could.

Well, what's happened to us? said Phil. Ruth and I got married, and we moved to Wolverhampton.

And your dad died, Phil, added Ruth.

Of course, mustn't leave that out.

And Maggie's wedding.

Who's Maggie? asked Aysha.

She's our older sister in Australia, said Phil. She's been in Australia all these years, and then she suddenly announced she was getting married. But then dad fell ill, so you couldn't go, could you, mother?

So you've got an auntie in Australia, Charly, said Aysha.

Yes, and two twin cousins, said the grandmother who'd been silent for a while. Two little one-year old toddlers. Two other grandchildren who I've not seen yet. Only I have now seen you, Charlotte.

She wants to be called Charly, said Aysha, in a huddle with her sister.

What? I can't help thinking that you're Charlotte.

You did see her as a baby, right? said Katy. And she was Charlotte then, right?

She was.

So you don't have children of your own? Katy turned to Ruth.

The woman, quiet and thirtyish, looked embarrassed. She turned to her husband with a blush.

Not yet, said Phil, clearly used to answering for her. We have tried, haven't we, but it hasn't worked out yet.

I had a miscarriage the first time.

Oh that is sad, said Katy, trying to empathise. My mother had a miscarriage between my older sister and me.

But we're keeping our fingers crossed, said Phil. Ruth is pregnant again. Early days. We only told you, mother, didn't we, on the car ride over here.

Yes, was I pleased! Too much to take in, though, all in one day.

Quite, said Katy, still doing her best to empathise. Well, I do hope this time it's straightforward.

Another little cousin for you, Charly, said Aysha, giving her sister a nudge.

Can you go and bring the puddings, Aysha? asked Katy.
Puddings?

Yes, there's a rhubarb pie in the oven and a bowl of strawberries in the fridge. And there's ice-cream or cream.

Wow, Katy, you's done us wicked for lunch.

Yeah, well it were only Zoë that helped, so give a hand with it now, will you? And it'll be you and Charly washing up, after our visitors have gone.

No way, Katy! I said I'd meet up with friends outside.

There'll be plenty of time to do both. Now go and get the puddings. Charly, can you take the plates out, and the cutlery. And Zoë, you take the vegetable dishes. I try and keep these kids in order. She smiled at her three guests.

You seem to manage them well.

Don't you believe it. Only now and again.

So tell us more about you girls. This time it was Ruth who spoke, when all three of them were back at the table, and Katy was fully occupied serving the second course and asking who wanted what.

Charly and me's at the same school, said Zoë, piping up for the first time. But Charly goes to High School in the summer.

The same school as me, said Aysha. That is, we hopes.

Which school is that?

It's called Andrew Wheeler High School. But I's only just started myself, me. Before, I went to a Unit.

Well, you still do, actually, Aysha, said Katy.

Only one day a week, Katy! replied Aysha querulously.

Tell them what you're doing at your High School, then.

Aysha looked blank. Mostly English and Maths, catching up, she muttered under her breath. But I's starting more subjects next term.

And tell them what else are you doing at Andrew Wheeler, prompted Katy.

Athletics, running that is. And music, and choir. See, I wants Charly to come too, so I's gotta try and do good at school. And them's things I can be good at. But I does like them too.

She's doing amazingly well now, said Katy, turning to Ruth. Compared with, say, a year ago.

Shut up, Katy! Don't embarrass me!

Why, what were you up to a year ago? asked Joan.

See, you shouldn't've said!

Tell them what happened, it's best they know.

I kinda went off the rails for a few years, muttered Aysha. See, I were put in care and I hated it. And then everyone used to have a go at me and it made me worse.

A downward spiral, said Katy.

Shut up, Katy, you don't know the half.

What about you two? Charly's grandmother turned directly to her.

We was in care, too, wasn't we, Zoë? Foster-homes, and then a kids' home.

And then we moved here, to live with Katy and Aysha, said Zoë.

Did you get in trouble too?

No. Only a bit.

Tell them what you get up to, prompted Katy. In school and out.

Swimming and dance, I like, said Zoë. And games.

What sort of games?

Board games. And computer games.

And you, Charlotte?

Music. World music, guitar bands, indie bands. And ecology.

Ecology? Do you study that at school? asked Phil.

I like science, geography, history, environment, reading and writing, painting, music.

Goodness, is there anything you don't like?

'Rithmetic.

But you's quite good, even at that, put in Aysha.

Charly's the academic one of the three.

Charly's expression was both puzzled and pained.

And you loves studying wildlife, Charly, doesn't you? Aysha turned to the visitors. In the summer, she's gonna go to Scotland on wildlife study.

Shut up, Aysha, I dunno if I's going yet.

Ruth seemed to sense an awkwardness. One of my friends went to Andrew Wheeler High School, she said. It's a good school. I wish I'd gone, in some ways, only I don't now, because I might not have met Phil.

Did you meet at school?

Well, yes and no - not exactly. Phil was four years above me - we hardly knew each other. But later, when we met, we did kind of recognise one another, well I recognised him anyhow, that helped break the ice. But I must get back in touch with my friend and tell her Phil's niece is about to start at Andrew Wheeler.

If she's accepted -

Joan interrupted. My grandson in Australia's called Andrew.

Andrew Wheeler? queried Aysha.

No, no - Andrew Tanner. It just reminded me.

What's the other one called?

Clarissa.

So it's boy and girl twins?

Yes. We've brought a photograph. Do you want to see a picture of your cousins, Charlotte?

Charly.

Let's clear the table first, suggested Katy. Shall I make some coffee?

When she got back to the table with the coffee, she found the girls staring politely at some photos. All three in their different ways seemed nonplussed.

Who are these children? queried Zoë.

They're Charly's cousins. Katy looked over their shoulders. These are the parents, yes?

Where're the photos of my dad, I mean Charly's dad, I mean Kenny? asked Aysha, struggling to speak.

Stupid of us, said Phil. We only brought recent photos. We do have some old photos, of course, stashed away somewhere, with Kenny on them. It might take a while to dig them out, but we didn't think.

Have you never seen any photos of him? asked Ruth.

We do have one or two photos, said Katy. Go and find them, Charly. You go and help her, Aysha.

Me too, said Zoë. I'll go get them.

Just the ones with Kenny on, mind!

Why?

Don't ask why, just do it!

But I ain't on any of them! complained Zoë. I weren't born then.

No, no, it's ok, bring the ones of Kenny and the one of you three girls together when you were small, said Katy, adjusting.

For a short while Kenny became the focus of attention.

He was a kind man, with a great sense of humour.

But he lacked direction in his life. Sort of never quite settled down.

He were good to me, said Aysha.

You could rely on him. Never let you down.

If our mam were out, he always stayed in with Charly and me. He took us to the park a lot.

He took more care of others than himself, said Joan.

We should go see his grave, said Aysha.

He don't have a grave. But I think there's a wooden marker. Have you been to the crematorium? Phil turned to Katy. We haven't been for years.

No, not yet. Maybe in the summer holidays. Is there just the one crematorium in Bursfield?

Ah, that's a point. Do you know, mother, if that were the only one? Anyway, it's the one out on the Vale Farm Road, that's where he were cremated.

Do you know that road, Aysha? asked Katy. I don't think I've been to that part of Bursfield yet.

No, nor me.

I thought you were familiar with the whole city?

Nearly all. Aysha was unusually abrupt, and Katy wondered if the photos on top of the occasion as a whole had got her upset. She would never show it.

You must come and visit us, said Ruth. Charly, you could come and stay over a weekend. Or two of you even. We wouldn't have space for more than two overnight. But you could all come for a day.

We don't have a car. Day trips are a problem. But we'll think about it and let you know. But now that Charly's met her uncle and grandmother, we'll make sure the contact is kept up.

Good.

Now, it's washing-up for you, Aysha, before you go out again.

Oh, Katy, don't be so cruel!

Charly, you go and see our visitors out, and then join

Aysha.

It had gone well, Katy thought, after the awkward beginning. Not easy to be sure how important these people were going to be in their lives, or Charly's at least, but they seemed nice enough. But she was struck at the hole in the children's lives. What little they'd been willing to admit of their lives between Kenny's death and Katy's arrival, had conspicuously left out mention of the mother's downward spiral towards addiction and prison, the years with Vic, the abuse ....

More important than ever to press on with the Life-Story work, she thought. Especially now, with this visit, this ordeal, completed and behind them. Start as soon as possible. Not tonight, though, she was too exhausted.

But it was Aysha who came to her. Later, after she'd changed back into her teenage gear, spent half the evening outside with Greg in the warm glow of the setting sun, she came in to see Katy who was reading a course book in the front room, after the two younger girls were in bed.

Katy?

Aysha? That went all right, didn't it? You did brilliant, kid.

She was always trying to recapture something of their earlier times together. It rarely worked. This time Aysha just shrugged.

Katy, it's about Charly going with Neil on this wildlife trip.

Oh yes?

Like, can I go too?

Why? You've never been interested in wildlife.

But I am, right, cos Charly's showing me, like I's learning it off've her. But thing is, Katy, Charly wants to go but she's like shy of going on her own, right, cos she hardly knows Neil.

But you don't know him either.

Well, a bit more than her, right. But that don't matter, it's like she'll say yes if there's me as well. And it'll get us off your back for part of the summer and Zoë can get all the attention.

Oh sure, thought Katy. It's Zoë who gets my attention now.

I'll think about it, she said. I'll have to discuss it with

Ruth Barnes anyhow. I haven't said anything to her yet cos Charly hadn't made her mind up.

Oh, Katy, you don't wanna say anything to her, protested Aysha. It ain't nothing to do with her and she's only gonna say no anyway, right.

I've got to check with her. It would be extremely irresponsible to send either or both of you away with a single man like Neil without getting permission first.

Why? You's our carer now.

Only on behalf of Social Services. They've entrusted me with your care.

Oh.

She went up to say good-night to Aysha in her room, something she rarely did because she knew it embarrassed the girl. She usually tried to have a quiet word with her before Aysha went up to bed, but if she didn't catch her, she normally just left it. But now she had reached a decision of sorts. She would do a deal with Aysha. She and Charly could go on this wildlife trip, provided Social Services gave permission, and as long as they both agreed to do some more Life-Story work first.

As soon as the girls had left for school the next morning, she phoned Ruth Barnes. The social worker had been to visit them at their new home, just the once, about a week after they'd moved in. Cassie had been to see them as well, and two or three other members of staff and volunteers from the children's home, who'd been to help with babysitting. Katy was still registered as a volunteer with the home, and she couldn't help sometimes thinking that if her chance encounters with Aysha hadn't happened it might have been the other way round, with her helping to sit for other children placed with carers. So there'd been a reasonable stream of callers since they moved in, but mostly helpers within the care system like her; the Harrisons were the first 'real' visitors, or at least this would be according to Aysha's take on the world. She did her very best to avoid seeing Ruth Barnes, and Katy knew she had to out-manoeuvre her protégée in order to bring about direct contact between the girl and her social worker.

She was fortunate this time to get through directly to Ruth, and she told her about the planned trip to Scotland with

Neil, and about her wish to start dealing with the sexual abuse as part of the Life-Story work.

With both Charly and Aysha, if possible, she added. After Zoë's in bed, asleep.

Do you think it's a good idea to be doing this at bed-time? Ruth Barnes queried.

Because it might give them nightmares? I have thought of that, but I don't see what the alternative is. I'd be happy to hand over to someone else, if there was someone available.

Well, I'd be willing to take it on myself, said Ruth. With you or on my own, although I don't have the time just now, it would be at least a month before I could free up enough time.

I think it needs starting now, said Katy.

Anyway, I don't think Aysha would co-operate with me, Ruth continued. Charly might, but not Aysha. And the same would apply to any other professional we referred her to, not that there are any who don't have massive waiting lists. But I think it has to be you with Aysha.

Is there anyone I could turn to if I hit problems?

Well, there's only me, really. Try me first, and if I can't handle it I promise I'll take it further, as far as consultation goes. But do you want to use one of the interview rooms here? You could perhaps drop Zoë off with Cassie and come on here.

No, no, said Katy hastily. That wouldn't work at all, too much of a big deal. Anyway, can you see me getting Aysha vol-untarily into a Social Services office? No, and I can't use the hour when Zoë has her dance class, because Charly stays on at school reading or using the school computer and they come on home together. Mind you, I could do work with Aysha on her own during that hour, provided she gets in promptly herself which she doesn't always. Or I could do the work soon after school and just plonk Zoë in front of the television and hope that works. But really, I don't see that it's a disadvantage doing it just before they go to bed. If they get upset I'm gonna have to deal with it somehow, whatever time of day. I'm not likely to be able to get hold of you till the following morning.

Fair point. Now as to this other matter, how well do you know this man?

Quite well. I'm sure he's ok. But he's my sister's brother-in-law and they, my sister and her husband, know him better than me and they'll vouch for him.

We'll need to run police checks.

Yes, I know that. I'll get you his full details.

You'll need to get his consent first. Send a form for his signature.

Oh, can't we bypass that bit? demanded Katy, her heart sinking. I'll tell him about the checks, I promise I will, but I don't think he'll take kindly to official bits of paper and signatures and all that, and it might blow the whole idea.

You mean he's not fully committed to this?

Well yes, he is, but it's like getting away from official-dom is part of it, if you get what I mean, and for the girls too, that's why they hit it off, or partly. I think so. Katy finished lamely, having got thoroughly confused and worried she'd said too much, or the wrong things.

I don't know if the police would agree to run a check if we don't get a signature first, said Ruth Barnes. But I'll see what I can do.

Oh thanks.

Katy realised she always had the upper hand. They, Ruth and her superiors in her department, would bend over backwards to make sure this placement continued to work.

She phoned Marcus at work. She had to get the phone number from Directory Enquiries, she knew the name and address of the factory where he worked but not the number. She hoped, as she was put through to him, that he worked in an office on his own.

Marcus, it's Katy. I'm sorry to phone you at work. Can I ask you something in confidence?

Yes? Marcus sounded doubtful, and anxious.

It's nothing too serious, well I hope not. It's about Neil. There's this plan been hatched for Charly to go off with him on one of his Scottish wildlife trips this summer. And now it's Aysha too. Both girls. Do you know about it?

No.

Well, I thought you and Sam should know.

And you want to put a stop to it somehow?

No, no, I think it's a really good idea, for both the girls, as long as Neil can handle it. I mean, they need a bit of handling, the two of them. But it's probably better, safer, two than just one.

272

Why don't you discuss it with Sam and me at home? I don't know what she'd think, mind.

Well, I could do, I mean, I will. Even though it's not really her business.

Nor mine neither.

Yeah, but you know Neil better than anyone, you're his closest relative, his next of kin. I need to know now, at this early stage, whether there's anything would make him not suitable for taking two girls on holiday, if you see what I mean. Anything in his background I don't know about. That's why I'm phoning you at work, in case there's something even Sam doesn't know. Please tell me in complete confidence if there is anything.

No, said Marcus. There's nothing at all, that I'm aware of. He's very good with Lara, she likes him, trusts him, and Liam as well of course. He is of course, shy and awkward with people, especially women, never has much contact with them unless he's rescuing them off mountains. He's happier with animals and birds. But, as I said, he's good with Lara.

Do you think he'd handle two troubled older girls for two weeks or however long it is?

I honestly can't say, Katy. They neither of them seem too troubled to me, or Aysha at least, I don't really know the other one.

Charly? She's ok, just quiet and withdrawn. Aysha could be more unpredictable.

Well, talk to Neil a bit more. Talk to Sam and me. You know Sam, she'll want to have her say.

Yeah, I will do. But Social Services will be running a police check on Neil unless I call them today to cancel it, and if nothing shows up on that then I think the trip will go ahead.

I'm quite sure there's no police record on Neil.

Good. OK, Marcus, thanks.

Will we see you soon? Haven't seen you for ages.

Maybe this coming weekend. There's nothing happening, I'll talk to the girls.

After she put the phone down, she remembered she had meant to get Neil's details from Marcus, but on reflection it was better that she spoke to Neil himself. The only problem was, it was difficult to get through to him except in the evenings when the girls were home. But with the evenings long and warm and

Aysha out so much, there should be opportunities. She tried to gear herself up to the work with the older two.

Well, as long as Neil doesn't turn out to have a police record, it looks as if you'll be going on this trip, she told them. And you and me, Zoë, we'll have a special trip of our own.

Where?

It'll be a surprise.

But we need to do this work. Talk about the missing years in your childhoods.

Zoë as well?

We'll start with just you two. After Zoë's in bed.

It wasn't easy to be sure how much their hearts were in this, but there was no desistance, no avoidance.

So after Kenny died, and you were with your mum, how much do you remember? she asked.

Not much, said Aysha.

Nor me, echoed Charly. They both had their Life-Story books in front of them, Aysha fingering hers restlessly, Charly's open on the floor by her feet.

Can you try and remember something?

We came into care, ventured Aysha.

Zoë were born, said Charly.

Yes, good, said Katy. Do you remember the first time you came into care, Aysha?

I remember one time it were just Charly and me. I think Zoë were a baby then or p'raps she weren't born yet.

I think there were two times when it was just the two of you, Katy said to them earnestly. One time before Zoë were born and another time when she were a little baby. Do you remember what happened?

Our mum were out of it with drugs, said Aysha with a peremptory shrug of her shoulders. It were me had to look after you, Charly, after Kenny died, nearly most of the time.

Yes, and how old were you then?

Five?

Yes, I think so. You should have been starting school. Do you remember starting, Aysha?

No.

I think you'll find the first time you went to school was when you were in a foster-home for the first time.

Oh my god, is that true, Katy?

I think so. D'you wanna write that in the book?

Why?

Well, we want to put something in from that time, don't we?

S'pose so.

Do I have to? asked Charly. There's no space in my book.

That's why you've got a separate bit of paper. It's up to you what you write down, but there is a gap of about three years in your story.

Not in mine, remonstrated Aysha.

That's because we've only just got to this bit. So you were in care, just for a few weeks, you were five, you started school. How old were you, Charly?

Two? suggested Charly, trying to work it out.

Yes. Nearly three by now, I think. So what happened when you went back home to your mum?

She had Zoë.

I don't think she had just yet.

No, I remember now, really I do. Aysha became some-what more animated. I remember Mum coming to take us from the foster-home and she had a fat belly, Zoë were in her belly, she got the both of us to feel the baby moving.

Was she on her own? asked Katy.

No, she were with that man, that Vic, and he had a car. An old car. But he stayed in the car and then drove us to her new flat.

OK, well write that in the book. And leave a space to draw a picture of the old car you went home in.

No way, Katy, I ain't doing a picture of that fucking car!

Why not?

Because, because ....

Aysha was agitated, unable to speak, close to tears. Katy had never seen her like this before.

I ain't putting this in the book, Katy.

No, ok, you don't need to. Putting what in?

The car .... Vic .... something between a whisper and a splutter.

What happened in the car?

He collected me from school.

Once? Twice?

Every day. Our mam couldn't.

Because of the baby?

Yeah. Or the drugs.

Was she back on the drugs?

Soon after the baby were born, yeah.

So Vic used to collect you from school?

Yeah. And take me. Only I wouldn't go.

Why?

Cos I were needed to look after Charly. And, cos of .... what he did.

He did things to you?

Yeah. And Charly.

What things?

Aysha could hardly speak. Bad things, she mumbled under her breath. Like touching and stuff, right.

In his car?

Yeah, but only coming home, right. He were sly, right, he knew if he did things going to school, the teachers would find out.

So every day you were at school, this happened on the way home?

Yeah, but sometimes I ran off before school so's I wouldn't have to go. But he still did things anyway, and he would hit me as well if I missed school. But if I were home I could stop him doing it with Charly, like this bad stuff. Or try to. But then he hit me even worse and I had to stay off school.

Because of bruises?

Yeah.

What did your mum do?

Nothing. She said I were making it up, like the touching bit, so I deserved a beating.

No wonder you don't wanna see her. What about the teachers?

Aysha hesitated. I think they knew. Cos I never wanted to go home with Vic. I wanted to go home, but not with him. I remember once a teacher took me home, but he used to shout at the teachers and, like, threaten them, so after that I had to go home with him, there weren't nothing they could do, right?

They could have contacted Social Services.

I think they did, in the end. Cos Charly and me were took back in care, and everyone had to go to court, and Vic went to prison.

Do you remember any of this, Charly?

The younger girl, silent all this time, shook her head.

You must have been three. Were you home the whole time, or did you go to nursery or childminder or anything?

I doesn't remember, muttered Charly.

I think Charly stayed home with Mum and Vic, said Aysha.

And Zoë?

Yeah.

And that time, Zoë didn't come into care?

She were only a tiny baby.

So, Aysha, you tried to protect Charly from the abuse?

Yeah. Aysha was becoming agitated again. But it were no good, like I just got hit worser.

Do you remember Aysha looking after you? said Katy, turning to Charly.

Yeah, said Charly. Right through, it were Aysha, not mum.

Well there, said Katy. I think you did your very best, Aysha, under appalling circumstances. Now listen, I'll tell you something about me when I was that age, five and six, right?

The girls stared.

Nothing really bad happened to me like happened to you. But when I were that age, my dad, my real dad, had gone off and left our mum on her own. And she got, like depressed, really bad, had to go in hospital a few times, I don't remember how many. And Sam, my older sister, used to look after me, right, even though we had our grandmother to help, it were Sam what looked after me. She were eleven then, or twelve, just starting high school, and I know how hard it were for her. I remember how she got in bad moods and shouted and used to throw her homework on the floor and I thought it were all my fault, but I know now it weren't. It's hard for kids when they have to take on responsibility and Sam did her best and it weren't no-one's fault, only my dad's for running off. But it were me five and Sam eleven. But with you, Aysha, you was five and six and you was the one doing the looking out for Charly, and no-one could expect you to do more than what you did. So you mustn't feel bad cos you did your best, right? Now we'll leave it there for tonight, and next time we'll talk about when you came back in care.

Now what about putting something in your books? she went on as the girls didn't move or speak. Cos it's really important to help you understand what's happened to you.

Could you write something, Katy? Aysha whispered. I can't do it myself, no way.

Yeah, ok, I'll do that.

Only write it on a bit of paper and show me first, right, before you puts it in the book.

OK. And you, Charly?

The same.

That night, Aysha had a nightmare. She screamed in her sleep and Katy had to go in to wake her up and calm her down, even though she knew Aysha hated her private space being invaded.

Aysha had switched off and was cold and hostile while Katy tried to soothe her back to sleep, but the next morning she was friendlier than normal towards her carer.

You came in my room, Katy, she said, as though not quite sure if she had been awake or dreaming.

Yeah, you were having a terrible nightmare.

Oh my god, were I really?

She didn't actually thank Katy, but the look she flashed her lifted Katy's heart more than any words could have done.

That Aysha's a funny kid, Sharon said to Steve. It was Sunday evening, Katy and the girls had caught the afternoon train back to Bursfield, and Steve had made a light salad supper for the two of them, as they'd all had a big cooked lunch together earlier.

They're all a bit strange, replied Steve.

Well, I know, Charly is, very - scowling and silent and so like a boy, but you never know what she's thinking, do you? That Zoë's the most normal. But at least with Aysha, she comes out with things. D'you know what she said to me?

No, said Steve, only half-interested, but more than willing to encourage his wife to talk. Sharon, he'd noticed, seemed to have gone into her shell quite a lot in recent weeks, and only the visits from her grandchildren or, this weekend, Katy and her girls, brought her out of it.

She was asking about Katy's dad. Rodney. Said she thought someone should help Katy find him. Sharon paused.

Is it any of her business? asked Steve. Aysha, I mean.

Sharon knew that Steve would be at the least lukewarm about the idea, which was why she'd resisted saying anything before. Coming from Aysha, it made it seem a safer topic, although Sharon could see this was, perhaps, feeble, cowardly, on her part.

Maybe not, she answered. But she did have a point.

Which was?

Well, Katy's been working hard at finding relatives and re-establishing contacts for all the girls. I don't know if you knew, but she took the two younger girls to visit their mother in prison, and last Sunday they had Charly's grandmother to lunch. And an uncle and aunt, apparently.

Yes, well, when you've got kids with no family contact .... said Steve.

Aysha was telling me that Katy talked about her first dad leaving and how Sam had to look after her when I got depressed, said Sharon.

Yeah, well. Steve remembered that scenario as if it were yesterday, but felt uncomfortable that Katy was now sharing it with 'outsiders'.

When did you and Aysha have this conversation? he added.

This morning, after breakfast. Aysha was up last, if you remember, and I kept her company while she finished her breakfast on her own. She certainly has an appetite, that one. Went on and on putting more slices in the toaster. And talking all the time. She seemed to think Katy was still missing her dad, and it was unfair that she should be putting in so much time finding her, Aysha's, and her sisters', relatives, when she needs someone to find her dad.

Does Katy even remember Rodney?

She must have some feeling of having lost him.

I thought it was Sam who was closest to him. Who missed him the most when he left.

Oh it was, for sure. But I think Sam worked through all that in her adolescence, you know, teenage rebellion as protest against the adults in her life, Rodney for abandoning her, me for getting depressed, you for taking the place of her real dad. And there again, Sam has a husband and kids now. But Katy never worked through any of this.

She never seemed to need to, said Steve. She always seemed very balanced to me.

Seemed, yes! But who knows what feelings are lurking underneath? And who does Katy have to confide in? No-one.

That's nonsense. There's you, me, Marcus, and most of all, Sam.

It used to be Sam, that's true. And there was that friend of hers, Sophie. But does she confide in either of us? Hardly at all, and not for some years, I would say. I don't think she's so close to Sam these days, either. From what Aysha says, she seems to be confiding more in her now.

Well, said Steve. Perhaps you could ask Aysha to tell Katy she should talk with us if she wants to start hunting for Rodney.

That's exactly what I did say to Aysha. Except that if anyone's gonna search for Rodney, it should be me. Katy has more than enough on her plate, as it is.

Well, if it's a serious idea, I'll do it. Most of it.

In some ways Steve would prefer to let things be, as far as family histories went. But he could sense Sharon's discomfort in raising this, and he wanted to try and ease things between them. If he were ever to reveal his own family secret, it would be better if some of these other matters were resolved. There seemed to be barriers between him and Sharon just now, nothing too much, just that they didn't seem to talk much like they'd just been doing. They steered away from personal matters, mostly.

As for Sharon, she found herself feeling relieved that she had finally aired what had been preying on her mind for some weeks, and that Steve had seemed quite supportive about it. She was quite amazed that Aysha had brought this up, and therefore given her the excuse for mentioning it. It looked as though the girl had been able to read her mind.

26. OUT OF THE FIRE

Katy continued doing the work with Aysha and Charly as best she could.

What d'you remember about the second time you were in foster-care? she asked them.

How old was we then?

You must have been six, Aysha, maybe nearly seven, and Charly four I guess.

Charly missed our mum, pronounced Aysha. Well, four years old you would, right?

Yes, said Katy. What about you?

Me? I didn't miss our mum. But I did miss my baby sister lots.

And I did, put in Charly, one of her few interventions.

I remember our mum coming to visit. And Charly cried all the time. And I said I hated the foster-parents. And mum said she'd stopped doing drugs and she weren't gonna have Vic back when he'd done his time, so she were gonna get us back off've Social Services. And she did. But she were still doing drugs, and she did have Vic back, and they moved us away and changed our names and put me in a new school where no-one knew what had happened before. And, like, everything started up again just like before.

Aysha clammed up very suddenly.

The abuse, you mean?

Yeah.

Why didn't you tell anyone?

Cos mum and dad, I mean Vic, said Charly and me's gonna be killed if I snitched. And I didn't want Charly to die, right. And if they killed me, then who's gonna look out for Charly and Zoë? And anyhow, who could we tell, I mean, it were a new place and we didn't know, like, no-one, yeah?

That must've felt awful.

Yeah, well, you know what, Katy, it's like it never happened. It's like a year missing in my life. I don't remember nothing 'bout it, right, Christmas, birthday, nothing. I don't remember the school or the shops or the street we lived in or nothing. Do you, Charly?

The younger girl shook her head.

So I don't know what you's gonna write down, Katy. I just kinda blanked my mind all that time.

Katy had agreed she would have to write down this part of their life-stories. No pictures, no photos, no graphic details, just an outline in Katy's careful script, with gentle, bland words.

I'll just put that this was a missing period in your lives.

Yeah, you do that, Katy.

You've been very brave to bring it out as much as you have. Do you remember how Social Services got you back into care?

Yeah, a social worker came with three police and bust down the front door and took us away. It were, like a real heavy scene with screaming and shouting and stuff.

Was that Ruth Barnes?

Yeah, and someone else from Social Services, I think. They brought us back to Bursfield.

Must've been awful, ventured Katy.

Aysha gave her familiar switching-off shrug. Not really, I didn't care what happened no more 's long as they weren't gonna leave either of my sisters with my mum or that fucking bastard she were living with, she said in a cold, hostile voice.

Katy knew she should break off here.

So next time we'll look at what happened when you were all three in foster-care, she said. Now, Charly, you've already got all this in your life-story book, so you don't need to carry on with it if you don't want.

But I ain't gonna do it unless Charly comes too, protested Aysha, suddenly animated again. I mean, she can help me remember, right?

Katy desisted from pointing out that so far it had been Aysha who had done virtually all the remembering.

But what about Zoë? She was part of this too. Perhaps we should include her from now on?

Aysha still had nightmares, one or two a week, but not with any pattern and not necessarily immediately after doing the work. Apart from this, the last weeks of term passed calmly. Charly and Aysha seemed to be making a real effort, Charly had been accepted at Aysha's school, Zoë had been accepted at the school next door to their home. Katy found and purchased a second-hand pair of binoculars for Charly, although Aysha seemed just as keen to use them. There was another choral concert at which Katy and Aysha were singing and the two younger girls were in the audience. At school, Aysha played drums at an impromptu rock concert at the end of afternoon school, the Friday before term ended. They continued to go running together, all four with Greg, or on country walks. The end of term was soon upon them, and Aysha was given a farewell lunch at her unit which she only attended with great reluctance. The trip to Scotland was approaching, and Katy arranged for her, Zoë and Greg a week at a caravan site in North Wales, and persuaded her sister to let Lara come along too - actually, no persuasion was needed.

They just had one more Life-Story session. Katy asked each of them, Zoë now also present, how much they remembered of the first foster-carers they were with when they were all three back in care. Now it was the two younger girls who remembered the details, the other children in the family, their names, what they were like, what they liked doing, that Ellie, the oldest girl, had a boyfriend, that Snowy was the family's pet cat, that there was a playroom in the cellar.

And what d'you remember, Aysha?

Nothing, the girl said. I hated it yeah? Foster-fucking-homes and school and the lot, all my life was like, total crap. You don't know what it were like, right, none of you. She turned to Katy. Charly and Zoë was happy, right, they was getting on good in that foster-home, but I weren't. I was like, total misery, everything in life was terrible, home, school, everything, and everyone, teachers, kids, foster-parents, social workers, you name it, had a fucking down on me. So all them people, they only had to say one word, they never even had to say a word, all they did were look at me and I would throw a fit, right, and scream and swear and lash out or pick a fight at school and no-one knew how to calm me down, and it were, like no-one knew cos there weren't no way they could.

She paused, and Charly and Zoë looked at Katy who didn't know what to say.

So what happened then? she ventured.

It just got worser. Like this whole load of crap just got

bigger. I started cutting my arms and I took some pills. And everyone started saying I gotta see a shrink and I wouldn't. That's when I started doing a runner. I bunked off from the foster-home and I got into being the school truant.

Where did you go?

Nowhere. I had no place to go and I still weren't happy but at least I were free, like wandering round the streets, yeah. It were like the best I could find of all the crappy places I could be. Out on the streets in the cold and the rain, but they told me that like eight years old or p'raps I were nearly nine they couldn't allow that cos it were dangerous and I were like vul - vunnel -

Vulnerable?

Aysha nodded.

Well you were, I'm sure.

Yeah, everyone said that, but thing was, Katy, I couldn't care less what happened to me, right, it didn't matter no more 's long as I were free. So I just kept bunking off, yeah. And later I met these other kids and started going round the estates and got into the gangs and took stuff and ran errands and hung around down the city centre and all that stuff I were into when you met me. And that were it, story of my life, right?

Well, you -

Oh yeah, I got suspended from school, more than once, I got moved foster-home, more than once, I got banged up in the nick, more than once. You can put all that in, Katy, but it don't matter a fuck to me, none of it, cos all you need to put is Aysha's life were crap right from the time Kenny died.

And is it all right now?

No, it ain't, Katy, and it won't never be, and that's what no-one ever understands, not even you, Katy, and that's why it's worse than useless going to a shrink, and you think talking 'bout it helps but it don't. And it don't matter what I do, like winning races at running or playing drums in a band, or getting GCSEs, or having a boyfriend, or camping in Scotland with Neil and Charly or taking Greg for walks, none of it takes the crap away or makes it any less or any better, all it does is not make it worse. Like all the stuff I were into, like going to a Secure Unit, that's what they told me, and that would make it worse, right? And if anyone asked me one year ago, or two years ago, or three years ago, or four years ago, what my life would be when I were thirteen and a half, then I'd've told them to fuck off, yeah, because all I could've thought were like life went from bad to worse and I would end up locked up, or else dead, ok, and if someone'd said that I would make friends with a girl at uni who had a dog and was into sports and music and me and my two sisters would go and live with her, then I would never've believed them, nor that I'd be in high school and running for the school and singing in the choir, oh my god! So what's happened now is the best that could've happened, and better than what I or anyone else could've thought would happen, but it still don't make it right, what I mean is, Katy, my life's still a load of crap and always will be, it's just like I've learned to hide it better, and that's what I've learned from you, right, like acting straight and doing good at things is better cos it gets people off your back.

When Aysha finally stopped Katy couldn't find anything to say. In the end she turned to the other two.

What d'you think about what Aysha's just said.

I think, said Zoë after a pause. That Aysha feels saddest cos she's the oldest.

That's right, yeah, added Charly. And she feels sad cos she thinks she should have stopped it happening to me. But Aysha, you couldn't have stopped it. There weren't nothing you could do.

Katy's heart went out to both of them, to all three, and knew she would write those words of theirs in Aysha's book tonight.

27. RESTLESS SPIRITS

Dark clouds swelled up over the shore, and the water looked blacker than the land. Night fell late in July in the west of Scotland, but this evening it had arrived early on a sudden snarl of wind which was causing boats in the bay to rattle their rigging loudly and all the trees along the roadside to emit a ceaseless moan. There was a strange clarity in the darkness in which well-defined outlines seemed larger than usual, and were moving, and colliding with one another until they eventually disappeared.

Watching out of his window, as he often did, Duncan Keith felt sensations familiar to him from the days when he used to drink heavily, but there was no alcohol in him now. There was, however, a nervousness which might, more than the wind and storm, have accounted for the sense of swaying, the strange combination of blurring and clarity.

Neil was due to arrive. That in itself would not have caused Duncan any anxiety beyond the mild thrill of anticipation associated with the need to keep getting to know his newly-found son, familiar to him now in some ways which were to do with their likeness to each other, but still awkward in other ways because of past histories unshared and difficulties talking about them. Neil had not stopped by as often as Duncan would have liked, and when he had done he had not stayed very long, he had carved out a life for himself in which Duncan was only a brief staging-post along a series of journeys, or expeditions rather, in which, Duncan sensed, a restless spirit was trying to reach fulfillment. If he judged right, then how well he understood, from his own past, that spiritual need.

And now Neil was visiting again, after more than a month, and was bringing two young girls with him. This was for Duncan so unexpected and so much of a deviation from the already difficult process of father-and-son bonding, that he felt a shiver of unpreparedness which was close to fear and caused him to mildly tremble. He had even thought of asking Neil not to call, until he realised how stupid this would have been, selfish, cowardly, and possibly threatening the embryonic relationship they had established. And now they might arrive in the middle of this sudden evening gale, and might need to stay more than one night if the wild weather took a hold for the rest of the week as the forecast suggested it could.

He watched the road across the loch, trying to identify the vehicles entering the village, but little was discernible other than their lights. There was plenty of space in Neil's large Volvo for two passengers and all the extra gear, but space in Duncan's cottage was at a premium. The girls would be sleeping in the small spare upstairs bedroom which, now, he had started to think of as Neil's, and Neil himself would be on the living-room floor. Everything was prepared, beds made up, extra supplies purchased, but Duncan didn't feel ready for this himself. He knew he should be, after all he had worked with kids for most of his adult life, and not just in the classroom either, and he had been a successful teacher without a doubt, with an innate ability to establish good rapport with his charges. However, the disintegration of his personal life as heavy drinking began to take its toll was mirrored by a marked diminution in his teaching abilities in the years that preceded his inevitable retirement. If his memories of children gravitated to those years as they always seemed to, then it made him nervous of facing children now. If he forced himself to think back to his early years as a teacher, the successful and popular field-trips, all the kids he had helped, to exam success and in other more personal ways, then it was Marie who stood out from the others as though she had a halo around her.

But Duncan found it impossible to fix his thoughts on Marie as she was then. Everything had changed with that letter and with his visits to Marie as she prepared to die. The innocence (or was it so?) of Marie as his academy pupil seemed more than one lifetime away. Now there was a grown-up son to contend with, and an additional family secret that Marie had, for some reason, entrusted him with. Why had she done that? It clearly had been important to her, and he liked to think that she had died more at peace because he had been there to hear her out, but he had no idea what he was supposed to do with this secret knowledge.

One other person knew, and it was possible that Marie would have wanted him to contact this Steve, who clearly knew about him and Neil, but might not know how much he, Duncan, now knew. But Duncan didn't know Steve, had not made the effort to locate him at the funeral, and Neil wasn't going to be any help, hardly seeming to know him either. But the problem was, as he realised from piecing together the complicated family strands, that these two girls knew Steve a great deal better than either Neil or himself did. All of which increased his sense of awkwardness, of unease, as he awaited their arrival, and whatever he tried to think about to divert his mind always led back to this.

And sure enough, just as his thoughts had come full circle, he heard the car draw up outside, and sounds of laughter mingled with mild panic got louder as rapid footsteps and impatient banging on his door announced the arrival of his visitors.

They entered the cottage in a burst of raindrops and sparks of colour and noise, and then were suddenly quiet and shy, a teenager looking cold in her skimpy clothes and bare midriff, and a younger girl more like a boy wrapped up against the night in a padded jacket and baseball cap. Neil followed behind, labouring with bags and cases.

Let me get you hot drinks, said Duncan. And food, do you want some food?

I'm sure we'd all like something to eat, said Neil. Duncan, this is Aysha. And Charly. Aysha doesn't drink tea or coffee.

Oh, what will you have to drink then?

Water's fine. Wasn't you at that funeral? The teenage girl was staring at him. Lara's grandma, what were she called?

Marie. Yes, I was there.

You went a long way.

Yes, well, she was a good friend of mine. And so is Neil.

And he's our friend too. Ain't he, Charly?

The younger girl nodded. Duncan busied himself getting drinks and a snack. He remembered Aysha now, even though she seemed to have grown physically in the few months since. That one's a livewire, he had thought then, and she still seemed now. He hoped Neil could handle her.

The younger girl kept her face down and her eyes averted nearly all the time, accepted her drink with diffidence and only a polite modicum of Duncan's food. But the older one kept staring quite brazenly at either Duncan or Neil, and took as much of the food as she could, tucking in with a relish, and making kind of funny faces at Neil as she ate.

What is it? Neil eventually asked.

You what?

What are those faces about?

I like it here, right?

You didn't when it thundered, Neil prompted.

Aysha hates thunder, added the younger sister. Don't you, Aysha?

The older girl, still stuffing food into her mouth, gave her sister a funny look now.

288

It's lightning I hates. She put an exaggerated stress on the word 'lightning'. And, like, there were one rumble and that were it.

It still got you scared though, remonstrated the younger girl, in self-justification.

Oh yeah, for about two seconds!

The forecast is for more gales and storms, said Duncan.

I heard it was going to improve, countered Neil.

Maybe in a couple of days, and then get worse again.

Well, this is July in the west of Scotland, d - Duncan, Neil went on. You don't expect settled weather. I've told you that, haven't I, you two?

Both girls nodded happily.

So how long do you think you'll stay? Duncan asked them. Wait another night or two until this system's passed over?

No, we'll be on our way tomorrow. We want to be on the morning boat the day after.

Where's that to?

Colonsay. Could be having clear skies and sunshine over there.

I wouldn't bank on it, said Duncan, trying not to let his disappointment show. Anyhow, you're welcome to stay on longer here.

This is the west of Scotland in July, Neil repeated. We have to take whatever weather hits us, don't we, girls? I have warned them, he added, turning to Duncan.

Well, I hope you girls have strong stomachs, if you're crossing the water in this weather, said Duncan. And I hope you've got warmer clothes to put on, he said, turning to the older girl, who in turn looked at Neil with a What's-he-going-on-at-me-for sort of expression on her face.

Don't worry, Aysha's got lots of warmer clothing and waterproofs with her, said Neil. She just doesn't like wearing them, do you, Aysha?

Only cos it's warm in your car, right, Neil?

What about you? Duncan asked the younger girl. Are you looking forward to this holiday?

She nodded her head, with both enthusiasm and un-certainty, it seemed.

Charly's the real wildlife enthusiast, prompted Neil.

Will you call here on the way back, then? asked Duncan. And tell me all about it.

Sure, yeah, we'll be fed up of sleeping in a tent by then, won't we, Charly? said Aysha. We'll want, like a warm bed'll be wicked then.

Wait til you've tried my beds. You don't know yet if they're warm or comfortable, said Duncan.

You might not have had a bath or shower for weeks, added Neil. We might not be in a fit state to sleep in my - I mean Duncan's cottage.

We'll swim in the sea, protested Aysha. You said we could.

I only said it was a possibility. If the weather's right, and other conditions.

What conditions?

Like the state of the tide, and the currents, and the temperature of the water.

Duncan drew back into himself, waiting for the girls to flake out, for his own chance to retire, the possibility of returning fresh to some communication with them, and with his elusive son, in the morning.

Aysha was enjoying the trip, so far anyway. However much she liked Katy, which she did loads, she still felt sometimes that Katy wanted something from her which she, Aysha, didn't have to give, even if she didn't know what it were, and didn't want to ask, and had only ever said anything to Katy once. If only Katy could find someone, she kept thinking, boyfriend, girlfriend, someone, it would let her, Aysha, have more freedom. Aysha was used to freedom, it were the most important thing to her, and living with Katy gave her more freedom that she'd ever had before but even so, she were used to a different sort of freedom, and now she were enjoying having a break from Katy. Being with Neil and Charly, going camping in the wilds, this was a whole different kind of freedom again.

Aysha thought over things like this to stop the nightmares coming back. She would like to talk to Charly, or to Neil, not about the nightmares, but about anything else to keep the nightmares away, but Neil and Charly didn't talk much, and if they did, only about wildlife. That weren't fair cos they both knew loads more than her 'bout wildlife and stuff like that. The only thing she could talk to Neil about was dogs.

Why couldn't we bring Greg with us? she'd complained to Neil on their way up to Scotland.

Couldn't handle a dog as well, said Neil.

But you's good with dogs, yeah?

Yes, but handling dogs and watching wildlife don't go together. Nor camping either.

Greg's very good. He wouldn't wander off.

All the same, he had to stay home with Katy and . . . your sister, said Neil, struggling to remember Zoë's name.

So the only dogs you likes is rescue dogs, right?

Mountain rescue, said Neil, emphasising the difference. But no, I do like other dogs. It's just that dogs can help a huge lot on a mountain rescue, but they're not helpful when you're trying to watch, or photograph, wildlife, when you need everyone to be silent. And still. I hope you both will be.

'Course we will. Charly knows that, don't you, Charly?

Charly nodded, which Aysha thought Neil might have seen in his mirror.

If Katy got mentioned, or the conversation lapsed, she crept back uninvited into Aysha's thoughts. She couldn't help it, it seemed odd not to be with her carer. Even worse was how she couldn't keep the life-story sessions from her thoughts, she wished she could, all that was over now, sometimes she regretted she'd ever said Katy could go over all that with her. She'd decided a long time ago that talking 'bout problems was useless, but then she thought Katy were different. Now Aysha weren't sure. She'd gone and mouthed off 'bout stuff, not just to Katy but her sisters too, and now she kept having terrible dreams. Everything she'd blanked off were back in her thoughts and she didn't like it.

That year she and Charly were sent back to their mum and Vic, it were true in one way that it were a big blank in her mind, everything 'bout it were just a blur. But in another way she could remember, and she'd not wanted to tell Katy, but now she wished she had.

What she could remember was how she hated Vic for what he'd done to her, but it were more than that. Vic hated her too cos it was her he blamed for being sent down. They both hated each other and they both knew they did. And Vic carried on doing things to her and hitting her and beating her up and keeping her shut in the house cos he hated her and he needed to have all the power. He wouldn't let her have the tiniest bit of power or freedom, and when you live in all that hate and things is being done to you all in hate and you ain't got any power at all to do anything 'bout it, then that were the most terrible thing for a kid. And the worst of all were how Vic and her mum had moved them away from Bursfield so there were nobody they trusted or places they knew that she could run away to if she ever decided to take the risk of leaving her two sisters for a few hours to get help for them. All of it filled Aysha with hate for the world, until Katy came along. Apart from her sisters there were no-one she didn't hate, not the kids on the estate or the drug-pushers and street-sleepers, certainly not the teachers or social workers or care workers what were s'posed to help her. Even after she got in with Katy, she still hated most people, even when Katy'd learned her to try and go along with them. Like Katy's sister Sam. She hated her, but she pretended not to cos she liked them two kids of hers. But the dad weren't so bad. Marcus. And this Neil were ok, he were like her and Charly, he didn't like people. Most men were horrible, evil, but there were some men were ok. Like Kenny, her dad. Neil were with her when she said good-bye to Kenny. And this old man were ok what they'd just stayed with. Duncan. Like Neil but older.

It were funny what Charly said. She never said much, but after they left the old man she said to Neil, Was that your dad?

And Aysha said. 'Course it's not his dad! His mum died and Katy and me went to the funeral, and his dad were already dead, they said so. Didn't they, Neil?

That's right. He died a few years ago, in the mountains. An accident. It was after that I decided to work for mountain rescue.

Why does they have dogs for mountain rescue?

Mostly because of their sense of smell. They can find missing climbers in snowdrifts, or in inaccessible gullies, where human rescuers couldn't find them.

But then, when they got to this port with boats they found the campsite and put their tents up, and they went to this café and had some chips. And then they went back to the camp-site and Neil brewed up mugs of tea for Charly and him and made cuppa-soup for her, and while they was just sitting there in the tents drinking, he told them.

He said it were something they must keep secret, Neil said "confidential" which Aysha knew meant they had to keep it secret. He told them that Duncan, the man they'd just met, was his real dad, but he'd only found out just before his mum died. He said soon as he met him, he knew. But it were a terrible thing, Neil said, to not never have known his real dad all the time he were growing up, and it were much harder getting to know him now.

If you ever have a child, said Neil. Or if I do, but I don't think I ever will, then you must make sure you never let that child grow up not knowing that it's your child.

And after that he shut up for the night and they got in their sleeping-bags and went to sleep, and Aysha didn't have a bad dream, at least not that she remembered.

28. DON'T STARE AT THE SUN

Katy locked up the house on the outskirts of Bursfield for the duration of the two girls' trip to Scotland. There was no real rea-son for Zoë and her to stay around, and while she didn't want to be a burden on her mum or Steve, she thought it would work best for her to be based in her home town. Zoë was moving to a new school, had said her goodbyes to friends at her old school and at the children's home, had no-one to play with in the summer holi-days apart from Lara and Liam. The caravan holiday and any day-trips could be undertaken from Longworth, and so too could a visit to Stella in prison, Katy deciding that to go with just the one child, while the other two were away, would work better. A visit to Phil and Ruth in Wolverhampton would have to wait for Charly's return.

The truth was that she was scared of how much she might miss Aysha. It would be much worse if she stayed in Burs-field, she was sure. She kept telling herself that it would be good for both of them to have a few weeks away from one another, but reminding herself of that did not fill the emptiness of life without her charge, who had become so much part of her life over the last nine months. What made it worse was that there was no fixed day for their return, about three weeks had been agreed, but she was going to have to rely on Neil to let her know by phone when he decided which day he would bring them back. Neil had a mobile, she had checked that, so she'd decided not to entrust Aysha or Charly with hers. Neil would let them use his if they needed to phone her for any reason, but of course it meant she couldn't phone Aysha, except through Neil, and she didn't want to do that.

She couldn't help worrying, wondering what they were up to. Charly she was less concerned about, partly because she still didn't know Charly well enough to have taken on her problems, but also because she knew Charly's interest in, enthusiasm for, the main activity of the trip, was genuine. But Aysha? Katy knew she needed to say something to Neil about the child, had seen the importance of it, and realised that would be almost impossible when he came to Bursfield to collect them, so she'd managed to speak to him on the phone after several attempts during the last few days of the girls' term.

She mentioned Aysha's nightmares, her burgeoning adolescence, her damaged fragility beneath her outward spiritedness. She asked Neil to be aware of the qualities he would need to show, care, understanding, responsibility. It seemed odd to be saying this to someone fifteen years her senior, but she wasn't sure how much experience of the world Neil had compared to her, although in all truth she had little compared to Aysha herself with her worldly-wise ways hiding all the pain and fear. But she couldn't be entirely sure how much of this Neil had taken in, he might have thought she was just a young woman fussing unduly.

Katy tormented herself over the work she had just done with Aysha, and the nightmares it appeared to have brought on. She wanted to help Aysha recover from the sexual abuse, not have it hanging over them both like a cloud, but it should have been someone else, she did not have the experience or skill. She had no idea whether to come out with the things she had come out with had helped Aysha or not, and even if it had, it was probably not a good time for it to happen with Katy not being around now to help her through any repercussions or find additional help if she needed it. It was unlikely that Neil would be able to offer what Aysha needed, although knowing Aysha, it would be someone like Neil she would turn to, if she couldn't turn to Katy. She would probably have to be dragged along kicking and screaming if she were ever to get help from a professional psychologist or psychiatrist. Katy could not help smiling as she thought how Aysha had latched onto Neil, someone who was about as far as it was possible to get from the systems of professional care, legal justice, and remedial education which had engulfed Aysha for most of her life. This perverseness was what Katy found so attractive.

However, she wasn't able to dwell on Aysha too much. Looking after two small children and a dog in a caravan and on the nearby beach gave her little chance to relax. Lara could be a handful when she chose, more than Zoë in fact. They did drop off to sleep quite early, compared with the older girls, but they constantly demanded her attention in waking hours. And Katy had course-work with her that she needed to get on with once she had the evenings to herself.

They splashed around in the sea, built sandcastles - huge ones a couple of times - played frisbee and ball games. Although Lara was a good walker for her age, and therefore giving Greg his walks was not a problem, both girls were reluctant to leave the beach unless it rained, which it only did once. So Greg ended up with most of his exercise on the sand. It was a lifeguard-patrolled beach and the four of them soon became familiar presences. A young male lifeguard seemed to be taking quite an interest, in Katy, they all hoped, much to the amusement of the two girls. He bought them drinks in the beach café at the end of his shift and clearly wanted to spend more of his free time with Katy. This was another problem she had to deal with.

His name was Gareth Rhys, he spoke with only a hint of a Welsh accent. He had a shaven head and a golden tan, a slim build and about the same height as her. She told him that Lara was her niece and Zoë the younger sister of her friend, she could not face referring to her as a foster-child. It was accurate enough. It turned out he was at Uni. also, Bangor in his case, and had just finished his second year. His family lived at Denbigh. When she needed to replenish supplies on their last-but-one day, he drove them into Rhyl, took them to the best supermarket according to him. She would have loved to have given him the caravan key, trusted the girls and shopping to his care and run back along the sand with Greg but she didn't dare, didn't know him well enough, it was too much of a responsibility. She did invite him back for a meal and a cup of coffee on their last night in the caravan. She hoped he wouldn't misread this, but was fairly confident she could handle it, what with the girls asleep the other side of a thin partition and Greg by her feet.

It wasn't much of a meal, she'd only been buying the basics this week. Spaghetti and something out of a tin, the girls had had the same earlier. But they did talk, on and on into the night, that he was on the rebound from a relationship with a student in his year who'd broken up with him just before term ended. She told him she was still a virgin, had never had a serious boyfriend, was unsure about her sexuality, and she told him about Sophie. And Aysha. Perhaps that was a mistake, it seemed to be understood that some physical contact between them, some sexual exploration, should follow.

But Katy knew she must not lose control, not let it go all the way. In the end, she felt, it had not satisfied either of them, Gareth left frustrated, herself tempted, interested, but no nearer having an answer to her dilemma. They did, however, exchange addresses and phone numbers and promised to keep in touch.

Katy texted Sophie on the train journey back to Longworth, when Lara fell asleep and she persuaded Zoë to read a book. She knew Sophie was into boys now, or rather one boy in particular. She wrote to Sophie every month or so, texted her if the news was more urgent or exciting, received letters or texts back. She wished her old friend, with or without the current boyfriend in tow, would visit her and meet her new friend, maybe Aysha would not then think of her as such a solitary person.

After they were back in her home town, Katy tried to get back to how it had been before between Sam and her. She had Lara and Liam up at her mum's house, or babysat them at theirs, to give Sam some free time, and she tried to talk to Sam, to reassure her about the three girls, reported on their progress. But it was Zoë who nearly scuppered these plans, and made Katy realise that the youngest of the three girls also had her problems and her needs, and could not be relied on to play the docile helper as she had been up to now.

It started with a day-trip. Steve offered to drive Katy and her niece and nephew, and Zoë, to Anglezarke Reservoir for a picnic. The kids were excited, and helped Katy pack the car while Steve saw to Sharon, made sure she had everything she might need for the few hours on her own.

Lara and Zoë jumped into the back seat when everything had been packed, but Zoë sat sideways with her feet on the seat and wouldn't allow any space for Liam. The small boy got upset and started crying, while Katy became more and more annoyed with the tight-lipped, obstinate Zoë.

Having physically forced Zoë to give way, and with Liam finally in the car, Katy sat down herself in the front passenger seat and turned round again to find Zoë attempting to push Liam away from her, to squeeze him against the side of the car.

What is all this about? she said to the three children crossly. She'd very rarely lost her temper with any of them but was close to it now.

Zoë's gotta sit between me and Ambrose, said Lara eventually, in a somewhat weary tone.

Who's Ambrose?

He's Zoë's friend. Only he ain't a real boy.

He is real! He's just invisible, protested Zoë.

Zoë's invented him, concluded Lara dismissively.

I won't be your friend then, said Zoë to Lara, manipulatively.

You has to include my little brother, said Lara in response. It can't be just us and Ambrose like at the caravan cos Liam's here as well. And Liam's a real boy, so he's gotta have a seat in the car.

Lara's right, said Katy very firmly, and she kept a very close eye on the back seat while they waited for Steve and throughout the journey, and when they arrived she watched all of them when they were playing and actively involved herself in their games to make sure that Liam was included, and there was no further trouble that day.

Katy knew she needed to talk to Zoë about this, but the visit to Stella in prison was only a few days off, so she decided to wait until that hurdle had been surmounted rather than have a confrontation just before they went. Meanwhile Lara, after having got on so well with Zoë at the caravan, made it clear that her loyalties were with her brother, and with Aysha, whom she constantly compared Zoë unfavourably with. In turn Zoë blamed Liam for turning his older sister against her, so that whenever those two children were in the same room there was a poisonous atmosphere, emanating almost entirely from the older child - Liam being the unwitting victim - and it took all of Katy's effort, skill, and close attention to prevent violence erupting. It was in some ways a relief, when the day of the prison visit arrived, to get on the train for the long journey east and have just Zoë on her own. The child was no trouble on the trip to see her mother, or at the prison itself. In fact it was the best visit there'd been yet. Child and mother enjoyed each other's company, and Stella was full of gratitude towards Katy. Well that's one thing I've got right this holiday, she thought as they took the short bus ride from the prison gates to the station, going with Zoë on her own, and with a very reasonable explanation concerning the other two. She wished she could be as confident about everything else since the summer holiday started. The week in the caravan, Zoë drawing Lara into some sort of exclusive, collusive twosome, it seemed. And that guy, Gareth, distracting Katy just when it seemed she should have kept her attention on the two girls. Zoë now hating Liam. And, in the background, how were the two older girls getting on? Aysha, most of all?

She decided she and Zoë might need to return to Bursfield. But first she would try and talk to Zoë - about her pretend friend, about Lara and Liam. It was so important that her new charges should get on well with her nephew and niece. That had been one of the really heartening things about Aysha. They got to the station with only a minute before their train came in. And once they settled in their seats, Zoë promptly fell asleep. Despite having to change trains twice, she slept almost all the way back to Longworth, so the talking was going to have to wait.

29. BITTEN BY THE NIGHT

Charly loved the boats. So did Aysha, even more than her perhaps. Crossing to the islands on a rough sea, with the sun beginning to peep through the clouds after the storm. After that first ferry ride the sea were calmer, but they still liked it. They neither of them had been on a boat on the sea before.

Charly stayed by Neil. He kept looking out to sea with his binoculars and Charly did too. He told her what all the birds was. That big white one's a gannet, watch to see if it dives in. Those little ones on the water are guillemots. That grey one's a fulmar, flying low, nearly touching the waves. If you see a black and white bird doing that, it's a manx shearwater. There was big gulls, medium gulls and little ones called terns. The terns dived in too like the gannets, from the air. The little birds what sat on the sea and then dived was puffins or guillemots or razorbills. If they was swimming on their own near the harbours or rocks they was black guillemots, they had red beaks and feet and a little patch of white on their wing. The big black birds called cormorants and shags dived in too. Aysha thought that birds called shags was a hoot. She thought Neil were having her on. When she found he wasn't, she announced shags was her favourite, but Charly thought they was the ugliest birds she saw. Oh look there's a shag, Aysha would say real loud, showing off, when anyone could have told her it were a seagull. Aysha could be like just so immature sometimes, it made Charly feel grown up. Aysha would quickly get bored looking out to sea, and would wander round the ship and then come back. She never sat down except to eat her lunch. This is just so awesome, she kept saying but because she couldn't stay still, she missed seeing the dolphins. Charly thought it would be terrible to have missed the dolphins but Aysha didn't seem to mind.

Wow, that's so awesome, she said, pleased for Charly.

The first island they left the car behind at Oban. A landrover came and fetched them and their camping-gear and other stuff from the pier. The driver of the land-rover knew Neil. Neil said they was gonna cross over the sands at low tide and camp on another island, which was why they needed to go by landrover. It were high tide so they had to wait. The driver took them to another place by the sea. It were a good place to watch for sea otters, Neil said. They sat on some grass looking over a bay with rock-pools and rocks what was covered by dark brown seaweed. They kept watching for ages and it got warmer. Aysha half stripped off and lay on her back sunbathing with her eyes closed. Then Neil and the other man heard something. They got up and scrambled across the grassy slope, Neil with his telescope and camera, the other man watching with binoculars. They waved Charly to follow and she did. On a grassy field covered in flowers sat a small bird singing on a waving stalk. Neil got his telescope on it and Charly could see it clear. It weren't singing like any other bird, it made a kinda fast high-pitched rattle.

That's a grasshopper warbler, said Neil. We're very lucky, they're very rare birds and they don't usually sing this late in the summer. What does the sound remind you of?

Charly weren't sure. A grasshopper? she said, doubtfully.

Quite right, said Neil. That's how it got its name. But it's also like the sound of a fishing reel being wound in, don't you think?

I never done fishing, said Charly.

Nor me neither, said Neil.

It's a young bird, I think, said the other man. They must have bred successfully somewhere near here. It thinks it's grown up, it's showing off, like teenagers today making out they're adult.

Like my sister, said Charly, and wished she hadn't, because Aysha was calling urgently.

Neil! Charly! Come here!

They rushed back quick as they could to where they'd left her.

Look! She pointed to a movement, a slithering among the seaweed.

There's your otter, said the man.

Aysha were fascinated and acted like she wanted to go play with it, like it were some kind of dog. As she got up to go nearer, Neil grabbed her arm.

Don't go any nearer, stay here. They're very shy and we might frighten it away.

I'm surprised it hasn't gone already, said the other man.

What with the shouting and us running back.

Charly watched it for ages, but then so did Aysha.

I saw it first, Neil, she said when they finally went back to the land-rover. Lots of the time she were like a little kid, proud and excited and happy.

But Charly was taking it all in, and taking it seriously too. They crossed the wet sand in the land-rover and put their tents up by the shore. Neil put his telescope up pointing out to sea and watched with his binoculars.

What's you looking at? queried Aysha, trying to show interest, Charly thought.

Checking if anything's around, on the sea. Do either of you know what we might see, round here?

Shags! Aysha were still obsessed.

No, not here. Charly?

Dolphins?

Possibly, but not very likely. No, ducks and divers is what I'm looking for.

Like gannets? said Charly. Or terns?

Could be both. Gannets will be further out. But there are birds <u>called</u> divers. They're a bit like cormorants but paler and smaller, more like the size of a duck. There are three types, red-throated, black-throated and great-northern. Great-northern is bigger than the other two, more like the size of a goose. But they're quite rare. What you're more likely to see, close in to shore, are one of two types of ducks, eider or merganser.

What are they like?

Eiders are big and quite plump, the males are mostly white with a bit of black, but this time of year you're more likely just to see the females with their young, and they're brown. They might be in quite big family groups, but the mergansers usually hang around in twos unless they've still got young. They've got dark heads and are slimmer than the eiders.

You may also see some wading birds down on the sand there, Neil went on. Waders spend their time on the shores and on estuaries and mud-flats. You might see a biggish wader with a red bill called an oyster-catcher, or smaller ones called ringed plover or dunlin. Watch for another otter down there too. But what we really are looking for here is a very special bird that breeds in the grass the other side of that fence, called a corncrake. We'll go looking in the evening, after we've eaten. And Neil went off to get them some food.

The two girls watched the sea and the shore, guarding the telescope and Neil's binoculars. Some gulls flew past and a crow. No otter, not even a shag. The wind was getting up and it started to cool down. Aysha shivered.

Bugger this, I'm frozen.

Well, put something else on then.

Nah, I'll go and help Neil. She drifted back to the tent.

Charly stayed watching. Suddenly she saw three birds on the water, a little way out. They sat on the water only for a few seconds, then dived, one, two, three. She kept watching. The same thing happened, only in a different place. One, two, three. Were they the same birds? They must be divers, she thought. She called out.

Neil, come and look at these divers!

He came out from the tents. Have you got the telescope on them?

No, I can't work it! But she had seen the birds in his binoculars, which she now handed to him, pointing to near the shore. They keep diving and coming up somewhere else!

Yes, diving birds do that. Impossible to get the telescope on them for more than a second. He studied them for a minute or so, adjusting the instruments as the birds reappeared.

Mergansers, he said finally. Easily mistaken for divers. Just as worthwhile seeing, though not quite as rare. Beautiful ducks, one of the finest. Tiny tuft on the top of the head. Female and two young. The male is more striking, but the female is beautiful too. Good sighting. There's also an oyster-catcher just flown onto a rock very near them. He pointed it out, and said, I'll go back to the food so that Aysha can see them.

Aysha sauntered over, mildly interested but hardly bothering to show it.

So it's only some ducks.

Mergansers, Charly corrected. And there's an oyster-catcher too.

Where?

On that rock, look.

I'm never gonna remember all the names.

I will.

Good for you. I'm gonna help cook, while you watch wildlife. It ain't so cold by the tents.

She pranced back to the tent like a frisky horse, swinging her arms around.

After the meal Charly and Neil went looking for corncrakes. Aysha switched her stereo on, put her earplugs in and stayed in the tent, lying on her sleeping-bag. Charly could hear the croaking of the corncrakes everywhere, but even with Neil's help couldn't get sight of one. She could still hear them back at the tent when it were nearly dark and past her bedtime. Only when it were totally dark they stopped their croaking and she fell asleep.

They stayed on that island a few days. One day a wind got up and it poured with rain most of the day and they had to stay in the tents. Another day Neil borrowed the land-rover and drove across the sands with the two of them in the front beside him, and they drove round the rest of the island. They saw golden eagles and black birds with red bills called choughs, and some wading-birds, one small and brown called a common sandpiper which flew off with high-pitched alarm calls, another oyster-catcher and a few lapwings flying above the fields. They went back to the place they'd seen the otter and the grasshopper warbler but they couldn't find them again. Then they went to the shop near the pier to stock up with more food. There were only the one shop on the island. Aysha went in to get the food they needed while Neil and her watched a black guillemot swimming near the pier. Neil got the telescope out and she got a really great view of it - she were getting used to the telescope now.

Aysha were beginning to help Neil a lot with the cooking and breakfasts and shopping and stuff. Charly were more than a bit surprised cos Aysha'd never shown much enthusiasm for shopping before, even though the two of them shopped regular at the supermarket in Bursfield and, Charly knew, Katy used to take Aysha when it were just the two of them. But still, seeing as Aysha weren't into wildlife so much as her, it seemed good of her to help so's Neil could spend more time watching with Charly. What did bother her a bit more was how, after the rainy day had gone and the sun came out more and it got warmer, Aysha got to stripping down to her bikini and just wanted to sunbathe by the tent listening to music instead of looking for corncrakes like Neil and her. Aysha tried looking for corncrakes once and said it were boring cos all you did was hear them and never see them. This was true in a way. Neil and Charly looked lots of times near where they camped and in another place the day he had the land-rover, but they never saw one. Instead Neil told her the names of butterflies and wildflowers.

They went back to Oban and got the boat to a different island. Two islands next to each other. This time Neil took his own car and drove to where they camped. Like the last place, it were near a kinda big house, a hostel or nature centre, where there was toilets and water and stuff. It were by a beach. By now it was staying warm and Aysha, as well as helping with cooking and stuff, and staying by the tents, wanted to swim a lot. The sea were still a bit rough. Charly and Neil weren't so keen.

But we gotta swim to keep clean.

There's a wash-room in the centre over there.

Yeah, I know, but it's manky and gross. The sea's miles better.

But I need to make sure you're safe, said Neil. Are you a strong swimmer?

Yeah.

How many lengths can you swim?

I never goes in the pool back home.

Why not?

Cos of this. The scratches on Aysha's arms were hardly visible any more, but she went right up to Neil and put her bare arm close to his face so he could see the faint scars. Charly hated the way she did that.

When did you get those?

I were always cutting myself. But not since I moved in with Katy.

So how did you learn to swim?

I just did. When I were a little kid.

Can you swim, Charly?

Yeah, but I don't like the pool either.

Have you seen Aysha swim?

Not for ages.

Well, you can only go in when we're there to watch, Aysha.

That's not fair. I wanna swim while you two's birdwatching.

Well, we can bird-watch by the beach sometimes. And it is true, we will all need to bathe in the sea to keep clean if there are no showers nearby.

So Aysha swam while Charly and Neil watched. But Charly knew that when they went off to watch wildlife, Aysha was going in the sea. She was always back by the tents when they returned, but Charly knew. She wondered if Neil knew too, but she said nothing.

Sometimes Aysha came with them. They stopped in the village, and dropped her off to go in a café and do some shopping and just wander about. They went to look for red-throated divers on little lakes that Neil said were called "lochans", and they saw two swimming so quiet you hardly knew they was there, and they saw big fast aggressive birds called skuas flying over. Neil were pleased to see these birds, he said you had to come to the Scottish islands to find them. But still no corncrakes showed up. Aysha was always there in the village waiting when they got back.

Halfway through the expedition, Neil felt reasonably content. At times he wondered why he had let himself in for this, because it was hard work for him, being with two youngsters, he wasn't that used to being with people at all, and when he was, it was usually adults rather like him, somewhat solitary and with similar interests and enthusiasms. And girls, too, well, the female of the species had always been a closed book to him, one he had never dared open. But he felt glad, even proud, he had taken it on, it was only two and a half weeks, three at the most, after all, and Katy had the responsibility of these girls all the time.

Charly's interest and enthusiasm was the most gratifying factor. Neil felt there was a kinship between him and her, more than just the shared passion for wildlife, something more meaningful and deeper. Much stronger than the link he'd once felt with Aysha, that time they'd walked her dog, or Katy's dog rather, after his mother's cremation. Aysha was odd, but in a way he couldn't quite work out, whereas Charly's oddness chimed with his own, she could have been his child, and if he ever had a child, his hopes for that child would be modelled on her. She was so willing, so keen to learn, absorbing all he could tell her.

Aysha wasn't like that, but he had to admit, she'd presented no problems either, which considering her background - and Neil was only just beginning to realise just how troubled her background was - he felt gratified about also, and with a hint of pride. She was helpful, and willing, in all aspects of the trip apart from the most important one, the wildlife discovery. But she wasn't hanging around them all the time trying to distract them, no, she was happy, it appeared, spending time on her own, whether by the tent, on the beaches, or in the few inhabited places they called at when they needed more supplies. Of course Neil hadn't been quite sure if he should leave her on her own for any length of time but she wasn't a little kid even if Katy had called her a vulnerable one, she herself seemed happy to spend the odd hour or two on her own, and, most importantly, these were some of the safest places in the British Isles, nothing much could happen to her unless it was of her own doing. He'd had that nagging doubt about Aysha, what she might get up to if unsupervised, but he'd tried it out and it seemed ok, apart from the fact that he was pretty sure she'd bought the odd pack of cigarettes, and with his money probably, and had a smoke or two when she'd been left on her own. But as far as he could tell, she wasn't coming to any harm, or doing any, and, it seemed, she was almost as happy as her sister despite not sharing their interest.

Conversation, that was hard work, that was when he sometimes asked himself if he was cut out for this. Neil was, he knew, lacking the usual social abilities, including conversation. Charly didn't mind at all, she was like him, all she wanted to do was look at, learn about, talk about, wildlife. But Aysha, he thought, would have liked to talk more, and the fact that most of the talk was about wildlife, and she, he suspected, wanted a different sort of communication, perhaps that was why she sought her own company, time apart from them, every now and again. Neil had thought about this, and decided that the evenings in or beside their tents ought to be more interesting for Aysha. To begin with, the evening light lingered so long that he and Charly could look for birds and otters - it was the best time of day - right up to her bed-time. But this was a bit unfair on Aysha, he realised. The nights were drawing in a little more now, so maybe when they got to Mull, with its woodland and forestry, they could make a campfire, or even before they got to Mull if they could find driftwood on a beach nearby. And attempt to talk, tell stories about their lives. Dogs was an interest they all three shared, Neil suddenly remembered. So one evening on Tiree, Neil raised the subject of dogs, and sensing Aysha's enthusiastic response, tried to get everyone telling their real-life dog stories.

You tell us 'bout the rescues, said Aysha, perking up. The ones the dogs did.

It's in the mist they're at their most essential, he started off. There's a mountain called Sca Fell, one of the really high ones. It's easy grassy walking to get up from the west or the south, but on the north and east sides it's sheer crags with lots of difficult gullies. Two climbers went up one of these but just as they reached the top the mist came down. They intended to come down by a route called Lords Rake, but they missed the entrance to that way down and ended up in an impossible gully. One of them fell, the other got stuck. He couldn't see where his companion was, couldn't hear him, and their mobile was in the pack of the one who fell. In the end he managed to scramble his way up to the top again, and found his way down the grass to Wasdale Head, from where they called us. Well, it's a long way from Grasmere to Wasdale Head, and we needed to find the missing man as soon as we could, so we went to another valley called Eskdale and made our way, with two of the dogs, up the mountain from there. We didn't have a lot to go on, the man who'd raised the alarm was exhausted and confused about location, we had nothing belonging to the missing climber, we had no idea how far he'd fallen and whether he'd be more easily located from the top of the mountain or the bottom of the crags. We had to rely entirely on the dogs, see if they could pick up his scent after nearly three hours. So we went to the top, and they did find a scent, and they led us to the missing man.

Was he OK?

No, he wasn't, but he did survive. He was badly injured and unconscious. But even after the dogs found him, it was a nightmare trying to get him out from there. It was getting near dark, and still misty, but we couldn't risk leaving him there until daylight. We couldn't lift the man out, at least not without a whole platoon of soldiers, so we called for a helicopter and paramedics. It was almost impossible terrain and conditions for a helicopter, and even with our experience of rescue, we couldn't be sure whether we should guide the copter in from above or below. In the end we left one dog guarding the injured climber while I took the other dog down the side of the mountain and up to Mickledore, the rocky col below the crags. My colleague stayed at the top. Well, the helicopter came close by where I was, and with my powerful torch I was able to wave him in closer. With the barking of the dogs to guide, the helicopter was able to get an arc-light onto the spot where the man was lying. Even after that, it was difficult, but there were paramedics on board, so as long as they could winch him on board before he snuffed it, he was ok.

Neil paused. Aysha stared at him, while Charly looked down at her feet.

Wow, when did that happen, Neil?

About two years ago, I think.

Are they all like that?

No, that was one of the hardest. Perhaps I shouldn't have started with that one, the others might seem tame now.

No way! said Aysha, all fired up. You must tell us more!

Well, another evening. No more than one a day, or I'll run out. You tell us about your dog, now.

My dog? You mean Katy's dog, Greg.

Yes, of course. Sorry.

No, it's ok, but there ain't much to tell. Aysha started telling Neil about the first time she'd taken Greg for a walk on her own, but she soon petered out.It's boring compared with you.

No, it's not. It's interesting.

You're only saying that. Anyhow, Charly's nearly asleep.

He felt the need to engage Aysha, and this seemed to be doing the trick. They were on Tiree, paradise for a bird enthusiast, which Aysha wasn't. But they saw quite a few seals at the north end of the island, and that did captivate the older girl. She spent hours watching them crawling on and off the flat rocks, bobbing around in the sea nearby, while Neil occupied himself getting photographs of arctic terns, purple sandpipers and twite, which he thought might be less interesting to the beginners, but he misread Charly who moved between Aysha and the seals, and him with his equipment, keen to discover what he had seen.

It was windy on Tiree, and showery for the first two days, but then the wind dropped a little, the sun stayed out, it got warmer, and Aysha, forgetting about the seals, wanted to swim and sunbathe. They'd camped just above a wide sandy bay, so they left her guarding the tent and looked for corncrakes again.

They saw little terns plunging down into the sea, as well as gannets, and there were waders everywhere on Tiree, running on the rocks and the beaches, flying up from the machair-land with their shrill, anxious calls. Those that had bred were still around, but were augmented by birds passing through from further north, or even the first ones returning that wintered on the island. Neil taught Charly to distinguish the different species from their habitat, their calls, and their breeding and migrating patterns, as well as by sight.

After he'd told the second mountain-rescue story, Aysha asked him if women could do it as well as men.

I don't see why not, he answered. As long as they were fit and strong and didn't mind the unsocial hours.

What's that?

Unsocial hours? It means a lot of the work is in the evening or during the night or at weekends.

Well, that's ok, said Aysha. See, I think I wanna do mountain rescue. D'you get paid?

I'm afraid not. Just a small allowance.

What's an allowance?

Just a bit of money to cover your expenses - cost of petrol from your home to the rescue centre, and your meals while you're on call - you've got to keep well fed, because you could be out all night.

Well, I'd be all right at it, don't you think, Neil? I'm a good runner, I'm strong, and I'm good with dogs.

But there's one other quality you'll need.

What's that?

Experience of the mountains, sometimes called mountain-craft. Have you got any?

Nah, I'll have to learn me that. Can you teach me?

Well, some things like map-reading can be taught, a bit at least. But there's nothing like experience, getting out in the mountains on your own, or with someone more experienced, in all weathers, and learning the best ways of coping with the different conditions.

Could I come and stay with you, and join in a rescue, like just to learn from it?

When you're a bit older, and have a lot more experience in the mountains, then yes.

But how do I get the experience, right?

You'll need to go camping with some friends, or on your own. Or stay at youth hostels in the mountain areas, there's lots of hostels. But there's one thing I can suggest now.

What's that?

Well, we've got one more island to camp on, and that's Mull. It's much bigger than the others we've stayed on, and it's got mountains on it. Proper mountains. It also has buses. So I was going to suggest that we leave the car in Oban again and we do proper backpacking on Mull, carrying all our gear with us. And that could include going into the mountains and camping one night there, or possibly two. Real wild camping that would be. Are you on for that?

Yeah! they both responded, echoing each other.

But it will be hard work. You'll both have to carry heavy packs. You'll have to carry one of the tents, Aysha, I can only manage one. I'll take the stove and water, but you'll have to take your own sleeping-bags and a share of the food. But it will be good experience in the mountains.

Will there be animals and birds?

We should see some new birds, possibly some quite rare and exciting ones. And maybe deer and hares.

What d'you think, Charly? Are you on for that?

Sure am, said Charly.

Me too, said Aysha.

Before they left Tiree, Charly and he did finally get to see a corncrake. It was moving slowly and secretively in a ditch almost covered with vegetation about five yards from the track they were walking on. Neil got the telescope on it, let Charly have a good view before it moved into thicker cover.

Now that is a rare sighting, he told her.

And then on the boat from Tiree, they watched endless Manx Shearwaters flying parallel with the boat, some of them quite close. Initially Neil had to point them out, help Charly identify them.

They turn and glide, and you see their long black wings. Very graceful, sometimes almost touching the water. Look, there's one! And another!

In fact, there were thousands, a continuous stream, passing the boat, effortlessly fast. Even Aysha seemed fascinated by the sight. She and Charly stood together for ages, pointing them out as they went past, There's one! There! And another! And there, look! until finally Aysha grew tired and wandered off to a different deck, to have a surreptitious cigarette, Neil thought.

On arriving on Mull, the three of them with their heavy packs caught a bus to the far south-west corner and camped there. They took boat trips over to Iona, and to Staffa to see the last remaining puffins, many of them having departed out to sea. There were still some puffins on the waters close to the island, among other seabirds, but they found one on the island, still guarding its burrow, and they got close up with a good view in the binoculars - Neil had left his telescope hidden under blankets in his Volvo. Aysha as well as Charly was fascinated to see the puffin, which took over from shag as the bird she most liked to refer to.

Mull was where the three of them stayed together, worked together, shared the load. The good weather continued and Neil's confidence grew. The wild camping was next, the bus dropped them at a lonely spot at the foot of the mountains, and they set off with their heavy packs over rough ground towards a valley where they could see a stream tumbling down from the peaks. Neil said they would set up camp about half-way up, spread the climb over two days.

Aysha asked if they'd be camping up at the top of the mountain.

Near the top, he replied. We'll take most of tomorrow getting up the top, and we'll walk around the mountain-tops for a couple of hours, and then set off down for about an hour before we camp again.

Charly wanted to know what birds to look out for.

Look out for any birds you can. Tell me if you see any-thing, and I'll tell you if I do. But especially watch the sky, be-cause we're particularly looking for birds of prey like golden eagles and peregrine falcons, and the weather conditions are just right.

It was slow going, but the girls plodded on gamely. They saw some deer on the skyline, and for Charly the ordeal was brightened when she spotted a large bird in the sky, a buzzard, it turned out to be, but the first one they'd seen on their trip. Later they saw hen harrier, merlin, golden eagle.

They found a grassy place by the stream to pitch their tents. Neil told them the water he was carrying in a large flask was for drinking cold only. For cups of tea, cooking and washing, the water had to be taken from the stream. That was exciting, but of more concern, and a little embarrassment to Aysha and Charly, was the instruction to find a large rock to hide behind when they needed the toilet.

It did not seem to him unexpected that Charly's enthusiasm should be sustained, but he kept waiting for, dreading, the point where Aysha would become fed up, especially now with her heavier load - the second tent - than the younger girl, but her willingness astounded him. She seemed to have become more helpful, more mature, more willing, since the expedition started. And he was able to begin telling her something of his knowledge of mountains, the respect you needed to show them, and to begin helping her learn to map-read, so that whenever they paused to rest their load, he would bring his map out, and point out the various visible features and how they showed up on the map. Charly took an interest in this as well.

But still Aysha perturbed him. The way she flaunted herself around the place, wearing so little. The way she'd insisted on packing her stereo and earplugs even on the crossing to Mull, when space in the packs, and weight, was at such a premium. OK, he knew she liked to listen to her music, but couldn't she have gone without for a few days? And, helping her pack, he'd noticed she'd squeezed in a small pack of cigarettes, he hadn't made a fuss about any of this, and indeed he didn't think she'd smoked since they landed on Mull, since the one she'd sneaked off for on the boat over. But what did concern him most was when she started trying to come into his tent in the night, lonely, frightened, sleepless, scared of bad dreams. He had to send her back, firmly, quietly, not wanting to make a fuss about this either, and hating to have to seem so rejecting.

He related a different mountain rescue incident each evening, but omitted those where one of the casualties had died.

So far, he told them the first night they camped in the mountains. So far, I've told you about rescues where the dogs have helped to find injured climbers, or walkers. But this story's a bit different. Sometimes we get a call when a walker's gone missing. Usually they've gone walking in the mountains on their own, and maybe the mist's come down, and they've got lost. Now since I started doing the rescues, it doesn't happen anything like as much as it used to. Can you think why?

The girls looked puzzled, and shook their heads.

Well, it's because of the mobile phone. Most people heading into the mountains take a mobile with them, and if they get lost they can call someone to let them know. Sometimes we're still needed, and the dogs are needed, but it happens a lot less often that it's just someone getting lost, and it's usually quite easy then. The difficult ones are heart attacks or injuries, especially injuries.

However, he went on, we had one very difficult rescue Easter of last year. This middle-aged guy had set off to do the Fairfield Horseshoe - that's a walk you can do from Grasmere, but it's a tough one - while his wife and two teenage daughters had gone shopping in Keswick. He hadn't taken a mobile, but otherwise he was well equipped, map, compass, warm clothing, waterproofs, plenty of food and drink. Not a situation where you'd expect any worries. When he was on the top the mist came down very suddenly and he got disorientated. He tried to make his way down off the top by the route he'd planned, but he ended going down in the wrong direction, either his compass wasn't working or he hadn't used it correctly. He lost the path, and when he finally came out of the mist, he realised something was wrong. What he should have done in that situation was to continue on down until he came to a cottage or a farmhouse, and then found out where he was and called someone to collect him. But he made the mistake of first trying to make his way round the side of the mountain, and then, when he ended up on a very steep slope in thick mist again, he retraced his steps and tried to make his way back up to the top of the mountain. Although he was well-equipped, he was beginning to get exhausted, and I think probably even more disorientated than he had been before.

What's disorientated? asked Aysha.

It means not just not knowing where you are, but also becoming confused and losing your sense of direction and your ability to make the right decision.

So this guy made a bad decision?

Yes, more than one in fact.

So what's the dogs do then?

I'm just coming to that. While he's back up on the mountain, darkness has fallen. He's lost, it's thick mist, it's night, he's running out of food and water, and although he's got warm clothes it can get freezing up high on a mountain in April.

So he's in a bad way, right?

He sure is. Meantime, his wife's called us when it's got dark and he hasn't got back to the place they're staying. So I get the dogs together and the first thing I do is go round to the holiday flat - do you know why?

No, said Charly.

I do, said Aysha. It's so the dogs can get his scent.

Very good, that's it exactly. Find some item of clothes he's worn a lot recently, let the dogs have a good sniff, take it with us if possible. Fortunately it was Grasmere they were staying. But even so, this wasn't going to be easy.

Fairfield's a big mountain, not too dangerous, not too many crags, but large in area and height. This man could be anywhere up there, he could even have strayed onto a neighbouring mountain. Even with the dogs, he was going to be impossible to find in the mist and the darkness.

Did you find him? asked Aysha.

Yes, we did, but it took us most of the night. We used whistles and torches, but most of all we relied on the dogs following the man's scent. But a thick mist tends to block out all the senses, not just sight but hearing and smell too. And the man must have crossed over his own trail several times, stumbling about lost up there, so it was really difficult for the dogs, but they did find him in the end. And when they got near him, they got eager and excited, despite the long hours they'd put in, and we did too, we started blowing hard on our whistles and shining our torches, but it wouldn't have made much difference. The guy was in a state of complete exhaustion, we had to stretcher him off.

Did you, like, take a stretcher with you?

Yes, we always do, unless we've got helicopter support, but in those conditions a helicopter would be no use at all.

So how many of you was there, y'know, on the rescue?

Five of us, two dog-handlers, two stretcher-carriers, and a para-medic. Plus the two dogs of course.

Was the man all right? asked Charly, still awake.

He was. He was given a good checking over the next morning, and he didn't even need to go to hospital. Just needed one day's rest. But that's why, said Neil, turning to Aysha, you need to experience the mountains, you need to understand the dangers, the formidable challenge they present. Any mountain, if conditions are bad.

But I am learning now, ain't I? pleaded Aysha.

A start, yes.

Is this mountain dangerous?

Quite often, it can be. At the moment, not too bad. But we still need to be careful.

What about?

Finding the best route, keeping an eye on the weather, making sure we don't get lost, or get separated from one another. Very important to stay together, read the map carefully, watch for signs of the weather deteriorating.

What do we do then?

We get down off the mountain as quickly as we can, by the safest route. And we don't pitch camp until we're off, or nearly off, the mountains.

He couldn't help be impressed, and gratified, by the active interest the older girl was showing.

The next morning they were up quite early, and continuing their slow ascent of the mountain. When they finally reached the col on the ridge leading up to the summit, they stopped for an early lunch. The weather was warm and the extra breeze on the ridge was welcome, even though it was from the south. The girls were hot and tired and thirsty, and Neil had to be firm about rationing water. Aysha had stripped down to as little as possible, even Charly had, for the first time on the whole trip. When Neil took some time explaining to the girls where they were on the map, what they could see in the distance, where they were going next, he began for the first time to feel uncomfortable about the closeness of the teenager's body right next to him, but he was also gratified at the girl's keenness to study map-reading and didn't want to put her off.

He told them they would spend about three hours exploring the summits of the mountain and the ridges connecting them. When he saw their faces drop, he said they would stow the packs by a rock on the col they were on now, and explained the route they would be taking when they dropped down off the top later in the afternoon.

Why does we have to walk all the way up there?

How many reasons do you want? One, because it's always good to make it to the very top, two, because the views are fantastic and we'll see more of the outer islands, three, because it will help you understand more about mountains, about the summit ridges, four because it's cooler up here than if we tried to explore lower down, five,

OK, ok, Neil, I get it right. You doesn't need to go on like that.

Aysha seemed to have quickly recovered her enthusiasm, Charly seemed the more reluctant. But after leaving their packs and continuing a gradual ascent for about half an hour, Neil spotted what he'd hoped to see but hadn't said. He signalled Charly to look, get her binoculars lined up.

What are they? she whispered.

They're very rare and unusual birds. Dotterel, they're called. If you look carefully, you'll see there are two chicks as well. He handed his binoculars to Aysha.

Yeah, I see them, said the older girl. Look in Neil's binoculars, Charly.

But in helping Charly switch binoculars, Aysha knocked one pair against the other, making a sharp tapping sound, which alarmed the up to then quite tame birds, and one flew off a little way with a sharp call, and then the others ran along the ground towards it as the first bird continued calling.

Neil was busy attempting to take photographs.

I wish I'd brought my bigger camera, he said. But then, if I had, what's the betting we wouldn't have seen the dotterel.

Where is it? asked Charly. The big camera?

I left it in the car in Oban. With the telescope, hidden under a blanket. Now let me tell you something special about the dotterel. It's the male that hatches the eggs and rears the chicks. The female lays the eggs, and then if it's not too late in the season, she'll go off and find another mate, leaving the male to do everything. And unlike most birds, it's the female who's the most brightly coloured. So with these two, it was the female who flew off and raised the alarm, leaving the male to stay with the chicks. The male does almost all the parenting.

But she ain't gone off to find a new mate this time.

No, but that's because it's late in the season. No time left to breed again.

So what does she do now, while the male looks after the chicks? asked Charly.

She might help with the feeding a bit, otherwise just hang around until it's time to migrate. They fly south to Africa in August or September. The female usually goes first, and the male will wait until the young are ready. In fact, it's likely this female will start her migration very soon.

They continued on to the main summit of the mountain, with a renewed spring in their steps.

The dotterel's the only breeding bird in Britain which has that... what's called a gender reversal. Unless you count a bird called a red-necked phalarope which has a few pairs breeding in the Shetland Islands ....

Has you ever been to see them? asked Charly.

I did see one once on migration, at Morecambe Bay. But I've never been to the Shetlands. Maybe I should one day, see them breeding.

Can I come if you does? said Aysha.

And me! added Charly.

Well, yes, if you wanted.

They walked over high ground to three summits, and then back to where they'd stowed the packs. Near the most remote summit they disturbed a ring ouzel which Neil was able to point out to Charly as it flew onto a rock and then darted out of sight. Having collected their packs, they set off on a narrow path down the mountain, while Neil pondered suitable places for their overnight camp, and how far down they should go, as he sensed thunder might be brewing, though he said nothing. About half way to the lake at the bottom, the ground levelled out for a while so they stopped there, putting their tents a little way from the stream, in which the girls paddled while Neil cooked up some supper and the brewing storm kept its distance. They were too tired for talking.

This trip were wild, Aysha thought to herself. This were the real wild, not the stuff she used to get up to on the estates and places, that were kinda pretend wild. She convinced herself she liked it, though once in a while a doubt crept in. No people, no-one her own age. Not that she liked people much, and she were with two she did like, Neil and her sister Charly. 'Part from Katy them was the two she liked best in the world. P'raps even better than Katy. Whenever she thought it were getting too lonely and boring up here, she thought how a long summer holiday with Katy and her folks was gonna be even more boring, and there was still three or four weeks of that to come. There was them two wicked little kids, Liam and that Lara, but even so. Nah, this were the right thing to do, come up here, see how great it were for Charly, into all this wildlife stuff with Neil, help them out, watch that Charly were ok.

Aysha went swimming most days after the weather were better. Sometimes Neil and Charly knew but most of the time they didn't. She didn't care, she loved it, she didn't actually swim that much, just splashed around. One time she swam with some seals. Not exactly with them but near them. She saw three seals come in close in a corner of the bay by where they were camping. Aysha was there on her own, minding the tent, and she already had her bikini on, so she just ran down the beach. She thought the seals were making for some rocks to go and lie on, but when they saw her, they stopped and just bobbed around in the water with their heads showing. Aysha swam near them but they never let her get too close, and she weren't gonna get too close to the rocks, or out too deep. So after a while she went back up the beach, but she still watched them and they watched her, and in the end they did climb up on the rocks and went to sleep. She didn't tell Charly or Neil, but she were gonna tell Charly after they got back home.

Charly still didn't talk much but when she did she were happy, Aysha knew. She, Aysha, were never gonna be happy, but it meant a hell of a lot to her to see that Charly were. Neil was good with Charly, so she, Aysha, was gonna be good to Neil, help him out and stuff, show an interest. She liked the seals and the otters and some of the birds. She loved watching all them black birds gliding past the boat like slow music but still faster than the boat, and the boat went fast after it got out from the shore. But she could never remember all the names of the birds, and Charly could. Aysha still loved dogs the best. Seals was like dogs swimming. Seals was dogs of the sea. She missed Greg loads.

When Neil started telling stories of how his dogs helped with the mountain rescue, Aysha loved that. She were wide awake listening. She were more into that than Charly, Charly always got tired in the evenings, it must be tiring watching wild-life all the time, Aysha thought. And carrying their packs up the mountains, that was tiring too. Charly got tired from that by the evening. But even though Aysha found her heavy pack tiring, she were determined not to give up, she wanted to prove herself tough, physically strong, show Neil that in a few years she could do mountain rescue, with dogs like he did. Show him that she could learn about mountains. She had to work hard concentrating on things he said, liking learning about maps, and she thought that must be even harder than watching wildlife nearly all day. But even so, Charly were tired in the evenings and she weren't. Her legs was tired but her brain weren't.

She loved it on the top of the mountain on a hot day. She only wished Greg could be up there with them, she knew he would've loved it too, racing around in the open space and the breeze. But he would've scared off them birds. There was them two mountain birds they saw, she forgot their names but there was the black ones in among the rocks and the browny patterned ones with their babies in the open grass. It were quite something to see mountain birds, specially for Charly. Even for Neil it were special to see them, she could tell from the way he was. Even for Neil who went up mountains a lot to do his rescue. Mountain birds was shy and you don't get to see them every day. It might be years before Charly saw them kind of birds again. It would be terrible if she hadn't got a proper look at them cos Greg scared them off before she could see them.

Aysha wanted to come to mountains again, to learn more about them. With Neil, or with someone else, or even on her own. With a tent and stuff, and a map. Always bring a map, Neil said. Always study the map carefully, he said, it's easy to get lost on a mountain. Well she, Aysha, weren't never gonna get lost. She would help people who'd forgot to bring a map and had got lost. She remembered that first time she'd took Greg for a walk and she were lost in the woods and had to get Greg to show her the way back. Even though she knew that city better than anyone and lived there loads longer than Greg, once she were out in the country a mile or so, she needed a dog cos she never had a map. If she'd had a map and learned how to use it, she wouldn't have got lost. Maps and dogs was both good, she thought, but maps is better specially if you's watching birds.

   She really worked hard at the map. Up on the mountain she worked out what was what on the map. The high bits and the bits between. Neil said them were called features. He told her all different words for bits, no features, of mountains, there was col, which was a dip between two tops, a top were called a summit or sometimes a peak or in Scotland Ben, there was crags and scree and a defile which were a flat passage between crags. And how you could tell the valleys and where the rivers went. You could work these out on the map. Neil wanted to show her things further away and where they were on the map, but she were more interested in the mountain they was on, and it were hard to remember anything else. She thought Neil understood.

   He told her that sometimes it were too windy up on the top of a mountain to get out your map. He said you could put it in a plastic cover and hang it round your neck so it didn't blow away or get soaked in the rain. But today weren't like that, they could open the map and spread it out no problem. Like, it felt good. Using the map she'd learned how to find the path off've the mountain. Neil helped her but she done it. They walked down a path what followed a stream and turned into a valley. Neil wanted to get a long way down before they pitched tent. He never said why but Aysha knew it were cos he thought there were a thunderstorm brewing up. Aysha were trying to be brave while she helped with putting up the tent and cooking the meal but inside she were scared. She knew she weren't gonna get to sleep.

   Truth was she already had a problem with sleeping. She hadn't when they started this trip, in fact she'd slept better in the first week of the trip than she had for a long time, since the first weeks she'd moved in with Katy, when she'd caught up on years and years of missing sleep.

Aysha knew what it were now. This holiday had given her chances to think, and she could see now that the night had a hold over her. What was the word, a fascination. An addiction, like a drug. She were a person of darkness, and drawn to darkness like a magnet, however scary it were, and it was scary, lots of the time. She couldn't work out if she'd been born like this, or whether it were the things what had happened to her, but there was bad in her, and the bad in her craved the night. That was why she kept running off, it weren't for stuff she took or people she got stuff from, it were so's she could be out in the dark. She could never sleep at night, foster-homes, children's homes, was like prisons, and there was loads of times when she'd stayed in and wanted to get out when it were too late, when the doors was locked and the windows wouldn't open far enough and she were trapped in. Sometimes it were so bad she got up and rampaged round and smashed things up for not being able to get out to the night outside. She'd soon learned when one of them moods was coming on and she made sure she ran off before they locked the doors. They couldn't stop her then. And she were out all night then with people like her, kids in gangs, drug-takers, drug-pushers, drifters, dossers on the streets down town, all of them like her with badness inside and addicted to darkness. And all of them grown-ups, foster-parents, care-workers, teachers, social workers, magistrates, police, the lot, none of them were like her, they was daytime people and that was why they never understood, that was why they told her off all the time, tried to make her the same as them but she never could be.

Why had she only just understood this? Until now she'd just gone out to meet the scary, evil darkness, embrace it even, without thinking what she were doing, it were just an instinct, a passion, a need deep inside her, sometimes like a pain, a craving, but she'd never once thought about it. And then Katy'd come along.

She saw what it were now, clear as anything. Katy were a daytime person too, even more than anyone else, she were an angel of the morning, surrounded by the glow of daylight. But Katy saw the night in Aysha, right from the start she did, and she understood it and accepted it and even liked her for it. It were, like, how do they say it, attraction of opposites. They never said anything about this but Aysha could tell, now, how Katy understood her craving for darkness. And that made all the difference. That were why their best times were going out at night, going to gigs, coming back home together, how at them times there were a wicked magic in the air between them. Even taking Greg for his late night walk. Having a dog helped, you could go out late at night and no-one could say what was you doing out so late when you had a dog.

Sometimes Katy and her took Greg out together, but soon Aysha started taking him on her own. And that were enough, just that taste of the darkness and she'd get back satisfied and calm and ready for sleep. She would never have run off, got hooked into her old life, when Greg were with her. Katy understood all this, even if she never said, Aysha could now see. And in those first few months with Katy, and with Greg being allowed to sleep by her bed, even on her bed sometimes, Aysha had slept like she'd never slept before.

But the darkness never left her, the pull of the darkness. When they moved, and Charly and Zoë came to live with them, it got stronger again. Now she wanted to be out at night on her own, like before. The demons was getting in her again, or something. She took Greg out late at night every night, and if there was other kids round the places they hung out, like the entrance to the sports-field or the pub car-park or outside the station, she would hang out for a while and have a smoke, or a swig of beer if another kid offered her, or a drag of blow. But Greg was with her so she always went back and Katy never said nothing except goodnight as Aysha scooted up to her room so's Katy wouldn't smell nothing. But she was getting restless again, and then the nightmares started.

Greg couldn't understand the nightmares. A dog wouldn't, would he, cos for a dog all stuff what happened in your past, well that didn't mean nothing now, it's only the present what counts for a dog. So when she had the nightmares, Greg thought she were in pain like on the outside, not the inside, and he wanted to find the hurting place and lick it with his slobbery tongue, and she just wished she could get all that hurting out from inside onto her skin somewhere for Greg to lick it clean. Maybe that was why she cut her arms but it never helped.

Now she was scared of having nightmares again. They went away when Neil brought her and Charly to Scotland, even without Greg she slept peaceful and she liked Neil for it, even liked him better than Katy for the first few days, cos she actually made Katy take some of the blame what with those life-story sessions and getting her to talk 'bout all that stuff what happened when she were a little kid what she'd never talked 'bout before and weren't never gonna again. Now she couldn't sleep at night again and when she did sleep she had these horrible dreams, they weren't nightmares, she didn't wake up screaming, thank fuck, but she usually dreamed of working in a place where they trained dogs for mountain rescue, and Kenny was there teaching her, or Neil, or sometimes both. And then a bad man took over the running of the place, it weren't that man, she never could say his name, or maybe it was him, or someone like him, and he started being cruel to all the dogs, and there were nothing she or Kenny or Neil could do. But Katy were gonna come soon and put a stop to it cos Katy would never allow dogs to be treated cruel, so they was waiting for Katy to arrive, but she never did, and she, Aysha, began to think something must've happened to Katy. She were dreaming a dream like this nearly every night, and when she woke she still had a horrible feeling left over from it. And it were getting harder and harder to sleep, were it cos of these dreams, or were it cos she was spending all the time with Neil and Charly now and not getting time on her own, or were it that the nights was getting quite hot now, even halfway up a mountain, or were it other feelings she was getting pulsing around her body like drumbeats, she didn't know what it were. She missed her drumming, she missed Greg, but most of all she were missing Katy now. She could go to Katy 'bout this, Katy would understand. Neil she always thought understood her but now she weren't so sure, she weren't sure he'd understand about all this. And Charly, right, she just got so tired by the middle of the evening and she were out of it, into a deep sleep all the way to morning. No use turning to Charly.

The last few nights Aysha got up in the middle of the night in the pitch black and walked around. That helped but only a bit, cos it were dead scary and sometimes she heard spooky animal sounds and it were dark with no moon and she were too scared to move very far from the tents. And if Charly did wake up she might notice and call out.

Now as she lied awake hearing the sound of the river quite close and sometimes other noises further away, and rumblings of thunder getting closer, Aysha could feel the fear mixed up with a load of other feelings rising up bigger and bigger inside her and taking over her whole being. Thunder scared her a bit but lightning was worse. There were a place in Canada called Thunder Bay. Charly told her that, she'd found it in one of her wildlife books or on a website. So whenever it thundered, they used to sing this song together, "We're on our way / To Thunder Bay" over and over and it helped, and they'd sung it in Neil's car when it thundered just before they got to that man's house, and that were a lot better singing it in the car, and where the man lived was by a sort of bay. But Charly weren't awake to sing it with her now, and it prob'ly wouldn't help anyway.

Then the flashes of lightning started, and soon after that the rain. The rain came sudden and fast and loud, ever so loud, hammering on the tent. And then the thunder got even louder, fighting with the rain to see who could be the loudest. The tent were gonna explode, it felt like she were inside a bomb, Charly and her the both of them, she wanted to wake Charly up but that weren't fair on Charly who was sleeping through it, best thing by far. She wondered if Neil were sleeping through it too. Everything inside Aysha were shooting like electricity through her skin and her head and her chest. Fear and aching and energies made her brain hurt and her heart thump like fast drumming. She were trapped in this little tent which seemed to get smaller like the rain and thunder was beating it into the ground but she couldn't go out, how could she, she would be soaked through in an instance and she were too scared to be outside in the lightning. She were gonna explode if she stayed here, she were gonna die, all the bad in her had taken her over shooting around like guns like she were in a war like flashes from bombs like hails of bullets splatter splatter on the tent bombs explosions right outside like that man doing those terrible things to her no escape no escape get out of here Katy Katy get me out ....

The morning after the storm it were all quiet again. The tents were dry and only the stream what were now a river, louder and

324

fuller and faster, told you there'd been a storm in the night. That and Aysha. Charly had woken up once, but pretended she were still asleep, and now she felt bad that she never helped her sister out, knowing how scared she must've got. And now Aysha were quiet, never saying a thing. She still helped with breakfast and with the tents and stuff, but she wouldn't talk. They was nearly running out of food and water, so Neil said they had to go to the nearest village what had a shop, which they did, catching a bus when they got down to a road, and Aysha went in to buy the shopping like she usually did while Charly and Neil stayed outside scanning the sky with their binoculars, hoping to see something more interesting than the big gulls which was everywhere, some high up, some squawking from rooftop to rooftop like they must've been bothered by the storm too.

Where do birds go in storms? she asked Neil.

If they've still got nests, young birds in the nest, they'll stay on their nests, he answered. At other times they'll find the best shelter they can, although some birds, that are strong and fast flyers, like swifts, for example, actually try and escape from a storm by flying away, but that doesn't always work.

Why not?

Because storms are unpredictable, thundery build-ups can occur in more than one place at the same time, and can merge together and then split up. Even birds, with their much more highly-tuned instincts about the weather, can't predict which areas will miss a storm and which will catch it.

Aysha had come out of the shop with her purchases and was listening eagerly. She also lit up a cigarette which was a total surprise to Charly, since although she knew Aysha had been sneaking an occasional smoke on this trip, she'd never once done it in front of Neil or her. Charly guessed it would've helped Aysha to have had a smoke in the storm, but you can't ever smoke in a tent so she were having one now instead. Maybe she'd run out and had to wait til they got to the shop. But while Aysha lit up, Neil were carrying on talking.

There's one bird I want us still to see on this trip, he were saying. And it's the best of them all, the rarest and the most magnificent. So I want -

What is it? asked Charly. This bird, what is it?

I won't tell you just yet. We do have a good chance of

seeing it, as long as we keep a good watch out. So I want us all to be watching the sky, including you, Aysha. Even while we're on the bus.

Are we catching another bus? Charly asked.

Just for about three miles, said Neil. To save us walking along the road. And to get us quicker to a good place for lunch. It's already past lunchtime.

That shop's shut at lunchtime, said Aysha, the first time she'd spoken all day. Twelve-thirty til two.

I know, they usually are round here. We timed it right getting here.

How long do we have to wait for a bus? asked Charly.

Ten minutes.

D'you know all the places round here? Aysha spoke again.

Yes, I know them well. My grandparents used to live near here and I used to stay with them in the holidays.

How old was you then?

Right through my teens, I think. And a few years after.

Will we go past their house?

We'll be camping very near it. I'll show it to you. But, of course, someone else lives in it now.

Why?

My grandparents died a few years ago now.

Was you sad?

Yes, very.

Was that man sad? asked Charly.

Which man?

Y'know, where we stayed on the way up?

Ah no, not his parents. These were my grandparents on my mother's side.

That's Marie, right? suggested Aysha, turning from Neil to Charly. Like, Marie, what I went to the funeral of, and Lara and Liam were there, and that's where I met you, right, Neil?

That's it. Marie was Lara and Liam's grandmother. And these people were Marie's parents, and my grandparents, and Lara and Liam's great-grandparents.

Did Lara ever see them? asked Aysha.

No, unfortunately they both died before she was born.

After their short bus journey, they walked up a track

into the hills again, only these were not mountains but woods and lakes. They stopped for lunch at a bridge over a river what roared and foamed, Neil said after the storm in the night. Then they came to a big lake and Neil found a place to pitch camp near the shore. Then he pointed at a house quite near, at the edge of the woods. That's where my grandparents used to live, he said. And where I stayed all those holidays. I just want to go there and tell them we're here. While I'm gone, keep a watch out for a very big bird.

Charly watched and watched. She saw pigeons and ravens and crows and gulls and what she now knew were buzzards. She saw an oyster-catcher land by the shore of the lake. Then she saw something different, only it weren't that big. It flew over the grassy hill by the side of the lake. Low down, nearly touching the ground, then up again. She watched it in the binoculars. It were an owl, she could now tell. It were the first owl they'd seen the whole trip. But it were daylight, weren't even starting to go dark yet, so what was the owl doing flying about?

She told Aysha, who weren't interested. She'd helped with the tents but now she were listening to her music with her eyes closed. She hadn't lit up again since that one she'd had by the shop.

Neil came back, so she told him.

That must be a short-eared owl, he said. You get them round here. Is it still there? He seemed quite excited.

Nah, it's gone away. What were it doing, flying around in daylight?

Well, they do, short-eared owls. They hunt more in daylight than by night. We call that diurnal. It's the only truly diurnal British owl. You did very well to find it, that's excellent. We'll keep a look-out in case it comes back.

What about that big bird?

Yes, we'll watch out for that too. It's a white-tailed eagle I've been talking about, one of Britain's biggest birds, bigger than a golden eagle even. And one of the rarest. And there's a pair nesting near here, at the far end of the lake. And I just checked with the people in the house, they are still around, the male and the second chick. The female and the first chick left earlier in the week, though they probably haven't gone far. So we might not see them today, but we should get to see them tomorrow.

What I thought was, Neil went on. We'll camp here two nights. Then we can have a rest from carrying the heavy packs tomorrow. Because we've been lugging them around for three days, haven't we?

Not when we were up the top of the mountain.

No, that's true. Even so, we need a rest. We'll walk to the other end of the lake tomorrow, and we should see the eagles. But we must be careful not to disturb them. Are you on for that?

Yeah! But Aysha might not be.

She's had a lot of weight to carry. I'm sure she'll welcome a rest. And when we're at the other end of the lake, we're quite near the sea. She might want to find the way to a cove where she can swim.

So they set off next morning walking along the side of the lake. Neil told Charly to watch out for the eagles while he and Aysha studied the map and he explained where they was going. Charly kept forgetting to concentrate, but then she suddenly saw this huge bird flying over the lake.

Look! she whispered, grabbing Neil's arm. The bird had a brilliant white patch on its tail, shining in the sun. The rest of it looked dark, nearly black.

That's it, all right, said Neil. Try and get the binoculars on it if you can, get a good look!

But it were hard with the binoculars. It kept flying this way and that, across the lake, up and down and back, so in the end she let Neil have the binoculars and just watched it like Aysha was doing. Finally it landed somewhere on the far side.

That's the young bird, said Neil. Practising flying. The nest is somewhere over there. We should be able to see the nest, and the other bird, the adult, from a bit further along.

So then he asked Aysha if she wanted to take the map and find her own way to the cove while he and Charly spent half an hour watching the nest.

Yeah! said Aysha.

I've marked the place on the map, the cove, said Neil, pointing it out again. You see how to get there?

Yeah, you just follow the path from the lake to the road, right, and then take that track down to the sea?

That's right, it's almost opposite when you get to the

road, but be careful crossing.

Course I will, but what happens if I gets lost?

Well, you shouldn't if you've been learning to map-read as well as you seem to have been doing. But the advice is - if you're lost. always retrace your route, exactly the way you've come. So remember your route, and come back to the lake.

But what if you and Charly's not here?

Well, you've still got the map, so try again. Or otherwise go back along the shore of the lake until you come to the tents. You can't go wrong, really. And when you get to the sea, there's only one sandy cove, and it's quite small, so we won't miss each other - but remember, don't go in the sea until we get there.

But how will you find it, Neil, if I've got the map?

Oh, I know this area very well, I know all the paths, remember I used to come here nearly every holiday.

What's we gonna do tomorrow? Aysha then asked.

We'll discuss that on our way back to the tents.

So while Charly and Neil watched in their binoculars the two eagles on and around the nest, Aysha set off on her own. Charly got worried that Aysha would go off somewhere, or get lost, and they wouldn't find her. In the night she'd heard her and Neil having an argument. Charly had put her hands over her ears so's she wouldn't hear, and snuggled down into her sleeping-bag and pretended she were asleep when Aysha came back in the tent. Now Neil were being extra nice to Aysha and trusting her loads, but Aysha'd been a bit funny since the storm and you couldn't always trust her in a funny mood. But when they got to the cove, Aysha were there, lying on a rock sunbathing, even though there were a cold wind today, mind you, it was more sheltered down on the beach. Charly felt such a relief.

They ate their lunch and then Aysha swam for a bit, and then they walked, led by Aysha with the map, by a different path back to the lake and along the lake to the tents. On their way back, Neil said that tomorrow they would pack up the tents and stuff, and walk after breakfast to a little town called Tobermory which was about four miles, and buy something for lunch there and then catch a bus to the ferry, and they'd be on their way home.

When will we get home? asked Aysha.

329

The day after tomorrow. Do you want to phone Katy?

Aysha shrugged.

Well, I've got my mobile with me, but we probably won't get a signal here. You could try from the ferry, or while we're waiting for the ferry at Craignure, although the bus doesn't normally give you long to wait.

Where's we gonna stay tomorrow? With that man?

Yes, with my - I mean with Duncan.

You's told us he's your dad, Neil. You can say it now.

Yes, but we mustn't keep saying it. Remember not to let anyone know, you mustn't tell Duncan that you know.

Why not?

I don't think he'd be very happy that I've told you.

Oh. OK, we'll remember, won't we Charly? Keep it secret.

Aysha was back to her usual self now, it seemed, and back at the tents was now keen to phone Katy but couldn't get through as Neil had thought. But in the night Charly heard another argument, and Aysha seemed in a mood again in the morning and said very little, even though she was as helpful as ever, even more so, with breakfast and the tents and the packing.

30. ANGEL OF THE MORNING

Two days after the prison visit, Zoë and Katy travelled back to Bursfield. The child was still being difficult and Katy's attempts to have a talk with her had come to nothing. It was impossible to arrange any activity with Lara and Liam, and Katy did not want her mother or Steve to notice what a struggle she was having. She might be able to sort things out in the quiet of their own home, although she would have preferred the other two girls there as well, indeed was desperate for their return. In the absence of any firm arrangement with Neil, she thought it would be better to be back in Bursfield, where he'd collected Aysha and Charly. He'd said they would phone, and both he and Aysha had her mother's address and phone number, she was sure, but they'd probably phone Bursfield first and she didn't want them to keep ringing with no answer. And, just in case they decided to spring a surprise and return without phoning, it would be awful if there was no-one home.

No, she felt happier now to be going back. While she'd been on the prison visit, that guy Gareth had phoned her at her mother's and now her mother was pestering her to call him back. She hated that sort of pressure, she wanted to put more distance between herself and Gareth, not because she didn't like him but because she thought she did, and she needed to work out what to do without her mother keep going on. Not only about this possible boyfriend, future husband even, to Sharon's fevered imagination, which Katy had been trying to avoid letting her mother know about, but in addition her mother had, on the night before they departed, and with obvious disappointment in her voice that they were returning to Bursfield earlier than expected, tried to explain to Katy that she and Steve were about to start trying to find Rodney, Katy's father.

It was too much, on top of everything else. She'd told her mother that was fine, but she wasn't that interested, herself. She had other things on her mind and was glad to escape her mother's intrusive concerns. As well as sorting out Zoë, she needed to start getting on with coursework, and most of all she was missing Aysha more desperately as each day passed with no news.

There was a whole pile of mail waiting at their house when they got there. Sifting through quickly, Katy found postcards from the girls in Scotland, one addressed to Zoë and one to her. This cheered her up a little, and after reading them through she passed them for Zoë to look at while she attempted to read the rest of the mail.

Most of it was junk. As well as the cards, there seemed to be only three items of interest. There was an envelope from Andrew Wheeler High School addressed to her, an envelope from the Sri Lanka High Commission, and a personal letter for her in handwriting she didn't recognise. She opened this first, but Zoë seemed determined to continue obstructing her.

It was no good trying to talk to Zoë about this imaginary friend of hers. Somehow Katy had got it wrong, touched a raw nerve, turned a normally friendly and compliant child into a whining and unbiddable one. And it was no good handing her a book or plonking her in front of the computer or television, or trying to involve her in helping to make the tea, or even in taking Greg for his walk. Zoë had decided to refuse to co-operate on all fronts, but would not leave Katy alone either. Apart from getting their meals and feeding and walking Greg - and even those activities required firmness and determination on Katy's part, she found she couldn't do anything until the child, after stubbornly fighting everything in her life, would finally drop off to sleep by the middle of the evening. Then Katy dealt with her mail, but she had no energy left for her coursework and it was too late to make phone calls.

The personal letter was from one of the viola players in her college orchestra. She played in a local string quartet, all young women graduates in the music faculty, but the cellist was expecting a baby in the autumn, and they needed someone to fill in for about 9 months or a year. They were all impressed by Katy's playing and wanted to ask her.

Katy wanted to oblige but wasn't sure she could. At the moment everything seemed impossible, but at the same time this seemed like a fantastic opportunity not just for her as a musician although mainly that of course, but as a chance to make closer friends with a few of her musician colleagues. She wrote a short note straight away saying she'd only just received the letter and would need a bit more time to think about it, she was flattered and grateful they'd thought of her and would let them know soon.

The envelope from the High School contained next term's time-tables for Charly and Aysha, Aysha's school report from last term, and an individual learning plan for next term for Aysha. It also contained details of a four-day drumming event in Devon over the bank holiday weekend. It sounded just right for all of them, Aysha could develop her drumming skills further, Charly could listen to a range of ethnic musics, Zoë could have supervised play activities with other kids her own age, while she, Katy, could just have a break from responsibilities and maybe read a book for a change. So she filled in the application form for tickets straight away and posted it with a cheque for a deposit - hoping she could persuade Social Services to pay the rest.

Then she turned to the envelope from the Sri Lankan High Commission, wondering what news would be in it, but decided it would be best to leave it, wait until Aysha returned.

Zoë did not give her any respite the next day, and, desperate to find time to get on with some college work, Katy phoned Ruth Barnes. She explained how she had Zoë with her and needed some time to herself, and were there any playschemes available or anything similar that she could book Zoë into.

Haven't you booked her into something already? I gave you the info, didn't I?

Yes, you did, but you see, I didn't think we'd be spending much of the summer holiday in Bursfield, and when we were here, that we'd be doing things together, she said, hesitantly, a little feebly, but determined to stay calm, for Zoë was close by and she didn't want either Ruth or the child to sense how desperate she was.

Well, unfortunately I think it's too late. I have to put the names down, and sort out the money, before now. Most of them have nearly finished now anyway.

Oh well, I'm sorry I bothered you, said Katy, her heart sinking while she realised the disappointment must be evident in her voice.

I could see if there's a child-minder willing to take an older child, Ruth went on, obviously reading the signs in Katy's voice. Or a respite foster-carer if you want an overnight break. Or you could try phoning the children's home. They have a range of activities organised in the summer holidays which might be open for other kids, especially as Zoë has only recently left there.

Cassie, thought Katy. Come to my rescue now. Yes, that's a good idea, she said to Ruth. I'll phone the home. That's the best thing.

What were that about? asked Zoë.

Just wait, kid. I'll tell you in a minute. And she picked the phone up again. Cassie wasn't on duty, but Teresa told her that in two days' time there was an outing to Ironbridge which involved a boat trip and some time at a fantastic adventure playground, and Zoë would be very welcome. They had spare places because quite a few children were with their families at present. They would collect Zoë in the minibus, early, straight after breakfast, and would give her an evening meal at the home when they got back. All Katy would need to do was to make sure she had about 5 pounds pocket money with her, and collect her some time in the evening before bed-time. She also mentioned that the day after they would be going swimming at the Leisure Centre and Zoë would be welcome to come to that too.

So, I've arranged for you to have a day out, a fun day, she said to Zoë. Would you like that?

Who with?

Some of the kids and staff from the children's home. You'll know a few of them, they used to be your friends.

When?

The day after tomorrow. And the day after, you can go swimming at the Leisure Centre.

Will they let Ambrose come?

I don't know, you'll have to ask them. Do your friends at the children's home know about Ambrose?

No.

Well, I think it's best not to say anything, then. You can just pretend he's there, or you can go without him, and wait for another time when it's just you.

Just me, Charly and Aysha.

Yes.

All right then, Katy, she said a little wearily, but was clearly brighter, less clinging and more willing to occupy herself from that point on.

So Katy finally was able to get on with her work, and also to make a few phone calls she needed to make. She belatedly called Gareth back and explained her situation. It wasn't going to be easy to meet up again, but she and all three girls would be up in Longworth later in the school holiday and if he could travel over that might work out as it was easier to get away when she had all three girls than if it were just Zoë as at present. When Zoë went off for the day, she finally had the chance to go running, to take Greg out for the exercise he'd been needing so much. Then she settled down to college work for the rest of the day. And then in the afternoon Aysha phoned.

Hi, Katy, we're on our way home!

Aysha, hi kid! Where are you?

We're just getting into Oban, on the boat. Tonight's our last night in Scotland, then we'll be back tomorrow.

That's great. What time, do you know?

The phone went quiet, as the girl appeared to be consulting.

Neil says, for evening meal. Around six o'clock. Can you make enough for Neil as well, cos he's gonna be driving all day.

Yes, of course. How's it been? Are you ok?

Yeah, it's been brilliant. Charly and me'll tell you all 'bout it later. Did you get our card?

Yes, I did, and Zoë got hers, thanks very much.

Could I speak to Zoë?

Well, she's not here just now. I'm here on my own.

Where's Zoë?

She's out on a day-trip.

Who with?

With some other kids, with the children's home in fact.

You've not sent her back there, has you, Katy? She could sense a distinct cooling in Aysha's voice, or was it just her imagination?

No, I haven't, she protested indignantly. They'd organised this trip, and they had spare places in the minibus, and they offered to take Zoë along. It was good for both of us, cos she's been bored stiff the last few days just with me.

How did they know?

They must've just guessed. She couldn't quite bring herself to come out with it and say, Well actually it was me that phoned them.

Tell Zoë we'll see her tomorrow, right?

Sure will. Love to Charly, and have a safe journey home.

Her heart was just brimming up, from having spoken to her protégée at last. But she wished Zoë had been there when Aysha phoned. She had not thought of that, she had been so desperate to arrange something for the youngest child, that the oldest one might phone while her sister was out, and be perturbed at her absence. She must make sure she got Zoë back from the swimming trip tomorrow before the others arrived. She must check the timing carefully when she collected Zoë tonight.

Should she tell Aysha about Gareth? All sorts of difficult issues seemed to be trying to undermine her pure straightforward joy at anticipating Aysha's return. And Charly's, of

335

course, she mustn't neglect the middle child. She wasn't sure how she felt about Gareth. He was a hunky guy, and there was a physical attraction, for sure, but in no way was she emotionally drawn to him in the way she was to Aysha. She had tried to explain that to him, and it didn't seem to have put him off keeping the friendship going, so maybe she should continue to see Gareth when it was possible, and tell Aysha about him. And tell Charly.

It was hard getting on with her coursework. Thoughts kept buzzing around in her head, and her feelings seemed to be swelling in her chest. She made a quick meal and then took Greg out. She walked him across the city suburbs to the children's home, taking in as many footpaths and grassy areas as she could. The evening was cool, windy and dry, and the walk cleared her head. Then she took the bus back with Zoë, having checked the times for swimming the next day. It was in the afternoon, and again they would collect Zoë in the minibus after lunch. But this time she arranged to call at the Leisure Centre to collect Zoë, to make sure they were back in time. In the morning she and Zoë shopped, stocking up with supplies as well as buying for the meal tonight, then Zoë helped her prepare the meal, a lamb casserole with lots of vegetables, and an apricot crumble and a big tub of cream. The child was almost back to how she was before the holidays, willing and amenable; it was definitely the right thing to arrange a day out for her with other children, Katy decided.

After Zoë had been collected in the minibus, Katy went out for a run with Greg, showered and changed, put the meal in the oven, and still found she had almost an hour before the train into town to collect Zoë, the Leisure Centre being close to the main railway station, and it only being ten minutes, two stops, from High Chapel to the town centre as long as you knew the times.

They got back relieved that they were ahead of the Scotland contingent, who in fact didn't arrive until nearly seven.

There were broad smiles and waves, but when she went to hug both girls Katy sensed an awkwardness, maybe shyness, maybe embarrassment. Both older girls seemed more natural, more affectionate, with their younger sister, but of course they would, Katy told herself. And with Greg, of course. The dog was beside himself to see Aysha again, and she had to be pulled away from a long canine embrace, all tongue and nose and tickles.

With Neil's help, Katy got them round the table and tucking into food. Then the talking started. To begin with, it was mainly a fragmented account of where they'd been, what they'd seen.

And you were camping the whole time?

Yeah, wild camping on one island, said Charly.

Mull, that were, added Aysha. And I learned map-reading, didn't I Neil, and if I can get more experience in the mountains, I can learn to do mountain rescue with dogs, like Neil.

And you'd like that would you?

Yeah, right I would!

Well, you both look very clean after three weeks camping.

Yeah, but we had baths last night, didn't we, Neil, said Charly.

At this friend of Neil's, added Aysha. But we've got loads of dirty clothes for washing.

Especially me, said Charly. Cos Aysha didn't wear much, did you?

Like it were hot, right, most of the time, y'know, like the last week and a bit anyhow. And I swam quite a bit.

In the sea?

Yeah, well, there ain't nowhere else to swim on them islands, right?

Probably there are pools, said Neil. In some of the hotels. We never went in those, too expensive.

The boats was wicked, said Aysha. Charly and me loved the boats, didn't we, Charly?

You see heaps of birds from the boats, said Charly. I never would've thought. And dolphins.

And one time we saw all these birds with long black wings, thousands of them, passing the boat, said Aysha. The boat were going fast, right, but these birds just kinda glided past, turning one way and the other and dipping their wings like they was dancing on the sea. They passed us ever so quick, and then more kept coming.

Manx shearwaters, they were, added Charly.

And what did you do about food? asked Katy.

We cooked our own, didn't we Neil? said Aysha.

Aysha helped an awful lot with the cooking.

Oh, that's good, said Katy, turning to look at the over-awed Zoë.

But that don't mean I'm gonna help out here, protested Aysha, suddenly concerned. Everyone laughed.

We had picnic lunches, didn't we, Neil? said Charly.

Most days.

Even on the boat, went on Aysha. Charly and Neil had sandwiches cos they wanted to watch the birds all the time. But I had chips on the boat coming back. I had chips twice yesterday, right, once on the boat just before I phoned you, and then we all stopped for fish and chips in the car, what's that place, Neil?

Lochrana. But you must ask Katy and Zoë what they've been up to.

Well, I'm glad I haven't made chips tonight, said Katy.

You don't never make chips!

I mean lots of vegetables, right, you probably haven't had many while you were away.

We have, haven't we Neil, out of tins. Anyhow, Aysha went on, you tell us what you've been up to, Zoë.

We stayed in a caravan, me and Lara and Katy. By the sea. And Katy got a boyfriend.

What? queried Aysha. You didn't, Katy?

He seemed to like us, didn't he, Zoë? Very friendly, and he's phoned me up since.

Oh wow, this is, like, the big news of the holidays.

It's no big deal. I might see him when we next go up to my mum's.

Why? Does he live there?

No, he lives in North Wales, but it's easier for him to get to Manchester than Bursfield.

When's we going up there?

I haven't worked that out yet.

I'd've thought you'd wanna get up there double quick.

No, it's not like that. Zoë, tell them what else you've been doing.

You went to see your mum, prompted Katy, when the younger child could only mumble, tongue-tied.

I went swimming today, didn't I Katy, and yesterday I

went on a boat ride ....

A boat ride? queried Aysha.

Yeah, on the river Severn by an old iron bridge. With Teresa and some other kids.

From the kids' home? asked Charly.

Yeah.

Are the same kids still there?

Some of them. There's two new kids, same age as me.

What's their names? Charly continued asking.

I dunno, I've forgot. It were fun, anyway, so was swimming.

Zoë was beginning to enjoy having some attention.

Well, that's ok, Zoë, if you liked it, interjected Aysha. But me, I would never do anything with them children's home kids again. I don't want anything more to do with them, right, staff or kids, or any more organised trips or fun days or stuff like that, me.

You've been on school outings, suggested Katy.

Yeah, that's different, that's like work, right, that's to help with exams and projects and stuff. That's just instead of sitting in a classroom all day.

I see.

Charly's the same, ain't you?

So what are you two going to do the rest of the holidays? asked Neil.

I dunno, go to gigs, take Greg for walks. What I'd really like to do is more mountain rescue training.

Well, that will have to wait. You've learned plenty for one holiday.

What's that about? asked Katy.

Yeah, like I said, I wanna do mountain rescue when I'm older, Katy. Train dogs like Neil. He's been telling us all about it.

Well, what I've fixed up, said Katy. I hope it doesn't sound too much like an organised activity, but I'm sure you'll all enjoy it....

Well, what is it? asked Aysha impatiently.

A drumming weekend.

Oh cool!

The confirmation came today. It's in Devon at the end of the month.

How will we get there?

By train. I thought we might try and call on your uncle Phil, Charly, on the way to Devon or on the way back, to save us making a separate trip.

When's their baby due? asked Aysha.

I dunno, but not yet, I don't think. You wouldn't have known she was pregnant when they came to see us.

When can we go to another gig, Katy? asked Aysha.

I don't think there are any at the moment. They take a rest in August.

That's stupid, Katy, there's gigs all the time, there's bound to be something if you really look, right.

Well, I dunno, they mainly have these weekend festivals at this time of year.

Well, we could go to one of them.

Maybe, but there's not many weekends available, and you'd have to camp, and I would've thought you'd want a rest from camping, since we'll be camping on the drumming weekend.

Oh cool. How will we take tents to Durham on the train?

Devon, it is.

OK, Devon then.

They provide tents. I've booked two for us.

Oh, wicked! Can I share with Charly?

Yes.

Well, could we just go for a day to one of them festivals?

That's possible, yes, but can you dish some pudding for Neil, I'm sure he'll be wanting to get back.

That's ok, said Neil. I need a rest.

What's for pudding? asked Charly.

Apricot crumble and cream. It needs to come out of the oven now. And the cream is in the fridge. You get the cream, Zoë, she added hastily as the youngest headed towards the kitchen. One of you bigger girls get the crumble.

So can we definitely go to one of these festivals? Aysha pleaded with Katy while her two sisters were in the kitchen. Just for a Saturday?

We'll need to think about it. If there's one the right

weekend, and if there's a late bus or train back, and if Zoë doesn't want to come, can we make arrangements for her?

She will wanna come.

We don't know that. And the other thing is, I've been invited to play cello in this string quartet -

What's that?

It's four musicians, a bit like a rock band only it's violins instead of guitars and it's classical music and no vocalist.

And a drummer?

No, it's just two violins, a viola and a cello. It would just be temporary while their regular cello player's having a baby. It's four women, young women at uni. I haven't said yes because I wanted to discuss it with you first, but it is quite an honour.

She started to serve the pudding.

Well, you must say yes, insisted Aysha.

Quite right you must, reinforced Neil.

Look, it ain't nothing to do with you, Neil! said Aysha.

I'd need to start going to quite a lot of rehearsals. And some of them might clash with things you want to do.

Well, that's ok, pronounced Aysha. I'll just go on my own. Me and Charly, or all three of us. And I'll look out for gigs, right. And for festivals.

Where will you look?

On posters in town, yeah? And in newspapers.

D'you have enough money to buy all these newspapers?

I won't buy them, Katy, right. I'll just go in a newspaper shop with one of my school notebooks and a pencil, and copy stuff down, ok?

OK. Katy couldn't help smiling as Aysha seemed to be back to her usual self but with her already precocious sense of independence enhanced even further by the three weeks away. Charly, too, seemed to have benefitted, brought out of herself a bit more. And Zoë seemed to be over her recent problems.

After Neil had left, soon after the meal finished, some sort of normality appeared to be returning. Aysha recommended her role as late-night dog-walker for Greg, and generally took over most of the responsibility for his feeding, grooming, and exercising.

341

She also started spending a lot of her time with Zoë, sometimes taking Greg for a walk or a run just the two of them while Charly stayed in, on the computer or studying her wildlife books. At other times all three children took Greg out while Katy studied, or there were occasions when they went out as a foursome, a family, as they had most weekends during the previous term. Even indoors, though, Aysha took it on herself to occupy her younger sister, and with Charly always able and willing to occupy herself, this enabled Katy to really work hard at catching up on course work. She couldn't remember saying anything to Aysha, but it seemed uncanny that the girl must have sensed that this was a problem between her younger sister and her carer.

Katy wanted to have some quality time with the older girl now that she was back, and hoped that to thank her for taking so much time with Zoë might bring them closer together, but before that could happen, one night when the other girls were in bed and Aysha was on her way out with Greg, she came into Katy's room first.

Katy, you lied to me. Aysha was never one to beat about the bush. She would either shut up, or come right out with something.

What? Katy murmured, startled and worried. She had genuinely forgotten the telephone conversation the previous week.

When I phoned you, went on Aysha. From Scotland, on the boat. I wanted to speak to Zoë and she weren't there. You said they'd spare places on their trip and they, like, offered Zoë one. You didn't say you phoned them up 'bout it, right.

Well, it weren't really a lie, explained Katy defensively. They did have spare places and they did offer Zoë one when I phoned Teresa.

Well, the way you told me, right, it meant she phoned you up. That's what I thought and that were a lie.

Well, a white lie perhaps. I'm sorry if I misled you.

And Zoë's been telling me how you were getting mad with her over her friend Ambrose.

Well, yes and no. It were a bit more complicated than that. D'you want me to tell you the details of what happened?

'Slong as you ain't gonna lie to me, then yeah.

I promise I won't lie, OK. I took Zoë and Lara on this

caravan holiday, right. And they got on brilliant. I didn't know about this fantasy friend of hers, this Ambrose, but it appears that Zoë drew Lara into her fantasy that week we were away. I'm not a hundred per cent sure but I think so, ok. That's not a problem, I wouldn't have minded if I'd known. Then we went back to my mum's and we were going to spend the rest of the time in Longworth until you got back. But that meant Liam joining up with Lara and Zoë, and Zoë didn't seem willing to let him. For instance sitting in the back of the car. It was like Ambrose had taken Liam's place, and she wouldn't let Liam join in. And it seemed to me she was trying to set Lara up against Liam, and if there's one thing I'm not gonna stand from any of you three girls, and I know you accept this, Aysha, it's causing damage or difficulty for Lara or Liam or between the two of them. You understand?

Yeah, course I does.

Yeah, well, that's why I was getting cross with Zoë. To be fair, Lara's a strong kid for her age, and knows what's what, and she wasn't gonna let Zoë drive a wedge between her and her brother. But I could foresee the situation getting uglier, so I thought it was best to return here. D'you understand?

Yeah, I would've agreed with that. But not phoning the kids' home.

But she just became more difficult after we got back here. I needed to get on with work for uni. and it were really getting to me. She wouldn't watch TV or go on the computer on her own like she used to. I don't think I'm good with kids her age.

You's good with Lara and Liam, and with Charly and me.

I'm not even sure of that any more.

Lara's told me how brilliant you was when you used to babysit her. You was her favourite.

Oh sure, I was just very willing, that was all. She hardly ever had anyone else.

No, you's good with her, Katy, I can tell, right. And you's good with Zoë. You would've won her over.

I wish I had your confidence about that.

Well, I'll talk to Zoë, right. But I don't like you phoning up the children's home, ok, Katy.

Aysha, I try and consult all of you whenever I can, but in the end, it is me that runs this family, you know.

Yeah, but I'm just giving you my opinion, right. That's only fair.

Quite fair, but you don't mind me contacting the home to ask for one of their volunteers to babysit for us.

That's different, right.

No, it's not, it's the same thing. Zoë ....

It's different, Katy, said Aysha emphatically, her voice rising and causing Katy to put her finger to her lips. Baby-sitting's, like, normal. It could be anyone babysitting.

The only difference is it allows you and me to go to gigs, while this was to find something good for Zoë.

No, that ain't fair, Katy. All I'm saying is, having a babysitter in is like any kid in a family, it's like Lara and Liam having you go round so's their mum and dad can go out. It don't matter where the babysitter's from, it's just, like, normal. But what you did were a bit like sending Zoë back in care. Just for the day, right.

OK, I take your point. Katy still felt she was in the right but Aysha's ability to argue was improving so much that it caught her off guard. But are you saying, she went on, that it would have been better to have got a sitter in and gone off to the library at uni to do my work?

No.

I think all the volunteers who were available were on this day trip anyway.

You could get someone else to sit with Zoë, not from the home.

Oh sure, a complete stranger. What would that have done to her?

I don't mean, like, now, I mean in the future. Like, she's starting at the school next door, right, and she's gonna make friends, and get to know their mums and dads -

Aysha stopped and looked sheepish.

You think we could ask other kids' mums or dads to babysit?

Well, she could go round other kids' houses for sleep-overs, right? Loads of kids do that.

It's possible, but what about Charly?

344

Well, if it's gigs, Charly could come too. To some of them, right. And when it's your cello, or your, what's that sport you do?

Basketball. Something that hadn't been mentioned for such an age that she couldn't blame the girl for forgetting the word.

Yeah, basketball, right, I could babysit them two, I'm old enough now.

I'm not sure, maybe when you turn fourteen, I'll have to check.

Why d'you always have to check these things?

You must remember you are still in care, all of you. It might seem quite a lot different, with me as your carer, but a lot of the same rules apply as when you were in the home. It isn't that different. And getting back to Zoë, you must remember that she's a more sociable kid than you or Charly. She likes doing things with other children. She liked going on the trips when she lived at the home, and she still likes that sort of thing now. That's why I invited Lara along to the caravan, so that Zoë would have another kid to play with. She wouldn't have been happy just here with me, even if we hadn't fallen out, she wouldn't have been happy having a babysitter in, especially someone she didn't know, and what is clear, and I'm sure you know this, is she was very happy going on the day-trip the other day, and the visit to the swimming-pool, with a group of kids, most of whom she knew, and those she didn't she got on with because they were around her age. It made all the difference, it changed her from being a miserable kid to being happy again.

Yeah, said Aysha. But what I'm saying is, we wanna get her so she's happy, like, here with us, so's she don't have to go back to the home to be happy. That's what's bad, Katy, that's what I'm trying to tell you ok, it ain't right if you gotta send a kid back there, even if it's just on a day-trip, to make her happy. And this Ambrose thing, right, it's important to Zoë, I don't know why, but it is, so it ain't no good getting mad at her 'bout Ambrose, you gotta go 'long with it til she, like, gets over it, right?

Right. And while we're on the subject, I've found there is a rock music festival in Cheshire the first weekend in September. That's quite near my mum's house, so I'm thinking we can combine it with going there for a few days, and maybe my mum and Steve would look after Zoë and Greg if you, Charly and me went to this festival for the whole of the Saturday. And Steve might come and collect us so we won't need to worry about the last train or bus.

Cool. But what if Zoë wants to come too?

I really hope she won't. She's much too young to enjoy that sort of thing, and she'll be happier staying with Greg.

You see dogs at them festivals, too.

How d'you know?

I've seen pictures, right. Glastonbury, right. Loads of dogs.

Well, I don't know about Glastonbury, but I think it's cruel on dogs to take them to festivals where there's loud music and flashing lights and strobes and stuff. Which I think this one in Cheshire will have.

Wicked! So when's we going?

Well, we go to the drumming camp the weekend after next. I've arranged to call on Charly's Uncle Phil and Auntie Ruth on the way down, on the Thursday, for lunch. An early lunch, so we won't be late getting there. I said coffee, but they insisted on lunch. Then when we get back, on the Monday evening, we'll just have one day, the Tuesday, to unpack, wash dirty clothes, pack clean clothes, and then set off for Longworth on the Wednesday morning. And after we get back from my mum's it will be nearly start of term. So tomorrow I'm gonna work out with all of you what you need for school, clothes, books, equipment, whether there's any work you need to have done, so we can start getting it organised cos it won't be no good leaving it to the last minute.

Aysha pulled a face. I have found two gigs, she pronounced. You was right, there's hardly any in August, but I has found two.

Well, let's just go to one, ok. We'll sort that out tomorrow cos look how late it is, and Greg's been sitting waiting patiently for his walk all this time.

Who's playing this festival we're going to?

I dunno, I've got the list somewhere. We can talk about all this tomorrow, right. And have you read that letter from the Sri Lanka High Commission? Cos we'll discuss that tomorrow too.

No, where is it?

I left it in your room for you to look at. So tomorrow morning find it, and read it at breakfast-time. We'll spend the morning sorting lots of things out - and now you take Greg for just a short walk, cos it's way past your bedtime. And mine.

She would have liked to have had some physical contact with the child after what seemed like the most important and meaningful communication they'd had for a long time, but she knew Aysha was completely resistant to that now, so she contented herself with giving her warmest, most affectionate smile, and knew that the frown which the girl gave in return was a made-up gesture, her way, the only way she now had, of returning the affection.

Life's gonna be really busy next term, it was anyway, but now with this chance I've got of playing in the quartet, then even more so. So we've gotta talk about all this, all of us, plan things carefully, right.

Right, yeah. And you must do your quartet, Katy, ok?

31. SPOOKY

Goodbye, Ambrose, Zoë said yesterday, when they went to the station to catch the train to go stay with Katy's mum and stepdad. Goodbye for a long time, cos I'm a big kid now.

It was Aysha who told her saying goodbye were important. Aysha did lots of things with Zoë after she and Charly got back from their camping holiday. When they took Greg out for walks, it were sometimes just the two of them, and Aysha talked to her. When they stayed home, they sometimes watched TV together, although Aysha never bothered with TV before. They sat at the computer together, and Aysha didn't know much about how to work the computer, so she got Zoë to teach her how to play some of the games. And in the evenings, Aysha read stories to her. Zoë didn't need them read out, she could read stories on her own, in fact she thought she could read better than her big sister, what with Aysha bunking off school so much and being sent to this Unit, but it were a surprise for her to find out

347

how good Aysha were at reading. Although she knew Aysha would always look out for her, Zoë had got used to Aysha never spending much time with her up to now, it was always other kids who lived on the estates, and then it were Katy, and after they moved in with Katy, it were Charly. And she and Charly had gone off for a long time, so Zoë had taken Ambrose with her on her holiday in the caravan and had found a new friend in Lara. That was only fair. But then Katy took her away from Lara cos Ambrose couldn't be friends with Lara any more and she, Zoë, got mad with Katy.

Aysha talked about all this with her when they was together, and Zoë felt happy 'bout seeing so much more of Aysha and talking with her. Aysha talked 'bout her new school and making new friends. She said it weren't like at the children's home, she might get invited to her friends' houses and meet their mums and dads and brothers and sisters, and that were a good thing if it happened, but it wouldn't be fair to take Ambrose along too. The same at school, Aysha explained, she might get laughed at if she told a friend about Ambrose and the friend told some of the other kids. And the same with Lara. Aysha liked Lara too, and they would see her again when they went up to Katy's mum's house, but not with Ambrose. Aysha talked 'bout this again and again, which were also a funny thing, cos Aysha knew 'bout Ambrose but she'd never bothered that much 'bout him before. But now they talked and Zoë could see that her big sister knew what were what, even after all the bad things had happened to her and the bad things she'd done and all the places she'd never fitted in, foster-homes, schools, the children's home, still Aysha had good knowledge of people. Zoë thought it must be Katy had helped Aysha learn things and stop being so bad, so's now Aysha could be kind and helpful to her, Zoë, her baby sister. Zoë'd got on well with Katy before the holiday, but then she got mad with her, and it were Aysha what told her she must get to like her again and do things to help out.

Zoë and her two sisters were at Katy's mum's house now, and this afternoon Lara and her little brother Liam were coming over to play and staying to tea. Aysha said she was sure Lara would still be her friend, as long as she allowed Liam to play too. And then Katy were gonna take Aysha and Charly to a whole Saturday of music gigs, and she, Zoë, would stay here and look after Greg and have Lara and Liam up to play, as long as she was good friends with Lara again now. Katy's stepdad Steve would take them to the park, as long as it weren't raining, so's they could play on the swings and so's Greg could have his walk.

Aysha were trying just to think 'bout the music, nothing else. She and Charly was going to a whole Saturday of bands, and it were gonna be seriously wicked. Charly were excited thinking 'bout it too. Aysha weren't sure how Katy felt 'bout it, cos Katy didn't seem to get excited 'bout the same things as her any more like they used to, but it might be that Katy had other things on her mind. She'd got the three of them together, one day, before they went to that useless gig which Aysha had found in the paper, and before the drumming weekend, and she'd made a list of everything they needed to sort out for next term. Aysha hated lists, and hated having to sort out stuff, there was loads of things to do with school, work, timetables, clothes, sports stuff, choir, bus and train times, blah blah fucking blah, then there was stuff 'bout activities and babysitting and working all that out, and then there was calling on Charly's uncle and auntie and granny, and then there was replying to the Sri Lanka High something in London 'bout her real father who they was still looking for. And then there was the stuff to take with them on the drumming weekend and stuff they were gonna need when they went to Katy's mum's, and had the Saturday at this music festival. Well, the drumming weekend were good, she'd done a lot of drumming and learnt quite a bit more 'bout different styles of drumming and different rhythms which was gonna make her a better drummer when she went back to school. And Charly liked listening to the different music that were playing, from all different places in the world, and Zoë liked playing in the play area, and it meant they all of them, 'part from night-time, got out of each other's hair for a few days which were good for Katy, Aysha could tell. But it were good for her, Aysha, too, cos she'd spent loads of time with her sisters this holiday, sharing a tent with Charly on that long camping trip with Neil, and then taking Zoë under her wing when they got back. And Aysha by the end of it had got so it were doing her head in so's all she wanted to do were taking Greg out and meeting up with some of them other kids what hung around in the village. Even gigs was no use in August like Katy had said, for once Katy was right. But it were all this other stuff was getting to her. School, right, now school weren't that bad, nothing like as bad as she used to think, but when you was on holiday from school you shouldn't be made to think 'bout it at all, you wait til school starts again, and here was Katy trying to get them organised and force school on their minds when it's only half way through the holidays. And then there's baby-sitting, which is a bad word cos none of them's babies or any-thing like, but it's the word everyone uses, and Aysha thought she should be allowed to babysit her sisters now, she were grown-up enough, after every-thing she'd done to turn her life around the least they could do was let her babysit. But Katy said she'd need to check with the social worker, fucking Ruth Barnes, they didn't even need a social worker none of them, and course what were the answer from Ruth Barnes, only that Aysha were still too young, fucking hell, she might be allowed after she were fourteen, well that was only less than one term. But even so, that were so fucking annoy-ing, and now Katy had that other music thing she'd joined, what were it called, a quartet, which Aysha knew she'd said yes, Katy must do it, not let a chance like that slip by, but that were extra babysitting needed, although Katy said if it were daytime on a Saturday or Sunday or half-term that they fixed a practice, Katy didn't say practice, she used a funny word, re something, reher something, anyhow she said she would agree leaving Aysha in charge then, but not evenings. So Aysha was gonna hide away in her room listening to music or doing homework or both when the babysitter was there cos she didn't wanna have nothing to do with no babysitter, and Greg would be up there with her and would have to wait for his late-night walk til Katy got back.

And then there was gigs. Katy said they was gonna try and go to one gig a week, but some of them, she said, would be like halls or theatres or places where they all could go, and that meant no smoking or booze for her like she could do at the smaller places like clubs, so she weren't too happy 'bout that and 'bout Katy saying she were still much too young to go to them places on her own. She thought about just going anyway cos Katy couldn't stop her, but she never had much money, and Katy might think she'd run away and call the cops which she'd really hate, it would be like the bad old days, and anyway they prob'ly wouldn't let her in on her own like Katy said, she had to admit Katy were prob'ly right 'bout that, and anyhow the clubs down the town centre were right crappy, all the best ones was further away, but even so this was one more thing to make her mad.

Everything was weird this summer holiday, the weather, Katy, her sisters, the funny yellow moon at night, the fact that she wanted to make things work out, for everyone else more than for her, and she were making an effort, but everything were getting to her at the same time. She were turning out like Katy, she kept thinking, oh my god, where's Aysha gone?

Well somewhere there was the old Aysha there waiting for her chance to peep out from the shadow of the new Aysha. The old Aysha were darkness and excitement and bad stuff. She were still there at night when she took Greg out and sometimes met up with other kids, if it were boys then something might happen, they might do something, or one of them, or her, it were that funny old yellow moon up there, it were true what they said, the moon could make you feel strange or p'raps it were just her, there was something weird happening to her and it made the night feel electric and the moon creepy. Or spooky, that was the word for everything at night, that were the old Aysha, the real Aysha, showing herself again, and it were spooky.

Nothing happened, prob'ly it never would cos she had Greg with her. Greg liked her the same whether it were the old Aysha or the new Aysha, it didn't matter to a dog, nor did it matter what she did but if it hurt her and bad things usually did, then it would matter to Greg. He would see to it, even before Katy. One of these days though the real Aysha would burst through, show herself again. It would be like a bomb, blowing apart all these people's lives. It would be mega stuff. Only thing was, she would never hurt Katy, cos Katy'd done so much for her, without Katy she'd be locked up in a secure unit by now, she couldn't bear the thought of letting her down, and she weren't gonna hurt her sisters either, and Greg even less. And then when she thought 'bout it, there was Katy's mum, and stepdad, and there was little Liam and Lara, and their dad Marcus, and there was Neil who'd given her and Charly that wicked holiday, no they was all on her side and she weren't gonna let them down neither, none of them. It were just that Samantha, Katy's sister. Aysha knew she couldn't stand her, they neither of them liked the other one, and if only the chance would come for Aysha to come out with the old Aysha right in front of Samantha and blow apart her world. But she couldn't see how that could ever happen. If she hurt Samantha it would hurt Marcus, it would even more hurt Lara and Liam, and what was worse it would hurt Katy too something terrible. And it would prove Samantha right about her too, and she weren't never gonna let that happen. No, she were gonna stand up to Samantha whenever she saw her, look her right in the face with an expression what said, think the worst of me but I don't care cos you'll never prove it and you'll never get one over on me. And all the bad stuff would just have to stay hidden for a while yet, the old Aysha stay stuffed away inside her like she was now, and just allowed a peep out when she took Greg out at night or went to gigs and maybe this festival on Saturday.

She were still trying to think about the festival and nothing else. Other thoughts got in the way. Everyone else in the house were asleep, must be. And Greg were asleep by her bed. And it weren't even Saturday tomorrow. Another whole day, fucking hell. Mind you, Katy was meeting up with this boyfriend tomorrow, only Katy kept saying he weren't a boyfriend, just a guy who'd took a liking to her, and that should've been really something if it weren't for the festival the day after. A whole wicked day of live bands, live acts, some big, most of them not so big, some she'd seen already, some she'd heard the music on radio or CD, some she knew 'bout but never heard before, some she'd never even heard the name. She went through them in her head for the hundredth time, in the order on the programme, that were always starting with the biggest names, that's how they did it -

K.T.Tunstall, Turin Brakes, The Delays, Idlewild, The Coral, The Magic Numbers, British Sea Power, Ed Harcourt, Guille-mots, My Morning Jacket, Broken Social Scene, The Evinrudes, Engineers, Jim Noir, Meridian, Bikini Atoll, Doctor Robert, James Yorkston, Hush The Many, Tilly and the Wall, My Latest Novel, Fionn Regan, The Beauty Shop, The Bright Space, Howling Bells, Tom McRae, Memory Band, Rose Kemp, Dustin O'Halloran, Aberfeldy, Proud Mary, The Young Knives, Sunny Day Sets Fire, Merz, Metronomy, Midlake, The Autumns, Roddy Woomble from Idlewild doing a solo set and the same for

Amy Millan from Broken Social Scene. And there was prob'ly more she couldn't remember or hadn't been announced yet, or on the acoustic stage. And she weren't gonna get to see nowehere near half the acts cos some weren't gonna play on the Saturday and cos there was two stages. There was a main stage and an acoustic stage, Charly and Katy would prob'ly stick with the acoustic, but she were gonna try the main stage mosta the time 'part from when Roddy Woomble and Amy Millan was on. The only ones missing was fucking Testicles, she hadn't heard anything of them for an age.

Sharon couldn't sleep that first night the girls were there. She talked to Steve in whispers, although Steve's responses indicated that he was close to dropping off most of the time. She still couldn't help worrying about Katy. Life for her daughter seemed to revolve around the three girls and fitting her studies and her other activities around them. Why was she taking the older two all the way into Cheshire, nearly half way back towards Burs- field, for a whole day, starting early and returning late, for this music festival, when she had so much else to do, to think about. She knew girls were mad about music these days, but she could- n't understand what was so special about the music they were going to be hearing all day. It was clear how much Aysha and Charly were looking forward to it, that was true. Maybe it would be a break for Katy also. But to Sharon it seemed that this young man who was coming over to spend Friday evening with Katy was far more important, but Katy didn't seem to think so at all. And then there was the business of trying to trace Rodney. Katy made it quite clear she didn't have time to even think about this, even when Sharon told her that she was thinking of employing the services of a private detective, which of course would cost money. No-one she knew, knew much about them, not even if there were any in the town. Of course Katy probably knew even less than her, but nevertheless she would have really really liked to have discussed this with one of her daughters. Samantha had just said she thought they were a waste of space. Steve, on the other hand, had been quite positive about the idea, even willing to help out himself to save a bit of money if that could be part of the deal.

But Katy just didn't seem to want to know, and Sharon felt sad that her younger daughter seemed to have so many responsibilities that a night out with a young man was of minimal importance to her and finding her real father was of no interest whatever.

How does Katy seem to you, my love? she asked the soporific Steve lying next to her. I do worry about her, me. But there was no answer from her husband.

So she talked to Aysha instead, the next evening when Katy was out with Gareth. The other two girls had gone up to bed, and Aysha was about to take the dog out. Steve was in the kitchen.

Katy doesn't seem to want to talk about finding her real father, she said. So I'll fill you in, Aysha. You can mention this to Katy, if you like, but please don't tell anyone else. Will you promise?

The girl nodded her head gravely.

He's not missing, you see, in the way that the police or the Salvation Army look at it. He packed his things and left to start a new life. If he's still alive he may be married with more kids of his own, and he may have changed his name.

Steve came into the room.

I'm talking about finding Rodney, she said to her husband. We've thought about hiring a private detective, haven't we, dear? She turned to Aysha. Steve fancies the idea of acting the detective himself, but I think we need someone with qualifications and experience, a professional in other words.

Well, I think I know where to start, the right questions to ask, said Steve. For instance, I asked you, didn't I, Sharon, what was the last address you had for Rodney?

And I said, I haven't had any address for him since he left here.

So, I said, went on Steve. Wasn't there an address on the divorce papers?

Oh, now you're getting personal. Not in front of Aysha, Steve.

Aysha was looking more and more uncomfortable. I never wanted to start an argument, she said. I just thought it would be good, like, to find Katy's real dad. Shall I go out with Greg now?

Yes, my love, that's a good idea. Katy could be back any time now and I don't want her finding us talking to you about these things.

Is she bringing her boyfriend back here?

I don't suppose she will, although I told her she could if she wanted. And you mustn't call him her boyfriend, she won't have that.

What do we call him then?

She wants us just to refer to him as Gareth.

I wish I could meet him, said Aysha.

Oh, so do I, love, so do I.

After Aysha had gone out, not without some trepidation on Sharon's part, as her daughter and Aysha usually did the late-night dog-walk together, and Steve was available on the nights Katy wasn't, but she'd been assured that this was part of Aysha's daily routine, Steve returned to the previous topic.

Why have you not answered, about an address on the divorce papers? he pressed her. A private detective will want an answer.

There was no divorce, she said slowly and painfully. She had presented herself as a divorced single parent when she'd first got to know Steve.

What? You don't mean our marriage was bigamous?

No, no, of course not. There was no divorce because Rodney and I were never legally married. We pretended we were, for the sake of the girls, but we'd never actually bothered. We'd gone off for a short holiday, and came back saying we'd got married. I took the name Owen, and that was that. It used to happen a lot in the old days.

So Owen isn't actually your name?

Yes, it is, I changed it by deed poll after Sam was born.

But you've kept the name of someone you were never married to, even though you've married me.

But that was because of the girls. Rodney is their father, so Owen is their rightful surname, and it seemed right for it to stay mine too. But when he left us, that were it. No need for a divorce or anything. He might have changed his name, of course, if he's remarried, I mean, just married, he could've taken his wife's name.

Well, it beggars me, said Steve. How we're going to

track him down. But let's start trying detective agencies on Monday.

And then a few minutes later, Aysha, Greg, and Katy all came into the house together, and there was no Gareth with them, and Sharon could hear Aysha whispering to her daughter as they went upstairs over how she should have brought Gareth back as she, Aysha, and Katy's mum were both dying to meet him.

It were new school for Charly tomorrow. A new school were always full of worries, but this one weren't so bad as when she'd gone to a new school before. She had been to see it once, but even better, Aysha told her this school were ok. That was quite something, for Aysha to say that, cos her big sister had always hated school. But now she quite liked it, and did things like running and choir and drumming. If the other kids and the teachers thought Aysha were ok, surprising as Charly thought that were, then that would make it better for Charly on her first day, tomorrow. And all the other kids in her class would be new, too. And Aysha would come to school with her and they'd go home together, cos Aysha promised they would, and that meant there weren't likely to be much trouble on the road outside school or on the bus. Aysha were a good older sister when it came to protecting Zoë and her, she looked out for them in foster-homes, and at the children's home, when she was there, and she'd look out for her at school, Charly knew.

For a girl, Aysha were strong, stronger than lots of boys even. Her legs was strong, otherwise how could she be a good runner, and even more her arms was strong. Charly thought about Aysha carrying that heavy pack with one of the tents in all the way up that mountain and never complaining once, never asking for a stop, only stopping when Neil did. Charly felt proud of her sister when she used her strength like that, or when she took control of Greg on his lead, or when she did well at running. In the old days, before Aysha met Katy, the only way Charly knew her sister were strong was when she got in fights or busted things or fought off the p'lice or staff when they tried to calm her down, and Charly hated that, not so much because it were Aysha putting her strength to the wrong use but cos it made her frightened 'bout what were gonna happen to her sister, and if she got sent away what would happen to her and Zoë without Aysha around to see they was ok.

And now there was drumming too. At the drumming camp, Charly and Katy went to watch Aysha on the last morning, before the camp finished straight after lunch. Aysha could drum fast or slow, loud or quiet, she kept going for ages without a break. Her arms could work in a rhythm so's it seemed natural and at the same time they could control the drumsticks without no easing off. That meant strength in them arms of hers. Charly were gonna join Aysha in her music. If she played drums at school, then Charly were gonna try and join the band, or the group, or the ensemble, or whatever it were. It might take a few years yet, but she would. Charly's birthday were coming up, and Katy'd just bought her a guitar, and arranged for her to start guitar lessons. She were gonna start singing in Katy's choir, too, and if she did ok, she would join the school choir, just like Aysha did.

Charly were getting to like Katy more now. Or getting to know her, was that it? She had, in one way, always liked her cos she had a dog and cos of the good influence she had on Aysha, but there was always other people, it were never just Katy, or even just the four of them, and Charly found that a problem. It weren't people so much, it were talking. Charly hated talking, what she liked were reading, or listening, or watching, or learning things. People meant talking, or being s'posed to, even with Katy, so Charly stuck with her sisters. But now she were getting to know Katy, since she got back from the expedition with Neil and Aysha. Like she'd been with Aysha so much, and then they wanted to have a break from one another. Charly thought Aysha would wanna see Katy lots and she, Charly would be with Zoë, but that weren't what happened, Aysha saw to Zoë and Charly started helping out Katy around the house, she didn't know why, it just happened. Then at the drumming camp, Aysha were practising her drumming, and Zoë were in the supervised play activities for kids, which meant Katy sometimes came with her to listen to the music she liked. Sometimes she didn't, she stayed in their tent instead, but mostly she did. Katy didn't talk much, but when she did, it were about the music from different countries they was watching being played, and they found they liked the same music. The same thing happened at the festival where they went for the Saturday all day, Aysha liked mostly the bands who made great walls of sound, but Charly and Katy both liked the acoustic stage where it were guitar music and quieter. Aysha came with them to the acoustic stage to hear Roddy Woomble and Amy Millan, but 'part from that she went off to the main stage so they had to tell her where to meet them for lunch and supper and going home. Aysha liked doing things on her own, and talking to other kids she never even met before. Roddy Woomble was from Idlewild and Amy Millan from Broken Social Scene, they was two of Aysha's fave bands along with Test Icicles which she called Testicles and was such a stupid name. It were funny how Aysha could remember all the bands she went to see or heard the music of or read about and even the names of who was in the bands, but she couldn't remember the names of the birds they saw in Scotland, which Charly could remember. It weren't having a bad memory, it were just, like, bands was the most important thing for Aysha. It were what she talked 'bout with other kids she met. That and smoking. Aysha smoked weed sometimes, Charly knew, that were cannabis, and she hated that cos it were a drug and drugs were what their mother had a problem with ever since Charly could remember and what her dad Kenny died from, ok that were worse drugs than weed, but it were drugs all the same and Katy would never have allowed Aysha to do this, and Charly thought Katy didn't know and she mustn't tell her. That were why Aysha liked going off on her own and talking with older kids. Charly would hate that, trying to talk with strangers. It was good being with Katy cos she didn't have to talk to anyone, even Katy. Katy knew she didn't like talking, but sometimes she did try and get her to, like when they went to see Charly's uncle and aunt and grandmother. Charly liked going to see them but didn't like it that they wanted her to talk to them.

She was only a little bit worried 'bout school tomorrow, but still she couldn't get to sleep. She'd heard Aysha going out with Greg, and coming back in - Katy told Aysha she must go out a bit earlier tonight cos of first day back at school. Zoë were fast asleep, she had one more day's holiday, and she were lucky, she were going to the school next door to where they lived.

Charly started thinking back to Scotland and the birds she'd seen with Neil, and the otters and seals, and the wild hares on the machair grass, and before she knew it she was fast asleep.

32. LAND OF HOPE AND DREAMS

The next term was over almost as soon as it had begun, so it seemed to Katy. The girls played their part, too, all of them getting on with their busy lives with only minimal disruptions, an occasional failure to complete homework or disciplinary problem at school on Aysha's part, or Zoë making a friend and then falling out very quickly. Charly turned eleven at the start of the term and quickly got stuck into her academic subjects and homework, all of which had a salutary effect on Aysha, who started tackling homework more assiduously. Aysha herself turned fourteen before term ended, declining the offer to have a few friends round after school or have a night out somewhere. Zoë, despite a few expected ups and downs, gradually settled in and made some progress at the school next door.

Weekday evenings were taken up with Katy's activities and a babysitting rota. Aysha walked Greg when she got home and again later, washed up and did homework, Charly and Zoë took it in turns to help Katy with the evening meal. If there was time before the babysitter arrived, Aysha practised drumming and Charly her guitar. Katy needed to put in quite a bit more cello practice now that she was in the quartet but she was able to do this during school hours, taking a break from course-work where before she might have gone for a run. Being in the quartet brought her into a whole new social world of musicians and music aficionados which she'd hardly been aware of from the orchestra, but she had no time to take advantage of this even if she'd wanted to. Just keeping up with the new pieces she had to not only learn but develop to a higher level of performance, was difficult enough on top of her other commitments.

Aysha turned out to be a tremendous help. Every Saturday morning she, with Greg, took Charly and Zoë into town where Charly had a guitar lesson and Zoë her dance class, and she would, whatever the weather, walk Greg in the main city centre park until it was time to collect the younger girls. On the way home the girls would shop for the week, Katy having decided that she would risk entrusting Aysha with the sizeable amount of cash that went with that responsibility. Katy herself was usually rehearsing with her quartet on a Saturday morning and then playing in a basketball match in the afternoon, sometimes seeing the girls briefly for lunch, sometimes going straight from the one to the other and not seeing them from breakfast-time until later in the day.

Sundays were the only days they could relax and be a family together, although she did try and take them all out on a Saturday evening, for a meal out, or a film, or occasionally a concert, with seating and suitable for all of them, and then fish and chips afterwards. She tried to avoid the other sort of gig at weekends, at places more like clubs, just her and Aysha, although once in the term it had seemed the best option. But on Sundays she tried to make sure none of them needed to work, apart from a bit of music practice and cooking and washing-up. She tried to give them quality time as a family together and took them all on country walks, or they went running in poor weather, or if it was really atrocious stayed in and played board games. Aysha quickly lost interest in these, and would opt for walking Greg however awful it was outside.

Aysha never helped with the meals, but she did with virtually everything else, washing-up, hoovering, shopping, and feeding and brushing Greg as well as being principle dog-walker. She even started offering to help in the garden which had up to now, during term-time, been the province of one of the teachers and a few of the year 6 children from the school. But the autumn was not a time for much interest in the garden from that quarter, and after half-term it stopped altogether. Instead Aysha threw herself into short but frenetic bursts of tidying up and digging.

Katy tried to get most of the housework done during the week when the girls were at school, but she did appreciate Aysha's willingness, since once her own term started coursework and cello practice took up a large slice of her available time between breakfast and Zoë's return, which before long involved inviting friends in for tea or to play on the computer or both.

At half-term they all went back to Longworth for a few days. Katy herself didn't have a half-term, but she worked out which lectures and classes she could most afford to miss and arranged a mid-week visit, since both Charly's guitar lessons and Zoë's dance class didn't have a break either.

She arranged another evening out with Gareth while she was back at her mum's, but he was pressing to visit them in Bursfield which bothered her a little. Eventually she said, yes, he could come for lunch one Sunday in November and scheduled this in. Aysha and Charly had never met Gareth and Aysha took a great interest prior to the visit, but when he came they both became totally tongue-tied and it was left to Zoë to resurrect her acquaintance with him by trying to be as friendly as she could. As for Katy, she was on edge from the start, and was sure Gareth must have been aware. The longer he stayed, the more nervous she became. Sunday evenings were supposed to be the most relaxing times of the whole week, when she might try and find a TV programme they could all enjoy, or play a game, or read, write a letter, talk gently together, even the computer was discouraged.

But Gareth stayed on, talking to her, with one or more of the girls in the room listening, it was clear he was waiting for them all to disappear to their beds so that he could be one-to-one with Katy, but he hadn't realised that Aysha had never gone to bed before her carer and wasn't going to change that now.

She sat with her ear-phones on, and with Greg at her feet as almost always, glancing at Katy quite frequently. Finally Katy indicated with a gesture that it was time for Greg to be taken for his night-walk. And as Aysha left the room with the dog, Katy followed her to the front door.

What shall I do, Aysha? she whispered. He doesn't seem to want to leave. Should I let him stay the night?

You go for it, Katy, if you wants, the child whispered back, with little doubt what she meant. Y'know, this guy really likes you, ok, so you gotta like take a chance here, right. But only if it's what you wants, yeah.

Katy went back to her guest, her mood lightened, almost laughing.

She's a funny kid, that one.

She seems very protective of you, observed Gareth.

Perhaps. She certainly likes to know what's going on. Charly's the same. I'm sorry they've both been so uncommunicative. Charly always is, but Aysha can be talkative when she wants.

Does she resent me coming?

Oh no, not at all, it's just a strange situation for her.

They don't know what to make of me, suggested her visitor.

I think that's it, or something like. Aysha probably doesn't know what to say in a situation like this, doesn't want to put her foot in it. She'd be mortified if she said something which put you off staying.

Gareth looked at Katy and took her hand. She could sense how keen he was.

I can tell how important to you these kids are, he said. Aysha most of all. You've got something really good going there.

It doesn't feel like it a lot of the time.

But she knew she was ready now, and that was Aysha, her doing. She had given the girl so much, had helped her grow, blossom into adolescence, and now she could feel Aysha's vitality, her strength and maturity, her sexuality even, flowing back into Katy's own body. She felt good about herself physically, she no longer felt doubts, and she responded to Gareth's tentative advances. When Aysha came back in with Greg and popped her head round the door of the sitting-room before retreating upstairs, she found the two of them curled up together.

It happened on the floor of the downstairs room. They slept closely entwined in the single bed in Katy's room, but she'd already lost her virginity by then. Gareth was gentle, curbing his eagerness unlike the evening in the caravan. She came with a start, not quite realising what was happening, not quite prepared for this. She felt Aysha was there, part of her, inside her soul somehow, as though their beings had merged, but she knew as soon as it had happened, she knew without a doubt, that it was Gareth she wanted physically, and her love for Aysha was of a different order entirely.

Gareth slept better than her, and indeed might have slept on in the morning if she'd let him. But there was still a part of her uptight about all this, and the need for Gareth to leave early, before all the other kids at Zoë's school and their parents, got to see him, took on a disproportionate importance. So she was up early and busying herself with breakfast for all of them, and rousing a somewhat bemused Gareth, who asked her if she wanted him away before the girls got up.

Not at all, she said. I'll go and call them now to come down and watch you eat breakfast. Aysha and Charly have to leave early anyhow.

There were some furtive glances and hidden smiles. Katy went out to the road with Gareth, arranging for him to visit again soon, this time on a Saturday, and just as she was kissing him goodbye the two older girls traipsed out with their schoolbags, slamming the front door behind them.

Don't shut the door, she called out too late. I haven't got my key!

It's ok, Katy, said Aysha in a mock older sister tone. Zoë's in there, right. She's just got up and she'll let you in. Don't worry, yeah.

She knew what Aysha meant, she was so knowing, that kid.

But she still felt troubled about Aysha. Despite the support and encouragement the younger girl gave her over Gareth, and would continue to do on his subsequent visits, despite on one level feeling the child was almost part of her soul, something didn't seem right between them. Of course, Katy told herself, how could she have expected things to remain the same when the younger sisters moved in? But she was sure it wasn't just that.

She wondered if Aysha was depressed. It would not be surprising, after all, considering her terrible childhood, and remembering what she'd come out with when the abuse had been talked through. On the one hand, she rarely smiled, or showed any enthusiasm for anything when with Katy. She'd taken to wearing black nearly all the time like she used to when Katy first met her. She no longer bothered about freaky styles for her hair. She was often last to bed and first up, rarely having peaceful lie-ins like she used to at the bedsit. Her appetite seemed erratic, too, sometimes she was as hungry as she always had been, even more so, but other times she would pick at her food, saying she felt a bit sick. She absolutely refused to go to the dentist in

363

Longworth at half-term when Katy had arranged check-ups for all four of them. But worst of all, she seemed unwilling to relate to Katy at all most of the time, and when they went to a gig, just the two of them, Aysha spent more and more of the time dancing with other kids and ignoring Katy.

All this pointed to the need to try and get her to a doctor, which in itself would have been almost impossible, but Katy had to consider the counter-indications. Aysha still communicated with her sisters and took an interest in their activities. She still helped Katy out with the same degree of willingness she always had done. She was continuing to work hard at school subjects and do her running and drumming with the same degree of enthusiasm. She still met up with other kids in the village whenever she could and, as far as Katy could tell, there was no change in her approach. Most of all, and perhaps crucially, she was as loving and caring and full of enthusiasm for Greg as she always had been, and every school-day, whatever she'd been doing, however tired she was and whatever the weather, girl and dog were always passionately excited to see each other and would embark on an energetic walk together. No, Katy decided, this was not the behaviour of a depressed kid.

But what was it, then? Was there something making Aysha miserable? Was she unhappy, despite her protestations to the contrary, about Gareth's appearance in their lives? Because he might take her, Katy, away from Aysha? Or just because she didn't like men? None of this seemed to offer an explanation, and in any case Aysha's mood had seemed to deteriorate way before Gareth's weekend visit.

Katy frequently tried to bring the disparate elements of Aysha's life into a meaningful whole. She longed to visit the school to watch the girl running for the team in an inter-schools match, or in rehearsal drumming with her band and, now also, with the school orchestra. But Aysha vehemently opposed this, she was working out her own position at the school, acting independently, and Katy had to respect that, and in truth had little time she could spare. Instead, she constantly tried to encourage the girl to bring one or more of her mates from the village in to have biscuits and coffee, or juice, while listening to music, but this too was declined. So Katy concentrated her efforts on Aysha's birthday, which fell on a Monday. Making sure Gareth didn't come that weekend, she arranged for the four of them to go to a film and have a meal out the night before, and on the Monday morning there were presents and cards, and after school a magnificent cake which Katy baked herself that morning after Aysha left for school. But Aysha did not want a piece of her cake, even though she was always starving hungry when she got in from school. Nor did she respond to Katy's suggestion that she could invite her 'mates' in to share her cake.

Katy thought she should try and talk to the girl, but not tonight, not on her birthday, maybe tomorrow evening, but then it was Aysha who came in to see Katy, after she'd returned from Greg's late night walk. Katy was in her room, undressing, getting ready for bed. She stood by the door, a little hesitant.

Thanks for the birthday, Katy. Y'know, all them presents. And thanks for the cake, right. Sorry I never ate any.

Yeah, why didn't you, kiddo?

Just weren't hungry, ok.

Is anything bothering you, Aysha? You don't quite seem your usual lively self?

Aysha shut the door behind her, but did not advance any further into the room.

Is it Gareth? Katy continued.

Oh god, no, Katy, it ain't that?

What is it, then?

It's, like, doing good's real difficult, Katy. It's hard work, right.

Sure is, kid. I do know that. But it's worth it, yeah?

I dunno, Katy. It's kinda boring too. There's no buzz, right. Like I'm missing my old life. Sometimes.

You really mustn't throw it all away, you know, after all the effort you've put in.

I does know that, Katy, and I ain't gonna run off or anything, right. I loves you all too much, my sisters and you, and Greg, 'course I won't never hurt Greg. But just don't think you can make me happy, right.

Aren't there enough good things going down to compensate for your unhappiness?

That's why I wanna do mountain rescue, right. Stuff at school ain't really exciting compared to mountain rescue.

Yes, but that will have to wait a few years. You must be

patient and get your GCSEs first.

I don't go for waiting, Katy, I ain't never liked it. That's what's boring, is when there's something you really wanna do and you've gotta wait.

So that was it, thought Katy. Aysha was caught between missing elements of her old life and her dreams of doing mountain rescue.

Christmas, the second one the girls had spent at Katy's mum's, passed in what seemed like the briefest of pauses in their busy lives, Katy taking coursework with her to catch up on, and her cello to practise for an important concert the week after New Year. Gareth, who now visited every alternate weekend, arranged to come over on Boxing Day, just for the day, but it was Sam who Katy most wanted to see. It seemed ages. She, Marcus and the kids were over on Christmas Day. As well as their own presents for everyone, Sam brought a parcel addressed to Katy which had arrived the day before care of Sam and Marcus. It was from Neil. There were packages for Aysha and Charly, and a card and a postal order which Neil said was for Katy to buy something for herself and for Zoë. Aysha and Charly opened their presents to find books - Birds of Sea and Coast by Lars Jonsson for Charly, and Winterdance (the Fine Madness of Alaskan Dog-Racing) by Gary Paulsen for Aysha - both second-hand books, but both enthusiastically received, which in Aysha's case surprised Katy, as the girl had never shown any interest in reading books before aside from her schoolwork, and even with that it was tenuous.

Why hasn't Neil come for Christmas? Charly asked Marcus.

He's busy with his mountain-rescue, interposed Sam.

Can we phone him? she asked.

Of course, if he's there.

So some time in the late afternoon, after the Christmas dinner finally finished, and more presents were opened, and Charly helped Marcus wash up, while Aysha and Steve gave Greg his second walk of the day, and everyone else helped the younger kids play with presents, Charly and Aysha made a phone-call to Neil and got through to him. Katy moved as unobtrusively as she could to the edge of the play area, away from the noise of children, to try and hear what was said.

.... for the book ....

.... and mine ....

.... go camping again?

.... are you doing mountain-rescue? This was Aysha, mumbling less now, sounding a little clearer.

....

Have you done one today?

....

Can't I, like, come and help?

....

But when, then?

....

That's ages off!

....

Bye, Neil. Happy Christmas. That was Charly taking over again.

Yeah, ... and New Year. Aysha finished like she started, in an almost inaudible mumble.

And then an almost identical day, but with Gareth instead of Sam and her family, and with Aysha keeping her and her sisters out of the way, Zoë occupied with new computer games and Aysha and Charly absorbed in their books, so that Gareth could spend the day with Katy and her mum and step-father, both of whom, and Sharon most of all, were wanting to get to know him.

And then before she'd hardly had time to blink, it seemed to Katy, it was the start of the new school term, fortunately with a week before her own term started, and a chance for serious quartet rehearsing and further catching up on coursework and taking Zoë out of school for a day to visit her mother. And life continued very much as it had in the autumn term with Gareth visiting every alternate weekend and Katy continuing to extend her sexual education and the girls seeming to accept this. But with one difference: Aysha now became absorbed in the book Neil had sent her (Charly as well, but this was nothing new, Charly had always absorbed herself in wildlife books since Katy had known her) and she wanted to frequently go to libraries, the public library in town and the university library, and find books on Alaska and on husky dogs and sled-running and most of all on the Iditarod race, and all the choices she had at school, in geography and science, were focussed on projects related to this subject. And of course she was determined to one day complete the race herself.

Women can do it, Katy! It says so in the book, right.

Grown-up women, yeah. But not kids, not teenage girls. I bet you need to be, what, at least twenty.

Surprisingly, Aysha agreed with this. Course I know that, Katy. But when I leave school, yeah, I'm gonna go over to Alaska and buy some dogs and train them into a team and practise for the race and all that stuff. And, like, by the time I've done all that I'll be twenty, right.

Where will you get the money from for all this?

I'll get sponsors, right.

Sponsors? What do you know about getting sponsors?

I can find out, ok?

What's happened to you wanting to do mountain-rescue?

That as well, Katy. It's the same kinda thing. It's dogs in the mountains, right, and snow and ice and all that. Mountainrescue will be good practice for the Iditarod race.

But it was clear that Alaska and Iditarod had taken over pole position in her enthusiasms and that Neil had not been willing to respond immediately to her keenness to involve herself in mountain-rescue.

33. ARMS OF SIN

One afternoon at the end of January Katy had a phone call from one of the secretaries at Andrew Wheeler High School. Aysha had collapsed at the end of a cross-country run, and had been seen by the school nurse. Could she now be taken home by car? Charly would wait with her.

Katy immediately ordered a taxi. The two-way journey

to the other side of town would cost a packet, but no doubt Social Services would refund her. She found her cheque book, and while waiting for the taxi slipped over to the school next door where Zoë was due out in a few minutes. They agreed to look after Zoë until Katy returned.

Sitting in the back of the taxi, Katy felt a mixture of motherly tenderness, anxiety and puzzlement. What could be the matter with her charge, so tough normally, so fit? Could it be hypothermia, she wondered, in the absence of any other satis-factory explanation. If so, she felt herself to blame. Aysha had already started making long lists of everything she would need to run the Iditarod race, including all the thick Parkas and other arctic winter clothing for herself. She showed this to Katy with the suggestion that a start could be made on these supplies on birthdays and Christmases from next year on. Katy could not stop herself laughing.

But it's years off, yet, Aysha.

Yeah, but I wanna get used to wearing the gear.

But you might grow heaps more in the years between.

Nah, I'm like nearly fully grown. I just need them a bit on the big side, right.

But if you wear all this arctic gear in a mild British win-ter, it's like you might lose its effect when you go to Alaska.

Yeah, but look, Katy, right, I can wear the stuff in mountains in winter, ok. Like, that's gonna be good practice for Alaska, right.

But it then seemed that Aysha had thought about Katy's words, and taken the message too much to heart, because she stopped wearing her usual tracksuit for her running, and took to going off in shorts and sleeveless top, claiming this would toughen her up for Alaska (as if she weren't tough enough already, Katy thought to herself). And now the weather had turned very wintry with a fine dusting of snow on the ground, and so Katy guessed hypothermia.

But her explanation was wrong. Aysha had worn her tracksuit for the run - it was only a practice run, not a match - and was not cold at all, if anything she seemed, when Katy saw her, somewhat hot and flushed.

The school nurse took Katy to one side. I'm afraid we might have a problem. Unless I'm very much mistaken, I'm pretty sure this girl is pregnant.

What?

I advise you to get it checked out as soon as possible. And please let the school know as soon as you have confirmation.

School had finished a few minutes earlier, Charly had collected Aysha's gear from her classroom, and the taxi was waiting outside, so they then left promptly. Neither girl seemed willing to talk, and Katy couldn't think of what to say. Termination was the first thing that went through her mind. So much seemed to be going well in their lives, all four of them, but Aysha most of all, this was the last thing they wanted. Minimal disruption, that was best, surely. They had covered abortion on her sociology course, and Katy had found herself the only one of her year-group who didn't have strong views either way. They were all fervently pro-life or pro-choice. She didn't like the idea of abortion but could see that there were circumstances where it was necessary, and believed in a mild, pragmatic way in the woman's right to choose. What would Aysha think about it, she wondered. She knew the most important thing was to talk to Aysha, but she was dreading it. But then, perhaps the nurse was wrong.

Aysha, back home, was even more sullen and morose than Katy could remember her ever being. Even her greeting to Greg lacked her usual spark, though she did want to take him for his walk, which Katy refused, ordering Aysha to rest and Charly to walk Greg while she collected Zoë from next door. Then she set herself to getting the evening meal, awaiting the babysitter, going off to her basketball practice, all the while her mind mostly elsewhere. Tomorrow she must call at the college medical centre, with or without Aysha, try and get an appointment with a woman doctor as soon as possible. She had only been there a few weeks ago, at the start of her term, on her own account, asking to go on the pill, why hadn't she thought that Aysha might be as much in need of this as herself, or more so perhaps. But again, she told herself, the nurse might be wrong.

There was no escaping from confronting Aysha. When the girl had returned from her late-night walk with Greg - she seemed fully recovered by now, physically at least - Katy entered her bedroom.

Aysha, she blurted out. Have you been having sex?

What?

Have you, in the last few months, had sexual inter-
course?

No.

Katy was trying desperately to be stern and serious, but
it wasn't quite working.

The nurse said she thought you were pregnant. So I've
gotta ask.

She noticed a flash of panic in the girl's eyes, then it had
gone again.

Nah, can't be, Katy.

We need to get it checked out.

What for? I ain't going to no doctor, right.

I think you'll have to.

No way. You can do it with one of them kits.

How d'you know about them?

I just do.

They're not very reliable.

How d'you know?

I just do. You must go to a doctor, Aysha. Because if
you're not pregnant, there may be something else the matter. And
if you are, we'll need medical advice on what to do next.

You can't make me go to a doctor!

Katy remembered how not so long ago she'd been
unable to get Aysha to a dental appointment. The signs weren't
good. The other two girls had kept the same doctor they'd been
registered with when at the children's home, but Aysha had adamantly refused this, and in the end had agreed to be registered
with Katy's family GP and dentist in Longworth. Katy herself
had registered with the college medical centre as almost all students did so that she could get medical help in term-time if needed, but she hadn't thought to register Aysha. It might need a bit
of persuading, but she had to try. Not as daunting as getting
Aysha there.

I'll try and get an appointment for you at the student
medical centre where I go in term-time. With a woman doctor. It
is important, kiddo.

She got one of Aysha's most sullen looks in reply.

In the morning Aysha went to school with Charly as

371

though nothing had happened. Katy went to college early and called at the Medical Centre.

I'm Katy Owen aged twenty. Second year. I'm guardian of a fourteen year old girl who lives with me. Social Services have approved me as her carer. She's registered with my GP in Longworth, Lancashire. I never thought to register her here as well. But I need her to have an urgent appointment.

Is she ill?

No, but the school nurse thinks she may be pregnant.

The secretary raised her eyebrows. What about the Pregnancy Advice and Information Service?

I just need, I mean she does, a definite diagnosis. I mean, an appointment. Urgently. With a woman doctor.

Katy was getting increasingly flustered. Her power of persuasion seemed close to zero. It wasn't working out as she'd hoped.

But the woman seemed more sympathetic now. All right, I'll arrange an appointment with Dr Yeo. But she can't see you until next week, as long as that's ok.

Yes, yes.

Any special time preferred?

Well, after school if possible, four-thirty or later. She's got enthusiastic about school for the first time in her life.

All right, next Wednesday at five. Could I have the girl's full name?

Aysha Jewel Stanton.

Date of birth?

12.12.91.

Address?

The same as mine. You have my address and phone number.

Any medical history?

No, I mean yes, I'm not sure. I haven't seen her medical notes but there is some history I'd like to mention to the doctor if I could see her or talk to her before Wednesday.

Well, she's here now. Will it only take a couple of minutes?

Yes.

Well, I'll ask her to come out and see you between patients.

So she told the story over again to the doctor, but added the information about Aysha's history of abuse.

When did this happen?

Between the ages of about five-and-a-half and eight. I think.

Who by?

A guy called Vic. Her mother's live-in boyfriend at the time.

Ok, I'll keep this in mind when I examine her.

Should I let her know I've told you?

It would be better to, yes, but not if it will cause her to refuse to co-operate.

So she arranged yet another babysitter, set off with Aysha as soon as she got in from school, walked with Greg the two miles across town to the university. Katy often walked or ran, so was used to the route. Taking Greg made the crucial difference, persuaded Aysha along quite willingly, although getting her inside the building would be a different matter, as Greg would not be allowed inside.

For the first time since she collapsed at school, Aysha seemed friendly and talkative, though in a rather childish and nervous manner.

Katy?

Yeah?

I did have sex.

Did you? When?

At that rock festival. No, I mean, at the drumming weekend, no -

Well, which was it then? Surely you can remember?

No I can't remember. I think it were the drumming weekend.

So what happened?

What d'you mean, it just did, right.

Who with?

I dunno. Just a boy. Between drumming sessions.

D'you know his name?

No.

Anything about him? What he looked like? Where he were from?

He had blonde hair and a ponytail, right. Not very tall.

Hot.

Hot?

Y'know, he were dishy, right.

How old was he?

I dunno, Katy. Fifteen, ok.

Fifteen, he'd be still at school. With a ponytail?

Well, it were summer holidays, yeah. P'raps he'd just left school?

Well, he'd be sixteen then.

OK, sixteen, whatever.

You don't seem too bothered. Don't you wanna see him again?

No.

Even though he's got you pregnant. Father of your child if you go ahead with it.

I might not be.

It's beginning to sound as if you will be.

Don't tell anyone else, Katy. Like, if I am.

We'll have to tell Social Services and school, whatever happens. If you agree to a termination, we probably won't need to tell anyone else.

How do I get a termination?

It has to be done through the doctor. That's one of the reasons it's important to see her.

But Aysha was still unwilling to enter the Medical Centre. She stayed outside the front door, cradling Greg, while Katy went in to await the appointment. While she was waiting, she tried to calculate the weeks. Last weekend in August, Thirteen weeks took them to late November. Two months, or a bit over, since then, was another nine, nine and a half, possibly ten weeks, twenty-two or nearly twenty-three, should just about be possible for abortions, in this sort of case.

She was explaining this to Dr Yeo while she took her to the front entrance to meet Aysha. The doctor talked gently to the girl, for some time, eventually persuaded her in to undergo some tests.

Aysha nodded, sad and silent.

Do you want your carer to come with you or stay here with your dog?

It's Katy's dog.

Katy, yes. But you're very fond of the dog, too, am I right?

Aysha nodded.

What's the dog's name?

Greg.

So will Greg be all right on his own while Katy comes in with you to get these tests done?

Katy can stay with Greg, the child whispered.

Standing with her anxious dog, shivering a little in the cold darkness of an early February evening, Katy puzzled over the girl in her charge, her guardianship, her care. How come she suddenly seemed reassured and willing to talk to a woman doctor she'd never met before, not needing Katy with her, when she was normally so unwilling to say anything unless it had to do with one of her sisters, going to a gig, mountain rescue dogs, Alaskan sled dogs, or Greg. Katy would have given anything to be there with her, listen to what was being said. She tried not to feel left out, rejected, tried to believe that it was Greg Aysha was thinking of when she'd asked her to stay outside. How long would she have to wait in this freezing cold? She started pacing up and down but this only confused the dog.

Finally the doctor appeared and summoned Katy inside. Ordering Greg to stay put, she entered eagerly but then saw Aysha with her head lowered.

Aysha is pregnant, said Doctor Yeo. But there are details from the test results that won't be available until tomorrow. There doesn't seem anything to worry about other than the fact that a girl her age shouldn't be expecting a baby, and that she smokes, which she really should stop immediately whether or not we refer her for a termination. There's no reason why she shouldn't continue her normal activities, including the running. She collapsed last week because she hadn't eaten anything and went for her run on an empty stomach. Half way round she slipped and fell on frozen snow. The combination of mild shock and an empty stomach brought on nausea and this caused the collapse because she finished her run feeling so unwell. So if you do continue running, Aysha, don't push your-self too hard, stop running if you feel unwell, and most of all make sure you've eaten first. If you can't eat any food, then you're not in a fit state for running anyway. Now can you both come back at the same time tomorrow for the results?

Yes, said Katy.

Can't we come lunchtime? said Aysha, raising her head a fraction.

Why? Katy asked her.

Cos it's unfair on my sisters if you and me ain't there after school again tomorrow, right, and they gets their tea late. And it means less time waiting.

How will you get here?

I'll get the bus into town and then another bus out here.

What if I met you at the bus station, and we got a taxi. That would be quicker.

OK, that's fine.

What time d'you finish morning school?

Twelve-fifteen.

So will you be available at one o'clock, Dr Yeo?

Sometimes morning surgery over-runs, but I'm usually finished by one. I'll wait for you to turn up here.

OK. I'll give you a note, Aysha, to say you'll be late back for afternoon lessons. What is it tomorrow?

Games, so it won't matter.

Will you be running again?

Yeah, but it's only practice. It don't matter if I starts late.

I'll be at the bus station at twelve-thirty, right. And I'll have a packed lunch for the both of us.

Will you bring Greg?

Not in a taxi, no.

When they returned for the test results, Dr Yeo informed them both that there seemed to have been some misunderstanding. She had checked and double-checked and the foetus, a male, was clearly about 26 weeks in development. This, she advised, made a termination very unlikely, very risky, not to be recommended. She suggested Aysha think instead about carrying the child through to birth and then having him adopted. Otherwise there was no cause for concern, but she reiterated about the importance of no further smoking.

They ate their lunch in silence on the bus back to town. Katy knew she had to talk to Aysha, but she wanted time to reflect, take this in. As for the girl, she was sullen, her head down

376

and avoiding Katy's eye. She insisted she would take the bus back to school from the city centre on her own, but she said nothing else. Katy went over things in her head, again and again. At first she thought she might have miscalculated, but she soon saw that the conclusion was inescapable. Aysha must have got pregnant on her trip to Scotland. She had to confront her that evening, after the other girls were in bed.

So what's this, then? Twenty-six weeks? Beginning of August? Can't be the drumming weekend.

Yeah, ok, Katy, you don't need to go on, right. I did meet this boy on one of them islands, right. Charly and Neil had gone off bird-watching and left me in the little village, yeah, for like shopping and stuff and I met this boy and it like just happened, ok?

So why did you say it were the drumming weekend?

Cos I got mixed up, right.

It seems like a funny thing to get mixed up about. Did you have a sexual relationship at the drumming weekend?

I had sex, yeah, I wouldn't call it a relationship.

And at the rock festival?

No, not then, I were thinking of the drumming.

What about other times? Are you being promiscuous, Aysha?

No, I ain't, Katy, she protested, her voice rising with a hint of anger. I promise you, it was just the twice. I could've done it loads of times, but I ain't.

What d'you mean, loads of times? Where?

School, here in the village, playing-fields ....

At school? What on earth d'you mean? Are kids your age having sex in school?

Nah, Katy, calm down, for fuck's sake. Aysha was giggling now, and Katy couldn't help it, despite the seriousness of the situation. What I meant is, there's boys up for it in school, round here, all over the place. They'll give you a couple of smokes or share a bottle of booze or whatever, and they wants a good screw in return. I can tell, nearly all boys is like that. But I've always said no, ever since I met you, 'part from those two times. I used to say yes before, but I were only twelve then and they left me alone. They might start something and then change their minds and leave off.

What age boys are we talking about?

I dunno, fifteen or something.

And no protection?

What? When?

These two times this summer. You can't have used protection or you wouldn't have got pregnant.

Yeah, I did actually, Katy, only one time it didn't work, it came off, but I forgot which, that's why I got mixed up.

OK, said Katy, attempting to summarise. You were left alone in a small village on a Scottish island while Neil and Charly went birdwatching, you met a boy, fifteen, you say?

Yeah, about that.

So how did it happen? Where did it happen?

Down on a beach.

On a beach?

Yeah, by the harbour, only out of sight. We got talking and he seemed ok, and I kinda liked him, and he said he knew this secret place he could show me, so we went there and it just happened.

D'you know his name?

Nah.

Was he a local lad?

Nah, he were on holiday too.

With his parents?

Yeah.

Did they know this happened?

How do I know? I never saw him again. But I don't s'pose he, like, goes round telling his parents that sort of thing.

D'you know where he was from?

Nah. Somewhere in Scotland, but I don't know where.

Didn't he say where he was from?

Nah, he never said. He talked Scottish though. Like, an accent.

What did you talk about?

Y'know, all sorts of stuff. Things about the island, where we'd been to, who we'd gone with, which boat we'd come on, which boat we was gonna get back to Oban, and music and stuff like that.

So you talked a lot?

Nah, just a bit.

Well, if we're going to apply to place this baby for adoption, we have to let them know as much as possible about the father, and if possible get his permission. So anything you can remember about him will be important.

There ain't nothing else.

Well, try. And this does mean we will need to let lots of people know now.

Why?

Well, because they'll start to notice, right, when the baby starts to cause a bulge in your belly.

But s'pose I lose it, y'know, before it starts to show.

I think that's unlikely. We have to make decisions on the basis that the baby will be born.

When?

Well, early in May, we expect. That's what I mean. In the Easter holidays, anybody we go and see will be able to tell that you're expecting.

Who?

Well, all my family for one. Charly's grandmother and uncle and aunt. Then there's Gareth, he'll probably notice before the Easter holidays start. And Neil - he might be arranging some mountain experience for you at Easter, he'll need to know.

No, not Neil, said Aysha, vehemently with her face turned away. He don't need to know, why should he?

Well, as well as this mountain rescue training he might be arranging for you ....

I can still do that, right.

That might be difficult if you're heavily pregnant. But also, he was s'posed to be in charge of you when it happened.

That's why I don't want him to know, Katy, right! And everyone else, right.

Well, we've gotta tell Social Services and school, that's definite. And if they know at school, the word's probably gonna spread slowly around. So I think we should tell Charly, she don't wanna first hear about it at school.

Ok, but I'll tell her, Katy, yeah. And Zoë.

Sure thing, kiddo.

Dear, dear Sophie, I'm really sorry I haven't written since

Christmas. Read on and you'll understand why - I hope. I thought of texting but there's so much I need to get off my mind. Instead I'm scribbling this in some desperation whenever I can between lectures and classes. I only go to Uni two and a half days a week now, you'll see why on that too.

The main news is that Aysha's expecting a baby. Early May. We only discovered it when she collapsed at school after a cross-country run. It's too late for an abortion, so we're going for adoption. Apparently it happened while she was on this camping trip in the summer hols. When this guy Neil - my sister's husband's brother, you may remember he was best man at their wedding when I was bridesmaid - was supposed to be in charge of her. I can't let her out of my sight, can I? I need to talk to Neil about it but Aysha absolutely refuses to let me tell most people. I'm desperate to tell people, friends, family, Gareth - but she won't have it, although some time soon she'll start showing so she can't hide it then. That's why I need to tell you. (Not the only reason I'm writing, ok?). The only people who know are her two sisters, who she told herself, fair enough, and her school and Social Services who I had to tell. That led me to a busy few days. First of all the school were very negative. They wanted her to go back to the Referral Unit she attended before. To my mind that would have been a complete disaster. Aysha is doing so well at school, it's quite amazing, she sings in the choir, runs for the junior cross-country team, and most of all is playing drums both in the school orchestra and an embryonic rock band. She's also working really hard at her academic subjects and is catching up fast, which started when her middle sister Charly started at the school in September. It would have been a real kick in the teeth for her to go back to the Unit. So I phoned the head at the Unit, who fortunately I knew quite well and got on with, and she absolutely saw eye to eye with me. She agreed to talk it over with the school and so she saved the day on that one, but it was a few days of high anxiety for me. Social Services insisted on calling a meeting to discuss the pregnancy, but Aysha wouldn't attend, totally refused, I couldn't even have dragged her there. So I went on my own and it was agreed to refer to an adoption agency. Fortunately I had the good sense to say it should be an independent agency, not Social Services, or Aysha would never have cooperated. But I fear she still won't, she just won't talk about anything to do with having a baby. I never understood before how these teenage girls sometimes gave birth without even knowing they'd been pregnant but now I do. Aysha's in denial, she lives her life as though nothing's changed, she leaves it all to me, to do with the baby (it's going to be a boy, by the way). I sometimes feel as though it's going to be me giving birth, and I'm sure unless I can be incredibly firm with Aysha that it'll be me who does most of the looking after. That's why I feel such a need to tell my folks and most of all to tell Gareth.

I can't remember how much I told you about Gareth but since late autumn he's been part of my life in a big way. All our lives, in fact. He comes every other weekend. He's really supportive about the girls. He's incredibly keen on me, physically and in other ways. It feels good to have someone who loves me so much and it makes the sex amazingly satisfying. And I'm keen on him too, but I have to admit that it's only in response to him loving me, or mainly anyway. He's the one who's made all the running. I guess this doesn't matter too much, and I tell myself, and him, because we do talk quite a bit, although talking's not really his thing, like with most men I guess, so I'm the one who's made headway with discussing stuff, so I say that I've had so much else on my mind, other emotional commitments, which limited what I could give him, and to a smaller extent still does, and he understands that.

I'm just so glad I've got Gareth around, because between Aysha and me is just about zilch right now. Don't get me wrong, she works hard at her new "straight" life and is very helpful with me and the other two kids, but there's nothing emotional between us like there was in the early days when we had this really exciting and very slightly subversive chemistry going on. I miss it, and I know that even with Gareth around, Aysha's still more important, the most important one for me, but it's like she's my twin sister or possibly my own child, which makes this thing of her having a child really strange. I mean I'm twenty for god's sake and is this boy going to be my nephew or my grandson? Or my own child, even? And now Aysha and me live these kind of parallel lives, co-operating but never meeting or touching in any way and hardly communicating even, just relying on timeworn routines to get by. I'm desperately sad about it, but the more I try, the more she resists, so I've just had to harden my heart, or pretend to, so she won't see how I'm affected deep down.

Well, it's the kids' half-term next week, and I've got three concerts coming up, two with this quartet I'm temporarily in, (did I tell you about that?) and one with my orchestra, so I don't think we'll be heading back to Longworth unless I can fit in a flying weekend visit in March, which might be better because then surely Aysha will have to accept that people must be told, most important Gareth, because being intimate, having sex, with him, feels wrong when I'm keeping this big secret from him, also Neil, who must bear some responsibility for all this mess.

Write back or text me, and I'll keep you posted.

I hope your love-life is going well, and less complicated than mine.

Lots of love from Katy.

34. HEADS WILL ROLL

I tried to phone Neil today, Katy said to Aysha. It was the first day back at school after the February half-term, it was late in the evening, the other two were in bed and asleep. The older girl had just returned with Greg from his late-night walk and, as she always did these days, had gone straight up to her room. Katy followed and entered after a brief knock. Normally she was more circumspect but today, after the frantic activity of the half-term week, her frustration over the pregnancy had reached breaking point and she'd become determined to confront her wayward protégée.

I told you not to phone him, Katy, said Aysha, eyes bright and blazing. I don't want nobody told, right, him most of all.

I needed to know if he's got any mountain activity planned for you in the Easter hols, so's I can plan what's happening, and if he has, he will need to be told, you must know that.

OK, but not if he ain't.

So why's his phone number not working, nor his mobile either. Why's he changed his numbers, do you know?

No idea. But Katy saw that flash of panic in Aysha's eyes before she turned her face away, panic with a hint of anger, a touch of fear, which she'd noticed once or twice before. If he's on a mountain rescue, the girl went on. Like, he prob'ly switches his mobile off.

I'd've thought he'd need it switched on.

But not for, like, outside calls.

But anyhow, that don't explain why his landline's no longer in operation.

It could be out of order, or he might have changed his number.

This all seems odd to me, said Katy. I'm gonna start telling people, Aysha, whether you like it or not. You're bound to start showing a bump soon. I'm not prepared to keep it a secret any more. When Gareth next comes, I'm gonna tell him. And when we next go up to Longworth, I'm gonna tell my folks.

OK, it's fine to tell Gareth, Aysha relented. I totally don't mind if he knows. Or your mum and Steve even. But please don't tell your sister. Or Neil.

Why, Aysha? What is this? If I tell my mum Sam is bound to find out. And I'm gonna need to see her and Marcus to ask how we can get hold of Neil.

No, Katy, no, please!

Don't you wanna carry on with mountain training?

Aysha shrugged.

Katy planned a short twenty-four hour trip to Longworth the first weekend she could fit it in. Sharon sounded overjoyed that they'd be coming. But meantime something else had changed. There'd been an appointment with an adoption worker the Friday morning of half-term which Aysha had missed, much to Katy's annoyance. The girl had gone out with Greg straight after breakfast and hadn't returned until lunchtime. Katy had to field the appointment, which considering that she had the second of her quartet concerts that afternoon, and the following day both a basketball match in the afternoon and her orchestral concert in the evening, and that Gareth had arrived the previous day for a long weekend, and they both wanted time together, as he would be looking after the girls quite a lot, including taking them to both concerts (he'd been vetted by Social Services by now), and that she had only agreed to the appointment with reluctance, she was furious with Aysha, and told the worker from the agency to call about five o'clock any school day without prior notice. But when the lady finally did catch up with Aysha, the girl had changed her mind, she said, and wanted to keep the baby now. The reason she gave was that if everyone was going to be told about it, she might as well keep it.

This seemed a most unsatisfactory argument to Katy, who decided that before they burned all the bridges to the adoption agency, she needed to talk it through with Aysha. So shortly before the visit to Longworth, she made another late-night knock on the girl's door.

Do you really think you're ready to be a mother, Aysha? To care for a tiny baby night and day? Because, rest assured, it won't be me doing it, it will have to be you.

I know.

Have you thought it through?

Yeah. I never liked the idea of adoption anyhow. Nor abortion neither.

Well, no-one does. But adoption can be the kindest thing if you're not ready for motherhood.

I am ready, ok.

So that's what I can tell people, right?

Aysha shrugged.

Remember I'm gonna be seeing Sam and Marcus to ask about Neil.

Why ain't you phoned them?

I have phoned them. But I want to see them in person.

Did they say 'bout Neil?

No, I didn't ask them. I just asked when they were available. I'm going round Saturday evening, a few hours after we get there.

The girl shrugged yet again, and her look, cold and hostile, which it seemed to be so often now, was slowly breaking Katy's heart.

Sharon felt overjoyed to be seeing Katy and her gang again, but as soon as they arrived she sensed something was wrong. If there was one thing Sharon could be sure of, it was those emotional antennae of hers, even in her times of deepest despair, even since she'd become crippled with her debilitating illness. It was something she shared with both her daughters, she knew, Sam more obviously, but Katy in her quieter more introverted way, also had the emotional measure of a person or situation, and that was why, Sharon was sure, she'd done so well taking on these three girls of hers.

But now something was wrong as she'd not seen before, and this was particularly frustrating for Sharon, because she had her own news she wanted to share with her family just now, and this must include Aysha and her sisters as well as Katy and Sam, for it was Aysha who had first set her on this path. Sharon thought that she had found Rodney. Or rather, Justine Palmer, the woman private detective who had undertaken the searching, had come up with a Rodney Andrew Owen, living on the island of St Clair in the Scillies and running the island shop there. Of course, it might not be him. The woman had been there, had taken a photograph, but she couldn't be sure, it did bear some resemblance, but so many years had passed, this man had a moustache, didn't much look like the man Sharon had lived with all those years ago and whose two children she'd borne.

What to do next? Now she'd reached this point, Sharon found she was baulking at the possible next steps to take. Someone should go there - or should they? Steve didn't think it should be her. The journey would be too much, the feelings possibly too fraught. Steve himself couldn't go, he was needed back home. Justine Palmer could be asked, and paid, to make another trip and this time talk to the guy, but, as she said, her job was done now unless it turned out not to be him, and it would be a lot of money extra for Justine to go again, and not the best way of reintroducing Rodney into their lives.

So Sharon wanted to discuss this with her two daughters, although she realised that Sam might not be too happy if the issue was discussed in front of Aysha, but that was hard cheese, Aysha was part of their family now and Sam must accept it. But things seemed to conspire against Sharon from the moment the Bursfield contingent arrived.

Aysha announced straight away that she would take Greg for a walk before the rain came on. It certainly did look like turning wet. The child walked off with no coat, and the rain started, and got heavier, and neither dog nor girl returned. Katy was going spare, but kept saying out loud, as though reassuring herself more than any of the others, that she was sure Aysha wouldn't do a runner if she had Greg with her. Then she turned to her mother and Steve.

I think I know why Aysha's disappeared. We have some news for you, or rather Aysha has. I wanted her to tell you, but I think her actions are saying loud and clear that she wants me to impart the news. The fact is that she is expecting a baby.

Sharon blinked, not sure if she'd heard right. For a moment she'd thought of Gareth, of another grandchild.

You say <u>Aysha</u> is, darling?

Yes, Aysha is. Early in May. I thought we'd be able to tell by now, but we certainly will by Easter. Hardly anyone knows yet, only these two. She smiled at Charly and Zoë.

The teachers at school know, said Charly. And a few of the kids.

We had to tell school. And Social Services. And Gareth knows now.

Of course, dear. But what's going to happen about the baby?

We had thought about adoption. But now Aysha's saying she wants to keep him. It's a boy.

But how will you manage?

We'll just have to. Between us. But mostly it will be Aysha. Must be.

Of course, dear. But where is she? It doesn't seem a good sign, her being out in the pouring rain all this time.

I know, she's going through some difficult times. She's in denial a lot. She might come back if she knew I'd spilled the beans.

But how will she know?

I think I need to go round looking for her. Steve, could you drive me round this end of town? I'll take my mobile and keep it switched on. Please could one of you phone me straight away if she does come back?

Of course, my darling, said Sharon, very worried.

But when the phone did ring, it was Marcus, and he needed to speak to Katy urgently, so Sharon asked him to phone her on her mobile.

Is it about Aysha? she couldn't help asking.

Sort of, he replied, more abruptly than she'd ever known Marcus to be, and hung up.

Marcus also had a bad feeling about today. He knew his wife had just about reached boiling-point. Back on Christmas Day she had struggled to button her lip and stay cheerful in the presence of Katy and her girls. Now Katy and the girls were coming back to Longworth for the first time since then, and Katy had said she would come round, on her own Marcus presumed, after Lara and Liam were in bed, to talk. And Sam had been getting herself worked up all day, and who knows what stuff would be said and what feelings would be roused, and Marcus was sure he was going to have to intervene and calm things down while at the same time giving his wife the support she needed and indeed deserved in these difficult times.

But before the kids were in bed, indeed they'd only just finished their tea, there was a knock on the door and Lara jumped up like she often did and peered out the front window.

It's Aysha! she announced gleefully. She's with Greg and soaking wet in the rain. And the child made a run to the front door.

This was not expected, thought Marcus, adjusting. This was not in the script. But that Aysha never played to any script.

Meanwhile Sam was both shouting at Lara and rushing after her.

That bloody slut! What's she doing here? Lara, you know you've not to see Aysha any more! Come back here!

Why not, mummy? wailed Lara.

Sam yanked her back into the room.

Don't ask why, you're just not! She made her way to the front door and Marcus could hear her raised voice. Aysha said something that he couldn't hear, and Sam was telling her to bugger off in no uncertain terms. Marcus, reacting rather late, remembered the occasion when his wife had almost hit Aysha, and fearing it might happen again, moved quickly to the front door. Lara was still wailing.

Take the kids upstairs, Sam, he said, gently, calmly, firmly. You go back home, Aysha, get back to Sharon and Steve's as quickly as you can. You're soaking wet and the dog shouldn't be out in this either.

Don't tell Katy, stuttered the child. She seemed genuinely frightened, but was she afraid of his wife? Or something else to do with Katy?

We'll tell Katy what we like, shouted Sam who had heard. You're not telling me what I can and can't say to my own sister!

Just go, Aysha, said Marcus.

After he'd shut the door, Sam said to him, Can you phone Katy and tell her to get round here straight away. I'll put the kids to bed.

What was all that about?

Katy's trying to contact Neil. I think she needs to know. As soon as possible.

Can she be trusted? asked Marcus.

I think so, yes.

So Marcus spoke to Sharon, and then phoned Katy on her mobile.

Where are you?

In Steve's car, looking for Aysha.

Well, Aysha's been here. I've sent her straight back to your mum's.

Couldn't you have driven her? In this pouring rain.

No, I couldn't. I'm needed here, said Marcus peremptorily. Sam wants to see you straight away. We both do. Get Steve to drop you off here, and then he can find Aysha and get her home. No-one asked her to come here in this rain.

Don't I know it!

Marcus didn't like taking that tone with his sister-in-law, but this was no time for tea and sympathy. Tea, perhaps, yes. He put the kettle on, hoping that Sam had calmed down sufficiently to get the kids to settle down to sleep.

He was listening for the car to pull up, was quick on his feet to the front door before the bell rang or the kettle boiled. He ushered Katy in with a finger to his lips while he saw Steve driving off.

He made the tea, carried it through.

Sam will be down.

What's happened to Neil?

Wait for Sam.

Well, you're his brother.

Katy wasn't a happy person either just now, Marcus realised with a sinking feeling. This was all going to be even harder than he'd thought.

Sam came in the room and was determined to shoot from the mouth.

It's that slut of yours. I knew she was nothing but trouble! What's she come round here for now? Telling us not to say nowt to you! What's going on?

You tell me what's going on, Sam! said Katy vehemently, urgently. Aysha's pregnant, and Neil's disappeared, and Aysha's been determined to keep it a secret, so why's she rushed round here?

Katy needed to say what she'd come to say, Marcus realised, and wasn't going to let her older sister stop her.

She's pregnant, oh my god! You know, then?

Know what?

There was a pause.

Marcus tried to explain, diffuse the ticking bomb.

While Neil and Aysha were in Scotland, there was an incident ....

What sort of incident?

A, sort of er, physical encounter.

They had sex! blurted out Samantha, with no patience for niceties. They had sex, and it was all the doing of that slut of yours!

What? Yet Marcus could see, as soon as the momentary horror of the discovery crossed Katy's face, it was as though a cloud had lifted and everything made sense.

Didn't she say it was Neil's?

No, she didn't. She gave these confused stories of boys she'd met up with in the summer.

Well, it might not be Neil's, said Sam. Knowing that little whore, it could be anyone's!

389

I'm sure she'd do anything to keep Neil out of trouble, said Katy. But what the hell was he thinking of? How d'you know all this anyway?

For god's sake don't blame Neil, Katy! He's the innocent party in this. It was that little slut led him on, all the way, you know Neil, he's a complete innocent as far as women are concerned, he was easy prey for a whore like her to get him into her knickers.

Marcus saw Katy wince. Neil came to see us, he told her. Some time last autumn. He'd felt terrible ever since it happened. He couldn't cope with the guilt any more, he said, he had to tell someone.

Why the hell couldn't he have told me? It was me he were responsible to!

You must see how he couldn't! He couldn't be sure what you'd do.

Neil felt bad enough anyway, Marcus continued. But when we told him how old Aysha was ....

That bitch had been going round lying about her age, making out she was seventeen, interrupted Sam. Neil believed her, he really did.

No, no, that can't be right, said Katy. He must've known her age, I'm quite sure I gave him all the details about both girls.

Are you making out Neil's a liar? We know he's not, don't we Marcus, he wouldn't lie about something like that.

He genuinely believed she was seventeen, she was doing the shopping for him, buying cigarettes, so of course he believed she was old enough.

Yeah, but that's not quite the same thing, I know she often makes out she's older to get cigarettes or alcohol, admitted Katy. But anyway, it doesn't justify what Neil did. She's a very vulnerable teenage girl, and he had temporary responsibility for her, I'd made sure he knew that, he was kind of in loco parentis.

Vulnerable my foot! exploded Sam. She's a total menace that kid, and it's the rest of us is vulnerable when she's about. I knew that right from the start and I wish now I'd taken more notice of my instincts and not listened to you lot but made you take notice of me! And to think I let my own kids make friends with her!

For god's sake, Sam, she's just a kid, mixed up and vulnerable, yeah ....

But she don't show it, Katy, she acts all grown-up, it's when kids have problems but no-one would know it, that's when trouble starts ....

But I told Neil that!

Well, from what Neil said, he did his best, but the way she came on to him ....

What d'you mean, came on to him?

Well, let's face it Katy, she's been running after Neil ever since she first set eyes on him, hasn't she, Marcus?

This was something Marcus and Sam had discussed over and over again. It wasn't something he would have thought wise to raise yet again in front of his over-wrought sister-in-law, but his wife would not be put off, however much he tried.

Remember the funeral! That bitch doing her best buttering up to Neil? Getting him to move you when you moved to a bigger place? And it was all her idea, this trip, let's face it, all that little slut wanted right from the start was to get inside some man's trousers, and it was Neil she chose, worst luck, who was the least able to resist of any man I know. I'll bet the little vamp knew that!

Marcus could see Katy visibly wince.

It's not like that, Sam. She liked Neil, yeah, but that was all. There must've been a reason why it happened. What did Neil say?

Well, it's not just going round making out she's seventeen, she's also flaunting herself in front of him all the time, wearing virtually nothing. And after a while she started trying to come in his tent at night ....

But he didn't let her, did he? Katy was going pale.

No, said Marcus. He was very firm about that.

But then one night there was an almighty thunderstorm, tipping it down with rain, and what should happen but that little slut comes rushing into his tent, soaking wet and stark naked, and jumps right on him. What could he do, she's soaked through, making out she's scared stiff?

It just happened from there, added Marcus.

She WAS frightened, said Katy. He took advantage.

No! said her sister. If she were, then why did she keep trying to come to him at night. After that, as well as before?

Katy had no answer.

He did everything he could to keep some distance between him and that whore, she made him feel really uncomfortable ....

Oh, come on! exclaimed Katy. He liked Aysha, the same as she liked him.

Don't even mention her name! I won't have that slut's name spoken in this house, I won't have her anywhere near my house, or my kids or my family, and ....

And she did make Neil feel uncomfortable, added Marcus. That's quite clear. Not to begin with, but the second half of the holiday. It seemed like he realised there was a danger things were getting too personal.

Well, there was no sign of him being uncomfortable when he brought them back to Bursfield.

He'd just be relieved to hand them back to you, I should think, said Marcus.

Well, anyhow, if Aysha were making him uncomfortable, he should have been even more on his guard then, said Katy.

For god's sake, Katy! Sam's fury was beginning to boil over. Can't you just take the wool from your eyes for one minute! Neil did what he could, but he shouldn't be in that situation!

So you're blaming me?

I'm blaming you for not seeing what that girl's really like! She's the sort of kid puts everyone at risk that can't see through her, and that means nearly all men, and it also means you, Katy. You've let her walk all over your life, you've gotta see that now! You've gotta pack her off before it's too late. She should be in one of them places, what's they called, Marcus?

Secure Units.

Yeah, for her own sake, but for other people's sakes most of all, including yours, Katy. And have the baby adopted or fostered or you can bet it will be you ends up looking after it cos that bitch has no morals and never thinks of anyone but herself and she'll just carry on chasing boys or older men! I don't know about the two sisters, they don't seem so bad.

You don't know her, Sam, like I do. Your picture just don't square up. She's no angel, but basically she's a frightened, vulnerable kid trying to face up to a very different life than what she were used to before, and doing amazingly well in the circumstances. This pregnancy's a setback, sure, but Neil must face up to his responsibility for that, and in any case sending her to a Secure Unit would be a thousand times worse and I just won't let it happen, Sam, whatever you say!

Well, don't say I didn't warn you. You watch your back, Katy, don't let the bitch ride roughshod over you any more.

Don't worry, I won't. I never have done and I never will. So where can I contact Neil?

Why d'you need to contact him?

To give him a piece of my mind, for a start! And to ask him what he plans to do about the baby.

But you don't even know it's his!

I don't think Aysha's been sexually active since I've known her, probably not even before.

Don't mention the slut's name! Samantha screamed. Of course she has, Katy, she's fooling you even more than I thought!

How do you know? Katy shouted back at her sister.

Because she told Neil! She was full of it with him!

But that's just her bravado! It's like the smoking and alcohol, she wants to make out how grown-up she is.

Well, she does smoke and drink alcohol!

That doesn't mean she's sexually active! It's all a front!

No, it's not, Katy, Neil could tell. He may be naive, but he does know a bit about human biology. and that slut was no snowy-white virgin, that's for sure!

No, of course she's not! She's been abused since the age of six, and then was running wild and probably taken advantage of by other men loads of times! And I know her hormones have been all over the place since last summer term, and that might have been because of what happened before. But I do know her, Sam, and I'd swear to god that she's not been sexually active since she's lived with me. That's why I think it must be Neil's baby now I know what happened.

Well, why've you brought such a damaged kid into our lives and not told us this before?

There was a momentary pause. I have tried to tell you. Marcus could sense that Katy was finally on the defensive.

You've told us in general terms, but not the specific

detail of the sexual side, he added, supporting his wife.

If you were a kid, would you want those details broadcast around to everyone?

I think we all have a right to know. Neil had a right to know.

I did warn him.

That she was a sexually mixed-up kid with her hormones running loose?

Not in so many words, but I would've hoped he'd have got the message. Just because Neil fails in his responsibility, you're starting getting at me, now. Katy sounded angry and hurt. You still haven't told me where Neil is.

We don't know where he is, said Marcus.

When we told him how old the kid was, he got really scared about being sent to prison. It can happen, said Samantha. That would've been the worst thing, the most unforgiveable thing to come out of this. I mean, can you imagine Neil surviving in prison? It would destroy him! And I'd've killed the bitch then, I promise you I would!

But you're happy to send a child to a Secure Unit?

That's different, that's for her own good. But we decided we couldn't trust that slut to keep her mouth shut, so the best thing would be for Neil to disappear for a while.

Disappear?

Yeah, just go off somewhere. Just after Christmas he went. None of us knows where.

We thought it best we didn't know, added Marcus. So we're under no pressure to tell. If the police do get involved, we don't have to pervert the course of justice, or whatever it's called. He may have gone abroad or he may be still in the UK, we just don't know.

But he'll contact you?

No. Or not for a long time, at any rate, Marcus added.

That's one of the worst things, said Samantha. That bitch has caused my husband to lose contact with his brother.

She would never tell on Neil, said Katy. You must know that, she's very loyal. The last thing she'd want would be to get him in trouble. That explains her secrecy in recent weeks. And please understand however much I disagree with you about where the blame lies in this, and Aysha I'm sure would agree with you, and is blaming herself, I would never say anything either to get Neil in trouble. The last thing I'd want is Neil up in court facing a possible sentence, and Aysha would never forgive me anyway.

But is there anyone else might report it? What about the sister?

No, she never would either. I've already reported the story Aysha told me to Social Services, and I'm just going to stick with that.

Well, we're grateful for that, Katy, said Marcus, seizing a chance to calm things down. I'm sorry we both got so angry earlier.

Well, some of the comments were uncalled for, said Katy. I have learned to defend myself now, when faced with such vitriol.

I'll give you a lift back to your mother's, said Marcus. His wife sat looking worn out and red-eyed.

Marcus drove Katy across town in silence.

I won't come in, were the only words he said, as he dropped her off outside her mother's house.

Katy was relieved to be silent. She felt she'd had enough talking for a lifetime. She hated the verbal assaults from her sister, the fact that defending Aysha meant arguing back, but she also recognised that what the child was about, to the very core of her being, indeed what had most led Katy to love her, was bound to cause argument, that some would take against her to almost the same degree that she, Katy, was for her and would always defend her, and would never ever, whatever she did, allow her to be sent from her, as Sam was proposing, to secure accommodation.

She was still seething inside, she knew, and she needed some time to herself, some peace and quiet, to think things over. She needed to talk to Aysha, but not yet. She had to sort this out in her confused mind. She couldn't entirely dismiss her sister's accusations, but still she mostly blamed Neil.

She walked into a cosy domestic scene at her mother's, but it was soon clear that she wasn't going to get the quiet she desired. The girls with her mother and Steve were sitting round the kitchen table, Aysha towelled and changed into dry clothes and finishing her meal, the others already finished. Greg, still a little damp, lay peacefully in front of the stove, and Katy stroked him tenderly, longing for the simplicity in the soul of a dog and the heartstrings of those who loved him.

We saved some tea for you, pet. Have you eaten anything yet? What kept you so long?

Nothing. It's ok. Steve brought her the last piece of bacon and egg quiche, fried potatoes, a mixture of vegetables in a bowl.

We started talking about something after our tea, while Aysha was finishing hers, didn't we, girls? Sharon continued.

Oh yes? said Katy, her heart beginning to sink.

Yes, you see, this woman we paid, this private detective, Justine Palmer she's called, well she thinks she might have found your dad. Yours and Sam's, Katy, your first dad, Rodney.

Part of Katy would have chosen to ignore this, to just carry on eating. If she'd been someone else she might have rushed upstairs and slammed the door of her room, but she wasn't that sort of person. In the end she did her best to show some interest.

Have you told Sam?

No, not yet. I wanted to tell all of you together. But when I knew that wouldn't be possible tonight, I'm just telling you and the girls, and I'll tell Sam tomorrow. Or maybe I could phone her later tonight.

I wouldn't phone her tonight, if I were you. But anyhow she ain't gonna be very pleased that you've told us lot first. I didn't know my dad, and she did.

Still, he's birth dad to both of you. And Sam worked through all that business of losing him, and don't seem so interested now, but maybe you didn't.

Didn't what?

Get over him going off.

There weren't nothing to get over, mum. I was what, one year old at the time.

Nineteen months, love.

Well, I'm glad you can remember it to the month. It sounds like it's you who still hasn't got over it. Have you spoken to him since this woman found him?

No, not yet. Someone has to check out it is really him.

Well, not me, if that's what you're asking. How would I know when I can't remember him?

We've got a photo. I think it's him but I can't be sure.

Well, that's not much good. Can't you get that woman to check it out a bit more?

We've already forked out quite a bit on her. It really needs someone to ask him now, and that's best not her but one of us.

Why?

A private detective might put him off. She said, Justine Palmer, that they usually work best just doing the background investigation.

So where is he, this guy who might be my dad?

He's on the Isles of Scilly. He runs the island shop on the island of St Clair.

Well, that's out then, ain't it, said Katy peremptorily. How's any of us gonna get there? And with a dismissive expression she'd copied off Aysha, she turned to the three girls and then went on eating her meal.

Well, Steve and I can't, that's for sure, persisted her mother. It's a helicopter flight and then a boat this time of year, according to Justine. And you've got to get all the way down to Cornwall first.

I don't think you'll get Sam to go, said Katy. Unless the four of them take a holiday down there some time.

They've already booked their holiday this year, said Steve. And they went to Cornwall last year.

I was hoping someone could go down there soon, said Sharon. Easter holiday time. It's no good for me, waiting longer. I want to find out quick, if it is him.

You won't get Marcus to go around Easter, put in Steve. It's the busiest time for his football teams.

Can't you ask Sam and the kids to go with you, Katy? If it's Rodney, he'd want to see his grandchildren, I'm sure. Aysha could go with you, she wants to go and gets on so well with Lara and Liam. You two younger girls could stay here with Steve and me if you preferred.

Now hold on a minute. Katy was beginning to get the sense of a fait accompli, and it alarmed her. Did her mother not realise the impossibility of getting Sam and Aysha even in the same room together, let alone a trip of several days to an island at the other end of the country? Nor would she let her children travel in Aysha's company at present, that was clear. Indeed it was doubtful if she'd be willing for her and her kids to go anywhere without Marcus just now.

For one, I'm pretty sure Sam wouldn't go, from the conversation I've just had with her. Nor the kids. And as for me, I've got far too much on my plate in the next few weeks. There's no way I could spare a few days to travel to the Isles of Scilly! Why don't you just phone this guy up? I'm sure you could find his number.

Don't be stupid, my love, would you like to be just phoned up out of the blue in his situation? How would we know what we were interrupting or who was listening or whatever? He'd probably just put the phone down and we're none the wiser. Or we speak to a wife or son or daughter – what are they going to think?

I don't know, mum, but it weren't me started this, remember. Katy felt on the defensive yet again. I don't see that it makes that much difference between phoning or calling in person myself, but if you think it does all I'm saying is it's not gonna be me goes down there, not until the summer holiday anyhow, and I'm sure it won't be Sam either.

Well, I can go, me, said Aysha. There's nothing to do in the Easter holidays, it's gonna be dead boring. I can go on my own if no-one else wants to go.

Oh, would you, love? That's very good of you.

Just a second, Aysha. You seem to have forgotten a few things. One, you're in care and I'm your carer. Two, you can't go off on your own unless Social Services agree. Three, you're expecting a baby, and by Easter time it'll be getting close to being due. Four, you won't have nothing to do in the holidays. You might be getting some more mountain experience with Neil ....

Only if he knew I'm pregnant he ain't gonna take me and anyhow he ain't around, is he?

But he might be back by then. And the other thing is you'll need to attend Pre-Natal Classes in the school holiday.

What's that?

Preparing you for having a baby.

I ain't going to no classes. You never told me that!

If you'd gone to any of the meetings we'd had about you being pregnant, you'd've found out. I haven't booked you into anything yet because of school, but all the more reason to attend regularly through the school holiday.

Aysha made one of her peculiar frowning expressions. They all involved clamping firm her mouth, widening her eyes, and screwing up her nose and her brow to various degrees and in slightly different ways. Katy had gradually learned to distinguish the varying situations. There was one which was instead of smiling, another which stopped her crying, another meant she was controlling a temper outburst and involved hardening her mouth a fraction, and there was this expression she had now which meant that she hadn't decided how she should react and was still considering what she should do or say next.

Well, there won't be these classes Easter itself, right? she finally announced. I mean, like the holiday weekend, everything's closed, ok! I could go then!

Where would you stay? All the accommodation will be booked up that weekend, for sure.

Well, I'll take a tent, then. I'm like used to camping now.

I don't think Social Services will be happy if you go off camping on your own. And where will you get a tent from?

There was a brief pause for thought again.

Gareth! I'll lend a tent off've Gareth. Or one of his mates. And I'll take Greg for protection so no-one's gonna need worry.

I still don't think Social Services would agree when we ask them.

Fuck Social Services! It was rare for Aysha to swear at all these days, certainly not in front of Sharon and Steve, but in her increasingly animated state she let it slip and then immediately realised and paused, turning her head this way and that, then looking at Charly with a hidden grin which was even rarer. Why d'you have to ask them, Katy? Can't you get me adopted so's we don't have to ask them any more?

Me adopt you? Deep inside Katy felt a glow of anticipation at the words. I don't think I'm old enough yet. Anyway, it takes ages, it won't help for the Easter holidays.

Well, just don't tell them, right!

I've gotta tell them, that's part of the deal, kiddo.

Well, I'm gonna go anyway, ok! I mean, no-one can stop me, right?

You mustn't go without my permission. Or Social Services.

You can't stop me. You don't own me, Katy.

Don't be too hard on her, Katy, my love. She's only trying to help, said Sharon.

She could have done without her mother's intervention. It made her, Katy, seem like the one who was hard on Aysha and drew others in to defend her, and she wished they could have seen her an hour ago, defending Aysha from the verbal assaults of Samantha, of Marcus even.

Well, let's see what the social worker says. One step at a time, she added, closing the discussion for now, but wishing it had never gone this far, aware of how serious, how determined, Aysha was about this, that it was yet another difficult matter she would have to deal with in the days and weeks ahead.

Back in Bursfield, Aysha tried to switch off. She wanted just to live from day to day, do her schoolwork, practise drumming, take Greg for his walks, stop off at night and join other kids she knew with whatever they was into. That was it.

She knew everything was different now. Too many changes had happened in her life, always had done, and if she thought she could do what she wanted, if she thought her life was hers now to choose, then things happened to prove her wrong. She hated that. It weren't entirely her own fault. How was she to know she were gonna end up with a baby inside her, just cos of what happened in that thunderstorm with her and Neil?

Sometimes she wished the baby would go away, then she hated herself for thinking that. It weren't the baby's fault. She tried to pretend none of this were happening, for as long as she could, but then she would feel something inside. She didn't feel sick any more, but sometimes she felt something move. But there was a worse feeling sometimes which was like it weren't her own life any more. Her body was being taken over, and her life shared. It came over her at night when her sisters were in bed asleep and Katy too, and she couldn't sleep. She would get out of bed and give Greg a hug but a dog didn't understand, he couldn't see why she weren't sleeping like the rest of them. The thing was that this had been going on since last summer. Not every night but lots of nights. Well, the baby might explain it. But Aysha's mind was too mixed up with other stuff, was how she saw it. That trip to Scotland had stirred up a whole load of stuff in that crazy head of hers, and she still hadn't sorted it out and most likely never would, now a baby had come along off've it.

She'd got drawn to Neil, that were one thing. And Neil had gone off, not even knowing there was his baby coming along. She didn't love Neil, but she liked him for the way he hated people like she did and the way he'd chose a life for himself which were independent and didn't need people, which she wanted to do but with her it hadn't worked, not yet. She was drawn to Neil's life more than Neil himself. Then there was dogs. She wanted a dog of her own, not now, but soon. Katy got Greg when she were fifteen. Aysha could get her own dog then, she was sure Greg would be ok about that, another dog for him to play with, maybe a girl dog, but one that were Aysha's own, not Katy's really like Greg was. She were nearly fourteen and a half now. In two and a bit years, she would've taken GCSEs and could leave school. If she worked really hard, she could make up for missing a bit of school next term when the baby were born. She'd already shown she could work hard and catch up. Two years weren't too long to wait.

When she left school Aysha weren't gonna go to college like Katy or get a boring job. She would travel around. A bit like Neil, but even more. In Scotland to start with, and then foreign countries. Scotland weren't really foreign, only a little bit. There were lots of countries she could go to, but Alaska were the one she wanted to go to most. She could talk to people and find out about the dog race more than she could learn from books. And when she weren't in Alaska or Scotland or another country, she could go round festivals in England, with her drum and her tent and perhaps a guitar as well, and join in and make a bit of money. She could sing a bit, her voice were quite good, and maybe learn guitar off've Charly. It didn't matter having a little kid with her. Or a dog. Well, it might make things a bit harder, 'specially with a kid, but she weren't gonna let it stop her. Things was different now, all that was ok.

If she were back in England in the autumn or winter or spring when there weren't festivals, she could help with mountain rescue. 'Specially with the dogs. She wouldn't get paid, but Neil said there was a small allowance. It all would help. And when she weren't doing festivals or mountain rescue, she could stay back with Katy. Wherever Katy was, whether it were this house at High Chapel or another house in Bursfield or at her mum's or even if she'd moved to another town, whether she still had Charly and Zoë with her, whether she lived with Gareth and maybe were married to him or even had kids of her own, if she had a job or whatever, she knew Katy would find space for her and her kid and her dog, a bed and some food and a bit of dosh to keep them going until she felt like wandering again.

Whenever Katy came into her thoughts it made Aysha feel bad. Somewhere inside her Katy meant so much, nearly everything to her, but the life they was leading now kept making Aysha fretful, needing something different, even wanting to be back in her old life sometimes. The Scotland trip, that helped, even though this baby what came out of it weren't gonna, and now soon Aysha would have the chance to disappear off to the Scilly Islands on a mission to find Katy's real dad. That would help too, like a kinda adventure. She was quite determined to go, but she didn't like it when there was so much stuff causing bustups between Katy and her.

It weren't Katy's fault, she did know that. She, Aysha, oughta be willing to talk to Katy more, that's what her carer wanted, but somehow Aysha couldn't. It were all too difficult, too many problems, and Aysha were never someone to talk when there was problems, she just had to show her hard side, like she weren't bothered when deep down she were. And then Katy would insist, get so she had to talk to her, answer these fucking questions, and that was when she hated Katy and switched off all the more. And that just made her life in the house with the three of them, or four with Gareth, Greg didn't count in this, all the more unhappy and it weren't that much better at Katy's mum's either, 'specially with that sister of hers living in the same town. It just made Aysha wanna get away all the more. It weren't like that when she first went to live with Katy, in that bedsit. Then she was, if not quite happy, at least as near content as she thought she were ever gonna get. Cos something had changed in her life then, and all the bad went away. But good kinda faded and bad started giving her a buzz again, and nothing much happened in her life. A little kid coming along, yeah, but what good were that to her life? The good in it were gonna be for Neil, had to be, but they wasn't letting her tell Neil. At first she never wanted him to know, it were just so awful, but now she did.

Sometimes she thought she would tell Katy all this but then she never did. She acted hard with Katy most of the time cos she knew Katy didn't like her being like that but still cared for her, loved her, all the same. And Greg. She got out of bed and gave the dog a hug. She weren't hard with Greg but he would love her anyway too. Tomorrow at school she would be collecting her tickets. Three tickets, one for Charly, one for Zoë, one for Katy. It were gonna be a surprise. P'raps Katy would be happier then, with her, Aysha. It were Gareth, not her, what made Katy happy now. Now she saw, all of a sudden, how she wanted to make Katy happy even more than Gareth did. So's they could talk 'bout all this stuff together and have a good laugh like they used to and not get in arguments 'bout it all the time.

A big greying man with a beard came on stage, talking in slightly broken English. He held a very odd looking guitar which had no body to it. All sorts of other instruments were decked out leaving, it seemed, not much space for musicians. But other musicians came on, two black-haired, brown-skinned men behind the drums, a young guy in a baseball cap on bass guitar, and a thin woman with a violin that was like the front man's guitar. They were all from South America, apart from the woman who was English. The front man came from Chile, the other guys from different countries, and after they'd launched into their first, fast number, the guy from Chile talked about how they played folk music, roots music, ethnic music, from all over the Americas and from Africa, and Britain, and Europe too, and how they worked in schools and tried to bring together different cultures from around the world. Then they played a slower ballad from Chile, with words by a woman poet, and then they said they would start introducing kids from the school to join them.

They were in the school hall of Andrew Wheeler High

School. Katy was sitting with Charly and Zoë. On Monday evening, when Aysha had carefully laid out the three tickets by their places at the meal table, Katy had thought for a moment that Aysha had decided not to come herself, to take herself off somewhere, with Greg, to meet up with other restless spirits like herself. *QUIMANTU present an evening of folk music from around the world*, the tickets said. Well, Charly and her had always been more into that sort of music than Aysha. She'd had to reorganise a quartet rehearsal, start a bit earlier, cut it shorter, and phone Gareth who was due to turn up half-way through the concert, ask him to come to the high school, or if he didn't want to walk in while the music was playing, arrive later, after they got home.

No ticket for you, Aysha?

Aysha looked shy and turned to Charly.

She's in the concert, Katy, said the middle sister.

Oh Aysha, that's brilliant! But Katy felt remorseful that she hadn't twigged. Why didn't you tell me before?

.... a surprise, Aysha mumbled.

Now Katy sat waiting, not knowing when Aysha would appear, which pieces she was playing, but only thinking of her charge, and the new life inside her, with tenderness and pride. She had made no attempt, yet, to talk through the issues around the pregnancy, and all Aysha had talked about between Monday and now, Friday, was how she was going to the island of St Clair and no-one would stop her.

So before the third number, the Chilean man said they would be introducing students from the school, one by one, as they joined in the band. First I would like to introduce one of the most promising young drummers I've come across in recent years, Aysha Stanton, ladies and gentlemen.

Katy was only half prepared, for Aysha appearing so soon. The girl stumbled across the back of the stage, took her place behind one of the drums, and bowed slightly, shyly. She wore a white sleeveless top and her normal school skirt. Katy wondered if any of the rest of the audience would notice the slight bulge in her belly that was beginning to appear.

She seemed small, half-hidden behind instruments and other musicians. No-one would see that much of her. But when the music started, none of that really mattered. Her hands and fingers worked the skins of the drums, as she followed, Katy could see, the other musicians intently. On some numbers she picked up sticks, moved to a different drum, changed places with the other two percussionists.

Other musicians from the school were brought on, one by one, a flute player, a cello, a keyboard. Then several more, the whole school ensemble, while the visiting band members slid off to the side during the first number of the school ensemble. Two more numbers, on the last of which Aysha's music teacher, whom Katy had met a few times, came on to conduct. Then the interval, and there was Gareth, waiting outside.

Katy tried to spend time with Aysha in the interval but she couldn't keep her alongside. Like a slippery fish Aysha would slide away, like a small black-and-white bird she would flit silently between her 'family' and the other musicians, and it was Charly, not Katy, whom she wanted to introduce to the visiting band members. Katy held tight to Zoë's hand and told Gareth what they'd heard so far, but it was her feeling of immense pride for Aysha, not just in the few minutes the child was with her although particularly then, that took her over, almost overwhelmed her heart.

The second set started with some African influenced pieces, then one Mexican, one English, one Hungarian, one Amerindian folk song before two South American pieces, one instrumental, one sung, and a third for an encore, finished the gig. Aysha played on all of these, her face a study in concentration, her arms and fingers and indeed her whole body in a mesmeric oneness with the music playing in front of her. Katy realised she had played on all but the first two numbers, more than any other musician. Everyone then left very quickly, Aysha letting herself be ushered into Gareth's car, still seemingly in a trance-like state. But she walked Greg as usual when they got back, and stayed out ages, even longer than usual.

Events were conspiring with Aysha, Katy could see, to delay even further the thrashing out of issues concerning the baby and his paternity. There were now only a few days of term left and now was not the time. Easter would very soon be upon them, it was important to get Aysha started on pre-natal classes before having a further confrontation. And to sort out this trip to the island of St Clair which was the only non-school, non-drumming matter on Aysha's mind at the moment, a very convenient avoidance, diversion tactic, Katy was sure. Katy had already telephoned Ruth Barnes about it and had been told quite firmly that there was no question of giving approval for Aysha to make the trip on her own. When Katy had pleaded, saying that Aysha would go anyway so wasn't it better for her to go with everyone's blessing, Ruth had said quite brusquely that that was the worst possible reason for saying yes, and in theory Katy had to agree with her.

It was hard enough getting hold of Ruth Barnes the once, but Katy decided she must try her again. At least the social worker did phone her back, seemingly sensitive in some way to Katy's dilemma even if the message was still the same. She did offer, this time, to call round herself and lay down the law with Aysha. But this seemed to Katy worse than useless as Aysha was not receptive to even the friendliest of Ruth's visits, and avoided the social worker whenever she could. She didn't say that, however, but simply asked what would happen if and when Aysha did take off.

Just don't give her any money. She won't get far without.

But she would. She'll get there without if she wants to enough, said Katy, thinking that Ruth didn't know Aysha that well if she thought lack of money would put her off.

What will she do about accommodation?

Well, she's asked my boyfriend to loan her a tent. She's got quite keen on camping now.

I hope he's said no.

I don't want him getting drawn into these arguments, said Katy. She will insist on going, and I'd rather she had a tent than slept rough. I'd rather she went with our blessing than without.

There was a pause.

Well, there's only one solution that I can find, said Ruth Barnes finally, and with some reluctance it seemed.

What's that? said Katy, after another long pause.

You'll have to all go down there. Make it a short holiday.

But I haven't the time. Or the money. The only few days when there's nothing else happening is the Easter weekend itself.

Well, go then. Social Services will pay, we'll call it part of your holiday grant.

But everywhere will be booked up. And desperately expensive. Katy didn't want to go, and she knew Aysha wouldn't be too happy either, the kid was wanting to branch out into independence, have time on her own.

I can't see any other way round the problem, said the social worker.

So Katy was stuck with this. Against her will, she considered it, talked to Gareth, talked to the girls, all the rest of them were enthusiastic, even Aysha, it seemed. Gareth pointed out, first to Katy, then to Charly, that April in the Isles of Scilly was good for birdwatching (part of his course had been a project on tourism in Cornwall and the Isles of Scilly). They decided to avoid the hassle of booked-up accommodation, and take tents. Gareth appointed himself in charge of stores and equipment. He drove back to Bangor and returned with tents, sleeping-bags and back-packs, stoves and cooking-gear. He booked camping-space at the main campsite on the main island, on the hill just above the harbour, and at Penzance, and he booked their ferry tickets. Katy sorted out train times and, finding that they had to change at Wolverhampton with a forty minutes wait, phoned up Charly's uncle and aunt and arranged for them to come to the station with their new-born baby, so's they could have a drink together, half-an-hour if they were lucky and their train was on time.

So it all got planned, more or less, happened before they could draw breath. And still Katy hadn't found time.

The train for Penzance, when they boarded at Wolverhampton after a brief rendez-vous with Charly's grandmother, uncle and aunt and new baby cousin, was very crowded. Fortunately they'd reserved seats. Katy sat across the aisle from the others who were playing a game of rummy, or something similar. Gareth was nearest to her, Charly sat at the window, next to Gareth, Aysha sat facing Charly and Zoë was next to Aysha. Somewhere at Aysha's feet, though invisible to Katy, lay Greg, whom Aysha had briefly exercised at Wolverhampton. Aysha had little interest in card-games, and only joined in now in a very desultory manner. In fact, she had no interest in games of any sort, if you asked her to list her interests she would have said dogs, music, running, travel, mountain rescue, map-reading, in that order, with nothing else counting at all. She had been taught some computer games by Zoë but, unlike most kids her age, she only joined in for her sisters' benefit, not her own, and it was the same now with the cards. She sat with her earphones in listening to her music, glancing down at Greg from time to time, fondling him with the hand not holding the cards, joining the game only when Zoë nudged her to remind her it was her turn. Egged on by Gareth, the two younger girls played noisily, competitively, prompting mildly disapproving expressions from the other passengers on Katy's side of the aisle. She looked up from time to time, smiled at them, but resisted the temptation to get involved in conversation. She used to enjoy playing cards, with her mother and stepfather, sometimes her sister too, but that seemed a lifetime away. She had chosen to sit apart from the others and not get involved in their games, though with pangs of regret now, so that she could try and catch up on some of her coursework, which she was getting more and more behind with. But she couldn't concentrate on the work at all, and it wasn't just the noisiness of the card game opposite.

Looking at Aysha in the opposite corner, with her earphones and her hand reaching out to reassure Greg, reminded her so much of those first weeks together in Katy's bedsit, when she, Katy, would try and do coursework and Aysha seemed more relaxed and peaceful than Katy had known her before or since. It brought thoughts and feelings flooding back into Katy's mind. Aysha seemed to have changed so much, she had grown, looked more mature and older than her years, and of course she was visibly pregnant now, though this was not obvious from the way she was seated in the carriage. But she was still the same Aysha, and whatever had happened, and was going to happen, to disrupt their lives with the arrival of a baby, she, Katy, was still needed to keep her life on track. She should have talked to Aysha, confronted her, before now. All these other events in their lives had given her easy excuses, but the longer she left it, the harder it would be. As soon as they got back, as soon as Gareth had returned to Bangor, she would clarify what had happened.

She blamed herself mostly now. Though she remained furious with her sister and adamant that her view of Aysha's situation was mistaken, she couldn't help remembering some of the words Sam had used and knowing there was a grain of truth in there. A sexually mixed-up kid with her hormones running loose - that exactly described Aysha last summer and she, Katy, should have seen it and never allowed the trip to Scotland to go ahead. And Sam was probably right that whatever transpired between Neil and Aysha, it was the girl's doing, though Katy still clung to the view that it remained Neil's responsibility to have prevented anything like that happening. She still couldn't under-stand where Aysha was at with all this, and berated herself for not un-derstanding the child better. Outwardly she claimed to be the one who understood her protégée best, but inwardly she felt full of doubt. Why had she followed the received wisdom and been fearful of Aysha taking out her sexual hurt on children younger than her? Lara, for instance - there had never been any sign of risk there. Why had Aysha sought physical intimacy with a man who must be about the same age as that of her abuser at the time of her abuse? Nothing in the books explained this. Could she have used Neil for a displaced revenge - surely not? More likely, perhaps it had been a kind of working through, a catharsis, by finding a mature man who was an alternative, about as far away from the nature of her abuser as it was possible to get. Of course, she would never get Aysha to express any of this, even if she did successfully confront her about what had happened, and of course, as she raised her eyes from her papers and sneaked a glance at the girl by the opposite window, what she loved most about Aysha was her unpredictability, her refusal to follow any of the normal stereotypes, psychological or otherwise.

35. SMALLEST WILD PLACE

The crossing from Penzance took them alongside the Cornish coast on a bright, breezy day. The coastline looked vivid green, fields sloping down to low cliffs, dotted with cottages and occa-sional larger farmhouses or manors, interrupted by wooded val-leys - chines as they were called in some parts of the country - and bright yellow patches of gorse. The sea was flecked white but not too rough, and Katy watched the ever-changing white of breakers against the brown of the shoreline below the low cliffs. She sat on the deck with Greg and Gareth, who had found them the seats. Charly stood by the rails with her binoculars, scanning. The other two girls explored the ship, the Scillonia, and frequently scampered back to the adults, bringing hot drinks, bacon baps or bags of crisps. Aysha would stay a few minutes to comfort Greg or interrupt Charly and ask what she'd seen, feigning interest, Zoë was fascinated by everything, on the boat and around them, never having been on the sea before. For Katy, too, and for Greg, it was first time on a boat, when she was a child she'd been to the Isle of Man twice on holiday with her mother, stepfather and sister, but both times they'd flown from Manchester airport. All the other family holidays and school trips had been within mainland Britain. She bowed to Gareth's greater experience, and was glad she could relax and let him be in charge. While queueing to board the ship, they'd tried to plan a schedule for the four days on the islands, to try and spend some time all of them together, allow Aysha some time on her own, and for Gareth to take Charly birdwatching.

She was having mixed success with the birdwatching now, on the ship. It was mainly gulls, wheeling above and across and behind, with their harsh, drawn-out cries. She couldn't quite remember how to distinguish the different gulls, and sought the help of her book, and of Gareth. Cormorants and shags she knew, their dark shadows low over the waves, seen as they left Penzance, and again as they approached the islands, and gannets, which she was very excited to spot after they passed Land's End and crossed the open water. Fulmars, which she'd seen many of in Scotland, still proved difficult to distinguish from gulls.

They were all excited to disembark, but struggled with their packs, slogging up the hill to the campsite. But the views, right across the channels to the smaller islands, were amazing and made it all worthwhile. Only Aysha was disinclined to gaze out to sea, impatient to get her tent up and take Greg for a walk around the ramparts of the fort. Then it was a matter of going into the town to buy food and find out times of the boats out to the other islands, and when the stores on the island of St Clair, would be open.

On the morning of Easter Saturday, Aysha went on the boat across to St Clair, on her own with Greg. The others saw her off at the quay. There had been the suggestion that Charly go with her, but Aysha wanted to do this on her own, and so the others were booked on a boat-trip round several of the islands, to see the seals, which Aysha might also have enjoyed but would not have suited Greg.

On the St Clair ferry the two boatmen were young and virile. Aysha half-noticed this, but would not have attempted conversation. When the one guy came round she proffered money shyly.

You staying on the island, or coming back tonight?

Coming back, she mumbled.

So don't pay now, pay on the return. And he told her the time the boat back left St Clair.

First time on the island?

Yeah. What's it like?

Magic place, really is. But you can't see all of it in a day. There's a hotel, a pub, a shop, a café. A couple of farms, a few growers, one or two fishermen, some holiday cottages, and that's about it. Two beautiful sandy beaches, and the far side of the island is really wild. Here, come through to the wheel.

He beckoned her to follow, and she pulled Greg to where the other guy was nonchalantly steering the boat through the channel, avoiding several rocks.

This is my mate Pete. I'm Brian. Here, have one of these. He handed her a leaflet. There's a map inside.

Give her a ciggy, Bri, said the gruff silent one at the wheel. That's what this kid wants, not the usual tourist bumph.

Aysha accepted gratefully as Brian lit her a cigarette, but still felt nervous.

Shouldn't be smoking, y'know, not really.

Don't worry about it, said Pete, as Brian started pointing out places on the map.

This here's the best place for a swim. But not this time of year.

Nah, too cold now, Aysha agreed. I'll only swim summer holidays. But Greg'll swim now, won't you?

Are you at college, or still at school?

College, she lied. Y'know, sixth form college. She decided she'd never pass for being at uni like Katy. There was one sixth form college in Bursfield, but it mainly took kids from the high schools that didn't have sixth forms. Her school did have a sixth form, and the sixth form college only took in a few from her school. Lots of year eleven kids she knew from music or cross-country had applied to the sixth form college but without much hope of getting in. There would be no chance for Aysha herself even if she did decide to stay on after GCSEs, but it felt good to pretend.

You come back August, said Brian. Let me know when you're on the boat, I'll come and join you for a swim down South Bay.

You, Bri? You can't swim! joked Pete.

Can, too. Learned when I were a little kid.

Never saw you swim in my life!

Well, that don't mean I can't. You don't always watch over me, Pete! complained Brian.

Well, I'll watch then, I'll sit on a rock on the beach. And I'll not be watching you, Bri, I'll be watching the young lady.

You won't be watching neither of us. You'll have to be minding her baby.

When's your kid due?

May, like less than a month off.

You done well, bringing it to St Clair, said Brian.

You tell the kid in a few years' time, how it got the very best start, breathing in the island air before it popped out of the womb, said Pete, finding his voice.

Make sure the kid comes back, before it turns five, said Brian. And you too, of course.

He's a boy, gonna be.

Wow, you know, do you? Many don't.

See, a cigarette don't do no harm here. Not when all the time there's fresh sea air and healthy Atlantic winds, said Pete.

You go to Hounds' Point and breathe deep, said Brian.

Catch that Atlantic spray on your face.

But don't go too near the edge, mind. Brian showed her the headland on the map.

Why's it called Hounds' Point? Is it good for dogs there? asked Aysha, turning to the neglected Greg with affection.

It is good for dogs, but that's not why it got its name.

Well, why did it then?

Cos the roaring of the breakers off the Atlantic, said Pete. Sounds just like the baying of hounds.

Aysha mumbled her thanks after her encounter with the boatmen, and set off with her light pack on her back, Greg on his lead and the map open in her hand, up the road from the quay. It was hardly a road, little more than a narrow track, and whenever a land-rover, tractor or farm-buggy came past, ferrying people or goods from the boat she'd been on, she and Greg had to squeeze tight into the hedge to let them by. She took a sandy trail which brought her down to the nearest of the two beaches on the map. Then she let Greg off the lead, and he ran on excitedly, splashing in the breakers. A variety of gulls and oyster-catchers (she would check those with Charly) scattered in alarm from the water's edge, some flying off, others wheeling out to sea and landing further along. Shags (she remembered those) were sitting on a rock at the far end of the sand and some flew low over the water. She looked for seals but could see none. A fishing-boat with one large black-backed gull perched on its mast sat a little way out, rocking gently. Aysha had her lunch in her pack and she had two hours before the assignment she'd taken on. She felt happy, happier than she'd felt for a long long time and Greg, she could see, was ecstatic, running and jumping into the waves as they broke on the sand. It was too cold to sit so she walked slowly to the far end and looked at her map. She followed paths which would take her across the island in the direction of Hounds' Point. The paths were sometimes sandy, sometimes stony, sometimes grassy, or a mixture of all three, but they always ran between hedges, often hedges growing on low stone walls, higher and bushier hedges than the ones around the fields outside Bursfield. Even on such a small island, she had no idea where she was except by following the map. It was good practice, she told herself. Then she climbed uphill and the hedges came to an end. The sea was in front of her again, and some cottages. To her right was a farm, and to her left the creamy-coloured buildings of what she could tell from the map was the island's hotel. She walked straight on with Greg following. The wind was getting stronger and colder and the sun kept going behind clouds. She came to the sea and followed the edge of a bay round to the start of Hounds' Point. There was no sand here, but there were lots of gulls and other birds on the stones and rocks, and there were shags flying further out, and there were seals here, one or two bobbing in the water of the bay. The wind howled and screeched and chattered like a million different creatures and Greg ran this way and that and she hoped she wasn't going to need to call him over the racket of the wind, nor put him on the lead while clutching tight the map in her frozen fingers. Her plan had been to eat her lunch at Hounds' Point and she still wished she could, for this place was wilder than anywhere in Scotland and the boatmen were right, she should stay and let the air from the ocean course through her and around her and the baby. But she worried if the baby inside would catch a chill and wished she had warmer clothes and gloves most of all.

Then she thought about Alaska and doing the Iditarod race, and told herself how could she do that if she let a wind off the ocean put her off sitting on this headland to eat her lunch and watch the waves and the sea everywhere and all the birds wheeling on the wind and crying out over the noise. She carefully stuffed the leaflet into her pack, checked the time on Katy's watch, put on her waterproof jacket which she'd stowed in her pack, and then started her lunch. After a few minutes she retreated behind a rock but even that hardly helped. She called Greg to have the last bit of her sandwiches, knowing he must be ravenous by now.

This is Hounds' Point, she said to him as she handed the piece of food over. It's the best place in the world for a dog. But the sound got carried away on the wind, even if he could have understood.

She took a quick swig of her drink, left her piece of cake in the pack, stuffed the banana and chocolate bar in the pocket of her waterproof to eat while she walked, and set off at as fast a pace as she could, with Greg scampering alongside, to warm up a bit. She might have run, but she knew she couldn't run now, not for a while, a cross-country race about two weeks before the end of term was the last run she would do until after the baby were born, and her bulge were hardly showing then.

Looking up the coast ahead, giant fountains of sea-spray burst up over the rocks and cascaded down again like fireworks. All the strength of the Atlantic Ocean thundered against the shore. She had chosen a different bit of the island to walk on now, and when the path divided, she took the right-hand one which led her uphill away from the sea. Greg trotted by her side. It was too windy to get the map out of her pack. The path climbed upward for a while and then levelled out. There were no hedges or fields or cottages or farms up here, there weren't no people anywhere although she'd seen quite a few walking about earlier. Apart from her and Greg, all there was were a few cows, eight or nine, on lower ground to her right where the grass looked greener. Up here it was just grass and rocks, rocks not much bigger than stones really and no way big enough to shelter her from the wind. This was a wild place she thought, it reminded her a little bit of one of the Scottish islands she'd been to, but she couldn't quite think which. Scotland was a wild place, she thought, and so was Alaska, but both, especially Alaska, miles bigger than this island. She thought this must be the smallest wild place in the world, and was pleased with that idea.

But however small, she didn't quite know where she should go now, and got worried she weren't gonna make it in time. She could see for miles, sea and other islands everywhere, but she couldn't make out where this island ended and the next one started, and she couldn't see any buildings close by, nor the place where she'd come off the boat. Wind or no wind, she knew she had to get out her map. Thank god Neil had showed her how to read maps - Neil, fuck she were trying not to think of him, wherever he was. She got out the little one Brian had given her, not the big orange one which would be impossible to open up in the wind.

Stopping to look at the map made her cold, and she thought of Alaska again. All good training, she told herself, trying to brave the conditions. She could see on the map the path she was on. There was a hill ahead, not a mountain like in Scotland but marked on the map, the highest point on the island, Beacon Hill. The shop was down the other side of that hill, there was a path going over it which she could see, although the path she was on took her to the north of the hill, so she was gonna need to turn off further ahead. Reassured, confident again, she stuffed the map back in the pack, took a swig of drink, took first the banana and then the chocolate from her pocket and walked along munching the rest of her lunch.

The path dropped very steeply down the other side of the hill to a few buildings clustered along a sandy track. Quite suddenly the wind had dropped and the sun was out again. Aysha felt warm, hot even from her exertions, and took off her waterproof, stuffing it back in the pack. She could see the shop now, one of two larger buildings scattered among a few small cottages. The other one was the island's pub. She checked Katy's watch, there was still ten minutes till the shop closed. She reached for the ten pound note. Five pounds to keep for the boat. She wondered why they hadn't taken her money this morning, and what would happen if she spent more than five pounds at the shop or the pub. There were people sitting outside the pub but the shop looked quiet. It was down a short gravelly track, and there weren't high hedges here but low walls with fences built on them. Behind one fence some chickens rooted around in dark earth, on the other side flowers grew. The shop was just a house with a big window in front and a double door. There was signs outside and notices in the window by the door. Back from the house was a shed, and by the shed stood a rusty, broken-down car and an old tractor. One of the chickens had got out from the fenced patch and poked around the front wheel of the tractor.

Aysha tied up Greg by his lead to an ice-cream sign that stood solid and heavy out the front, and went in, clutching her money. Going out of the sun made it seem very dark in there at first and she had to adjust her eyes. She could see it was self-service like most shops, just smaller than the supermarkets in Bursfield. There were two smaller children in there, whispering, and a woman at the till. It seemed very quiet. Aysha was unsure of herself for a moment, having hoped, expected, to find a man running the shop. She slowly sauntered around, looking and thinking. She picked up a can of pepsi, a chocolate bar and a packet of crisps, but didn't immediately move to the till.

We're closing in a couple of minutes, called out the woman, but Aysha wasn't sure if it was for her or the kids. She waited.

The children went up to the till with a few sweets. Aysha followed, stayed back. She waited for the children to leave the shop, but they stayed in the doorway, watching her surreptitiously. After she'd paid for her things, Aysha said to the woman as quiet as she could without it being too much like a whisper,

Is Mr Owen here?

I'm Mrs Owen, said the woman.

It's Mr Owen I wanna speak to.

What about?

It's kinda private.

Does he know you?

No, he don't. My name's Aysha, Aysha Stanton. Is he here?

I think so, he may be out the back, or upstairs.

I'll be out the front, said the girl. I'll wait for him out there.

The children still stood and watched her as she untied Greg and sat on a low wall holding him by his lead. She heard the woman lock the shop from the inside and change the sign on the door from open to closed. A few minutes later the woman's face appeared at an upstairs window. Aysha felt uncomfortable that she was being looked at, and then a man came round the side of the house and approached her somewhat aggressively. He was a burly, rather red-faced man with dark hair beginning to grey, and a moustache of similar colour. The two little children had suddenly vanished.

Who are you?

Aysha Stanton.

Have I met you before?

No, never.

Oh. She could sense the man's mood relax. So you're not trying to make out I'm the father of your unborn child?

Oh no, I know who the father is, it's something else. Aysha relaxed too, sensing now what everyone had been bothered about, staring at. There was a pause, during which she thought the man had glanced up at the window and then glanced again at her.

So what can I do for you?

Are you Rodney Andrew Owen? She had rehearsed this, many times.

Yes.

Did you used to live in Longworth near Manchester and have a wife called Sharon?

No.

417

And two kids called Samantha and Katy?

Oh my god! The man's face crumpled as though actually this might have been even worse news than the allegation of fatherhood. Are you Katy? he asked hoarsely.

No, no, it ain't me who's Katy, Aysha said in a great hurry, beginning to stutter and garble her words. I mean, she's like, my friend, my best friend, she's like my carer, my guardian kinda, she looks after us. Me and my two sisters.

The man looked at her and seemed to be having difficulty taking this in. You're part of Katy's family?

Yeah, kind of.

So who are you then?

I'm Aysha, Aysha Stanton.

And Katy's your guardian, you said?

Yeah, kinda. She's gonna adopt me, and my sisters, only she ain't quite old enough yet.

How old is Katy now then?

Twenty. She thinks she might be able to apply to adopt us after she's twenty-one. She turns twenty-one in July.

Is she married?

Nah, but you don't have to be married no more to adopt kids. She's got a boyfriend called Gareth.

So you don't have your own parents to look after you?

Nah, our mam's in prison, and Charly's dad's dead, she's the next sister to me, and Zoë the youngest, her dad's a child abuser.

My god! And your father?

He were from Sri Lanka, but no-one over there can find him so we think he must have died in the tsunami.

Jesus wept! And you're the eldest?

Yeah, I were like running wild and getting in loads of trouble and so Katy kinda rescued me off of the streets.

And your sisters? Were they on the streets too?

Nah, they was in a kids home but they neither of them liked it. Nor me, even less than them. I were s'posed to live there but I kept running off.

There was a pause, as both girl and man seemed to have run out of things to say, and in the case of the man he was clearly having trouble taking all this in. Aysha looked rather desperately around her as though seeking inspiration but unwilling to meet the gaze of the man who was staring at her with some degree of disbelief. In the end she looked down at the dog.

This is Katy's dog. He's called Greg and he's brilliant.

In what way?

Next to Katy, he's the best friend I'll ever have.

So why have you come all this way to find me instead of Katy?

Are you Katy's real dad?

Well, I thought that would be clear by now. Yes I am.

D'you have another family now?

Yes, that was my wife who served you just then. I've been married fifteen years now, and there's five children. She had three kids already, and then we had two of our own. A girl and a boy. I don't know why, but I always wanted a boy. So we tried twice. The oldest two of my stepchildren have left home now, but the youngest still lives at home with our two. They're all three at high school now.

Is there a school here, on this island?

God no, there isn't even a primary school any more, there's one High School on St Mary's and our three go there. They board during the week, but of course it's school holidays now.

Yeah, I'm on holidays from my school. And Charly, she goes to the same school, it's called Andrew Wheeler High School. And Zoë from her primary school. But I won't be going back to my school until after my baby's born.

The man looked at her again and she turned away.

When's it due?

Next month.

You haven't said why it's you who's come to find me. And how did you find me, by the way?

It were Katy's mum who wanted to. It were someone told her you was living here, I don't know who, and so I said I would come and find out if you was, y'know, like Katy and Sam's dad. Katy didn't wanna come, I think she were, like, shy or embarrassed or something, I dunno, uncomfortable, whatever, so I said I would. I mean, after all Katy's done for me, then this were one thing I could do to help her, right?

Sure. You get on well with her, then?

Kind of. She's brilliant, Katy, but I kinda disappoint her

loads. Like, not talking to her when she wants me too. I hate all this talking 'bout stuff, me, so does my sister Charly. We should talk, but it's always, like, heavy stuff. But we does help out in other ways.

I know how you feel, said the man. I have that problem too.

Did you tell anyone, y'know, 'bout having a family before?

Well, I did tell Donna, my wife, soon after we first got together. Even that was very difficult, as you could imagine. But we never told any of the children, I'm not quite sure why, thinking about it now. Well, I think the reason was that they were very insecure then, living in a caravan near the Cornish coast when I met them, they'd moved around different temporary addresses, nearly homeless in fact, and we thought if they knew I had another family it might increase their sense of insecurity, thinking I might leave and go back. And for me, it seemed best if I tried to put Sharon and Samantha and Katy out of my mind completely.

Did you do that?

More or less. Well, I tried, but, of course, I did sometimes wonder how they were all getting on. And I had dreams about them, which I kept to myself.

Well, Sam and Katy's ok now. Sam's married to a guy called Marcus and they have two great little kids what's your grandchildren. Lara and Liam, they's called, and I really love them both, 'specially Lara who's just turned six. And Katy's got Greg. And Gareth. And us.

What about Sharon?

Sharon ain't too well now, she's got this, kinda disability, I don't remember what it's called, but she's in a wheelchair nearly all the time now. But she's got a new husband called Steve who's really good to her.

Good, I'm pleased to hear that. How long's she been married?

The girl furrowed her brow. I dunno that. But Katy told me 'bout when she were a little kid, like just starting school, how it were Sam what mainly looked after her cos her mum was bad from depression.

Oh, I'm very sorry to hear that. But then Sharon was

depressed just after Katy was born. And indeed, before that.

So why did you leave her then?

Katy's father looked at her, and Aysha began to feel she might have already said too much, although there was a lot more she could have said and she had been trying to be careful.

There's no simple answer to that one, said the man. Lives get complicated and don't work out as planned. People change, feelings change. I wasn't ready to cope with a needy, depressed partner. I'd already begun seeking sanctuary with Samantha, and that wasn't right. She needed her mother and baby sister more than me. Of course I should have stayed, I know that now, but I was feeling pushed out. I'd no idea what to do to make things better. I went as far away as I could and then I met Donna. She was also in an unhappy situation but she seemed stronger, with more experience of working through the tough times. Once I hitched up with her there was no going back. We looked around for something to do, some place to go. We'd thought of these islands, though we were prepared to stay in Cornwall, or even move to some other place. Then we heard they were look-ing for someone to take over this shop. They were looking for a family, and it was ideal for us too, the accommodation came with it. We none of us looked back. So where is Katy now?

Where? She's in her second year at uni.

No, I mean has she stayed home, or come down with you?

She come with us, her and Gareth and my sisters, we're camping on the big island.

St Mary's?

Yeah, the one the boat come from this morning. And they've all gone on a boat tour to see seals.

So when are you all returning to the mainland?

I ain't sure. Soon.

Look, just wait a minute, will you, said the man, and disappeared round the back of the shop.

Do you want to come up and have a cup of tea? he said, returning very quickly.

Nah, said Aysha. Thanks, but I never drink tea.

Something else to drink? Piece of cake or a biscuit or two?

Oh yeah, thanks. She realised only then how hungry she

was. A cold drink would be cool. Juice or something, she added.

Well, come on up and I'll introduce you to Donna.

What about Greg?

Who?

Our dog.

You can bring him up. That's no problem.

What about your kids? What shall I tell them?

They're not at home. The eldest is on a school trip and the younger two are visiting friends on St Mary's. In fact, they would have got off the boat this morning when you got on, and when you go back, they'll be waiting to board when you get off. But you won't approach them, will you?

Nah, course not.

Please make sure you don't.

They went up some stairs at the back of the shop, and she met Mrs Owen again.

You're welcome here, but this is a shock, she said.

We're not sure what to do next, said her husband.

About telling your kids? Aysha asked.

Yes, and - well, I'd like to meet Katy. While she's here, otherwise it would be a missed opportunity.

But we don't want to rush into anything, said Donna Owen, presenting Aysha with some food and drink. Even photos, that will be difficult. Maybe we could just hear a bit more about your family while you're here.

Katy's family, prompted her husband.

Apart from us, there's just Sam, and Marcus, her husband. And Lara and Liam.

I have these two grandchildren, said Rodney Owen to his wife.

Yeah, and the thing is, went on Aysha. They don't have no other grandparents, 'part from Katy's mum. Their other grandma, that's Marcus's mum, she died a year ago. Marie, her name was. I looked after the kids at her funeral. And the grand-dad, he died before that. Jack, his name was, I never knew him. In a mountain accident. And Neil, that's Marcus's older brother, Lara and Liam's uncle, he took up doing mountain rescue after his dad died that way. He trains dogs for it. She clamped her mouth shut. She was in danger of saying too much, probably already had.

422

So you're saying the children just have one grand-parent?

Yeah, and she's in a wheelchair.

What about her husband?

Steve? Yeah, he helps out with Lara and Liam, but he ain't related, is he, and you is. I think that's why Katy's mum wanted to find you, and that's why I said I'd help her, cos I likes Lara and Liam a lot.

Does Katy have a mobile with her?

Yeah.

Do you know the number?

Yeah, course I do. She always tells me to phone if I needs her.

Good. Could you phone her from here and maybe she'd let me speak to her?

Aysha hesitated.

But what if she feels too shy or awkward?

We'll try and get over it.

The thing is, said Donna Owen. We could tell you all about our family, but then you'd have to tell Katy.

I know, and then, like, I might forget and get it wrong.

And if there's a chance for me to actually meet Katy, it will be best to tell her direct. Or we might not have much to talk about.

Yeah.

So Rodney Owen showed Aysha the phone and she dialled.

It's switched off, she reported. She must still be on the boat trip.

Yes, that must be it. What a pity.

Why don't you show Aysha round the island? Donna Owen asked her husband.

Oh no, said Aysha, a little anxious. I've seen some of it already.

Which bits have you seen?

Hounds' Point. And the hill just behind here. And that big stretch of beach, y'know, this one .... she pulled out the leaf-let she'd been given on the boat, and pointed out the beach on the map.

Well, that's good. And did you walk all of that?

423

Yeah, well Greg needed a good walk.

Sure. But there's more of the island to see.

Yeah, I know, I wanna see South Beach if there's time.

And there's all the north-east. Spectacular coastline and an old castle.

Aysha took out Katy's watch. I've only got an hour and a half now.

I could drive you down to South Beach, well nearly, or you ....

Drive? queried Aysha. What d'you mean, drive?

We've got a land-rover, we need one to collect stock from the boat.

How d'you get it out here? The boat's not big enough, said Aysha.

There is a bigger boat will take vehicles across to the smaller islands, if you book it in advance. Expensive though. We never take the land-rover anywhere else. It came with the shop.

Aysha was feeling a little anxious. She didn't really know these people, and Katy's dad had said something about getting too close to Samantha. Could she trust him? she wondered. But then, she did have Greg.

Would Greg be allowed in the land-rover?

Of course. It'll only take five minutes, and I'll take my mobile with me and we'll try phoning Katy again when we get to South Beach. It's the best place to get a signal.

So which other islands are you planning to visit? he asked, as they jumped into the land-rover.

I dunno, but my sister Charly's into birdwatching and stuff and she wants to go to the island what has a lake and some bird-hides.

St Luke. Good, well maybe I could meet Katy there.

So he parked the land-rover at the end of a track and they walked towards South Beach. Aysha dialled Katy on Rodney Owen's mobile and Katy answered, but wouldn't talk to Rodney direct. With Aysha as intermediary, they arranged to meet by the pier on St Luke the following morning.

Aysha spent a few minutes on the beach and then walked back to the pier with Greg, briskly at first but then she saw she still had loads of time and went by the other beach which she'd visited in the morning, and dawdled along it. On the ferry, an older man was at the wheel, but it was still Brian taking the passengers' money.

Where's Pete? she asked him.

He's on the fast boat this afternoon.

Why's he doing the fast boat?

So that he can finish earlier. We had an early start this morning.

Don't you wanna finish early too?

Well, I would, but I haven't got my navigation licence yet so I have to work on this boat. I hope they'll let me have it next year. And then he got busy with other passengers, but they did wave at each other as she disembarked on the main island, and Katy was waiting for her and she noticed the two kids, dark-haired, a girl about her own age and her younger brother, and she realised later they were Katy's half-brother and sister and had been on the quay together and never known it, but she didn't say anything.

The next morning on St Luke while Gareth took Charly off to look for birds and seals and visit the hides, Aysha helped introduce Katy to her father, and so he then told them more about his new family and why things had happened as they did all those years ago, and started asking Katy about her life, now and in the past, and Katy gradually thawed, until Aysha took Zoë and Greg and quietly slipped away for a while.

When they'd got back, and all met up again, and Rodney had gone back to St Clair, Katy seemed numbed by the experience, or perhaps just exhausted.

Who's gonna tell your mum about this? Aysha whispered to her back at the camp-site.

You can, Aysha, the older girl replied. And she spent the next two days and nights in Gareth's arms.

Shortly after their return to Bursfield, Gareth departed for Bangor where the final term of his degree course was about to begin. Katy pulled herself together after the shock, the emotional bombardment of an encounter with someone she'd never met before, that she could remember, yet who was so much part of her. A flying visit to see her mother was coming up before term restarted, she still had a lot of coursework to complete, she still had to cajole Aysha into attending her pre-natal classes, but most of all, she needed a real talk with the girl. Aysha still felt more a part of her than this new person in her life, this Rodney Owen, ever would, and she could not imagine rebuilding any link with this man who had resurfaced on the horizon of her life without Aysha being part of that connection.

She had put off visiting the girls' mother for the moment. Aysha didn't want her to know about the baby until it was born, and Katy hoped Aysha might be willing to come along with the baby for Stella to see. But another expedition to the cemetery to see Kenny's memorial was called for, they had only been once so far and it took more than half a day. Fortunately Katy's other commitments had reduced. There was only the choir now, basketball and orchestra had finished for the summer. The quartet's regular cellist had had her baby some months before and although she would have taken a longer maternity leave if circumstances allowed it, she was now willing to rejoin the quartet and relieve her replacement. Katy had mixed feelings about this. It had been hard work in the quartet, practising, raising her level of playing to what was required, and there had been one piece (the Bartok 4th Quartet) they'd had to temporarily discard from their repertoire because Katy could not master the cello part. But she'd loved it in so many ways, becoming so much more intimate with the music and with other musicians, all the encouragement the other three had given her, the sense, especially at performances, of being a real musician now, a fully committed, full-time one. But the experience, however brilliant, had in the end, she now knew, not been really her. She had had a glimpse of how real musicians worked, and she could never be one, even if she hadn't taken on her commitments as a carer. She lacked the intensity, the passion, the single-mindedness. She had, and would always want to have, too many other strings to her bow. And the wider contact with musicians which being in the quartet brought about more than the orchestra, and which she'd been unable to make best use of, well that had an exciting element to it, but she knew she would never be entirely comfortable in that element. At the same time there was real sadness at departing from the quartet.

So she snatched a few moments with Aysha when the other two girls were asleep.

Thanks for finding my dad for me. I'm sorry we haven't been able to find yours.

Aysha mumbled something along the lines of it was ok, he was probably dead.

Now we need to have a talk about the baby, and what really happened last summer.

There ain't nothing to talk about. The child continued to mumble, but the tone had changed, and she'd put on one of her insolent, "up yours" sort of look.

You can start by telling me what happened between you and Neil.

Nothing.

I know something happened, and I want your side of it. Don't worry, I won't tell the authorities or get Neil into trouble, but I need to hear what really happened.

Aysha now looked a little startled and also disbelieving.

Why won't you tell? Why should I believe you?

Because you've gotta trust me, Aysha, and I absolutely promise I won't tell.

All right then, so how d'you know something happened?

Because Neil told Marcus and Sam, and they told me.

When did they tell you?

In March, when I went round there and you'd already been there in the pouring rain.

What did Neil say?

Something about a thunderstorm and you'd rushed into his tent soaking wet and scared. Seems to be a thing with you and pouring rain.

It weren't Neil's fault, she said, annoyance, dismay and pleading mingled in her tone.

Why, was it yours?

No, it weren't mine either. It were just one of them things what happens.

Babies don't just happen.

They did this time.

It is Neil's then?

Yeah, I s'pose it is.

And were you trying to seduce Neil, make him feel attracted to you?

No.

What were you doing, going about with hardly anything on?

It was hot, right. We was carrying heavy packs, and before that we was by the sea and I wanted to sunbathe.

I've never known you sunbathe before.

Well, we ain't by the sea here, are we?

And trying, lots of nights, to go in his tent?

Aysha struggled for an answer to this one. Look, I were mixed up, right, Katy. I kinda felt lonely and I was missing Greg. And you, Katy. And I needed, like -

Hugs?

Yeah.

Why not Charly?

Cos she were always asleep when this, like, feeling lonely came on. Anyhow, I ain't never gone in for that with her.

But you thought you could with Neil?

Yeah. No, I mean I don't know, Katy, I were mixed up. But it weren't his fault, I promise you.

Why did you go running into his tent with no clothes on?

Cos it were pouring with rain and I didn't wanna get my stuff wet. Most of it were just, like, so disgusting by now and I only had one t-shirt to wear for coming back and I needed to keep that dry.

So you had time to think, it wasn't spur of the moment?

No, it just happened, like, it were spur of the moment, yeah. What I mean is, like, that's why I never had nothing on at night them last few nights.

Did you have some sort of crush on Neil? Or still do?

No, Katy, I don't, I promise. I like Neil and I thought he were really wicked with Charly and me. But it ain't a crush, I don't want anything like that to happen again.

Well, I still think he must be largely held responsible for this. Did you know he'd told Marcus and Sam?

No.

So why did you go round there before me?

Cos I thought, y'know, like, I thought they was gonna tell you where Neil were, and I didn't want you chasing after him.

Why not?

I didn't want him to know I were pregnant. Not if I were gonna get it adopted.

What good was it gonna do for you to rush round to my sister's?

I dunno, I got mixed up.

OK, so we're sure as can be that this baby is Neil's. What about these other sexual encounters you told me about?

What about them? Aysha seemed unprepared for this change of tack, and even more disgruntled than before.

The boys you told me about. In Scotland and at the drumming camp. Did that happen?

What?

Did you have sex with other boys? Katy was also getting exasperated, having to spell everything out.

Oh. Nah. I mean .... She paused.

You made that up?

She nodded.

So you're not being promiscuous, going round having sex with all and sundry?

Aysha just hung her head.

Is that a yes or a no?

No, I made that up.

Well, I'm glad in one sense. But why did you lie to me?

It were only a white lie, Aysha claimed defensively.

You think lying about how you got pregnant can be dismissed as a white lie? It seems like to me it's a serious matter.

Well, you lied too, Katy. You're like so hypocritical.

When did I lie?

Last summer, about Zoë, you said the home had phoned to offer to take her on a trip when it were you what phoned to ask them!

I don't think you can compare the two, that was a white lie, it was only a tiny difference.

No, Katy, you got that wrong! protested the younger girl. A white lie, right, is when you don't tell the truth to save someone else from getting in trouble. That's why I lied, to save Neil. But you never, what you said were to make you look good, or kinda not so bad, when you knew it were the wrong thing, right.

I knew you'd be upset, ok, I mean disappointed in what I'd done, I just kinda wanted to let you down gently. That counts as a white lie in my book.

Well, same with me. But it were Neil you was gonna get mad with, I knew, so that's why I said what I did.

Did you know Neil thought you was around seventeen years old?

Nah, I never told him, it were you should've told him.

I know that, and I thought I had done. But were you acting like you were seventeen?

Aysha shrugged. I dunno, do I, right?

He still shouldn't't've let it happen, even if you were. But you know he later found out your real age?

No.

Well he did, so he's disappeared. He's gone into hiding.

Where?

I don't know, nobody does. It wouldn't be in hiding if we did.

I bet you Sam and Marcus knows!

They've promised me they don't.

How can we let him know 'bout his kid then?

I thought you didn't want him to know.

Not me getting pregnant, right! But when I've got a baby I'll want him to know, yeah, like he's the father, he's got a right to know.

Maybe leave it a while, ok, we don't want to arouse any suspicions.

Katy couldn't work Aysha out, her mixture of secrecy and openness, but she knew this was a time when she, too, was having to give confused messages, introduce an element of collusion, try and keep her charge on board. She would probably never find out exactly what happened but at least some things were clearer now. And Aysha was going to her classes more regularly and a little less unwillingly, though still needing Katy to take her.

Sharon was always pleased to see them all, her younger daughter and her new "family", but this time her anticipation was even keener. She knew Steve was puzzled, anxious about this, she hadn't been able to hide it from him, she wanted to hear all about Rodney. She knew they'd met him, that it was him, that it was Aysha who'd made the initial contact, but neither the girl nor Katy had been able or willing to say much over the phone, they'd kept her on tenterhooks until this flying visit, one night only. She and Steve were expecting them now.

She had told her elder daughter and they'd fallen out over it. If Sharon's excitement had been hard to contain, then even more so was Samantha's anger. Sharon knew that Sam had never taken to Aysha, but she hoped that by doing this, stepping in where Katy felt too awkward and shy to proceed and so in some way making up for all Katy had done for her, that Aysha might bring about some softening in her elder daughter's attitude. Sharon herself liked Aysha, had quite taken to her almost from the beginning and hoped the feeling was mutual although these days with girls her age it was almost impossible to tell; but Sam's hostility had clearly grown out of all proportion, and her fury when she found out that it was Aysha who'd made the first contact with the father who she still remembered from her childhood, seemed to know no bounds. Not only was this going to mean that Lara and Liam were unlikely to see, or even know about, this grandfather of theirs, at least in the foreseeable future, but it seemed that even she, Sharon, might not see them for a while.

She asked herself many times whether she'd done the right thing seeking him out, and attempted to talk to Steve about this, but all Steve said was it was done now, you can't undo what's done, you have to make the best of it, and he really didn't want to get involved in any family disputes about it.

So Sharon pinned her hopes on Katy now. Her younger daughter was not one for disputes or shows of anger unless it was absolutely necessary. She could hold her ground now, for sure, but wasn't she doing well with these three kids on top of her studies and her other activities, ok this pregnancy was a bit of a worry, but Sharon felt proud of Katy, and the three girls as well, and the fact that contact with Rodney had been established. Despite the falling-out with Samantha, she was determined to welcome them with open arms, hear what they had to tell with genuine appreciation.

They arrived for a late lunch. Steve busied himself getting food onto the table. Aysha was quite enormous now and very hungry. Everyone wanted to concentrate on food rather than talk. Sharon got frustrated. After what seemed an age to her, Steve started clearing the table and Charly helped him, and they both went into the kitchen to wash the dishes.

Aysha can tell you more about Rodney now, said Katy.

I'd prefer Steve to hear as well.

Charly never really met him, her daughter went on. She went off bird-watching with Gareth, while we talked.

She ain't really interested in that sort of stuff, added Aysha.

It's a pity Gareth hasn't come with you, said Sharon.

Well, he had to go back to uni himself, it's his final term about to start.

Sharon was aware how disjointed the conversation was. She looked at her daughter, at Aysha, even at Zoë, appealingly. Katy seemed just as uncomfortable.

Aysha can tell you about it, mum. I'll go and see if Steve wants to hear about it. And Charly. Katy went to the kitchen door and Sharon could hear a muffled conversation starting up. Katy stayed, helping the other two at the sink, while Aysha started talking. The three of them returned to the table a few minutes later.

See, I went to this island with Greg, and I had a walk, and I went to this wild place called Hounds' Point. Then I got to the shop just before it closed and I went in. There was a woman at the till, she was his new wife, and there was two little kids in there, like, on their own. So I said could I speak to Rodney Owen and then I sat outside and he, like, came round from the back.

Sharon was already a little impatient. What was he like?

Quite old, with a moustache. Hair going grey. He were suspicious at first, then friendly. His wife's called Donna. She had three kids of her own when they met, and then they had two more. He met her when she were living in a caravan in Cornwall. He said she were kinda homeless or had been but he didn't say why.

What are the children's names?

He didn't tell me their names, but I did see two of them, they was waiting on the main pier with Katy when I got back from the island.

They were waiting with Katy?

Nah, what I mean's they was on the pier too, standing close to one another and not even knowing. Cos he told me, that Rodney, they'd be on the boat, and there was only two kids that age, on their own.

What age are they?

A girl my age, and a boy a bit younger.

Did you speak to them?

Nah, I wanted to, right, cos they's Katy's half-sister and half-brother, yeah, standing right by her and not even knowing they's related. But he made me, like, promise not to talk to them, cos they don't know nothing 'bout Katy or anything. His wife does, but not the kids.

He told me quite a lot about the kids, said Katy, back in the room now taking over from Aysha who by now seemed quite played out by it all. But not their names. And I told him all about us, and what had happened in our lives, and I gave him our addresses, yours, mum, and Sam's and mine. He's gonna write to us and let us know when he's told the kids about us. It ain't gonna be easy for him. He asked us to wait til we hear from him.

Is that all?

Well, what more d'you want? Katy protested to her.

Best leave it there, said Steve. The initial contact's been made, that's the main thing.

I can tell you some more about the island, said Aysha, perking up. He's got a land-rover which came with the shop. They use it for collecting stores for the shop from the boat. If there's big things there's a trailer too. There ain't, like, proper roads on the island, just sandy tracks. And the ferry don't take cars so the land-rover stays on the island. There ain't no garage so if they wants petrol or repairs they take it to the boat-yard, right. All there is on the island is a pub, a café, a hotel, a few cottages and one or two farms. They's got hens and cows and they grows flowers and, like, produce and stuff. And the shop, right, with a post-box and phone.

How big's the shop?

Quite small, but it's got a till like a supermarket, right.

On the other island, piped in Zoë. Where we met Katy's real dad, there's a big shop, much bigger. And Katy's real dad went in there to get some things for his shop what he'd run out of.

 So where did you meet him, Katy?

 I met him on this other island, what's it called, Aysha?

 I forgot.

 So do I. So only Aysha saw him on his home patch. This is all thanks to Aysha, mum.

 I know, dear, I'm really grateful, my pet.

 Aysha squirmed off, looking really embarrassed, mumbling something about taking Greg for his walk.

 She won't be able to do that much longer, will she? Sharon said to her daughter.

 No, Katy said with a slightly uncomfortable laugh. I don't know how she'll manage when she doesn't have this ready excuse for avoiding situations she finds difficult.

 But this hasn't been difficult for her, surely?

 Quite difficult at times, I think. You do embarrass her sometimes, mum.

 What about this baby, then? Is she going to cope with it?

 We none of us know for sure. We've just got to help her, all of us, the best we can, and hope.

36. FAILING MOTHERHOOD

He was called Peter Kenneth Rodney Stanton and he popped out into the world just before two in the morning on May 9th, 2006. Katy was there, at Aysha's bedside, she'd gone back home a bit earlier in the evening and the hospital called her just before midnight and she came in by taxi. The birth was straightforward and either Aysha was incredibly stoical or she had it easier than most. She made more fuss about having to be in hospital for a few days and Greg not being allowed on the maternity ward, than about the birth itself.

 But there was no option other than the hospital. Katy had a bag packed for her well in advance but Aysha needed little apart from her personal stereo. Gareth agreed to come over before the birth to look after the younger girls after school, so that Katy could stay with Aysha in the hospital, in the daytime at any rate. Soon after he arrived in Bursfield, it appeared that contractions were beginning so they phoned the ward and then set off in Gareth's car with Aysha in the front passenger seat and her sisters and Katy and Greg all squeezed in the back. Greg wasn't allowed in and Aysha got upset. Katy stayed with Aysha, as she did all the subsequent days, and Gareth would drive the other two girls over for the end of evening visiting hours, after which Katy went back home and returned the following morning after Charly and Zoë had left for school.

On the first day in the hospital, Katy asked the younger girl, once she seemed a little calmer, if she'd thought about a name for her baby and Aysha said she hadn't.

She had thought of Neil but decided against it, quite rightly, Katy said, so then Aysha said she thought his name should begin with P or R.

Why?

Cos there's a lot of S's and O's and K, L and M. In our family, I mean your family, right.

Katy puzzled this. Who's M? she asked.

Marcus. And his mum. Marie. And your mum and Steve, M's their surname, right.

Actually, my mum still calls herself Owen, even though she married Steve.

Well, it don't matter, it's still all O and S. And L for them kids and K for you. P and R's missing, right. 'Part from Rodney.

I don't want you to call the baby Rodney.

OK, P then. Peter, right, and then either Kenny or Rodney. Kenny I guess, if we can't have Neil.

You can have three first names if you want.

So they settled on Peter Kenneth Rodney.

Katy stayed with them the whole of the first day. Gareth brought Charly and Zoë straight after school to see their baby nephew, and Katy returned with them to try, not very successfully, to get some sleep. She returned to Aysha the next morning, and later that day baby and teenage mother were discharged home.

In the beginning Katy felt the signs were good. Aysha

held Peter close, seemed happy with him, frequently put him to her milk. She stayed home and received visits from midwife, then health visitor and social workers without, it appeared, any reluctance. She took Peter to the well-baby clinic, Katy accompanying initially. She refused to give any further thought to adoption, and nothing more was said about the baby's father. She made a great fuss of Greg when she first got home and helped the dog befriend the tiny child. And from the first day back, she, Greg and Peter slept in her room upstairs where Katy could hear her rising in the night when the baby awoke and cried, feeding him and getting him quiet again.

By the time Peter was two weeks old, the clinic was recommending that the breast milk be supplemented by the bottle. Aysha grew less and less willing to put him to the breast during the daytime although she still did so evening and morning, and as far as Katy could tell, during the night as well.

Gareth returned to Bangor and Katy was on her own with the kids. She arranged to go to her mother's for most of the half-term, partly because her mother was desperate to see the baby and them, partly because she herself wanted some support. She desperately wished she could see her sister, heal the differences with her. And she arranged to go and visit Stella in prison from Longworth, hoping Aysha would come, or at least let Katy take the baby, so that Stella could have contact with her grandchild. But Aysha would not agree, and that was the first real argument. Katy went with Zoë on her own and a folder full of photographs, of which Gareth had taken loads.

When they got back in the evening, exhausted, Katy found that Aysha and Charly had taken Greg for a long walk, during which they had visited her sister's. What was particularly annoying was that they'd left Peter with her mother and Steve, although it was clear her mother had been a more than willing accomplice. Marcus was at work, and Aysha at first claimed she'd gone because she wanted to see Lara and Liam, but it then transpired her main purpose was to ask Samantha where Neil was. Needless to say, Katy's sister was furious at this intrusion, both with Aysha at the time and later with Katy and Sharon. At least, Katy thought, Peter wasn't with them but then she wondered if in fact the presence of the baby would have softened, rather than exacerbated, Sam's reaction.

Aysha was asking about returning to school after half-term, but Katy, backed by every professional she spoke to, including the teachers at the school, felt it was too early. Peter needed to continue to bond with his mother, it would not be good for Katy to become principal carer nor for the baby to be farmed out to a child-minder so soon. Not much happened in the final period of the school year anyway, September would be the better time to go back in. And the school certainly did not want the baby brought along there.

Later, Katy came to the view that this had been a mistake, that everything might have worked better if Aysha had returned to school as soon as possible and resumed her normal life, the positive progress she was making. As it was, life seemed to go rapidly downhill from the moment they returned to Bursfield after half-term.

The teenager was getting restless, the days were long and warm. Katy organised walks for Aysha, pushing the baby in his buggy, and Greg, and at the weekends, and sometimes after school, for the other two girls as well. She even bought a little backpack for when Peter was six weeks old, so that she and Aysha could jog gently around, or walk on paths not suitable for the buggy, when Charly and Zoë were at school. But none of this satisfied Aysha's fretful soul. She didn't seem to want to be around Katy that much, she wanted to be with friends her own age or even out on her own. And when she did meet up with friends, whether she had Peter with her or not, Katy noticed with horror that she was using tobacco and alcohol again.

She seemed to develop an aversion to nappy-changing. In the daytime, it fell more and more to Katy to care for the baby at home. Aysha still looked after him at night, or at least fed him and soothed him back to sleep, but most mornings Katy found an unchanged nappy which Aysha just hadn't bothered with, leaving it to her. She tried to confront the girl, tried to reason with her but none of it seemed to work. Yet Katy was very reluctant to seek help, inform the authorities, fearing that Peter would be taken off them and that would break them apart, with Aysha unable to forgive and set on a downward spiral. So she struggled on, giving as much as she could to the baby and hoping for a breakthrough.

It never came. Aysha started going out more and more

in the evenings, leaving Peter to be babysat at home by Katy. She never said much about where she'd been, but it was clear she'd got closer to some of the other teenage kids in the neighbourhood and often, if not always, was going to gigs, possibly clubs or bars, with some of them. When she got back she always took Greg out, even if it was late and dark, and took Peter with them if he was still awake. But booze and tobacco often reeked off her, and Katy didn't like this.

Katy did still go to her choir once a week, with Charly, and on these nights Aysha happily stayed in with the baby and Zoë, and looked after them, although it became clear from things Zoë said later, that they didn't always stay in those long light evenings, but nevertheless nothing on those occasions gave Katy any real concern. But the more she tried to intervene with Aysha, set her right, the less the child wanted to be with her, Katy, the more she wanted to escape from the house, and Katy just didn't know what to do.

One thing Aysha pestered for was to take Peter up to the school to show her friends. Katy hadn't thought that Aysha had any particular friends there, and was in any case rather concerned at the way Peter was being shown off like some sort of trophy among Aysha's teenage peer-group. But in the end she and the school relented, and she took girl and baby to the High School in the lunch period. It was mostly the musicians Aysha wanted to catch up with, and Katy wondered if that was the reason she'd been keen to return to school. She would never show any concern, but perhaps deep down she was bothered that someone else would take her place on the drums.

They also, at Aysha's request, took Peter to Kenny's memorial stone at the crematorium. What was in Aysha's mind was never quite clear, but it appeared she had some strange idea that Kenny's spirit still stayed on there and that she wanted, indeed needed, some of that spirit to be conveyed to her small child.

Her strongest desire though, was to contact Neil. Indeed it often seemed to Katy that a lot of Aysha's behaviour, her shifting of the burden of responsibility onto her carer, was designed to force Katy to do something about Neil. In vain did Katy keep telling her that no-one knew where Neil was - Aysha was convinced that Sam and Marcus knew, and that Katy should be able to persuade them to divulge his whereabouts.

There was one occasion where she was almost explicit about this.

I should only go halves looking after Peter, she insisted.

That wasn't what we agreed, said Katy. You must be the main carer, the amount you're loading onto me isn't right. It was an argument she'd used with Aysha many times.

I mean Neil should do his share, said the girl. He's the dad and he should get to know his baby boy. He would want to, if only we could tell him.

It would be too risky, said Katy. Peter is the responsibility of Social Services, just as you are. They have to know who's caring for him. If Neil's caring for him they might realise he was the father and prosecute him and put him on the sex-offender register or whatever it's called, and then he wouldn't be allowed to care for kids, even Peter.

Aysha considered this for a while. We don't have to tell no-one he's the father, right. He could be a, like a family friend, or a godfather or something.

I still think the safest thing is to leave it a while. And since no-one knows where he is, we don't have any choice.

But nothing she could say satisfied the girl.

One Friday night at the very end of June, Aysha stayed out very late and was eventually returned, very much the worse for wear, by the police. By two officers in uniform, one man, one woman. The girl was not violent as she was escorted into the house, possibly she wasn't physically capable of it as she could hardly stand up, but she was very loud, shouting and laughing and swearing and then, as the officers released her once inside the front door, she somehow summoned Greg and lurched unsteadily up the stairs with him, clutching the bannisters to prevent her falling, not shouting now but still cursing under her breath in a slurred voice.

It's ages since we had any trouble from that one, said the policewoman.

She hasn't committed any crimes, has she? asked Katy, anxiously.

Drunk and disorderly? Breach of the peace? said the policeman in a somewhat sarcastic tone. No, we won't be pursuing anything, he added more gently.

Katy was embarrassed. Let's mark it down as a one-off aberration, she said. I'll do my very best to make sure it doesn't happen again.

Later she heard her protégée stumble into the bathroom and vomit copiously.

In a sense that incident marked a low point. Nothing as dire happened again, and within two weeks Gareth, having finished his degree, had arrived and moved in with them. Struggling with Aysha and her child was still a problem for Katy, but she no longer felt quite so alone.

Gareth suggested she attempted to meet half-way Aysha's constant insistence on finding Neil. Katy tried to remember from Marie's funeral who else was there that Neil might have fled to. There were Marie's two brothers, and they both lived in Scotland, or did they? And then there was an aunt on his father's side whom she had been introduced to, but what was her name? Ellen, was it?

She finally got round to phoning Marcus and Sam, and received a very hostile mouthful from her sister. No way should either she or Aysha be attempting to contact Neil, and she was really surprised at Katy for pursuing this. Sam made it clear that Marcus would absolutely forbid any contact to be made with any of his relatives concerning Neil's disappearance.

Katy felt totally caught in the middle. She told Aysha of her attempts and how they'd come to nothing, but it seemed nothing would satisfy the desperate child, who was convinced Katy's sister knew where they could find Neil.

Why is it so important now? Just leave it a little while, wait for everything to calm down, she repeated the advice she'd given many times already.

No, it can't wait, I ain't no good with a baby, not all the time, every day and night. It'll drive me, like, mental, Katy. If Neil took over half the time, that would be, like, ok.

How d'you mean, half the time?

Like, one week at a time, or something like that. Or him looks after Peter in the term and me in the holidays. He always said mountain rescue was busier in holiday times.

She seemed to read the dubious expression on Katy's face.

No, look, Katy, I don't wanna live with him or anything

440

like that, no way! I don't want nothing to do with him only to help look after Peter and to learn me mountain rescue, that's all, I promise.

How's he gonna teach you mountain rescue when there's Peter to look after?

I dunno, Katy, you could look after him a few days now and again or if not, then someone could look after him up in Grasmere or in Scotland.

Who?

Y'know, someone. Neil does know people, right, he does have some friends.

You do know these people would have to be approved by Social Services?

Fuck that! What's important for Peter is how he should have a dad, right, how he should be with his dad, get to know him. If Social Services don't understand that, they can fuck off!

Katy tried to explain, as she again had several times before, that Social Services might regard Neil as a paedophile if they knew what happened, and that would mean he would be forbidden contact.

You know he's not like that, Katy! pleaded Aysha. I know what them men's like, right, and Neil ain't one of them.

I know that, but I don't know that either you or I could convince the police or social workers, Katy responded. Just wait a little while, right.

He needs, like a dad now, ok?

He's got alternative father figures, hasn't he? What about Gareth? Or Steve?

It ain't the same, right? He needs his real dad. Gareth and Steve ain't connected to him like Neil is. I know what it's like, growing up without a dad, right.

But Kenny was a good dad to you, even though he wasn't your real dad. And I'm in the same position, ain't I? I never knew my real dad, but Steve was a good substitute.

Yeah, but look how hard it's been for you, getting to meet up with your real dad again, and look what happened to me after Kenny died and that tosser came along instead and look what that bastard did and our mam never said a word to stop him, and I never had no real dad I could've gone to what would've stopped all that stuff happening and .... and ....

But Peter's never gonna get abused, Aysha, you must know that.

But I'm too much like my mam, I'm gonna turn out a bad mother to him just like she were to me and my sisters.

No, you can break the cycle, Aysha. Please believe that, cos I do.

The only way to break the cycle, right, Katy, is for Neil to take charge of him. Look, if Neil don't want to help out with Peter, if he ain't interested, ok, then I'm gonna put him up for adoption, yeah, well, I'll like think about it, right. But I ain't gonna do it without finding Neil first and letting him know, ok?

But we're getting to know Peter more all the time, bonding with him, how can you say that?

That's why it's important to find Neil now, right. I know you's good with Peter, Katy, but it's for his sake, cos I'm a useless mum with him, I know I am. But if we leave it, it'll be harder giving him up, either to Neil or for adoption, and it'll be harder for Peter, right.

It was by far the most important talk she and Aysha had had since the baby was born, but it still left Katy feeling anxious and strangely disturbed about her charge.

Before Peter was born, in the days when she was at home in that short period that Katy, smiling in a good-humoured way, called her confinement, because she was too heavy to go out even to take Greg for a short walk, Aysha had a dream in which she gave birth to a dog. Not a dog like Greg but a child-dog, still a puppy but wild and able to run along with her, wild and free. In the dream she was running in a forest in the snow, and she had to find the hut where she had firewood to get warm and food for her and her child-dog and blankets where they could sleep. But it wasn't easy to find where the hut was because everywhere in the forest seemed the same and the paths were covered by snow and the child-dog couldn't help because he'd only just been born. In the dream Aysha was beginning to panic but then she did see the hut a long way off, across a river and a big clearing, but she woke up before she could get there. The dream stayed with her and became both liberating and confusing at the same time, and after Peter was born, she continued some nights to have variations on this dream.

Sometimes she was a human mother with a dog-child, sometimes a wild dog mother with a human child, sometimes a dog, wolf even, with a wolf child. Nearly always she and her child would run feral in forest or mountain, snow-covered or bare earth and rock, crossing big rivers or rushing mountain streams where she as wolf mother would hold the child in her mouth as she battled her way across. Yet she always searched for something, there was some place she had to get to, with the child, not food or even shelter but something more within her, some place of origin, village or burial-ground, she could never be sure until she got there which she never did. And when she got woken by her real baby and his need, for the breast whether feeding or just for comfort, and she soothed him and got him back to sleep eventually after a while, she had a desperate need to return to the dream she'd just left, even though she was troubled by it, but she never could.

She never woke Katy in the night, never handed Peter over, though she wished to often. She got very mixed up between trying to be a good mum and knowing she couldn't be and just giving up. At night there was nothing else to do but try. In the daytime, in the warmth of the long evenings, all the other possibilities gave her the rush of excitement which drew her away from failing motherhood.

She knew she could rely on Katy. Her carer would not abandon either her or her sisters or the baby. Katy loved her, she knew, and because of this loved her baby and her sisters too and she was taking advantage of this and she hated doing it but she couldn't help it. Katy was a better mum and she knew how to look after babies better than Aysha. She didn't have kids of her own but she'd looked after them little kids Lara and Liam, her niece and nephew, all them times she'd babysat for them. Aysha'd had two baby sisters and she'd tried to do her best for them but it weren't the same, she were too young herself then. She'd looked out for her sisters but looking out for weren't the same as looking after, there were a big, big difference. She were gonna look out for Peter ok, all the rest of his childhood, but that meant finding Neil, his dad, that were the best thing she could do for him. Neil would be a good dad, and if he said no, she might have Peter adopted. She weren't a good enough parent herself and it weren't fair on Katy to land it all on her. She already had enough on her plate with Charly and Zoë.

Aysha felt bad how she were going off the rails and meeting up with other kids and leaving Katy to cope with her sisters and her baby and causing her grief. But she, Aysha, were full of grief too. All her life and her dreams had been turned upside down, she'd no idea what she were gonna do next. She did know a bit about depression, how it could come on after someone died or after a woman had a baby. Katy's mum had talked about how she got depressed after Katy were born and after Katy's dad went and left her, and that sister of Katy's had to look after her when she were a little kid cos her mum couldn't, and then Sam herself got depressed after that Marie died and her husband Marcus had to look after Lara and Liam. Aysha couldn't remember if she were depressed after Kenny died but she did know how terrible she felt those years with that bastard and the years after, when she got took in care, all those years till she met Katy. Now she felt awful again but she had no idea why or if this were depression or what, she were just mixed up like hell. Staying home with the baby just made it worse, going out with other kids, taking stuff gave her a rush which helped a little bit though not for long. It only made her more and more sure of how she were a bad mum like her own mum who'd got into taking more and more stuff when she should have been looking out for her kids.

So she hung onto the dreams of the dog child or the dog mother. She hung onto how she loved Greg. Dogs was better than people, they could live free and wild like wolves, ok it were hard, finding shelter and food and getting across rivers, but it weren't all the complicated stuff that people got into that hurt other people. She thought back to being with Neil last summer and she wished she could escape all the problems.

Katy weren't like other people. She were a good person, really good, not pretend good like all them who criticised people who went off the rails like her. Katy might not like what she, Aysha, did, might be disappointed and hurt, but she would always stand by her and not even criticise. She knew she should talk to Katy about how she felt and about the dreams she had, she wished she could talk to her but she never could. Katy wouldn't be bothered about her dreams, most other people might think she were mental but Katy wouldn't. But still she couldn't say nothing, only the once or twice she did it all just came out about Neil and how she needed to find him and Katy were no help at all with that and that just made her stop talking about everything else.

Katy hoped against hope that the summer holidays would change life around. That they could all be a family together, it was what she desperately wanted and maybe Aysha did too. She'd not planned any holiday away, but she and Gareth decided day-trips to the coast would be a good thing to do, even perhaps a day at one of the weekend rock festivals. Anything to draw Aysha back in, make her happy again. Gareth had moved in and was trying to negotiate with the university to pursue postgraduate work in sports studies. He'd found temporary work at the city's Leisure Centre. And he had a car.

The school holidays started in a blistering heatwave. Whenever Gareth had a day off they squeezed into the car and set off for North Wales, the nearest coast. The two younger girls were happy and the baby seemed content, Katy and Gareth enjoyed playing mum and dad, and Greg was in his element. But Aysha still wasn't happy. She stood out from the others as the moody, angst-ridden teenager, taking Greg off for walks on her own, showing little interest in her son and constantly pestering Gareth for an early return to Bursfield, so that she'd have time for her evening out. They didn't, usually, bow to her pressure, the rest of them all wanting to stay by the coast as long as possible. Most times they picked up a takeaway meal in town on their way home. Aysha would stuff hers down as fast as possible and whatever time it then was, she went off into town to find kids she knew at pubs, clubs or bars, or at least that's what Katy and Gareth came to assume. They would prefer the teenager to meet up with her mates first and go into town in a group rather than disappearing on her own. So they did start returning a bit earlier with this in mind. They also considered leaving Aysha at home, something she regularly requested, citing how much of a squash it was in the car for all of them. But squash or no squash, Katy was wedded to the idea of all the family having days out together, and she didn't want to leave Greg or Peter behind, nor did she want to leave Aysha entirely on her own. More arguments developed, and Aysha went out more frequently, came to spend less and less time at home.

By the second week in August the heatwave had well and truly broken, and Katy suggested they go and visit her mother. Gareth would have to stay in Bursfield some days for his work, but it was mostly Aysha she was thinking of. She'd phoned Steve and asked him to find out if there were any gigs or concerts at the Old Mill Arts Centre, and yes there was some folk music. Later in the month they might go for the day to the same Rock Festival they'd been to last summer. So towards the middle of the month they all set out in Gareth's car - he would commute back to Bursfield for his job, sometimes staying at the house there according to his shifts. Aysha made hardly a murmur about this journey, but then, as Katy so often told herself, she did seem to get on well with her mother, and perhaps she was thinking it would be a further step towards finding Neil, something she was still fixated about.

37. INTO THE DARKNESS

The baby lay on a blanket by her bed. Not a bed exactly, for Samantha was resting on a downstairs couch. The baby was fast asleep now, but Samantha didn't sleep. The rest of her family, she hoped, were asleep upstairs in their beds, but over the last few hours she had only dozed intermittently. She kept looking at the baby to check if he was still there, for what happened still seemed more like a nightmare than reality.

How had it ended up like this? Samantha tried to retrace in her mind the sequence of events, as she had tried several times, but it all still seemed confusing and she knew she needed to get the story clear. Now that it was light there could be a phone-call any moment, in fact she was surprised there hadn't been already, and that was one reason she couldn't sleep. The phone-call might be from her sister or her mother, her sister most likely.

What was not in doubt was that they'd all four of them been woken at some godawful hour of the night by banging and shouting. And then screaming and wailing and barking. Not just them but the whole road. When they'd peered out of their bedroom window it was that scrawny bitch Aysha outside with her baby in its buggy, and Katy's dog. Banging on the door with her fists and screaming blue murder. Picking up her baby and looking as if she was about to throw him against the window. The dog barking like hell. Lights going on up and down the road. Lara and Liam awake and crying and wondering what on earth was happening. Samantha's first reaction was to shout out of the window to order the hysterical kid away and refuse to open the door, but Marcus had had the sense to see that that would only make things worse, so he'd gone down and let them in the house.

After that, it all seemed a confused blur to Samantha. She remembered cursing the fact that the girl had ever been to visit them, had learned their address. She cursed the fact that the girl had ever met her brother-in-law. That she'd made such an impression on her two kids. Most of all, Samantha cursed her sister for ever meeting such a deranged child, for thinking that she could somehow reform her, for taking her under her wing, and, without a doubt, allowing herself to be dominated by this kid. Katy had little knowledge or experience of damaged kids, she was studying sociology, sure, but why on earth did she think she had the ability take on a delinquent girl hardly even in her teens? Katy was a quiet, gentle person with a bit of an idealistic streak and that was her fatal flaw. She'd taken on this hussy and it was now quite clear that she had no control over her whatsoever. Samantha had always maintained that a leopard couldn't change its spots and now this girl's true nature was clear. She was a total head case, she'd completely lost it as far as any semblance of reasonable behaviour went, and how could anyone possibly think that she was a suitable person for raising a child?

None of this she said out loud though. She didn't know how much of it was going through her mind once Marcus had brought them into the house, or if it was only afterwards that she had sought to justify to herself her actions in removing the little boy from his teenage mother. She could remember the state that the girl was in, screaming at them after she came in the house as well as on the doorstep, waving her baby around with her arms fully stretched in her and her husband's faces, going on and on about finding Neil, the delinquent seemed to have a total fixation. Marcus kept trying to calm things down, suggested that Sam should take Lara and Liam upstairs and try and settle them down, not easy when they both liked that Aysha, had even looked up to her before now, and there was still the noise of screaming and shouting and the wailing of the baby and the barking of the dog downstairs. And Samantha remembered reading somewhere about shaken baby syndrome and the phrase kept going through her head.

I promise you we don't know where Neil is, Marcus was trying to explain to the teenager, as calmly and firmly as he could, when Samantha finally returned downstairs. If he does contact us, we'll let him know. About your child. I promise that.

He needs to know now! the girl screamed, still totally beside herself.

Look, I'll take care of the baby, Samantha had found herself saying. What's his name? Peter, isn't it? You're in no fit state to look after him just now. Leave him with us, and you get back home. He'll be fine with us, just for now, for a day or two. She took the baby off the teenager and held him close and calm. She was good with babies, everyone had said.

The girl hadn't resisted, but she was shaking uncontrollably and her voice had started choking. You find Neil and give him Peter, it's his kid, not yours. Everything about the wayward teenager was totally out of control, her voice, her movements, but she had left then, with the dog following her out. All the baby's things she'd left behind.

Samantha looked at the little boy. He slept peacefully now after all that fracas. Lara would love having a little baby in the house to help look after, especially the baby of that older kid she used to think so much of. Surely he was better here at present than with his highly disturbed mother. Katy had taken on too much. She, Samantha, could surely help out here. But she feared her sister wouldn't see it that way, and was dreading the phone call. Perhaps it should be she who made the call, but when? She didn't want to wake anyone up at her mother's.

She still couldn't work out how it had happened like this. Sometimes she thought that the girl had come round expressly with this in mind, to hand the child over to them, to give

Samantha no choice, and like a sucker she'd fallen for it, but then she told herself the kid was in no fit state to have planned things out so cleverly. On the other hand, why did she have in his buggy a spare outfit, a small pack of disposable nappies and a bottle filled with milk?

The baby woke up and started crying. Samantha roused herself from the couch and picked him up, rocking him gently. She decided she and him both had better get dressed. Holding him tight, she crept upstairs and collected some clothes from the bedroom. Her husband and children slept on. Returning downstairs, she undressed the child, wiped him clean, put on a clean nappy, dressed him and gave him the bottle. While he sucked hungrily she got dressed herself, looking at the little one all the time. She was growing fond of him already, even though, she could now see, there was a strong resemblance to his mother in his tiny face. The child couldn't help who had given birth to him, she couldn't blame him for the circumstances of his birth or the deranged behaviour of his mother. Anyway, he was her nephew, her husband's in fact, and cousin to her two children, though she couldn't tell them that, not yet. She was more closely related to him than Katy was. She picked up the phone.

Katy heard the phone ring and Steve go to answer it. Then the knock on her bedroom door.

It's your sister. Wants to talk to you.

She picked up the phone. Sam? Hi, why so early?

The baby's here, Samantha sounded very unlike herself. Almost whispering.

What?

He's fine, Katy. Don't worry. Didn't Aysha tell you?

Where is Aysha?

Hasn't she come home?

Aysha, Greg, and the baby slept in the front room now. Aysha seemed happy on a makeshift bed. Katy and Gareth were back in Katy's old bedroom. She put down the phone for a second and opened the door. There was no-one in the front room.

She's not here. What's happened to her? Katy spoke down the phone in a panicky voice.

She turned up here in the middle of the night, said her

sister. She was in a terrible state, you know I've never liked her, always thought she spelled trouble, but this was much worse than anything I've seen before. She'd totally lost it. I was really worried for that baby, I felt I just had to take him from her.

What? You took the baby off Aysha?

But she was waving him around the room, shaking him, looked as if she might throw him through our front window at one point. She let me take him, I think she knew she couldn't trust herself with him. She'd totally lost it, she was screaming and shouting all the time. Marcus was trying to calm her down, but he didn't have much effect.

When was this, did you say?

Some time in the dead of night, for godsake. Half past three? I've had no sleep since. I was furious with her, you can imagine.

Did you say she had Greg with her?

Yeah, she had the dog and the baby, and the buggy and some of the baby's things ....

So what happened to her?

I don't know, do I? She'd just flipped, gone mental.

No, I mean Aysha and Greg, where are they?

I don't know, Katy, I'd assumed they'd come back to you. They left here in the middle of the night. But the baby's safe, he's here.

Well, thanks, Sam, I appreciate that. I'll come and collect him some time this morning, but I've gotta try and find Aysha and Greg first.

Katy, don't worry about the boy. We can look after him here for a while. It's that girl you've gotta sort out, you really have. I don't know what the best thing to do with her is, but something must be done. She's a total liability. I don't think she should have care of this baby in the state she's in, not until you've sorted something out.

She's fine with Peter, nearly all the time. With my support, of course, I can make sure he's well looked after ....

But you can't, Katy, let's face it. You can't supervise all the time, look what happened! You were asleep, and that kid decides to go off the rails, not only that, but she comes round our house, disturbs all of us in the middle of the night, traumatises my two kids.

It's our business, Sam, it's between her and me. We need to have Peter back.

It's not just your business, it's her what keeps bringing us into it. Ask her why she does that? I feel very strongly Peter should stay here until you've sorted something out.

And how'm I supposed to know when?

I don't know, Katy, that's your problem. But what I would say is I think you need to be tougher on that kid. I think you let her walk all over you too much. That's my opinion, for what it's worth, and I think Marcus agrees with me.

It was all entering familiar territory now, Katy could see. She was torn between the need to retrieve the baby from her sister, for Peter was an integral part of family life, of all their lives now, not just hers and Aysha's, and a wish to avoid any further friction, any more terminal falling-out with Sam. But first of all, even before breakfast, even before waking the girls, she had to try and find the recalcitrant teenager and the dog.

She slipped out after a quiet word with Gareth. She hoped the fact that Aysha had Greg with her could be a re-assurance. Surely she would not have taken the dog back to Bursfield or anywhere else for that matter. Nor have taken any other extreme action while she had Greg there with her. Her heart ached with anxiety, nevertheless.

She found them quite soon, in the nearby park. It was Greg she saw first, sitting alongside a figure on a park bench whom she might not have immediately recognised. Aysha wore her hooded top with the hood up, and was slumped forward. The sun was quite well up, breaking through the thin dawn mist and beginning to dry the heavy dew, and the figures stood out darkly against everything around them green and sparkling. She could have been a homeless drifter who slept with a dog on a park bench. As Katy started running towards them, Greg recognised her and yelped, pulling on his lead. But the girl had a firm hold, or perhaps had tied the lead to the bench. It was only when Katy got right to her that they made eye contact.

Peter's with your sister, the teenager whispered. She seemed lifeless, totally played out. Her face was smeared, her eyes bleary, and Katy couldn't be sure if it was just lack of sleep or if she'd been crying. She had never known Aysha to cry.

Yes, I know, she phoned me. What on earth made you

take him round there?

So's she'd let Neil know. I thought if she really saw Peter, got to know him, it would, like, make a difference.

I don't think it will. But even so, why in the middle of the night like that? It only makes people anxious or furious or both.

But I knew you'd never let me go.

Since when have I been able to stop you doing anything?

The girl made the faintest of smiles.

You gonna get Peter back?

Sam don't wanna hand him back just yet.

Why not?

She thinks .... Katy paused momentarily. She thinks you want a break from him. She thought you were ok about her taking him off you, that that was what you wanted.

The girl just stared at her.

Did you? Is Sam right?

Just a faint shrug of her shoulders.

Should we let her keep Peter for a few days?

Only if she lets Neil know.

I don't know about that. They swear they don't know where he is.

I don't believe them.

There's the folk concert tomorrow night. And we thought we'd go to that festival for the day on Monday. Perhaps we could leave Peter with Sam and Marcus till Tuesday morning. Then we don't have to leave him with Steve and my mam.

She nodded faintly.

You wanna go to those gigs?

Yeah. Who's going?

All of us tomorrow night. Just you and Charly and me to the festival, like last year. Zoë'll stay with my mam.

What about Gareth?

He's working all the bank holiday weekend. He'll drive up here late that Monday night, collect us from the festival on the way. We'll keep in touch by mobile.

Aysha had stayed slumped on the bench, as if welded to it.

Come on, let's get home, said the older girl. Why didn't

452

you come straight back?

The teenager shrugged again. I dunno, just needed to be on my own. Like, y'know, to think.

Think about what?

Nothing. I mean, like, what a mess I'm in. Like, what a load of crap life is.

Oh, come on, come on, it's not as bad as all that.

It is, Katy, you don't know, right.

Something had snapped, been lost between them. It might have been the baby they were both missing. Katy had hoped they might get closer, back like they used to be, but too much between them was unspoken. There were too many other people around, needing her in their different ways, concerned about Peter's absence. They went to the folk gig and the festival, but Aysha seemed a shadow of her usual self. She had almost vanished into the darkness and she hardly said a word in the days that followed. Then on the morning after the festival, everyone was up late. Katy rose first and she heard Greg whimpering downstairs. She opened the door of the front room and found Aysha gone.

38. GONE TOMORROW

Aysha caught the first bus into Manchester, from the bus-stop just up the road from Katy's mum's house. She'd found out the time, she knew where in Manchester the bus went, how close to the Piccadilly main-line station. Once they'd had to go by bus to Manchester to get home because the local line was closed for track repairs. She'd packed her back-pack and written a note after everyone had gone to bed, before she went to sleep, and she slept in her clothes, so all she had to do in the morning was keep Greg quiet, find some money, and leave the note on her pillow. The note said:

IM GOING OFF FOR A BIT I WILL COME BACK
DONT TRY AND FIND ME
VERY SORRY ALL THE BAD IVE DONE AND TOOK YR
        MAMS DOSH I WILL GIVE IT HER BACK
PLEASE GET PETER FROM YR SISTER AND
LOOK AFTER HIM AND GREG AND MY SISTERS
I KNOW YOU WILL
IM NO GOOD WITH A BABY PLEASE DONT WORRY
        SEE YOU SOON WHEN I GET BACK
                AYSHA

Once she was on the bus it felt like an adventure. Freedom! She felt better than she'd done for ages. In Manchester she made her way to the rail station. She looked at a street map of Manchester. Then she bought a ticket to Lancaster, and boarded a train going north.

At Lancaster she got off the train, looked at the time-table, and bought another ticket, this time for Carlisle. Then she walked out into the centre of Lancaster. She hadn't eaten for ages so she found a café and ordered an all-day breakfast, the biggest they could do, with a glass of juice. The waiter wanted to be chatty but she tried to talk as little as she could. Then she found a clothes-shop, a cheap one she hoped. She looked through tops and skirts, bought a pink top and a yellow skirt, and after she'd paid for them went back to the changing booth and put them on, packing her old clothes into her pack. She also bought some bright red tights but she didn't wear those for now. Then she went to a shoe-shop and bought a pair of stiletto-heels, and then she went to a unisex hairdresser. She said she wanted her hair pink, and she ended up buying a pink wig because it would have taken ages otherwise and she'd have missed the next train and it didn't cost that much more.

She'd never worn these colours before and she was no longer Aysha and it felt strange. She'd never wanted to change her identity before, but she'd grown to hate her old self so much. When she got back to Lancaster railway station she bought a bottle of water and a bit more food for the rest of the journey, and she boarded a train for Glasgow Central.

She tried to stop herself thinking of what she was doing, but sometimes the thoughts crept back in. Her sisters and Katy.

Greg most of all. It used to be a better life with them, better at least than anything she had since Kenny died, but she'd fucked it all up. She was no good any more. Specially not with a baby. Everything she tried turned out bad. Going round Katy's sister's in the night and losing it like that was the worst thing. She'd gone and sat on that park bench and she'd cried and cried her eyes out. She wondered if Katy knew. Greg would've told her if he wasn't a dog. She'd never cried like that, even when all that terrible stuff happened when she were a kid. She would fight it then. But now she just cried and she didn't know what was worse. It were no-one else's fault now, that was the thing. Only hers. She hated crying but it seemed right in a way. Or was it just sitting on the park-bench with Greg? That was her now, the only way she could be. She had to be on her own.

She didn't get off the train at Carlisle but stayed on. She'd noticed the ticket inspectors normally only asked to see tickets of people who'd just got on the train. She'd nearly run out of money but if they stopped her she'd just have to offer to pay the rest with what she had. When she got out at Glasgow the sky was grey and it was beginning to get dark. She felt hungry again and it was very cold for end of August, she thought, much colder than it had been in Lancaster. She didn't want to put her old clothes back on, but wished she'd known how cold it would be so's she could have kept them on under her new clothes. It weren't anything like as cold as this last August in Scotland. She found her way through the streets of central Glasgow to Queen Street station, but she had missed the last train to Oban. While she thought about what to do, she spent the last of Katy's mam's money she'd took on a sandwich, some crisps and a carton of juice. Then she thought she'd hang around the station all night and sat down leaning against her pack and wondering if people were out looking for her. But then a man wearing railway uniform told her she couldn't stay there all night and there were laws against her type hanging around in stations. Then another man came up and said he could offer her good money and find somewhere they could go. Then she suddenly understood what this meant and she fled from the station, running as fast as she could go. Perhaps she shouldn't have bought a pink wig or pink and yellow clothes, perhaps in Scotland it meant something she didn't know. It couldn't be just pink, surely, lots of girls wore that. Out on the cold streets of Glasgow, she was scared of the men everywhere. Nearly all of them looked at her. She'd no money left and she couldn't walk the streets all night, she needed to find a doorway or something where she could doss without getting molested by men only out for one thing. It wasn't that this was new to her. Many nights she'd dossed in doorways in Bursfield or down the underpasses, she'd met that sort of man before, but it were nearly two years and her life had turned out very different since, and she thought she must have gone a bit soft about all this. For the first time she felt sadness for Katy and Greg and the homes she and her sisters had lived in since she met Katy, but she wasn't Aysha now and she had to be tough. Safety in numbers were what it was, had always seen her through on the streets and that's what it would be now.

The young kids, though, was all in groups, or gangs more like, and looked scary as hell. No chance of a weird stranger from England hooking up with them. Then she saw a woman on a corner leaning against a doorway smoking a ciggie and, though, she looked quite a bit older, wearing bright punkish gear like her. And a friendly kind of face.

Have you got a light? she asked the woman, taking her pack of cigarettes out of her back-pack, and putting one in her mouth.

Sure.

Aysha pulled a second cigarette out. Here, you have this one for later.

Thanks. You're not from round here, are you? said the woman, in a broad Scottish accent.

No. I just arrived tonight.

Where you from, love?

Manchester.

What brought you up here from Manchester?

Personal stuff, to do with my baby and the baby's father.

You looking for them?

Yeah.

In Glasgow?

Somewhere in Scotland.

D'you know where?

Nah.

Scotland's a big place.

I'm trying to find someone who might know where they are.

And where's this person?

I dunno exactly. Somewhere near Oban.

How old are you, kid?

Eighteen and a bit.

You look rather young for eighteen.

I am, I promise. It's what I'm wearing.

You need some dosh to get to Oban?

She nodded.

You might make a bit round here, said the older woman. I can make a bit, and there's more men these days like 'em young like you.

I weren't ....

I can look after you, kid, there's no need to be nervous. We could make a good pair, us two, some men like an older more experienced hand like meself and then there's them'll want it fresh and that's where you come in. Trust me, we'll do well together. Just for a few days, you understand, til ye've got the cash to continue your journey. Ye'll be safe with me till then. Have you got a name?

Yeah ....

Don't use your real name, now, that's for sure. You take a new name, fresh as yerself is.

OK.

And there's one other thing, lass, I've gotta tell ye.

What's that?

You don't get mixed up with the druggies, will ye? There's nearly all the girls now is out of it from all the stuff they's taking. I've always stayed clean from all that, and I always will. And the booze too, stay off the drink. If you promise me that, I'll keep ye from any harm.

OK, I promise that, yeah.

Good. Now I'm Marcia. My real name's Martha, but you call me Marcia. Everyone calls me that now. I don't have any family, I've lost all my friends from when I were a kid, so I'm always Marcia.

Hi Marcia, the girl mumbled, proffering her hand.

Marcia took the girl's hand. So what's your name?

She paused for a fraction to think.

457

She collected the baby from her sister. They all packed up their things and set off after lunch in Gareth's car, back to Bursfield. Katy thought that's where Aysha would be, that was her home patch, she never really considered anything else.

She knew she had a lot to do. Try and explain, or at least give some reassurance, to Charly and Zoë. Look after Peter as best she could. Inform the authorities. She had to get money back off them to repay her mother, that was one of the most dispiriting things, that the girl had betrayed the trust of her mother who had come to like her so much, take her side; and she'd never known her steal once in the time they'd known each other. But overriding all this, find Aysha. Maybe Gareth could help out, but she couldn't, mustn't, rely on that. Suddenly Gareth seemed the least important thing in her life.

She called their house several times on her mobile while Gareth drove, but she knew Aysha wouldn't be there. The house was in darkness and empty but Greg clearly thought Aysha would be there and eagerly chased upstairs to her room, becoming very distressed at her absence.

In the evening Katy went out around the neighbourhood, with Greg, and asked all the local teenagers who were out and about if they had seen her, if they knew where she might be hanging out, but she drew a blank. Now she started wondering if Aysha had returned to her old haunts, her old habits, her old allegiances.

The next day she informed Social Services, as she knew it was her duty to do. Ruth Barnes said this was always a possibility, that the surprise was that it hadn't happened before, that Katy had done amazingly well to keep her on track for so long. Katy said that whatever happened she would have Aysha back, and would look after her sisters and her child meantime. The social worker agreed to place Aysha on a missing persons register, inform the police, and apply for a grant to refund Katy's mother.

They all hoped against hope for the girl's return, for that knock on the door, any time of the day or night. Katy slept very little and only went out if Gareth was home. He was back at work at the Leisure Centre, several evenings in the week, and the two girls returned to their schools. She phoned Aysha's new Year Head to let the school know what had happened.

Greg spent nearly all his time in Aysha's bedroom, or sitting mournfully outside the door. At night Peter slept in there and Greg sat with him, guarding the small child. The dog knew the baby was Aysha's, Katy realised, and devoted himself to protecting the mite. He no longer came for walks eagerly like he always used to, unless Peter came too. Everyone they met, of course, thought the baby was Katy's, even more than had been the case before Aysha went, and she could no longer face up to disabusing them. She became as devoted a mother as if he were her own.

In the day time if she was on her own with the small child and the dog, she sat with them up in Aysha's bedroom and called back the girl to her mind. She played some of her music, she cast her eyes around the room, on the posters of her very favourite bands, on the bottles of lotion and mascara, the clothes and bangles scattered untidily around, she buried her face in the unmade bed to recall the faint scent of her body, the perfume which lingered on some of her tops. She was always sparing with scents and lotions, and with make-up even more so. Katy sobbed tearlessly in these hours of summoned memory but she forced herself not to cry at other times. It was hardest at night when she would while away her sleeplessness by remembering everything she could about her protégée. She remembered the first time they'd seen each other, at the front of the children's home, the first time they'd spoken, the first gig they went to, that band with the ridiculous name matching their uncomfortable noise. She remembered all those happy months in the little bedsit together, with Aysha content to sleep, eat, listen to her music and look after Greg, seemingly finally at peace after all the traumas of her young years. And Katy asked herself, tormented herself, wondering where it had gone wrong. She summoned recent memories to her mind. Sometime over the Bank Holiday, after Gareth had returned to his job but before they went to the rock festival, she had asked Aysha if she were missing the baby, and Aysha said no. She then asked if she were missing her friends in High Chapel.

They ain't exactly friends, was the reply. Just kids I hangs out with sometimes.

But are you missing them?

No.

Something in the tone of voice as Katy recollected it now, though she hadn't noticed it at the time, meant that the answer was yes but no-one would get her to admit it. The baby most of all. She had said virtually nothing else that whole weekend, certainly nothing of importance, nothing about her feelings, nothing apart from thanking Steve for a meal or saying which band she wanted to hear at the festival. She knew something was seriously wrong but she should have seen it was building up to a crisis, Katy now told herself.

But when, oh when, had they started drifting apart? Was it Peter's birth? Or when she first found out she was pregnant? Was it the camping holiday with Neil? Her anger about Zoë's day-trips with the home? Or was it even before then, when they moved home, for instance, or that week and a half when Katy was unwell and Aysha didn't like it that Katy attempted to draw her so close, lean on her for support when she felt so physically low? She came up with no answers, just constant questions which lay there every night between her and Gareth like a barrier, preventing closeness, preventing sexual fulfilment.

She resented Gareth because he was so little affected by Aysha's disappearance, not directly at any rate. All the rest of them were. For Zoë, it was mainly the not knowing. Not understanding why. Katy tried to reassure, but was unable to satisfactorily explain. Both the sisters had, of course, been used to Aysha's frequent running away, but she had always returned within forty-eight hours, had never abandoned them like this before.

Charly seemed to have more understanding and indeed a belief, an optimism that her sister would soon return which even Katy found hard to match, but Charly's problems were in the present, and particularly at school, where she was the focus of constant questions which gradually developed into personal probings and then teasing and finally verbal intimidation. She was trying, in her own right and not just because of her sister's disappearance, to follow Aysha in cross-country running and particularly in music as her guitar skills improved, but all of this was becoming too much for the girl to handle despite Katy's awareness of the problems and best attempts to support Charly.

Katy herself was taking it particularly hard but was able to disguise it, keep the suffering at bay, through effort and activity. Not just her attention to the two girls and the baby and all the routines to keep the household functioning, but she continued to search for Aysha whenever she could. She always took Greg with her, partly for protection but also in the faint hope that the dog might pick up Aysha's scent. But Greg did not seem to understand the purpose of this and was reluctant to leave the house and the baby. They first went into the city centre late in the evening, on a number of occasions, searching among the drunks, the druggies, the dossers and beggars and hookers, but with no sign of the missing teenager. So then Katy phoned the children's home, to ask which housing estates Aysha used to frequent before Katy met her. Cassie had moved on, found another job, but she spoke to Teresa who remembered well enough and sympathised with Katy, and gave her some details, though she thought it unlikely that Aysha could be hanging out there without having come to the attention of the police. But Katy had to take her courage into her hands, and go round there, with Greg on his lead, searching, asking, swallowing the humiliation, the frustration, the disappointment, as she again drew blank after more than one attempt.

Gareth had some sense of how much she was crucifying herself and tried to stop her, but for Katy that didn't work. He may have resented her for the degree to which Aysha's disappearance had drawn her away from him and caused her to lose interest in the sexual relationship, but then she also resented him for thinking that life could carry on as before, for not suffering like the rest of them were, for trying to divert her from her suffering and her ways of dealing with it.

Her resentment of him came to a head when he let Greg escape and the dog disappeared too. For perhaps of all of them it was Greg who was affected the most severely. He must have had some sense of what had happened, for the previous summer when Aysha and Charly were away for nearly three weeks, he hardly pined at all. But now he had lost interest in everything except Peter and his protection. One time Katy had to go out with the baby but not the dog. It was to a meeting at Charly's school in the afternoon, Gareth drove her there but he had to work that evening, he'd been unable to change his shift. Zoë had arranged to have a sleepover at a friend's. Greg came in the car with Katy and Peter, but had to stay in the car as Gareth drove back. Katy had suggested Gareth took him in the car to his work rather than leave him in the house, but Gareth let him out when he went back in the house to change and grab a bite to eat. When he went back out to his car, Greg ran off. It was more than an hour later, when Katy got home, that she found out.

Now she truly despaired. She knew that if Aysha returned or made contact, she would disappear again or do something worse on finding that the dog she so loved was gone. She phoned the police, the RSPCA, the local dogs' home, and she took to the streets again but it seemed a hopeless cause. That night Katy slept in Aysha's bed and left Gareth on his own.

However, by the following afternoon Greg had turned up. There was a call from Teresa at the children's home. He had turned up there and she had recognised him. He was thin and exhausted and his coat was dirty and matted, but he was alive and safe. A relieved Gareth drove them over to the home to collect the runaway dog.

If only finding Aysha had been as quick and simple! Katy realised how Greg needed to visit the places he identified with Aysha to check whether she was there. He may have gone to her old bedsit first and then to the children's home. Perhaps he had sat all that night by the gate of the house where they'd first lived.

The police had not visited her since Aysha vanished, which led Katy to think they weren't doing much to investigate. When she reported Greg missing she flagged this up with them, which resulted in a visit from two policewomen and Ruth Barnes. They were as ever sympathetic but also quite blunt. They did not think Aysha was in Bursfield. They thought the bright lights of a bigger city had lured her away, and although she was on a Care Order and therefore there was a statutory duty to find her, in practice this would be very difficult if she'd drifted into the underbelly of a large city and no-one even knew which. Katy really feared the worst now, she began to think the child would never return, that she'd seen Aysha for the last time. But even more terrible was not knowing for sure, the faint glimmer of hope, of possibility that there would be a phone call or a knock on the door, but which, as week followed week, never came.

She slept in Aysha's bed now. Greg's return did not really ease things between her and Gareth. He became increasingly angry, something she'd never seen in him before, and she couldn't be sure if it was sexual frustration or jealousy that fuelled this. They tried to talk to each other but communication had almost broken down. She wasn't happy that he slept alone in her bed, and she knew he wasn't happy either, but she didn't want to ask him to leave mainly for selfish reasons, it was useful having a car, he could babysit when needed, and he did have a good relationship with Charly and Zoë even though he had developed no bond with Aysha or Peter. He had been asked to prepare some classes at the local Further Education College for next term. It wasn't as high powered as he'd hoped, but he said yes and this would keep him in Bursfield. So if he moved out, he'd have to find a place nearby.

Katy had given up nearly everything. She'd already stopped her art course when the baby was due, and now she negotiated to skip a year on the other two subjects as well. And she gave up orchestra, indeed stopped playing the cello entirely apart from improvisations when she was in the house on her own. She only continued with choir because Charly went too and was doing well. But she did continue playing basketball. She played frenetically, psyching herself into some kind of physical over-drive. She became feared by all the other teams, and indispensable on hers. But she needed Gareth to babysit in order to continue with basketball, she wasn't happy having volunteers, often strangers, in the house though that still was necessary occasionally if Gareth couldn't change his work rota to fit with her.

And she took up painting again. She set her easel up in Aysha's room and used a lot of black paint. She tried to paint the child as she remembered her at different times, but more often she worked at abstract or expressionistic shapes and colours in an attempt to convey the darkness in Aysha's soul, or the mixture of dark and other colours in her own. She did not show anybody what she'd painted, and none of the others dared ask to see them though they must, she thought, have known what she was doing.

When she'd stopped searching for Aysha, and wasn't painting or doing housework or looking after Peter or seeing to the other two, she wrote a letter to Sophie.

My dearest friend, life has become unbearable for me. I'm sorry to sound so dramatic, but it's true. Aysha ran away at the end of August and has been missing since. I'm looking after Peter (her baby) and her two sisters and that's keeping me going on a surface level. Gareth has been helpful, in one sense, but our relationship has fallen apart due to (as I see it) his unwillingness to let me grieve in my own way. I fear the worst but it's the not knowing anything for sure which is so crucifying. I would do ANYTHING for her to come back. But for her sake I must carry on, and for the other three kids, however terrible I feel. I don't really know who to turn to, the professionals are sympathetic but that's all, Gareth's ability to support is less than I'd hoped, but that may be unfair, it may be me who's driven him away (he does still live here but things are only one step above zilch between us), and what with Aysha and the other two girls and the baby and Gareth, I haven't had the chance for other friendships here since my first term (the only people I got close to were the other three women in the string quartet I played in for a few months, but since I stopped playing in both the quartet and the orchestra I haven't seen them at all.)

So I'm hoping I can resurrect (a bit) our old friendship which perhaps will make me feel a tiny bit better, shine a few rays of warmth, if not light, onto my cold dark existence.

Please tell me about your life and relationships and I hope they're much better than mine. I don't want this all to be about me.
Do write soon, (or text or telephone), love from Katy.

She got a short text back at once in which Sophie said if there was anything she could do to help, Katy must let her know.

With the autumn half-term approaching and still no word from the missing girl, Katy told Gareth that she'd decided to take the family to stay with her mother and stepfather for the whole of half-term and leave Gareth minding the house at High Chapel, to give them a week and a half apart. She thought this might help them mend their relationship, and Gareth agreed. He had to work that week, so there was no need to reveal anything to anyone else. Katy only came to this decision with great reluctance, because she hated the thought of Aysha finally returning to the house and finding her not there, none of them there except Gareth, and not even him when he was working. However, she saw that she couldn't spend the rest of her life tied to the house waiting for Aysha's non-appearance, and if it took her to go away to induce the child's return then that would be a happy out-come. The teenager had a key when she left, there would be a note in her bedroom, and Katy would keep her mobile switched on with clear instructions for Gareth or Aysha to phone immedi-ately if there was any news whatsoever, and for Gareth not to let the girl out of his sight until Katy got back.

There was another thought going through her head. It was from her mum's house that Aysha had absconded, and it might be there that she went if she did return. And, too late as it probably now was, it should have been around Longworth that she searched for any clues, neighbours, bus stations, train sta-tions. She had been too hasty in dashing back to Bursfield. She was convinced now that Aysha wasn't in her home town. If she had got drawn to the big city lights, maybe it was in nearby Manchester, and oh how she wished she'd had the forethought to think of that in the first days of the child's disappearance. But late as it was, perhaps it still wasn't too late to follow up these possibilities. She couldn't just stop searching and wait passively, she had to stay active to stay sane.

39. EACH ONE LOST

Colleen Paterson drove into the centre of Glasgow as she had done hundreds, thousands, of times in the past. It was mid-October and she hadn't been here all summer. She had been with her husband to the USA and Canada, on a lecture tour, but also on a long and much-needed holiday. They had departed at the end of June and been away nearly three and a half months.

The organisation had not stayed in good shape during her time away. The woman they'd employed to bridge the gap had left after little more than half her scheduled time. The volun-teers, who didn't seem to like this replacement, now appeared dispirited. There was no-one in Sanctuary House at present and

465

they, the volunteers, seemed to have spent little time on the streets, so no-one had much idea what was going on. Colleen knew she needed to get working, pick up the momentum again.

She drove carefully. When she first started coming to this part of Glasgow, she had no car and no licence. She had caught the bus in, and often, having missed the last bus or train, she'd had to catch a taxi back to her home. But that was quite a long time ago now.

Colleen had started working with Glasgow's street-girls in her late twenties. Initially it was just her, trying to help them, listening to their stories. Big flasks of tea and coffee and soup helped, and several warm shawls to wrap around their shoulders on winter nights. Many times she stayed with them until dawn. She did not judge, she did not even try and persuade, but she did call herself Street-Rescue, because she soon became aware that rescuing was what some, maybe many of the girls longed for. In the early days she was tempted to bring them home, but she knew that was taking befriending a step too far. So she set up her organisation, set about raising money and recruiting supporters, with a view to finding a property which could be a safe house for the girls who wanted to get off the streets but had nowhere to go.

It all started when she was on holiday with her husband on the south coast, in a holiday flat. They'd been married, what, about two years, and she'd given up her clerical job as soon as she married because she hated it and her husband's income could easily suffice for them both. But she was bored at home without work. She tried sports and hobbies but nothing provided the rewards she wanted. In the holiday flat she started reading an autobiography of Father Joe Williamson of Stepney, who had worked with prostitutes in the East End of London in the late fifties and sixties with the aim of getting as many as possible off the streets. She was aware of the problems in Glasgow's red light district, occasionally when she had passed through those streets but mostly from newspaper reports and the radio and TV news. As soon as she finished reading the book, she knew she had found her vocation. If Father Joe could do it in late 1950s London then surely she could make a difference in Glasgow in the early 1980s. She talked to a very dubious husband but convinced him to give her his moral support, at least on a trial basis.

The first lesson she learned was surviving the hard

knocks. Many of the girls she attempted to befriend just didn't want to know a so-called 'do-gooder', and more than a few were abusive. The vileness of their tongues shocked her, and there was even physical violence on one or two occasions. But she pressed on and in time a small number sought her help. The numbers grew, and although many returned to the streets, there were others who were reunited with their families or made their way independently to a new life. She still got abuse from time to time, but her presence on the streets came to be accepted, even valued, and to assault or take advantage of Colleen led to ostracism from the community of street-workers, such as it was. One of the most appalling things was how young many of the girls were, and how many were runaways from the care system, or had been cast out at sixteen. Helping girls such as these was particularly difficult since they had lost all faith in adults who claimed to care, yet Colleen felt a strong need to stay with these teenagers on the streets until they were ready to trust her. And when, after many years, she finally raised the funds to purchase, adapt, and then open Sanctuary House, it was the teenage girls who were given priority for places there. The house had space for four girls, but only very rarely was it full. Two or three was the optimum residency, Colleen soon found. It was unusual to be empty like today.

Of course it had never been as straightforward as she'd in her naivety first imagined. Even in the 1980s many of the girls on the streets had problems with alcohol or drug abuse, and the proportion that were addicted to heroin or crack had increased markedly since Colleen had started her work. And the lines between the girls who were working the streets for sex and those who were just on the streets had become increasingly blurred. When she'd first got to know the red-light district, there were plenty of beggars, dossers, winos, meths-drinkers and other down-and-outs in the centre of the city, but these were nearly all men, adult men, and the working girls kept to entirely different streets. But as drugs became an increasingly major factor both in prostitution and homelessness, she noticed that the street-dwellers were getting younger, more and more teenage girls were among them, and some of the girls moved between the sex-workers and the homeless groups, intermingling in both in order to score their drugs where they could find them cheapest and easiest. So Colleen had found herself rescuing some young teenage girls off the streets who hadn't been selling their bodies at all, but who probably would have started doing so once they'd settled to a life on the streets and addiction had taken hold. She had even helped some teenage boys, though it was a firm rule that the places at Sanctuary House were for girls only.

There were of course many other organisations in Glasgow working with the homeless and with drug-users. For homeless people there were hostels, there were the churches, and in drug rehabilitation there were Health Service facilities, private facilities and voluntary organisations a bit similar to hers. So for many years another aspect of the work for Colleen was learning to liaise, to avoid treading on other people's toes, and as she grew more confident, to fight for her corner and for the girls who needed her most. Because most of the time people providing for the homeless didn't want to know if there was a drug problem, and people providing support for drug-users didn't want to know if the user was homeless - there was too much pressure already on their service and the priority was to help clients who were still living at home with their families. Until Sanctuary House was up and running it had been impossible for Colleen to persuade the Drug Abuse Unit at the Royal Hospital to even look at any of these girls and even then, she'd had to use all her powers of persuasion.

Now she was a well-known figure at the hospital, both at the specialist unit and at Accident and Emergency, but it hadn't always been like that. Her commitment and seriousness of intent had finally won through the doubters, and the fact that it was the teenage sex workers that her organisation was primarily dedicated to helping gave her Street-Rescue organisation a distinct role. She had become respected, well-known, even famous, throughout the city, and beyond, with an OBE and frequent requests to give talks or appear on radio or television news and current affairs programmes.

None of this was in her mind now. She was only concerned about the girls on the streets, the ones she knew and any she didn't know, and what had happened while she was away. She parked her car in a side-street - she knew the best streets to find a space - and continued on foot. It was still early evening, dark and a cold wind as so often in Glasgow, and everything was familiar but in a strange way. Once it had felt really strange here when she'd nervously set foot on these streets, a young woman with a sweet smile and a firm belief, large-boned though not tall, broad-shouldered in more than one sense, prettier in her face (or so her husband would tell her) than her figure. As a girl the only thing she'd liked about herself was her hair, very dark and wavy, but it was turning silvery-grey now, and she was thinner than she used to be when she'd started her project.

She looked around cautiously as she reached the usual streets. The first woman she saw was Marcia, and she felt a certain relief. They'd got to know each other well over the years since Marcia first appeared in the red light district, she couldn't remember how many years ago now. Even when she first started at a young age, Marcia seemed like an old-fashioned pro of the sort one rarely found any more. She had offered Marcia refuge at Sanctuary House many times, and eventually the woman had started accepting Colleen's offers, but had made it clear that it was only to give herself a break, respite from the cold streets, to which she would always return after her two weeks or however long she stayed. But even Marcia couldn't go on forever and Colleen wondered what would happen to her when her ageing body made it impossible to carry on.

Hi Marcia, she greeted her, thinking that even now she seemed to have aged quite a lot since they last met.

Colleen, you're back. They hugged one another.

Yeah, said I would, didn't I? What's happened while I've been away?

Not a lot, Colleen. The streets was lively in the summer but me, I kept well outta it, y'ken. Quiet an' steady for the likes o' me.

The house is empty just now, said Colleen. You wantta get a roof over ya head for a whiles?

Nah, not me. Aill wait fo' th' winter to set in, me. Tell ya what, Colleen. There's this kid ya's needing to look out for. Jade Owen's her name an' she's nah fro' round here. Manchester, she's fra. Told me she's eighteen but I'm sure she's a younger kid tha' eighteen. I looked ou' fo' hers a while, tried ta take her unda me wing, y'ken, but she werena tha' kinda girl. She got in wi' the kids what's using an' I never saw much of her afta tha'. Last time I saw her she looked in a bad way, an' tha' were over two weeks back. I'm telling ya, Colleen, she's who ya should be looking fo', Jade Owen's her name.

40.   I'D FOLLOW IF I COULD

For Charly it only got worse and worse. At first she was sure her older sister would come back, within a week probably, ready for the start of the new school term. When she didn't, it meant she was just a few days late, delayed, maybe she'd lost track of the date. But when she didn't come back, and didn't, and still didn't, then it meant something terrible must have happened to her. Aysha wouldn't have stayed away all this time, causing them all to worry and get upset if she could've done anything about it. She might've got lost but not for this long, she could find her way back home in the end, however lost she got. It could only mean she was either dead or being kept prisoner against her will.

If she'd known Aysha weren't gonna find her own way back, Charly would've told Katy before. Very early on. But it were s'posed to be a secret and Charly knew she wasn't s'posed to say anything, and it had gone on longer and longer and it got harder and harder to tell Katy and now she knew she'd done the wrong thing. She must tell her.

Charly didn't know for sure where Aysha had run away to because she never said anything. The only thing her sister had ever said to her about that man they called to see when they was with Neil who Neil said was his real father but they must keep it secret, was how Charly must never tell no-one about him cos they'd promised Neil. But Charly knew how something had happened that night of the thunderstorm on the mountain and how that meant that little baby Peter's real dad was Neil and how he'd run away in case he got into trouble and how desperate Aysha were to find him so's she could tell him like he told them they must if he ever had a baby of his own.

It were Charly who said to her big sister one day that the best way to find Neil were to find that man they'd gone to see in his cottage by the sea who were Neil's real dad. But Aysha said how could she find him, she didn't know his name or where he lived or anything, and the best way was to get his brother Marcus to tell her where he was cos she were sure Marcus knew. But Aysha were good with maps, Charly thought, surely she could find that man, but she didn't say so. And it was then that her sister said how they must always keep it a secret. But now, finally, she were gonna break that secret and tell Katy. Everything was going wrong since Aysha left, Katy and Gareth weren't getting along, and Charly liked Gareth a lot, everyone was miserable.

Katy took them to her mum and Steve's house at the start of half-term, straight after her guitar lesson and Zoë's dance class. They went on the train like they used to before, but this time there was no Aysha. Katy went upstairs to change Peter and give him the bottle and get him to sleep, cos he'd been awake all the time on the train, and Zoë stayed downstairs with Katy's mum so she went up to help Katy and it were then she said.

Katy, she said. I think I might know where Aysha's gone.

Colleen drove her car very slowly along the streets, among those who slept in alleyways and doorways, looking for the girl called Jade Owen. Asking, young girl, drug user, asking. She hardly knew anyone here now, such was the transience of this population. They looked at her blankly, two or three gave her a mouthful of abuse. She expected nothing different, she'd done this many many times before, she was inured to it now. These people, most of them, did not take kindly to interference from anyone who was not one of them. But still she needed to find the girl. On and on she went, covering all the narrow wynds and entrances, every corner of the city centre, asking wherever she could.

Finally a young man who knew her, and knew who she meant. Yeah, her name's Jade, but all of us here call her Amber. Yeah, she's in a bad way, should be in hospital, don't wanna call an ambulance, ye mind me, don't want her dead on the streets. It was the nightmare scenario for these homeless street-dwellers if one of them pegged out, as very occasionally one did, and finally police and ambulance services arrived and they'd all be herded up and grilled. A nightmare for the police too, information was never forthcoming. Those, like this young man, who knew Colleen, recognised the value of her efforts. She could get the drug-overdosed or injured or sick from any other cause, to medical help with a minimum of fuss. No need to call an ambulance. Hardly ever did anyone on the streets want to call an ambulance because they knew the police would come along also to provide protection.

She followed the young man around several corners, she at the wheel, he hurrying on foot. She found the child, for she seemed no more than a child, huddled in a blanket, her body rocking, her eyes glazed. She seemed out of it, unconscious, comatose. Colleen talked to her, but there was no sign that the girl heard. The young man helped lift the deadweight figure into the passenger seat, held her steady while she was strapped in. Colleen would take her to the hospital herself. She knew them very well at the Royal Infirmary, not just the Drug Abuse Unit, but A and E as well. She was already calling them on her mobile as she shut the passenger door and walked round to the driver's side.

They were ready for the emergency admission when she got there but they couldn't tell her how long it would take for the girl - Jade Owen's her name, possibly aged eighteen, I don't know anything else about her - to be examined, diagnosed, treated. Prognosis uncertain.

I'll keep in touch, said Colleen Paterson. I don't know if she has anyone else.

Katy studied the face of the girl standing by the closed door. A number of emotions were playing across her mind and heart, disbelief, excitement, anger. Something was telling her not to get too worked up. Charly was a child of few words anyway, and the slightest hint of an emotional scene always caused her to clam up completely. Katy knew her quite well by now, though she'd been by far the hardest of the three girls to get to know.

Did Aysha tell you where she was going? she asked her.
No.
How do you know where she's gone, then?
I don't, I mean, I think I might know.

472

Well, why didn't you say anything before?

Because, like, because, I thought she would come back. I never thought anything else, only she would come back.

So where d'you think she has gone?

Charly hesitated.

What is it?

I ain't s'posed to say, muttered the child.

Why not?

It's kind of a secret.

Who told you not to tell anyone? Was it Aysha?

Yeah. No, I mean no.

Charly was clearly having more and more of a struggle to know what to say, and Katy was becoming increasingly exasperated.

Look, this is no time for secrets, Charly, your sister's been missing nearly two months and anything you know which might help to find her, you must tell me, ok?

Yeah.

So tell me where you think Aysha is.

At this man's house.

Which man?

I don't know his name.

Where does he live?

In Scotland. But we ain't s'posed to say, it's a secret.

Why?

Cos Neil told us. Neil told Aysha and me it was his real dad, and then said not to tell anyone.

Katy thought the girl had got mixed up.

No, that can't be right, Charly. Neil's dad is Jack who died a few years back in a mountain accident, that's why Neil took up mountain rescue.

No, this was his _real_ dad. Neil only found out, like, not long before he took us camping. And we called in to see his dad, only we wasn't s'posed to know that's who he was.

How did you know?

Cos, Neil said. After we went there.

So you've been to this man's house?

Yeah. Twice, coming back as well. But we weren't s'posed to know.

And you think Aysha might have gone there?

If she could find the way, yeah. Cos she wanted to find Neil, and that man might know where he was.

And would you be able to help us find this man?

Charly shook her head. I dunno, she mumbled.

D'you know his name, or address, or anything?

She shook her head again. Only he lives in a little cottage by the sea, and it's on the way to Oban.

Well, we're gonna have to try and get there, then, yeah? But why couldn't you have told me this before, Charly?

I don't think she can have got there, or she would've phoned, said Charly. Or the man would've phoned. Or he'd've brought Aysha back.

But it's the only lead we've had in all this time, so we've got to follow it up, and I wish we could've done this earlier.

But will Neil get in trouble?

Let's try and find Aysha first, and then we can start worrying about Neil.

Her first instinct was to jump on a train with Charly, and leave the rest of them here, but she soon saw how wrong that would be. Nor could she face asking Gareth to come up and drive them, abandoning his rostered duties at the Leisure Centre, nor wait however many hours or days while he tried to rearrange his duties or take some emergency leave. No, the first thing she would do was to find Sunday morning train times to Glasgow, and then she would phone Sophie. She'd said to let her know if she could help in any way, she owned and drove a car, and she probably wouldn't be working on a Sunday. And after that she would ask her mother if she knew anything about this strange and hidden secret of Charly's, Neil's "real" father.

She phoned Sophie rather than texting. She needed to speak to her and needed an answer straight away.

I do need your help like you said. I've got a possible lead on Aysha which I must follow up. Are you free tomorrow?

I could be, came the rather faint and bemused voice down the phone.

I need you to drive us. We're looking for a cottage near Oban but we don't have the address. Can you bring any maps you've got?

What sort of maps?

Road maps of Scotland, or any other maps that include

474

the Oban area. We're gonna try and get an early train from Manchester to Glasgow Central. Can you meet us there just after 12? We'll have food with us. It's all of us, Aysha's two younger sisters, the baby, the dog, and me, right? Hope that's ok.

I've only got a small car.

I know, but don't worry. We'll squeeze in.

The girl in the hospital bed stirred. Pain washed over her semi-consciousness in waves. Acute, like night terrors, then drew back into empty numbness, then came again. Nothing else, only the pain. She did not know where she was. She did not know who she was. She had only the faintest consciousness of time. Only the slightest sense of life or death. There was some sense of waking into the pain, but no awareness of sleep. Slowly she realised she was alive, pain meant alive. Where had she been? Had she died and come back alive again?

For a long time she couldn't open her eyes. She couldn't think who she was or how long she had been, what, dead, out of life in some way, the long sleep. Nothing came into her mind except the numbness and the pain, alternating, the numbness and the pain.

Then she was aware of someone else close by. She tried to speak, call out, scream, but she couldn't find words, or even sounds. She tried to move, but the pain seared through like a knife, like a gasp. She couldn't see, but she could hear. She heard the person close by call out, call to someone else.

She's waking up!

Who is?

Jade!

Can you hear us, Jade?

We'd better call Colleen!

Isn't she due in soon anyway?

The girl in the bed tried to stir. The sounds were all a blur, and the names, if she'd heard them right, meant nothing. But she still felt trapped in the numbness and pain and wanted to try and break out into the aliveness that these other people signified. A world out there which was less like death and less horribly full of pain than the one she inhabited.

She heard them come and go but still she couldn't speak

and couldn't see. But she found she could begin to think. She was Jade, they had called her Jade. There was something vaguely familiar about the name, but still she couldn't place it. She couldn't place herself. Had she lost her memory? Who was she?

Finally she could speak.

Where am I?

The Royal Infirmary. Intensive Care Ward.

Are you a doctor?

A nurse.

Who am I?

Don't you know you are, Jade?

Jade who?

Jade Owen.

Where is this? she asked again. She tried to open her eyes, see the other person.

A hospital ward.

Yes, but where?

Glasgow. Glasgow Royal Infirmary.

Have I had an accident?

No, drugs overdose. Listen, Colleen will be coming in soon, she'll talk to you about it.

Who's that?

Colleen Paterson, don't you know her?

No. It was all too much, none of this made sense. She tried again to open her eyes, but the daylight hurt too much and she shut them tight again. She could not see. Perhaps she was blind. Perhaps the nurse got it wrong. She must have been in an accident.

The other person sensed her pain and confusion.

Try and rest and sleep now, until Colleen comes in. If you get some rest, maybe your memory will come back.

But that didn't work. There was too much pain to sleep, and as she sank back into semi-consciousness, she re-entered a world of horrors. New horrors, or were they, in fact, old horrors? In the nightmare, the semi-awake nightmare, she was a terrified child trying to resist two people, grown-up people, who wanted power over her to do awful things to her. But she was too weak and her resistance was futile, it only made it worse. Was that what had happened to her? Was that what caused all this terrible pain? Was she still a small girl even though she felt grown-up

476

now? The man came at her again and again, all-powerful, crushing and hurting and breaking her down, time and again, and the woman too, but mostly the man, robbing her, taking her, jerking her, mocking her, piercing her, overpowering her, leaving her a limp doll too weak to move on a cold floor with no energy to escape before it happened again. She felt sick, horribly and nauseatingly sick but she couldn't be and she knew she had to be. And then she knew she had died and this was another life which she didn't know and which surely couldn't be worse than the other one. Were they both real and if not which was real and which was a dream? Then she was sick and it wasn't a dream and she was choking and she couldn't breathe and she heard what seemed a long way off a shout and the nurses come running and then nothing.

41. THE GUILTY WILL PAY

Everything in her life was falling apart, so it seemed to Sharon. The only thing holding it together was Steve, her husband. He was still devoted to her, willing to devote his time to her care, and he seemed to understand how if she couldn't reciprocate, then that was her condition speaking. But with everyone else close to her, it was all falling apart, and there was nothing Sharon could do. The only way was to try and find solace in the past. She had thought a lot about Rodney, her first love, and how to find him again. Well, he had been found, but that really hadn't done much good. Leave him to make contact in his own time, Katy had said, but that was back in April and it was now nearly November and there was no word from Rodney. Maybe he would write a letter at Christmas, that's what a lot of people did, but if not, she would have to think again. Should she have gone herself to find him, despite her condition? She frequently asked herself that question these days.

Sometimes at her low points she saw her disability as a long slow dying. That would explain the need to find Rodney, reconnect herself with the past. It was like her whole life passing through her mind, very very slowly, month after month, in reverse. Family life with Steve and the girls. Katy's teenage years, when Sam had left home and it was the three of them. Four of them with that friend of Katy's. Sophie. Then further back there was the four of them. Sam going through teenage rebellion, Katy at primary school. Then Sam as a pre-teen, when Steve had just moved in, and Katy not long started school. Meeting Steve and falling in love. Then the years she skipped through, that she couldn't face up to revisiting, the long years of depression, in and out of hospital, death of her mother who'd helped out until the sudden heart attack, though she could see now it had been the ten, eleven year old Samantha who'd kept the family together. Then it was difficult pregnancies, death of the taxi business, Rodney's disappearance, Katy's birth. Only when she went further back than that could she reconnect with light and happiness, the joy of their first child, Samantha, the happy years of running Owen's Taxis, the years of first living together, of first meeting, of falling in love.

But she was now winding the memories back beyond their sixties courtship, back to her fifties childhood. Her beloved grandfather in his little old back-to-back, boiling a black kettle with a spout on his old-fashioned stove, how she loved going there, as a small child on her own, the stories he would tell her of life at the mill, or the one week a year holiday they had, Wakes Week he called it, when the whole town it seemed would relocate to Blackpool, on a fleet of coaches or specially laid on trains. And the trips to Blackpool later in the year, for the illuminations, a Saturday night and Sunday morning in October. He'd died of old age, or so she'd been told, when she was what, twelve? She'd always taken the deaths of those close to her hard, her father in 1985, a few weeks before Katy was born, knocked down by a car on the main road out of town while he attempted to deal with one of his friend's cars having broken down, her mother about five years later. Then Jack's death, and then Marie's, even though she didn't know either of them particularly well, but Marie's she'd taken hard, but then so had Samantha, and she was so like her older daughter. She wondered if there would be any more before the inevitability of her own.

There were little moments in her childhood she remembered, not all associated with her grandfather though most were.

One or two holidays by the sea just the three of them, mum dad and her. At Morecambe they would walk to the harbour at Heysham and watch the boat come in from the Isle of Man. They never went across there themselves in her childhood though her father promised her they would, and later she and Steve had taken the two girls over there for a holiday. After her grandfather died they got some compensation from his house which was pulled down for redevelopment, and she remembered them moving to a bigger house, and her father setting up his own business at the back. When she was on school holidays, or sometimes on Saturday mornings, she liked to go out and watch, help where she could. Her mother worked from home, repairing cushions, making cushion covers. It seemed a dull job to Sharon then, and still did now, thinking back. She never had the inclination to help out her mum. Maybe she was always more interested in the men's world of cars and people. Maybe that was why pregnancies and births and the death of her father, and then Rodney going, all sent her spiralling downhill. Maybe it would have been different if she'd had a son. There was only Liam, her grandson, whom she probably wouldn't live to see grow up. Although, of course, there was also now Peter.

Perhaps she'd been closer to her father than her mother. She'd never thought so at the time, she could talk to both of them, about leaving school, her job at the grocery store, about Rodney, about getting married - she pretended to her parents that they'd gone off and quietly wed. But it wasn't the same, her father gave advice, friendly cheerful advice, but still just advice, her mother gave support, or did her best to. It had been an ordinary childhood, limited in many ways, but happy enough.

How much more complicated her life had become since. And little Peter seemed about the most complicating factor of them all. Katy tried to joke about it, now that she had the responsibility for him, with Aysha still missing. She was going to adopt the three sisters, she said, she should have set the wheels in motion in July, as soon as she turned twenty-one. She didn't know if they would agree now that Aysha was missing. But if she did turn up, it was the first thing she would do. That would make Peter her grandchild, she laughed, almost certainly the youngest grandma in the country, maybe in the world. And Sharon thought, yes and that would mean Peter was part of the family too, another male heir as well as Liam, though not through blood.

How she wished she was in better health, she so much loved to take care of her grandchildren. But Peter was too small, she couldn't really cope. And Lara and Liam, well she hardly saw them. The falling-out with Samantha was such a painful thing. But even worse was what had happened to her younger daughter. Katy tried to make light of it, for sure, but Sharon could tell how hard she was taking the disappearance of her foster-daughter, protégée and friend. She was struggling on, for the sake of the baby and the other two girls, she was friendly enough with her and Steve, but what about Gareth, she didn't seem to have much time for him any more. Sharon liked Aysha, had grown to believe in her, was disappointed on her own as well as her daughter's account, that the teenager had let them all down, proved Samantha right in a way. But most of all she felt terrible for Katy, life should not be like this for a twenty-one year old, she should be out enjoying herself, and all of them, including Sharon herself, who'd seen the warning signs, now felt guilty that they should have taken more notice, made Katy herself take notice.

And now one more bombshell. Katy had only just arrived, only been in the house a couple of hours, when she announced she was going to Scotland first thing in the morning, her and the two girls, the baby and the dog.

Why on earth?

Charly's given me a possible lead for finding Aysha. I've gotta go, mum, you must see that.

Can't you phone or something?

No, it's not like that, mum, this isn't straightforward, I wish it was. I've arranged to meet my old friend Sophie at Glasgow Central station, and we're going to look for a cottage that Charly and Aysha have been to before.

When, my love?

When they went to Scotland with Neil last summer. Mum, I've gotta ask you this, did you know Neil's real father wasn't Jack?

What! That can't be right! exclaimed Sharon. Marie and Jack were happily married, everyone looked up to them, both boys are their own, I'm sure. There must be some mistake.

Well, Charly seems quite definite. And Aysha knew too, Neil told both of them that he'd recently met his real father.

Kids can get mixed up about these things, love, but why is it so important now?

Because Aysha may have run away to this man she believes to be Neil's father, that's why we're trying to find him.

Oh goodness, dear, well, maybe you should phone Marcus and ask if he knows.

I don't think I should do that, said Katy.

Why not?

Because I don't think he knows, and things are difficult enough with that branch of the family as it is.

But without knowing, it's a wild goose chase, Katy. Surely, any chance of getting more information -

She turned to Steve, who'd sat there in silence so far. It was not like him, and when Sharon looked at him, she could see he knew something. In his body he was squirming, as though trying to disappear into his clothes, and his face was pale and twitching.

Steve, do you know something about this?

Katy's right, said Steve, clearly with a great effort. Marcus doesn't know anything.

But you do, I suppose?

He nodded, minimally, reluctantly, painfully.

Well, tell us for god's sake, Steve, exclaimed Katy impatiently.

All I know is that Jack isn't Neil's father.

How do you know?

Because Marie told me, many many years ago, before I met any of you. I felt I had to keep her confidence.

But Marie is, was, Neil's mother?

Yes, of course.

There's no of courses any more, Steve, said Katy crossly. Do you know who Neil's father is?

No, I don't. He was someone she had a relationship with before she married Jack. I think he came to her funeral, though, there was an older man there who looked a bit like Neil.

Well, did you speak to him, Steve? Did you find out who he was?

No, of course not. I didn't know if he knew anything. I

tried to speak to Marie before she died, to find out who else knew, but the chance slipped by.

Someone must know who he is, complained Sharon.

Don't worry, said Katy. We'll find him, just going on what Charly remembers about visiting his house.

42. DARK ANGEL

It was the news Colleen had been waiting to hear. The girl, Jade, her life hanging by a thread in the intensive care ward for more than a week, had finally stirred. Maybe Colleen could start talking to her, find out a bit more about her, enough to alert her family, commence the process of reuniting her with those closest to her, for surely there must be someone. It was all Colleen ever wanted for these girls.

She got to the hospital as soon as she could. The ward staff informed her that the girl appeared disturbed in her semi-consciousness, and in physical pain. Colleen soon realised that she wouldn't get much out of her today, that she would need to keep coming to see her many times.

She took the girl's hand but it was quickly withdrawn. She seemed to shrink from all physical contact.

Hallo, Jade, I'm Colleen.

Who?

Colleen Paterson, I brought you here.

Where am I?

Hospital, Glasgow Royal Infirmary. You were in very bad shape. How are you feeling now?

Still in bad shape.

Can you tell me anything about yourself?

No.

Can you remember?

No.

Nothing at all?

No.

Anything about a baby?

The medical staff had alerted her to a number of points.

That she was almost certainly some years younger than the eighteen Colleen had been told. That there was evidence of sexual abuse as a younger child. That she was HIV positive. That she appeared confused and her sleep patterns were disturbed, suggestive of earlier trauma being recalled. And that recently, within the last six months or so, she had given birth. Colleen was used to these sorts of details. Rescuing girls like this was what she was about, she as an individual and her organisation. Her confidence in these cases had grown over the years, but she wasn't entirely confident with this girl.

Do you think we should get a psychiatrist in? she asked the ward staff.

I think you'll do as well as any psychiatrist could just now, she was told. Wait and see how she is as she recovers further.

Is she going to recover?

I think she's over the worst.

The baby seemed to be the best way in. None of the other issues seemed appropriate to raise at present. So Colleen kept on coming to the ward, every day almost, just to be there with the girl, try and gain trust, or at least some familiarity. At present, until she gleaned some more information, Jade had nobody else.

When she did venture to speak, the girl spoke in confused snatches. Not her own baby but a baby sister. Protecting her, removing her from harm. Run from the house, she said, more than once, as though Colleen was that sister in her bedroom at home. But where was that home? Manchester, Marcia had said. The girl repeated the word with a faint sense of recognition – Manchester.

That's where I caught the train, she said, in a rare moment of lucidity.

As the days progressed, she started mentioning dogs. Dreams of dogs, one dog, many dogs. Colleen encouraged her to keep talking. Who were these dogs?

Pulling sleds in Alaska. It didn't seem to make sense. In her subconscious mind, the child seemed to identify with dogs, a human child raised by dogs. Could she have been a feral child? And if so, what was she doing on the streets of Glasgow?

The staff reported she had called out two names, Katy,

Greg, in her dreams. This was after about a week of Colleen's visits.

Who are Greg and Katy? Are they dogs or human beings?

Silence.

Is Katy your sister?

Jade turned away, refused contact.

At times she seemed more with it. She asked what year it was, what season of the year.

It's 2006, middle of the autumn. What year were you born?

1988.

What month?

September.

Colleen wished she could be sure how much was memory loss and confusion, or was Jade deliberately hiding and obscuring details.

We need to think about what will happen to you when you don't need to stay on this ward any more, she told the girl. If you can remember anything about your home or your family, we could transfer you back home. Or you could move to a rehabilitation ward at this hospital. The drug rehabilitation unit would be best, but there's a huge waiting list for beds. Or you could come to the house I run called Sanctuary House. You'd still get treatment from the medical staff here and from the drug dependency team. But you'd be looked after in an ordinary house by me and some of my volunteers.

The next time Colleen went to the hospital to visit Jade, the girl told her she'd prefer to come to Sanctuary House.

They met Sophie off the train at Glasgow Central, but Katy would not have recognised her. It was Sophie who recognised them, and not just, she said, because of the two school-age girls, baby, and dog she had with her.

You haven't changed a bit, Katy, only maybe a bit taller.

Well, you've grown up a lot, said Katy.

Oh, stupid me, I didn't mean that.

Isn't it me looking worn down with all these problems?

484

No, Katy, honestly, you don't. Well, what about introducing me to your friends?

But she hardly had time for the introductions when Sophie exclaimed,

Look, we must run to the car – I've left it on a yellow line. There's never anywhere to park in Glasgow.

She'd always been like that, Katy remembered, impatient, happy-go-lucky, always rushing from one thing to the next.

They squashed into her little car, and Sophie started negotiating the city traffic.

Where are we going then? Oban, did you say?

Katy turned to Charly.

Near Oban, Charly says. She's the only one who's been to this house.

Charly whispered to her again.

Before we get to Oban. And it's by the sea. Have you got maps?

Yeah. Just like you asked.

Once they were out of the city, Sophie pulled into a lay-by and reached for the maps.

See, this would be the normal road. You don't hit the sea until a mile or so from Oban.

How far from Oban was this, Charly?

Quite a few miles, said Charly. But her anxiety made her sound far from certain, Katy could tell.

Are you sure it was the sea and not an inland loch? Sophie asked her.

Charly could only mumble.

She's sure, said Katy. They were driving near the sea for a long way.

Before you got to this man's house, or after?

Before, said Charly. You could see lightning out to sea. And then after we left him, the day we came back.

Lightning again?

Nah, you could see the sea, I meant, said Charly crossly.

OK, you go and give Greg a few minutes' exercise, while I feed Peter and get the lunch out. Zoë was already out of the car with Greg, but was having difficulty holding onto the straining dog's lead.

Have you had lunch, Sophie? asked Katy.

No, but I had a big breakfast before I set off.

So did we, and some elevenses on the train. But we may as well have lunch now, save us stopping again. She handed the carrier bag over to Sophie. Help yourself to whatever you like, while I feed the baby. There's plenty for everyone.

Sophie was still studying the map. It sounds like they went round the coast and approached Oban from the south. It's not the quickest route, but we'd better go that way. There's only one main road we can follow, but if she doesn't recognise any-where from the main road and we have to start turning down every little lane to every bay or harbour, we're in trouble.

Was this cottage on a main road, Charly? Katy asked when they started off again.

Charly couldn't answer that one. It's near a little town, she said after a long pause. It's a cottage, not a house, and it's just outside this town and it's on the sea. Well, not the sea but a bay.

An inlet, a sea loch?

Yeah.

And the town is by the sea?

Yeah, and the cottage.

Well, this is very helpful – should narrow it down a lot. Do you remember if you went through Glasgow? Or did you cross the Clyde by the Erskine Bridge, or the Clyde Tunnel?

Charly looked blank.

The river Clyde, said Katy. Do you remember crossing a wide river by a big bridge?

I think we did coming back.

We're now passing the Faslane Nuclear Submarine base, said Sophie. Where they have all those protests. Was the cottage anywhere near here?

No.

Well, we are still a long way from Oban. Do you remember passing here?

No.

Katy, squashed in the back with the baby and Zoë – Greg at Charly's feet in the front alongside Sophie – glanced every now and again at her long-lost friend. Sophie was always open, full of laughter, a little scatterbrained. But always willing

486

to help out. Now her dark features were resolute, focussed on the task. Her face in mid-autumn was still quite tanned, reminding Katy that her friend had always liked sunning herself, even back when they were bosom buddies at aged thirteen. That was one thing that hadn't changed. She decided she needed to tell Sophie the full story.

I'd better explain what this is about, she said, loudly, above the noise of the car on the road.

You think Aysha's run away to this cottage, right?

It's a bit more complicated than that.

Yeah, well wait till we get past Arrochar, ok, said Sophie. We're nearly there, and it's one place the cottage could be. Keep a watch out, Charly – we're just coming into it now.

But this was only a small village along the shore of the loch.

It were a bigger place than this, the town was, said Charly. And the sea was more like real sea.

OK, well, I didn't really think so, said Sophie. We're still a long way from Oban.

Katy had never visited Scotland before. Occasionally she was struck by the scenery – high mountains on nearly every side, and dark brooding water glimpsed below, or lapping alongside, close to the car. But she was too preoccupied with other matters to give the scenery much thought. Sophie seemed familiar with it.

Have you been here before? she asked her.

After we moved up here, we had lots of holidays in the Highlands, she said. With Mum and Dad.

You still go on holiday with your parents?

They let me go on holiday with my boyfriend this year. Big deal. We split as soon as we got back.

You still live at home?

Oh yeah. Too cushy by half.

They left the water's edge – sea, loch, it got Katy confused – and climbed up towards the mountains. A thick mist surrounded them and Sophie slowed down to a crawl.

We come to the top of the pass soon, she said.

How will we find the cottage if it's like this? asked Katy.

We should come out of the mist as we drop down the other side, said Sophie. And they did.

So what was this story you were going to tell me, prompted Sophie, putting her foot down and relaxing her concentration.

Well, said Katy. Where to begin, right? She looked at the other kids, Charly alert and all ears, Zoë cradling the sleeping baby and drowsy herself.

You know Aysha and Charly went on a camping trip to Scotland with this guy Neil?

Yeah, I know, best man at your sister's wedding.

Yeah, and little Peter resulted from that trip. Neil got Aysha pregnant.

That was careless of him.

You're telling me, but he was careless about something else as well, which Charly only just told me about. Maybe not as dastardly as implanting his seed but still pretty dire.

What was that?

He'd had a double shock, so perhaps I should never have given him the responsibility. His mother had died of cancer, and he'd found out that the man he thought of as his father wasn't his real father. Although none of us knew this second thing, we don't know how Neil found out, Marie must have told him before she died.

Marie?

Yeah, Marie, his mother, she died a year and a half ago.

What about the other guy?

What other guy?

The one who he thought was his father, but wasn't.

Oh, Jack, yeah, he'd died already, right. I thought you were around then.

No. Well, if I was, you never told me.

Well, I hardly knew Jack. But he was my sister Sam's father-in-law. And my niece Lara's grandfather. Although she was only just born when he died, too young to understand. But she was just about old enough to understand about Marie.

But perhaps he wasn't her real granddad either, suggested Sophie.

Who, Jack, no of course he was. It was only Neil turned out to have a different father. And that's the guy whose cottage we're trying to find now. Neil's father, Charly can't remember his name. But that summer Neil called on this guy when he was with the girls, didn't he, Charly?

Twice – on the way to Oban and on the way back.

Not only that but he confided in them about him being his father. Wasn't that stupid? And he told you to keep it a secret, Charly, is that right?

Yeah, and he said if he ever had a baby we should make sure to tell him before it were too late.

Too late for what?

So's they wouldn't grow up not knowing 'bout one another.

So we think that's what's prompted Aysha, Katy went on. Neil had disappeared before the pregnancy was discovered. Aysha seemed desperate to find him, I couldn't understand why, but I think that was it. So this guy, this mystery real father, is our only hope.

They were close to the sea again, but a drizzly rain had started. Sophie put the wipers on and peered ahead through the windscreen.

We won't get much of a view of cottages. But this is Scotland for you.

Katy was feeling more and more tense. She wanted to ask Sophie, a confident and fairly sophisticated young woman now, it appeared, compared with the last time she'd seen her, to tell her story, but instead she sank back into silence, for some reason suddenly acutely aware of Aysha's absence, as she glanced at the alert but also now silent Charly, and at Zoë, wondering how much she'd heard or understood. From time to time she could make out the sea to their left through the rain and the light now beginning to fade. They passed the entrance to a castle, imposing gateposts painted white facing out across the water, bright in the gloom. The road climbed up and left the coast behind, then dropped down and they'd be travelling along the shore's edge for a mile or so. Several times this happened, as they progressed in silence for a good twenty minutes, Sophie entirely focussed on the road ahead.

Finally, she turned to Charly and said, Now look very carefully here. We're about to hit Lochrana, and I can't think of any other place on this road it could be. If the cottage isn't near here I don't know what we'll do, because it must be on a different road.

Katy could sense Charly's pain and apprehension as she peered out of the car windows. They entered a little town on the edge of the sea, an inlet, small boats anchored in the bay, a few pulled up on shingle. A dark place, the buildings, the water, the shore-line all dark, in this light at any rate.

This is it, exclaimed Charly suddenly. I know it is, I remember this!

Where? asked Katy.

That's the chip shop where we stopped to get fish-and-chips. I remember it! she said with a mixture of enthusiasm, relief, and a sudden surge of pleasurable memory.

Can you direct us to this cottage, then? asked Sophie.

That seemed more difficult and her mood rapidly deflated again.

Have we passed it? Katy asked.

No, I don't think so.

And you say it's by the sea, a short distance out of the town?

Yeah.

Well, we just follow the shore round, said Sophie, gently putting her foot down again.

The streetlights were just coming on in the town as they followed the road round the curve of the bay. When they left the town lights behind it seemed almost night and Sophie slowed right down and pointed to the outline of various buildings faintly visible in the gloom. But Charly couldn't recognise any of them.

I don't remember all these houses, she complained.

They might not be houses, Sophie prompted. They could be farm buildings, or boat-sheds or caravans. Or houses only just built. She slowed down even more. Which side of the road was it, do you remember?

Charly seemed to be getting more and more confused, and there were very few lights other than vehicles on the road.

I think we just passed it, she said in a kind of urgent whisper.

I didn't notice any house.

Just back there. It didn't have any lights on.

Sophie stopped the car and turned to Katy. How do you know he'll be in? He might not be there. She negotiated a u-turn and crawled back.

I didn't think of that, replied Katy truthfully.

There it is!

Where do you park the car?

Just by the side of the house.

It was a cottage in darkness. Sophie pulled the car alongside, a space of gravel, grass and mud.

Is this it?

Yeah.

Everyone was whispering in the darkness. But Greg was suddenly excited, straining on his lead and yelping. And Peter started to wail. They all emerged from the car in chaos and confusion. To add to the disarray, a frantic barking of a dog sounded from inside the cottage, and lights went on.

Katy knew she had to get a grip. Is this the place? I didn't know he had a dog, she said to Charly.

Yeah, he does. But I never heard it bark before.

OK, you go in front then. She had to push Charly forward. Zoë, you hold Greg. Katy picked up the crying baby from the back of the car and they all headed for the cottage door.

43. PRINCE OF DARKNESS

The hospital staff called her Jade, but the girl in the intensive care ward began to realise that it was not her real name. Very slowly her memory started to return as her health became less critical.

To begin with she survived with waves of darkness and pain washing over her. The only sense of people were strangers who did her harm or meant to. Added to the hurt. Flashes of something else in her life came and went away before she could grasp what it was that might end the pain.

Then she remembered a small child, but the distress only got worse. She had to protect the little girl from all those grown-ups who meant her harm, she had to run out of the house with her, but she couldn't, or if she did, they only got found and were taken back and hurt even more. It wasn't easy to tell if these were memories or nightmares.

The nurses looked after her and a woman called Colleen came to see her several times but she didn't know who any of these people were or what she was doing in this place or if she could trust them. All she had the sense of was how the world was a terrible place and if there was anyone out there she could trust, doing her good or trying to, it didn't seem to make any difference.

There were some days in this half-conscious, half-remembering state when she thought she must have been trying to kill herself and wished she had done, or could still do. The physical pain was still excruciating but worse were the half-formed memories merging into nightmares. Darkness like a river she could drown in was almost a comfort.

Then dreams of dogs began to percolate through into her conscious mind. Sometimes a pack of dogs, sled dogs, and she a small child, running free with them. As she clung to this moment of possible happiness, individual dogs began to come clearer into her mind. She was a teenage girl looking after dogs, training them – for what? – and she was a mother with a tiny puppy to look after. Gradually one dog stood out clearer in her mind than all the others, and she knew this was the dog she loved more than anything else in the world. Greg!

Greg! she called out, seeing the bundle of brown fur in front of her eyes. But it was only a dream. Still, she was beginning to remember now. Katy, Greg, her two sisters, the house at High Chapel in Bursfield, she'd been living there. Katy! she called out again, wanting above anything to see that tall blonde angel and her dog again. But the hospital ward was silent and in darkness, it was the middle of the night.

She would tell them about Katy in the morning, tell the nurses or tell that woman Colleen, they would contact Katy, she would come and collect her, take her home. How long ago was it she'd left them? And why, why for fuck's sake had she gone? Had Katy carried on looking after her sisters? Of course she had. And what about her baby?

At first she didn't want to remember the baby. And when she did, she couldn't think of his name, and tried not to. A baby without a name could be brushed out of her mind easier. But she couldn't keep him out, his name was Peter and she'd been crap at looking after him. Fucking hopeless, just like her own mother. History was repeating itself, even if Katy said it didn't have to. Her mother had her when she was just a kid and never learned how to look after her and her two sisters, and now she was the same with her baby. That was why she'd left, because she was a lousy mum and she needed to find Peter's dad and tell him. Tell him he had a kid and tell him she couldn't look after the baby and it weren't fair on Katy for her to have to, and so he'd gotta do it or else she would get him adopted. It were no good waiting like everyone else told her she should, cos Peter would start getting too attached to Katy, to Charly and Zoe, even to herself, she knew that much, and it would make it harder for Neil to take over, or to hand the baby over for adoption.

Neil, that were his name, Peter's dad. She remembered Neil now, and she remembered he'd gone off somewhere, no-one knew where he was, or they wouldn't tell her. But she did know someone who might know and that's why she was in Scotland, to find Neil's real dad. It were a secret Neil had told her, Charly and her. What had happened to her, why hadn't she found Neil's real dad? Why was she stuck in this hospital? Why hadn't she brought the baby with her?

It was still dark in the hospital but she was wide awake now and her mind was racing. She could remember all the terrible things that happened to her many years ago, and more recently how it had all gone wrong again, how she wouldn't look after her baby, how she and Katy stopped talking to one another, how she'd taken the baby round to that sister of Katy's, Sam her name was, and left him there. So she'd ended up coming to Scotland on her own. And she'd run out of money so she'd tried to earn a bit on the streets, that woman said she could. Once she'd made enough for her train fare, she should have carried on with her journey. How dumb could she get, staying on the streets and ending up in hospital?

They'd taken her off the drip now and they came round with some breakfast once it was daylight. But already she'd changed her mind. However much she wanted to see Katy, and Greg, and her two sisters, she knew she had to complete her mission. If she went back with them, she could never run away again and Neil would never get to know he had a baby boy, not until it were too late. No, she still had to get the message to him soon as she could, soon as she were well enough, soon as she could get out of this hospital bed. She could wait a few more days, a week or two perhaps, before seeing them all again. Until then, she mustn't let that Colleen woman know who she was.

Herself she knew now, she wasn't Jade Owen, she were Aysha Jewel Stanton, a hopeless person whose whole life sucked, who couldn't do nothing right, least of all look after a little baby. All she could do, when she were grown up, was race sleds with dogs and do mountain rescue with dogs. But she had one thing she must do first, and she'd nearly failed in that too. This was the best and most important thing in her life because the future of her baby was at stake. If she gave up on this, what hope was there for the other plans in her life? So she would still be Jade Owen, to the staff here and that Colleen woman.

She always pulled a face when they told her Colleen was coming to see her, and the nurses ticked her off.

Don't be like that, she saved your life, you know.

It were Katy who saved my life, she kept wanting to say, but she kept her mouth shut. She would go to that house, though, the one Colleen told her about, anything to get out of the hospital.

Duncan had very few callers. But he had been half expecting, half dreading a knock on the door for nearly nine months now. His feelings about what had happened were very mixed. On the one hand, he was encouraged, flattered by his son's need of his help, turning to him in the absence of anyone else suitable, and how their relationship, in the few weeks they had been together, had grown stronger, been cemented. But there was also the terrible anxiety, that the son he had only just got to know, would be taken from him for an act of stupidity which the outside world and the forces of law, if they ever found out, would view as a heinous crime.

His son refused to blame the girl, but Duncan did blame her. When she'd first set foot in his cottage, she'd given him the impression of a provocative kid, sexually aware, streetwise beyond her years. And she'd told Neil, as far as he could recall, or at least given him a very clear impression, that she was older than in fact she was. Even Duncan found it difficult to believe, when his son had told him, how young she was, and he'd had more experience of teenage girls than Neil had, though not in the last ten years either of them.

It reminded Duncan of him and Marie, back in the first years of his teaching. He knew how these attachments could happen. But the age difference between him and Marie was much smaller, and anyway, nothing had happened between the two of them, not until a few years later. That was the 1960s in Scotland, and times had changed a lot since. And this girl, Aysha, was from a very troubled background, so Neil had told him earlier in the year. She'd made no long-term attachment to Neil, perhaps just as well, was probably incapable of it, and similarly his feelings for her were nothing like Duncan's for Marie. It all seemed to have been a spur of the moment thing, a needy girl, a sexually repressed man. The trip seemed a good idea at the time, but clearly, Duncan could see now, it had been a big mistake putting the two of them together, even with the apparent safeguard of another girl with them.

So for about three weeks in the winter he'd sheltered his son, and helped him make various arrangements to become a fugitive. Duncan wasn't happy about this, but recognised the necessity and was glad he could help. Nowhere had he claimed Neil was his son. Robbie Keith, the name his son had assumed, was a nephew who had re-established contact with Duncan, according to what he'd told his Bank Manager, when they'd set up a joint account.

In fact Duncan Keith had no nephew or niece. His only sibling, a sister eighteen months older than him, had died tragically from meningitis in her early teens. The family never recovered and an idyllic childhood near the coast of the Moray Firth was lost to Duncan. After a while his parents split up and they'd both been dead now for some years. He himself moved to Oban and immersed himself in teaching and associated activities, trying to distance himself from his childhood. Even now, with not too many years left to live, he believed, and with the past constantly sweeping through his mind like a film on rewind, he always seemed to press the stop button at the point of arrival in Oban, focus on those early years there, and allow himself only the most fleeting glimpses of his life earlier where his own family was a more dominant feature. There were other more distant relatives he'd met as a child, he could just about remember them, uncles, aunts, and cousins, possibly some of the latter still alive, but he had long ago lost touch with them. But none with the surname Keith, his father only had two sisters, until Duncan's son had now assumed that family name.

It appeared not just on the joint bank account they had set up, but as the named driver on the insurance for the old van that Neil had bought with some of the money from the sale of his estate car. Duncan had taxed and insured it while Neil fixed it up as a rudimentary camper-van. All this happened up in Lochrana after Neil effectively shut down his life in Grasmere and told people there he was going to travel abroad for a year or more. But he hadn't gone abroad, he'd come to his father for help. Now Duncan was the only link between his son and the rest of the world, and he had dreaded the day when that link would be put to the test. No-one knew about the connection, apart from the two girls, and Neil seemed sure neither would say anything. So tracing the fugitive was unlikely. Duncan was surprised that Neil had divulged their secret to the girls, but his son assured him that this had actually provided an added safeguard since the girls were now much less likely to speak out.

However there was, of course, one other person who knew of the secret. Neil didn't know this but Duncan did. And that man was, Duncan realised, connected to the two girls who had visited with his son. Katy, the girls' carer, was this man's stepdaughter, as was Samantha, Neil's sister-in-law. Duncan still hadn't worked out why Marie had such a profound need to tell him this, nor what he should do with the knowledge. He had only crossed paths with this man once, at Marie's funeral, when he thought he'd identified him among the mourners, and he'd been tempted to seek him out, speak to him on the quiet, but had resisted that temptation, and now was very glad he had. He had also resisted saying anything to his son about this during the extended contact with him last winter.

It may have been unlikely, but the thought of his son being traced through him was always somewhere in Duncan's conscious or subconscious thoughts, and so he'd found himself, as if by a form of transference, acting the fugitive in his own

home. Dreading the sound of a car pulling up outside or the unexpected knock on the door, and frequently keeping the lights of
his cottage turned off as he sat in darkness these autumn
evenings alone with his thoughts and memories and his elderly
dog. A bevy of young females emerging from a small car, a wailing baby, a yelping dog, was something he would never have
expected and felt he could not hide from. Deal with in some way,
even welcome, perhaps. But even without recognising any of
them, he suspected this must be to do with Neil and was on the
defensive even as he opened the door.

A young woman holding a baby pushed a girl forwards,
while behind them another young woman held back, holding the
hand of a smaller girl who clutched the lead of the straining dog.

Is this the man? the woman with the baby asked the girl,
who nodded.

Do you recognise this girl? she then addressed Duncan.

Duncan could not speak, caught on the defensive but
knowing he could not now shut the door on them, and aware
suddenly that he did indeed recognise the girl at the front.

The young woman with the baby was trying a different
tack. Is it right that you're Neil Sullivan's real father? she asked.

Duncan shook his head, but knew it was in no way
convincing.

Look, please don't worry, said the woman, changing
her tone again. Can we come in and talk? We're not here to get
anyone in trouble, I promise you, we just wanna find Aysha and
Neil.

Aysha? Duncan stuttered, half to himself. Yes, come in,
please do. Sit down. He roused himself, moved chairs and cushions, rekindled the fire, heaped on wood.

They trooped on in after him and sat. One young
woman with the baby, the other with the younger girl on her lap,
Barney no longer barking but intermittently growling, the
visiting dog nervously settling itself at the feet of the woman
with the baby.

She was the one who continued to take charge. OK, so
this is Charly, she said, indicating the girl who sat on her own,
the one Duncan recognised. You've met her before, right? That's
Zoë, Charly's younger sister. I'm Katy, we haven't actually met

before, but I do recognise you because we were both at Marie's funeral, weren't we? This is my friend Sophie ….

I've just come as chauffeur, cos Katy doesn't drive, the other woman piped in nervously. You must learn, Katy.

This is our dog, Greg. Duncan remembered the dog now, watching Neil and Aysha bundling it into the back of his son's car, after the funeral.

And this is Peter. The young woman, Katy, held up the baby as she now adopted a slower, stronger voice, a more serious tone. If it's true that Neil is your son, then this child is your grandson.

Duncan was already struggling with the idea of the two missing people. Somehow what had come across was that the two of them had gone missing together, but that would mean that his son had been deceiving him which he refused to believe. Now the mention of the grandson was the sucker punch which had him reeling, and clearly Katy could tell.

Neil doesn't know about his son, she said gently. But the poor kid has both his parents missing, and his only other living grandparent is in prison, so we hope you will agree to do your best for him.

There was a pause. I don't know if I could cope with a baby, he finally said. I'm not a well man, you know, quite disabled really.

No, we're not asking that. We just hope you'll be able to see him regularly and all that. No, what we've come for is to find his missing parents. Can you help us? Do you know where they are?

How can you be sure this boy is Neil's?

Oh, I'm sure all right. Without going through a DNA test, which I'm sure you'd agree would not be a good idea, I'm as certain as it's possible to be. Aysha was – is – quite clear about it, so much so that ever since Peter was born she's been determined to find Neil to tell him.

But is she reliable? Duncan had a nightmarish vision of the troubled teenager pursuing his son for another reason entirely.

In this matter, yes. But do you know where they are? The woman was losing patience and insistence was getting close to aggression.

Neil, yes. Well, not exactly, but we're in touch by phone. Every now and then.

And Aysha?

No, not Aysha. I've not seen her since that summer with Neil. I'd no idea she was missing.

In the silence that followed, Duncan could almost hear the air escaping. Katy's face sagged like a punctured balloon. The younger girl started to cry.

It was the other woman who spoke, clearly needing to break the gloom that had descended.

Did you say you were in telephone contact with your son?

Well, only every few weeks. But I can leave a message on his mobile phone.

So you could ask him if he's seen Aysha?

Well, yes, but I don't see how he can have. There's only me knows how to contact him.

Please try and phone him, she said.

But shall I make you a cup of something first? Duncan roused himself. Tea or coffee? What about something to eat?

Now it was the first young woman, Katy, the one with the baby, who forced her face back into shape.

We'll go and get some fish and chips! she said with false brightness. Is that chip shop in town open on Sundays?

It's open every day. But not until six-thirty.

The woman looked at her watch. How long will it take us to walk?

Fifteen minutes, ten if you're quick.

Well, we'll go in a minute, you and me Sophie, give Greg a walk, and Peter some air. Will you two girls stay here? Will that be all right, Mr - ?

I'm Duncan Keith. Call me Duncan.

Why can't we go? asked the younger child.

Well, maybe Duncan would prefer us all to go, and eat down there. But I thought we could bring some back for you as well, Duncan, save you cooking for yourself....

Oh no, none for me, said Duncan. I'll just have a slice of bread. I have to be strict with my diet and I don't eat much these days. I'll make a big pot of tea for when you get back.

Bring your chips back here, there's nowhere in the shop to eat them.

Where did you eat yours, Charly, the last time?

In Neil's car, said the nearly silent girl.

OK, well we don't want to eat them in Sophie's car, so you two girls stay here, then we can walk back really quick before the chips cool down. And while we're out –

Yes, I know, said Duncan. I'll phone Neil.

Steve understood Sharon well enough to know that, even though she had said nothing since his admission of being aware that Neil's biological father wasn't Jack, she was expecting some further explanation from him. But how much should he now divulge to her?

He ought to tell her everything, he knew. He ought to have done so long before now. But the chain of circumstances arising from the moment Marie first took him into her confidence was growing more and more complex and involving an increasing number of participants, and this made it more of a problem for him, when to tell Sharon, how much to tell her, and how to explain it in ways which would minimise the potential damage. He wished he'd found the chance to talk to Marie before she died, to find out how much she herself wanted revealed.

I'd better explain how I knew about Marie and Jack, he said to Sharon, when they'd just finished breakfast.

It would help, said Sharon, calm, but biting back her emotions, Steve could tell.

We were good friends, said Steve. This was quite a few years before I knew you. I had no real ties. Jack and Marie were probably my closest friends, and apart from Jack I was Marie's closest friend. She never went in for women friends after she married, not on a personal level. She'd had girl-friends at college but already they were becoming more distant to her. So she began to confide in me.

Why couldn't she confide in Jack?

Because it was about him, the paternity of his child, his possible infertility. She began to suspect Jack couldn't father children. And if her fears were true, it meant Neil wasn't Jack's child.

Couldn't she persuade him to take the tests? They did have them then, didn't they?

Yes, but if Neil wasn't his child, she didn't want Jack to know. She thought it would be better to hide it than for Jack to know the truth.

So what about Marcus, then? asked Sharon.

Yes, said Steve, suddenly unsure of himself. That's the thing.

Is his father the same guy as Neil's?

No. Marie didn't want to get back in touch with that guy. It was someone she'd known before she got married.

But she must have contacted him, Sharon asserted. Or else how would Neil have found him?

Yeah, but that must have been just before she died. All these years later.

So who is Marcus's father?

Steve found he couldn't go on with it. He was floundering and had no mental strength left.

I don't know. Maybe it was Jack after all.

But Sharon, despite her condition, was now fired up. She wasn't going to let it go at this half-way stage. Marcus was her son-in-law after all, nothing would stop her pursuing this to the end.

You must know, Steve, if you were that close to her, she must've told you.

It was Jack, he said. Or that's what she believed, anyway.

But his reluctance had been a dead giveaway, and the horror of the sudden realisation swept across Sharon's face.

My god, don't tell me it was you, Steve! She paused. It was, wasn't it? That's why Marie confided in you, so's she could get you to father her next child. Oh my god, you're Marcus's father. How could you, how could you?

Steve knew the family secret was out, he couldn't hold onto it any longer. You must not tell anyone else, Sharon, please! Remember it happened a long time ago, I was young and naïve, and it was many years before I met you and the girls.

But you could have told me, she said in a hurt voice.

I honestly thought it was best not to. I didn't think you were ready for a bombshell like that, and as the years went on, it

501

never seemed possible. And there was Marie's confidentiality to take into account. I'm sure many people would have felt the same.

Bugger Marie, said Sharon dismissively. You let them get married without saying anything, how could you? <u>She</u> let them get married, even worse.

How could either of us say anything then? They were really happy together, and it might have destroyed their relationship. There's no blood connection, is there?

But they are, like, stepbrother and stepsister, in a sense.

Why should that matter? Please, please, Sharon, you mustn't say anything, not to anyone.

But, Steve – it means you're Lara and Liam's grandfather! She said it with a sense of finality, as though she'd been building up to this.

Yes, but that's ok isn't it? I mean, I've taken on the grandparent role anyway, up to a point. And I'll continue with that, I don't love them any more or less.

Any more or less than what?

I mean, the same whether I'm step-granddad or real grandfather.

But I've been making all that effort to trace Rodney when it's not been so vital.

What on earth do you mean?

You know, Steve – Marcus's parents are dead, I might die quite soon, I really wanted to find their other grandparent.

But he still is their grandparent.

But now there's you.

I told you, I love them anyway, we must leave it the same as it's been. And you, you're not going to die soon, you mustn't think that.

I might if you give me any more shocks like this, she grumbled. But Sharon appeared to be more sad than angry now. Well then, yeah. She paused. I do wish Rodney had contacted me by now.

Maybe he will at Christmas. Remember he had to talk to his kids first.

But it's over six months now. I really feel like contacting him.

You mustn't. Be patient, give him more time.

It had only been a faint hope, but it seemed like the last one. Katy walked the half a mile into the small town slowly, feeling deflated, no energy left, nothing she wanted to say, desperate to do something more but lacking any sense of what. Greg pulled on the lead continually and Sophie, pushing Peter in his buggy, walked ahead. She tried to keep up, walk alongside even, out of a mixture of duty and affection towards her old friend, but the occasional car, its headlights sweeping the road and them ahead of its arrival, forced them into single file. It was hard enough to keep up with life before, it was even harder now without the two younger girls present, perhaps she should have brought them.

The sound of waves lapping on her right might have soothed her, but as they reached the edge of town she knew she was close to tears. There was a grassy area between the main street and the shore, a few seats facing out to sea, and she stepped onto it, let Greg off his lead, walked to the nearest seat.

Can we sit here for a few minutes first, she called to Sophie who followed her, but Katy felt her voice breaking as she called out and when Sophie sat beside her, there were tears dribbling down her face.

What are you going to do now? Sophie was trying to be sympathetic.

I dunno. Go back to England, I guess.

Are you still gonna search for Aysha?

I would, if I knew where.

She must be somewhere.

Dead most likely.

No, she would have been identified, they would have contacted you.

Katy nodded unconvincingly.

Could she be with this Neil guy?

It's just possible that he contacted her without me knowing and she left to meet up with him. And they were still worried about trouble with the law so they've continued being fugitives. It's possible – I know Aysha liked him, got on with him, but I believed her when she said she didn't want a relationship with him. She only wanted to let him know about the baby.

Maybe I'm wrong, maybe she was having me on, but I can't believe they would just forget about Peter.

Perhaps she never told him?

No, I can't believe that.

Well, if the guy in the cottage gets hold of Neil, you might get an answer.

Or I might not.

Will you wait here until he turns up?

Who, Neil?

Who else.

No, I won't! No way! It's funny, I really wanted to see him, to give him a right telling-off. Y'know, when I found out it was on her holiday with him that Aysha got pregnant, before I knew it was actually him. And even more when I found out he was the dad. But not now. Not unless he knows where Aysha is, of course, which I doubt. The thing is, I've been thinking about all that, every night I do, and I don't blame him any more. He's a good man, just a bit naïve.

You think she used him?

Not really, not in the way you mean. You see, none of us really know what it's like for abused kids when they reach adolescence. Her flow of tears had stopped now and she looked round to check that Greg was nearby before girding herself up for what she needed to express. I didn't have a clue but then neither did the professionals. One guy told me she might be a risk to younger kids, so of course I was worried sick she might abuse my niece or nephew, she'd already met them by that time and they got on really well. But Aysha would never abuse a younger kid, I know her well enough to say that now with complete confidence. But she was reaching adolescence, her hormones were kicking in and she needed to work things out her own way. You don't mind me telling you all this, do you?

No, of course not.

She used to hang out with the teenage boys who lived locally, and the girls, you know, the way teenagers do. They used to smoke, dope I think as well as cigarettes, but I don't think anything else happened. I don't even know what they talked about, apart from music, like, the latest rock bands you know, and all that. If they talked about sex, or any of them tried it on, she never said anything to me. She gave me the impression she knew all about sex, but she may have been putting it on to hide the problems she had with it.

What problems?

Well, all the pain resulting from the abuse. I did go through that with her, it was called her life-story book, and she did say quite a bit, she did express her feelings, and I really hoped that meant she'd worked through it all, that she was normal now. But what is normal?

Quite.

She never expressed how she felt about her sexuality now, in the present. But teenagers don't, do they, except among themselves, maybe not even then. Maybe she wasn't sufficiently aware in herself. But how I wish she could have talked to me. I can see why not, I wasn't the person to guide her through that minefield, I was very inexperienced, I hadn't met Gareth then, she may have suspected I was lesbian, I mean I had some doubts myself.

Really?

Yeah, but not any more. But Aysha, she found herself in close contact with this guy for nearly three weeks. A different sort of guy, not like the one who abused her so badly, not like the professionals who had such a down on her because of her rebel-liousness. Not easy to talk to, but she was all the more drawn to him because he's shy, a social misfit, but her need for support got mixed up with her sexual needs and she lost all sense of boundaries. He should have kept the boundaries of course ....

He bloody well should of.

Yeah I know it was his responsibility, not Aysha's, but thinking about it now, I can't blame him too much. He's not a paedophile is what I'm saying, he shouldn't be hauled up in court or sent to prison, in fact he's the opposite of the guy who abused her, as different as you can get. I would trust him with Peter, totally, with any kids in fact. He's fine with his niece and nephew, who are also my niece and nephew, I know that for sure. He tried to resist Aysha's needs, but at one critical moment he failed. She didn't use him, it was her vulnerability. I blame myself, they should never have been together all that time.

Will you leave Peter here then?

For Neil to take over? No, I can't. He's my responsibility, I have to keep Social Services informed. I've already failed in my responsibilities far too much.

She started sobbing again. At the same time a few drops of rain fell. Heavy drops, but only a few. The sound of waves on the shingle seemed to get louder all of a sudden. The night was pitch black, heavy cloud blanketed the sky, apparently only a few feet above them. Greg had stopped scampering about and sat by Katy whining occasionally. Peter woke up and whimpered.

Let's go for our chips, said Katy.

You shouldn't have to cope with so much responsibility, not at your age, said Sophie, as they crossed the road to the chip shop. What will you do?

About finding Aysha? I don't know.

No, I meant about Peter, if Neil wants to see him.

I'll work something out. I'm not gonna stay in this godforsaken hole just for that.

It probably looks beautiful when the sun's out, like nearly everywhere in Scotland.

There was a queue at the fish-and-chip counter, almost to the door. The two young women had to squeeze themselves and the buggy inside to get out of the rain.

Who would've ever thought? said Katy. That when we two met up again, it would be in a place like this.

Not many other visitors in winter, Sophie laughed under her breath.

Why should being a carer have got so difficult? Is it just my age?

I'm sure it's not just that.

Did your mum and dad have these problems?

My foster-parents? I think they might have done once. I guess they were lucky with me. But I would never do fostering myself.

Tell me more about yourself. We've talked long enough about me. Do you still see your real mum and dad?

I haven't seen them for ages, but we do keep in touch. My dad's still in Bolton, but Pauline, my mum, she's gone to New Zealand now. I get an e-mail every now and then, and a card at Christmas.

Are you still getting on with Roy and Andrea?

Yeah fine, only they want me to go to college, get qualified.

In catering?

Yeah, only really I'd like to be a dietician. And that's what they want me to do, but they say I should be studying for it now, not wasting my time working in a college cafeteria. But I say it's all good experience, and anyway I need the money. And what better place to work than a college when you're twenty-one and fancy free?

I thought you had a boyfriend?

Not any more. Well it's a bit off and on, shall we say. More off than on just now. What about Gareth? How are things between you and him?

Still not good. But I need to sort something out. I'm gonna apply to adopt the girls if I can. I should've done something about it before. I need to know if Gareth wants to be part of that. I must phone him tomorrow. Remind me to get a top-up for my mobile. She took Peter out of his buggy and held him close to quiet him.

What? You really think adopting them's best? Roy and Andrea never adopted me.

Well, their mum might not agree of course. But I have a feeling that if I'd started the ball rolling as soon as I'd turned twenty-one, Aysha might never have run off. She lowered her voice.

Why d'you think that?

Because she'd have the prospect ahead of her of not being under Social Services any more.

They reached the counter and ordered their portions. Katy passed the now quiet baby to her friend while she paid, and Sophie put him back in his buggy.

Let's rush back quick as we can, said Katy.

You know I'll have to set off back, soon as I've eaten, said Sophie. I have to be at work tomorrow.

Sure. I mean, I wish we had more time to talk, but there we are. You've done more than enough already to help out.

How will you get back?

Oh we'll manage. There must be buses.

It's more than four hours drive for me. I'll be lucky to make it home by midnight.

507

They scampered back through the threat of heavier rain. The two girls were solemn and quiet, but perked up with the arrival of their supper.

Have you managed to contact Neil? Katy asked as soon as she had the chance.

I've left a message on his mobile, said his father. I don't think he'll phone now, he usually phones just as it's getting dark.

Will he phone tomorrow?

I hope so, I've said it's important.

Sophie has to drive back tonight, said Katy. Could we stay on for a night, go back tomorrow some time?

Sure, said Neil's father. But I'm a bit short of beds and space. And food. But we'll manage. One person will need to sleep down here on the couch.

Will we be able to catch a bus back to Glasgow?

There's two buses a day, but the morning one is quite early, and the afternoon one won't leave you much time for the rest of your journey. I mean, if you want to get home the same day.

Oh, I think there'll be trains from Glasgow to Manchester through the evening, said Katy. And I'm sure Steve will collect us when we get there. She turned to the two children. So how's about it, you two? We can go shopping for – for Neil's dad, I'm sorry, I've forgotten your name – tomorrow morning –

Duncan, he said. Duncan Keith.

Yeah, I'm sorry, Duncan. We'll cook Duncan a good lunch tomorrow, won't we kiddos, and then we'll catch the afternoon bus.

You can't wait for Robbie, can you? said Duncan. I mean Neil. Did I tell you he calls himself Robbie Keith now.

No. Why's that?

Well, you know, just part of his – his –

Disappearance?

I guess that's the word, said Duncan. Robert is his other Christian name: Neil Robert.

Well, I don't mind him changing his surname, said Katy. But me and the girls, we won't be able to stop calling him Neil. And no, we can't wait for him to get here if he's going to. But I will speak to him on the phone if he calls back.

The last thing she wanted to do now was to meet Neil face to face. She had been determined to not so long ago, but things had changed, so much she had had to go through. Most of all, she wanted to get some normality back into her life, be more like Sophie. Mend some fences, try and get back on track with Gareth, if he would still have her, there was so much she was missing of her life with him, why had she been so stupid to cut him out. Not just Gareth, but her sister too, and Lara and Liam, she missed them all. It was still Aysha she missed most of all, but she mustn't let it destroy how she felt about the other people important to her. She would make some phone calls tomorrow. She must remember to top up her mobile when they went shopping in the morning.

So have you decided? Are you leaving tomorrow? the old man, Duncan, was asking, bringing her out of her reverie.

Yeah, like I said, the afternoon bus.

So you'll leave the wee bairn, will you, for Robbie to see?

No, said Katy. I'm sorry, I can't do that. You see, I'm responsible for him, to the authorities. I can't hand him over without their agreement, and I'd have to explain why. Anyway, we don't even know if Neil wants to see him.

But I'm sure he will, and if he does – then how will he be able to?

I'll sort something out, Duncan, I promise I will, I'll let you know, I'll make sure I've got your phone number and I'll let you have mine.

Sophie had finished eating, and rose from her chair.

Well, good-bye everyone. I must rush off now. Great to have met you all. Sorry I didn't meet Aysha but I do hope she turns up soon.

Katy went out with her. It was pouring with rain now, but they hugged each other by the car door for several minutes.

Thanks for everything, Sophie. It's just been such a help being with you, right. Helped me get a better perspective, done me a world of good.

Only wish it could've turned out better. Sorry I can't do more.

Don't worry, you drive safe through all this rain. Keep in touch.

Colleen found herself working many weekends. The streets were at their most active on Saturdays, she usually found. And many of her volunteers were women with families, they didn't mind giving up a weekday evening or even a whole night every now and again on the sleeping-in rota at Sanctuary House, but at the weekends family came first. If there was work required at a weekend, it usually fell to Colleen. One thing she did make sure was that she never slept at Sanctuary House, she would insist on relying on volunteers for that. However late into the night she worked, she made sure her husband would find her sleeping alongside him when morning came.

She planned on moving Jade into the house on the Monday. It was early November now, and it was going to take most of the weekend to get the place prepared, warm and comfortable, clean and well-stocked, the sense of being lived-in, although in fact it hadn't been for many weeks. One of her volunteers worked hard on this on the Friday, while Colleen herself decided she wanted to seek out Marcia.

Can I persuade you to come into the house for a week or two? she said when she found her.

I told ya, Colleen, not just now, all right. Later, when the real winter sets in.

It's just that young kid, Jade, she's moving in on Monday. She's made a good recovery in hospital, but I think she'll be lonely on her own in the house. You get on with her ok, don't you?

Well, I did once, said Marcia. But I don't know as I could be much help to her now.

I'm sure it would be better for her if you were there too.

So after some reluctance, Marcia allowed herself to be persuaded. She would move in on the Sunday. Colleen would need to visit each day that week, to check how Jade was, try to get to know her a bit better, make sure she was taking her medication, link up with the doctors who were treating her, take her to clinic appointments. But she couldn't be there all the time, and she felt Marcia would be a stabilising factor for Jade, complementing what she and the volunteers could offer.

She fully expected to be working almost full-time over the first weekend Jade was there. But outside events intervened. In a large industrial town in the south of England, a number of prostitutes had gone missing and a body had been found. The police there were struggling, and they called a consultation meeting, and invited Colleen. She didn't feel she could turn them down. It was short notice, the Monday after Jade moved in. So she and her husband decided to have two nights in London, and travel down the Saturday afternoon. She would spend the Saturday morning at Sanctuary House, and get back there some time on the Tuesday, arranging for volunteers to cover in her absence. During the week she would spend as much time as possible with Jade, helping her, getting to know her, but then there would be three days when she depended on her volunteers, and on Marcia.

44. MAKE ME LONELY AGAIN

Neil, or Robbie Keith as he now called himself, hurried back to his tent, dived in and shut the flap tight behind him. As it so often did in the Scottish Highlands, heavy rain had come on quickly. He had been exploring this area up Strath Kanaird for some weeks now, and full days of dry weather had been very occasional. All the autumn, for two months now, he had woken himself at daybreak, and if the cloud was not down and it wasn't raining, he would be out early to explore the hills around, the Cromalt Hills to the north, the smaller but steeper and nearer hills to the south, and the wilderness plateau of the Rhidorroch Forest further off to the east and south-east, but all too often he was driven back as he had been this morning, by the driving rain and the cloud closing in.

Despite the weather, he was beginning to enjoy the fugitive life now, and had decided to make the attempt to stay up in the mountain wilderness of the Highlands right through the winter. It hadn't been like this to start with, all the anxieties about the new life he was starting and the regrets about the one he was leaving behind, combined to make the first winter months difficult for him. He had driven up to his father just after New

Years, had got from him the promise of help and support he'd asked for, they'd drawn up plans together, and then Neil had driven back to Grasmere and shut down his whole life there. He'd sold his estate car, terminated the rentals on his flat and workshop, had his deposits back, and told everyone who knew him that he was going abroad for at least two years. He'd then travelled back to Scotland by train and bus with the few last belongings he needed to keep, and a moderately fat wad of cash in his pocket. He'd spent nearly a third of this buying an old van at Lochrana, which he worked hard at converting so that he could live in it, while his father taxed and insured it in his own name. They visited his father's bank and set up a joint account in the names of Duncan and Robbie Keith, which enabled him to have his own cash card, and the rest of his money was deposited in that account.

But there were still anxieties that haunted him those first months. Only three documents remained from his previous life, and they were all hidden away at his father's cottage – his passport, his birth certificate, and his driving licence. It was unlikely that his passport or birth certificate would be needed at present. But he drove around northern Scotland always fearful that he might be unwittingly involved in an accident, or some other matter such as a faulty brake light might cause the police to stop him, ask for his licence. It was better to use his van as little as possible. Early on, however, he had not adjusted to living in a tent, and he spent the rest of that winter and much of the spring keeping to the north-west coastal areas, parking the van in remote lay-bys, trying to avoid stocking up at the same stores too much, phoning his father from call-boxes when he could, limiting the use of his new mobile phone (also in Duncan's name) to the minimum. He'd soon rejected the thought of crossing to any of the islands. He was already known on quite a few of them, and soon would get to be on others, the crossings were expensive even if he left his van on the mainland, and if the authorities did catch up with him, he would be trapped on an island, with no escape routes.

So he stayed on the mainland, and by the late spring he had taken to the hills with his camping equipment, his binoculars, telescope and camera. Quite a weight to carry around but he didn't want to leave anything precious in the van. He had found himself reaching the hamlet of Altnaharra and leaving the van there, using the store now and then to replenish supplies, while he explored the northern and eastern slopes of Ben Klibreck where he studied dotterel on the higher slopes and whimbrel and golden plover lower down. Then he had spent many weeks of high summer exploring the lochs to the east of Ben Hee where greenshank bred and several species of raptor were frequently seen. Eventually he moved the van round to Strath Oykel, and spent the rest of the summer high up on the massif of Ben More Assynt, to keep away from midges for one reason, and where he found himself camped at one end of a high defile below the mountain ridge, close to where a stream came tumbling down from the crags above, and where he could study at close quarters several families of ring ouzels preparing for their autumn migration. Only occasionally did he drop down to the valley to drive to Lairg to stock up.

Finally he had travelled south-west to here, where he had to content himself with watching herds of deer, ptarmigan at the higher altitudes, dippers on the streams, and an occasional mountain hare running on the hill above him, or golden eagle flying over, to keep him with his camera at the ready.

He was less anxious now, but felt committed to continuing this fugitive lifestyle. He had wondered if anybody might try and trace him through the two girls. He was fairly sure Aysha would say nothing, a little less sure about the younger sister, how much she knew, how easily she might be pressured into talking. But he still had the denials of his father as the final line of defence, and his father had received no calls enquiring after him. It would seem the secret was safe. Now he was keeping the girls as far from his thoughts as he could, and was mostly successful in doing so, even though the older one had been the unwitting cause of this whole enterprise. He did not blame her, she was a troubled child and he had not hardened himself enough to resist her advances. Dreams about her had occasionally troubled him, and that startling vision of her entering his tent at the height of the thunderstorm, her wet skin shining bright in the flashes of lightning, had from time to time returned to haunt him, but not for some time now.

The rain had set in for the day, so there was little for him now to do, once he had made himself a bite of lunch. He had been into Ullapool yesterday, walking the five miles in the rain to the road where the van was parked, to get provisions. So he checked his mobile, something he didn't usually do until darkness had fallen, and found there was a message from his father, nothing unusual there, but this one sounded a little more urgent, so he decided to phone back straight away.

Robbie, he heard the anxious tone in his father's voice. We have some news for you here. Some young women have turned up looking for you, and they have a baby with them that they say is yours.

Nothing could have prepared Neil for this, although he soon came to see that he should have been. He reeled, sat down, but could say nothing.

Are you still there, Robbie?

Yes, yes – who are they, these women?

Katy, she's called, I think you know her.

All his worst fears overwhelmed him. Yet something made him hang on to the phone call, knowing he should speak to her.

Shall I put her on the phone? his father was anxiously asking.

Yes, yes. There was impatience in his voice as well as fear and anxiety, and the image of the girl flashed through his mind one more time, after all these months freed from it, Aysha there at his father's cottage with a child, product of that awful, awe-full deed. But a woman's voice was already speaking down the phone-line, and he had to jerk himself into the present and do his best to concentrate.

Neil? Is that you? A voice sounding more impatient than him.

Yes. Is that Katy?

It is. Listen, Neil, we've not come to make any trouble, I promise you, for you or with the authorities. I know Aysha would not want that.

Is Aysha there?

Is she there with you, Neil?

What? No, of course not, I haven't seen her since I dropped her and her sister at your house that summer.

Are you sure? Please promise to tell me if you know where she is! The woman sounded desperate more than impatient now.

I promise you I've no idea where she is. But what's this about a baby my father mentioned?

Yes, there is a baby, we have him here with us, he's Aysha's baby, and yours, we believe, he's a boy, nearly six months old, he's called Peter.

Well, it's a shock, I don't know what to say.

The thing is, Neil, Aysha's gone missing, over two months. She was desperate to let you know about the baby, and I think she ran away to try and find you. That's why I was asking. We're urgently trying to find her, and we're beginning to fear the worst.

I'm really sorry, I do hope she turns up ok.

We've got to go back to England in an hour or so. Do you want to have contact with your son?

What? Of course I do. I'll get down to Lochrana as quickly as I can, but it could be midnight or after before I arrive. Can you leave the baby with my father?

I'm afraid I can't do that, Neil. I hope you'll understand, but I'm responsible for him, to the authorities, and I can only leave him with family or approved carers.

But I am family, and I was approved, last summer.

He immediately realised the implications of what he'd just said.

No, Neil, none of that counts, we have to keep quiet about all of that. I'm hoping to adopt the girls, and in the future it might be different. But if you do want to be a dad to Peter then that's fine, I know Aysha would want that, and I would be very happy about it too, especially with him not having his mother around at the moment. Please leave it with me and I'll sort something out.

So what shall I do?

Well, I'll keep in touch with Duncan about it. It's up to you whether you stay up there in the mountains or you come back to this cottage, but just wait until you get a message about contact with Peter. Oh, by the way, his full name is Peter Kenneth Rodney Stanton.

Tell my father I'll come down to his place, Neil was beginning to say, but the woman had rung off and he wasn't sure if she heard.

Samantha Sullivan gently removed the baby from the cradling arms of her six year old daughter and started feeding him from his bottle. She was feeling strong now even though a whole range of emotions had been running through her mind in the last few days. She had been right about that kid Aysha, for a start, no question about that. Everything that wayward girl had done since she came into Katy's life, all of their lives, had just spelt trouble with a capital t. She had seen it coming but she hadn't been able to convince her sister or her mother and the girl had let them down badly, caused a lot of hurt and upset. Stealing nearly all the money in her mother's purse, how could she? Not only had she shown herself to be a slut who seduced Neil and caused him to disappear out of their lives for a while, but she was a thief and a runaway too, who couldn't face up to the responsibility for what she'd done. It was better that little Peter was with her family, after all he was Marcus' and her nephew, cousin to Lara and Liam, though she hadn't told her children this just yet, to them he was still Aysha's baby. When Neil arrived and started spending time with the boy, getting to know him, well that would just be a natural thing for him to do.

She was a good mother, Sam knew that now. She was very like her own mother who had not coped well when Sam was a girl, and had put most of the responsibility of running the home and caring for her younger sister onto Sam herself, and Sam had worried for a time that the pattern might repeat itself. But she had broken the cycle, and Lara, who was so much like her mother just as Sam was like hers, was going to turn out ok, Liam too. Lara was already such a strong and sensible kid, and family life for her was stable and secure. Of course, she had to thank Marcus mostly. She'd had a troubled childhood and adolescence, and more recently there was that bout of depression, but with the help of her husband she'd pulled through. But what she'd come to regret was the falling out with her sister and in consequence, her mother too, to some extent.

Lara was wanting to feed Peter from the bottle.

Please let me have a turn, mummy, she pleaded. But Liam had got tired of playing on his own, and wanted his big sister to join in.

He's had quite a lot already, Samantha said to her daughter. Don't try and force it in, if he closes his mouth or turns his face away it means he's full. And don't complain if he sicks up a bit on your lap, cos he sometimes does at the end of a feed.

I do know that, mummy, I've watched you feed him loads of times.

Mummy, said Liam. Can you tell Lara to play with me now?

It's ok, Liam, said his sister. Peter's nearly finished his feed and I'll play with you straight after.

Yes, thought Samantha. Lara's good with both of them, no question. Again she thought of her own childhood and how Lara seemed so like she was at the age of about seven when she had first taken an older sister interest in her baby sister Katy. And how that interest in Katy had grown into caring, and then into a deep-seated and reciprocated love which had reached fruition when Lara was born and Katy had become a devoted aunt and baby-sitter. What had happened to their relationship since, why had Katy taken on that Aysha and her sisters? Why had they gone looking for her and Katy's first dad, who Sam could never forgive for leaving them just like that and causing all that misery and despair? It was Aysha who was instrumental in that, too, going in search of Rodney, and finding him. What a waste of space!

Are you all right, mummy? Lara was trying to hand baby Peter back to her.

Yes, I'm fine. Just thinking. Her daughter skipped off to join Liam's games.

Her sister, her mother, and her brother-in-law, hardly speaking to any of them. And such a loss to Lara and Liam. How much she'd wanted, over recent weeks, to repair the relationships in whatever way she could, but something had held her back, was it her stupid stubborn pride, or was it all the anger, hatred, hostility which had already been expressed and might resurface again? Too much water under the bridge? It seemed her sister felt the same way, because on that day back in August when she'd come round to collect Peter after that slut of a girl had run off, Katy hadn't said a word, but then she was probably too upset or in shock or something. Stupid woman, getting so devoted to a no-good kid like that. But Sam felt bad that she'd not been there to support her sister when she'd clearly been so distressed.

She'd discussed this with her husband. Marcus held the view that she should let it be for now, let time be the healer. That was his usual position. It might be that what with the new football season bringing ever-increasing commitments, and with an expansion taking place at his factory, new contracts to meet, new machines being installed, he didn't have the time to think out anything other than his usual response. But that was being a bit harsh, he had continued to support her as best he could, he was always a devoted father and husband.

He continued to do the main supermarket shop on a Saturday morning, taking the kids with him. Even if there were football matters to attend to, people to chase up on the phone, checking the availability of one or more of the kids on the team, doubts about the state of one of the pitches, he always found someone else to do these Saturday morning tasks. He gave her the chance to have her friends round, it wasn't every week now, but the coffee mornings continued, and how glad she'd been to sound off to her friends. Of course, she hadn't said everything, she'd missed out the bit about Neil and Aysha, Neil being the baby's father. No, it was her sister she wanted to talk about, what could she do to get her sister back in her life? There was a range of views among her friends, and various suggestions had been made.

But then there'd been the call from Katy and all suggestions became superfluous. Katy had sounded nervous, but she'd spoken clearly enough, and there might have been a time when Sam would have reacted furiously to her requests, but that time wasn't now. She was overjoyed to be able to help her sister out, especially when it meant having little Peter to care for again, but most of all having her brother-in-law back in her life. Neil was on his way down to stay with them, he would arrive tomorrow. The kids would be overjoyed to see him again, just as they were to see Katy yesterday, although Lara was still asking after that Aysha. Samantha was good with babies, was happy to have the care of another one, and Katy had got the agreement of the authorities that, subject to police checks, she and Marcus could take on Peter's care. And it meant Neil could get to know his son, the very son that she was cradling gratefully just now and was falling asleep in her arms.

Zoë knew a lot of things now. She really really wanted Ambrose to come back so's she could tell him all the things she knew which she didn't when she last saw him.

She knew that Neil was the father of baby Peter and he'd disappeared. She knew that Aysha had run away because she wanted to find Neil and tell him about the baby. And she knew that Katy took them to Scotland and met her friend who had a car, because she wanted to find Aysha. Charly helped them find a house where she and Aysha and Neil had been before, because Katy thought Aysha and Neil might be there, but they weren't. The man phoned Neil and told him about Peter and Katy spoke to Neil too, but nobody knew where Aysha was, and Katy was upset and nearly cried.

Zoë really wanted to tell Ambrose all about this. She was sure it would be all right because Ambrose would never tell anyone else.

And she knew some more things. She knew that Katy loved her and her two sisters and Gareth. But when Aysha ran away Katy had to love Aysha twice as much to try and make her come back and she still loved Charly and her, but she couldn't still love Gareth because she didn't have enough love left. So she went to sleep in Aysha's bedroom and Gareth didn't like it. And everyone was sad twice over, because Aysha had run away and because Katy and Gareth weren't getting on.

Zoë liked Gareth and she wanted Katy to marry him and adopt her and her two sisters and she was sad when it didn't look like this would happen. When she told Charly, her sister said it was never gonna happen anyway, and so she wanted to tell Ambrose.

And Katy also had a falling-out with her sister who was Lara and Liam's mother. That was something to do with Aysha and baby Peter, but Zoë didn't understand much about it, except that Katy adored those kids and would never have wanted to stop seeing them.

Zoë learned to listen to things people said and sometimes watch their faces and that way you got to know things about people – that was something Charly told her and now she wanted to tell Ambrose.

But Aysha had said to her, before Zoë started her new school, High Chapel Primary, how if she wanted to make new friends at school, and have sleepovers and stuff, how she'd better say good-bye to Ambrose cos the other kids might think she was babyish for having a pretend friend. So Zoë did say good-bye to him, and she did make friends at her new school, and now she wanted to talk to Ambrose again.

And she knew this one last thing. If people had a falling-out they could say sorry and get back together again, if they tried very hard. Katy had done it. Zoë had listened and watched her. She had made it up with her sister and now the baby was staying at her sister's house and Lara was helping to look after him and Neil was there, being dad to him. And Katy had made up with Gareth too, so now they slept in the same bed and they might get married and adopt her and her sisters. All it needed now was for Aysha to come back.

She needed to tell Ambrose all this, and tonight she would. She would make it up with Ambrose, just like Katy had with Gareth, and pretend she was his friend again, just for one night, so she could tell him all these things she knew.

Colleen took the evening train back to Glasgow, the conference with the police having finished in time to allow this. She thought she would have to stay another night in the hotel, return on the Tuesday morning, but she was on her own now, her husband having travelled back earlier in the day, and the last thing she wanted was a night on her own in the dull, featureless London hotel, so she collected her things, checked out at reception, took a cab the half mile to Euston, and caught the train with a feeling of great relief. She was longing to get back to her home, her husband, and her work at Sanctuary House.

She had phoned the volunteers at least once a day while she was away, and heard that everything there was as it should be, and she phoned again now. She'd get there tomorrow morning, she said, a bit earlier than planned. She felt very tired, so she didn't promise to go first thing, she might need a lie-in. She phoned her husband too. Then she felt she could relax, opened a book, and despite the crowded train, she slipped in and out of sleep all the way home.

By morning she felt restless and decided to call in at the Social Work office on the way to Sanctuary House. All her efforts at tracking down Jade Owen's family had so far come to nothing. The national missing person's register was computer-ised and there was no Jade Owen on it. She'd gone through the Scottish list of missing children and she'd phoned Manchester too, more than once, but there was no-one answering Jade's description. But suppose she was from somewhere else in Eng-land, and using a false name? Colleen had thought about this, more and more leaning towards this conclusion, but was there no record in the Social Work Department which could help her?

I'm still trying to trace this girl Jade, she said to the clerical support officer whom she'd spoken to a number of times in recent weeks. She's not showing up on any of your computer systems, but do you still have a manual filing system too?

Well, we've tried that, said the young woman. There's no Jade Owen on any of the Missing Person Registers or any open case system.

But suppose it's not her real name? Don't you still get written notification of missing children in care?

Yes, we do, but we put them on the computer unless the papers clearly state that's already been done, which most of them do.

What do you do with the papers then?

Well, the Scottish ones we keep in an open file for two years.

And the English ones?

They get filed in a closed file. We don't find much use for those normally.

Where are those files?

There are box-files in the store-room. But it will take you weeks to go through them all.

In what order are they filed?

By year. The 2006 box-file is still here in my filing cabinet. I'm adding something to it nearly every day.

Well, can't I have a look through that?

Yes, of course. She retrieved it for Colleen.

The papers had been filed in date order, the most recent at the top of the pile. Colleen set to work eagerly, questioning why on earth no-one had thought of doing this before. When she worked back to the beginning of October, she started looking through the notifications more closely. As she worked backwards through the September ones, she picked out two or three that might possibly be Jade, and put them to one side for further study later.

After half an hour she had gone through almost all the September notifications when she came to one dated September 4th:

MISSING YOUNG PERSON

AYSHA JEWEL STANTON   (date of birth 12.12.91)

Aysha is subject to a Care Order to Bursfield Social Services Department and normally lives with her foster-carer Katy Owen at The School House, High Chapel, Bursfield, Staffordshire. She disappeared from her carer's mother's house in Longworth, Greater Manchester, on the morning of Tuesday August 29, 2006, and has not been seen or heard of since.

Aysha is of medium height and slim build. Her hair is a darkish blonde and is normally short to medium in length. Occasionally she has worn her hair beaded or in unusual styles such as afro or other punk styles. Her ears are pierced and she has worn a nose-stud in the past. She has tattoos on her upper arms and faint scars from earlier periods when she used to self-harm.

When she disappeared Aysha was thought to be wearing a white tee-shirt, blue denim skirt, black jacket, and black-and-white trainers. She did not apparently take any other clothing with her, but her normal preference is to wear black. She is physically well-developed for her age, and because of this and her streetwise characteristics resulting from earlier experiences, she could be mistaken for an older girl than her 14 years 9 months.

Aysha has two younger half-sisters who live with the same foster-carer. Her mother is in prison and there are no other close relatives. In May 2006 Aysha gave birth to a baby boy. The baby is currently being looked after by her foster-carer.

Aysha was placed with her current carer in December 2004, and since then has appeared to settle down. She is a young person with a very troubled history and with patterns of behaviour prior to late 2004 which included frequent abscondings from placements, truancy, self-harm and crime. This is the first instance of running away from her present carer.

Aysha Jewel Stanton has been reported missing to Police and Social Services throughout the country and is placed on the National Missing Persons Register and other websites. If you have any contact with her or know of her whereabouts or she comes to your attention in any way please notify your local Police or Social Services or contact direct her carer Katy Owen on her landline or mobile phone numbers.

Everything seemed to fit, the names she'd given, the history of abuse, the recent childbirth, the fact that she'd passed herself off as eighteen but seemed younger. But what clinched it was the photograph, it was Jade without a doubt, though she seemed a lot younger.

Snatching up the piece of paper, Colleen was about to head for the door but then she picked up the other papers as well, she didn't want to have seemed to have jumped the gun.

Can I borrow these? I'll bring them back, she gasped, almost out of the door as she was saying it, leaving the box-file on the desk.

She reached for her mobile phone, found it was switched off – which it hardly ever was – switched it on but then decided it was more important to get to Sanctuary House, confront Jade about this, attempt to talk to her. The phone call would have to wait.

She was met by a tearful volunteer. Jade's gone, they've both gone, but not together. Marcia left last night.

When did Jade leave?

Early this morning, when I was still asleep.

How did she get out?

Through the toilet window. I thought I checked it but it mustn't have been locked.

Why didn't you phone me?

I tried to, I phoned your house, your husband said you'd just left, you were on your way in.

My husband? He left before me.

He'd forgotten something. He'd just popped back, he said.

Well, I'm sorry, but I called in at the Social Work office first. I've just found out who Jade really is.

Yes, I know, she's left a note telling you. And Marcia's left one too.

Has Jade got any medication with her?

No.

When did she last have it?

Bedtime last night.

Bloody hell. We've got to find her. What does the note say?

Something about her baby. It says don't try and find her, she'll get back in touch, she says.

That might be too late unless we can get her medication to her, said Colleen, her voice betraying both resignation and despair.

She took the hand-scrawled notes from the terrified volunteer and while attempting to read them, moved hurriedly to the phone in her office, retrieving the Missing Person papers from her bag at the same time. She knew she had to make, and without delay, one of the most difficult calls in all her years of effort, struggle and dedication.

She sank into a seat on the train at Queen Street station, bound for Oban. She was Aysha now, Jade no longer, and that felt good, but she was already beginning to feel terrible. The events of the last twenty-four hours were buzzing through her mind, but she was also remembering more of her brief time in Glasgow. It started when she and Marcia were talking one evening at the house, in Jade's bedroom when she still was spending most of her time in bed.

She told Marcia she couldn't ever live her kind of life. They were so alike in lots of ways, they didn't like the sort of life most people led, with a house and a family. Marcia didn't have a home to go to and she never wanted one either. But Marcia liked living and earning money on the streets of Glasgow, while all she, Aysha, wanted was to travel and wander the world, and make her money from training dogs and playing music.

She told Marcia that to her music was better than sex, she got more of a high from a gig even if she was just in the audience, and playing a gig would be best of all.

I canna understand that meself, lass, said Marcia. Ye did tell me that already, d'ye remember.

And she recalled then how she'd been keen to get into the Glasgow indie music scene and how she'd met one or two kids who were on the fringes of that scene. So she told Marcia how she preferred music to sex and she went off with these kids and they got her into two or three very small-scale gigs in tiny upstairs bar-rooms or rehearsals in garages or cellars. She even got to take over on the sticks now and again, and once had a turn at the mike. It could've been great if this had carried on but the problem was dosh. There was no money to be made from any of this, in fact everything cost something and it was a lot of dosh to get to see the better-known acts. The kids she knew all went to those gigs, and wanted her to go with them, but she couldn't lean on them for too long, already she was staying free in their flats and going short of food. All the other kids had money coming in, some had jobs or student loans, one or two still lived at home with generous parents, some were on benefit. And a couple of them made a bit of cash from small-scale drug-dealing.

So she ran some errands, as she'd always preferred to call it, just like she'd done before. Warehouse to crack house, crack house to street dealers, and so she ended up staying at the crack house. Horrible place it was, never cleaned, no running water, rats showing up most days, easier to find the stuff to take, and booze, than any decent food or clean plates and mugs.

But she'd only been there a few days when she heard the banging on the door. Dawn raid, first light, and everyone else in the house out of it completely. She weren't using much then, she was still alert to every slightest sound like Greg would've been if he were with her. She knew who were outside and she were out of there like a flash, only taking a second or two to grab another layer of clothes, put her trainers on, and kick the nearest slumbering body to try and give a warning, and then she made for an upstairs back window. Down a drainpipe, onto the roof of a coal-house, into a next-door back-yard, vaulting walls and fences. The fuzz were everywhere, but she'd had years of prac-tice at giving them the slip. Many times she'd ended up in their clutches in her past life, but it was different then, she had a home of sorts to be taken to and she was too young to be sent any-where else even if she did sometimes spend an hour or two in a police cell and be read the riot act or faced a charge. Now, no way was she gonna end up in custody so she fled with desperate determination from that place and even so she had some luck – when she finally found her way onto a main road there were crowds hurrying to work, a nearby bus-stop with queues waiting and one bus letting out a whole stream of passengers onto the pavement that she could lose herself among. And another piece of luck, or she thought so at the time, she found herself in that part of the city centre she knew and found Marcia there and turned to her again. But it was worse now than when she first met Marcia, she had nothing but what she stood up in, her train-ers and a few odd items of clothing some of which weren't even hers. The little bit of dosh and few possessions she still had were back at the crack house. And she had the taste for crack and her-oin now, and the stuff was easy to find among the street-dwellers. It weren't good stuff at all, if it ever is, but it were cheap and available. So she didn't stay with Marcia long.

Thinking back, she still couldn't work out whether she sold her body to pay for the drugs like so many of the girls did, or whether, with her, she took the drugs to escape from the awfulness of the sex.

Her reflections about this were interrupted by the ticket inspector. The train had started and was rattling uncomfortably through the suburbs of Glasgow. She couldn't take in anything outside the train window, but she did, with difficulty, find her ticket. She noticed the train was crowded. She hoped she didn't look as bad as she felt, that no-one would single her out for attention. She went back to thinking about Marcia and the house they'd shared for a week.

She'd talked with Marcia because the older woman liked her and seemed ok, but mostly because Aysha knew she would need her help. So she told her about the music she liked, the gigs, the drumming, the choir, though she didn't say anything about Katy. She needed to ask Marcia how to get to the centre of Glasgow and she needed her to lend her some money. When she first moved to the house, Aysha thought it would be much easier to run off from there than from a hospital ward, but it turned out to be harder than she expected. For a start, all the doors were locked at night, and the windows too. The woman called Colleen told her it weren't to keep the girls prisoner in there but to keep undesirable visitors out. She said when it first opened men used to visit the girls for sex or to bring drugs, in ones or twos or sometimes larger groups which meant the police had to be called. One girl had tried to run a brothel from the house, and another time some drunks had trashed the place, and windows had been smashed more than once. So it were reinforced windows and doors and everywhere locked now, after dark. And most of the daytime, Colleen or one of her volunteers sat in the little office which looked out into the hallway through a big window. All the cash, keys and medication was locked away in that office and impossible to get to.

The hallway was big and was called the Reception Area. There was lots of soft, comfortable chairs, two small low tables with magazines, and reports and information sheets, and on the walls were photos of the house when it first opened, and two large maps. There were three doors, one to the outside, one, alongside the big glass window, into the office, and one to the rest of the house which could only be opened from the inside, or with a key.

The maps on the wall were a stroke of luck. One of them was a street map of Glasgow, but the other had all the central part of Scotland on, right to the coast, including Oban. And you could easily tear them off the wall. The other fortunate thing was that Colleen had got her some clothes because she had to take her to these appointments at the hospital. Before that, she thought she might have to ask Marcia to lend some of hers. And there were always snacks, crisps, biscuits, chocolate, and bottles of water and other drinks available in the kitchen cupboards and in the fridge. No, all she needed was to find a way out of the place, and to persuade Marcia to lend her a bit of dosh.

Please, Marcia, just a bit, she pleaded on several occasions. The answer was always no.

I dunna have any money. I'm na earning when I'm in here, y'ken.

But you've got a bank account, right. Can't you go and get some out?

But that's my savings, Jade. That's for when I'm too old to carry on with this, so's I've got a wee nest-egg to keep me goan.

But I'll pay you back, I promise, she pleaded urgently. You won't lose any savings cos you'll get it back, right.

Oh, sure, everyone says that. How're ya gonna get it back to me?

I'll send it Colleen to pass on to you.

What d'ye need this money for anyway? Ya's not thinking of leaving here, are ye?

Jade kept silent.

Where're ye gonna go? Ye still wanna get to Oban and find yer bairn?

She nodded.

But ya're not well enough. I'll be in trouble if I help ye leave.

I won't say nothing, I promise. I'm better now.

Look, why dunna ye ask Colleen? She's always willing to help, she'll drive ya over to Oban when ye're well enough and she has a free day.

I ain't gonna wait for her. Anyhow, it's private, right, it ain't no business of hers.

With Marcia she wouldn't give up, wouldn't allow any alternative suggestions. But the older woman's idea had stopped her in her tracks mentally. When she weighed up whether it would indeed be better to ask Colleen, it made her think of Katy. If only she could remember Katy's phone number, she could ask her to take her. Katy knew about Neil being Peter's dad, she couldn't tell Colleen, she couldn't be sure what she'd do. She couldn't talk to Neil's dad in front of Colleen. She'd have to make Colleen wait in the car outside and Colleen wouldn't like that, she'd get suspicious, she might be good in lots of ways but she was an interfering old so-and-so, always wanting to find things out. Nah, if anyone took her it must be Katy, but then that would mean breaking her promise to Neil to keep it a secret about his father.

Well, it were too late now, anyhow, she was going on her own, she was on the train. Whenever it stopped at a station, she was jerked out of her reverie. She could hardly open her eyes but she was aware that lots of people had got off and the carriage was much emptier. But she felt awful and returned to her thoughts.

The night before her last day at the house, Aysha had a dream. She was with Greg in some snowy woods and Greg was pulling a small sledge with her gear on. She was walking alongside, reined to the sledge, half pulled along by Greg's eagerness, half slowing him down by using her rein like she used to control him on his lead. The woods was very beautiful but also huge. You could easily get lost but Greg knew his way through. In the dream she felt happier than she'd ever felt in her life and when she woke up she tried to get back in the dream again.

After lunch that day she went out with Marcia. It were the first time she'd been out of the house except in Colleen's car. Marcia had finally agreed to get her a bit of dosh. They went to the nearest café and Marcia had a coffee and she had a juice. Then Marcia left her to go to the post office, and she sat there slowly sipping her juice and watching people walking past along the pavement. The sun was shining and the sky was blue and she was outside in the world and the world felt real for the first time in ages. She tried to recall the dream of her and Greg while staying awake. She felt a bit better than she had but knew there was no way she could do sled races with dogs, or mountain rescue, not for years and years, the way she was now. She couldn't even take Greg for a walk. She'd really blown it, she had. And sitting there in the café, suddenly it all seemed unreal. This weren't her life, this were part of her nightmare, Marcia and Colleen, however kind they tried to be, weren't part of her real life, which was back in Bursfield with Katy and Greg and Charly and Zoë and that boy Katy took up with and the High School and the band and orchestra and the cross-country team. What was she doing here now except yet another big fuck-up in her life?

On the train now she remembered vividly sitting in that café yesterday and how she felt. And with a great effort of will the dream came back to her too, in the snowy forest with Greg and the sledge. She was free now and travelling back to her real life. She'd got away from Glasgow. She'd got Marcia to show her the bus-stop for the buses into the city and she'd remembered. When they got back in she'd taken the map off the wall and studied it, she were good with maps now, and marked the place where she thought that man's cottage were. She'd found a plastic carrier bag and put a bottle of water in and a few snacks and stuff and the map folded up, and hidden it in her room. She'd closed the downstairs toilet window and left it unlocked but so's the volunteer would never notice. It only opened a little bit but it were enough for her to squeeze through. She had a tenner and a few coins from Marcia.

Marcia told her that after tea she was gonna leave the house. She couldn't bear to be there and know Jade was going and not stop her.

She said to Marcia was she gonna write a note to Colleen and Marcia asked if she were and she said yes if she could get some paper. So Marcia found some paper and a biro and said, Jade, could you tell Colleen, y'knows, why I've gone? And she said, Why are you going, Marcia? And Marcia said, Tell her one of my reg'lars needs me badly. And she said, Can't you write it yerself? And Marcia said, You do it, Jade, I'm hopeless at writing. So that evening when she were in her room and Marcia had gone and she was on her own in the house with the one volunteer, she wrote two notes, one from Marcia and one from her. The notes were for Colleen and in her note she explained who she really was and how Colleen should let Katy know that she were in Scotland and would soon phone her. And she said sorry for taking the map and she'd get it back to Colleen soon, and Marcia's money. She folded the notes and put them under her pillow. Colleen was gonna be back in some time tomorrow but she'd be miles away by then.

In the morning she forced herself to wake up while it were still dark and she silently slipped on her clothes and shoes, left the notes on her bed, picked up the carrier bag, and tiptoed downstairs. She peed in the downstairs loo quietly as she could, opened the window, put the carrier bag over her arm and squeezed her way out. She made her way round the side of the house to the street, and caught an early, nearly empty bus, which dropped her almost at Queen Street station. She had half an hour before the first train to Oban and she was already feeling terrible and some of Marcia's money gone on the bus fare. But she forced herself to study the timetable, make a mental note of the stations she could remember and pronounce, Tyndrum, Helensburgh, Dumbarton, working back from Oban.

At the ticket office she asked how much was a single to Oban. It was more than she had and her heart sank.

How much to Tyndrum then?

Single?

Yeah.

Eight pounds fifty.

I'll go to Tyndrum.

Make your mind up, will you.

I'm going to Oban, but I'll have to hitch the rest of the way, she explained, knowing she would do no such thing.

She had nearly two pounds left and her mouth was dry as a bone. But she needed to get on the train and sit down, she'd buy another drink on the train or when she got to Oban.

It was much worse now. She forced herself to drink a bit more of the water she'd brought from the house. She couldn't face any of the food. With great effort she opened her eyes and looked out of the window from time to time. There were mountains all around, and rivers and lakes and mountain streams. She could hardly look at them and she was in despair. She remembered learning about the mountains only one summer before, carrying the heavy pack up to the top, determined to help with mountain rescue. Now she felt so sick that she couldn't take more than a few steps up a mountain and none at all with a pack on her back. Now it was her what needed rescuing, as she had done all of her shitty life. Police, social workers, carers, people like Colleen, all thinking they knew best. Rescuing her but never making her life one bit better. It still sucked and always would. Only Katy had made her life a bit better, and what had Aysha done? She'd fell out with Katy and run off, how dumb could she be? But there was this one last thing she could do, and she would do it, no matter what. She would get to that man in the cottage, Neil's real dad, tell him about Neil's baby, and he would tell Neil and he would find Katy's number and let her know.

She felt worse and worse now and every time the train bumped or jerked she thought she would throw up. She hadn't touched any of the food she'd brought and she couldn't face eating anything now. She took sips of water from the bottle which was getting near to empty. She was shivery cold and wished she could sleep. She tried to recall the dream of her and Greg in the snowy forest. She wondered if she would see Greg again. Horrible memories kept interrupting her picture of Greg. She lost any sense of whether she was asleep or awake, only that life was terrible whichever it was. The abuse was happening again, the pain was real, and she was too sick to stop it.

The ticket man was talking to her.

Hey, lass, are ye all right?

She struggled to take him in, his presence, his words.

Yeah, she mumbled, wondering how long he'd been standing there, what sort of noises she'd been making.

Ye's missed yer station. Ye should've left the train at Tyndrum.

She shook her head. Nah, Oban, she whispered hoarsely.

Yer ticket was for Tyndrum.

Didn't have enough money, she managed to explain, too weak to invent excuses.

Where are ye goan, lass?

She succeeded in pulling out the map and prodding her finger at the place she'd marked.

Lochrana? That's miles off, lass. How's yer getting to there, d'ye think?

She struggled to think, find an answer. Taxi? She croaked unconvincingly, convulsed in shudders.

Are ye sure yer fit to travel? the man persisted. Shouldn't ye be seeing a doctor, lass? Shouldn't we be getting ya to the hospital?

Nah, nah. Aysha was at once horrified, springing to life, overcoming her nausea and shudders. Please not hospital, I'll be all right, I promise. I just need to get to this cottage. It's real urgent, right?

What's so urgent about it?

She dredged up the reason she'd given before.

It's my baby, I've gotta find my baby!

She seemed to be winning over the man's sympathy.

I've got a friend drives a taxi. I can call him, but how'll ya pay him, me girl?

This she had thought of. He'll pay the fare, the man I've gotta see.

Are ye sure, lass?

Sure as anything.

So the official on the train phoned ahead and helped her off at Oban station into a waiting taxi. She could hardly speak now but pointed again at the mark on the map, and lay on the back seat of the taxi feeling near death but willing herself to stay alive over the long, bumpy, swervy drive and the taxi man looking back at her with concern and now and again attempting to speak to her without success.

After an hour or more of drifting in and out of painful consciousness, she heard him say, We're now approaching Lochrana. Where is it you want to be dropped?

She raised her head as much as she could and made one final effort.

It's a cottage where a man lives. An old man with a stick. Just outside the town, by the shore.

What's his name?

I don't know, she mumbled, so much wishing she did. He's kinda half-crippled and has an old dog. Lives on his own just outside of town. If you ask anyone, they'll know.

She sank back and could say no more.

The taxi-driver stopped his car, got out, and soon returned.

Got it, she just about heard him say. Duncan Keith, that him?

Hoot when you get there, she croaked.

She could hear the horn, the dog barking, doors opening, all very far away. She tried to crawl out of the taxi but fell.

She heard voices, the two men got her to her feet.

I've been waiting a long time for you to arrive, she heard the man, Neil's father, say.

You gotta pay the taxi, she whispered shakily as she was carried into the cottage. And you gotta tell Neil 'bout his baby.

She knew she was inside the cottage now and everything blacked out.

He already knows, was the last thing she heard the man say.

46. ANCHOR OF FORGIVENESS

Katy had made herself an early lunch and was finishing it when the phone rang. The morning's rain had just cleared and she thought she would take Greg for a walk before collecting Zoë from school. The dog seemed to know this and sat, alert and expectant, in the doorway.

Sometimes Katy felt she was beginning to adjust to life without Aysha, sometimes she thought she never would. At least she recognised that Gareth had a point in thinking that she should, and trying to help her with it. And he in turn had recognised how hard it would be for her. So the wedge driven between them had been removed and their relationship was back on track. She no longer slept in Aysha's room.

Greg did sleep there still. His sadness each night was a pitiful thing, for he was now mourning not just the absence of Aysha herself but of her baby also. He had watched over that baby on Aysha's behalf, for he understood Peter was her child, with loyalty and determined persistence. Now he seemed to want to guard the spirits of the two of them that still remained in that room. Each evening he had an eagerness to enter the bedroom, a sad, joyless eagerness born of devotion and loss.

Katy was sorry on Greg's behalf, but still believed she'd done the right thing about Peter. She missed the small child too, but if Neil wanted contact with his son, there was no way she would have him visiting here at High Chapel and even less staying over. She was also sure this would be what Aysha wanted, ok there had always been those difficulties between her and Sam, but they were not of Aysha's instigation. Katy always believed Aysha when she insisted she didn't bear her sister any ill-will, and she knew how much she liked Lara and Liam, and would surely be happy for Peter to be with the other two small children.

As for Katy herself, she hadn't yet resumed her college studies, or the orchestra, but she felt she might soon be ready to. She spent a lot of time with Charly and Zoë, helping them through, she kept house, went running and walking with Greg, she went to choir with Charly, and played basketball, as long as Gareth could arrange his work schedule to fit in with her matches and practices, for there was no way she would revert to babysitters. Greg was always happy to join her on a walk or a run, but he always kept close by her now, as though fearful that she too would disappear from his life. Katy would have continued to spend more of her time searching for Aysha but she had no leads. She had been to Manchester from her mother's house for a whole day but it was hopeless, Manchester was such a huge place, it would be a chance in a million to run into the girl even if she was there.

When she and Greg were alone in the house with nothing else to do, she still spent many hours in Aysha's room. She kept her canvasses and paints in there, and her cello. Sometimes she played music or painted, as she had been doing this morning, slow mournful pieces on the cello punctuated by the occasional fast fervent piece which she played badly but with an outpouring of pent-up feelings. Canvasses and large sketch-pads were filled with brooding "abstracts" – so some would have called them but she did not consider them abstract – in which mixes of colours were overshadowed by strange black shapes of foreboding. Greg sat there with her, usually on the bed, seeming to understand her need to play music but with no comprehension about the paints.

Sometimes, though, Katy just sat, looking at Aysha's things, not that many in truth, summoning memories as best she could, knowing that the living presence in the room, the smells and warmth, had all but drained away.

She picked up the phone and heard a Scottish accent, female.

Is that Katy Owen?

Yeah, that's me.

I have some news about Aysha Stanton – am I speaking to her carer?

Katy's heart jumped right out of her body, as she heard herself stammering impatiently, Yes, I am, please tell me, is she alive?

She's alive but the news isn't good. She ran away this morning. My name's Colleen Paterson and I've been looking after her for a while –

What? Why didn't you let me know before?

Because I didn't know who she was until just now. She's been using a false name. Listen, she's been in a very bad way, she nearly died. She's recovered well, but she's on a cocktail of medication, very carefully worked out, and she's gone off without it. It's really important she has her medication –

Why has she gone without it?

Why? Well, all medication is locked away in our medicine cabinet, she couldn't have taken it without asking me or one of my volunteers –

Who are you? asked Katy abruptly, beginning to feel very confused.

I run a voluntary organisation for street-girls and run-aways in Glasgow. My name's Colleen Paterson. We have a house called Sanctuary House where Jade has been living for just over a week –

Jade?

I mean Aysha. I know her as Jade Owen.

Owen is my surname, said Katy.

Yes, I know. I picked her up off the streets of Glasgow nearly a month ago. She was in a coma, she was on the intensive care ward for over two weeks. I tried to find out who she was, I wanted to contact someone –

It's all right. How long since she left you?

536

Four hours or so. Look, it's very important we find her, her health could be at risk, she really does need to take her medication. Have you any idea where she might have gone? The woman pleaded with Katy.

I think I might know actually, but it's a long shot. I just wish I'd known earlier she was in Glasgow.

She just disappeared off the radar for a while. Tell me your hunch where she's gone, said the woman.

Oban. Or quite near Oban. But I've no idea how she would get there.

Yes, I think now that Marcia mentioned to me something about Oban.

Who's Marcia? asked Katy, hanging onto every detail.

An older woman, in her thirties, who befriended Jade for a while. I mean Aysha, the woman corrected herself. Anyway, listen, I'm now going to try Oban. Bus station, train station, police, hospital, I'll do my best to find her. Here's my office number, and my mobile, which I'll keep switched on. She gave Katy the numbers.

I'm gonna set off for Scotland straight away, said Katy. I wanna see Aysha as soon as I can. I'll catch the first train to Glasgow. I'll keep my mobile switched on too. Do you have the number?

Yes, I do. I would give you a lift over to the West Coast, but I might have to go sooner, depending on how quickly we can locate her, and what arrangements I can make about her medication. We'll speak again soon.

As soon as she put the phone down, adrenaline kicked in and Katy started rushing round the house. First she put her mobile onto battery charge. Then she looked up the train time-table to find the first main-line train heading north. She already knew the times of the local trains into town. She collected food, bowls and a blanket for Greg and put them into a plastic super-market bag. Then she picked up her back-pack and stuffed her toothbrush, towel, and a few spare items of clothing in, and then she went back into Aysha's room, Greg following her, and picked up some of Aysha's clothes, her personal stereo and headphones, a few of her favourite CDs. She might try and find the latest music magazine at a station bookstall if she had time when changing trains. There were two second-hand books she'd

found for Aysha in a store in the centre of Bursfield while looking for her early on – The Snow People by Marie Herbert about
the Inuit of the high Arctic, and Terra Incognita by Sara Wheeler
about Antarctica, which was Aysha's next geography project –
and she stuffed these in the back-pack too. As an afterthought
she picked up the three photographs – copies of those borrowed
from Stella on that first prison visit – which Aysha kept on her
dressing-table. Then, remembering to collect her mobile, she put
Greg on his lead and hurried out for the next train.

We're going to find Aysha, she said to Greg, who
clearly had been expecting a walk and was perturbed about the
turn of events. She hoped the dog might have understood, wished
she could make it so.

She decided to wait until she was on the main-line train
before she started making calls. On the short ten-minute journey
into town she made a mental list of who she needed to call. She
wanted to contact Duncan Keith first, but knew that most important was to phone Gareth at work, give him as much notice as
possible to arrange cover so that he could collect Zoë from
school, be at home for Charly's return. Later she would phone
and speak to the girls – she knew they would have wanted to
come, but she couldn't justify taking them out of school on what
might turn out to be a wild goose chase. And if they found Aysha
in Scotland, alive, then Katy would stay with her, forever if necessary, wherever she was, until she was well enough to return to
Bursfield. Having the other two girls with her wouldn't allow
that possibility. Gareth could bring them up to see Aysha at the
weekend, it was his turn to be off duty. After Gareth and Duncan
she would speak to Colleen Paterson again, and after that?

She pulled out her mobile, switched it on, as soon as the
train pulled out of Bursfield main station, heading north. It took
a while for her to be put through to Gareth. While waiting, she
glanced along the carriage. Half of the other passengers seemed
to be using their mobiles, and she wondered if any of them had
such urgent business as her. But then who was to say what was
urgent for someone else? How had people got by before they had
mobile phones, how could she have dealt with all this crisis this
afternoon without one?

After she spoke to Gareth, sorted out the girls, she tried
Duncan.

I've been trying to get hold of you, he said. But there was no answer at home and I couldn't get through on your mobile. Aysha's here at my cottage. She turned up half an hour ago.

How is she?

Not good at all. She's in a bad way, semi-conscious, drifting in and out. I'm not sure what to do.

You must get a doctor to see her. Should she be in hospital, d'you think?

She won't go, said Duncan. She's adamant about staying here. All she's said is to contact you and ask you to come and not to put her in hospital. Oh, and the reason she's come is to let me know about my grandchild.

I thought so.

Well, to let my son know, really, more than me. And tell me to pay her taxi fare.

We'll pay that back, Duncan, don't worry. Listen, this is important. She needs medication, urgently. There's a woman called Colleen who's been looking after her and who has her medication. I'm gonna give this Colleen your number. She will phone you about the medication. You'll probably need to call your doctor and get him to sort it out. If he says she should be in hospital she'll have to go. D'you have one in your town?

In Lochrana? No, only a cottage hospital. And a health centre. Emergencies have to go to Oban.

OK, well leave it between Colleen and the medics. Listen, I'm already on my way to Scotland. Tell Aysha I'll see her soon. Tell her I'm bringing Greg – you remember Greg, our dog. Try and keep her spirits up.

I've given her some sips of water. Should she have anything else?

I don't know, Duncan. You'll get advice about that soon. Just stay by the phone, right.

Concern clouded Katy's sense of enormous joy and relief. She would see Aysha soon. But there was no time for her feelings. Responsibilities were foremost. She dialled Colleen's number.

I've been tracking Jade down, said the Scotswoman. Aysha, I mean. A girl answering her description got off a train in Oban and was put into a taxi.

Yes, I know, she's turned up at a cottage just outside Lochrana. A man called Duncan Keith. I know him slightly, I'll explain the connection later –

Something to do with her baby?

Sort of. Here's the address and phone number. Can you phone him and sort out her medication with him?

Well, it'll need to be a doctor or nurse. Is there a hospital there, or a surgery?

A surgery. And a cottage hospital. But emergencies have to go to Oban.

I don't think there's time to get her to Oban. I do wish they'd taken her to the hospital straight from the train. I'll do my best to sort something out.

What's the medication for, exactly? Katy couldn't help asking.

There's a methadone-based treatment to help wean her off the heroin. Then there's anti-retroviral drugs – did you know she was HIV positive?

Oh my god, no! She's not, I mean she wasn't, not when she was with me. She had all the tests before her baby was born, and after.

Well, she is now, I'm sorry to say. But she doesn't have full-blown AIDS, and with the new treatments she could stay well, stay clear of it, for years and years. She's made a really brilliant recovery, did I tell you that less than a month ago she nearly died, the doctors were amazed at the strength she showed to pull through so well.

Yeah, she is a strong kid.

Particularly considering she's HIV. If she'd developed the AIDS, she wouldn't have stood a chance. But the medication is absolutely vital.

Just those two treatments?

They're the most important. But there are others, to reduce side-effects, and to boost her general physical functioning in addition to her immune system. It's all very carefully planned and monitored.

What should she be eating and drinking?

Lots to drink, and as much solid food as she can manage. She has been eating quite well for several days now.

She's in a bad way now, apparently, said Katy. Only semi-conscious. Can you phone Duncan Keith and advise him about giving her food and drink –

Yes, of course. But I must sort her medication out first. I'll do that now and get back to you.

If my mobile's engaged you can leave a message and I'll call you back. I need to phone Aysha's two sisters. Will you still be in your office?

I hope so. I don't want to have to drive like greased lightning over to the west coast.

There were other people Katy would like to be phoning, her mother, her sister, Sophie, and yet others she knew she should be contacting, Ruth Barnes, Andrew Wheeler High School, Charly's uncle Phil, Stella even. But they would all have to wait, at least an hour or more. She needed to keep the phone line open for further calls from Duncan or Colleen, and make sure neither her battery nor credits ran low. But Charly and Zoë were really important. When she was sure both would be home she dialled her own landline number.

They've found Aysha, she told them. I'm on my way to see her now, but she's not well, she's in a bad way.

What's the matter with her? Charly asked.

Why can't we come with you? That was Zoë, already getting quite querulous. Katy had been prepared for this.

She hasn't been looking after herself. She's turned up at that cottage we went to, and she's collapsed. She might end up in hospital.

But you could take us with you. We wanna see her too.

You'd have to miss too much school, it isn't allowed. And there isn't room in the cottage. I might have to stay with Aysha for quite a while. You can come up and see her at the weekend when you're not in school. Gareth will bring you. If she's better we can all travel back together.

Is she gonna get better? demanded Charly.

I don't know for sure, but I really hope so. We must all pray for her to recover. When she wakes up I'll get her to speak to you on the phone.

But what if she doesn't wake up? Zoë still sounded upset and anxious.

Don't think that, said Katy. I'm sure she will.

It ought to be one of the happiest days in recent years, Sharon thought. Since her diagnosis, in fact. Two significant events, both of which she'd been hoping for. In the morning there had been a card from Rodney. He had finally found the courage to tell his children about his previous family, and now all of them, his wife, himself, and his kids, would be happy to meet up with Katy, Samantha, and his grandchildren.

Of course Rodney had already met Katy, and the three girls. Perhaps not all three, but certainly Aysha and Zoë. Aysha had met the wife as well. They were part of Sharon's family now, those girls, all the more so since Katy had started steps to adopt them. That had been the main topic of her last phone call. This would mean more grandchildren for her, and for Rodney, and as for little Peter, well she supposed once the adoption had gone through he would become her and Rodney's great-grandson, although she couldn't really think of him as such – now that he was with Sam and Marcus, he was more like a baby brother to Lara and Liam. In any case, it was impossible to think of Aysha as Katy's daughter – the other two girls perhaps, well certainly Katy seemed motherly towards Zoë, but Aysha – no, they were more like sisters, that had been the impression that first time Katy had brought the girl to the house, the younger sister she'd never had, and Aysha herself wanting an older teen-age girl as a sister, a role model, someone she could look up to.

Could her daughter adopt Aysha, Sharon had asked her-self, if the teenager was still missing, and what if she was dead? She tried to dismiss that thought. But would Katy adopt Peter instead, perhaps? Or maybe Sam could adopt him. All these questions were buzzing through her head while she started to write a reply to Rodney. How much should she tell him? About Aysha going missing, about baby Peter – well, he knew Aysha was pregnant, didn't he? – about Katy's plans to adopt. Of course she wouldn't say anything about Steve and Marcus. That bombshell was something she was still struggling to adjust to. It hadn't been easy between her and Steve since, but the thing was, she knew she couldn't live without Steve, and it wasn't just her illness either. He had helped her in crucial ways earlier in her life, brought love and stability to her and her kids, been good to her in ways she needed. Katy had benefitted enormously from his presence. Steve was a good man, and so was Marcus, something in the genes had been passed from father to son. He would never desert her as Rodney had done. It had not been sensible for her to hanker so much after Rodney.

Nevertheless she wanted to write a prompt reply to her children's father and she wanted to do it herself. Writing was something she found very difficult now, she couldn't steady her hand enough, and Steve would usually help her. But this time she was trying to write her own letter and it was a struggle, knowing how much to put down and getting it onto paper. And in the middle of this attempt there was the call from Katy.

Steve had answered it, and perhaps sensing that this was not the normal social call, had brought the phone straight to Sharon. Katy came straight out with it, she was back in Scotland, on the train, would be in Glasgow in half an hour, she was heading for the same cottage, and this time Aysha was there. But the girl was in a bad way, had been in hospital, had nearly died, something about missing her medication. There was an urgency to Katy's voice, mingled with the relief that her foster-child had turned up and was alive, but Sharon could tell that there was a desperation there too, to get to Aysha, to see her, and that all the emotion behind that urgency was threatening to break out, only just being held in.

They hadn't talked for long, Sharon did not think there was much she could do or say, and Katy seemed in a hurry to get off the phone. But now she knew what she should have offered to do, and that was to phone Sam and Marcus. They were looking after Peter, it was only right they should know straight away. Sharon was on good terms with them again now, but she wasn't sure if she should give them the news without Katy's agreement. She called Steve who had gone back to preparing the evening meal in the kitchen. She told him the message from Katy and how she'd failed to offer to pass the message on.

Should I tell Sam and Marcus anyway?

Best wait, said Steve. Phone Katy in a bit to ask how Aysha is. Ask her then if she's let Sam know and offer to do it if she hasn't.

I'm also struggling with this letter to Rodney, Sharon admitted. There seems to be such a lot to tell him.

Perhaps wait a bit for that too, until we know more about how Aysha is. She's the one who first met Rodney, after all. I'll give you a hand with the letter later this evening.

Steve was usually right about these things, she had to admit.

After she'd finished eating, and Steve was washing up, Sharon was overwhelmed with painful feelings. She couldn't help thinking of Aysha, confined to hospital, close to death. She had a soft spot for the kid and knew she hated hospitals, just like Sharon did. She was dreading the arrival of that time when she would have to start spending periods in hospital herself, although Steve kept trying to reassure her that even if she required assessments and treatments which could only be done in hospital, this could be on a day-patient basis and he would bring her home each evening. And now her thoughts were returning to that period of her life which she'd blocked from her memories up to now. Life on the psychiatric ward of the local hospital, the nightmare of trying to live her life in close proximity to manic or paranoid people, the periodic admissions when she couldn't muster the energy to resist, to challenge the medical decisions, the fear of what it would be like, who would be there, which only got worse with each subsequent admission, rather than the familiarity providing some comfort. And the shame when Sam and Katy came to visit, usually brought by her mother who was quite infirm and not good on public transport, although she seemed to remember a social worker bringing the two girls on at least one occasion. Much of that time was a blur now. She did remember first meeting Steve – or perhaps it wasn't the first meeting? – when she was taken home from the psychiatric ward on a Friday afternoon for a trial weekend at home. And somehow, even though her mother died soon after this, things had started getting better, or at least she'd started fighting the depression, had grown more determined and confident that she could beat it. She couldn't have done this without Steve, she reflected. She started crying, convulsed by loud sobs. Steve came hurrying through.

What is it, darling?

Poor dear Aysha, she said. She's had such a tough childhood, and now all this.

Well, I know how fond you've grown of her, and me too, said Steve. But really she's her own worst enemy. And giving Katy such a hard time, it's Katy deserves our sympathy the most.

I know, I know. But I must phone Katy soon and find out how Aysha is.

You want me to help you finish that letter to Rodney?

No, no. That can wait till tomorrow. Give me a hug, Steve. You've taken on so much, and I don't always appreciate it. I do so wish I could do more, for my family and for you.

47. A SOUND LIKE ANGELS WEEPING

Colleen waited on the platform at Glasgow Central. She was fascinated to meet in person the young woman off the train.

I've got a back-pack and a medium-sized brown dog, she'd said on the phone. Long-haired with one or two white patches – that's the dog I mean. She had laughed nervously. Me, I've got shortish blonde hair, quite tall, quite young. This last she'd spoken with some reluctance, as though it was the dog she had wanted to be the main identifying feature.

It was already dark out on the streets of the city. Cold and miserable, but throbbing, thronging and alive. The world carried on working, walking, shopping, playing, queueing, driving, well into the hours of darkness at this time of year. The station was crowded with commuters going home and people arriving for their city nights. It was a time of year when the conventional life of the city mingled unobtrusively with the debauched underbelly in which she had worked all these years, though less so now on a Tuesday than on Fridays and Saturdays. It was also a time of year of depression, suicide, higher crime figures. Before she had her work Colleen used to hate this time of year, she used to feel half-dead. Now she felt tired, very anxious to the point of desperation, but alive in every fibre of her body and keyed up for this meeting.

Through a network of numerous interconnecting phone conversations, with doctors and nurses in Lochrana, Oban, and here in Glasgow at the Royal Hospital, and with the man at whose cottage Jade had holed up, she had succeeded in getting the more vital elements of her medication out to her with the urgency it required. The girl should have already received it, they would have called her if there'd been any delay or other problem. Colleen had the rest of Jade's medication in her bag, which she clutched tightly to her while at the station. The only other items for her to bring, which were in her car, were slippers, pyjamas and toothbrush. The girl had so little!

When she met the girl's carer off the train, it was indeed the dog that identified her. The woman looked so young, hardly more than a girl herself.

Colleen mentioned this at the first opportunity, as they set off in the car.

You said you were quite young, but you look very young to be caring for a kid like Jade. You must be, what, early twenties, mid-twenties at the most.

Early twenties, came the sheepish reply. But I must have aged five years in the last few months.

So how come you took this on?

I was doing voluntary work in a children's home as part of my sociology degree. Aysha kinda latched onto me. Well, to be honest, I grew attached to her too. It was because I wasn't yet out of my teens, I think – I wasn't an authority figure, I was just an older teenager, more like a sister to her. There was no other adult she'd made any relationship with, well, apart from super-ficially a few criminals and drug users, y'know, belonging to gangs off the nearby estates. And they, Social Services I mean, were desperate to get her out of the children's home, they needed her place for kids who would make better use of it. But for her age, the cost, and her two sisters, they would have sent her miles away or locked her up. Approving me as her foster-carer seemed like a better option at the time.

Yes, I can see that, said Colleen.

And the thing was, it did seem to work for a while.

I know, I read the missing person report, but I only found it this morning. I do feel really bad about that. If only I'd realised that using the Social Work department's manual system would have found me the information so quickly, of course I should have known, I should have looked through it earlier, found your name and number....

Colleen found herself getting caught up in the distress of the situation, she could sense the younger woman's accumulated pain of these months of not knowing, and she, Colleen, did feel genuinely remorseful and found herself stammering with confusion, something that used to happen a lot but rarely these days.

They moved us to a bigger place, a house instead of a bedsit, and the other two girls moved in. Katy, perhaps realising how difficult it was for Colleen to explain, continued where she'd left off. They must have thought we were doing ok. But after the baby was born, it all began going downhill. I thought Aysha had started bonding with the baby, but I must've been wrong.

I must remember to call her Aysha, Colleen reminded herself. She still instinctively called her Jade.

Is the baby there now, at this cottage we're going to?

Oh no, just Aysha.

Where's her baby then?

You won't get to meet little Peter I'm afraid. He's being cared for by my sister in Longworth. But please tell me how Aysha's been, like, with you in Glasgow.

There isn't a lot I can tell, actually, said Colleen. She was on the streets, semi-comatose, when I first met her. I took her to hospital, she was in a coma, in intensive care, on a drip, for quite a few days.

What was the matter with her?

Too many drugs of various sorts. Probably alcohol as well. And sex. Not enough food or shelter. And of course being HIV.

Oh my god, said her carer. Aysha!

There was something in the way the young woman spoke the name. Colleen wanted to find the words, to say more.

She was close to death. No-one was very hopeful. She's shown a lot of strength to pull through.

Yes, she is a strong kid, the other woman agreed. Does she know she's HIV positive?

I have told her, said Colleen. I've explained about the medication, she seems to accept it, but I'm not sure how much she's been taking in these last weeks. When she first came round she didn't even seem to know who she was. But later it wasn't too clear how much she couldn't remember and how much she was deliberately withholding.

What did she talk about?

Very little, actually. She told me she wanted to move to Sanctuary House when she was ready for discharge from hospital. She was willing to discuss day to day matters but otherwise she kept things to herself. But she was always friendly and co-operative and I got to like her. Dogs, she talked about dogs.

What did she say?

Just that she liked dogs, better than people she said. How does she get on with your dog?

Oh, she's fantastic, said the young woman, visibly brightening. She has a brilliant way with Greg, who absolutely adores her. She'd be good with any dogs, I can say that with confidence.

She said virtually nothing about family or other people in her life, only dogs, Colleen went on. Of course, I thought that was because she'd been abused and had a terrible childhood and couldn't talk about it, either that or she had genuinely lost her memory....

Well, she did have a terrible childhood, she had been abused, it affected her very deeply.

Yes, ok, but there were some bits of her life, clearly, that had improved for her, weren't there?

When the other woman didn't reply, Colleen went straight on.

You see, Jade had been very clever, I mean Aysha. She'd given another name on the street, Amber, so of course I thought Jade was her real name, Jade Owen....

She used both her sisters' middle names, said her carer. Charlotte Jade is the middle sister and Zoë Amber the youngest. And my surname.

I still think of her as Jade, I was so convinced that was her name. It took ages before I realised she might be hiding her real name. I kept searching the missing persons websites for Jade Owen. If I'd realised I might have got to you much sooner.

Well, you got to Aysha in time, that was the main thing.

Only just. And now we have to hope that recovery won't be undone.

What d'you mean? asked the other woman in a very anxious tone.

Well, she should really have stayed in hospital longer. Sanctuary House, the place I run, can sometimes be used more like a recuperation ward. They nearly always are desperate for beds in the hospital, as I'm sure you know. She should have stayed in bed another week at least, but she was up and about yesterday when I was at a conference. Colleen paused, wondering if it could really be only yesterday afternoon that she was in the south of England. And then today she's made this journey and gone without medication for several hours. She would never have left hospital except that she had the regime of regular medication worked out and she promised to stick to it.

In the silence that followed, Colleen sensed that her passenger had finally reached some understanding of the critical nature of much of her work.

Don't worry, she's strong as you say, she was beginning to eat soundly, she really was doing well. Loch Lomond on the right now, she went on, motioning with her arm across the darkness. She was keen to change the subject, to leave talk of Jade on that positive note.

I did this journey about two weeks ago, the other woman said. My friend drove us out to the same cottage we're going to now. Me and Aysha's two sisters, that is. But I don't remember Loch Lomond. We went past that nuclear submarine place.

Ah yes, that's an alternative route. But this road alongside Loch Lomond is quite new and makes the journey faster, I think. Will you find the cottage when we get to Lochrana?

I hope so.

Why were you going there two weeks ago?

We hoped Aysha might be there, or that Duncan might know where she was. It was Charly, Aysha's sister, who suggested we tried to find the cottage. It was a long shot but worth trying.

How did you find it?

Charly and Aysha had been there before, with Duncan's son Neil. We hoped she'd remember, and she did.

What was the connection with her baby? Jade, I mean Aysha, seemed to be trying to find her baby.

It's a very long story, said Katy. She sounded very weary. I can't tell you now, maybe later when we've got there, or another time, if we keep in touch, which I hope we will. She raised her voice and sounded more positive. I want to hear more about your work, I'm very interested. Do tell me what you do and how you got started.

So Colleen, for the rest of the long drive through the November darkness of the west Highlands, found herself telling the young woman whom she'd only just met but no longer seemed a stranger to her, all about her organisation and why she'd started it and how it had developed. Twice she had to pause when the woman beside her needed to phone ahead on her mobile phone to check how her foster-child was, and once when she received a call, which turned out to be from the young woman's mother, sounding even more anxious than she was.

Duncan attempted to keep some sort of vigil as the semi-conscious girl lay in his house. Interrupted only by the many telephone calls to ask after her, to let him know what was happening, to sort out this business of the medication, and by the arrival of the nurse to administer this.

The girl was passive, she accepted drinks of water and juice and she accepted the medication. She lay on the couch downstairs, for Duncan had no way of carrying her up to a bed, it was hard enough to get himself up his narrow staircase these days. She seemed frail and childlike, very different from the somewhat provocative teenager he had met before. But she also, paradoxically, seemed older now, bruised and worn out by her experiences, with little fight left.

She drifted in and out of consciousness and Duncan asked himself if he should try and keep her awake. She seemed very weary and in need of sleep. Once she had established that Neil knew about his son Peter, and had insisted she wouldn't go into hospital, all she asked about was Katy. Katy was on her way, with this other woman who knew the girl in Glasgow, and who had with her the main supply of the girl's medication. They would arrive as quickly as they could. He tried to reassure the girl but it was he who was praying for their speedy arrival. He didn't really know what to do and was terrified the child might die on him. Not finding many appropriate words, he let her sleep.

Once or twice he tried to wake her and found it impossible. The nurse who came did so without a problem, got the medication into her. Duncan was relieved he wouldn't have to administer the next dose, the others would be here well before then. He'd never been much good with medical matters, and it was more than enough now to cope with his own needs.

It was hard for him to keep in mind that this was the girl who had borne him a grandson, the girl who had visited his cottage twice, with her sister and his son, the girl who had appeared a nervous and shy, but somewhat brazen creature, the girl who must have been, he realised now from his own recollection and from things his son had said to him, like a wild animal on heat for the whole of the period they had spent on the Scottish islands. And such a sad creature now.

His routine today was disrupted. Barney had had his short walk in the morning, but not his afternoon one, and nor had Duncan made his daily phone call to his son, asking after his grandson. Neil would know by now of Aysha's reappearance. Katy had phoned her sister to tell her. She was phoning him, Duncan, every hour or so to check how Aysha was, and one of those times she told him that she had let everyone know and had asked them not to phone Duncan so that the lines could be kept open for sorting out Aysha's medication and for Katy to satisfy her anxieties. But Duncan had his own anxieties, not just about the girl lying semi-comatose in his cottage, but about his son and his grandson, how they were getting on together, and how he, Duncan, could play an active role in their lives. He wished they could come and live with him, though he understood the reasons why not. Regular visits, perhaps, but even these were not under consideration at present. If Duncan was to see his grandson, he would have to make the journey to Longworth himself, and this he was reluctant to do. He hardly knew Robbie's, Neil's rather, brother and sister-in-law and their children, nor how much they knew of the things Marie had told him. It was all a very murky area. He wished he'd taken more notice of his grandson during those hours the small child was at his cottage, but there was so much else to get his mind around at the time.

His reverie was interrupted by a knock at the door which caused him to start even though he was expecting it. He leaned over to the semi-comatose girl to check she was still breathing and attempt to wake her. At the same time dog noises erupted. Barney gave three or four low growling barks and Katy's dog, at the door of the cottage, started yelping uncontrollably with excitement. It was this that woke the girl, not his own attempts, Duncan felt sure as he hobbled to his front door.

The dog rushed in, dragging Katy behind on its lead as she desperately tried to restrain it. It knew where the girl was and leapt over her on the couch, licking her frenetically. The girl was wide awake now and overjoyed to see the dog again but unable to cope with its energy. Katy knew this and kept saying, Greg, Greg, calm down please! After no more than a few seconds, however, the young woman was overcome. She herself pressed her face against the child and began to weep.

It was a sound Duncan was sure he'd never heard before, beyond pain or grief. It was the sound of pure love, from another world or the soul's deepest place in this one. It kept on and on, until Aysha herself seemed uncomfortable, or embarrassed, or perhaps remorseful.

The other woman who had entered his house had spoken to him on the phone but never met him. She now did the sensible thing which was to usher him out of the room. She then introduced herself as Colleen Paterson, and she asked Duncan if there was a bed made upstairs for the girl, whom she called Jade. They crept upstairs quietly and made one up. Later she and Katy would carry Jade up the stairs, she said. All this time, though, Duncan was haunted by the sound. He had only ever loved one person not directly related to him. But nothing in his feelings for Marie, or hers for him, would have caused the angels to weep like this.

Katy tried to talk to Aysha. She needed to, quite desperately. But first, she and Colleen carefully carried the child up to a bedroom. Katy washed her fragile body, put her into pyjamas, and tucked her up in the newly made bed. Then Greg was allowed up and clambered onto the bed, gently nuzzling the patient. Katy had stopped crying by now, but tears welled whenever she tried to say anything.

You're gonna be all right, kiddo, she kept repeating.

The child spoke in faint whispers.

Where's Charly and Zoë?

They're at home with Gareth. They'll come up and see you at the weekend. D'you wanna speak to them now if I can get through on my mobile?

Is Peter there too?

No, he's at my sister's house. And Neil's there too, getting to know him. He wants to be a dad to him. Peter's coming on fine.

Are those two kids ok?

Yeah, they're fine. Lara's enjoying helping to look after little Peter.

Good, whispered Aysha. What about your mum? I'm sorry I took that money from her purse.

Don't worry, she's been paid back from Social Services. She ain't too bad. She heard from Rodney this morning.

Who?

My real dad. Y'know, the man you went to see who runs the shop on that island.

Aysha turned to Greg, fondled him, but seemed to have no energy left. Her head sank back into the pillow.

Colleen Paterson knocked and entered the room. I've got to drive back to Glasgow soon, she said. But first I could go into the town and get food. There's very little in this house. Do you want something to eat, Katy?

She suddenly realised how famished she was. She'd had nothing to eat, hadn't even thought about food, since her early lunch back home in Bursfield.

I could murder a plate of fish-and-chips from that chip shop in town.

What about Jade – I mean Aysha?

The enervated child shook her head.

Don't you want anything? asked Katy.

Juice, she whispered weakly. No food.

Could you get Aysha some fruit juice, if they have it at the chip shop, or if there's a store open? Katy said to Colleen. Any sort of juice, but quite a bit.

And a big portion of fish-and-chips for you?

Sure thing.

There's a bag I had with some stuff in, said Aysha to Colleen. There's a map I took from the house. You gotta take it back, the rest of the stuff can be thrown out. And there's money I owe Marcia. Katy, can you give it Colleen to give to Marcia.

How much?

Twelve quid, I think it were.

She lay back, and Greg crawled even closer.

After Colleen had left the cottage, Katy pulled out her mobile.

Will you speak to Charly and Zoë if I can get through?

The girl brightened a fraction and Katy dialled.

They didn't seem to know what to say to one another.

Hi. You ok?

Not bad, Aysha said. I gotta stay in bed for a few days. You come up and see me, right. And be good, yeah? Don't mess up like me.

She could find no more words, or strength to say more.

Katy put her head on the pillow, alongside Aysha's, competing with Greg for closeness, and started to cry again.

I love you, kiddo. I've missed you so much.

I'm sorry, Katy, said the child. I fucked up, right. I always fuck up.

You won't any more. Promise me you won't.

Katy looked into her eyes from no more than an inch away and saw a faint affirmation before the eyes closed.

I'm gonna adopt you, she said, insistently. All the things she needed to say before the girl slept. I'm gonna adopt the three of you, soon as I can. I've already started it.

Why?

Why? I thought that's what you wanted, kiddo. Katy couldn't help sounding affronted and raising her voice a little. Because you won't need to be under Social Services any more, none of you, nor Peter either. I'll get an allowance for you, and sign a form once a year to say I'm still looking after you, but that will be the only Social Services contact. Of course your mother's got to agree first but I think she will. We'll still allow contact with her for any of you that wants it.

She paused. But most of all because I love you, all of you. I want you to be my family.

Aysha looked at her and seemed satisfied, but immensely weary. Her eyes closed again. Greg nuzzled her with a little squeak.

Five minutes later, Colleen returned with food, and juice for Aysha.

I'll have to set off back after I've eaten, she said to Katy. But before I go, I'll give Jade another dose of medication, and I'll explain it to you.

D'you wanna share my fish and chips? asked Katy, wondering what the other woman was going to eat and reaching into her bag to pay her.

No, I've got my own downstairs. I'll go and keep Duncan company.

Oh, my god, Duncan – I've been completely ignoring him, exclaimed Katy, guiltily.

No, no, he understands, we both do. You stay here.

Katy gave Aysha some juice, but she didn't want much. Aren't you hungry, kiddo? she asked her. Have some chips.

Aysha gave another weak smile and shook her head.

Go on, try and eat something.

Just one chip then.

Katy picked out a fat one and proffered it. Aysha took one or two bites but struggled even with those. She gave the rest to Greg.

Have you fed Greg? she asked Katy but was hardly able to speak.

No, I will soon.

Aysha slept, and for the first time Katy began to be seriously concerned. It was so unlike her to refuse to eat, even yesterday, so Colleen had said, she'd been eating well. She seemed to have lost the fight in her, not just her appetite had gone but her appetite for life.

The next time she stirred, Katy tried to encourage her to hope and believe. To fight for her future.

You'll soon be well, Aysha, you're a tough kid, right. Back at school after Christmas, playing drums, in the rock group, the choir and orchestra, the cross-country team. Two months, you'll be fit again. Mountain rescue, dog-sledding, the Iditarod race, you can still do all those things in a few years time. You can live for ages with HIV, lead a normal life, as long as you keep taking your medication.

Aysha looked at Katy for a long time, and her eyes brightened a little. Then she closed them again and sank back.

Colleen came up and explained about the medication while Aysha slept. There was a note with the details folded and tucked in among the containers in the bag of medicines. Colleen then wanted to wake the child but Katy asked her to hold on a minute. Suddenly she was desperate for a pee, she hadn't been, she realised, since she'd left the house in Bursfield, and there was also Greg to feed. She took her empty plate downstairs to the kitchen, greeted Duncan, brought Greg's things up, and went into the bathroom. After she'd peed she attempted to feed Greg, but the dog wouldn't budge from the bed.

She woke her foster-child and with Colleen instructing, medicated her. Then the older woman said good-bye to both of them, and made to go.

We'll keep in touch, both of us, said Katy. Thanks for everything.

Did you give her Marcia's dosh? whispered the girl.

Yes, I've got that, and the map, said Colleen. Bye-bye for now. Get well again soon.

Katy thought of asking her to stay with Aysha while she took the dogs out for a few minutes, but Greg seemed unwilling to leave the sick child. Colleen, Katy knew, had to get back to her home, her bed, her husband. She mustn't be asked to stay longer. For a fraction of a second, Katy thought longingly of sharing her double-bed with Gareth back home. But Aysha was here, and wasn't able to move for a while, and this was Katy's place to be.

Aysha drank water to swallow down her tablets and then drank lots of juice to take the taste away, and now she needed a pee also. Katy carried the fragile adolescent in her arms like a toddler and sat her on the loo-seat, wondering as she did so whether there were special precautions she should take. She'd had no instruction about this and had not thought to ask. Be careful to flush, yes, but what about wiping the seat? She quickly gave Greg some food, and then took his other bowl to the bathroom door and knocked.

Can I come in to get some water for Greg?

Yeah, it ain't locked.

She was planning to ask, but found Aysha painstakingly wiping the seat, putting the paper into the bowl, then flushing and washing her hands. She'd not given up yet then. Good girl, Katy almost said as though to a toddler, as she carried her back to the bed, before retrieving Greg's water.

You're such a good kid, she finally did say, tears brimming again as she kissed her on the cheek and the exhausted teenager sank back into sleep.

She is a good kid, Katy thought, as she watched her closely. All right, she'd done some wrong, in a minor sort of way, she'd caused hurt to a few people here and there, but haven't we all, most of us? And those people who'd done less harm than Aysha, hadn't they come, mostly, from more stable backgrounds, happier family situations? When you looked at the balance of the harm done to her and what she'd given to others, there couldn't be many people who came out better. She'd given so much to her, Katy, joy and fun, support and good advice over Gareth, and to Katy's family, helping Lara and Liam, going to find Rodney for her mother. She'd made Charly's uncle and aunt and grandmother feel at home that awkward Sunday lunch, and most of all she had over the years supported her two sisters so much. Not all the time but whenever they were in need, Aysha knew it and was there for them.

She slept on peacefully, with Greg beside her. After several hours she woke and seemed better. Her eyes were very very bright and her voice was stronger. She drank lots, both water and juice, and Katy gave her the next dose of her medication.

I'm gonna do that race, Katy. The dog-sleds.

The Iditarod?

Yeah. I will do it. Two years.

Good.

And I'll do mountain rescue. And train dogs.

Yeah, course you will.

I've only ever climbed one mountain so far.

Is that right?

Yeah.

Well, it's one more than I've ever climbed.

But I'll climb lots more, Katy.

Good.

And drumming. I'll do more drumming, get even better. Play drums in bands.

Yeah, that's the way, kiddo.

Aysha turned to Greg and let him lick her face.

Are Charly and Zoë gonna come and see me?

Yeah, at the weekend.

And my baby?

Maybe him too.

That man downstairs is his granddad.

Yeah, I know.

She looked at Katy with her bright, bright eyes.

Miss, she said. D'you remember when I used to call you miss?

I sure do. And that first gig we went to.

Yeah, wicked, that were, right.

Tomorrow you could listen to music and read a bit. I've brought you a couple of books and a few of your CDs.

Did you bring my stereo?

Your CD walkman, yeah.

Can I listen to something now?

Well, ok, but you must be quiet, it's the middle of the night.

Have you brought Arcade Fire?

Yeah. Katy knew they were her protégée's most recent favourites, even though Aysha hadn't talked music with her for quite a time. She still tried to follow the teenager's tastes. In fact, this current band she liked was easier on Katy's ears than the Test Icicles or Idlewild.

Just track seven, right.

The child listened to the one track right through and seemed happy. When it finished, she switched it off and looked at Katy. Her eyes had changed now and Katy had never seen the expression before. She had seen a whole range of emotion in those greenish-brown eyes she loved looking into – anger, fear, anxiety, doubt, courage, determination, rebelliousness, gratitude, hatred, self-loathing, despair. Much of the time Aysha's eyes conveyed the fretful nature of her soul, the challenge and struggle that life always was for her. And evasiveness was frequently there too, that glazing over, that shifty quality that resisted a head-on challenge, which was her most common form of defence. And always, alongside whatever other emotions she showed, there was that restlessness which was her true spirit.

But her eyes were different now, all those old expressions gone. Peace had entered her soul at last, and something akin to love. Katy knew then that for Aysha the long struggle was over now, the restless spirit was restless no longer. For a moment Katy wished she had not given her that CD track to hear, that she might have held out longer for the prospect of hearing music tomorrow. But she rejected that thought, could not have begrudged the girl her last wish, could not contemplate the possibility that she might not have honoured that wish. All that was most important had been put in place, a track of music, a few words with her sisters, and Katy and Greg there by her side.

She continued sleeping for some hours. Twice she appeared to momentarily wake, and Greg nuzzled closer and Aysha touched his nose. She looked at Katy with that same new, pure expression, and the sense of deep reassurance that her carer was there. An hour or so before dawn, the breath finally slipped away from her. Katy held her limp hand and laid her head against her still face, and there were no tears now, only a sense that the inevitable had happened and a mustering of strength for the difficult and important tasks ahead.

Greg, however, coming to his own way of knowing the life had gone from her, did mourn now. His wailing and his howling continued well past dawn.

48. TOWARDS HIGHER GROUND

Aysha is crossing a vast snowfield. She has been standing on the back of the sledge, but now she has stepped off and walks alongside. She is not attached to her harness, but the dogs are tired and pull the sledge very slowly, allowing Aysha to keep pace alongside.

Aysha is twenty-three now. She is not sure how she knows that, but she does. Past months, even years, have been a blur to her. All she can remember is that she was living for several months in a place where she got to know the dogs and learned how to handle them and the sledge.

Along with a tent, sleeping-bag, blankets, extra clothing, food and water for her, food for the dogs, and replacement parts for the sledge and harnesses, all of which are stacked on the sledge, she has a map, an instruction sheet, a mobile phone and an emergency number in the inner pocket of her parka. She hopes she won't need to use the latter, but just in case.

Ahead of her is a chain of mountains, high, snow-covered, with peaks and passes, stretching in both directions as far as she can see. She is approaching them at an angle, the mountains are nearer to her left than to her right. She has to cross these mountains, find the best way over them. There is a route, which others have taken, on foot or with dogs or mules, she has been told this, and the map will help her find it, but the snow makes it difficult to pick out and she cannot at present see it.

All she knows is she has to cross the mountains and reach a place on the other side. She's not sure what the place is or why it's so important, but it is. She has some sense she won't be alone then.

Until then it's just her and her five dogs. The dogs are Dusty, Bonnie, Shadow, Hector and Finn, and she knows them all well now. They all have their different personalities. The two male dogs, Hector and Finn, are the heaviest and strongest and are harnessed next to the sledge. But even those two are very different. Finn is more excitable, his energy shows itself in bursts. At the moment he is relaxed and quiet. Hector is more of a plodder, he will pull all day but would never run at speed unless the other dogs or Aysha herself gave him that message.

The pair in front of Hector and Finn are strong wiry bitches who as well as contributing a lot of the pulling effort, also provide a vital channel of communication between the lead and the male dogs. They could not be more different, Bonnie is a friendly, cheerful husky, almost white, attentive to the other dogs and to Aysha, while Shadow, the darkest coloured of the five, is a quiet, moody loner. But Shadow has a loping, apparently effortless run, and an intuitive understanding with Dusty up front. Dusty is a grey-brown highly intelligent female husky who is happy to take the lead. She knows the terrain, the safest places, has an intuitive awareness of danger, and an ability to think and adjust direction quickly with lightness of foot. The other dogs know this and respond to her, nor do they mind that Dusty expends the least energy, for they understand that her senses must stay alert. Aysha is happy to have five dogs whom she has got to know and trained to work as a team, and she trusts them all, individually and collectively, but Dusty she trusts, she has to trust, most of all. It will be Dusty she looks to for help in finding the best route up the mountain.

At first she thought she was dreaming. The last thing she could remember was lying in a bed in a cottage in Scotland feeling happy and peaceful but very very tired, with Greg lying on the bed next to her, and Katy sitting by the bedside. Whenever she woke up she felt Greg nuzzling her and saw Katy watching over her, and if she wakes again she expects them still to be there. However much she is enjoying this sledging trip with her five dogs, she desperately wants to wake up and see them again. But she can't seem to wake up, and by now she's decided she can't be in a dream. For one thing, every night she goes into a magic heavy sleep and dreams of being back there, in her old life, with her sisters and Katy and Greg. Or she dreams, very occasionally, of being a small child again. Charly is crying in the night, and she finds her bottle and puts it to her mouth. Then Charly's quiet and content again, or if she isn't, Aysha has to go and wake her dad, Kenny. And then she wakes up and she's back on the snowfield with the sledge and her dogs. She can remember everything about that old life, all the good things and the bad. But the funny thing is, the bad things don't seem so important now and she only really ever thinks about good things and that's all she dreams about too. So she came to think that maybe she's in a coma. She was in one before, she remembers, but she doesn't remember any dreams like this when she was in that coma, all she remembers is when she came out of it she felt terrible and couldn't remember who she was, but she doesn't feel bad now and she knows she's Aysha Jewel Stanton.

She is a bit confused, though, about where she is and where she's going. The map she was given doesn't help her. Also it seems like summer here, with the sun low in the sky all through every day, although it does dip down close to the horizon for a few hours, but she knows from when she studied the

Arctic in her geography project that the snow and ice thaws in the summer – that's why explorers trying to get to the North Pole on foot or on sledges had to go in the winter or early spring. She's already crossed a few rivers, including one big one, that were still frozen over, she doesn't know how she'd have got across otherwise. She's been trying to decide whether she's in Antarctica, she knows there's a long chain of big mountains there, the only other thing she knows is that penguins are the main wildlife there, but she hasn't seen any penguins. She has a pair of binoculars which are mainly for looking ahead to find the route or to spot any danger well in advance. The only binoculars she's used before were that pair Charly lent her now and again on the trip to the Scottish islands and when they went for walks in the country near Bursfield. Using the binoculars she's spotted a couple of polar bears a long way off to the right, a small herd of caribou a bit nearer, apart from that the only wildlife has been a fox crossing the trail ahead of her, a hawk-like bird drifting overhead, and a few white gulls now and again following her tracks. All of this, she thinks, means it must be the Arctic, and maybe it's still spring, before the snow and ice melts, but there again, she remembers about global warming and how the ice in the Arctic was melting earlier each year and if she's eight years older now and global warming was going to get worse like they said it would, then why is everywhere still frozen and snow-covered? And whether it's Alaska, where she knows there are big chains of mountains, or somewhere else she doesn't know so much about, like Greenland or Svalbard or Siberia, she just isn't sure. Most likely it will all become clear when she gets to the place she's going to.

As she gets closer to the mountains, the sun goes behind them for a few hours and she's in shadow, and decides this is the best time to sleep, rather than when the sun is closest to the horizon. She had thought she was going north, towards the pole, because all the famous polar treks went north, or south if it was Antarctica, and because the Iditarod Race also runs south to north, ending at Nome in Alaska, one of the furthest north towns in the world. But she's worked out that she's not going in the direction of the lowest point of the sun. She seems to be travelling east to west, or west to east, she can't work out which. And she's not in any race, she does know that, although she's following a route others have travelled, there's no-one else around just now, she's on her own with the dogs, and the sky blue all the time, and the reason it's getting colder is because the sun is hidden behind the mountains part of the time and she's beginning to climb to higher altitudes. Today she's put on an extra layer of clothing under her parka, put a woolly hat on instead of her peaked cap, found a thicker pair of gloves, and only needs to wear sunglasses against the glare of the snow, for part of the day. The dogs will go for longer now, but stopping is getting more difficult because of the cold. She has to get a fire going, thaw out the dogs' meat and her own food, get her tent up, before she gets too cold or tired. She needs to walk more now, to keep warm, but then she's more tired at the end of the day.

Going across the mountain range is going to be the really difficult bit. To lessen the weight on the sledge she knows she will have to walk almost all the way over, and because she is less sure-footed than the dogs, she must harness herself to the sledge the whole time. In addition the load on the sledge will have to be carefully allocated and fixed by ropes to avoid sudden shifts and overbalancing. There might even be the need to halt progress and adjust the weight balance as they go along. The most difficult part though will be the degree of cold at the higher altitudes. They won't be able to stop once they reached a point about two-thirds of the way up. As it will take well over two days to climb from the bottom up to the pass that will take them across the main spine of the mountains, she will have to judge carefully on the way up where to stop for food, rest and sleep. The last leg, over the pass, is going to be a very long day of continuous effort and while she'll be able to eat and drink as she goes along by carefully packing cartons of food and drink in inner pockets of her parka, close to her body, the dogs' food will be frozen solid on the sledge and she will have to heat up double portions for each of them before they set out on that long leg over the pass, and they will then have to get by on licking frozen snow until they reached a low enough altitude to stop on the other side.

The other side of the mountains is very much an unknown proposition. She has to assume the terrain will be similar to the way up, and that it will be faster going because it's downhill. Care would need to be taken, though, to avoid the sledge swinging about or reaching an unstoppable momentum and losing control. She will be very tired by then but it would probably be safer for her to keep walking, harnessed to the sledge, rather than hitch a ride which her legs would no doubt be demanding at that point. But there might be some easier, safer stretches where it would be ok for her to ride on the sledge.

She will be very dependent on Dusty, her lead dog, to help get them safely over the chain of peaks, to find the best route, to maintain a safe speed. And to know the direction to head in once they reach the lower slopes on the other side. She remembers the first time she was out with Greg on her own, and how she'd depended on him to find the way back to the city. Dogs are good like that. The place they're going to is many miles away even when they're down from the mountains. She doesn't know what the terrain will be like. Maybe, if the weather stays clear, she will be able to see this place with her binoculars as they make their way down the slopes. If not, she has a compass, but it's Dusty she will mostly rely on.

Aysha has only just come to the thought that maybe she's died and this is another world. It's hard to believe this because she's never ever believed in God or Heaven or life after death or anything like that. Whoever let Kenny die and made life so terrible for her when she was a kid is not the kind of God she could believe in, and the few times she went to church she hated it. Because of this and all the bad she's done she always knew she would never go to Heaven, and it always seemed better not to believe any of it. There are other things not right about it too. For one thing, if she makes a mistake on a steep bit of mountain she could be killed, and the dogs could be too, she's been warned about this, but in the heaven and hell she was taught about as a kid you never die. And another thing is about phoning, there were never supposed to be any mobile phones in heaven, and although on this dog-sledging journey she can only use the emergency number on her mobile, they've told her quite clearly that once she reaches this other place she can phone the people she loves, and that only means Katy and her sisters who are back in England. Well, you can't use a mobile to phone from one world to the next, can you? She knows now for sure that Katy loves her as much as Charly and Zoë do, and she loves her too. Back when she was nearly fifteen, the last thing she can remember, is what Katy said to her and how she looked at her when she lay resting in that man's bed.

And then there's Greg, who she loves most of all. If it's really more than eight years since Greg lay on that bed with her, then Katy's dog will have probably died by now. And Katy must've been really devastated, and her sisters too, to lose him after losing her, Aysha. He was five when Aysha first met him, two years she spent with him, and fifteen is too old for a dog. And she has this real sense, more than hope, more than belief, this faith is all she can call it, that the main reason she has to get to this place beyond the mountains is that Greg will be there. And if she meets Greg again there, it must mean Greg has died and gone to a different world, and that means she must have too. That's why she can't wake up from this dream, that's why when she sleeps now she dreams of her old life. All death must be is a dream you can never wake up from, and when you die it means you live in your dream and you dream of your life.

Thinking of this, and of seeing Greg soon, and that Charly and Zoë and Katy are still part of her life, she feels a certainty and a contentment in her life she never remembers feeling before, and a hope and a determination, and she concentrates on the five dogs she's with now, urging them on towards where they will start climbing the mountains.